Echo Springs

LEISL LEIGHTON

DANIEL DE LORNE

TJ HAMILTON

SHANNON CURTIS

mira

Published by
Mira
An imprint of Harlequin Books Australia
Level 13, 201 Elizabeth St
SYDNEY NSW 2000
AUSTRALIA

MIX
Paper from
responsible sources
FSC
www.fsc.org   FSC® C001695

A catalogue record for this book is available from the National Library of Australia
www.librariesaustralia.nla.gov.au

Printed and bound in Australia by McPherson's Printing Group

Contents

Dangerous Echoes   1
Leisl Leighton

Embers and Echoes   145
Daniel de Lorne

Echoes of the Past   255
TJ Hamilton

Hope Echoes   385
Shannon Curtis

Also by Leisl Leighton

Available in ebook from Escape Publishing

The Pack Bound Series

Pack Bound
Moon Bound
Shifter Bound
Wolf Bound

Dangerous Echoes

Leisl Leighton

To Helen, my best friend always. You give me the courage to keep
on trying even when things are at their worst.
And to Alex, the best agent a writer could have.
Without you this book would never have been written

Chapter One

Erika looked down at her hands. The handcuffs clanked against the bar on the table. Sighing, she lowered her head to the cold surface. It smelled of stale coffee and sweat. And was sticky.

She shot back. The stickiness—god only knew what it was—was now on her nose and forehead.

Perfect! Just perfect.

Where were her wipes when she needed them? Not that she could grab them even if her backpack was next to her and not out on the sergeant's desk. She pulled against the handcuffs, a little kernel of desperation overtaking the self-pity. And the exhaustion she'd been fighting. Unable to get a flight to Bourke, she'd flown in to Sydney and driven the eight hundred odd kilometres to Echo Springs, not arriving until the middle of the night. She'd been ready to drop.

Then she had been arrested for breaking and entering.

She couldn't believe Sergeant Cooper was still working, let alone dispensing his Jurassic-era small-town justice. What a joke! A heavy sigh burst from her lips. She could be here for hours waiting for someone to realise she'd been telling the truth and set her free. The waiting might drive her insane, let alone the stickiness on her nose.

Don't think about it, Erika.

In an effort to focus on something else, she let her gaze wander around the interview room. It hadn't changed much. The walls were still the hospital green they'd been, the black and white linoleum squares were still on the floor, the white squares now kind of browned. She clenched her glutes and shifted, trying to get more comfortable. The chair was new—moulded grey plastic—but just as uncomfortable as the old wooden one. The table was different. Stainless steel with handcuff bolts in the centre rather than the old dented wooden thing she'd scratched her initials into when she was younger.

There was no way she could work the bolt out so she could lift her hand and wipe the sticky stuff off her face. Oh god, now she was thinking about it again. Okay, think of something else. Anything else.

Peter. Where was he? Why had he sent her that text? And why on earth had she come back to Echo Springs, the place she'd vowed to never return? Of course, she knew the answer to that: to find Peter. And now look what had happened. Bad things always happened to her here. The town hated her, and she hated the town in return.

The handcuffs clanked as she moved. Her nose twitched and tingled. She ached to wipe it. No, best wait for the wipes to do the job properly rather than get it on her hands too. Jenny would say look on the bright side. Okay. What bright side was there to this? Perhaps she wasn't here at all. Yes, that would be a bright side. Maybe she'd fallen asleep on the road and was now ploughed into the red soil on the side of the Mitchell Highway, hallucinating this nightmare due to a serious head injury. Oh god! She could be dying. Just like her parents… No. No. She couldn't think of that. She wouldn't. It was this place. It brought it all back, the memories, the nausea, the tension headache, the shortness of breath.

No. She wouldn't let this happen. Not here. Not when at any moment one of them could walk in and see her losing it.

Her head spun. She was breathing too fast. She needed to calm down. She hadn't had a panic attack for years, and she wasn't chancing having one here. She closed her eyes and forced herself to breathe. In. Out. In. Out. In. Out. She could hear Jenny's voice in her head telling her to go to her calm place. She pictured a meadow at the top of a hill, rolling green hills and valleys stretched out around her as far as the horizon. She turned, letting the blue of the sky sink into her soul, the sun warm her face, the scent of jasmine and eucalypts tickle her nose, the light breeze curl around her and lift the hair from her sticky neck, cooling the perspiration that panic had left behind.

She let go of one more breath as the peace surrounded her and opened her eyes. Okay. She was no longer shaking or hyperventilating. She was in control and reason had returned. Someone would be in here soon and this whole mess would be sorted and then she could get on with finding Peter and discovering why he'd sent the text asking for money. And why the hell he hadn't told her Mabel had sold the family property. She frowned. It could have saved all this hassle. She never would have got the key from the shed to let herself inside and been caught in the kitchen by Mrs Patterson—an absurd echo of the past—as she'd been raiding the well-stocked fridge.

It was kind of funny, really. She might even laugh if she wasn't so tired and worried about Peter. She only wished she could see Sergeant Cooper's face when he found out her 'story' was true. That she was actually working on his side of the law now. Wouldn't he feel like a dick? A part of her couldn't wait to see him eat a little bit of crow when he finally did come in here to release her. It would even make the ribbing she'd get from her colleagues back in Melbourne when they heard about this—and they would hear about this—worth it. She was often astonished at how quickly gossip travelled to interested ears at work. One would think, being involved in the justice system, people would be used to keeping information to themselves, but that wasn't the case at all.

The door opened. She looked up, expecting Sergeant Cooper and the brand of bluster she'd come to expect from him, but instead found herself looking into jade eyes, a colour she'd only ever seen on one person. Her mouth dried as her gaze dropped to the full lips, now outlined by a five-o'clock shadow and spread in a grim line she'd never seen on that laughing mouth before. His once-tousled brown curls were cut into a short back and sides with only a hint of curl on the top. The style emphasised the slash of his cheekbones and the squareness of his jaw. Her gaze took in the uniform, the blue a stretch across a chest that was much broader than the last time she'd seen it, the drill material of the dark blue pants emphasising just how long his legs were. He'd grown tall. Taller than she'd imagined. And he was a Detective Senior Constable by the stripes and insignia on his shirt. A policeman. It took her a moment to comprehend the fact. He'd been so savvy about people and given finesse to all their plans. She supposed it shouldn't surprise her that he'd become a police officer. But here? No. She'd never imagined him still here, in this town. He was staring at her, as if waiting for her to move or speak first. She opened her mouth to say something, but all that came out was, 'Harts?'

'Well, well, well. Erika Hanson. I never thought to see you back here again.' He tipped his head on the side, skimming his gaze over her in much the same way she had when he'd walked in the door. That look made her forget the stickiness on her face or the fact she was handcuffed to the table. 'What was it you said to me before you hopped on that bus? "I'm never coming back to this hellhole again. There's nothing worth coming back for."'

Her head was buzzing. He remembered her words? 'I had no choice.'

His lips moved into something that could have been a smile if not for the fact his eyes were cold. So cold she couldn't repress a shiver.

'We all have choices, Miss Chief.' The way he said it slurred the words together so they sounded like mischief. Her super hero name. The one he'd chosen for her that nobody else knew. He was Cooperman and she was Miss Chief. They'd done everything together. And now he was looking at her like she was a stranger.

Something ugly crawled through her chest but she didn't know what to do with it, with the feelings his attitude raised in her, so she simply shrugged. 'I had to leave. I thought you knew that.'

Something flashed across his face before his expression blanked. He looked down at the manila folder in his hand. 'It doesn't matter now. Sixteen years have passed—it's all water under the bridge, right?'

She shifted uncomfortably, certain she was missing something behind his words. 'I put the past behind me.'

'I got that when you never tried to contact me or anyone else here to tell us you were okay.'

'I contacted Peter. And Daphne and Pip knew where I'd gone.'

He looked down at the folder again, his lips twitching, as if he was holding something back. 'They didn't tell me.'

'I asked them not to.'

His gaze whipped up to collide with hers. 'I see.' His fingers drummed against the folder. 'Not that any of that matters now. What matters is you breaking and entering Mrs Patterson's house and stealing her food. Some things haven't changed, right?'

'This is a misunderstanding.' If she was reading him right—and there was no guarantee she was—he looked unamused.

'That's what you always said.'

'Well, half the time that was true. You know it. But this time, it's completely true. I didn't know Peter and Mabel had sold the house.'

His lips thinned. 'I see.' He crossed his arms and sat back, gaze raking over her in an unflattering way. 'How did you get into the house? There was no sign of forced entry.'

'I used the old key hidden under the flower pot near the back shed. It was still there.'

'Why didn't you ring the front doorbell?'

'It was one o'clock in the morning. I didn't want to wake them when I could let myself in. I was planning on talking to them in the morning after I'd had some sleep.'

'Why did you come back?'

'That's not really any of your business, is it?' He simply stared at her. She shifted again, more aware than ever of how uncomfortable the seat was. She didn't like him looking at her like that. It reminded her of the way Sergeant Cooper, his dad, looked at her. 'Peter sent me a text saying he needed my help.'

Hartley sat up straight. 'What kind of help?'

She shrugged. 'Something to do with money. I don't know what. He didn't respond to my latest texts, so I came here to see what the problem was. Now I'm here and given the family home's been sold, I have to assume it's a serious financial problem. If you just call Peter, he'll be able to clear this up.'

He leaned forward, his hands moving across the table, almost as if to hold hers, but then he stopped. There was something in his eyes she didn't like. She swallowed hard. 'What? What is it? What's happened to Peter? Where's Mabel?'

His brows hitched. 'Your gran's in Coolabah Nursing Home, Erika. She's not well.'

'What? Peter never said anything.' She looked at the door, almost as if expecting Pete to walk in, her heart banging loud and fast in her chest, making her take quick little sharp jabs of breath. She shouldn't ask. She knew she shouldn't ask. But she had to. 'Where's Pete?'

'I'm sorry, Erika. Peter is dead.'

Chapter Two

Erika jerked as if she'd been punched, her dark auburn ponytail—so dark as to look like blood—flicked over her shoulder. Hartley waited for her to flick it back in irritation, something she'd always done in the past when her ponytail didn't stay where she'd put it, but she didn't move.

Crap. He really shouldn't have been so blunt about Peter's death, though, in his experience, there was never a good way of telling someone a loved one was dead. But he'd really screwed it this time. Seeing her again after all these years had done something to his head, like the world had tipped and his footing wasn't quite steady. Which was why he'd been too blunt. And now look what he'd done.

'Ms Hanson?' He sat forward, concerned about how pale she'd turned. Concerned about the way she was staring at him but didn't seem to be seeing him at all—a big difference from the way those astonishing hazel eyes had connected with his when he'd entered the room. Concerned about the way she was shaking her head, almost like she had water in her ear. Her lips were moving, but no sound was coming out.

He reached for her hand, touched her briefly. 'Ms Hanson?'

Nothing. She looked right through him—very disconcerting.

'Erika?'

Her lips kept moving, head kept shaking, and she was even paler now. He touched her again, this time covering her hand with his. It was icy. 'Erika?' He squeezed, thumb brushing over her wrist.

Her gaze was like a slap. 'He can't be dead. You must be mistaken.'

'We're not mistaken.' He squeezed her hand again, holding tight when she tried to pull away.

'But…but…he sent me a text. It's why I came up here at the last minute like this. He can't be dead.'

'His body was found,' he glanced down at his watch, 'a few hours ago. There was a fire.'

'A fire? He was burned? Then how can you tell it was him?'

'His car was found at the scene and we found his wallet and identification in a jacket we found just inside the door. It's him.'

'You found his car? Are you saying this didn't happen in his home?'

'No. Your brother has been living at the Echo Springs Hotel for the last year.'

'He has?' She seemed completely baffled. How could she not know where Peter was living or that he'd sold Hanson House?

'Yes.'

'So, where was this fire?'

He coughed. He didn't want to tell her what Peter had been doing when he'd managed to blow himself and his friend up. He let go of her hand and reached for the pad and pencil he'd brought with him. 'Can you tell me about his text?'

Her gaze zeroed in on the pencil hovering over the paper as if accusing it of her brother's death. 'Why?'

'It might help.'

'Help who?'

He swallowed. 'Us. To figure out what happened. Why Peter was… where he was. Did he ask you to come back here?'

'No.' She shook her head, throat working, mouth tight. 'He asked for my help.' Devastation filled her eyes. 'If I'd got here faster, he would still be alive.'

'Don't do that to yourself. There was nothing you could have done. It was an accident by the look of things.'

'An accident?'

'Yes.'

Her eyes clouded with something painful. 'A car accident?'

Shit. Of course she'd think that. 'No.' He reached out and touched her hand again, trying to get her attention back on him. 'The text?'

She nodded slowly, swallowed hard. 'He texted me asking for money.' She shook her head. 'But he couldn't have been having money problems. Mabel was loaded and he had access to her accounts—he was her accountant and financial planner. At least, that's what he told me.' Her frown deepened.

'If he'd sold Hanson House and the property, then there should have been even more money.' Her fingers curled into her hands, making the handcuffs jingle. 'I thought he was having a joke with me about needing money. I texted him back telling him I didn't get the joke and I wasn't amused.'

He almost smiled. She'd never been good with jokes. 'You didn't think he was being serious?'

'With my family's fiscally sound background? No. But then I got another text a few days ago, saying he was serious. He needed a hundred grand ASAP for something important. I texted him back, but he didn't respond. I called him, but only got his messages. It was then I realised he was being serious and needed my help. Given he wasn't answering any of my attempts to contact him, the only thing I could do was come up here and find out what was going on.'

For a moment, he thought she was going to drop her head into her hands and give in to a bout of tears, but her eyes became emotionless, like she'd shut herself off behind a wall. 'I should have just sent him the money. I should have known he wouldn't have asked if he didn't need it. This is my fault. My fault.' Despite the cold look on her face, her voice wavered.

He went to reach out to touch her again, to comfort her, the instinct so strong, but she jerked back as far as the handcuffs would allow.

'What are you doing? Why do you keep touching me?'

'I'm just trying to comfort you.'

'Why?'

'To show you I'm sorry for your loss.'

'Oh.'

She looked so bewildered. His heart ached for her despite the anger he still carried. 'What can I do?'

She nodded briefly and looked down at her hands. 'Can you take these off? And get my backpack. Your dad took it. I have something sticky on my nose and I'd like to wipe it off.'

'O...kay. Let me get the key.' His father should never have arrested her in the first place. She hadn't been breaking and entering. She'd just been going home. After all these years. And now this. He had to get those cuffs off her ASAP. He stuck his head out the door and waved Constable Leila Mayne over. 'Can you fetch the keys for the handcuffs from the Sarge and get Ms Hanson's backpack out of the evidence lock-up for me? She's just had an upset and I don't want to leave her alone.' She nodded and headed off. He took a deep breath and walked back into the room.

'Thank you,' she said quietly. 'But if you're busy, you can go. I'm fine.'

He didn't answer, simply sat back down. Silence rose between them. He began to tap the manila folder, wishing he'd opened it and had a look before coming in here. But the moment he'd heard, he'd just had to come inside and see her.

'What's that? Is it the report on my brother?'

He frowned and looked down at the report, the edges of the folder now curled up where he'd been playing with it. 'We don't have a file for your brother yet. This is your file.'

'I want to see the autopsy report when you get it.'

'What?'

'I want to see the files on the investigation. I want to see what you're doing to figure out who murdered my brother.'

'There's no evidence your brother was murdered.'

'Of course there is. He texted me he needed money and now he's dead.'

His frown deepened. 'That isn't proof of murder.'

'Proof? No, it's not proof. But alongside the other evidence it suggests my brother's death wasn't an accident.'

Despite the tone of reasoned practicality in her voice, he knew her well enough to know it was the grief and the guilt talking. He'd seen it plenty of times—people trying desperately to find a reason other than 'just because' for the death of a loved one. It was much easier to point the finger and place blame on a human than to shriek up to the heavens asking why and never getting back an answer. But because it was Erika, because he felt sorry for her, because he'd always admired how Peter had given up his career to look after Mabel when things got dicey, he decided to play along with her and let her reason her way through it herself. 'Evidence? What other evidence?'

'You said he died in a fire.' He nodded. 'Peter didn't smoke, so he couldn't have set himself alight in bed. You said he was living at the Echo Springs Hotel, so it couldn't have been a kitchen fire or others would have been involved too. If he'd been at work, there might have been an electrical fault, but unless he had been knocked unconscious or there was a sudden explosion, he would have been able to get himself out in time after the smoke alarms went off. So, that means he must have been knocked unconscious or there was an explosion, which points to foul play, even if you don't take into account the texts I got from him about suddenly needing all that money.'

'He wasn't at work. But there was an explosion.'

Her gaze drilled into his, the golden flecks in the hazel suddenly more apparent. 'An explosion? Then why on earth aren't you looking at this as a homicide?'

'Because nobody else was involved in the explosion. Just Peter and Tyler Montgomery.'

She blinked rapidly for a moment, her mouth working. 'Tyler Montgomery? Was he killed as well?'

'Yes.'

'But…' She blinked again—it was like she was computing something, seeing things with that remarkable brain of hers that nobody else could see. It could speed through information in a way that was virtually inhuman, but it had also caused more problems than it helped. Particularly in this town, where nobody was prepared to be called to account by a rambunctious youngster who made everyone around her feel stupid. So he shouldn't have been surprised when she said, 'Are you saying that Peter was involved in a gang?'

He looked for a way to stall. 'How did you come up with that conclusion?'

'I may have been gone for sixteen years, but some things around here don't change. Tyler's family has always been involved in the shadier side of things. Mabel hated that Peter was friends with him when we were at school, but she could never make him drop Tyler. Peter always said, "He isn't his father", and Mabel would say, "The apple never falls far from the tree", and Peter would say, "But that doesn't mean that apple is rotten at the core".' She smiled softly, her eyes losing that piercing clarity.

'Peter was more open minded than most.'

Her gaze came back to him, lips curled in a small, sad smile, and he thought she was going to say more, but all she said was, 'Yes.'

Then, as her gaze stayed on his, the mistiness cleared and he was being assessed again with that intelligence that had once been everything in the world to him. Nobody looked at a person like Erika Hanson. He missed it. He cleared his throat, unnerved by the thought. 'Tyler was involved in his family business.'

'Drugs.'

'Yes. We think they were starting up a new meth lab and because of Peter's chemistry background, Tyler roped him in.'

Her frown deepened. 'Peter is an accountant now. He said he'd never do any chemistry ever again when he came back here.'

It seemed she was just as mystified as everyone in town had been when Peter gave up his PhD in biochemical engineering to come back and become an accountant. The mystery had deepened when it got out that he'd been offered a contract at one of the most respected infenctious diseases labs in Australasia. But because of the middle-of-the-night phone complaints and call-outs to disturbances around town, he and a few of the other police officers knew exactly why Peter had come back home.

He'd come back to look after their grandmother, Mabel Hanson.

Why hadn't he told Erika about it though?

Sympathy stirred in his gut. No. He didn't want to soften toward this woman. Not after she'd left here so abruptly, leaving him with a broken heart and in so much trouble he'd been grounded for a year. He'd vowed to forget her and he had mostly managed until—

'Why would Peter have got involved in a meth lab?'

Her question made him start out of his reverie. He jumped, knocking the manila folder off the table, the contents spilling out onto the floor. The chair legs squealed noisily as he pushed it back and bent to pick up the papers that had spilled out of the file. Words jumped off the page as he fumbled them back into the folder—coroner, forensic pathologist, Melbourne, medical degree—but he didn't really register any of them because Erika was pummelling him with questions in a way that was far too familiar and far too intuitive. Shit, her mind moved fast. His mind was reeling in the same way it had when they'd been children and she'd managed to both scare the crap out of him with how far beyond him she was, and make him want her all at the same time.

It seemed nothing had changed despite all his vows to the contrary.

He dropped the folder on the table and put his hands up. 'Whoa. Just hold up there. Mere mortals like me need time to process information, so just slow down.'

Her lips twisted, but not in a smile. No, her expression was far more complicated than that, just like the rest of her. 'Sorry. I'm upset.'

'I know.'

'And confused.' Which explained a lot. Erika never liked being confused about anything. Especially when emotions were involved.

'That's to be expected,' he said softly.

Her lips pressed together. 'Is it? I wouldn't know. I've never had a brother die before.'

He almost wanted to laugh at that, but this wasn't funny. 'You lost your parents.' He was one of the only people who could mention that, because he'd lost his mum around the same time. It's what they'd bonded over, that shared loss. 'This must be similar.'

'No.' She moved her head in a way that made him think of a curious puppy. 'I was there. I saw them die. It was senseless, but there was a reason. This…' She waved her hand. 'Peter being dead. There's too many questions. Too many confusing parts of the story. All the bits don't add up.'

'Sometimes life is like that, Erika. It's not a puzzle that can always be solved.'

'But you're a policeman.'

Now it was his turn to frown in puzzlement. 'What does that have to do with any of this?'

'It's your job to solve the puzzles, to bring order out of chaos. So why aren't you wanting to solve this?'

He lifted his hands off the table a little. 'Because there's nothing to solve, Erika. Peter was cooking meth with Tyler. You said yourself Peter had money problems. He probably thought this was a quick way to solve them. Help his friend make some drugs and pay off his debts in one go. Unfortunately, something went wrong with his chemistry and he blew Tyler and himself up.'

The cuffs rattled as she lifted her hands a little, pointing at him. 'Peter wouldn't have made a chemistry mistake.'

Before he could comment on that there was a knock on the door. 'Yes?' he called out.

Constable Mayne walked in, Erika's backpack in her hand. 'I'm sorry, sir. But your fath…Sergeant Cooper has left the building and isn't responding to his radio. He has the keys to the cuffs on him and Constable Fields hasn't been able to find any of the spare keys.'

'That's because the sergeant probably has them with him,' Erika said matter-of-factly.

'Why would he do that?' the constable asked.

'Payback.'

Chapter Three

Hartley growled. Erika was right. He loved his father, but he could be a stubborn old bastard when he chose to be. Obviously the file he'd brought in with him and failed to look at had proved her story true, but his father didn't want to let her go so quickly. This was his way of teaching Erika Hanson a lesson and paying her back in some small way for what she'd done to Hartley when she'd left all those years ago. They had no reason to keep her here.

He growled. If his father was here, he'd strangle him. 'Constable, call the sergeant again and tell him to get his arse back here. We have no reason to keep Ms Hanson a moment longer. If he doesn't answer the radio, tell him that I'm sure he won't like the paperwork he'll have to fill out and file if Ms Hanson decides to sue us for wrongful imprisonment.'

'But if he doesn't answer the radio, how can I tell him that?'

'Because, if I know the sergeant,' and he did, 'he will be sitting beside his radio waiting for a call-out. He'll hear.'

'Okay, sir.' She turned to leave, but hesitated, turned back. 'Wouldn't it be simpler to let Ms Hanson out of the cuffs?'

'Obviously it would, Constable, except we don't have the keys.'

She cleared her throat, her face going a little pink, her gaze meeting his shoes. 'I might be able to undo them.'

'Constable? Do you have a set of keys?'

Her gaze flew back up to his. 'No sir. I would never copy a set of handcuff keys. It's against regulations.'

'Yes, it is.'

'But…' a little pause as she cleared her throat. She reached up and took a pin out of her tight bun. 'I could use this to undo the cuffs.'

'You know how to undo the cuffs with a hairpin?'

The pink in her cheeks deepened to sunset red, but this time she met his surprised gaze. 'Yes. My ex taught me.'

'TMI, Constable,' he said, hands raising.

'Sorry, sir. But you did ask.' Her cheeks now flamed so brightly she could heat the room.

'Yes, I did. More fool me.' He stepped back, waving toward Erika and the cuffs. 'Let's see this unexpected skill of yours.'

Constable Mayne stepped briskly across the room, back ramrod straight, her air one of crisp professionalism. She dropped the backpack on the floor next to Erika and inserted the pin into the cuff, her brow set into a line of concentration, tongue poking out a little between her lips as she jiggled it. There was a click and one cuff slid open. She did the same with the other until there was another click and Erika was free. 'There,' she said, stepping back as she jabbed the pin back into her still slick bun, an air of supreme satisfaction surrounding her. Hartley couldn't help but smile. She was still so green, not long out of the academy and an absolute stickler for the rules, more so than he'd ever been. Possibly had to do with her family background and wanting to prove something. Despite all that, she'd just opened a set of handcuffs with a hairpin, a dubious trick probably learned from her ex, Hayden Terrence, and despite the embarrassment of the situation—he tried not to think about all the reasons there could possibly be for Hayden to have taught her that trick—he could see she was proud of herself. Erika wasn't the only one good at surprising people.

'Thank you,' Erika said, giving the constable a brief smile while rubbing her wrists. 'I must remember that trick.'

And she bloody well would too, Hartley thought. Although, why she'd have to know how to get herself out of handcuffs again was beyond his ability to imagine. At least, he hoped it was beyond his ability. Maybe she had a boyfriend like the constable's ex. An icy sensation prickled down his spine at the thought, but he shoved it away. What she did in her private life was none of his business. 'Thank you, Constable. That will be all.'

'Yes sir.'

Mayne nodded and left the room.

There was an uncomfortable silence as they stared at each other. She was the first to break the moment when she grabbed her backpack, rifling through it quickly to pull out some wipes and using one on her face. Once done, she folded the wipe up into a neat square, put it in a plastic bag and placed everything back in her pack. Then she stood, straight as a pin, and met his gaze. 'If you could show me the case file on my brother's alleged death, then I can help you work out what happened.'

'Why would you do that?'

'I have a degree in forensic pathology, with PhD in forensic anthropology and a secondary degree in forensic science. I work with the coronial office in Melbourne as well as the police, so this is what I do. I can help.'

Words his eyes had skimmed over when he'd knocked the file to the floor came back to him now.

Well. Hell.

A wash of pride filled him at what she'd accomplished. Which was stupid. She'd turned her life around and it had nothing to do with him. And yet, he couldn't stop his lips from spreading into a stupid grin. He shouldn't have been so surprised that she'd surprised him. She had always surprised him. It was one of the things that had always been so addictive about friendship with her—she was constantly knocking his feet from under him in one way or another.

'What are you staring at?'

'Nothing.'

'Okay.' Erika picked her backpack up, slung it over her shoulder and stared at him. He stared blankly back.

'The file?'

'You know I can't give that to you.' Hartley picked the folder up off the table and gestured to the door. 'You're free to go.'

'Cooperman.'

He froze, registering the plea, the need, the pain and grief all wrapped up into that softly uttered word. Everything but sorry. He should know never to expect sorry from her, and yet disappointment jabbed at his heart. 'Don't call me that.'

'You called me Miss Chief.'

'That was mistake. It won't happen again.'

'What can I call you?'

'Detective Senior Constable Cooper is fine.'

'That's a bit of a mouthful. How about Harts?'

The muscles in his face twitched. Nobody except his mother had ever called him Harts, and after she died he never wanted anyone to call him by that name. Everyone, including his father, called him Coops, but then Erika had come along and refused to call him anything but Harts. Or Cooperman.

For some reason, he'd liked hearing both names on her lips. His heart clenched. 'Detective is fine.'

'Harts.'

He shook his head. But not in denial. It was that shake of 'why should I be so surprised you're still arguing with me' or the 'I give up' shake that had been a common part of their friendship. Erika would do what she would do and there was no arguing against it. He wasn't sure why he was even trying. 'Call me whatever you want.'

She nodded, smiled, an apologetic smile. Then, before he could compute what that apologetic smile might mean, she said, 'I want to see the crime-scene photos.'

'As I said, you know I can't show you those.'

'No, I don't know that. As I've told you, I work for the coroner and the police. This is my job.'

'In Melbourne.'

'Well, if you're going to make it into a cross-jurisdictional issue, then I can simply call my boss and ask him to call the NSW Police Commissioner—he owes my boss favours because of help I've given them, so I know he'll let me see the files. Of course, that will involve plenty of paperwork neither of us needs, so we could bypass all that and you just give me the files.'

'Blackmail, Erika? That's not like you.'

She frowned as if confused. 'No. I'm just stating the obvious.'

Of course she was.

She crossed her arms. 'So, for me to help, I'll need to see a copy of the report as well as a copy of the post-mortem report that's been done on Peter.'

'There hasn't been an autopsy done.'

She couldn't have looked more surprised if she'd tried. 'Why not? Oh, of course. The forensic pathologist probably only works office hours in this godforsaken town.'

'That's not the reason. There's no proof of foul play.'

'You have two bodies found in an explosion at a meth lab. That should be enough by any state law to ensure a post-mortem is done by the coronial office at least. You don't need to shield me from the report or photos. I've seen plenty of dead bodies before.'

'None of those were your brother's body.'

'Yes. But two of them were my parents'.'

'That was different.'

'I want to see the post-mortem report when it's done.'

'Then you're going to have to wait a while.' Her brows rose and he could see she was going to argue with him some more, so this time he raised his hand. 'Dr Metler has retired and we haven't been able to employ a new forensic pathologist—apparently there's a sparsity of them.'

'I know.' She sighed. 'Then what are you doing for post-mortems?'

'The bodies are going into cold storage until someone can come up from Sydney to do them.'

'But…doesn't that severely hinder you closing your case files?'

'This isn't the big city. We don't have many murders up here. Or even suspicious deaths.' Most sudden deaths were caused by vehicular accidents, but he wasn't about to mention that to her.

'So, you're admitting Peter's death could be murder.'

He blinked rapidly. 'No. I didn't say that. What I was trying to say is that given there is no true case here that suggests foul play…' She went to open her mouth, but he held up his hand again. 'Nobody in Sydney will be in a rush to get up here to do an autopsy on a case that virtually closes itself.'

Her mouth moved as if she was chewing the inside of her lip. 'Then put me to use while I'm here.'

'What?'

'I'll do the post-mortem on Peter and Tyler.'

'But…what? You can't do that. He's your brother.' And he wasn't a very pretty sight. She didn't need that to be her final memory of him.

Her chin lifted. 'Are you saying you don't think I can remain professional because of my relationship with the victim?'

'Yes. You'd have to be a robot not to be affected.'

She stiffened even more. 'I've been called worse.'

Shit. People had always accused her of being unfeeling because of her intelligence and the way she processed information and was a bit socially awkward, but he knew better and hadn't meant to bring up those bad memories with his careless words. 'Erika. I'm sorry…'

She shook her head. 'Let me do it.'

'You're not registered in New South Wales. I can't just let you do it.'

'Exemptions are made in justifiable circumstances. As you said, there is a sparsity of forensic pathologists, particularly ones with my excellent level of skill and range of degrees. My office has lent out my services to other states—including the New South Wales coroner and police. This would be no different, especially as you have nobody else. As I said, it would be a simple matter of making a call to my boss.'

'But he's your brother.' They wouldn't let her work on her brother.

'I don't see why that should matter. I know how Peter must look. I've done post-mortems on fire victims before. Believe me, my imagination is far worse than reality could ever be.'

'I'm not sure that's true in this case.'

Her gaze snapped to his. 'This isn't about what *you* think is true. It's about Peter. About discovering the facts of his death. That's more important to me than anything. Do you understand?'

Her gaze was piercing again and he knew she wasn't going to give up. Wasn't going to stop getting in his face about it as long as she was here. 'Fine. You can do your autopsy. But then, when you prove it was an accident, you have to go.'

'Done.' She held out her hand.

And fool that he was, he took it.

Chapter Four

Erika pulled her car up on the edge of the Echo Ridge Lookout. The spur of rock was the southern tip of the plateau that came to an abrupt stop in a crescent-shaped ridge that ran from the springs that gave Echo Springs its name, around the west of town and up to the north to peter out around Bulls' Run station. She'd always loved the view here, the empty spread of land before her that made her feel like she could be somewhere as distant as Mars. She'd never minded that sense of endless space and emptiness; it had always been kind of soothing.

Thankfully, nobody else was here. It was too early in the day for sightseers or for the teenagers who came at dusk to play tonsil-hockey with each other. She was alone, the way she preferred. Especially now. There was too much to think about and process. Too much anger to push down before she could show her face back in town again.

It seemed that when Hartley said 'done,' he hadn't quite meant it. He didn't have the authority to give her permission to do the post-mortem on her brother and Tyler—he had to ask his superintendent. He'd told her to go home and get settled in and he'd call her later.

The only problem was, she didn't have a home to go to. Hanson House was now owned by Mrs Patterson. Mabel was in Coolabah Nursing Home according to Hartley, so she couldn't go stay with her even if she wanted to. She supposed that left only one place—the Echo Springs Hotel. Daphne and Pip might be happy to see her. They'd helped her out all those years ago, numerous times. Had given her Jenny's details in Melbourne and money to get there. But she hadn't spoken to them for years. Would it be strange for her to drop in on them now? She simply wasn't sure. Peter would know, but he wasn't here to ask.

She sucked in a sob, fingers itching to start up the car again and keep driving right down the Mitchell, all the way to Sydney, and hop back on a plane to Melbourne. But she couldn't do that. Fighting the urge to flee helped shove aside the clawing squeeze of her grief for a blessed moment. Only a moment. 'Peter,' she whispered.

What the hell had been going on here? Could Peter have been involved with drugs?

No.

Impossible.

She couldn't believe it. Wouldn't believe it. He wouldn't have done something like that, especially given the rumours about the car accident that killed their parents being caused by her mother taking drugs. It had affected him more than her—she'd caught him crying about it when he was bullied at school and it had confused her a bit because they knew the rumours weren't true. But it had upset him that people thought so badly of their mother. So there was no way he'd get involved in drugs. None. No, it was more likely he'd been trying to talk Tyler out of doing something stupid and been in the wrong place at the wrong time. Yes, that was more in character. Her brother was good man. Caring. Empathetic. He liked people and people liked him. It was something they'd never had in common, but she'd always admired it in him. And been a little jealous of it, in a proud kind of way. He was a good brother, and a better person than she ever could be. He'd probably been trying to save his friend right up until the end.

Tears stung her eyes as grief rose up and dried her throat. She wanted to let the tears pour out of her, to sob until there was nothing left inside. But she couldn't. Not when she had to go back to town soon. She also couldn't take the chance it would lead to a panic attack, or worse, an emotional fugue that could lead to a dissociative episode. The panic attacks were difficult enough, but the fugues were worse and not something she wanted to live through again.

But it was so difficult, now she was alone, to hold back these overwhelming sensations. She wanted to wail at the sky, to rail at whatever force was responsible for this—a god or fate or just simple dumb bad luck. She had never associated in any way with the concept of faith or belief or karma. She'd never been able to understand her mother's faith in her Jewish heritage and religion, especially given she was a scientist, a doctor. She, and nobody else, shaped her life. And yet, right now, she wanted to blame someone. Something. Peter was dead and it made no sense.

She slammed her hand against the steering wheel and screamed out 'Fuck!' It felt good.

She slammed her hand against the steering wheel and swore again. Harder. Louder. Again. Again. She slammed both hands against the steering wheel, stamping her feet on the floor of the car and screamed out every swear word she could think of and some she made up. She slammed and stomped and screamed until her palms stung and her throat was dry and sore. Then she sat there, panting, the ache in her chest somewhat lessened, the need to cry a small prickle in her eyes, and stared out through the windshield of her car, over the valley below, at the wide expanse of craggy red and purple rock and sand and the pale greenish-grey of the scrub scattered across the landscape.

Dry. Endless. Echoing. Empty.

No. Not empty. Something scuttled out from the brush down below—a desert mouse with a lizard hot on its tail. 'Run. Run,' she whispered to the mouse, watching, fingers curled around the steering wheel. Breath caught in her throat as the lizard leapt, pounced—it was going to have its dinner—but then the little mouse dodged left and disappeared into the earth where the lizard was too big to follow.

Erika took in a shuddering breath. She didn't know why it was so important that the little mouse lived—it was the circle of life, hunter and prey—but it was. It made her feel like...feel like...like she wasn't the only one always on the run from the thing behind her.

A little burst of laughter exploded out of her. She was being ridiculous. She wasn't on the run. She never had been. Moving to Melbourne, living with Jenny, it had been the sensible thing to do and it had changed her life. She had a home and job she loved, had the respect and friendship of her colleagues. She wanted nothing more than to get back there and forget all this.

But she couldn't. She had to find out what had happened to Peter. Sitting around waiting for permission wasn't going to get that done.

She picked up her phone and made a call. Five minutes later, she hung up the phone, took a deep breath, then started up the car and backed out. Mentally wishing luck to the little mouse, she drove back up the Mitchell toward Echo Springs and the Echo Springs Hotel.

Twenty minutes later she turned down Main Street and then onto Echo Parade. And there it was. Sitting on the corner where it had always sat. It looked the same, maybe a little worn, as did many of these Federation-style buildings in many country towns. But it was familiar, with its red bricks and the lacework on the wraparound veranda, the tower on the far right corner a beacon for the thirsty and weary. She'd always thought the sandstone trim around the front windows and the doorway made them look like eyes and a mouth, smiling at her, and even now, as an adult, she couldn't help but feel they were welcoming her as she drove past and pulled up in the car park.

She hopped out, trying not to cough from the red dust kicked up by her car. It was dry out here. Dryer than she'd remembered. Heat wrapped around her as she grabbed her bag from the boot, despite the fact that it was still early in the day. She'd forgotten how hot it could be here.

As she began to walk toward the front door, nerves danced in her stomach, a fine film of perspiration prickling her skin. She tightened her grip on her bag and marched up the stone front steps and across the black-and-white chequered tiles of the veranda. One of the wood and stained-glass doors stood open, and she edged through it and into the cooler, darker depths within.

'Erika Julietta Hanson! What a delightful surprise. Come here and give me a hug.' She was enveloped in warm arms—a little more fleshy than she remembered—and the familiar homey smell of baking scones and the slight sour smell of beer.

'Daphne!' For some strange reason, she felt like crying again.

'Pip. Pip. Come and see who is here.'

She was released from the hug, but not from the gaze of the slightly rounded red-head—red-head?—who was vibrating with excitement beside her.

A grey-haired, slightly more crinkled version of the strapping man she remembered came out of the storeroom from behind the bar. 'What's all the excitement?' His suntanned face creased improbably further into a wide smile as his eyes lit on Erika. 'EJ! Are you a sight for these old eyes.' She was enveloped in another bearish hug, the smell of ginger and dust swirling around her making her eyes prick again and a lump wedge in her throat.

Before she could manage to speak around the lump, she was held back from him, his endless sky-blue eyes glowing in the dark of the bar as his gaze roamed over her. 'You turned out just the way I thought you would.'

'And how is that?'

'As pretty and smart as your mother.'

Damn it. She was going to cry. She blinked hard, pulling away from him. 'I don't know about that.'

'Well I do. I'm sure Daph agrees.' He gestured to his wife, who was standing there staring at her, eyes a little bit weepy, sniffling into the apron she'd gathered up and was holding to her nose.

She nodded, her inplausibly red hair bobbing around her still pretty face. 'Wait until Peter sees you. He'll…'

Pip made a gesture and Daphne's eyes widened and she said, 'oh.'

Erika's gaze skirted between the two of them. She knew news travelled fast in this town, but this was taking things to a new level. Peter's body had only been found late the night before and it wasn't even eight o'clock in the morning. 'You've heard already?'

'That Peter was missing? Mac's a policeman now. He told us he was going to register a missing person's report so he could start to investigate Peter's disappearance officially.'

'Missing?'

'Yes. Nobody has seen him for the last few days and all of his stuff is still here, so we know he didn't go away suddenly and forgot to tell us.' Daphne tipped her head on the side. 'Is that why you're here?'

'Nobody's seen him for a few days?' Oh god. They hadn't heard. 'Perhaps we should sit down.'

'Of course,' Pip said, gesturing to the booth behind them. 'What is it, luv?'

She didn't know how to say it. She never knew how to say it—which was why she was a forensic pathologist and not a doctor. So she just said it the only way she knew how. 'I've been at the police station this morning. They told me Peter is dead.'

Daphne gasped again, pressing the scrunched apron harder against her mouth, her eyes wider than before.

'Dead?' Pip's deep voice vibrated through the air. 'Are you sure, EJ?'

'Yes. There was a fire or an explosion.'

'That must have been what all the commotion was late last night.' He looked over at Daphne. 'There were sirens from all the services going west out along Main Street and toward the Mitchell.'

'Yes. I was told it was an explosion at a meth lab. Police, firefighters and ambulance would have been sent as a matter of course.'

'But it couldn't be Peter. He wouldn't be involved in that kind of thing. Not after those horrible, untrue rumours about your mum.'

She slapped her hand down on the table, making Daphne jump. 'That's just what I said. Hartley was certain, though. They found identification at the scene and his car was there.'

'Hartley Cooper?'

'Yes.'

'He's a good lad. And a good copper. Better than his dad, I reckon.' Daphne and Pip shared a look, the kind of look that always left Erika feeling like she was in the dark about something essential. 'If he says it was Peter, it must be.'

'Oh, Peter.' Tears welled up in Daphne's eyes and Pip encased her hand in his, squeezing and stroking.

'There, there, Daphne, luv.'

Her gaze flew to Erika's. 'How did it happen?' She slapped her hand to her mouth. 'I'm sorry. I shouldn't have asked. You must still be in grief and shock yourself.'

Erika pressed her lips together to stop the squeezing ache in her chest and the prickling in her eyes. It didn't help. She could feel the emotions rising. She bit the inside of her lips, tasting the copper sting of blood, the pain bringing a moment of control with it, making her able to nod. In her mind, she began to create the mountain field, breathing in and out slowly, certainly. She had to hold it in. Hold it together.

'You poor thing,' Daphne said, patting her hand. 'Does your grandma know yet?'

Erika shook her head. 'Harts said she was at Coolabah Nursing Home. Is that true?'

'Peter never told you?' Pip asked.

'I told you so,' Daphne whispered in an aside that Erika couldn't help but hear. 'That boy was keeping secrets.'

'Shush, Daph. Erika doesn't need to hear about that right now.'

Erika managed a smile. 'It's okay. I've kind of figured out he was keeping things from me.' She squared her shoulders. 'I don't want to see her, anyway. Someone else can tell her.'

Daphne's grip on her hand tightened. 'We'll take care of it.'

'I find it hard to believe she's in a nursing home. How did Peter get her to agree to go there?'

'She didn't have a choice. Peter tried to look after her himself, but it just wasn't possible. Besides, he needed to sell the house to pay for her treatments.'

'Treatments? What do you mean?' They shot looks at each other again and she could tell they didn't want to tell her what was obviously more bad news. 'Please, tell me.'

Pip nodded slowly, took a deep breath, and put his hands on the table, palm up, met her gaze. 'Your grandma started to behave strangely about ten years or so back, but it wasn't until about six years ago things got worse. Got herself into some trouble financially and with the law. That's when Peter came home to help, and things seemed okay for a few years, but then she started to have fainting spells and fits. Peter didn't tell you any of this?'

She shook her head, numbly.

'No. Well. Anyway, Peter took her off to the doctor and she had lots of tests and was sent down to Sydney to see a specialist. When they came back, Peter sold the house and put her in the nursing home.' Daphne sighed sadly. 'She has an inoperable brain tumour. It's slowly eating up her brain, giving her a kind of dementia, changing her personality. She'd actually gambled away all her money.'

'Oh my god,' Erika said.

'He had to sell everything to cover her debts and to pay for a room at Coolabah, because he really didn't want her at the public hospital in the palliative care wing.'

'She's dying?'

'Well, she's hanging on. He's paid for all sorts of treatments that have kept the thing from killing her outright, and he's spent all his free time looking into new treatments, here and overseas. He recently found out about some trial in the US that could help, but he needed one hundred grand to pay for the airfares and hospital stay. He was desperate to get her over there, but he wouldn't take money from us. Just like Mabel—too proud. He went to the bank, but he already had a business loan and no collateral, so they said no.'

'That's why he asked me for money. Why didn't he tell me? Why didn't he come to me first?'

'Maybe he thought you wouldn't give it to him if you knew who it was for.'

Horrified realisation prickled over her. 'I thought he was pulling my leg. I had no idea about any of it.' Maybe he had got involved with creating meth to pay for the experimental treatment. He would do anything for Mabel.

'Poor Peter. He was such a good lad. How did this happen?'

Erika stared at Daphne for a long moment, feeling Pip's steady gaze on her. She straightened her back, shoving away the betraying thoughts. Peter wasn't making money from meth. Not even for Mabel. 'I don't know why he was there, but it wasn't for the money. Otherwise, why would he ask me for it?'

Pip shrugged. 'Perhaps Mac or Coops can help you with this, EJ. You should go and speak to them.'

'Detective Senior Constable Hartley Cooper doesn't think there's a crime here worthy of his time and effort.'

'I'm sure that's not true,' Daphne began. 'And even if he did, Mac wouldn't feel the same. He knew we loved that boy. He'd want to know what happened. He'd...'

Pip put his hand over Daphne's, stopping her. 'Mac isn't a detective yet, Daphne. It's not up to him whether to investigate or not. That will come down to Katherine. If there's no proof of any wrongdoing—'

Erika raised her hand, stopping Pip's words in their tracks and making the older couple look at her, their eyes widening in surprise. Fierce. That's how she felt. And avenging. Peter might be dead, but he wasn't going to be remembered as a foolish man who got in over his head with drugs and was killed in a stupid accident. Not if that wasn't the truth. And she was certain the truth was something else entirely.

'EJ—are you okay?'

She nodded, let her hand sink back down to the table with a faint slap. Then, turning to stare out the window that overlooked Echo Parade, she said, 'They might not think there's proof right now, but if there is, I'm bloody well going to find it.'

Chapter Five

'I'm sorry Coops, but despite her obvious credentials,' Superintendent Katherine Stuart tapped the open folder in front of her, 'I can't allow Erika Hanson to do an autopsy on her brother or Mr Montgomery.'

'But Boss, it's her brother...'

'Even more reason why this is totally inappropriate.' She raised a brow and gave him that look that somehow managed to be both authoritative and empathetic at the same time. She folded her hands in front of her on her desk and the empathetic look deepened. 'I understand that she would want to have some answers as to why and how her brother died, and she wants them sooner rather than later, but how on earth could she possibly be an impartial examiner with her brother's burned body lying there on the slab?'

'You don't know Erika Hanson.'

She frowned a little. 'Yes, I have heard from Sergeant Cooper already how much of an ... unusual personality she was and just how much trouble she used to get both herself and you into because of it.'

Hartley's mouth dried a little. 'It isn't as bad as the Sarge makes it out to be.'

'No, maybe not.'

'And most of the reason she used to get into trouble was because she was smarter than anyone else in the town by more than a country mile and that made her see things in a different way.' He had no idea why he had this sudden need to defend her against anything his dad might have said to the Boss. 'She certainly never responded to things in the ways others expected her to, and it caused a lot of misunderstandings and resentments, most of which weren't really her fault.'

'I don't see what relevance any of that has to the discussion.'

'I'm telling you because her intelligence and the way she looks at the world means she is actually quite capable of doing an autopsy on her brother and remaining completely impartial. It's strange, but it's the way she's wired. You'd understand if you met her.'

Katharine stared off into the distance, her dark brows slightly crinkled in that way that told him she was seriously considering his words, but then she shook her head and sighed. 'I know it's not what you wanted to hear and I wish I could give you another answer, particularly as it would speed up this investigation and allow us to close this unfortunate case, but it's just not possible. Even if I believed she could remain impartial, there's jurisdictional issues at play here, not to mention the whole politics of the situation. We cannot allow someone who is not employed by the New South Wales State Coroner's Office to do an autopsy on one of our cases. If there is any suggestion of foul play in this case, the defence could have a field day with the provenance of the evidence collected.'

'She says her boss would be willing to loan her out to the New South Wales Coroner's Office, that they've done so before. She could come on as a temporary replacement to Metler.'

'Detective, I do not want the New South Wales coroner being bothered with what will seem to him an insignificant case. Besides, I'm quite certain he will have the same reservations as me in regards to her ability to remain impartial, so it's not as guaranteed as your friend seems to think.'

'But Boss—'

She held up her hand. 'I have given my reasons why this can't happen and that is final. The autopsy can wait until a New South Wales-registered forensic pathologist is available to come up here and do the job.'

Katherine's jaw squared in the way that meant she wasn't about to change her mind. 'But if you don't allow Erika to do this, Boss, I know she's going to make my life a living hell.' Oh god, had he just said that? He sounded like a whiney arse.

'Then that is your issue to deal with, isn't it, Detective Senior Constable. It is hardly the role of this department to ensure Erika Hanson doesn't give you hell. Which right now, I'm quite sure you somehow deserve. Now, if that is all, I think you need to let Ms Hanson know of my decision and then you need to move on to the other cases that require your attention.'

Hartley shoved his hands behind his back. 'Yes, Boss.' He nodded curtly, turned and walked out, managing to close the door behind him without slamming it.

Katherine never liked her staff to exhibit what she called 'male posturing gestures'. If you wanted to stay on her good side—and he did, she was one of the best superintendents he'd ever worked under—you made bloody sure to keep that kind of shit out of the workplace. Gender politics aside, he actually thought it made the station a better place to work. He didn't particularly like the kind of workplace his dad often reminisced about and where he himself had worked in the city before getting the position here.

'No luck?'

He looked up to see Senior Constable Mac Hudson, leaning against his desk, arms crossed over his chest. Hartley twisted his mouth. 'Nope. It was a long shot anyway.'

'And yet you still asked.' Mac made a whistling noise. 'Well, well. I didn't think it was possible.'

'What?' Hartley asked, slumping down into his chair and staring morosely at the pile of paperwork on his desk.

'That you were still holding a candle for Erika Hanson. I thought that ship had sailed sixteen years ago when she skipped out of town, leaving you holding your sausages.'

'Eh-hem.' Hartley looked up to see Constable Mayne standing in the doorway. Her face was alight with suppressed laughter, lips twitching.

'Constable?' Mac asked. 'Can we help you?'

'I'm sorry to interrupt your serious discussion of...sausages.' Her gaze dipped down and then shot back up. A flush of red highlighted her cheeks as she cleared her throat. 'You asked me to bring you this as soon as it came in, Senior Constable.'

Mac ignored the package she was holding out toward him, his lips twitching. 'Constable, I'm shocked. Did your mind wander into the gutter just then?'

'No.' Her lips stopped twitching, her back ramrod straight.

Hartley stood abruptly. He was in no mood to let Mac have a little laugh at the constable. He took the package from her hand, and smiling, said, 'Mac was actually referring to the package of sausages from the butcher that Erika and I took from an order meant for Mrs Patterson. Erika wanted to give it to the wild dogs outside of town. She said they were starving and Mrs Patterson obviously wasn't.'

The constable made a sound that was like a choked laugh crossed with a snort. 'I think I like the sound of your Erika Hanson.'

'She's not my Erika Hanson.'

'Are you sure?' Mac drawled.

Hartley shoved the package at him. 'I think both Mayne and I have had enough of your particular brand of smartarsery today, Senior Constable. Don't you have something better to do than stand around making fun of your betters?'

'Perhaps I would if they were actually my betters.'

Leila made another choking sound.

Mac frowned at her. 'Aren't you supposed to be out on patrol, Constable?'

She snapped straight, all amusement leaving her face. 'Yes, Senior Constable,' she said as she marched from the room.

Hartley sighed as she disappeared around the corner. 'Give Mayne a break, Mac. She's not her dad.'

'Maybe not, but that doesn't mean I'm going to automatically trust her, given her history. Especially with that chip she's got on her shoulder.'

'She's got that chip because she thinks she's got something to prove.' Hartley raked his hand through his hair. 'It's hard enough being a country cop in your hometown without extra baggage.'

'You've got that right.'

'So just give her a break.'

Mac shrugged then shrugged again as Hartley kept looking at him. 'What?'

'Nothing. Just wondering what stick's crawled up your arse today—it's not like you to torment the newbies.'

'It stops me from punching a hole through the wall.' Mac's smartarse smile melted away to be replaced by anger and grief. 'I can't believe Pete's dead.'

'I didn't realise you were friends.'

'We were—kind of. Well, as much as anyone could be with a Hanson— we played a bit as kids because our parents were friends. That stopped after they died. But when he came back to town to look after Mabel, we played cricket and footy together. And he was often there for family dinners at the hotel when he moved in.' He scrubbed his hand over his mouth. 'Mum's going to be devastated. Especially given it looks like he was involved in drugs. How the hell am I going to tell her?' He shoved away from the desk, began to pace. 'How could he? How could he do that to them? They took him in. How could he bring that shit near them?'

'Erika doesn't think he had anything to do with the drugs. Do you think he could have?'

Mac stopped pacing and ran his hand through his hair. 'I don't know. I thought he was so straightlaced. I mean, the man barely even had a beer with the boys after a game. He'd usually just drink coke or one of those energy drinks before going home early to get a good night's sleep. And after all the rumours about his mum and the way it used to upset him … It just seems so improbable that he could be into making drugs.'

'People do all sorts of things when loved ones are on the line. Mabel was sick and he needed the money. I mean, what would you do for your loved ones?'

'Not that.' He shook his head. 'Pete should have known better.'

'Maybe he did.'

'You think Erika is right?'

Hartley pushed away from the desk he'd been leaning on. 'Maybe. We won't know anything until that autopsy is done and Toby gets back to us with the report on the fire and explosion.'

'So what's next?'

Hartley grabbed the file from his desk. It was still too empty for his liking. 'I need to make up a new case board with what we've got so far, then I need to find out who owns those warehouses and chat to the owners.'

'Putting off talking to EJ, eh?'

He shot Mac an 'eat shit' grin. 'Maybe.'

Mac chuckled. 'I can do the calls.'

'No, Ben's supposed to be working this case with me, I'll get him to make the calls.'

'Strawberry's not here. He headed back out to the meth lab to have another look around after the firies were done with their investigation—didn't want to miss anything.'

Hartley smiled. Ben Fields's surprise return to Echo Springs had turned into a good thing for them—he was a good copper. 'I'll radio him and let him know I'm heading out a bit later.' He headed toward the locked door that led into the detectives' case room. Mac followed him but hung at the door as Hartley began to pin what he had up on the blank board at the far end of the room. As he stuck a photo of the warehouses up, he heard Mac walk up behind him and turned to see him staring at the photo of the warehouses. 'What is it? Do you see something?'

'No, it's not that. It's just, those warehouses are pretty run down and filthy and Pete had a bit of cleanliness thing going on. You know he used to wash his hands all the time? It's hard to believe he'd choose to go out there and set up a drug lab.' He scratched his jaw. 'It's probably nothing.'

Hartley wrote it down on the board next to the picture. 'It's worth not-ing. Anything to help us with the wider picture.' He stuck the last bit of paper from the file on the board and stepped back to have a look.

'There's not much here,' Mac said. 'Pity about the Boss not letting EJ do the autopsy. There could be some critical evidence there.'

Hartley turned in surprise. 'You think she should be allowed to do it?'

Mac shrugged. 'She's the only forensic pathologist around. Besides, it's EJ. You know she was always a little … strange. All those rumours about her mum's death and she never batted an eye. Not like Peter.'

'There were reasons for that.'

'Maybe. But I was younger than you guys and I noticed it.' Mac raised his hands. 'Look, all I'm saying is that if anyone could do it, she could. Besides, it's not like we don't need help with this.'

'You're not wrong there. But it's all useless talk anyway, because the Boss said no.'

Mac folded his arms. 'So when are you planning to tell EJ the bad news?'

Hartley winced. 'Now's as good a time as any, I suppose. Then I need to go talk to Grim.'

'He won't have had a chance to do any analysis yet, will he?'

'Probably not. But he does have a feel for fires. It's in his blood. He might have something to add to what Erika thinks.' He clenched his fingers at his side. 'Maybe enough to change the Boss's mind.'

'Hey, Mac. Call-out for you.' Siobhan Graham, their dispatch, stuck her head around the door. 'Disturbance at the Taylor property. The Boss wants you to take Constable Mayne with you.'

Mac's brow rose. 'I'm on my way.' He picked up his hat. 'I'll walk you out.' As they got to the Patrols, Mac said, 'Good luck with EJ.'

'Yeah. I'm going to need it.' He hopped into the Nissan Patrol and started it up. There was only one place Erika would go now her family house was sold—the Echo Springs Hotel. Pip and Daphne, Mac's parents, had always had a soft spot for her. They were probably the only friends she had here—she'd specialised in alienating people in the years before she ran away. It was only a block and half behind the police station, but he got in his four-wheel drive and drove there. He might need a quick getaway. Not to mention, he had to go to the fire station afterwards and then had some people to talk to.

Erika was sitting in a booth having a cup of tea with Pip and Daphne. Pip had his arm around Daphne's shoulders and Daphne's hand was stretched across the table, patting Erika's hand as it clenched a serviette. Mac didn't have to worry about telling his parents about Peter—Erika had obviously already done it. He wondered if they'd filled her in on Peter and his situation with Mabel. He hoped not. A person could only take so much bad news in one sitting.

He gritted his teeth. He'd read the report on her, and an hour ago he'd talked to a homicide detective mate in Melbourne. Clearly, Erika was brilliant at what she did. A bunch of cases would have gone unsolved if not for her keen observations and the thoroughness of her autopsies. She saw things others didn't. If anyone could find out what happened to Peter and Tyler, it was her. Mac was right about that.

Except he wasn't here to give her the go-ahead but to tell her she couldn't do it. This day had started out shit and it was just getting worse. Sighing, he walked toward the intense trio.

Daphne saw him first. 'Hartley. How lovely to see you. Is there something wrong at the Cooee?'

Erika turned in her seat, her hazel eyes arrowing in on him with uncanny clarity even in the dimmed lighting of the bar.

'I expect he's here to see Erika about Peter,' Pip said. 'Horrible thing that.'

'Have you found out something more about poor Peter?' Daphne dabbed at her eyes.

He shook his head. 'No. This has to do with something else.'

'What trouble have you got yourself into this time, EJ?' Pip said, trying for joviality. It fell flat.

'Nothing that wasn't a misunderstanding. As usual,' Erika answered. 'Is Mrs Patterson still wanting to press charges?'

'No. It's about the autopsy.'

'Autopsy? What autopsy?' Pip asked.

'I asked to be allowed to do the post-mortem on Peter and Tyler.' Erika laid her hands flat on the table and met Daphne's horrified stare. 'If we wait for someone to come up from Sydney, any evidence found that proves he wasn't at fault will probably lead to cold trails and it could take even longer to track down the people truly responsible. Besides, I'm one of the best at what I do.' Her voice caught a little and she took a quick breath, chin rising. 'I do this for other people, so it's only right I do the same for my brother.'

The older woman looked at Hartley, stricken. He didn't know what to say to her. He understood why Erika wanted to do it, even though it made no sense to anyone else.

Pip patted his wife's shoulder. 'Erika knows what she's about, Daphne.'

'I'm not sure she does right now.' Tears spilled down her face. 'You have to tell her she can't do it, Coops. It's not right. It's not right.'

'I have to do the post-mortem on my brother. I can't leave him to someone else. You can't expect me to.' Erika slid out of the booth and stared down at them, expression harsh. 'Thank you for the tea. And the information about Peter and Mabel. I'm just going to talk to Detective Constable Cooper now. In private. In my room.' She brushed past Hartley and disappeared through the door that led to the stairs to the accommodation.

Pip and Daphne seemed rooted to the vinyl cushions of the booth, their eyes fixed on the door Erika had just exited through.

'Well, I better go talk to Erika,' he said, turning to go, feeling their gazes like arrows in his back.

'You're not going to let her do that autopsy, are you?' Pip's voice stopped him as he got to the door.

Sighing, he turned back to face them—he should have made a faster getaway. 'If it were up to me, I would, but the Boss said no.'

Pip nodded slowly. 'Sensible woman that.'

Daphne's expression brightened. 'Oh, thank goodness. I couldn't imagine anything more horrible.'

'I don't think Erika can imagine anything more horrible than having to wait for answers someone else has to give her.'

Pip's mouth twitched. 'She always did like to be in control.'

'I don't think that has changed at all.'

'No. Poor kid.' Pip stood and walked over to him stiffly. 'I gave her the key to room 102 earlier. Go and let her down kindly, Coops. It's the least she deserves.'

'Yes. Of course.'

He ascended the stairs, dread a hard lump in his chest. It was his job to make sure she saw reason. But how on earth was he to do that now when he'd never been able to before?

Chapter Six

He didn't knock. She should have known he wouldn't. The door opened
behind her and she turned and he was there.

Just as when he'd walked into the interview room, her body did that
funny thing, jolting as if she'd received a shock. It made her want to run.
From him, from the way he made her feel. Peter was dead. She shouldn't be
thinking of anything else. She needed to ignore the urge to smile at Hartley
Cooper as he walked into the room with that sexy, contained stride of his.
The need to reach out and touch him, to have him touch her with those long
piano-player fingers, to make him smile at her, not just with the sideways
curl of his mouth, but that glow that entered his eyes denoting something
more than true happiness… No.

Rational. Controlled. That was who she was. It was what everyone
always saw. It made her exceptional at her job. It was that and nothing else
that would help her find out what had happened to her brother. She needed
to focus on what was known, safe. Hartley was no longer either of those
things.

She folded her arms and didn't return his smile. 'Well?'

Hartley rubbed his hand across his jaw and turned to close the door and
she knew.

'She said no, didn't she?'

His shoulders stiffened before he turned to face her, his gaze…troubled?
Wary? Pained? She wasn't sure. 'It's the politics and protocol of the thing,'
he began.

She waved her hand, stopping his words short. 'I understand.'

'You do?' His frown deepened and she could see he was trying to read her. She looked away, back out the window. He'd always read her a lot better than she'd been able to read him.

'I should have known your superintendent wouldn't allow it. I shouldn't have asked.'

'That seems very…rational of you.'

'I'm a rational person.' She could feel his gaze on her, but still didn't turn back to look at him. She was afraid fury would show in her eyes or spill from her lips. He always brought out the emotional side in her. She'd never liked it. So, staring fixedly out of the window, not registering anything beyond the brightness of the sun outside, she said, 'Your superintendent doesn't believe I can compartmentalise and do my job efficiently without compromising the investigation. Which, given she knows nothing about me and currently has no forensic pathologist to do the post-mortem, is stupidly short-sighted of her.'

He made a snorty-laugh kind of sound. 'Not so rational then.'

She knew he was smiling at her, wanted to turn to see it, but couldn't let herself. Couldn't let herself be touched by his smile, or the understanding in his eyes. If she saw, she'd start to cry and then he'd hold her, like he had every time Mabel had made her cry. And just like she had in the past, she'd hate it and him in that moment, only to feel embarrassed and regretful for feeling that way later. It wasn't rational, and she needed to be rational.

'Erika? I'm sorry.'

He was. She could hear it in his voice. He moved toward her. Tears prickled harder behind her eyes. No. No. She wasn't going to cry. She wasn't going to lean on him. This was a setback, that was all. It wouldn't stop her. However, she couldn't involve Harts. Despite the fact they'd once been Miss Chief and Cooperman, she wasn't certain he would help her—they'd both changed a lot—but even if he would, she couldn't be responsible for getting him in trouble. And there would be trouble over this. She was planning to do an unsanctioned post-mortem of not only her brother, but Tyler, post-mortems she would then report to Hartley's superintendent to force them to investigate her brother's death. It didn't matter that she'd already put in the call to her boss in Melbourne so what was currently unsanctioned wouldn't be for long, because she couldn't even wait for that go-ahead. Vital evidence could even now be eroding away due to the fire and chemicals that caused it. The fact she was going to be even more unpopular because she'd gone over Superintendent Stuart's head to force more than a coronial investigation was just par for the course—she was used to being unpopular in this town—but that was even more reason not to drag Harts into her mess.

She stared out the window until her vision starred and her eyes dried and then she blinked once, long and slow. 'Thank you for trying.' She released her rigidly curled fingers, unfolded her arms, and with a placid smile plastered to her lips, turned. 'You didn't have to, but I appreciate that you did.'

He stared at her and then his head tipped on the side. 'Erika.' The word was a drawled question and warning all rolled into one.

It shuddered up her back, but she stood rigid, not letting herself react. 'I also appreciate you coming to tell me in person. You could have just called. I know that would have been easier. You must be busy.'

'Erika.' He took a step forward. 'What are you up to?'

'Nothing.' She was pleased her voice sounded so innocent.

'Now, that's a lie if ever I heard one.' Another step closer.

'I have no idea what you're talking about.' She wanted to back up, but was already standing against the window.

He smiled, but it wasn't the smile she'd longed to see only minutes earlier. It was knowing and intelligent and calculating. 'You're going to do it anyway.' It wasn't even a question.

Her brows moved—she couldn't help it—and his smile widened. Anger flared inside her, anger at the fact that even after all these years, he could read her so easily. 'You don't know me anymore, Detective.'

Another step and he was standing only a hand's span away. So close, she could feel the warmth of him along her front. 'Oh, I think I know you well enough.'

'I've changed.'

'Maybe.' He tipped his head again, gaze assessing. 'But not that much.' He tapped his finger lightly against her forehead. 'Your brain is as lightning fast as it always was, which means one thing. You knew the Boss would say no and you knew what you'd do about it when that happened.'

'And what is that?' She crossed her arms again, fists clenched under her armpits, hating that he made her react so defensively.

'That you were going to do it anyway, no matter what anyone said.'

'You're wrong.'

'I don't think I am.'

She floundered, her brain curiously sluggish with him this close.

'Can't think of anything to say to refute me? That's not like you, Erika.'

His smugness was what did it. Before she could even think about respond-ing verbally, she shoved him, hands against his wide chest, pushing as hard as she could. She caught him by surprise, because, given his size and hers, there was no way she'd budge him if she hadn't. But he stumbled back a few steps, giving her the room to move, to escape his closeness and get to the door, swinging it open. 'I want you to leave.'

He simply crossed his arms over his chest. 'Make me.'

She gaped at him. 'That's...that's... a child's response.'

He chuckled again. 'You want rational? Then convince me I'm wrong. Convince me you are not going to turn around and do an illegal autopsy on your brother and Tyler and I will happily leave.'

'I...I...'

'I didn't think so. Which means I'm staying right here, by your side.'

'But...you can't do that.'

'I can and I will to save you from yourself.'

'I don't need to be saved from myself.'

'I think it's precisely what you need. It always was. If I'd been capable of understanding that sixteen years ago, things would have been a lot different.'

'Sixteen years ago, you were my friend.'

'Yes.'

'You wouldn't have been my friend? Is that what you're saying?'

He lurched abruptly forward, expression intense. 'Never. Your friendship was the best part of those years.'

'But I got you into trouble. Often.'

'If I hadn't wanted to do those things with you, Erika, nothing you could have said would have made me. You know me better than that.'

She clenched the door handle, not understanding why those words thrilled through her. 'I don't want to get you into trouble now.'

'I know.' He was there, in front of her, removing her hand from the door, closing it with a soft click. 'I don't want to get you into trouble either.'

'I won't. I've already made the call to my boss. I'll have permission in the next twenty-four hours.'

He swore under his breath. 'But you're not going to wait until then, are you?'

'I have to do the post-mortem now, Harts. I have to.' She blinked rapidly, hating the betraying tears that just wouldn't stop invading her eyes.

'I know.' He touched her cheek, his fingers scraping over her jaw and into her hair, tipping her face so that she was forced to meet his gaze. 'What kind of friend would I be if I let you get arrested for B and E again? You could lose your job.'

'I don't care. Peter deserves action now.'

His thumb stroked across her cheek and his gaze warmed, heating her to her core, chasing lightning around her body. 'I know.' His smile was indulgent, as if he saw softness inside her.

She sucked in a breath. 'I'm not being sentimental. It's the right thing to do.'

'So rational.' He smiled, circling his thumb, making something flutter and curl low in her stomach. He leaned forward, his breath against her ear. 'And yet, I can see your big heart.'

'No.'

'Yes.'

And then his lips were on hers and that big heart he saw quite literally stopped.

Chapter Seven

This was so stupid.

She had no idea how she'd agreed to this.

Yes she did. She'd agreed because of a kiss. A kiss that had turned her mind to mush and made her promise to let him help her, even though she didn't want to do anything of the sort.

And now here they were. He was going to get into trouble with her when she handed in her findings and they knew she'd done the post-mortem before she'd had permission.

She should tell him to go back. To leave her to it. It wasn't rational to let him hold her to her promise, and yet she couldn't open her mouth and say the words that should be said.

He opened the door and waved her into the hospital foyer. No need for any kind of breaking and entering, no slipping past guards and nurses or stealing of hospital doctor's coats or scrubs. He walked up to the desk, a charming, harmless, butter-wouldn't-melt-in-his-mouth, mummy's-little-angel-boy smile on his face. She'd seen him use that smile on people multiple times when they were children. Now though, as he aimed it at the brunette nurse on duty, the smile was enticing, sexy, reminding her of his kiss. Little shivers shook her, then turned into something less pleasant when the nurse—Nancy, her nametag said—blushed and fluttered her lashes.

'Hartley Cooper. I haven't seen you in a while.'

'Not since that party at Smithy's.'

'That was quite some night.'

'It was…fun.'

Nancy's eyelashes fluttered again as she looked up through them at him, a coy smile on her lips that made Erika's stomach clench.

'Have you got something in your eye?' The words spat out of her before she even knew she was going to say them.

'What?'

'You were fluttering your eyelashes at the detective. I was giving you the benefit of the doubt suggesting you had something in your eyes. I didn't think you could possibly be flirting with him here given it's a hospital and not a bar.' Her lips tightened into a smile that felt as strange as the words coming out of her mouth.

'What?' Nancy's blush turned deeper as she shot a look at Hartley. 'I'm not fluttering my eyes.'

'You're not now I pointed it out.' Oh god, someone needed to shut her up. She had no idea she could sound like that.

'Okay, that's enough,' Hartley said, grabbing Erika's arm. 'Erika's just lost her brother, so isn't thinking very rationally right now. In fact, we're just going down to the morgue so she can do an official ID. We might be a while.'

'I'm sorry for your loss.'

Erika didn't have a chance to respond as Hartley turned and marched along the hallway, hauling Erika along with him. After they turned the corner and were out of sight of Nancy, she shook off his grip. 'I don't need you to make excuses for me.'

'Maybe not, but you need something.'

'Like what?'

'Like a clue. We're here to do something we shouldn't be doing. Would it hurt you to be nice and sail under the radar for once rather than acting all jealous?'

'I'm not jealous.'

'Really? Then what was that about?' He pointed back the way they'd come.

She shrugged. 'I just want to get down to the morgue and start the autopsy, okay. I don't have time to stand around while you pursue your social life.'

'Pursue my social life?' He snorted. 'Now I know you're jealous.'

'You're being ridiculous. What would I have to be jealous of?'

'You tell me.'

She tightened her lips and kept walking to the lift, all too aware of the smirk on his face as he pushed the call button and waited for the lift to come.

He'd always been such a know-it-all when it came to reading others. Sometimes it had been good to have a friend who could interpret people and their emotions—she'd learned so much from him. Sometimes it just annoyed the crap out of her. 'You don't need to come with me.'

'Yes, I do.'

The lift dinged and the doors opened. 'I'd prefer that you didn't.'

'I'm sure you do, Erika, but you should know by now, you don't always get what you want.'

She wanted to growl at him. Instead, she stepped into the lift just as he did. His arm brushed hers as they turned to push the button to the basement at the same time. Her skin prickled and heat surged through her. He glanced up, gaze clashing with hers, the green of his eyes brilliant in the dim glow of the fluorescent lights overhead. There was a look there that made her feel like he was reading her mind; like he was touching her soul.

She swallowed hard and turned swiftly, almost stumbling over her own feet.

'Erika?' Hartley's warm fingers gripped her arm, her shoulder bumping into his chest as he held her steady. 'Are you sure you want to do this now?'

Her throat felt tight. She cleared it. 'I need to find out what happened to Peter. To find the truth of his death. I need to do it now. Then I can get out of your hair and go home.'

'Okay.' His grip lightened, fingers brushing up and down her arm, the expression in his eyes one of sympathy and something else she didn't understand. It couldn't be worry, because all she really was to him was a bad memory from the past and a pain in his arse right now.

But the kiss…

The kiss meant nothing. It happened because they were both emotional. Because he was trying to make her feel better or prove a point or…

Well, she didn't know exactly why he'd kissed her. None of the reasons she'd come up with quite made sense. Men didn't kiss women simply because they were emotional or had once been close friends. Usually it had more to do with desire and passion created by a mix of chemicals in the brain that made reason and intelligent thought non-existent while sexual release was attained. And that definitely wasn't the case here. She wasn't attracted to Hartley and he most definitely wasn't attracted to her and even if they were, what did that matter? When she was done here, she would go back to Melbourne, back to her job that was everything to her and he would stay here. It didn't matter what either of them felt about the other, because ultimately, they both had their places to be. He was a country boy at heart and she was... Well, she didn't really know what she was. She supposed she liked living in the city, except she missed the open spaces, the echoing emptiness of the barren plains that rolled on and on beyond the far horizon once she made it out of the stifling enclosure of this closed-minded town. She'd not realised how much she missed it until she was driving here. Didn't realise how much she missed the places where the echoes lived. She'd had to leave them just like she'd had to leave Harts and Peter all those years ago. She hadn't much liked the picture of herself that had been painted here. It had taken running away to make her realise she didn't have to fit herself to that picture. She could create an entirely different one. And she had. One that didn't belong here with Harts or with the echoes that had once been her friends.

So she would go back to where she'd made a place for herself and he could go back to his normal life before she careened into town and turned everything upside down like she always had. He could return to flirting with Nancy if he wished.

She sucked in a breath as pain stabbed in her chest.

His worried frown deepened. 'Erika, are you sure...'

'Why did you kiss me?'

'I...what?'

She liked that she could catch him off-guard. It was nice to not always be the one who didn't understand emotions or thought processes. But then again, perhaps he looked shocked because they were heading to the morgue, about to do an autopsy on Peter's body. She should be thinking only of that. So, why wasn't she? Made uncomfortable by the question, she waved her hand. 'Forget I asked.' The lift door opened. 'Let's get this done.'

'Erika.' His hand was on her arm again before she'd made it to the doors into the morgue—she wished he would stop touching her. It was making it difficult to keep her mind where it needed to be. 'It's only natural not to want to think about the death of a loved one, let alone doing an autopsy on them. It's no wonder you tried to distract yourself from all of this by kissing me.'

'You kissed me.'

'I...' He frowned, mercifully letting go of her arm and folding his arms across his chest. 'That's not how I remember it.'

'Then you're remembering it wrong.' She turned away, reaching out to push the green button to open the morgue doors.

'Erika. Do you really think I kissed you first?'

She froze, hand hovering over the button. She shouldn't look at him and yet she couldn't stop herself. 'Yes.'

'I remember you reaching up for me.'

'You reached for me first.'

'You opened your mouth to me.'

'The kiss surprised me.'

He brushed his hand through his hair, the look of puzzlement increasing. 'If you didn't want to kiss me, you could have just pushed back, said no.'

'So could you. You pulled me close.'

'You raked your hands through my hair.'

He was standing close again, gaze skipping down to her lips and back to her eyes. Her chest tightened. The hot prickling intensified. 'I'm not talking about this.'

'You brought it up.'

'I've got an autopsy to do.' She hit the green button and fled through the opening doors.

A cool wash of air moved over her and she sighed with relief at the familiar landscape of the morgue—the stainless steel tables, the instrument trays, the compartments where bodies were stored until they were cleared for burial. She'd worked in a number of different morgues during her training and then in her job, but every single one, whether a simple country hospital morgue with bare-minimum equipment or the flashier technology-studded installations in the city, had an essence at heart that was the same. Cold. Practical. Clinical. She felt right at home.

The door opened again behind her, but she ignored it. She didn't want to think about or talk to Hartley Cooper right now. All she wanted was to find her brother's body and examine it with the care and precision she was known for. Then, and only then, when she knew more about what had happened, would she be able to breathe.

She found the clipboard with the locker allocations—no computerised system for logging the bodies in place here, obviously—and found the cool-locker he was in. She expected Hartley to hover in the background—usually the cops she worked with preferred not to see the working end of the post-mortem, despite, or perhaps because of, the horrors they saw out in the field, but he was at her shoulder when she reached the locker door.

'Here, let me.'

He opened it and pulled out the tray. Her brother's body was in a bag; not precisely usual, but not unusual given the circumstances of his death and the fact that they didn't have a coroner or forensic pathologist here. There would have been nobody to prep the body.

She angled the trolley in place and said, 'Help me lift the tray onto the trolley?'

He unclipped the tray and helped her lift it down, then pushed it over to the autopsy bed. 'On three?'

She nodded and together they lifted the bag, lowering it gently onto the metal table.

She stared at the bag for a long moment, then steeling herself against what she'd see inside, said, 'We have to get this off him.' She reached for the zip on the bag.

Hartley's hand covered hers. 'Shall I?'

She looked up at him, brows raised. 'I can do it.'

'I just thought...' He shook his head, a strange smile on his lips, and then lifted his hand away. 'Of course you can.'

She knew how Peter had died, could smell the burned flesh even if she hadn't already known, but when she uncovered his head, she couldn't help reacting to the sight. There was nothing here that was recognisable and yet her mind framed his face over the twist of features, so that she saw him lying there, eyes staring up at her, accusing. Pleading. Blaming. Blaming her for running away, for not thinking about him, for not helping him the moment he'd asked without question. Pleading with her to find out who had done this to him. Oh god. Peter.

No. She took in a sharp breath, blinking rapidly. This was why she never wanted to see a photo of the victim before she went to work. Why she never wanted to know their names. It made it all so much harder when she could see their smiling face layered atop the death on her table. Peter might be dead, but he could still speak to her if she could make herself forget who he was and find the clues left behind. But it was so hard this time, harder than she'd imagined it could be.

'Are you okay, Erika?'

Hartley's voice came at her from far away, but she heard it, and it was enough to allow her to blink away the accusing image of her brother's face, to suck in a breath laced with the scents of disinfectant, burned flesh and metal. And something else? Under the other scents, pungent and recognisable. She leaned closer, sniffed. 'I smell kerosene.'

'You do?' His face was twisted in an expression of distaste—dead bodies, even refrigerated ones, had a certain smell and it upset most people.

'Yes. I'll have to take a sample to do a chemical trace, but I'm quite certain there is kerosene here.' She looked up at Hartley. 'Why would there be kerosene at a meth lab?'

'Perhaps they were using it somehow?'

'No. With all the combustibles, having kerosene there would have been foolish in the extreme.' She frowned down at her brother's body, still mostly shrouded in the body bag. 'This smells like it was poured on him.' She glanced up at Hartley who was looking at the body in surprise. 'Did the firefighter in charge of the investigation mention anything about what caused the explosion?'

'No. I think they're still looking over the site. I was planning on speaking to Grim later today.'

'Grim?'

'Toby Grimshaw. He's one of the professional firefighters based in Echo Springs. He takes care of most of the fire-related investigations here, although he has to send most things to the police forensics teams in Dubbo or Sydney given we don't have our own unit. He'll be the man to talk to about this.'

'We need to ask him if he's found any kerosene containers.'

'Okay.' He swallowed. 'So, are you done? Is that all you need?'

'I haven't even started.'

She directed him to put some gloves on and help remove the body bag. He paled, but helped despite how it affected him.

'You can go now if you're squeamish,' she said, folding the bag up neatly and putting it on the bed behind her to examine for any evidence later.

He swallowed hard, hands jutting out from his sides as if he was afraid of touching himself with them. 'I'm fine. I need to stay here to ensure the chain of evidence is correctly handled.'

'Of course. Given the fact this post-mortem is not yet officially sanctioned.'

'I'm glad you didn't think I was questioning your abilities.'

Her brows rose. 'Why would I? I'm excellent at what I do.'

'Of course you are.' His smile widened.

Her stomach fluttered a little. Ignoring it, she looked down at the body. 'The fire was hot. His clothing has melted into his skin.'

'Problem?'

'No. It does make it more difficult to find particulate evidence that would normally be found in the fibres. Clothing always picks up a remarkable amount of evidence.' She looked down at his feet. 'Where are his shoes?'

'Maybe he wasn't wearing any.'

She shook her head. 'No, the skin here is almost intact indicating he was wearing shoes, probably leather. Someone took them off when they brought him here. I'll need to see them. They could have evidence on them.'

Hartley turned around and spied two zip-locked bags on a far table. 'Maybe that's them.' He walked over. Peter and Tyler's names were printed on the outside of the bags. 'Yep, this is them by the looks of things. Tyler's are here too.'

'Okay, while I take samples of skin and clothing for chemical analysis, can you please don a fresh set of gloves, and very carefully remove the shoes from the bags and put them on separate tables so I can look at them later.'

'Sure.'

There was a sound in his voice that caught her attention. She glanced up at him—he was already donning new gloves. He still looked a little green, but his gaze was fixed firmly on her and he moved his lips in a tight smile and nodded, as if she'd asked him a question. She nodded back and then, bending over the body, picked up an instrument and went to work.

Chapter Eight

It didn't take long to take the samples she needed—from under fingernails, remaining hair, skin, blood and scrapings off the teeth. She did a visual check of the body and pulled samples of glass and metallic shards that were embedded in the soft tissue. 'It's difficult to tell with the extent of necrosis, but I think there is evidence here,' she pointed at the frontal bone of the skull, 'here,' to the ribs, 'and here' to the phalanges, 'of trauma.'

'What kind of trauma?'

'I will need to take an X-ray to see.'

'Can't you see that with your X-ray vision?'

She looked at him blankly. What?

'You said Miss Chief would have X-ray vision like any true super hero.'

She looked down at the body and then back up at him. 'I'm not a super hero.'

Hartley smiled and shook his head. 'You are still so literal.'

'That was a joke?' He nodded. 'It wasn't very funny. You need to work on your material.'

He barked out a laugh. His face lit up when he laughed like that. There was a glow in his eyes that made her want to laugh with him, except she didn't quite know what was funny. But then he looked guilty, his gaze returning to the body. 'Sorry. I shouldn't be laughing.'

'Grief can do strange things to people.'

A shadow clouded his eyes as he looked at her. 'Yes, it can.' He gestured at the body. 'Wouldn't that trauma have been caused by the explosion? When the bodies were thrown?'

'I don't think he was thrown.' She looked back down at her brother's body. She shook her head a little. No. She couldn't think of it that way when she was working on it. He was the victim. The body. That was all. 'There is explosive debris, but not the kind of breaks I would expect if they had been at the epicentre of the explosion.' She glanced up at him. 'I need to X-ray the body before I go any further. The X-ray could help make cause of death clearer.'

He helped lift the body across to the trolley and then pushed it to a door at the far right of the morgue that had 'X-ray' written over it. 'You know how to work it?' he asked when they were inside.

'Of course.' He had come around the trolley and was now standing close behind her. Too close. She jerked the trolley in place and slammed her foot down on the brake, then turned to set the machine. 'You can't stay here,' she said. 'I'll call you when I need you.' She waved him away. He went, but not before saluting her with a 'Yes ma'am.'

The door swung shut behind her and finally she was alone.

She put on the apron that was hanging on a hook and breathed out a sigh of relief. Except it came out as a little stuttering gasp. She pressed her hands to her eyes and took in another deep breath before turning back to the machine. She pressed a few buttons, heard the familiar hum behind her as it jerked to life, taking the slow progression of photos she'd need to finish her job.

Too quickly, the machine gave one final groaning click and fell silent. Usually she liked the silence of the morgue, but now she hated it. She wished for some sound to distract from the push-pull of emotions she couldn't allow out.

She closed her eyes, clenched her fingers tight into her hands, and pictured the mountain meadow, the scents, the warm breeze, the rolling green of the hills that spread out before her reaching out to touch the blue sky that was fading to purple and orange and red in the distance. Yes. That was better. She took a deep breath, let it out slowly and shook out her hands. Nerves still kicked under her skin when she opened her eyes, but they weren't pulling her in all directions like they had been a few minutes earlier.

She hadn't felt this bad for years. It was this place. This town. It had always made her feel wrong. Peter had been different. He hadn't exactly fitted in, not like Harts, but he'd liked it here and been liked in return. And he'd been loved and cared for by Mabel.

Now he was dead.

Her fingers curled at her sides again, before she made herself press on, finish the array of X-rays necessary for a full and complete picture of the how and the when that could lead to a why.

The door swung open just as she finished. 'Are you done yet?' Hartley was outlined in the doorway, his expression hidden in shadow.

Her fingernails pressed so hard into the flesh of her palms, she wondered she couldn't feel them cut her skin. Even so, she managed a fair approximation of a smile and said, 'All done in here. We've got to get the body back on the autopsy bed so I can finish the post-mortem.'

'I thought you'd already done that.'

'I took samples. That is only the first step. I must remove, weigh and take samples of all the vital organs and brain—'

He held his hands up. 'Right. Got it. Let's get you back in there then.' He took the end of the trolley and pulled it back out the door. She steadied her breath, heart beating hard and fast in her chest, then, taking a moment to copy the X-ray files onto her personal memory stick where she kept all her back-up files, followed him back into the morgue.

★★★

Hours later, she finished the last stitch in her brother's chest—she'd weighed, examined and taken samples of his heart, lung, liver, kidneys, stomach and bladder, using her phone to verbally record the procedure given the morgue didn't seem to have a recording device. Any one of the vital organs could have evidence of what happened and would help to complete a picture of his last day. His lungs were pink and healthy—no sign of smoke inhalation, which meant he wasn't alive when the fire began that started the explosion. She would run some tissue samples, but she knew she was right. Hartley stood through all of it, arms crossed, leaning against the bench against the wall, as if he didn't have a problem with what she was doing at all. But he was a little green. She hoped he wasn't going to vomit. That had happened on more than one occasion when a detective had come down to follow up on the case and had caught her mid-post-mortem.

She began on the skull—Hartley turned away when she started up the small rotating saw, and busied himself with sorting the samples she'd collected, even though they didn't need to be sorted. She bent to her work. She weighed and took samples of the brain, noting the bruising on the parietal lobe and the pooling of blood on the inside of the skull at the same point. She could feel a compression in the bone of the skull as well which the X-ray would confirm. 'He was hit from behind in what would have been a killing blow.'

'Could something from the explosion have done that?'

She looked at the shape of the mark, the pattern of the fracture on the skull, and shook her head. 'Debris would be lodged in the back of his head from the explosion if that was the case. And he wouldn't have received this kind of injury from a fall. The angle is wrong.' She bit the inside of her lip and rubbed her hand over her chest where an intense burning sensation had begun to grow. 'Someone hit him in the back of the head and it killed him. This is cause of death.'

He came closer and looked over her shoulder. 'How can you tell from looking at that?'

'Intercranial bleeding and skull fractures tell the story. I just have to be smart enough to read it.'

He touched her shoulder. 'You are.' He stepped away.

Teeth-grindingly aware of that simple touch, desperate to ignore it, she methodically continued her work. Finally, when she was done, she stripped off her gloves and scrubs. 'The equipment here is somewhat rudimentary and can't give the kind of chemical analytics I need. I'll do some analysis on these,' she said, pointing to the clothing samples she'd pulled off the body and the boots, 'and some work on the blood and a few of the tissue samples, but there are others I want to courier down to my colleagues in Melbourne.'

'It will be faster if we send them to Sydney.'

'I want these handled by people I know are competent and capable.'

'The people in the Sydney labs are competent and capable too.'

'I want them to go to Melbourne.' She looked up at him, about to say more, but the empathy in his eyes undid her. She breathed deeply, trying to ignore the squeezing feeling in her chest, the rawness that dried her throat, the rising anger inside her. She now had proof that someone had murdered her brother. That they'd probably set up the explosion to cover the murder. It was enough to move this from a coronial enquiry to a murder investigation. But she would need more to help catch the murderer. Heat prickled behind her eyes as she tried to hold his gaze, but the longer she did so, the more she felt like breaking down, breaking apart.

She looked down at the floor and whispered, 'I need people I know to do the work-ups. For Peter.'

His hands were suddenly on her shoulders, pulling her toward him, arms wrapping around her, squeezing her against his chest. She stiffened, but he didn't let go, and after a moment, she let herself lean into him, wrapping her arms around his strong back, feeling the tension of his muscles under her hands as she gripped tight.

'You can let go, you know.' His chin moved against the top of her head as he spoke.

'I can't,' she said, her voice muffled against his chest. She knew she should pull away, but couldn't make herself do it. 'There are still things that have to be done.'

'They can wait, I'm sure.' His voice was a warm puff of breath in her hair. She shivered at the intimacy of the sensation. 'Cold?'

'Yes,' she lied—she was never cold in the morgue, the exhilaration and exactness of her work always kept her warm in a way she knew probably wasn't normal. She began to pull away from him. It was more difficult than it should have been. She shivered again.

'You should put a jacket on.' He moved his hands up and down her arms. The frisson of warmth that tingled over her skin made her want to lean back into him, but she couldn't. She still had the next post-mortem to do.

She shrugged away from his hands. 'I'm fine.' She set about copying all her work so far, making doubles of all samples, some to stay there for analysis and some to go into the special containers she kept in her backpack. In Melbourne, she had a secondary storage area in a different section of the morgue building where she kept the samples, but when she was out on the road she had her specialised backpack—double stitched, army-tough, waterproof with extra pockets and tabs and a combination lock—to use until she got back to her lab. She always kept it fully stocked and prepped and took it everywhere she went even when there was no reason to take it. Jenny called it her blanket. She called it being practical, and she was glad of that practicality now.

She printed out her findings so far and put them in a manila folder which went into her backpack along with her laptop—the morgue computer was too slow for her liking—and the medical USB with the X-rays on it.

Once done she turned back to Hartley, who had been watching her silently. 'I've got to work on the other body now. Can you help me to put this one away?'

They worked together quietly and quickly, the click of the lock as the door closed on her brother's body like a final goodbye. She pressed her hand against the door, swallowing down the grief aching in her throat, and turned back to Hartley. 'Let's get Tyler. Once I'm done with him, I'll look over both the X-rays and do what I can do here with the blood and tissue samples, while you organise a courier for the ones I need sent to Melbourne.'

He reached out to touch her again, but she moved away to open the locker Tyler was in. 'Help me here, please.'

'You don't have to do this now. You should take a break. Get some rest. We can come back tomorrow.'

'No. I want to do it now.'

'Erika. You don't have to prove anything to me. Take a break. Nobody will think worse of you for it. In fact, they might just think that you're human.' He winced as soon as the words left his mouth, before she'd even had a chance to understand the impact of them and why they hurt so much. 'Erika, I...'

She didn't let him finish. That ball of emotion she'd been suppressing had grown too large, too hot, too forceful, for her to keep it inside anymore. Pushed by his words, by the pain they brought, the ball exploded in sudden fury.

She leapt at him, a sound coming out of her mouth that wasn't words, wasn't a scream, her fists lashing out, hitting him, glancing off his shoulder, smashing into the locker behind him. She barely felt the pain. Raw anger and grief were finally flying free, aimed, rightly or wrongly, at the man who had tied her in knots ever since he'd walked into the interview room at the police station not twenty-four hours earlier. The man who had tied her in knots for more than twenty years, ever since they'd been griefstricken kids who found each other through mutual loss. She kept lashing out with her fists and knees and elbows and hands even though she knew it wasn't reasonable, even though she knew it wasn't fair, even though she didn't really want to hurt him. Some hurt-animal part of her had sprung free and didn't care. She just wanted somebody else to feel what she was feeling, because then, maybe then, it would mean that she wasn't all alone.

Chapter Nine

'Erika. Erika. Stop it.' His head smarted from where it had smashed into the locker when she'd launched herself at him, the copper tang of blood in his mouth, the sting of a cut under his eye from where her ring had cut him, but he didn't care about that. He managed to get his arms around her, pull her tight against his chest so she couldn't hurt herself more. There was blood on her knuckles. She struggled against his hold, the hurt animal sound wrenched from her soul grew louder. Hell.

He'd heard that sound before, once, when he'd snuck into her room one night and found her curled in a corner of her dark bedroom. She'd been rocking back and forth, making that sound, and he couldn't make her stop. There'd been blood that night too—not much, but enough to scare him. Her nails had cut into the skin of her legs as she'd held onto herself so tightly, almost as if she was afraid she was going to fly apart if she let go.

He'd been so scared for her that night and he was scared now. He hadn't been able to help her then, hadn't been able to get through to her, but he was damned if he was going to be as useless and helpless now. He had caused this emotional fugue with his unthinking words and it was up to him to fix it.

'Shh, shh, Erika. Shh. It's okay. It's okay. You're okay. You're safe. Nothing's going to hurt you now. Shh. Shh.'

He had no idea what he was doing but he kept on doing it, muttering soft, insensible words against her hair, rocking her gently, until slowly, slowly, she stopped fighting, that horrible sound changing into shuddering sobs until finally she turned in his arms and clung to him, burying her face into his chest.

It broke his heart.

Just like it had broken his heart all those years ago. *Shit!*

When she'd run away, his hurt and sense of betrayal had made him accept his father's version of events—that he'd been a stupid boy with his first crush, and she was a girl that had only ever used him—but even then, he'd known it was a lie. He'd tried to cling to that lie when he'd heard she was here, when he walked into that interview room. He told himself he didn't care that she was back. But then why had he come here with her and helped her? Why had he kissed her?

That kiss… It had felt like coming home, like the two of them had always, and would always, belong together. He'd been such an idiot! He'd believed in a lie to protect himself when the truth was, he cared more for this damaged woman than he'd ever cared about anyone else in his life.

He stood with her cradled in his arms for long minutes, expecting her to stop sobbing, to let go. She didn't. She didn't respond when he spoke to her either. Knowing she'd hate it if anyone at the hospital saw her like this, he picked her up and carried her away from her brother and his death, away from the science of the autopsy that she'd clung to as a way of holding onto herself, or her sanity, or whatever it was she was trying to hold on to. He carried her to the freight lift and then up and out the loading bay doors. He hurried across the parking lot to his Patrol, thankful it was quiet. When he got there, he tried to coax her to let go of him so he could put her in the car and drive her to Daphne, but she wouldn't let go. Shit, he couldn't drive like that. There was only one thing he could do.

He called Mac.

Mac didn't ask any questions when he got there, just helped Hartley get into the back of the four-wheel drive and then drove them back to the hotel.

Hartley carried Erika to her room and Mac went to get his mum.

Erika's sobs had stopped when he opened her door, but she was still clinging to him, her face almost welded to his shoulder. He sat on the bed, not knowing what else to do, Erika cradled in his lap. His shirt was wet and he was certain there would be bruises in his shoulders where she clung to him.

'Oh, goodness. What's happened? Oh, you poor dear.' Daphne, hand to her throat, rushed through the door, wearing a pair of Wonder Woman pyjamas that, in that moment, looked oddly right, with Pip hot on her heels. Mac came after his parents but stopped at the door.

Daphne sat beside them on the bed and began to stroke Erika's hair, her back. Pip stood a few feet from the bed, edging from one foot to the other, his white t-shirt half tucked into his crinkled pyjama shorts. He looked back at the door where Mac stood, then back at his wife. 'I'm going to call Jenny.'

'Yes. That would be good. Let me know what she wants us to do.'

Pip brushed past his son and was gone.

'Who is Jenny?'

'The lady Erika went to live with when she left here, a friend of her mum's. She's a psychologist. She'll be able to help.'

'I hope so.' Hartley's voice was hoarse. 'She hasn't spoken and won't let go of me.'

'What happened to her?' Daphne's gaze wasn't accusing, but he could feel her urgency, her worry, right down to his soul. It echoed his own.

'I'm not sure. It might have been something I said, but I can't remember anything specifically. She'd just finished the autopsies and X-rays on Peter when...'

'Oh, Lord. No wonder. It probably took her right back to her parents' deaths.' Her gaze piniomed him to the spot. 'You know she was there with them, in the car, when it was run off the road? She tried to save them.' Hartley nodded. She'd told him that much. He'd heard the rest in whispered gossip around town. She'd been twelve. Her mother's neck had been broken on impact and she died instantly, but Erika managed to keep her father alive until the ambulance arrived. She'd stuck her hand right in the wound in his chest and pumped his heart with her own little fingers. People had looked at her as if she was some kind of monster to have been able to do that. Hartley knew different. Her mind, her beautiful, brilliant mind, had probably read it in a book and given she remembered everything she'd probably just done it. To her, it would have been the only thing to do.

'Most adults wouldn't have been able to do what she did,' Daphne said, stroking Erika's head softly, surely. 'When Pip and I arrived at the hospital, she was still covered in blood and clinging to her father like she's clinging to you now. And she was making a noise. The most horrible noise.'

'I know that noise.'

Daphne's hand clenched, tangling in Erika's hair, dislodging the ponytail. A little choking sound erupted from Daphne's throat, then she pulled out the band gently and kept stroking Erika's hair, the wavy auburn locks falling over Erika's shoulders and onto Hartley's hand.

'I thought, I hoped, she would have grown out of these fits of hers,' Daphne said after a long silence. 'Poor, dear girl. You had no business letting her do something like that, Hartley John Cooper. No business at all.' She wasn't looking at him, her gaze glued to Erika, but it felt like she was.

'I couldn't have stopped her. She would have done it with or without me. Better I was there, right? And lucky she did do it because she found something almost right away.'

Mac stepped into the room. 'What?'

'Peter was murdered.'

Daphne gasped, but Mac said, 'How?'

'There was evidence of an accelerant as well as clear evidence that he'd been bludgeoned on the back of the head. Erika said it would have been a killing blow.'

'Oh my.' Daphne's hand stilled, trembled, but then returned to stroking. 'So it's lucky she did the autopsy.'

'She shouldn't have done it,' Daphne said, her voice low and hard. 'You shouldn't have let her autopsy her own brother. The other boy, fine. But not her brother. It's too much.'

'She's so damned icy, Mum. Who would have guessed it would flip her out like this?'

'I would have, Macarthur Hudson. She isn't cold. She just struggles to deal with her emotions. Which is completely understandable given what she went through.' Her hand trembled as she turned Erika's wrist over, fingers stroking over the white scars there. 'She feels more deeply than any of us know.'

Hartley's arms tightened around Erika as Mac stared at the scars on Erika's wrist and said, 'She tried to kill herself? I never knew that.'

Daphne sighed. 'Mabel refused to get her help and then, when it became a matter of saving face, sent her away for a few months to be dealt with elsewhere. It probably would have worked too if the poor dear didn't have to come back here afterwards. She got sent back a few more times to the asylum when Mabel couldn't take the "hysterical episodes" as she used to call them.'

Hartley squeezed his eyes closed. So that's what happened. 'She would never tell me where she went in those months she was gone.'

'Of course she wouldn't.' Daphne's eyes burned into him. 'She's too brave. Too independent and proud to have leaned on someone like she needed to. It got to the point where Pip and I said enough was enough. That's why we gave her the money to go to Melbourne. We sent her to Jenny. She'd gone to university with Erika's mum and while we didn't know her well, we knew her well enough to know she could help. Would want to help. And we knew Erika's mum and dad would want her to go to their friend.'

'You helped a sixteen-year-old to run away? Mum, you could have been arrested.'

Daphne waved her hand. 'Mabel didn't care. She didn't even write up a missing person's report. She said she didn't think it was necessary given everyone knew Erika had run away so she wouldn't get in trouble for stealing those sausages, but the truth was, she just didn't care.' She wiped her free hand across her eyes, sniffing.

'What happened when she got to Melbourne?' Hartley asked.

'Jenny took her in and helped her as we knew she would.' She sniffled again. 'Erika has built such a wonderful life for herself, something to be truly proud of. And while we missed her, we were glad for her sake she never came back given all the misery she left behind. But now, here she is, not only dealing with it all again, but doing autopsies on her brother and discovering he was murdered.' Her gaze bored into him again, accusing. His heart raced, his breath came more quickly, drying his throat, and he swallowed, looked away, prickling heat spreading over him. He thought she might berate him further—god knows, he deserved it—but she simply sighed and said, 'Thank you for bringing her back here,'

He nodded.

'Right.' Pip came back in the room, running his hand through his salt-and-pepper hair. 'Jenny said to give her time to grieve. She needs peace and quiet, but also to know someone is there for her. She wants one of us to stay here with her until she comes out of this. If she isn't better in the morning, then we're to call again and she'll arrange for us to fly her back to Melbourne where Jenny can get her the care she needs.'

'It can't be that bad.' Mac shot his dad a disbelieving look. 'She was fine only an hour ago.'

'Jenny said she hasn't had one of these episodes for years, and the last time she did, it only lasted for a few hours. Let's hope after a bit of peace and quiet that will be the case here.' Pip gestured with his head to the door. 'Come on, son, let's go downstairs. Let's leave your mum and Coops to it. They're the best thing for EJ right now.'

'Dear girl. Dear sweet girl.' Daphne cooed, leaning forward to kiss the back of Erika's head as her husband and son left. 'I'm here, EJ. I'm here for you, luv. Just like before you left. I won't leave you. I'm here. I'm here. I won't leave you. Okay? Okay, EJ? You're not alone.'

Hartley wasn't sure if Erika heard anything Daphne was saying, but she shuddered, let out a large sob, and in a fluid motion, moved from his arms and into Daphne's, sobbing against her shoulder as if her heart were breaking all over again.

Hartley could barely stand the sound. He could barely stand the empty feeling now she wasn't in his arms. He sat for long moments, wanting to pull her back to him, to deny her need of anyone but him, but that was selfish and more about his needs than hers.

It was Erika that mattered, not him.

He should leave Daphne to it. Erika needed a woman right now, female understanding and all that. He stood.

Erika's hand shot out, grabbing his hand before he made it one step away from the bed. She looked up at him with red, tear-stained eyes that were still achingly beautiful to him. 'Don't go. I don't want you to go.' Her voice was barely recognisable, a twisted husk of a thing, but he could read the need in her eyes, the question there, the fear of his rejection—he didn't need her words to ask him to stay. He sat, held onto her hand, not minding when she clutched it so tightly it was almost painful.

'I won't go. Not this time.'

She nodded, her breath hitching, and then she lay her head against Daphne's shoulder like an exhausted child and closed her eyes.

He thought she had fallen asleep except her hand never stopped gripping his. The empty feeling that had smothered him only moments before drifted away like mist in the hot summer sun.

Eventually, Erika's grip loosened on Daphne and she and Hartley were able to encourage her to lie down. She lay there for a long time, staring up at the ceiling, eyes glazed. She held on to Hartley's hand, her grip tight, as if she was afraid he'd disappear. Daphne stroked her hair over and over, fingers grazing across Erika's brow and slowly, slowly, Erika's breathing slowed, her eyelids drooped, and she was asleep. They both sat there, watching her, waiting for something to happen. But she had fallen into a deep, needful sleep and didn't stir, her breathing slow and deep.

Without a word between them, Hartley and Daphne moved from the bed. Hartley took off Erika's shoes while the older woman fetched a blanket from the cupboard in the corner. After placing her shoes on the floor under the window in the way she'd always done when they were kids, he returned to the side of the bed and stood there, staring at her, uncertain what to do. She looked so peaceful, so far from the uptight, cold, rational person others saw, that he'd tried to make himself believe she was. But he'd always known better than that. Her problem was, and always had been, that she felt too damn much.

'Daphne?' He turned to the older woman, but she shook her head.

'Not now. We don't want to wake her. What she needs more than anything is sleep.'

'You're right.'

'And so do you.'

He didn't want to go. 'I should help you make her more comfortable.'

'You should do no such thing.' She began to shoo him toward the door. 'Go stop my boys from coming back up here. I know they will because they're as bad as cats for curiosity. Tell them I have everything in hand, have a drink with them if you need a bit of relaxing, but then go and get some sleep.'

'What about you?'

She looked back at Erika. 'She'll want you rested and ready to help her find the bastards who killed Peter. Get a key from Pip for the room next door. I'll come and fetch you if she wakes.'

He sighed. There was little point arguing. He knew Daphne was right. He went down and got the key from Pip, but didn't stay to have a drink with the two men. Daphne was right. He should try to get some sleep so he was ready to help Erika in any way he could in the morning.

But after a couple of hours of lying there, staring at the ceiling, he got up and went next door. Daphne was almost nodding off. 'Go to bed, Daphne,' he whispered. 'I'll sit with her.'

Daphne sat upright, blinking rapidly. 'I'm fine. You should get some sleep.'

He shook his head. 'I'm not tired. You go and rest. If I feel tired, I'll come knock on your door.'

She smiled gratefully and vacated the armchair she'd been sitting in. 'Our room's the one at the end of the hall.'

Hartley nodded. 'Sleep well.'

Daphne took herself off, closing the door with a quiet snick.

Unable to sit, Hartley strode to the window and stared out, down Echo Parade to the heart of the town that was his home. There were only a few streetlights on to illuminate the quiet streets. A dust whorl whipped up under one of the pools of light across the way, disappearing into the dark of the vacant lot opposite. That lot had been vacant for five years since an investor had bought it to build a new set of shops, knocking down the Granger

Grocery and Hardware Store that had stood there for a century despite the protests of a local 'save our town' group. The builder had lost his funding after the old Federation-style building had been knocked down, and the block had been vacant ever since. Although he'd heard through the gossip mill that the town council was looking at building a new tourist centre in that very spot.

He hoped so. Vacant blocks right in the middle of a town never looked good. They started a trend and there was no way he wanted Echo Springs to go the way of so many other country towns. Echo Springs relied on the tourists who came to visit the springs and tramp through the national park to the south. But if the rains didn't come, the springs would become dryer, as would the park. If that happened, the tourists would stop coming and the town would lose the lifeline that had kept it alive after the mines closed thirty years earlier.

A sigh shook out of him as he stared at the outlines of the backs of the buildings that lined Main Street, the corrugated-iron roof of the police station standing out among all the other tiled and painted roofs, the silver glinting in the moonlight.

God he loved it here. He'd done the city living thing for a few years, thinking that he wanted to get away from his father and the constant feeling he was living in his shadow. But the moment a placement had come up here at the station, he'd jumped at it and never looked back. Home. It was his home and always would be. Like his father and his grandfather before him, both coppers here, he knew he would never leave. His life's blood was this town. He would never be the same man he was here anywhere else. He wasn't just a country copper, he was a country man.

He turned back to look at Erika, walked toward her, stared down at her beautiful face. She'd just got more beautiful in the last sixteen years. She was a bright star, forever out of reach, while he was like the red soil, firm and hard packed. She was one in a trillion. He was a grain of red dirt, just like the trillions of other grains that made up this harsh and exacting land.

He hadn't fully understood that until right now. Her past wasn't the only reason she couldn't stay. She had to leave and go back to the good, decent life she'd built for herself without him, a life where she could shine and be lauded for her brilliance, not brought down because of it.

He knuckled his fist against his chest. Damn. Knowing that shouldn't still hurt as much as it had all those years ago when she'd walked away from him and never looked back.

Chapter Ten

Erika woke to the sound of birds. And someone shouting.

'Shoo. Shoo. You're making a mess of my beautiful lawn! Shoo.'

She couldn't help but smile at the aggrieved voice and the unconcerned chittering of the birds. She pushed up from the bed but the room spun and she sat back down with a plop. 'Whoa!' She must have got up a little too quickly. She put her head between her knees until the room settled and she felt steadier. She stood up slowly this time and made her way carefully to the window to see what was going on outside. She pushed the heavy curtains aside. The bright light and vibrant blue of the sky blinded her. She blinked rapidly, eyes watering, and shaded her eyes. She'd need to buy a darker pair of sunglasses if she was going to stay for longer than intended. She'd completely forgotten how harsh and unforgiving the light was here.

Her vision cleared and she was able to see what the commotion was about. The trees lining the street were full of corellas, their white feathers brilliant in the sunshine. They were stripping the trees along the street of all their nuts and pollens, the detritus of their feeding showering onto the nature strip below. Two doors down from the vacant block, a woman in a purple kimono dressing gown, her hair up in yellow rollers, stood on the pavement in front of a brick Federation-style house. She was waving her hands, jumping up and down, yelling at the birds in the tree that sat in her immaculate front lawn—a front lawn that was being slowly covered in bits of shells and pollen.

Corellas weren't often seen in town at this time of year. They usually stayed out in the bush. Maybe it was the long dry that had brought them into town. Erika felt a little communion with them for being forced to come where they weren't wanted.

'Shoo. Shoo.' The curlers on the woman's head bobbed comically. They had to hurt, banging up and down like that. She touched her own head, feeling a sharp sympathy pain. Actually, it wasn't sympathy pain. It was a real. As was the ache slowly overtaking every part of her body. She hadn't felt like this since she'd had the flu two years earlier. And before that, the last time she'd felt this achy and tired was when...

No!

Memories flooded back in an overwhelming rush and she plonked down on the floor beside the window as her mind scrambled to keep up.

She'd had an emotional fugue. She'd fought for so many years to overcome them. Counselling with Jenny and a specialist friend of hers had given her the tools to help her cope with the dark memories and even darker emotions tied into the PTSD she had from the trauma of her parents' deaths. She thought she'd had control of them. She had control of them in Melbourne.

It was this place. Coming back here had been such a mistake—although, how could she have done anything else? And how could she leave now? Peter needed her to make things right for him, to prove he wasn't involved in drugs. She'd had to put up with the whispers, insinuations and outright taunts after her parents' deaths. She hadn't been able to do anything to save her mother's reputation and preserve her memory in this prejudiced and closed-minded town, but she could certainly do something to save Peter's memory from suffering the same fate.

She wouldn't let him down. Even though the thought of facing Daphne, Pip and Mac had chills racing through her, she would carry on and pretend it hadn't happened.

What about Hartley? She winced. He'd seen her like that once before, the year she'd left. He probably thought her crazy. She dropped her head into her hands. How was she going to face him? It was more than embarrassing. It was soul-destroying.

There was a creak on the floorboards beyond her door. The others were up. Which meant she should get up. Acting normal would make her feel more normal. Besides, if she acted like there was nothing wrong, they were unlikely to bring up her storm of crying and emotional overreaction. She hoped.

She made her way shakily into the bathroom, stripped out of her clothes and hopped into the shower. As she reached to turn the shower on, she saw the cuts and bruises on her knuckles. God, she had truly been out of control, still felt the echoes of it now, like she was emotionally raw. Before she faced the others, she had to regain her composure. As the hot water pummel her tired, sore muscles, washed the blood from her hands and soothed the stinging cuts, she closed her eyes and put herself in her calm place. She built the image of the mountain in her mind, but before she could sink into the image as she always did, it shifted, changed. At first, she wasn't sure where her mind had taken her and then she realised.

The Springs.

The sky was an endless blue, the crisp yellowing grass on the hill where she stood in her mind-image giving way to the heat of the red sand as it spread toward the purple-orange-yellow-red striations in the craggy rocks that hid the springs. The air around her was warm and full of spicy, mineral scents. How she'd loved that scent. She used to stand there, breathing it in, letting it fill her and wash away the bad. Then once she'd breathed in her fill, she'd run to the springs, sometimes alone, sometimes with Hartley.

Together they'd laugh as they ran, exclaiming over the colours in the rocks, the strange almost-greens of the shrubs and bushes, the scurrying nearness of the outback animals and reptiles. They'd strip to their bathers or to their underwear if they'd come unprepared, and jump into the cool springs first, gasping and laughing, then when they were ready, they'd slip into the hot springs, the effervescent water fizzing against their skin. Hartley would talk and splash about, but she would simply lay back and stare up at the vast blue sky, his voice muffled by the water lapping in her ears. Finally, Hartley would join her and there would be peace.

She smiled as she sank into the memory, into the image, a peaceful calm filling her even though the image wasn't the mountains and hills imagery she'd used for years. She let the image play over her, filling her, as the hot water ran over her body, mimicking the waterfall at the largest hot spring. She and Hartley had gone there not long before she'd run away. She'd remembered laughing with him when she hadn't felt like laughing. They'd looked at each other and smiled and he had stared at her in a way that made her stomach twist. The same way he looked at her now.

Her eyes popped open. Water from the shower filled them, her heart a loud beat in her ears. Heat flushed over her skin as her mind furnished her with an image of Hartley stepping into the shower with her, sun-browned skin glistening with the slickness of water as it rushed over his firm chest, arms, thighs and...

She turned the hot tap off with a jerk and hissed as the cold water bit into her heated skin. She forced herself to stand under the cool stream for two minutes and then, teeth chattering, turned it off and stepped out of the shower.

There. That had done it. Nothing like a cold shower to stop wayward thoughts. And before those thoughts could become wayward again, she grabbed a towel and dried herself, dressed her hands with the antiseptic and bandaids she found in the bathroom cupboard, then dressed and, chin held high, left her room.

She had to make everyone believe that she was fine. She had to be fine. If she was to help Peter, that's all there was to it. She must keep her mind on the job at hand and off anything that might make her lose control again—and that included thinking about Hartley Cooper.

She marched downstairs and found Daphne, Pip, Mac and Hartley in the kitchen having breakfast.

Tension skated over her skin as they all turned to face her. She waited for one of them to reference last night, but after long, silent seconds, Daphne hopped up from her chair and said, 'Oh good, you're up. I'll just get you a plate. You must be starving.'

Actually she didn't think she could eat a bite, but if she admitted that, they would worry. So she accepted the plate and sat at the table, forcing herself to swallow a mouthful of the scrambled eggs. Concentrating on the food also meant she didn't need to speak or look at any of them. Even so, she knew she was being watched, could feel it like a stroke on her skin.

She looked up, her gaze clashing with Hartley's. There were unspoken questions in his eyes, concern, fondness, and something else that made her heart hitch. She looked away.

'Do you want some tea?' Daphne reached for the pot in front of her. 'Mac, go and get one of the tea cups for me, dear.'

Mac pushed his chair back, but Erika held out her hand. 'It's fine. I'd just like some juice.' Her voice sounded normal, thankfully, as she reached for the carton on the table and poured herself a glass. After a long sip, the cool tartness zinging on her tongue, she managed what she thought was a decent smile. 'That's better.' She turned to Hartley. 'So, when can we go back to the morgue? I'd like to do the post-mortem on the other body.'

Worry shadowed his eyes as his gaze roved over her. Her hands trembled, so she shoved them in her lap, met his gaze, tried to make him see she was okay. She needed them to treat her like she was fine.

After what seemed an eternity, he nodded and said slowly, 'We can go this morning as soon as we've finished breakfast.'

She had to stop herself from slumping in relief. He'd understood. Or believed that she was fine. Either way, he was playing along. 'Good.' She picked up her fork and shovelled some more egg onto it.

'I don't think that's a good idea, luv.' Pip was frowning at Hartley, not looking at her. 'I think we should ring Jenny again and see what she thinks.'

She jerked, scattering egg across the table. 'You called Jenny?'

'Of course, luv.' Daphne gripped her hand, squeezed. 'We were worried and wanted to make sure to do the right thing. I mean, after what happened last night...'

'I don't want to talk about last night.' Erika dropped her fork with a clang then, seeing their shock, took a deep breath and calmed herself. 'I don't need therapy. I haven't needed it for years. I just need to get on with my work. Jenny will be the first to tell you that.'

Daphne moved her pleas to Hartley. 'Coops, dear. You can't possibly think this is a good idea.'

Hartley didn't even pause to think about it. 'Erika knows what's best for her, and if she wants to finish the autopsies, then that's what we'll do.' He looked down at her. 'If you're finished, let's go.'

She nodded and followed him out of the hotel, ignoring the commotion behind her of Pip holding Daphne back, saying, 'She's an adult now. Hartley's right. She knows what's best for herself.'

Hartley waited for her as she ran upstairs to get her backpack. It wasn't there. Of course. Hartley wouldn't have thought to stop and pick it up the night before. She went back downstairs. She'd be at the morgue soon and would make sure after that it didn't leave her sight.

They headed out to his car as hers was still at the hospital. The heat folded around her as they walked, the sky a cloudless bright blue that made the eyes squint even behind sunglasses. They climbed into his Patrol in silence. She knew she should thank him, but then that would mean acknowledging last night, and she couldn't do that.

As they drove out of the car park and onto Echo Parade, she turned to look at him, wondering why he had backed her the way he had. It was like the old days, when he always stood solidly beside her, his presence taking the bitter sting out of her life. As she watched him, she realised they'd fallen into that same pattern. Except she was more aware of him as a man than she'd ever been all those years ago. Her gaze jerked down to his muscled thighs encased in faded denim. She dragged her gaze away, only to be caught by the way his soft blue t-shirt pulled across the muscles of his chest and biceps. He had grown up. Changed. He was a man. One with undeniably lovely triceps and bicep muscles. Nicely defined without being overly large. She liked tall men, but she didn't like overly muscled men. They made her feel small and helpless, like that mouse she'd seen yesterday at Echo Ridge. Hartley was well built, tall, but not body-builder big. Fit. That's what he was. Athletic. He'd have to keep in shape for his job. He probably had a lot of stamina. In fact, he'd probably last a long time in b…

Her thoughts skidded to a halt and she jerked in her seat, forcing her heated gaze away from his body and out the window beside her. What the hell was wrong with her?

She stared blindly out the window, so it took her a moment to realise they weren't heading toward the hospital. 'Where are we going?'

'I thought we'd just stop by the fire station first and tell Grim about the kerosene and the blow to the head. See if they'd found anything that might help us with the investigation.'

She bit the inside of her lip. 'Good idea.' Not to mention the fire station was close, just a couple of blocks north of the hotel, and she wouldn't have to spend more than a few seconds longer in the car with Hartley thinking about just how well built he was and how much stamina he might have in bed.

She hardly saw the buildings as they flew past, and she tried to remember how to breathe properly.

Chapter Eleven

They turned left onto Waratah Street a minute later and came to the fire station half a block down. Like much of the town, it hadn't changed much in the last sixteen years, apart from a coat of paint on the exposed wood around doors and windows.

As they pulled in, an attractive man in a fireman's blues turned from washing down the fire truck sitting in the drive. He lifted a soapy hand and waved to Hartley as he hopped out of the Patrol, but didn't smile. 'Hey, Coops.'

'Hey, Grim. What did you do to get washing duty?' Hartley said, voice full of laughter. 'Did you put too much chilli in the stir-fry again?'

'Very funny, Coops. You know that wasn't my fault.'

He turned to Erika as she hopped out of the four-wheel drive, gesturing at the other man. 'He blames the station cat for upending an entire bottle of chilli flakes into the stir-fry he was cooking. There were flames of a different kind in the fire station that night. We heard the howls all the way down at the station.'

The man called Grim rolled his eyes. 'You've been spending too much time with Mac, I can see.' He wiped his hands on his pants and then held one out to Erika. 'Toby Grimshaw.'

Erika took his slightly damp hand in hers, shaking firmly. 'Erika Hanson.'

His eyes widened a little in recognition. '*The* Erika Hanson?'

She pulled her hand back, shifting from one foot to the other. She hated this, the moment people recognised her name and thought only of her past deeds and nothing of the person she now was. 'I don't know if I'm "*The*" Erika Hanson.'

'The one who put the teachers at school to shame because you knew so much more about every subject than they did.'

'That's her,' Hartley said, coming to stand at her shoulder.

Toby didn't smile as he looked at her with too-serious eyes. 'You know, I always wished you were in my year when I was at school. Anyone who could put old Mr Ashdown in his place like you did in maths and science is a legend in my books. People are still talking about it.'

Edging from one foot to the other, Erika said, 'I don't know why. I simply showed him the calculations he was preparing for his year twelve class during our year nine prac class were incorrect and set him a problem that would truly challenge them.' The school had suspended her for being rude and embarrassing a teacher, and as a result Mabel locked her in her room for a week with nothing to eat but bread and water each day—a classic punishment technique of her grandmother's. But they didn't need to know that.

Toby snorted. 'Brilliant. Just brilliant.'

'Wow, you almost made Grim laugh,' Hartley said. 'He's right. You are legendary.'

Erika wasn't sure this solemn young man had been anywhere close to a laugh—she kind of liked his seriousness—but they were both looking at her, expecting some kind of comment, so she simply muttered, 'Thanks.'

Toby gave her a short nod and then turned to Hartley. 'I guess you're here about the explosion and fire and what caused the deaths of those two idiots.'

'Peter wasn't an idiot. My brother was exceptionally intelligent and he was a good man.'

His eyes widened. 'Oh, I'm sorry. Peter was your brother...I...I forgot. I shouldn't have said that. I'm so sorry.'

'It's okay.' Erika held up her hand, making a little brushing movement. 'From the simple evidence, it did look like he was engaging in something idiotic.'

'No I meant...I'm sorry for your loss. I know what it's like to lose someone in a tragic accident.'

'As do I. We seem to have that in common.'

'Yeah, well, I'm sorry.'

'Thank you.'

He glanced between her and Hartley, his brow furrowing, and muttered, 'excuse me,' waved Hartley to follow him. Erika stayed where she was, but even though Toby lowered his voice, the acoustics of the cavernous fire station house, with the firetruck in the driveway acting as a rebounder, allowed her to hear every word. 'Should we be talking about this in front of her?'

'Erika is helping with the investigation.'

Toby jerked back a little. 'She is? Why?'

'She's a forensic pathologist. She saw some irregularities in the case and offered her assistance given we haven't been able to replace Dr Metler. She began the autopsies last night and found some interesting evidence.'

'You let her do an autopsy on her brother?'

'Let doesn't come into it. There's no stopping Erika once she's got her mind set on something.'

'But...her brother. It's just...how could she do it?'

Hartley's face broke into a smile as his gaze flickered to her. She turned away, looking out at the street, trying to act like she couldn't hear them, but she was desperate to hear his response. 'She is a consummate professional. Besides which, she doesn't believe the fire was an accident.'

'It's not.'

'What? Have you found something?'

Erika gave up any pretence at pretending she couldn't hear their conversation and joined them. 'You found evidence of an accelerant, didn't you? I found it on the body, too, with burning that suggested he was soaked in it and set on fire.'

Toby's gaze became even more intense. 'That backs up what I've found so far.'

'Which is what?'

'There was evidence that the fire started where the bodies were found. Yet the bodies weren't near where the meth equipment was set up. I thought it was strange as it looked like the bodies had been thrown where they were by the explosion and the fire had caught them there, but when I looked at the path of the fire, it didn't seem to fit the version of the story the scene was telling me. I believe the fire was set in the corner where the bodies were, given the marks on the concrete around them, then ran along a path on the floor from the bodies and made contact with the chemicals being used to make the meth. The explosion was the last thing that happened, not the first.'

'I knew it,' Erika said, excitement buzzing through her veins. She was so close to proving Peter's innocence. Closer than she'd thought. 'I'd like to look at the scene.' Toby's brows shot up in surprise. 'I often go to scenes in Melbourne to help build a case for the police because the crime-scene photos don't always show what I need to complete my work, to build the story of the victim's death.'

'But this isn't like those other scenes. This is where your brother died.'

She looked down her nose at him—although that wasn't that hard given he was only a little taller than her. 'I'm not squeamish, Mr Grimshaw. Nor am I maudlin. My brother is dead. I want to find out how it happened and catch those responsible. To do that, I need to see where they were found, how they were lying. The placement of the bodies and the way they fell will tell me if they were blown there by the explosion or placed there. Also, there might be blood sprays and splatter or pooling that you missed seeing in the fire detritus. If I don't have a problem seeing the evidence, I can't imagine you should have one.'

His brows rose again. She braced herself for the usual comments about her cold practicality, but instead he said, 'You really are legendary, aren't you?'

'Yes, she is,' Hartley agreed.

Erika snorted, not sure why she was so embarrassed by their approval. 'So, shall we go now?'

Toby nodded. 'Just let me grab my kit.'

As he hurried back into the fire station, Erika endeavoured to ignore the way Hartley was looking at her. It was too intimate. Too knowing. She didn't like it. 'He seems nice.'

'He's had some tragedy in his life, but he's a good man.'

She didn't like the silence that followed. Took a step away. 'I think I should go to the morgue first and send those samples off that I put aside last night.'

'I already did it first thing this morning.'

She looked up at him. 'You did?'

He nodded. 'There was a mail plane leaving at six, so I made sure they were on it.'

'Thank you.' Her throat felt thick.

He stepped a little closer. 'I knew it was important to you.'

'It was.' She swallowed hard. 'But I didn't think it was that important to you.'

His finger brushed against her cheek and she couldn't help but lean into the caress, her gaze fluttering up to meet his. 'It's starting to be more important by the second.'

Her lips opened on a gasp. He moved closer, leaning down toward her, breath brushing across her lips. She swayed forward.

'Thanks for finishing the truck, Carl. I should be back in an hour or so.' Toby's voice echoed out of the cavern of the fire station.

Erika stumbled back. By the time Toby reached them, she and Hartley were standing a few metres apart, Erika looking down the street, Hartley with his hands shoved into the front pockets of his jeans, rocking backward and forward on his feet, whistling as if he didn't have a care in the world.

'Whose car should we take?'

'Mine,' Hartley said, gesturing to the Patrol.

Erika hurried into the back seat before Toby could do the chivalrous thing and take it—she really didn't want to be sitting so close to Hartley again. Toby didn't seem to notice the tension in the air, but took the front seat and swivelled to face her as Hartley backed out and started driving down Waratah Street towards the Mitchell.

'Have you analysed any of the samples you took in the autopsy?' Toby asked.

'No. I haven't had a chance yet. You?' He shook his head. 'You don't do a chemical analysis yourself?'

'I can. We don't have the equipment. There usually isn't a need, as most fires out here are caused by old wiring or nature doing its thing. Anything that needed more analysis than that was usually sent to Metler and if he couldn't do it, it was sent to forensic units in Dubbo or Sydney.'

'I can probably do some of the tests for you, if you haven't already sent them off. Or you can come to the morgue and do them yourself.'

'I was hoping you'd say that. They were going with a courier later today, but we'll swing back and get them when we're done at the site.'

'Sounds good. Do you think...'

She was interrupted by a burst of static from the police radio followed by a voice hailing Hartley.

Hartley picked up the handset. 'Echo 4 here. Out.'

'Echo 4, the Boss wants you to come in and see her. Out.'

'Copy base. I'm just on my way to the explosion site with Grim and Dr Hanson. Can it wait? Out.'

'No. The Boss says she wants to see you now. Out.'

'Copy. I'll be there in five. Echo 4 out.' He put the handset back. 'Sorry folks. We'll have to do this later.' He pulled over onto the verge and then turned the car in a wide arc back the way they'd come.

She touched his shoulder before she could stop herself. 'My car's at the hospital. As is my backpack. I need both. I know it's out of the way, but can you drop us off there first? I can drive us out to the site.'

Hartley's gaze met hers in the rear-view mirror. 'I'm not sure that's a good idea.'

'Why? Mr Grimshaw—'

'Toby,' Toby interrupted, shooting her a serious smile.

'...Toby will be there for the sake of investigational integrity. And I'm hardly likely to do anything to damage the sanctity of the scene.'

'I'm happy for that,' Toby said.

She shot Hartley a 'see, what are you worried about?' look via the mirror. Hartley took a deep breath and she realised she was still gripping his shoulder. She dropped her hand back to her lap, her fingers tingling.

Hartley didn't say anything, but he took the turn down Main Street that led to the hospital. Ten minutes later, they were at her car. 'I'll meet you out there after I've finished with the Boss,' he said through the open window.

'Your superintendent has found out about me doing the autopsy, hasn't she?'

'Probably. Either that or your boss has got you assigned to the case and she knows you went over her head.'

'Sorry.' He waved away her apology and reached to put the car in drive. 'Wait. I've got something for you that might help. Stay here.' She ran inside the hospital and down to the morgue, grabbed her backpack and ran back to the lift. In the lift, she pulled out a pad and scribbled a note to add to the manila folder she pulled out of the backpack. She'd just finished when the doors dinged open and she ran out to the car. 'Give her this. It's my notes so far. It might make a difference.' She handed him the folder.

'Thanks.'

She wanted to tell him she was sorry for getting him into trouble, but couldn't. She wasn't sorry he'd been there for her. She pressed her lips together, nodded, then turned and went to her car. She hopped in—it was already boiling inside—so she turned it on to start the air-conditioning and watched through the rear-view mirror as the two men shared a few words before Hartley drove off with a little toot. She looked suspiciously at Toby as he got in but he just turned to put his kit on the back seat before securing his belt.

Consternation hummed through her. She couldn't help but think the two men had said something about her, but she didn't want to ask, so simply said, 'Where to?'

'The old warehouses near the railway line on Old Station Road.'

'Okay.' Pulling out of the hospital car park, she headed toward the Mitchell.

Chapter Twelve

Superintendent Katherine Stuart was pissed. Majorly pissed.

Hartley wished she was a yeller like the superintendant in charge of his old station in Sydney. That would have been easier to deal with. Her cold disappointment in him and how he'd ignored a direct order to help Erika flout the rules made him feel like crawling from the office and back into the swamp from which he must have originated. The only thing that saved him from immediate suspension was the fact that Erika had gone over the Boss's head and now had permission to work on the case, not to mention the folder she'd given him with the findings that proved murder.

If there were two things Katherine Stuart didn't like more than being ignored and overridden, they were drugs cropping up in her town and the murder of Echo Springs's citizens.

She sat in her high-backed chair, greying hair pulled back into a tight bun, her lips held in a steady line as she looked at the papers in front of her. After a long moment, she lifted her head. 'She is certain?'

'She would stake her reputation on her conclusions—and that's saying something.'

Katherine waved her hand. 'Yes, yes. I've read her file.' She splayed her hands flat over the report, her gaze flinty. 'So, this is a murder investigation.' Her lips pursed. 'You have put me in a difficult position, Detective Senior Constable.'

'I know. And I'm sorry for it.'

She tipped her head. 'Are you?' Her gaze was assessing. 'I think you are sorry for disobeying my orders, but as far as the rest...' She let out a harsh breath that could have been a laugh, except he knew her good humour would have fled to the Simpson Desert the moment she'd heard what he'd done. 'With Detective Charles on stress leave, we have nobody here with enough experience to take the lead in a murder investigation.'

'I am more than happy to take the lead.'

'I'm sure you are.' Her sarcasm was sharp enough to draw blood, but he stood still, hands behind his back, ready and willing to take whatever punishment she decreed was fitting for his crime. 'I know you couldn't stop Ms Hanson from calling her boss and going behind our backs, but there is still the little matter of you disobeying a direct order and helping her to do the autopsy before it was approved. If I give you this case, it would be tantamount to a pat on the back for a job well done. I really should put a request through for a detective from Dubbo or Sydney to come and take on this case.'

Ice ran down his back. He didn't want to lose this case, he couldn't. He had to be the one to work with Erika. He didn't let any of that show though. 'I understand.'

'However, there's the matter of what Ms Hanson has written here.' She held up a piece of paper. 'She states that she would prefer you to be the investigating officer on the case, that you disobeying my order was completely her doing and you being there was necessary because otherwise the correct chain of evidence wouldn't have been maintained so you were doing your job.' He brow rose as she looked up at him. He maintained the perfect poker face. She pressed her lips together and looked down at the file again. 'Then she says without her, we wouldn't know this was a murder and would miss the chance to follow the leads while still fresh. Then she goes on to praise your professionalism and state that without you, there would be no case.'

Hartley only just managed to stop the pleasure those words brought from showing on his face.

'I don't like to be blackmailed, Detective.'

That wiped the small smile from his face. 'I don't think she would have meant that as blackmail, Boss. You don't know her.'

She waved her hand again. 'Your father has told me about her.'

'My father doesn't like her.'

'I know. I also called her boss in Melbourne after I got the call from the New South Wales Coroner's Office approving her request to be loaned out for this case. He said Ms Hanson was the best at what she did and if anyone could help find the truth of things, it was her.'

'You called her boss?'

Her brow rose a fraction. 'Of course.' She looked down at the report again. 'She's as good as promised.' Her lips moved silently. Hartley stood still, waiting for her decision. Finally, she looked up at him, gaze still flinty, but her lips weren't still pressed in a harsh line. 'You have the lead on this, Detective Senior Constable.'

'Thank you, Superintendent.'

'Don't thank me. Given I apparently have no choice about allowing Ms Hanson to work on this case, and given I have no other detective at the moment and can't request another to be transferred without having to explain to my seniors how you and Ms Hanson jumped the gun on the autopsy, I have no choice.' She pointed her finger at him. 'Work with her and get this solved. I don't like murders happening in my town.' She held up her finger before he could respond. 'But from now on, everything by the book. Do you understand? One more show of "independence" on your part, and you'll be on immediate suspension with no pay.'

'I'm a bit surprised I'm not on that now.'

She huffed out a laugh. 'Quite frankly, so am I.' She closed the file and held it out to him, but when he went to take it, she didn't let go. 'Don't let me down, Cooper. I won't be so lenient next time.'

'Understood, Superintendent Stuart.' He saluted her.

She nodded, and let the file go into his hand. 'Constable Fields is still to work with you but rope Mac in as well—this case is turning into more than a two-man job. Update him on what you know and then get him out interviewing family and friends. One of them could be a suspect.'

'Yes Boss.'

'Now go. Catch me a murderer.'

'Yes Boss.'

Everyone was staring as he walked out and into the main floor of the station. Ben 'Strawberry' Fields shot him a sympathetic look. Hartley gestured back to the office he'd just come from. 'She wants you on the case with me. And Mac.'

'You're still on it?'

'Holding on like grim death.' Ben nodded his appreciation, but didn't laugh. 'Did you see anything else out at the site yesterday arvo that we missed?'

'No, but I was looking at it as a drug accident, not murder, so maybe there is something. Should we head out now?'

'No. Erika and Grim are on their way out there now. They'll let us know if they find something. Let's go over what else we've got.' He led Ben into the case room and together they went over the evidence on the board, adding the movements of the murder victims in the previous week that Ben had verified the day before and that morning as well as what Erika had discovered.

'I'll go out and interview again with this fresh information in mind,' Ben said when they were done.

'Good. Let me know what you find.' Ben left. Hartley looked down at his watch. It had been a good hour and a half since he'd left Erika. He needed to tell her they had the official go-ahead to investigate. Knowing her, she was probably still out at the site of the explosion collecting evidence. He was on his way out when Siobhan stuck her head out of the dispatch office.

'A 000 call just came in about your friend, Erika Hanson.'

'What?' Fear prickled down his spine. Had she had another episode while viewing the place her brother had died? 'Where?'

'Her car has been run off the road on Old Station Road near the abandoned warehouses.'

Before Siobhan could say anything more, he sprinted past her and outside. A minute later he was on the road, lights and sirens blaring, heart well and truly lodged in his mouth. Thoughts of her parents and how they'd died flooded his mind.

Bloody hell. It was taking too long even at speed, lights and sirens blazing, to get to her. Why on earth had he let her go out there without him?

Chapter Thirteen

Hartley drove over a rise. In the distance, where there was a tight bend in Old Station Road, the back end of a silver Holden sedan—Erika's car—stuck out of a deep, wide ditch. The ditch had been a measure to dissuade kangaroos from bounding onto the road when there'd been a lot of road-train traffic in and out of the area. For cars run off the road, it was a potential death trap.

As he drove closer, he saw two people standing on the far side of the car. The taller one was leaning against the upturned tail, and the shorter one was standing in front of him. Toby and Erika. Erika was holding something to Toby's head. She looked unhurt. A bit dishevelled, but otherwise okay. And playing doctor. If he wasn't so worried, he might have laughed at the picture of her tending to an obviously embarrassed Toby.

He took a deep breath, the first in the last few minutes, the tightness in his chest loosening somewhat. They were okay. They were both okay. He'd been so worried, not just that she might have been injured, but that the nature of the accident might have pushed her over the edge again. Her parents had died in a car accident after being run off the road, and Erika had been in the car. Yet she didn't seem to be affected, standing there calmly, doctoring Toby.

He pulled in beside them, turning off the lights and sirens. Toby pushed himself upright, but Erika said something snappy to him and he leaned back against the car again.

'Are you both okay?' Hartley asked as he climbed out of the Patrol. Erika turned. Her clothes were dusty and there was a smudge of blood on her t-shirt, and a small cut on her leg. 'You're hurt.'

'I'm fine.' She waved off his concern. 'But Toby isn't. Some idiot ran us off the road.'

She said it like she couldn't believe the audacity. Like it was the greatest insult that someone would not only try, but succeed in running her off the road. Laughter burst out of him, and he wondered if this was what it was like to feel hysterical. In fact, now that the panic and fear had subsided, now he knew they were both okay, he was furious.

'You could have been killed,' he said, reaching out for her, taking her shoulders in his hands and pulling her close. 'You could have been killed.' He buried his face in her hair, breathing in her scent—wildflowers with a hint of something spicy, mixed now with the road dust.

'Harts.'

At the husky sound of his name on her lips, he pulled back and seeing the life in her eyes, the slight hint of bewilderment, he took her face in his hands and kissed her.

This was nothing like the kiss they'd shared two days earlier. That had been anger and surprise and a 'you shouldn't have left' kind of kiss. This was relief and bliss and an acknowledgment of what was in his heart. He loved her. So much that he suddenly knew he couldn't let her go. He'd thought it would be best for her to leave this town, but it wasn't best for her to leave him. She was good for him and he was good for her. Or he intended to be. Intended to find a way to share this love between them. Because she loved him. He knew it with every fibre of his being in the same way he knew he loved her. He'd seen it in the flare of her eyes when he'd first walked into the interrogation room at the station, when she'd leaned forward and called him 'Cooperman', as if she still acknowledged that they were each other's superheroes. He knew it in the way she'd asked him if she could do the autopsy. She would never have asked anyone else. That was her leaning on him, relying on him—and Erika never leaned or relied on anyone. He knew it in the way she'd argued with him, showing emotion that she didn't show anyone else. He knew it in the way she'd broken in front of him and the way her gaze hadn't met his that morning when it had met Pip's and Daphne's and even Mac's, because his opinion was the one that mattered the most. He'd known it in the way she'd responded to their first kiss, but most of all, he knew it in the way she kissed him now. With no hesitation. As if she was ready for it. Needed it. Wanted it.

Exactly the way he was kissing her.

Warm, exploring, giving, open-mouthed kisses. Her tongue met his, licking, tasting, stroking. Her lips were soft and plump and lingered with every movement, as if she never wanted to let go of him.

Hell, he knew that feeling.

He slid his hands into her hair, completely dislodging the already messy ponytail, fingers sliding through the silky strands. She moaned, a little sound of pleasure in the back of her throat. He smiled against her lips, nipped at them. She moaned again then nipped his lips. Christ that felt good. He ran his hands down her back and pulled her closer, needing to feel the warmth, the life of her crushed against him. Her hands slid from his shoulders to his back and held him tight in response.

'Ahem. Just so you know, I'm still here.' Toby's voice infiltrated the fog of passion and need surging through Hartley, but only enough to make him slow down, to press lingering kisses to her lips, to stroke the hair back from her face.

'Despite the fact I'm a fireman, there are some fires I can't put out.'

'Who said I wanted you to?' Hartley said, unwilling to stop entirely. He was holding Erika. Kissing Erika. And she was right there with him. And it was bliss.

'Ah, you might be interested to note that those sirens you hear in the distance are the ambulance. And by the looks of it, another patrol car. I think it might be the Sarge, Coops.'

That did snap through Hartley's passion-fog. He pulled back from Erika just enough to turn his head toward the sound of the sirens. Damn it. He knew that patrol car. It was his dad.

Erika moved out of his arms, but he caught her hand, holding tight. She didn't fight him. Grim's lips almost twitched into a smile.

The patrol car overtook the ambulance and came to a brake-squealing stop on the dusty verge opposite them, a cloud of red dirt spraying up across the potted bitumen. 'Where's the fire?' he called out to the large police officer who exited the car and strode over to them.

Sergeant Harry Cooper ignored the fireman's joke, his gaze arrowing in on Hartley and Erika, their joined hands. 'Is anyone hurt?'

Erika's chin lifted and an air of calm descended over her that was truly impressive. 'Only minor injuries, Sergeant. The airbags deployed efficiently. Fireman Grimshaw here has a head laceration that will need to be checked. He fell over and hit his head on the bumper when he climbed up to the road to catch the license plate of the offending car.' Toby groaned and rolled his eyes. Erika turned back to him. 'Are you in pain, Toby?'

'No,' Grim said, his gaze flicking to Hartley and then the sergeant, before leaning in toward Erika. 'It would be nice if not everyone knew I was a klutz.'

'You're lucky Mac isn't here,' Hartley said. 'Where are you going?' he asked as Erika freed her hand from his and began to work her way back down to the car.

'I just want to get my backpack.'

'I'll get it for you.'

'No you won't. I'm quite capable of getting it, thank you,' and she was down the ditch before he could move. He frowned and made a noise under his breath.

'Did you catch the licence plate?' the sergeant asked.

Grim pointed to his head. 'No, just my head on the edge of the car.'

The Sarge pressed his lips together in obvious disapproval then pulled out his always present pencil and pad and asked, 'Can you tell me anything else?'

Grim scratched his head and winced. 'It was a white ute with a silver tray. Ford, I think. Quite new. I didn't see the driver. It all happened pretty fast.'

Sergeant Cooper grunted. 'That's not much use to us. There's about 100 white Ford utilities licensed to townspeople alone, and that doesn't include all the vehicles used on the properties for one hundred miles around.'

'This one will have a bit of a dent in the side, and possibly some silver paint from where it scraped against the side of Erika's car.'

'Hmm.' The Sarge flipped open his note pad and wrote a few scratchy notes.

'Help me up please.' Erika had her backpack over her shoulder, a first-aid case in one hand, the other outstretched. Hartley leaned down and helped her up the last section. 'Thank you.' She flashed him a smile he felt all the way down to his knees, and then flipping open the little case, began to get out gauze and saline solution. 'I'll see to your cut, Toby.'

'You should leave the professionals to do that,' the sergeant said as the ambulance pulled up. 'Besides, you should see to yourself. You've got a cut on your leg there, girl. I thought you said there were no injuries except for Fireman Clumsy over there.'

Erika greeted his father's words with a completely neutral expression. If he hadn't known better, he'd think she'd never met his dad before and that he hadn't made her life a little slice of hell. 'Thank you for pointing that

out, Sergeant Cooper. I thought you were referring to potentially dangerous injuries, like Fireman Grimshaw's.' She pulled the 'bandage' away from
Grim's head—it was the green shirt she'd worn over her plain white singlet
that morning and was now ruined—and began to clean the wound with the
saline. 'If you're interested, the car that ran us off the road was a white Ford
Ranger utility with a flatbed tray, license plate number C1S56G.'

'You saw the license-plate number while you were being run off the
road?' Sergeant Cooper asked, his tone incredulous.

'I have an eidetic memory,' she replied crisply. 'I remember everything I
see.' She returned to cleaning Toby's wound.

'Well,' the Sarge grumped, his pencil scratching across his pad. 'I'll follow
this up then. If you've got everything else in hand here?' he asked Hartley.

'I do.'

'I'll be off then.' He turned to go, but as Grant and Steph, the paramedics,
passed him, he said to them, 'Watch that one. Thinks she's smart enough to
take over everyone's jobs.'

The paramedics looked bewildered before they shrugged and kept walking. Everyone liked his dad, but they all knew he could be a grouchy old
bastard sometimes.

'You banged your head again, Grim? Patching you up is getting to be a
habit,' Steph said as she put down her kit.

Erika turned to face Steph. 'He hit his head trying to get the license-plate
number of the car. It had nothing to do with being a klutz.' She glanced back
at Toby, nodding and smiling.

Toby snorted. 'Thanks, Erika.'

Hartley laughed at his expression. He'd often felt the same way in the
past when dealing with Erika's cluelessness when it came to social situations.
Annoying and adorable.

'Toby not being a klutz. I'll believe that when I see it,' Grant snorted.

'It was very heroic,' Erika continued.

'Sure it was,' Steph said, smirking, as Toby groaned louder and Erika
looked even more clueless. 'Let's look at this heroic injury then.' A moment
later, Steph nodded at Erika. 'You did a good job here.'

'Of course I did. I am a qualified doctor.'

'Erika is a forensic pathologist,' Hartley explained as Steph's brows rose.

'Lucky there's nobody here for her to see later,' Grant joked.

'It's Grim's job to not be funny, Grant, not yours,' Steph said. Erika just
looked confused. Steph rolled her eyes and packed up her kit. 'Well, I think

we're done here. You should get that leg properly seen to.' She pointed at Erika's leg. 'And Toby, you should go to the hospital to get a CT done.' She held her hand up before Toby had a chance to protest. 'Standard procedure for head injuries as you well know. We can take you both back if you like.'

'That's the last thing I need right now,' Grim said. 'If Coops can take us back, I'm going with him.'

'Me too.' Erika took Hartley's hand again, which got eyebrow raises from the two paramedics. She pulled him toward his car. 'Are you coming, Toby?'

Grim waved goodbye to the paramedics, a resigned expression on his face, and followed them to Hartley's Patrol, hopping in the back seat.

As they drove down the highway, Hartley said, 'I'll organise a tow truck to come get your car.'

Erika waved her hand. 'That doesn't matter right now. What does matter is the reason why someone ran us off the road. It has to be connected to our investigation. But how did they find out so quickly?'

'It's a small town. Everyone knows everything everyone else is doing.' Normally that didn't worry him, but right now, given the town's gossip mill had endangered Erika and Toby, it worried him a lot. 'I'll talk to the Boss. We'll make sure nothing else gets out.'

'Let's hope the Sarge can track down that ute.'

Hartley nodded. A creeping sensation ran down the back of his neck. He had a feeling they would never find the ute. And that Erika and Toby being run off the road was just the tip of the iceberg. 'Someone has gone to a lot of trouble covering up the murders, and they've just shown us they'll go further to ensure we don't continue our investigation.' He took her hand in his, squeezed. 'You need to be careful. They wouldn't have expected you to be here or that you'd be so brilliant at what you do, but now they know, they might come after you again.'

She shook her head. 'I don't care. All I care about is catching those responsible for killing my brother. I'll trust you to take care of my safety.'

He stared at her for a moment before returning his attention to the road, his mind playing over her words. Was that true? Did she trust him? He had to know. Because if she did truly trust him, then what they felt for each other really stood a chance.

But first, he had to make sure nothing more happened to her while investigating these murders. Once that was done, they would see to the possibility of their future together.

Chapter Fourteen

The drive back was quiet. When they got to the hospital, Erika wanted to go straight to the morgue, but Hartley insisted she and Toby be checked out by a doctor first. She didn't argue. She could feel Hartley looking at her and had to work hard not to shake, to want to bury herself in his arms and lose herself to his kiss once more because now the adrenaline rush was fading, all she could think of was the horror of that moment when she'd been driven off the road. It hadn't been the same as the night her parents had died—it was daylight, she was driving, and the road was completely different. They hadn't rolled and there were no trees for the car to end up wrapped around, but even so, she'd still had difficulty pulling herself together. Emotions had rushed over her, her strength crumbling around her in a whoosh, the world moving and swaying, but then Toby hurt himself. Seeing his blood, his pale face, had snapped something inside of her. Fury enveloped her, filling the cold emptiness that had been growing bigger and bigger since she'd come back to town. The fury brought with it ice-like clarity and she'd been able to tend Toby, hands as steady as a surgeon's.

She needed to get back to that feeling, to not give in to the fear and the panic and the need, that huge, unquentiable need, she'd felt when Hartley had taken her in his arms and kissed her. It had swept over her, swept through her, wiping away all worry, all fear, all doubt, and she couldn't let it happen again because for that moment, she'd forgotten her purpose. And she was nothing without purpose. It was the only thing that had seen her through all the bad times and it was the only thing that could truly help her now.

She must solve Peter's murder. That had to be the only thing that mattered right now.

Hartley wanted to wait with her to see the doctor, but she made him leave – he had paperwork to finish and leads to follow. By the time Doctor Baker came to do the examination, she had herself under control, answering the doctor's questions as efficiently as possible.

'You're fine, but shock could set in,' the older woman said, the serious look in her pleasant green eyes belying the smile on her face as she finished. 'I suggest you rest up and take it easy for the next twenty-four hours.'

Erika almost snorted in her face. That wasn't going to happen. She had things to do. 'I'll take that under advisement, Doctor Baker. Thank you.'

She hopped off the examination table, slung her backpack over her shoulders and went in search of Toby, but he'd been sent off for a CT. Damn it. She'd been hoping he'd come down to the lab with her and help. She'd just have to go by herself.

She was almost at the lifts when Hartley turned the corner. She thought he'd still be at the station reporting on the accident. He must have rushed it. He really shouldn't do that. She changed direction and walked toward him.

A smile bloomed on his face as he saw her. 'So, how are you?'

'Well. And you?'

He chuckled and shook his head. 'What did the doctor say?'

'She said what I already knew. I'm fine. A few bruises and the little cut on my leg, that's all. So we can get back to work right away.'

'All right. What do you want to do first?'

'Go down to the lab and start looking at these new evidence samples.'

'Sounds good to me.' The lift doors opened and they entered. The moment the door closed he took her hand, holding it firm. She knew she should say something, but she didn't, just curled her fingers around his.

The lift doors opened on the morgue floor. Instantly, Erika knew something was wrong. There was a strange smell in the air—not the antiseptic scent she was used to. It was stronger, oily. Just like...

She began to move just as the siren went off.

'Erika, wait!'

She smelled the smoke before she pressed the green button to open the doors to the morgue. The sprinklers above her clicked and water streamed down over her head as the doors opened. Smoke billowed out of the room, but no flames followed. She couldn't hear anything over the siren and the noise of the water pouring down from above, but when she darted into the morgue, she immediately located the source of the smoke.

The boots taken from the bodies and the lab's computer, smashed and mangled, had been dumped into one corner along with a pile of files, and set alight. What looked like a selection of sample slides and culture dishes were scattered around the lit pile, most destroyed beyond use. But that wasn't the worst of it. Two of the doors were open in the refrigerated cabinets where the bodies were kept. The two drawers that held Peter and Tyler. They were empty.

'No. No!' Someone had stolen her brother's body. Destroyed evidence. This couldn't be happening. Things like this just didn't happen.

'Erika! What are you doing?'

She spun. Hartley was standing behind her, dripping wet. 'They've stolen Peter.'

He looked around, the fire in his eyes matching exactly how she felt. 'They couldn't have gone far,' Hartley said. 'We must have just missed them.'

His words were like electricity, lighting her up, pushing her into motion. She ran past him and out into the hallway. The body snatchers couldn't have taken the stairs. That left the lifts. And the only one that would ensure they wouldn't be seen was the freight lift. Dead bodies were brought in and out of the morgue that way as a matter of course. Nobody would even think to question someone taking out two bodies. She raced to the lift. The floor number on the panel indicated it was at ground level. They might still be up there, loading the bodies they'd stolen. The exit stairs sign glowed green in her peripheral vision. Hartley's heavy footsteps echoed behind her in the wet hallway. 'Up here,' she yelled over her shoulder. 'They might still be there.'

She slipped through the door, racing up the stairs, heart booming, as she took them three at a time. She was alive. She was flying. She needed to fly faster. She had to get them. They couldn't do this to Peter. They'd already taken her brother's life. They weren't taking his body too.

'Erika. Wait.' Hartley's voice, echoing up the stairs behind her. 'They could be dangerous.'

She didn't care. The cold fury was back. If they were dangerous, so was she. She was a box jellyfish. An eastern brown snake. A poison dart frog. They'd made the mistake of messing with her, and now their time was limited. She would find them, and she would make them pay. She would make them pay. She burst out of the door next to the loading dock.

It was empty.

Sirens sounded in the distance, getting louder, the whoop-whoop sound thumping in her head alongside the beating of her heart. Water-soaked hair whipped against her face as she spun around, her backpack thumping against her spine as she searched the horizon for a van speeding away. Water dripped into her eyes, her breath razored her throat. Hartley exploded out of the door next to her, gun in hand. He saw her. Must have read her expression. He lowered the gun. 'They've gone.'

Yes. The men who'd destroyed evidence, had stolen dead bodies, who had most likely been responsible for killing her brother and were now trying to cover it all up, who had probably run her off the road, were gone. Fury rode over her again as she spun to fully face Hartley. 'Your security here sucks!'

He holstered his gun. 'Yes. Although, in the hospital's defence, nobody has ever bothered to steal from the morgue before.'

'They've done more than steal from the morgue. They've stolen from me.' She hit her fist against her chest, filled to the brim with furious purpose. 'They've taken Peter. They've taken him and they're not going to get away with it. I'm going to catch the criminals who did this and then they're going to be sorry they ever made the mistake of stealing from me.'

'Erika. You need to calm down.' He gripped her shoulders.

'No.' She jerked away from him. 'I don't want to calm down. I want to work. I need to work.'

'How will you do that?' He pushed dripping hair out of his eyes and jerked his hand back to the door, to the mess they'd left downstairs, the burned pile of papers and melted plastic and splintered glass littering the corner of the morgue. 'The bodies are missing and the evidence is destroyed.'

She looked back out to the distance, to the endless earth and sky she'd always loved and yet had simultaneously thought of as a cruel glimpse of a freedom that could never be hers. She pushed those feelings down, under the fury, burying them in cold, sharp reason. Fingers curling around the strap of her backpack—thank goodness it was waterproof—she pulled it off her shoulder. Inside were her notes and the samples she'd taken from the explosion site and more, kept safe in a refrigerated thermos. But best of all, her memory stick with her back-up files and the X-rays were there. And her phone with the recording of the autopsy. She patted her bag. 'They made a mistake. They thought everything was in the morgue, all the evidence, but they don't know how I work. I keep copies of everything. And it's all in here.' She glared fiercely at the road that led from the hospital. 'If there's the slightest bit of evidence that leads to the people responsible, I will find it. I will track them down and make them pay.'

'No.' He stepped closer, gripping the hand wrapped around her backpack strap as if her life depended on it. He smiled down into her eyes, the green in his glinting with something she thought might be pride, pleasure. 'We'll track them down and we'll make them pay. Together.'

Oh god. His words. They threatened to unravel her, to sweep away the cold fury once again. And without that, she had nothing. She was about to pull away when the fire truck pulled up behind them.

★★★

Hours later, once the site had been cleared by the firefighters, they re-entered the wet, smoky mess that had been the morgue.

Everyone—police, firefighters, ambulance officers—who was free had come to help with the clean-up. They worked with clenched jaws and furious eyes, helping to put the morgue back to rights after all the evidence had been photographed, tagged and bagged. The place was too wet to dust for fingerprints, but everything else that could be done had been done. Now all that needed doing was to make a space where Erika could get to work. Most evidence she worked on helped to prove a case, but sometimes it also helped to find the perpetrators. Real life wasn't like television shows where DNA, blood, particulates and hair left at the scene inevitably led to the suspect, but sometimes, just sometimes, it did. According to Hartley, Ben had interviewed people of interest in the drug trade in the few days since the bodies had been found, but while he was certain they were lying, he had no proof. They didn't even have enough proof to link these people to drugs going through the town. They needed something, anything, to tie these people to these crimes.

Erika was their only hope to do that.

It was strange, but even in Melbourne, working with the coroner's office and the police, Erika had never felt so much a part of something before. She'd always found contentment in her job, had felt welcomed and esteemed, liked even, but not this kind of fierce sense of belonging to something so much greater than her. It would have been frightening, the kind of thing she would have instinctively run from in the past, except for the fact that she had to find Peter. That alone helped her to focus.

Finally, the morgue was cleaned up enough so that she could go to work. Thankfully none of the equipment she needed to use, aside from the lab's computer, had been damaged by the small amount of smoke and the water. She walked with Toby and Hartley to the door to thank everyone, but only Mac and Ben were still there.

As the door opened to show the two tall men, Toby halted at her side. 'Ah shit,' she heard him mumble. She turned to see what was wrong, but he was already walking away back through the morgue to disappear through the X-ray doors.

She would have followed him to check he was feeling okay, except Hartley pulled her forward.

'Where did the Boss go?' he asked the two other police officers.

'She's following up a lead from one of the hospital staff we interviewed,' Ben said, gaze darting to the closing X-ray door before snapping back to Hartley. 'One of the cleaners was outside having a smoko when he saw an ambulance back up to the loading dock. He just thought they were unloading another body to the morgue. He finished his smoke, so he went back inside and didn't see anyone get out of the ambulance. I called the station and apparently one of their ambulances is missing. The Boss is at the station now talking to the paramedics on duty at the time of the incident.'

Hartley rubbed his jaw. 'They stole an ambulance so they could steal the bodies without anyone asking questions?'

'Sounds like it.'

'They've got some balls. Can you let me know what comes of the interview with the paramedics?'

Ben nodded. 'Sure thing. I'll go and join the Boss now.'

'Aren't you going to the Cooee with the others?' Mac asked.

Ben looked down at his watch. 'I'm still on duty for two hours. Later maybe. Will you guys be there?'

'I'm going to stay and help Erika and Toby, wherever he's gone,' Hartley said.

Ben shuffled his feet, gaze darting back to the closed X-ray door as he stuck his hands in his pockets. 'You don't need me to stay, do you?'

'No. I don't like too many people around when I work,' Erika said. 'You'd be more of a distraction than a help. Unless you have any knowledge of the pathological or forensic sciences.' She looked between Mac and Ben.

Mac made a snorting noise. 'Afraid I flunked science. Grim in there's your man for that.'

'Yes, I already know of Toby's proficiency in the forensic sciences.'

'Yes, Toby is nothing if not proficient,' Ben said.

Erika observed a strange look cross Ben's face, but she couldn't understand what it was, or why Hartley and Mac were suddenly shuffling their feet and stuffing their hands in their pockets.

Mac broke the uncomfortable silence. 'We might not be able to help with the sciency stuff, but do you want us to stick around and watch your back?'

Erika frowned. 'Why would I need my back watched?'

'In case word gets out that you are still doing work on samples?'

'That's unlikely given Harts promised he'd make certain no further information got out about this case.'

Mac laughed. 'You've been away too long, EJ. Gossip is king here and secrets are never kept for long.'

'We didn't tell anyone else about the double samples I kept.' She looked at Hartley. 'If everyone does their job, there should be no gossip.'

Hartley's mouth twisted. 'What Mac is trying to say is, even if everyone keeps their mouth shut, it will still get out you are here working in the morgue. And if you're in the morgue, people will guess you're still working on something pertinent to the case.'

'I didn't think of that.'

'That's what we're here for. To consider the big picture so you sciency types can concentrate on the particulars,' Mac said, face splitting into an even bigger grin.

'Fine. I'll leave you all to organise guard shifts for the morgue. I'm going to work.'

She turned and left Hartley to discuss the roster with the other men and went back into the morgue. As the door swished shut behind her, Toby stepped out of the X-ray room. 'Everything okay?'

Face a blank, Toby said, 'Fine. I just thought I'd check we hadn't missed anything.'

'Good idea.' She turned away and then back again. 'Are you sure everything is fine? I feel like I'm missing something.'

'No. You're not missing anything.'

'Okay. Then let's get to work.'

'There's nothing I'd like more.'

She made a quick call to Stephen Thompson, her boss in Melbourne, asking him to prioritise the evidence she'd sent to him and confirm there was more on the way. She then explained to Toby what needed to be done and they set about working up the samples and sorting through the evidence they had from the explosion site, building a story of death and murder.

Finally, she plugged the medical USB with the X-rays into her computer and brought them up. The fractures in the bone around the parietal lobe were more severe than she'd thought. He'd been hit very hard peri-mortem and if she were to take an educated guess, she'd say it was something rounded and about four to five centimetres across. A pipe of some kind. Or a bat. He would have been dead in seconds. He possibly hadn't even seen it coming. Although…

She frowned.

The angle of the blow didn't make sense unless the person was nine foot tall. Which could only mean Peter was on his knees when he was hit.

She brought up the images of his legs. Yes. There was a fracture and tearing of the patella which suggested a hard fall to the knee. She looked at the images of his hands and arms. There was damage to his distal and proximal phalanges and the break across the metacarpals—they were all defensive wounds. Wounds you'd gain in a fight. There was no sign of remodelling, so these injuries had been sustained just before he died.

He even had a fracture of the radius on the right arm, suggesting he'd lifted his arm to stave off a blow. Although, Peter was left handed, so he would have lifted his left arm. Which was why he'd broken his arm all those years ago when he'd fallen out of the tree she'd dared him to climb. He'd put his left hand out as he fell and given himself a fracture of the ulna and radius. It had been bad. Except…

She frowned, flipping back to the image of his left arm.

This body had no indications of breaks on its left arm, either recent or healed.

This couldn't be Peter.

This body was somebody else!

Chapter Fifteen

'Are you sure?' Superintendent Katherine Stuart stared at her from across her desk, her expression intelligent, thoughtful. She wasn't questioning her ability to do her job, just simply asking for verification. Erika understood. Verification was everything.

'I am. But you can see for yourself.' She handed the Superintendent the USB.

Erika couldn't help but shift from one foot to the next, her fingers dancing against her leg as the other woman loaded up the images that turned the whole investigation around.

Her brother was missing, not dead. And the proof was currently taking way too long to appear on the superintendent's desktop monitor. 'You need new computers.'

'Yes. The requisition is in, but as always, these things take time.'

Erika felt like she was coming out of her skin. She was about to burst. Frustration. Excitement. They both felt the same.

Hartley grasped her hand, holding her fingers still, his breath brushing across her cheek as he leaned down and whispered, 'Take a breath before you pass out.'

She did. And another. He squeezed her hand.

'Better?'

She nodded. She was better. More centred. Less like she was going to crawl out of her skin.

Finally, the image blinked onto the monitor. Katherine looked up at her. 'What am I looking at here?'

Erika came around the desk and pointed at the image. 'Peter broke his left arm very badly when he was ten. He had to have an operation and they put plates and screws in so it would heal properly because it was near the growth plates.'

'So we would be seeing screws and the plate?'

'No. They took them out after it was properly healed. However, you would see evidence of the fracture through remodelling here.' She ran her finger across the screen. 'And you would also see indentations where the screws held the break in place here and here.' She looked up from the screen and into Katherine's slate-blue eyes. 'There is nothing. No break. No sign of any form of operation. This is not Peter's arm.'

'Which means this is not Peter.'

Erika nodded. 'This,' she said, poking the screen before standing upright, 'is somebody else. But even if this isn't enough proof, I asked Hartley to get Peter's dental file from Dr Bliss, our old dentist. They don't match.' She looked from Hartley to Katherine and back again. 'I don't know who this is, but it isn't Peter. My brother is alive.'

'Then where is he?'

'And why was his wallet found on the victim?' Hartley added.

Erika shook her head. 'I don't know. Maybe his wallet fell out of his pocket when he went to visit Tyler. I imagine he was going there to talk his friend out of doing something stupid.' She glanced at Hartley. 'That sounds like Peter, doesn't it?'

He shrugged. 'I didn't really have much to do with him anymore.' She glared at him. 'But yes, it does sound like something he would do.'

She nodded. 'Maybe he even saw the murders and got frightened and ran for it and is in hiding.' Although, that didn't really sound like him. She shook her head. 'I think if we can find out who this is, then we might have a better idea of what happened and where Peter might have got to.'

Katherine tapped the screen. 'I can't believe it's as innocent as that, Ms Hanson. The wallet wasn't just found on the floor. It was found in the burned jacket pocket of the deceased. It didn't get there by mistake. Someone put it there.'

'You think Peter had something to do with these deaths?'

Katherine's expression was grim as she met Erika's gaze. 'Without further evidence suggesting otherwise, it certainly looks like that might be the case.'

'Why? Because his wallet was found on the deceased?'

'Yes. The most likely reason for that having occurred is that he put it there to make us think he was dead.'

'An autopsy would have quickly proved it wasn't him. He would have known that.'

Katherine's gaze dropped to the computer screen. 'Yes. But Peter was aware we were without a coroner.'

'As was everyone else in town,' Hartley said. He gripped Erika's hand more tightly, held on even when Katherine's gaze flickered to their hands and her brows raised. He met her questioning expression with an implacable stare, and she gave a curt nod.

'Yes. That's true. But there is no evidence anyone else was there.'

'That we've found. Grim is still analysing those samples we took at the site.'

'Oh?'

'Hair and a piece of material that didn't belong to the two deceased, as well as the chemical composition of the accelerant. They might give us a clue as to who was there along with the deceased.'

Katherine sat back in her chair, staring at the screen. 'I'm glad your brother isn't one of those bodies, Ms Hanson, but this makes things even more complicated than they were before. It's also possible someone stole the bodies to try to keep us from finding out this isn't your brother. Why would they bother doing that if he wasn't involved in some way?'

Erika didn't know the answer to that question. 'I know he wasn't involved.'

'Mmm.' Katherine tapped her fingers on the edge of her desk. 'How is the rest of the investigation going, Detective?'

'I've pulled Mac in to help. He's tracking down the stolen ambulance. Ben and the Sarge are tapping their sources around town to see if there's any other information about Tyler or Peter we don't already know. And to perhaps shed light on who this is.' He pointed to the screen.

'Good. Well, until we have something more, I think it's time you two got some R&R. You both look like you've not slept for a week.'

'I'm fine. I just want to get out there and try to find Peter.'

Hartley's gaze roved over her face. She tried to steel her expression, but he obviously saw something there she couldn't hide from him, because he nodded. 'The Boss is right. Let's go to the Cooee, get a steak and a drink, and then get you back to the hotel.'

Erika followed Hartley out of Katherine's office after saying goodbye to the older woman, but as she hopped in his car, realised she didn't want to go to the Cooee. Despite the odd feeling of being a part of something earlier, she didn't feel like seeing any of them right now. She wanted things simple. Quiet. With Hartley. Without people staring at them and making comments about things they didn't understand. As he started up the car, she said, 'I'd rather go back to the hotel and eat if you don't mind.'

'Okay.'

They drove straight to the hotel. Even though it was only around the corner, it seemed to take forever. She was climbing out of her skin. Her brother wasn't dead. She wanted to jump for joy. She'd kept it together so far, but now she wanted to celebrate. To do something wild. To just feel the joy of life, rather than the heaviness of loss and death.

Hartley turned to walk into the bar to order drinks and food, but she stopped him, grabbing his hand. 'Thank you.' Before he could say anything, she went up on her tiptoes and kissed him. Even though the caress was brief, fire flared. His hands, which had come to her shoulders to steady her, gripped tighter. She leaned back a little, looking into his eyes.

It was like looking into a fiery blaze. Heat and desire and passion and something more, something almost frightening, stared back at her. Breath caught in her throat. Nobody looked at her like Hartley. Nobody ever had. It was…thrilling.

'Erika,' he breathed, his breath brushing over her face.

'Harts.' She knew what he was asking. Knew she should step away, stop this from going any further. Particularly given her decision at the hospital to concentrate solely on Peter. Besides, it didn't make sense. They were too different, despite everything they'd shared. He loved it here. She…didn't hate it anymore, but not hating it was far from wanting to stay. Nothing could ever come of what was between them.

But did it have to? They wanted each other. Here. Now. After the last forty-eight hours she'd spent thinking her brother was dead, after the emotional fugue she'd suffered the night before, surely she deserved something that would make her feel good, even if only fleetingly?

Besides, getting this need for each other out of their systems with a night of passion would be a good thing. It would allow her to concentrate fully on finding her brother and the murderers and then she could leave.

It made sense to allow this to happen tonight.

She didn't say anything, simply took his hand in answer to his question and led him upstairs to her room.

She inserted the key in the lock and turned, fingers as steady as when she held a scalpel even though her entire being was trembling with anticipation. Hartley stood close behind her, not touching, but his heat enveloped her, stroking her back, his breath heavy and hot against the nape of her neck. She opened the door, took a few steps inside, placed her backpack on the chair near the door. The door closed behind them, but before she could turn, Hartley had her up against the door, his body pressed against hers, his fingers scraping into her hair, his lips a hairs breadth from hers.

'Are you sure?' he breathed, breath a caress across aching lips.

'Yes.' She scraped her fingers into his hair and pulled his head down that final centimetre.

Lips meshed in a hot hard clash of teeth and tongue. Bodies pressed. Hands found purchase in muscle, on skin, fingers stroking, clenching, holding, as if to say 'mine'.

And he was hers in that moment. Just like she was his.

Before fear had time to catch her, his hand was on her breast, his lips tracing, hot and wet, down her throat. Sensations flooded through her, muddying her thoughts. Her head flopped back against the door, giving him access to trace nibbling kisses back up the column of her neck, sending flames of need licking all over her.

'Hartley,' she gasped, pushing into his hand, the aching nub of her nipple scraping the inside of her bra.

With a groan, he lifted her up. Her legs twined around his middle, her core pressed to the hard push of the erection straining his jeans. She writhed against him. Why weren't they already naked? Why wasn't he buried deep inside her, working away this sudden, horrible need? A need that had been building ever since he'd walked into the interview room—could it only have been two days ago? It seemed an eternity. Of waiting. Of frustration building. Of this need itching under her skin, bursting to get out. And now, now, finally, it was happening.

She was going to have sex with Hartley and hell! It was already more glorious than she could bear. More frightening. She had no control. No control.

She didn't care.

She tore her lips from his, breath a harsh slash in her throat. 'Bed. Now.'

They tore at clothes as they stumbled back toward the bed, fingers fumbling, lips kissing and laughing and nipping and licking. Then they were naked and he was staring at her and she was staring at him.

Beautiful. Just beautiful. Long and lean with just the right amount of muscle. Wide shoulders tapering into narrow hips with that sexy dip near the hip bone just above dark curls and the erection straining toward her. She reached for it, enjoying the hot silk of it, the jerk of his muscles, the hiss of breath in her ear. His hand came over hers, stilling the movement. She looked up. 'Later. I've got other things planned for now.' The smile in his eyes was too delicious and she reached up and drank it from his lips.

They fell back onto the bed, hands finding each other, his hard chest brushing over her peaked nipples. She gasped into his mouth as sensation shot through her, nerves on fire in a way she'd never felt before. She wasn't a virgin by any means. She'd been sexually active since the age of twenty and had a healthy sexual appetite. But nothing had ever been like this. This was wild. She had no control over him, over her. It was just happening, frighteningly, gloriously, with no constraints, with barely any thought.

She held tighter, bit down on his shoulder, the instinct to run, to pull away, burned in the fire of longing and need. He groaned and ran a hot trail of lips and tongue and teeth down her neck, to her breast. He took her aching nipple into his mouth. She arched up off the bed, the light behind her eyes flaring and turning to black as he sucked, his tongue flicking over the sensitised peak. Her hands streaked over his back, her legs wrapped around him tighter, pulling him in. He resisted, lifted his head to gasp, 'Condom.'

'I'm on the pill.'

'Thank god.' He bent to kiss her again, but just as she sank into his kiss, he flipped them, letting her be on top, gifting her control.

She laughed. The rumble through his chest as he joined her laughter, vibrated through her thighs and into her core. She gasped, knowing he couldn't help but feel how ready she was. She leaned down and took his lips with hers again, her fingers pushing into his hair. His arms came around her, but before he could pull her down to him, she sat back, took his hands in hers and placed them over her breasts. Something flared in his eyes as she raised herself over him. 'Now.'

'Now.'

She sank down on him in one glorious slide. Her eyes rolled back into her head at the feeling of fullness. Of rightness. She opened her eyes, her gaze finding the vibrant green of his in the semi-dark room and she rode him, a slow, long slide to start, but speeding up, their breaths coming faster and faster as the sensation inside her tightened, tightened. His hips met hers in a rhythm that seemed designed to touch her in all the right places. She wanted to kiss him, but she couldn't tear her gaze from his. She was captured. Beyond control. Beyond thought. Just feeling and an intense pulling need inside her that was telling her she belonged.

They moved, skin damp with sweat, breath a panting moan, eyes locked, hands grasped together over her breasts. The muscles at her core were pulling tighter, tighter, rising up and up, the tension of it almost pain. She could see the same reflected in his eyes. They moved harder, faster, oblivious to anything else but the need driving them up and up and on and on. The orgasm took her, vicious, pulsing, all encompassing. She lifted, lifted, then was released to fall, lights sparking around her, breath a harsh rasp in her chest, heartbeat thundering in her head.

Somewhere in the back of her mind, she heard Hartley cry out her name, spasm against her as his seed pumped into her, and then she was unaware of anything else for quite some time.

When she finally surfaced, she was wrapped in Hartley's arms, her cheek against his chest. His breaths were even and steady. Had she fallen asleep? It was fully dark now, only the faint glimmer of a streetlight shining through the window. They'd forgotten to shut the curtain in their need for each other. It was night. Huh. She must have fallen asleep.

'Are you still with me?'

She lifted her head, gaze finding his even in the dark. 'Yes.'

He smiled and kissed her.

Passion ignited again immediately, as if she'd not just had the most astonishing orgasm of her life. Without thought, she gave herself up to it again, to him, his name caught in her heartbeat, in the thrum through her nerves, in the twist of pained delight that was the orgasm he brought to her a second time as he used fingers and tongue and finally his hot, hard length buried deep inside her.

After, as she lay twined in his arms, breasts pressed into his side, his leg thrown possessively over her hips, she listened as he fell softly into sleep. She was happy. Happier than she'd ever been. Happier than she had a right to be with everything else going on.

Did that make her a bad person?

The thought was a dissonant chord in her mind. She moved a little away from Hartley's warmth. She didn't have a right to this belonging. It wasn't what she wanted.

His arms tightened around her and he mumbled, 'Stay with me.'

She went to answer him, to say something, but he was already asleep again. She didn't want to wake him, so she stayed where she was, eyes wide, staring into the night. And as she lay there, his slow, steady breaths and the low thump-thump of his heart beating in his chest reverberating against her cheek, something old and painful sparked to life deep inside her, digging the claws of fear into her heart. She should never have given in to this, because it meant something to him it could never mean to her.

As the pain tore little pieces of happiness away, she knew only one thing—she couldn't do what he asked. She could never stay with him, because this kind of happiness, it could never be hers. She'd learned that lesson and learned it well the night she'd failed to save her mum and dad.

Chapter Sixteen

Erika was gone when Hartley woke up. That wouldn't have normally worried him, except she'd tidied up, folding the clothes she'd ripped off him the night before and placing them on the chair by the window, his shoes neatly lined up under it. Crap. When they were children, she was pedantic about everything being tidy and orderly, even lining up clothes pegs in the basket a certain way. The most extreme bouts occurred when she'd had a hard time at school or home and she'd come over to his place after cleaning hers, climbing up to the window—there was no way the Sarge would have let her inside their house—spending hours cleaning and tidying every last centimetre of his room. She'd even make his bed to within an inch of its life, the sheet folded over the top of the doona, one corner turned back just so.

He sat up with a jerk. The doona had been over him, so it was rumpled, but the blanket they'd kicked off the night before was folded across the foot of the bed, the corner turned over just so. 'Ah shit.' If she wasn't covering emotional turmoil, burying it deep inside under control and order, then he was a monkey's uncle.

He threw his clothes on and was out the door and downstairs a moment later.

Voices came from the kitchen. He pushed open the door.

'Morning.' Daphne's bright smile met him as she looked up from the stove. 'Did you have a good night's sleep?' The knowing light in her eyes told him she knew what he and Erika had done in the night and that she approved.

'Do you know where Erika is?'

Daphne pointed with her spatula toward the bar. 'She's having a chat with Pip. Such wonderful news that Peter isn't dead. Although, I am concerned he's not contacted anyone to let them know he's okay. I'll have to give him a piece of my mind when he comes back.'

Hartley didn't stop to listen to the rest, just charged through the kitchen and out the western doors into the bar. The shutters still hadn't been opened to let in the morning sun, so the room was dark. Even so, he knew where she was. He felt the pull whenever she was near, a lodestone to him.

Erika's head snapped up. She could sense him too? He hoped that was true. Perhaps his worry was needless. They had a connection. Something special and unique. She couldn't walk away from it. It didn't make sense.

Comforted by this thought, he made his way through the tables to her side. 'Erika.' He bent down to kiss her.

She stiffened, lips trembling under his as if fighting against something. He pulled away, unable to stop from frowning. 'You were gone when I woke.'

'I'm an early riser. And I didn't want to wake you.'

'I'll always be happy to be woken by you.' He tried a smile. She didn't return it.

'Pip was just trying to think of something that might help us find Peter.' She turned back to Pip, her movements stiff. Was she embarrassed? Perhaps. This man had been a kind of father figure to her. Maybe she didn't want him to know they'd slept together. Although that didn't gel with the woman he knew.

The other man nodded, gaze skating questioningly between them. Hartley grabbed an upturned chair off a nearby table, righted it and took a seat at the head of the booth. Erika didn't so much as glance at him again, keeping her gaze steadfastly on Pip. Well, if she wanted to be all business this morning, that was fine. But if she didn't shake it off, they were going to have a talk later in the day.

He forced his mouth into a smile. 'So, could you remember anything?'

Pip shook his head, shoulders sagging. 'No. I have no idea where he might have gone or why. He was fired up trying to get the money to take Mabel overseas for the treatment. I can't imagine he'd just take off suddenly.'

Erika rubbed at her brow. 'There has to be a reason other than what the police think. He couldn't be involved in this.'

'He might have been helping Tyler. For Mabel.'

'No.' Erika's eyes blazed.

Pip raised his hands defensively. 'I'm just saying he would have done any-thing for your grandmother.'

'Not this. He knew what she was.'

'To you. But to him, she was different. He loved her and she loved him. It's why he came back to look after her.'

Her eyes shadowed with pain, she stared intently at him. 'You seriously think he could have got involved with drugs to pay Mabel's medical bills.'

Pip nodded sadly. 'It's possible. If it was the only way, he just might.'

She glared from him to Hartley. 'You think that too.' It wasn't a ques-tion, so he didn't answer. She stood up. Pointed her finger at them. 'You're wrong. He wouldn't do it. That's why he contacted me. He needed money from me. And I would have given it to him. I never touched the money I got from Mum and Dad. He could have had it all.'

'Even if you knew it was for Mabel?'

She paused, something painful twisting in her eyes. 'For Peter. I would have done it for Peter.'

'Do you think he would have known that?'

Her face screwed up as if she was fighting tears, but then she took a deep breath, her expression implacable. 'He is not a murderer.'

'Of course not,' Pip gasped. 'I'm not suggesting he is.'

'The police are.' Erika jabbed a finger at Hartley. 'If you believe that Peter was involved in making those drugs, and yet he's not one of the bodies, then you believe he had something to do with the murders.'

'I never said that.'

'But you're thinking it.'

Her glare was like a shove, a dare to deny what she was saying. 'It's part of my job to look at every angle, even those ones that aren't probable or popular.'

She made a choking sound in the back of her throat. 'I should have known it would be like this. I should have known you'd turn out exactly like your dad, always ready to jump to the conclusion the privileged Hanson kids are rotten to the core.'

Hartley pushed up from his seat, the chair skidding back across the par-quetry floor. 'Now, that's hardly fair.'

'Fair? What in all this is fair?' She threw her hands up, her face a snarl. 'I can't even look at you right now. I want you to leave.'

'No. We need to talk about this.'

'Leave!' She pointed at the door.

He crossed his arms. 'Not until we talk about what is really going on.'

'What is really going on? What is really going on.' Her voice was rising with every word. 'What is really going on is I slept with a man last night who thinks my brother is involved in drugs and could murder two men. And it makes me feel sick. Sick.'

He flinched as her words slapped at him, but it didn't stop him from saying what needed to be said. 'That's not what is really going on.'

'No?'

'No.' He took a step closer, not caring that Pip was sitting there, eyes wide, watching them. 'I think you are using that as an excuse. You know I don't really feel that way. I know Peter isn't a murderer. And I'm pretty sure he didn't get involved in the drugs Tyler was making. There is some other reason why his wallet was found on the other body. But you and I both know what I feel doesn't matter. Only the facts do. And the facts, at the moment, are pointing to Peter having been involved with what happened in that warehouse. So, it's my job to consider all scenarios and investigate, just as it is yours. Without emotion. Without prejudice. We need to let the facts speak. You know that's true as much as I do.'

She opened her mouth to respond, but he was too angry to let her. 'No. It's my turn to speak. You've said what you think of me, now it's my turn to say what I think about you.'

She folded her arms and lifted her chin, almost as if she didn't care, but he saw the fear dancing in her eyes, the pain she was running from, had been running from all these years. It made his fury wilder. He wanted her to stop running, to stop accusing, to stop fearing. Words came spilling out of his mouth.

'You come across as if you don't feel, but that's just an act. A cover. Just like this bullshit about me believing Peter a murderer. It's just an excuse so you have permission to run away, just like you did all those years ago, because you're scared shitless. Scared to let yourself feel. Scared to let go. Scared to hold on to something, someone, outside yourself. Even when that someone loves you more than life itself. You would rather make up some stupid, cowardly excuse and run away, than face the fact you feel something real and true and raw and full. And you know what that makes you, Erika Jasmine Hanson? A coward. You're a coward. And you know what else is true? I deserve someone who isn't too cowardly to face me the morning after the most amazing sex of our lives, who isn't too cowardly to hear me say I love you. I deserve someone with the strength to stand there and say it back.'

She was staring at him, arms still crossed tightly in front of her, expression shuttered more firmly than it had been before. He wasn't even sure she'd taken in a single word of what he'd said. 'Screw this for a joke. I've got work to do.' And with that, he marched out of the Echo Springs Hotel and away from Erika. He'd been an idiot, apparently, to think she felt for him even a skerrick of what he felt for her. She was like a cyclone, sweeping in and upending his life, twisting him this way and that until he didn't know which way was up. And he'd let her.

His dad was right. She was using him. She was heartless.

He swore again as he jerked open the door to his Patrol. That wasn't fair. He knew she wasn't using him. And she had a heart. It was iced over, buried so deep under fear and pain for so many years that no amount of his loving her could ever hope to thaw it. Not without some help from her. And she'd proved today that was never going to happen. She'd prefer to run away from the miracle of what they'd shared than face the fear and pain from her past. And there was nothing he could do about it.

'Fuck!' He slammed his hands against the wheel. He wanted to strangle Mabel Hanson for what she'd done to Erika. Instead of getting that poor, intelligent girl the help she needed after her parents died, she'd treated her granddaughter as if she was some pariah who didn't deserve anything more than harsh words and emotional and physical torment. She'd screwed her granddaughter right royally. And she'd screwed any chance for her to experience true happiness.

In essence, Mabel Hanson had screwed them all.

And now he'd just super screwed everything over again by losing his temper with Erika and saying some horrible things to her, that while having an essence of truth, were completely unfair.

His anger slipped away as suddenly as it had come and he leaned his forehead against the steering wheel. He felt sick. What had he done? What had he *done?* She'd never speak to him again. And he'd deserve it if she didn't.

His fingers curled tight over the steering wheel until his knuckles felt like they were going to pop out of his skin. Stupid. *Stupid.*

He sat up abruptly. He couldn't stay here.

Turning the key so hard it almost snapped in the lock, he started the car and with a squeal of wheels, roared off down the street, knowing nothing more right now than he needed to get away before he did something more he'd live to regret.

He drove out to Echo Ridge Lookout and stared out at the horizon, but was just reminded of Erika all over again. She'd always loved this spot. They'd come here often, especially after a big rain, and just sit and stare out at the empty horizon. She'd said it made her feel like there was a possibility of everything being wiped clear and clean. A blank slate. Tabula rasa. She'd left here to get her blank slate and she'd filled it with things other than him. Perhaps it was time he accepted that fact rather than rail against it.

He had no idea how long he'd been sitting there when his radio crackled.

'Echo 4, this is base. Come in.'

Shit. He'd forgotten he was supposed to be on duty. He picked the radio up. 'Echo 4, base. What's up, Dispatch? Over.'

'The missing ambulance has been found. The Boss wants you to bring Dr Hanson to the site to look over the ambulance for evidence we might miss, over.'

His heart leapt a little at the news the ambulance had been found, but then dipped at the thought of facing Erika. 'Copy base, but I'm not with Ms Hanson right now, over.'

There was a pause. 'Aren't you supposed to be guarding her? Over.'

Crap. He turned the Patrol around. 'Copy base. I'm heading back to the hotel now. Echo 4 out.' He only hoped his stupid need to run away hadn't given whoever was behind the murders a free run at Erika.

He called her mobile. She didn't answer. By the time he got back to the hotel, he was in a panic. He raced inside. Pip was at the bar.

'Erika?'

Pip gestured over his shoulder. 'In the kitchen with Daph. Do you want me to get her?'

Hartley leaned against the bar, relief leaving him a bit jelly-legged. 'Is she okay?'

Pip sighed heavily. 'She seems fine. Didn't even tear up after you left. Just turned around and went upstairs for a while. When she came back down, she was the same as always.'

Hartley's shoulders slumped. He wasn't sure if he was relieved or upset about that.

Pip pointed his finger at Hartley. 'What you said wasn't a lie, but I'm still disappointed in you, son.'

Wow. That hurt more than he thought it would. 'You can't berate me more than I've already berated myself.'

'Figured that might be the case.' He put his hand on Hartley's shoulder, squeezed. 'This town has had its fair share of tragedies, but that girl has been through more than anyone else I have ever met. She might never be able to give you what you want.'

'I know.'

'But she's worth fighting for.'

'I know that too.'

Pip slapped his shoulder. 'Good lad. You don't give up. That's how I got my Daph. And I've never looked back.'

At that moment, Daphne and Erika came out of the kitchen. Daphne frowned at him. 'Daphne.'

'Hartley.'

That was all he could manage without looking at Erika. She didn't meet his eyes, hers fixed on the window behind him. He deserved that. Just like he deserved her curt, 'What do you want?'

He knew it was pointless making excuses—there were none—so he just kept it simple. 'I'm sorry for what I said. I didn't mean it. I was angry. And hurt.'

She looked up at him, the surprise on her face so comical he would have laughed if the moment wasn't pregnant with tension. 'I hurt you?'

'You did.'

She looked so confused, like she couldn't understand how that would ever have happened. He wanted to explain, to tell her he loved her, this time without yelling it at her. Of course, that would get them nowhere, and right now there was a case that needed solving and her help needed to get them there.

'The ambulance has been found.'

The confusion disappeared as her keen sense of professionalism shone through. 'You need me to look for forensic evidence.'

'Yes.'

'Let me get my backpack and I'll be right with you.'

When she'd disappeared up the stairs, Daphne excused herself. 'I've got two hundred scones to get in the oven and the tea cakes and finger sandwiches to make for afternoon tea.' The Echo Springs Hotel had become famous among the retirees and grey nomads staying in the caravan parks around town for the high tea it put on every Thursday, so Hartley knew it wasn't just an excuse. She literally did have that many scones to bake.

When Daphne had disappeared back into the kitchen, Pip slapped him on the back again and said, 'I better get back to things too. The flowers Daph wants for the table settings won't get in those vases by themselves.'

'Thanks Pip.'

The other man pointed his finger at him. 'Just don't give up.'

Hartley nodded. Giving up on Erika was the last thing he would ever do, but he wasn't sure it was up to him.

Chapter Seventeen

On her examination of the stolen ambulance, Erika found hairs and a smear of blood and traces of a reddish-purple soil with a silica base. The colour was particular to the area around the springs and to the north and west of the town where the old copper mines were situated. A large area. Too large to search thoroughly with only the manpower of the Echo Springs police station. There were also some shavings of metal which, when she did analysis on them, turned out to be low-grade copper. The leaf debris she'd have to send to Melbourne to identify—plants and bugs and slime weren't her particular forte. It was important though. Knowing what it was and where it came from could narrow down a search location for where these men had come from or where they'd dumped the bodies.

There were also a couple of good boot prints but no fingerprints. They'd probably worn gloves.

Erika returned to the lab to work the samples while Hartley and Ben and Mac continued to question townspeople about Peter, the ambulance and anything suspicious they might have seen in recent weeks.

Hours later, Hartley called and said the Sarge had tracked down the registration of the ute that had run her and Toby off the road. It had been reported stolen from a local farmer, Jacinta Buchanan, earlier in the week, and was still missing. A dead end. Erika clenched her jaw as she bit back a sound of frustration. 'We need to find that ute.' They had a good amount of evidence, but sometimes that wasn't enough. The ute could be the solid lead they were missing. There could be evidence there that would lead them directly to the murderers.

'We'll do our best,' Hartley said, before hanging up.

Erika took a deep, steadying breath and then turned back to her work. She'd been about to look at the hair they'd found in the ambulance. She put it under the microscope. It was short, dark brown at the root, the majority of the strand bleached a white-blond. It was the same as the hair she and Toby had collected at the explosion site the day before. She'd been thrilled to see the root as they could get DNA off that, but she didn't have the equipment here for that, so she'd have to send it to Melbourne. However, she could type the blood and do some analysis on the sand while Ben was going through the database looking for similar treads to match to the boot print. If it was something unusual to the area, then it might help them pinpoint the owner.

The hair was probably their best lead so far. None of the ambulance officers had dyed blond hair—she'd met them all the day before when they took shifts to help clean up the morgue—so this was possibly their killer.

There couldn't be many men around with short, white-blond hair. Surely Hartley and the other police could identify a suspect from that. Until DNA was done on the strand, it wouldn't be enough to take to court, but it certainly was enough to bring someone in for questioning. She made a note and continued going through the evidence collected so far.

She finished jotting down her final notes, saved them and her findings on her computer and then copied all of it to two memory sticks, before taking care of packing away the evidence slides and bagged items in a new locked safe. The items that needed refrigeration were more of an issue, but they'd bought a sturdy lock for the cool-room door, which would have to be enough for now, especially given Superintendent Stuart had posted a police guard outside the morgue to stop any further incidents of burglary and vandalism. And to keep Erika safe. She hadn't missed the pointed look between Constable Smith and Hartley when they'd arrived earlier. She was one of their best chances to track down the murderers, and so the police weren't taking any chances. Or maybe it was Hartley who wasn't taking a chance that she'd run off again with no warning.

She bit her lip. Damn it. She wished she still had more work to do. It had stopped her from thinking of all the thing she didn't want to think about in any depth right now—Hartley, Peter, Hartley, her grandmother, Hartley, this town.

Hartley.

Damn it! She shook her head. No. She couldn't think about him. Thinking about him hurt too much in too many ways. His words kept circling in her mind now she had nothing to do. Words she thought might actually be true, no matter how much she might deny it.

She *was* a coward. She *had* been running and was about to run again. From this town. From him. From her feelings for him. The only problem was, she didn't think she could ever run far enough to get away from that. She had a horrible feeling her love for Hartley would follow her wherever she went. She'd tried to shield her heart for so long from this very thing happening, but it had happened anyway. She'd known the possibility of it when she'd been sixteen and had run away from here, from what he might come to be to her. It wasn't the only reason she'd run, but it was part of it. Nothing good ever came from loving people.

And yet, she loved him.

She leaned her head against the cool-room door. What the hell was she going to do about it?

She turned her face, pressing her cheek against the cool surface. She could reason this through. That's what she did. She turned further until she was leaning against the door, staring at the empty morgue. So, reason through it. Reason through what he said and why it hurt so much.

The two things that hurt the most were that he said she was a coward and that he deserved more.

He was right. She didn't deserve him. Probably never would. And that hurt more than she ever thought it would. She was strange and saw the world through a kind of clinical lens. She was also broken. She knew that about herself. Even Jenny's help hadn't fixed her. There was just too much about her that had shattered the night her parents died and there wasn't any way of putting those pieces back together. She'd kept going, kept pushing on, because that seemed like the only thing to do, but she remained broken.

Even though Jenny was a psychologist herself, she'd taken Erika to see a colleague of hers to talk through her issues in a private, safe space. There, she had discovered that she'd closed herself off from her emotions, relying on the cold clarity of reason and logic and facts to give her a touchstone with the world and the people around her. She might not have done this if her grandmother had been loving and gentle and got her the help she needed, but then again, her personality type was one that felt more comfortable taking care of herself.

The psychologist had made it seem like this was something Erika should change, or should want to change. She hadn't. It worked for her. Protected her. Look how far she'd come. She'd finished her VCE in one year, entered university as an early entrant and had two science degrees under her belt and a PhD by the age of twenty-two, before deciding to turn to medicine and forensic pathology where she'd fast-tracked her studies once again, so much of the work being easy for someone with her high IQ and eidetic memory. She'd turned all that into a successful career, one that challenged and inspired her, and she had Jenny and her work colleagues to socialise with. What reason was there to change?

What about love?

The words whispered in her mind. Hartley said he loved her. In fact, he'd thrown the words at her, like an angry javelin straight through the heart. He loved her. She loved him. It should work, and yet it couldn't. It wouldn't. He was just too good and kind and understanding for someone like her. He wanted to live here, in the town she'd always hated, near the woman who was her nemesis, whose hatred and bitterness had helped to keep her broken. How could it work if he was here and she was in the city? She couldn't leave the city. She had a house there, a job, people who were her friends. And what was here for her? They didn't know where Peter was. Their family home had gone. Only Hartley remained.

Was he enough?

She had a horrible feeling maybe he was. He was worth a lot of sacrifice. The only problem was, she didn't know if she could be strong enough to stick it out. He deserved someone who stuck. She'd never stuck.

Why? She'd been happy here when her parents were alive. She remembered that with perfect clarity in the same way she remembered everything. She had still been strange and too mature and way too intelligent for any adult's comfort. She'd been the object of bullying at school. And yet, she hadn't really minded. Her father and mother had always ensured she was engaged in her learning. They talked to her. They understood her. She'd never been in trouble with the law or a problem child before they'd died.

Perhaps their caring made all the difference. She hadn't had a problem getting along with Daphne and Pip, with Mac and Toby just recently. They'd all accepted her. Were glad of her presence. Mac and Toby could even become her friends. Perhaps even Katherine Stuart. The superintendent was someone who could keep her on her toes intellectually. It didn't have to be like it was before.

Yet...

She shivered, old fear clawing inside her. The memory of faces looking at her like she was some alien being that could never be understood, never belong. She'd never minded that before her parents died, but afterwards, without their love and support and understanding, those looks hurt. The memory of words said to her face, and the ones she heard whispered behind her back, had hurt. And there was Mabel.

Even though she hadn't gone to visit Mabel, hadn't seen her for sixteen years, it was as if she was always there, her words, spittle in her ear, the cane coming down on her back where no one ever saw the bruises, how she screamed at Erika as she pushed her into her room and locked the door. She remembered every single moment of abuse, verbal and physical, and each memory brought the crawl of fear shuddering up her spine, making her breath stutter in her lungs, her heart pound hard and fast in her chest, the scream she could never let out filling her ears. Why? Why couldn't Mabel love her? Why had Peter been loved and cared for while she had experienced the opposite? Was she such a monstrous creature that she couldn't be loved?

She'd been so frightened of the answer that she'd run. And in running, she'd let Mabel have power over her for so many years. Both Jenny and the psychologist said she'd never repair herself until she faced Mabel and took her to account for what she'd done. Both of them had suggested she come back here and confront her grandmother with adult eyes, adult perception. But she couldn't. She just couldn't.

She'd been the coward Hartley had accused her of being.

Mabel Hanson shouldn't have that kind of control over her anymore. She was a sick old woman, locked away in a nursing home, dying. She should be left to rot. It struck Erika suddenly that letting nature take its course was just another kind of running.

She had to face Mabel.

No, she didn't want to. Yet she'd tried to fill her life with science and facts and logic and reason, and ultimately none of it had helped. Maybe facing Mabel would finally give her what she'd been missing all these years—a reason why she was so hard to love.

The morgue was tidy. She had nothing left to do except courier the samples to Melbourne. It was time. She was going to do it.

She was going to face Mabel Hanson.

She reported her findings on the hair they'd found then organised the samples to be flown to Melbourne, waiting there until they were picked up and were safely away. After that, she called a taxi. Hartley had told her to call Constable Mayne to take her back to the hotel when she was done, but, even though Erika knew the young woman would take her to the nursing home if she asked, she didn't want anyone knowing she was going there. It could end up being a total disaster, but it was her disaster and she had to deal with the consequences herself. She told Constable Smith she was going to the toilet and then, once around the corner, took the freight lift up and walked out the front to hop in the waiting taxi.

She had to wait for a while when she arrived—it was dinner time. Then she was ushered down a hallway by a casually dressed nurse. 'My, you don't look like your grandmother at all. Not like Peter does,' the nurse—her name tag announced she was Sarah—said as they walked.

'I take after my mother's side of the family.'

'Mabel doesn't have photos of her daughter-in-law, so I wouldn't know.'

'That's not surprising. She and my mother never got along.'

'Oh, what a shame.' They walked a few more steps in silence and then stopped outside the door to a private room. 'I just want to let you know she's had a bit of a day. But I'm sure she'll be glad to see you after all this time.'

'I don't know about that. I imagine seeing me will make her have more than a "bit of a day".' Sarah's dimples disappeared in confusion at Erika's cold tone.

Even so, she managed to smile again as she asked Erika to wait while she went in and prepared Mabel for her visitor.

She could hear the brunette's low, soft tones as she told Mabel that Erika was here.

'Erika?' It was the strident, cultured voice she remembered so horribly well.

'Your granddaughter.'

'I don't have a granddaughter. Not anymore. She ran away. Ungrateful bitch. After everything I did for her, taking her in after her mother killed my son. My beautiful boy. His life was ruined the day he met that Eastern European slut. She came from nothing, from a nothing family who couldn't even stay in their own country, but had to come and contaminate ours with their accents and their smelly food and religion that was so much more important than mine. Do you know, my son would have converted for her if I hadn't put my foot down?'

'Mabel, maybe this isn't the best time...'

'And the airs she put on, as if she was too good for us. I know she thought she was too smart to stay in a country town, her flitting all over the country—reknowned heart surgeon my arse! They were leaving. Did you know that? They were leaving me. They were going to take my beautiful grandson away from me and leave me to rot in this town.'

'I'm sure that's not true. You have Peter and now your granddaughter is here...'

'Her? Ha! Exactly like her mother, she was. She should have died in that car with her mother, not my son.'

'That's a horrible thing to say, Mabel. She can hear you, you know.'

'Good. Tell her to come in. There's some things I'd like to say to her.'

Sarah came out the door, face a picture of apology. 'I'm so sorry about that. She's not in a good mood today. The tumour—it's changed her personality. She's not like she was at all.'

Erika was shaking, tears burning her eyes. 'She sounds exactly like she always was.'

'Oh...I...' Sarah looked uncertainly around her. 'Even so, perhaps another day would be better. When you're both not so upset.'

Erika laughed. 'I'm not upset because of what she just said. She's said far worse things to me over the years.' No, she was upset because it was becoming clear she'd let this woman have far too much sway over her life all these years. She swallowed hard. 'I need to see her.' She pushed past the nurse and into the room.

Chapter Eighteen

Her grandmother's gaze burned through Erika as she came to a stop a few metres from the chair the old woman was sitting in. The last sixteen years hadn't been kind to Mabel Hanson. She'd always been a handsome woman. Tall, with rich dark-brown hair done up in a forties style, and vivid blue eyes that stood out in her face. She'd never been pretty, her features were too square cut, jaw a little too pronounced, nose a little too long, lips a little too big. But those startling eyes—her dad's eyes, Peter's eyes—and the way she held herself had always made her seem more than she was.

Now that was all gone. The hair was a dull grey, her skin sallow, her nose had grown so it resembled a hawk's beak and her lips had crinkled up into something akin to a prune. It was pursed now, as if she'd eaten something distasteful as she looked Erika up and down. She looked rather like the evil witch she'd always been, the outsides finally reflecting the insides.

Neither of them said anything; they just stared at each other.

'Ahh, well, shall I get some tea and cake?' Sarah asked nervously.

'No thank you,' Erika said. 'I won't be staying long.'

'Pfft. That figures! Sixteen years and not a word and then you just show up out of the blue, probably to ask for money, and you can't even be bothered to sit and have tea with your sick grandmother?' She shook her head. 'I'd say you were a disappointment, but then that would mean I'd have to have thought better of you at some point.'

'Mabel!'

Erika held up her hand, and smiled. 'It's okay. As I said, it's nothing I haven't heard before.' She cleared her throat. 'I wouldn't mind a word alone with my gran.'

'Gran! You know I hate you calling me that.'

Sarah flinched, her expression filled with concern—not for Mabel, but for Erika. She smiled at the nurse. 'You can go. I'll be okay.'

'If you're sure. I'll just be down the hall though. If you need anything, just call.'

Erika nodded her agreement and the nurse turned, leaving the room quietly. She closed the door, but didn't completely shut it. She was probably listening outside, but Erika didn't really care if she heard every word. It seemed about time that the secret she'd been holding onto so tightly for so long was finally unleashed.

'Well!'

Erika turned to face her grandmother. 'Hello Mabel.'

'Mabel?' Her grandmother's mouth worked for a moment, spittle at the corners, nostrils flaring. Erika knew if Mabel Hanson could have got up and hit her, she would have.

'What else would you like me to call you? You've made it clear I'm not your granddaughter.'

'You've not changed.'

'You have. And not for the better.'

'Still rude. Exactly like your mother, you are.'

'Thank you.'

'I didn't mean it as a compliment.'

'I know. But thank you anyway.' Her mother had been a brilliant doctor and an amazing humanitarian. Her memories, memories she'd too long suppressed but had come back to her over the last few days, were of a kind, generous and funny woman who loved her family and always had time for anyone who needed her. She'd been brought up in Israel, her parents' families having settled there after the war, but she'd come out here to study and stayed after meeting Peter Hanson Snr at university. Despite what her grandmother had said, she knew her mother never asked her father to convert to Judaism, because, as she'd told Erika when she'd asked one day, religion was a personal thing and should never get in the way of loving someone. Her mother had always been so open minded. The woman Mabel described with such vehemence was nothing like the mother in her memories. Memories that were true and good and precious. She spoke one of them now.

'I remember dad saying that the day he met Timnah Finklestein was the best day of his life. He told everyone who would listen that she was the best woman he had ever known. So if I am like her even in the smallest way, that is the best compliment I could ever receive.'

'Hmph.' Mabel tried to hold her gaze, but after a moment she looked away, her mouth twisting. 'Your father was besotted with her from the first. He could never see sense after she got her claws into him.'

'He loved her. Just as she loved him.' The memory of that made her smile. She'd forgotten their love for each other, their love for their children. It had hurt so much to remember it, because with those memories came such loss and grief. But now, finally, in front of her grandmother, those memories came free, and they no longer hurt or made her feel small. They set her free. She'd come from love. She'd been loved, so, so much, by good people who had deserved much more time on this earth than they'd had. Her mouth twisted as she realised how much damage she'd done to herself by forgetting that.

'She loved him! A fat lot of good that did him in the end.'

'What do you mean by that?'

'She killed him.'

'No she didn't. They died in a car accident.'

'She was driving. She'd had too much to drink. And had drugs in her system.'

A creeping sensation crawled up Erika's spine. She'd never understood where that rumour had come from—the one that her mother was a drugged-out alcoholic who had caused the accident—but now she realised exactly where it had originated. 'Daddy was driving that night. Not Mummy.'

'No, no. That's not true. It was her. Her!'

'You forget. I was there.'

'So? You never remembered. The doctors said you couldn't remember. It was too traumatic. Some kind of stress-related amnesia they called it.'

'I remembered. I was just too traumatised to talk about it.' Horrifying realisation dawned. 'And you took advantage of that to blame my mother for something that was never her fault.'

'Yes! Yes I did.'

'But it was a lie.' She took a step forward. 'Why? Why did you lie about such a thing?'

'Because I couldn't have it out there that my boy was at fault.'

'He wasn't at fault. We were run off the road by a driver on the wrong side of the road. The police must have known Daddy was driving.'

'That's not what it says in the report.'

'How do you know that?'

Mabel smiled at her.

Erika's eyes widened. 'You had the police reports changed.'

'Of course I did. I couldn't have them finding out the truth.'

'The truth?' Images from that night flashed before her eyes like the staccato flickering of an old-fashioned news reel. They'd been at Mabel's house. She and her mother and father. Peter had been staying at a friend's place for a few days because they were going to Sydney to attend a fundraising event in Timnah's honour, and he would be bored to tears. Erika, on the other hand, wanted to go. They'd been so proud of her, wanting to show off their brilliant daughter. The memory of that was like a gasp of fresh air inside her.

They'd just found out the foundation her mother worked for had got funding to send her to Far North Queensland to set up a heart health clinic for the Indigenous communities, and they were all moving up there with her, to be a part of that community and experience a different way of living. Mabel had served drinks, fawning all over Peter Snr in that way of hers that had always made Erika feel edgy and sick. Her father had thrown back three drinks before mentioning Timnah's good news, the pride on his face shining in his smile, his hand stroking down her mother's back. Mabel had become hysterical. She'd said all sorts of horrible things about Timnah and was starting into Erika when Peter Snr had told his mother she was a hateful bitch and he never wanted to see her again. He'd thrown back his fourth drink, grabbed Erika and her mother's hands and marched them out of the house and into the car, Mabel's screams dying off in the distance as they drove away.

They'd driven down the Mitchell toward the airport at Bourke where they were chartering a flight to Sydney. She remembered her mother's softly accented voice, asking her father to slow down, to calm down, to pull over so she could drive. '*You've had too much to drink,* Motek. *You always do every time you see your* Ima. *You shouldn't be driving.*'

'*You're right. I'm sorry. I'll pull over after this rise and you can drive.*'

Her mother's hand on her father's shoulder, the smile they shared that made Erika's stomach fill with warmth. Everything was fine. They were going to be fine. They drove over the rise, the indicator on to pull over. Another car came flying toward them, lights off, in their lane. Her father saw it too late, swerved to avoid it. They hit the loose dirt at the side of the road, spun and flipped and the world turned into hell.

Erika blinked the memory away as realisation sank in. 'You were afraid it would come out that dad was over the legal limit. That maybe the accident wouldn't have happened if he'd not had those drinks you'd shoved down his throat.'

Mabel jabbed her finger into the air. 'Stupid girl. Of course I couldn't let anyone know that your father was drunk when driving. Another drunk Hanson, following in his grandfather's footsteps. And all because your bitch of a mother was trying to take him from me. I couldn't allow that to happen. Not after everything my husband and I sacrificed to keep everything going, to keep it together, to keep the Hanson family name one that was respected and looked up to. Your mother had taken everything else from me, she wasn't taking that too.'

'For the name? You changed the truth for the family name?' She shook her head, unable to comprehend Mabel's twisted thinking.

Mabel's mouth thinned. 'Yes. Except, it didn't work did it? Your mother had the last laugh. She lumped me with you and I was reminded of what I'd done every time I looked at you.'

'I am part of my father too. You could have seen him in me.'

Mabel barked out a laugh. 'You are nothing like my son in looks or nature. You were so awkward and needy.'

'I saw my mother and father die. I'd tried to save them, but they died anyway.'

'Yes. Your smarts weren't enough, were they?'

'I was twelve!'

'You delighted in making those around you feel stupid because you were so smart. Just like your mother. Sent to torment me and remind me that if not for you both, I would never have lost my precious Peter. She took him from me. She took his love and I can never get that back.' She began to sob, her hands coming up to cover her face.

Erika stared at her grandmother, something like sympathy stirring inside her. 'I would have loved you if you'd let me.'

Mabel looked up, hatred in her tear-filled eyes. 'I didn't want your love, Timnah. I wanted my Peter back. You didn't deserve him. You never deserved him! And where is he now? He's been gone for days. He's not been in to visit. He told me he'd visit. Where is he? Where is he? I want him back. I want him back!'

Her voice had risen to a screech and Erika took a step back. Insanity was staring out at her. She'd never realised it before, but it had always been there.

As her grandmother screamed and cried and the nurses rushed in behind her, something inside her shifted, lifting, a shroud of misunderstanding falling away to reveal a simple truth she'd always denied.

Her grandmother hadn't hated her because of anything she'd done. She'd hated her because she had a twisted and unhealthy mind. It wouldn't have mattered if her mother hadn't been a foreigner or Jewish—any woman who took her son from her would have been equally despised. Her mother's strange name, her religion, her intelligence that Mabel took as an insult, her accent, simply gave Mabel an excuse for her hatred. And she'd transferred that hatred to Erika when Peter Snr and Timnah died, simply because Erika was more like her mother than her father. Erika had never stood a chance to gain anything close to affection from a woman so horribly damaged. A woman incapable of loving anyone in any good way. Not even her son. Or grandson. Certainly not the granddaughter who reminded her of the woman who had won her son's love.

Only now, with the weight of Mabel's hatred lifting from her, did she remember her father's last words to her as he lay dying, his blood all over her hands. *'You are so special. So special. Your light is incandescent. Don't let anyone take that from you. Don't forget that, Erika. And don't forget you are loved. You are made to be loved.'*

Oh god! She'd allowed her grandmother's bitterness to make her forget those words, that feeling. To not let herself see that other people loved her too—Daphne, Pip, Peter, Mac, back then and now. Daphne and Pip had loved her so much, they'd given her the money to leave and had sent her to Jenny, who had also loved her and believed in her.

And Hartley.

He'd loved her when they were children. She couldn't accept his love then. She'd been too damaged, too unable to see her worth. All she could accept was his friendship. But even that, in the end, had been too much, and she'd run, because she'd believed what her grandmother said about her, that she wasn't worthy of love. She didn't believe that anymore. She wasn't strange and unlovable. She was remarkable. She deserved to have the love her parents wished for her with their dying breaths.

'Thank you for the truth,' she said to her grandmother's door, and then she turned and walked away from the past that had blighted too much of her life already. She was going to start to change that. Today.

She had to find Hartley. She needed to tell him she loved him. What happened next, she didn't know, but she was determined to make certain he knew beyond doubt how she felt for him and always had.

Chapter Nineteen

The taxi slowed down before they reached the police station. 'There seems to be a bit of a kerfuffle up ahead, miss.'

An ambulance and a MICA unit were pulled up out the front along with a firetruck, lights still whirling. And there was a crowd surrounding the police-station entrance.

Oh god. What had happened? Hartley!

She threw money at the taxi driver and leapt out before he'd even come to a complete stop. She ran, backpack banging against her back, pushing past the crowd of onlookers who were being held back by the firemen from the truck. One of them tried to stop her, but thankfully Toby was there and waved her through.

'Hartley?'

He gripped her shoulder. 'He's okay. He's inside with Mac giving his report.' He gestured behind him.

A man—a blond man—lay sprawled on the front steps of the police station, blood pooling around him, eyes staring blindly at the blue sky above. Steph and Greg, the ambulance officers she'd met, were working on him, but Erika could see it was too late. The man had what looked like multiple gunshot wounds to the chest. It wasn't likely he would survive, even if they got his heart pumping again. 'What happened?'

'I'm not sure. Coops and Mac were bringing a suspect in for questioning. I'm not sure why they thought he was involved.'

'The hair.' Toby's brows furrowed. 'I found a hair in the ambulance. It matched the hair we found at the warehouse. It looked like that.' She pointed at the man.

'Someone was worried about him being brought in.'

She looked down at the man. 'Did they catch the shooter?'

'No. A man rode up on a bike and unloaded a clip. You'll have to ask Hartley for more info.'

She stared at him, shock making her immobile for a moment. A drive-by? But this was a country town. Quiet and peaceful. This kind of thing happened in the cities, not in places like this. She had to make sure Hartley was okay. She ran inside. Hartley was coming out of the superintendent's office, in deep conversation with Mac. Both men had blood sprayed across their necks and faces, and blood on their hands. They must have been right beside the man when he was shot and then immediately tried to save him. She knew neither of them had been hurt—otherwise they'd be in the ambulance or already at the hospital. Even so, her heart was in her mouth as she called out Hartley's name.

He turned. His gaze met hers. He frowned and then with a quick word to Mac, who nodded and headed off to his desk, walked over to her. 'I'm okay. I'm okay,' he said as he neared.

'I know.' She couldn't stop herself from touching him anyway, to make sure. 'Toby told me there was a drive-by. What happened? Who was he?'

'Come on.' He took her hand and led her down the hall. 'I'll tell you while I clean up.'

She let him lead her to the locker room at the back of the station and stood as he stripped off his shirt, put it in an evidence bag, and washed his face, neck and hands. She waited as he put on a light grey t-shirt, strapped on his shoulder holster and gun, and then slung on a light charcoal jacket before asking, 'Who was he?'

Hartley gestured for her to sit on the bench in the middle of the room. She sat next to him. He took her hands. 'We were pulling him in on your evidence.'

'That was quick.'

He nodded. 'When Mac and Ben and I were looking over the evidence board earlier, Mac remembered seeing a guy with that hair colour coming out of the Springs Motel the other day as he was doing his patrol. Luck was on our side, because the idiot was still there. We got his name from the clerk—Tom Johnson—and ran his record. He'd been involved with the bikie gangs in Sydney with ties to drugs. He'd also been a suspect in a murder case but there wasn't enough evidence to stick. He seemed a good match, especially given the colour of his hair. Mac and I were bringing him in for questioning when this bikie came flying up the street, stopped in front of us, and unloaded a clip into our suspect.'

Erika's fingers clenched at her sides. 'It's a wonder you didn't get hurt.'

'He wasn't aiming at us.'

Erika stared at him for a moment, at the strange smile on his face. 'That's not funny.'

'I didn't mean it to be. He didn't even look at us. Didn't seem to care we were there. It was virtually point blank range. We didn't even have time to duck for cover or get in front of the suspect it all happened so quickly.'

'Did you get a license plate?'

'Only a partial. Ben's running it now with the make—a Kawasaki Ninja, but we're not hopeful.'

'Why?'

'Do you know how many black Kawasaki Ninjas there are out there on the road? It's one of the most popular road bikes in Australia and I can think of at least fifty people who own them in town.'

'There would have to be blood splatter on it if he was that close.'

'He was.' He crooked a smile at her. 'I thought you'd be upset our one lead is now dead.'

'He wasn't our only lead. There's more coming. I might find more when I do the post-mortem on Mr Johnson. Don't lose hope.'

'I won't. We've got you.' His gaze ran over her and the frown on his face deepened. 'Something's changed.' He stepped closer again, his warmth, his proximity, making her hairs stand on end, her skin prickle.

'Yes.'

'What is it?'

'I went to see Mabel.'

'Ah.' His frown deepened into worry and he reached out to touch her, but then pulled his hand back. 'Are you okay?'

'Better than okay.'

'She didn't say anything horrible?'

She snorted. 'Oh, she said something horrible. Many things that were horrible, in fact. She was the one who told everyone my mother was a drug addict and caused the accident. She told me I reminded her of my mother and that's why she hated me from the start. I never stood a chance. I was too much my mother's daughter. She even called me Timnah. She's a bigoted hateful woman. And insane. I think she always was.'

'And you're okay?'

'Yes.' The answer was slow. 'I'd never realised why she hated me and it was…liberating. My mother was brilliant and loving and caring and I am just like her. I never realised.' She swallowed. Hard. Now that the moment was here, she was reluctant to tell him. Not because she was a coward—she was frightened, but that was okay. She was allowed to be. No, it was because she didn't want to tell him here. In the empty locker room, the scent of old sweat and fresh soap heavy in the air, grey paint peeling off the cornices. But it was now or never. With everything going on, she might not have another chance to get him alone for days. Now or never.

Now.

'My mother was everything I am, but she was more. I want to be more.' He didn't say anything, but the aching hope in his eyes spurred her on. 'I never realised why I closed myself off from life until I saw Mabel. I thought it was because I couldn't feel. The accident was the catalyst, but Mabel's words, her actions, bearing down on me every day, became my reality. My parents had left me—'

'They died.'

'I know, but it felt like I was abandoned, especially because they'd left me with Mabel, who they knew didn't like me. I thought it was a sign that what Mabel said was true. That I wasn't deserving of love. That I never had been.'

'Shit, Erika, that's not—'

She raised her hand to his lips. 'No, please, let me finish.' His warm lips brushed against her fingertips as he nodded. For a moment, she forgot what she was saying. His nearness, his warmth, his touch, it was unnerving. And essential. But she had to finish explaining before she gave in to her need for him. Sucking in a breath, she started again. 'I forgot how my parents loved me, overlooked the love of those around me, all because Mabel didn't love me. I let her drive away the truth simply because she should have loved me but didn't. I made myself into what she said I was and even after I ran away, I continued to do that. It was foolish. Stupid in the extreme.'

'You were a little girl. You'd lost your parents. That bitch should have been there for you.'

'Yes. She should. She wasn't, and because of that, because of her, I have let my hatred, resentment and fear rule me for too long. I thought I had moved on from her, but running away isn't moving on. I ended up with a good life, but at heart, it's empty. Because I'm empty. And I deserve so much more.'

He reached out, touched her face, fingers lingering on her cheek. 'You deserve the best of everything.'

'Yes.' She leaned into his caress. 'I do.' She looked up at him, trying to put in her gaze everything that was in his—that way he had of looking at her like there was nothing else in his world as important as her. Inside her, the thing that had loosened, that same thing that had been tightly furled and long guarded since the night her parents died, opened further, began to bloom under the steadiness of his green gaze. 'I deserve love. I deserve to love and be loved. I deserve to be with someone who feels about me the same way I feel about him. I deserve you.'

'Erika.' He stepped into her. 'I…'

The door swung open and Constable Mayne walked in. Her eyes popped wide when she saw them. 'I'm sorry. I didn't realise anyone was in here.'

'We were just leaving,' Hartley said, pulling Erika toward the door.

Leila Mayne stepped back, giving them room to pass, a wide smile on her face. 'Have…fun.'

'Take this to evidence,' he said, handing her the bag with his bloody shirt in it. 'And tell the Sarge I won't be back for a while.' Hartley didn't give Leila a chance to respond, just kept walking, pulling Erika along beside him.

'Hartley, I…'

He glanced at her. 'No. This isn't the place to finish this conversation.' His gaze was heated, wanting, needing. 'And I want to finish it, more than I want to breathe. With you. Alone.'

'Me too.' Heat prickled under her skin at the force of his gaze. She felt undressed already.

She let him lead her outside to his Patrol and climbed in. The silence between them was palpable, stroking her skin, making her feel itchy with tension and expectation. 'Where are we going?' she finally managed to ask.

'My place.'

'You live alone?'

'Yes.'

'Good.'

He shot a smile at her, hot and needy.

They pulled up at his house—an old brick Californian bungalow with a neat front yard and massive ghost gum shading the veranda and right side of the house. She didn't see much more than that though, because he had her up the front steps and inside before she could look around.

The moment he had her inside—she had a flash impression of clean white walls and polished honey-red floors—he turned and backed her up against the door, his mouth on hers before her back had even hit the wood. Oh god!

She gripped on tight and matched him kiss for kiss, passion turning them into an inferno of need. It was shattering. Before Hartley, sexual encounters had been pleasant things she'd enjoyed, much like eating a good meal with a fine bottle of wine and good company, or maybe even with the adrenaline rush of going on a rollercoaster for the first time. She'd thought she had a healthy appetite and enjoyed sex, but with Hartley, it was something else. She was something else. A mindless puddle of need and want and desire.

She liked feeling this way. Liked the edgy lack of control. Finally, finally, she was going to give herself over to it and just let herself feel.

Lips parted, tongues tangled, licking, tasting. His hand stroked under her t-shirt, slipping over heated skin to cup her breast. She moaned, gripped him tighter. Held on to him. Something hard and cold pressed into her bicep as she wrapped her arms around his body. His gun. He was still wearing his gun. That and his jacket and t-shirt would have to go.

She wanted to feel him. All of him. Her hands raced under his t-shirt, over the hard silk of his warm skin. Nerves and muscles jumped and quivered at her touch. His breath was rasping in his throat, matching hers. Her fingers found his zip. She wanted to tear his jeans off him and impale herself on his thick length. She didn't think she could ever do without this again.

She couldn't do without Hartley ever again.

She had to tell him. She'd not said the words yet. She pulled her mouth away from his on a gasp of air. His lips immediately found her neck and he began to lip, nip and suck his way down the column of her throat. She arched against him, the motion begging for more. But she had to tell him first. She had to say the words. 'Hartley, I...'

'Don't move or we'll shoot you both.'

She and Hartley froze at the deep gravelly-voiced command that came from behind Hartley. She opened her eyes. Two men were standing in the dim hallway, only a few metres from them. One had a bat in his hand. The other had a gun, pointed at Hartley's back. She stiffened, her fingers tightening on Hartley's shoulders, stopping him from moving. If he didn't move, she might be able to pull his gun from the holster without them seeing. With everything in her, she tried to make him understand what she was trying to do. He'd been shot at once today. She could have lost him. She wasn't going to take the chance of that happening again.

He stilled.

'Aww, what'd you have to go and interrupt them for, Frank? I thought I was going to see myself some titty.'

'We didn't come here for a show, Willie G.'

The tension in Hartley's body increased to the point she could feel his fury pulsating through him. She could tell he wanted to move, to face them, but he didn't. His green gaze met hers, and he nodded, glancing down briefly as her hand began to slowly make its way up from where it had been on his zip toward the gun nestled under his armpit, hidden by his jacket and their pose. All the time, she looked over his shoulder at the two men. If one of them moved, she was going to be ready.

'What do you see?' he whispered leaning his head against hers.

'The one on the right has a gun. The other one has a bat,' she whispered against his jaw. 'They're both wearing leathers.'

'Bikies?'

She nodded slightly.

'We could have a bit of fun before we take 'em to the boss,' the one called Willie G was saying.

Hartley's fingers pressed into her skin, stopping her from responding to the man's words. 'Act frightened.'

She didn't question his instruction, trusting him with everything in her. She peered over his shoulder again, as if she couldn't believe what was happening and then screamed, 'Oh my god. He's got a gun! Don't hurt us. Don't hurt us.' She cowered into Hartley.

'Shh, shh, it's okay, EJ.' He pressed her head into his shoulder with one hand, the movement making it easier for her to get access to his gun. He turned a little as if trying to partially face the men behind them, the movement giving her free, unfettered access to the gun. As he said, 'Please, let her go. She has nothing to do with whatever this is,' she slipped the gun from the holster.

'Oh, she's the one we're here for. She and her bloody meddling,' the one called Frank said, waving the gun casually at them. 'We could have counted on old Metler not to do a proper job on those bodies, but her, she really looked like she was going to find evidence that pointed to us. The fact you were pulling in Blondie just meant she was close.'

'Did you kill him?'

'Of course. He wasn't one of us. Too new. We couldn't trust he wouldn't sing like a little blond birdie. We couldn't have that, could we, Willie G?'

'No, Frank. The boss would not be at all happy.'

'And who's this boss of yours?'

The one called Frank snorted. 'I'd have to have a death wish to tell you that, mate.'

Hartley turned a little more, still covering Erika's movement with his body so she could grasp the gun with both hands and remove the safety.

'Ah-ah, no sudden movements. Not that I mind shooting a copper, but I think we'll get less out of your girlfriend if we did.'

'I won't tell you anything. You bastards murdered my brother,' Erika said, raising her head enough to let the words wail out of her. If the situation wasn't so dangerous, she would be pretty impressed with her acting right now.

'The only thing I know about your bro, little girl,' Frank said, lip curled, 'is what that Blondie idiot told us after he screwed up getting rid of Tyler and that betraying son of a bitch Andy J for daring to set up a rival business in the boss's territory.'

'What did he tell you?'

'Don't suppose it will hurt to tell you given you're not goin' anywhere after this. What do you reckon, Willie G?'

'Might as well tell her, Frank. Might make her a bit more inclined to be friendly before we take care of her, if you know what I mean.'

'You won't touch her!' Hartley growled.

'Shh,' Erika whispered in his ear, fingers gripping the gun a little tighter as she edged it between their two bodies. She needed them to tell her what they knew. 'Let them talk.' She lifted her head a little. 'What else do you know?'

'Blondie overheard Tyler trying to talk your bro into helping, sayin' some stuff about how he was the best chemist he knew of and that together they could make some truly addictive meth that would put everyone else out of the market and make them rich. Your bro wasn't into it at all, but after hearing how good a chemist he was, Blondie decided to see if your bro would work for the boss instead, especially seeing he'd just offed Andy J for betraying the boss by working for someone else. Then the stupid bastard set it up to look like Andy was your bro, so no one would come looking for him while he worked on him, making him more … amenable to the situation.'

'He kidnapped Peter? So he's alive?'

'I've got no idea. Blondie never told us where he'd stashed him and quite frankly, I didn't care. I told him he should have just killed your bro in the first place and not tried to have a bright idea, 'cause if he had, half of this shit wouldn't have had to go down like it did and Willie G and I wouldn't have had to haul arse out to this dry as dirt place and help him steal bodies right out of the bloody morgue. Besides, the boss doesn't hold with kidnappin'—brings too much attention our way. It's one of the reasons we was sent up here—to clean up Blondie's mess.'

'So you don't know where he is?'

'We never even seen him, did we, Willie G?'

'Nope.'

'For all we know he's dead as those others you was workin' on. Now enough chatting about your bro. Time for you to tell us exactly what you know about us and our operation. We took the bodies and destroyed your evidence, but you still found Blondie, so we need to know how and also, what did Blondie say to you before we gave him a lead shower? We need to know what else we gotta clean up.'

'I didn't speak to him.' Oh god, Peter could be dead. And if he wasn't, he most certainly was injured given what they were saying. And if nobody knew where he was except for Tom, he could be dying from dehydration right now. Heartless bastards. Her grip tightened around the gun.

'He'll be okay,' Hartley whispered against her neck, somehow reading her thoughts.

She nodded, whispered back, 'If he isn't, I won't stop until everyone responsible pays for his death.'

'That's my girl.'

'What about you, copper? What did Tom tell you?'

'As if I'd tell you when it's our only bargaining chip for keeping us alive.'

'Nothin's going to keep you alive, copper. What tellin' us will do is stop us from goin' after one of your other copper mates to find out what you don't tell us and also, maybe we won't have too much fun with your girl before we kill her too.'

'If you kill us, the police won't stop. You know what they're like when one of their own is killed.'

'I don't think so. The boss told us after we finished questioning you, we was to make sure it looked like you ran away together, and died in a nasty car accident, right Willie G?'

'Right Frank.'

'Nobody will believe that.'

'Enough. Either tell us what we want to know, or get a bullet in the back.'

'Let me turn around first. I want to see who I'm talking to.'

'Fair enough, but no being a hero, Detective. Move nice and slow, hands where we can see 'em.'

Hartley shifted his head so he could look at Erika, his eyes full of love, worry, fury and trust. His trust in her at what would come next meant so much. He knew she could shoot—they'd stolen her grandfather's guns often enough and shot at cans in the paddocks when they were younger. Holding his gaze, she leaned up and kissed him gently. 'I love you,' she whispered against his lips.

'I know.'

At any other time she'd hit him for being so arrogant, but right now the little flash of humour was all she needed. 'Okay.'

He spun away from her quickly and lunged toward the one with the bat. 'What the fuck?' the man with the gun spat out, his gun moving toward Hartley.

Nobody was looking at Erika. She lifted Hartley's gun and fired just as another shot rang out.

Chapter Twenty

Erika drummed her fingers against the metal table and the file there.

The sticky section was gone, thank goodness. Although this time she wasn't cuffed to the table and could pull out her wipes from her backpack if necessary.

Drum, drum, drum.

How long were they going to be? She wanted to know what was going on. She should have gone to the hospital with Hartley. She would have been able to help. Instead, she was sitting here feeling completely useless and out of the loop. Worrying about Hartley. Worrying about what had happened to Peter. Was he even alive? Had they found out any more from Frank and Willie G? They said they didn't know where he was, but they could have been lying. 'Stay alive, Peter,' she whispered into the quiet of the room. 'Give me time to find you.'

She bit her lip, trying to stop it from trembling, trying to stopper the emotions that would cloud her thinking. Clear thinking was the only thing that could help Peter now. That and Hartley's help.

Hartley. Oh god, Hartley. Was he okay?

She looked down at her hands and her mind skipped to the moments after the gun blasts. The blood was gone, but she could still see it there. She'd not had blood on her hands since the night her parents died. On her gloves, yes, but not her skin. It was different. More…real. More like she was actually, truly in the moment, feeling everything. Emotion had pumped through her as the blood had pumped over her hands. Just like it had on that night when she'd held her father's heart in her hand and tried to pump it for him, to keep him with her.

Drum, drum, drum.

She thought that living through that again would have brought back horrible memories, but it hadn't. It had been different. She was different. She wasn't that traumatised twelve-year-old anymore. She was a grown woman, a qualified doctor of forensic pathology. She'd survived Mabel. Survived running away and starting over. Had survived coming back here and going through the grief of losing Peter only find out he was alive, then swinging back to not even being certain of that. She'd survived realising she loved and was loved and then faced losing it again.

She clenched her hands, stopping the drumming. If she could survive all that, she could survive this waiting without falling apart. She had to. To be strong for Hartley. To be strong enough to find out what had happened to Peter.

The door swung open and she looked up. It was Sergeant Cooper. She flinched internally, but came to her feet. 'Is there any news?'

He shook his head. 'He's still in surgery. The Boss, Fields and Mac are down there interviewing the other suspect.'

'Is he saying anything?'

His eyes narrowed. 'That's none of your concern.'

'It's exactly my concern.' She stood straighter. 'It's my evidence that can help to put them away.' She noticed then he had a manila folder in his hand. 'Is that from Melbourne?'

'Yes.' He stalked across the room and tossed it onto the table in front of her.

She grabbed it up, opened it. DNA results from the victims and from the skin cells found under the fingernails. Hair, soil, fibre and bug analysis. Blood work. It all told a story, a story she would be able to finish when they let her out of here so she could do a post-mortem on 'Blondie', as Frank had called him. She would match his DNA to these samples to prove he had killed Tyler and Andy J and with the other evidence she'd collected, she would then prove that Frank and Willie G had helped him to steal the bodies and destroy evidence and then murder him when he became too big a liability. She snapped the folder closed, looking up at the sergeant in triumph. 'I think we'll have them once I've done the autopsy on Mr Johnson and collected some more samples from Frank and Willie G.'

'That will have to wait. The Boss wants you to stay here for a little longer. She might have some more questions for you when she gets back from the hospital.'

She didn't want to stay here, thinking, waiting, worrying. She wanted to get on with the work ahead of her. The work that would help wrap up this case and possibly find Peter before it was too late. 'I should get on it now.'

'The Boss says you're to stay, so you stay.'

She opened her mouth to protest again, but he held out his hand to her before she could say anything. 'You saved my boy. Thank you.' He shook her hand briefly then turned and left before she managed to pick her jaw back off the floor.

He'd thanked her? She'd never imagined a time that would happen. Was he finally realising she wasn't who he thought she was? No. She didn't have that kind of luck. But maybe, just maybe, he wouldn't treat her like public enemy number one any longer. Which was good. She didn't want to cause more strain and trouble between Hartley and his dad than she already had.

She sat back down and read through the evidence workup a few more times, matching it in her mind to what she'd already found in the lab. Even without Frank's confession to them, when she matched their DNA to these samples they would have everything they needed to convict them. She only hoped they'd tell Hartley where they'd dumped the bodies, as the only thing that might help find Peter was some evidence Blondie might have left on the bodies that might give them a clue as to where he'd been. It was a long shot, but it was all she had. She just hoped it would be enough.

The door opened again. She looked up, expecting to see Constable Mayne—she'd already been in half a dozen times in the last two hours to ask if she needed anything. However, it wasn't the younger woman. 'Hartley.'

She met him halfway across the room, their arms locking around each other simultaneously, chest meshing against breast, lips locking, taking, giving.

Minutes passed, then they pulled back at the same time, Hartley's hands on her face, hers on his shoulder over the bandages.

'How are you?'

'You should still be in hospital.'

Their words tumbled over each other and then they just stopped, gazes colliding, searching, breaths mingling,

'I thought I'd lost you.'

'I was so scared for you.'

Their words overlapped again.

They both laughed. 'You first,' Hartley said.

Erika nodded, breathing in deeply, the warm, alive scent of him filling her. Citrusy with a warm undertone to cut the sharpness. Fresh. Clean. She wanted to breathe it in and cover herself with it. 'I love the way you smell.'

A laugh burst from his lips.

'What?'

His lips curled into that smile she loved. 'You always surprise me.'

'How?'

'I expected almost hysterical worry about my shoulder and you simply say you love the way I smell.' He ducked his head and sniffed her neck. 'I love the way you smell too.'

He kissed her lightly, a promise of passion, but she pulled away from it. 'Your shoulder. I was worried. I am worried. You need to be careful.'

'It's fine. The doctor said it would be a lot worse if not for you.'

'I did nothing. Just cleaned it up and bandaged it.'

'You looked after me. You saved my life.'

'Hardly that.'

'Yes, that.' The smile fell from his face. 'But I'm still worried about you.'

'Why?'

'You shot a man. And then you did CPR on him and kept him alive after taking care of my wound.'

She nodded slowly. 'You're worried how that would affect me.'

'Of course.' He looked down, his fingers stroking across her cheeks before his gaze met hers again. 'Especially after what happened to your parents. I know you tried to keep your father alive in the same way.'

She stroked her hand over the furrows on his brow. 'It isn't the same. Besides, I'm stronger now.'

'Yes, you are.' There was pride in his voice, alongside sheer joy. 'You're the strongest woman I've ever known.'

She blushed. His fingers lingered over her cheek, firing the heat of the blush into insatiable flame. She reached up for him and their lips met again, this time soft, longing. 'I love you.'

He leaned back, eyes bright, like the sun coming out over a crystal lake. For a split second, she could see the teasing 'I know,' in his eyes, but of course, because he knew her best, he said the words she needed most to hear.

'I love you too.'

Lips met again, and for a while she was able to forget her worry about Peter and sink into the rightness of his mouth on hers, his hard body pressed against her, the silk of his short brown hair against her fingers. Their kissing slowed, stopped, and he pulled her against him so she could hear the steady beat of his heart. Their arms wrapped around each other and they just held. It was good. It was necessary. It was everything she ever wanted. Well, maybe not everything. A bed and him inside her would complete the moment. And knowledge that her brother was alive and safe.

That thought had her pulling away, asking the questions that needed to be asked, even as she wished she could stay in his arms, hearing his heart beat strongly in his chest for the rest of her life and not think about anything else. 'What happened? Did you get to interview them?'

'Yes I got to interview Willie G. Frank's being kept in an induced coma for a few days while he recovers from his injuries.'

'Did he say anything more about Peter?'

'No, I'm sorry, he didn't.'

She sucked in a shaky breath. 'Do you think he's dead?'

He ran his hand through his hair. 'I don't know. I hope not, although, given what Frank said, it's not looking good.'

She nodded, swiping away a tear. 'I know, but until we find a body …'

He cupped her face in his hands, held her gaze. 'We're not giving up hope, okay?'

She nodded again, let herself be pulled into his arms, to be comforted for a moment, before she pulled away again. 'Did he tell you where they hid the bodies?'

Mouth pressed in a tight line, he gestured to the chair. She sat and he pulled the other chair around the table to be right near her so their knees were touching. He leaned forward and tangled his fingers with hers. 'He said nothing at first, but when I told him I'd let drop in Silverwater prison that they told us what they did last night, that they fingered their boss for drugs and kidnapping and murder, he said he'd tell us for a deal.'

'And?'

'He said they dropped them in the old CJ & Co. mine, although it was dark and he can't remember which shaft they went down.'

She stood up. 'We need to get those bodies. There could be evidence that leads us to Peter.'

'Mac and Ben are already putting a team together, so there's nothing you can do until they've gone in and found something.'

'I can help in the search.'

'Your time is better spent here doing the post-mortem on Tom Johnson. There's undoubtedly evidence on him that could help us tie this case together.'

'I care less about this case than I do about finding Peter.'

'I know. And as soon as we've had something to eat and you've rested a little, we'll get onto doing exactly that.'

'I don't want to rest.'

'Erika, we both need to rest. You can't tell me you're thinking as clearly as usual right now. And you won't be any good to Peter or anyone else if you drive yourself into exhaustion.'

Damn it, he was right. She loved and hated that he knew her so well. She folded her arms, afraid perhaps she was pouting a little. 'Fine. A few hours and some food then I can do the post-mortem.'

'Deal.' He didn't shake her hand, simply kissed her again, chasing some of the cold and worry away simply with his touch. After a moment, he leaned back. 'You'll find him. I know you will.' His eyes glowed with his trust in her, helping to warm some of the chill of worry over her brother. But then that glow dimmed a little, shadowed by a worry he wasn't sharing with her.

'What is it? There's something you haven't said.'

'I don't want to take your attention from finding Peter.'

God, she loved him for that alone, but if she was going to stay, if she was going to be with him, she needed to make him understand she was here for him too. 'It's important to you. Tell me.'

He scrubbed his hand over his face. 'I'm worried about what Frank said, about their syndicate. Drugs being run through our town is one thing, but murder and cover ups…' He shook his head. 'It feels like someone is escalating. Like they are planning to do more here, especially given Tom took Peter to try to coerce him to make drugs for whoever is behind all this.'

'We'll work the case together. We'll find Peter and then we'll find whoever is behind all this. They're not going to ruin our town any more than they already have.'

His fingers gripped hers more tightly, his eyes so full of emotion, it almost hurt to keep looking in them. 'Our town? Does that mean…'

The hope in his eyes, the love there, made her want to be closer, so she stood then sat on his lap, careful of his injured shoulder, before saying what she needed to say, what he needed to hear. 'I can't go back to Melbourne, not while Peter is still missing. But even if he was here with us and fine, I

going to stay. Hopefully with you. I'm going to go for
…nologist and local coroner here.'

…moved, almost spilling her off his lap as he pulled her to face
…re squarely. 'You can't do that.'

'Don't you think I'll get it?'

'No. Of course you'll get it.'

'Don't you want me to get it?'

'It's not that. I just… I don't want you to give up your career for me. And I know how much you hate Echo Springs.'

'I don't hate it anymore. I've come to realise in the last few days just how much I don't hate it. It was Mabel I hated, and everything she took from me. Everything else followed from there. But I don't even hate her anymore. I don't like her.' She shrugged. 'But I don't hate her.'

Hartley's brows rose. 'Huh.' His brows fell again into a slight frown. 'But will the job here be enough for you?'

She considered that for a moment, lips twisting. 'Probably not. I'm not foolish enough to think I'll get the kinds of interesting cases here that I'd get in a big city. This last week has been an anomaly. But you know, that's kind of okay. And it will give me time to delve into some of the research I want to do on cell degradation and bone pathology. I thought I might do a PhD in forensic science to back up my PhD in forensic anthropology. And there are more papers I want to write, not to mention I have ideas for a book.'

'You want to become an author.'

She sat up straight. 'I have authored some very well-received papers and have magazine articles to my name.'

'Impressive.'

'Yes. And a journalist once said to me that I should write a book using some of the things I've learned from cases, and I have been playing with the idea more seriously over the last year. Other forensic pathologists have done the same to great acclaim, so it's not something new, but that doesn't matter.'

'No. The public always has an insatiable desire to work out a murder.'

'Yes. I never had time to follow up the idea in Melbourne, but here, I would. And if I need more mental stimulation than that, get my fingers back into a good case, I can always consult. But of course, all that can wait until after we find Peter. I can't give anything else my attention until I know what happened to him—good or bad.'

He hugged her closer and she took the comfort, safe in the knowledge that regardless of what else happened, Hartley would always love her, just as she would always love him.

He kissed her temple and then pulled back enough to look in her eyes. 'But what about Mabel? She's here too. Can you live in the same town as her?'

She tipped her head to the side. 'Yes. It's not like I have to have anything to do with her.' She waved her hand in a little flicking motion. 'Besides, I called the nursing home while I was waiting and told them I'd pay for her operation. They had all the paperwork from Peter and just needed payment details to get it organised, so they're doing that now. She'll be away for a good six months while I settle in here.'

He almost spilled her off his lap again as he jerked upright in shock. 'You what? Why would you do that?'

'Because, it's the right thing to do,' she said on a big breath of air. 'Peter loved her. He never had the relationship with her I did.'

'He knew what she did to you though.'

'I think that's maybe why he never told me about Mabel and why he came back here. I think he always felt a little like he'd betrayed me or something because he loved her despite how horrible she was to me. I never expected him to hate her though. She loved him.' She looked down at her hands. 'Life would have been so different if she'd loved me too.'

'Do you wish she had?'

Her head snapped up, her gaze colliding with his. 'No. Despite the painful memories, if she'd loved me, I would have stayed here. I probably wouldn't have bonded with you like I did. I most certainly wouldn't have run away and gone to Jenny in Melbourne. I never would have got into medicine and become a forensic pathologist. So, in many ways, I almost have to thank Mabel. I wouldn't be the me I am now without the horrid bitch.'

Hartley shook his head slowly, a smile in his eyes. 'Fair enough. Still, paying for her surgery—it's a lot of money and not guaranteed to help her.'

'I know. But Peter wanted to do it and I need to see it through for him. I have the money my parents left me, which given I invested it in stocks at Jenny's insistence over twelve years ago, has grown to more than enough. Besides, I need to know I am a bigger person than Mabel ever was. Also, I want Peter to know that I didn't leave him saddled with everything. That I am here for him. I'll put up with her to let him know that.'

His stroked her cheek. 'Won't she refuse it if it's your money paying for it?'

'Possibly. More likely she'd think it was my duty to pay. That I owe it to her.'

'Doesn't that bother you?'

'Not as much as it would have even last week. What she will have a problem with is me going with her if Peter is not back by the time she's ready to go.'

'Are you sure you want to do that?' His thumb stroked over her hand. 'She's horrible to you.'

'I know. But I can't send her off by herself. It's not right and Peter wouldn't like it.'

'If you have to go, I'll come with you.'

'You will?'

'Of course I will. But we have to hope he'll be found alive and well and you won't have to deal with your horrid grandmother at all.'

'Yes. Hope.' She felt the tickle of tears at the back of her throat, but didn't try to swallow them down, just let them show in her eyes and in the huskiness of her voice. 'But I also have to be realistic. I know there's a possibility that he won't come back.' She faltered, panic rising as the emotions threatened to overwhelm her, but when Hartley hugged her tighter, his hands stroking up and down her back, she realised she no longer had to be afraid of that, that there was strength in emotion, in feeling the good and the bad and fighting on anyway. It was made so much easier when you loved someone and was loved equally in return for exactly who you were, faults and all. She wasn't fixed, she knew that, but she was stronger than she'd ever been and she was going to keep getting stronger for herself, for Hartley, for Peter. She let the emotion wash over her, but not take her away, allowing it to sink in, to become a part of her strength, of who she was. Voice trembling, she finished what she wanted to say. 'I just want to do what he would do.'

'We'll find him, no matter what. And I'll be with you every step of the way.'

'I know. We're Miss Chief and Cooperman.'

'Damn right we are. I love you, Miss Chief.'

She looked up into his eyes, leaned forward and kissed him. 'I love you too, Cooperman.'

He smiled against her lips. 'Always.'

'Forever.'

They kissed again in the interview room where they'd come back together after sixteen years of being apart, arms wrapped around each other, holding on to the moment, to each other, to the undeniable reality of the fact that they were meant for each other and always had been. It seemed horrific that twice now, they'd almost lost the opportunity to have this. To share this. There was so much sadness in their past, still possibly more in their future. Life could be so fleeting, taken in an instant—her job taught her that every day. But right now, she just wanted to be in this moment, to savour the joy she felt with Hartley, knowing she could share everything with him and he would always be her forever. Knowing that every day, she intended to make sure he knew she was his forever.

They might not be the superheroes they'd dreamed of being when they were younger, but Erika knew that together, if anyone could wrestle a happy ever after out of all of this, it was Miss Chief and Cooperman.

Right now, in his arms, she was pretty certain they could fly.

Also by Daniel de Lorne

Available in ebook from Escape Publishing

Beckoning Blood
Burning Blood

Embers and Echoes

Daniel de Lorne

To my sister, Donna

Chapter One

The chalky tang of ash coated the back of Constable Ben Fields's tongue the moment he stepped out of the four-wheel drive. Attending a fire was not how he'd planned on visiting the cemetery today.

He tried to work saliva into his mouth, but the taste spread. Red dust fell from the car door as he slammed it shut. The Sillitoe Tartan's blue-and-white had become a dull purple and pinkish-white marred by black flecks. Keeping the thing clean out here was impossible. He slipped his cap over his head, bringing small respite from the heat that trapped him between the midday sun and the scorched earth. At least his aviators kept back the glare.

One small win.

The fire truck—a light tanker—they'd parked beside dwarfed them. As he and Leila walked over, Adrian jumped out of the cab to greet them.

'Great timing as always guys,' he laughed, 'showing up when the danger has passed.'

'Nice of you to put out the campfire,' Leila said. 'Hope you didn't drown the sausages.'

Adrian's easy smile vanished. 'Does that look like a campfire to you?'

He turned away without waiting for a response. Ben scanned the blackened paddock. Nope, definitely not a campfire.

Smoke rose off what had once been grass south of the cemetery. In the distance, a second tanker was parked further up the road and firefighters encased in protective yellow checked over the sodden earth. One missed ember caught on the wind would wreak havoc elsewhere.

Man, he hated bushfire season.

At least the cemetery had been spared. The fire had crept close, sniping at some of the recent graves, but it had been halted before it could engulf it. The wind had been blowing gently south rather than north. A square two hundred metres of the paddock was now charred.

'Adrian, who's got the lead?' he asked, Leila having now gotten him off-side.

He jerked his chin towards the firefighter heading towards them from the field. 'Toby.'

His gut plunged faster than a diver at the springs. He closed his eyes, pulled off his sunglasses, and pinched the bridge of his nose.

Shit.

When he looked again, Toby-bloody-Grimshaw marched out of the plumes of remnant smoke like the devil rising from the brimstone pits of hell.

Grim by name, grim by nature.

One hand dragged the hose, the other lugged his helmet. Ash flecked his black curls. His coat hung open and heavy, his Echo Springs Fire Department t-shirt clinging damp to his body. He gave them a short, firm nod, his dark, hard eyes meeting Ben's for a heartbeat before he turned to the truck to help Adrian secure the hose.

Ben swallowed hard. At least Leila didn't give him a ribbing, probably because she knew what today meant.

They waited in silence and the tendons on the back of Ben's neck tightened enough to strum. The sooner they discussed the crime, the sooner he could get away from Grim. Almost a whole summer had passed without him being snared in one of Toby's disapproving, cold looks. Not that he'd tried to avoid him. In fact, Toby had been the one hiding, sticking to the fire station or at home looking after his dad.

The good fireman. The good son.

Ben massaged his neck. *Better get this over and done with.*

'Was it deliberately lit?' he asked, slipping his aviators into his vest pocket.

Toby's shoulders stiffened then relaxed. 'Accelerant has been poured in a straight line along the edge of the paddock. I'd say someone was trying to torch the cemetery.'

'But the wind stopped them?'

He nodded. 'Lucky for us.'

'So, we've got an arsonist on our hands?'

'Looks like. I'll finish up the investigation here, then send the paperwork to you guys. Hopefully you can catch whoever did this before it escalates. They've got a taste for it now.'

'No chance it was an accident?' Ben's stomach clenched and it had nothing to do with the taste of ash. He'd already been told the blaze was lit with intent, but being around Toby gave him a case of the stupids. At least Toby did him the favour of not rolling his eyes.

He shook his head. 'This was deliberate.'

'Can you show us where you think it started?'

Toby looked from him to Leila and back again. 'Sure, why not?'

He led them to a definite dark line in the grass. Ben could even smell the remains of the fuel.

'Footprints? Cast-off matches?'

'We've been busy putting out the fire. I'm hopeful we'll find something. I don't think we're dealing with someone who knew what he was doing. If he'd waited for a stronger wind, we'd have had a bigger problem.'

'Thank god for stupidity, huh?'

Stop talking!

'Yeah, it has its benefits,' Toby said.

Ben's heart jumped like a creek full of frogs on a full moon.

Toby didn't say anything more, just looked at him, and for once Ben didn't feel like he was under some malevolent examination. But whatever the look meant, Toby blinked and the moment passed. Ben's heart was slower to quit fibrillating.

'Look, I'd better get back to it. Go find yourself some witnesses. I'll collect what evidence I can, and give you a call if I need any help.'

Unlikely. Toby never needed anyone's help, least of all Ben's. He'd been clear on that long ago, and the few opportunities since then reaffirmed it.

Leila gave him a strained smile. 'We'll have a look around here first. *If* that's alright with you, Tobias?'

Toby's eyes narrowed, and Ben wrestled a grin. Too many memories of that name being called out across the back field as Toby's mother...

Time to get away.

'Thanks, Toby. We won't mess anything up. Come on, Leila.'

Toby gave a small nod and headed back to the tanker.

'He's such an arse,' she said when Toby was out of earshot. 'Nice arse, though.'

'How can you even tell in that tunic?'

'Good memory.'

He chuckled despite himself. 'So classy.'

'That's me.'

Tearing his eyes away from Toby's retreating back, he walked with Leila along the line where the fire started, snapping photos for their investigation. There wasn't much. No footprints, no dropped matches or rags. Perhaps Toby would find something, but Ben didn't think it likely. The arsonist might have been an amateur, but he knew enough not to leave evidence.

They searched the cemetery, passing the graves of town founders and the recently departed. Peter and Timnah Hanson—renowned doctors taken too soon and parents of the still-missing Peter Junior—lay not far from the graves of two people who mattered a lot to Ben. But for now he kept his distance.

The graveyard dirt was too dry and cracked to retain shoe-prints. They found nothing leading from the cemetery or the road to the point where the fire had started. Perhaps whoever it was had come from the other side, standing in the paddock, looking towards the cemetery and the town. Either way, the earth gave them no clues.

They walked back to the car. 'D'you mind if I check those last graves myself?' he asked.

She gave him a knowing smile. 'Sure, I'll start writing up the report.'

'Thanks.' He opened the back door and retrieved the bunch of yellow flowers. He scanned the scene for Toby, not really wanting to do this in front of him, but his one-time friend was back in the paddock.

He searched the final sector for evidence, which provided a good excuse for keeping his head down. He didn't want to see his mother's grave until he was standing in front of it. The sting of her death had faded years ago, when he stopped dwelling on the how and the why. He'd managed to separate today from *that* day, until now, when it was just him and a white gravestone. And a nose full of foul smoke.

Ella Susan Fields

Beloved wife and mother.

The grave was untouched. His dad hadn't been there yet, probably waiting for a cooler part of the day, like Ben himself had intended. He removed the dried twigs of flowers he'd left on her birthday, when, like every year, he'd promised he'd come more often, knowing he wouldn't. He placed the fresh flowers in the vase at the base of the gravestone. Looking at the chiselled letters and numbers, his eye was drawn to Toby working in the distance beyond. They hadn't been here together since the day of the funeral.

Funerals. Plural.

He released a long breath. Death was meant to bring people together, wasn't it?

His attention drifted to his left, to three graves down, where Toby's mother rested. The two women would have been buried next to each other if not for family plots getting in the way. Perhaps it was enough they'd died together.

While the ones left behind still suffered.

Losing his mother had hit seventeen-year-old Toby the hardest, perhaps because he was there when it happened. Certainly that was the reason Toby became a firefighter, even more of a reason than wanting to follow in his dad's footsteps and measure up to the big fire chief of Echo Springs. But he had shut Ben out completely, even when he was hurting too... They could have helped each other. Had the kiss they'd shared broken something in him? Was their love-making an act of shame Toby had wanted to blot out? Did Toby think it had been nothing more than a fling?

Every time he went near the springs, he couldn't help but reminisce. Swimming together after that footy match, hanging around with a few of the guys from the team and relaxing by the springs. Riding a winning high, he'd felt invincible and thought that after years of wondering what it would be like, of whether Toby felt the same, he'd decided to go for it.

Toby had gone with him when he suggested a walk while the rest stayed behind. And then, behind that big tree, he'd stopped and taken Toby's hand. There was a long pause as Toby looked from his hand to Ben's face. He'd tried to convey the question without speaking, fearful of being heard, but Toby understood and smiled.

And it had worked out better than he'd imagined.

Only it hadn't worked out at all.

'Idiot,' he muttered to himself, and refocused on the graves.

Roses lay at the base of Mary Grimshaw's headstone.

He frowned. It couldn't have been Toby. He hadn't known he was going to be here—unless he'd come earlier. Or maybe it was Toby's dad. Strange though that Bob Grimshaw, who didn't drive, would be out here by himself. Perhaps he'd walked.

Ben went over to the grave, his eyes landing on the set of shoe-prints beside it, heading towards the fire scene. Were they evidence? He lay a measuring tape beside them and took a photo from three angles. Bob's shoes? Toby's boots?

He couldn't leave without finding out, but that meant summoning Toby. No avoiding it; if Toby wanted to give him that contemptuous look, so be it. He had to follow this through.

'Toby!' he shouted, waving at him to get his attention.

He trudged over. He probably had to muster the strength to be in the presence of Blind Ben Fields.

'What's up?' he asked. His jaw barely moved.

'Did you bring these flowers?'

He glowered at them before shaking his head. 'No, wasn't me.'

'So I guess they're not your prints here and here?'

He pointed to his fire-retardant boots. 'Too small for mine.'

'Was your dad here?'

'Not that I know, but I've been out since early this morning. He could have come down.' He took a few photos of his own.

'I'll drop by on the way back to the station and ask him.'

'Can you wait until I'm there?' His words shot out. 'Please? He's...he's gotten worse lately.'

'How so?'

Toby chewed his bottom lip, an action that had Ben biting his own—for entirely different reasons.

Focus!

'He's forgetting more, and getting confused. If you guys rock up in that car, I'm worried how he might react. He hasn't had a cop car outside our house since...'

Neither of them wanted to think about that day, Ben was sure. 'How long are you going to be?'

Toby crossed his arms across his chest. 'What's the hurry? Do you think he's going to do a runner?'

Toby might have been shorter than him, but a stern look or word could make him feel like a lumbering idiot. 'What? No. But time is important and—'

'What are you implying, Ben? That this is somehow my dad's fault? You think he's getting around lighting fires, now?'

He rolled his tongue over this bottom lip. 'I'm not implying anything. These are the only footprints we've found that don't belong to someone here. I want to know if they're your dad's, and if so, whether he saw anything suspicious when he was here. The sooner I ask him, the sooner I can get on with the investigation.'

The rush of words had him breathing hard, but goddamn it, it was his job to ask these questions. The last thing he wanted to do was jump to any conclusions about Bob Grimshaw. But firefighters, even ones who had retired, were never above suspicion when it came to arson.

Like cops when it came to corruption.

He breathed deeply, expelling that thought before it had a chance to root itself in his mind. Toby's dark looks didn't help matters.

'I'll give you an hour. If you're not there by then, I'm speaking to him without you. Call your aunt if you think he needs someone familiar.'

He used to be someone familiar—to Bob and to Toby—but that changed long ago. And his longing for the man standing in front of him wouldn't get in the way of him doing his job.

Toby's fist clenched at his side. 'I'll be there.' He spun on his heels and stalked back into the paddock.

He watched Toby go, a spear of righteous anger driving up his spine. That's why he kept away from Toby. What was the point in being around someone who couldn't stand the sight of him? To hell with Toby Grimshaw. Whether he liked him or not was irrelevant.

He had an arsonist to catch.

Chapter Two

Ben Bloody Fields.

Why did he have to complicate things?

Toby wanted to finish his investigation in peace, in his own time, but now he had to rush or else deal with the consequences of his dad getting in a state when the police showed up. Why couldn't Ben wait?

But he knew the answer. If it were him, he wouldn't have even given Ben the hour. Whoever had done this needed to be stopped before they escalated. Putting his own family's interests above those of Echo Springs wasn't on. That guilt sat heavy and wet; even in this heat.

'You need a hand, Toby?' Adrian called, breaking him out of staring at nothing.

'Can you check the gully by the road? In case they dropped anything.'

Adrian and Lewis set off while Carl worked at the other end of the paddock, taking measurements and photos of the extent of the damage.

He needed to concentrate. He could still finish his investigation and get back to town to be there when Ben questioned his dad. As he brushed aside another bit of burnt earth in the hope of finding a match, he couldn't brush away the worry that his dad might have had something to do with this.

Which brought him back to what day it was.

No, he hadn't brought flowers. Ben had. Ben always did. Even when he'd lived in Sydney for those five years, he'd driven out here and brought flowers. When Toby had driven past—as he always did, driving past without stopping—he'd seen Ben with that guy he'd shacked up with, the one who'd almost ruined him. There he was putting down flowers, sharing that moment with that dickhead when it should have been him, when it should have been the two of them together.

Well, only if he ignored the fact that it was Toby's fault they were dead.

No, he didn't bring flowers. He didn't go near the graves if he could help it. Yet here he was, today of all days, and he'd been here with Ben.

He cast the thought away.

They finished forty-five minutes later and jumped into the tankers, heading back to town. He was cutting it close to Ben's deadline. Adrian swung past his house, let him out and drove off. Toby checked his watch.

Late.

Two car doors slammed and he turned. Ben had parked a few houses down, and he and Leila were now approaching the house. At six-foot-three-inches tall, Ben didn't so much walk as stride across the lawn like a giant roaming across the countryside. He filled every inch of the uniform, his thick thighs encased in navy, his light blue shirt barely covering the girth of his biceps. Rather than hiding his broad chest, the load-bearing vest accentuated it, adding more strength to his already formidable frame.

The only thing that didn't work was the aviators. They obscured his eucalypt-green eyes and stopped the smile—and the dimple in his right cheek—transforming him from the severe arm of the law to the friendly neighbourhood cop that the town loved.

I know which one I prefer.

As they came closer, Toby prepared to thank him for waiting, or at least give him a smile. Speaking felt too great a challenge at the moment.

'Ready?' Ben said abruptly, killing any notion that his good opinion could be so easily restored.

Toby's heart retreated beneath the lash of Ben's tone. It was no more than he deserved. He'd acted like a dick at the cemetery, but that would have to be another wrong to add to an already long list. He had to get this over with, then they could go back to avoiding each other. Not out of preference but necessity.

He nodded and led the two officers into the house.

The TV played down the hall, but that was no guarantee Dad would be there, not lately. His aunt usually came by to check on him but Fridays were tricky for her. 'Dad? You here?'

'In the kitchen.'

At least he responded. Perhaps he'd be coherent enough to answer Ben's questions. But what if he didn't like the answers?

Ben followed close behind him. Even with the smell of ash and burnt grass on his clothes and skin, Ben's scent of sun-infused leather got inside him and nestled in his gut.

His dad sat at the table reading the newspaper, a cup of tea beside him. A quick scan of the room showed nothing left running, no sign of blood, no kettle melted black. Not this time. The sooty smear running up the wall by the stove was still there. He should have repaired and painted it already, but other things had gotten in the way. And he expected something like that would happen again.

Bob didn't look up from his paper until the three of them got much closer. The movement in his peripheral vision caught his attention, and he lowered the paper as he spotted the two cops.

He blinked and shook his head as he focused on Ben. 'Oh, hello, Ben,' he said, cheering as he recognised him. He rose out of his chair, offering his hand.

Ben clasped it firmly. 'How are you, Mr Grimshaw?'

'Mr Grimshaw! I remember when you used to call me Uncle Bob.'

'And you used to call me Beanpole.'

They laughed. His dad's laugh wasn't something he heard often around here but Ben's laugh…that deep and strong and reassuring sound hummed inside him. One of many reasons he'd kept away from Ben since his return two years earlier.

'And how's your dad doing?' Bob asked.

'You know, the same.'

'Hard time of year, for all of us. You give him my best,' he said in earnest.

His dad always said he should see more of Bill Fields but he never did. And Bill never showed his face around here either.

Ben gave a strained smile. 'I will. Do you mind if we have a chat? It's important.'

'By all means. As long as it's not bad news.' His short laugh gave way to a scraping cough. 'Toby, put the kettle on. Let's go in here.' Dad led them into the family room, lowering the TV's volume. 'Have you been watching the cricket lately?'

Toby filled the electric kettle and strained to hear Ben's answer but it was lost. He flicked the switch and went into the room, standing back as Ben and Leila did their job. He'd step in if needed but he knew Ben—or had done—and had watched him around town, had listened to every little snippet of information about him. He knew Ben wouldn't treat his dad badly.

'You're here on official business, hey?'

'I'm afraid so,' Ben said. 'Were you at the cemetery today?'

Leila sat with a pen ready over her pad.

'Yes, I took some flowers for Mary's grave.'

'These the shoes you were wearing?'

Four sets of eyes looked at Bob's flat-soled, brown slippers.

'Wouldn't get very far in them, would I?' he laughed. 'I wore the white sneakers in the hallway. At least they used to be white. Bit red now. What's this about?'

'There was a fire at the cemetery today and we found some shoe-prints.'

Toby's shoulders bunched, exacerbating the knots that had locked into his back from the morning's work. Ben had effectively accused his dad of being the arsonist.

'Ahhhh,' Bob said, leaning back into his armchair and interlocking his fingers across his chest. 'Well, feel free to take a look.'

'Thanks, Mr Grimshaw. We will. What time did you go to the cemetery?'

Bob didn't answer. Instead he watched the television and the pause stretched.

'Mr Grimshaw? What time did you go to the cemetery?' Ben repeated.

He rubbed his palm with his thumb, thinking, watching, the rubbing becoming more insistent.

The knots in Toby's shoulders tightened.

'Dad!'

His head jerked up. 'Yeah?'

'What time did you go to the cemetery?' he asked, and for a second it looked like he'd avoided falling into the fog.

'Three o'clock,' he replied. 'You remember. You were there.'

His throat closed; he had to force the words out. 'No, I wasn't. You went by yourself.'

Ben looked at him.

'No, we were all there,' Dad said. 'Ben was there too. And Bill.'

His stomach went into freefall.

Same place, different decade.

'Dad, we're talking about this morning. Not the funeral.'

But it was too late. His dad's eyes shimmered.

'We'll give you a minute,' Ben said. They walked into the other room, leaving him behind to calm his father.

He sat and took hold of his thinning and weathered hands. 'It's okay, Dad.'

'Toby? Where's your mother?'

He sighed. 'She's gone out, Dad. She'll be back soon.'

He hated lying to him and wiping away the tragedy, but there was no point in hurting his dad. Reminding him of what he'd lost was cruel, especially when he'd forget again. He'd listened to his dad cry enough for several lifetimes. Better to keep quiet, keep it in.

'Her birthday's coming up soon. What should we get her?'

'I'll think of something,' he said. The tears had been held at bay. His dad settled back into his armchair. The television held him transfixed as he watched the cricket.

'I'll be right back. I'm talking to some visitors.'

But his dad wasn't listening. Toby increased the volume and returned to the kitchen.

Leila had gone but Ben was at the counter making the tea. It would have been such a homey image if he hadn't been wearing his uniform, that utility vest loaded with a gun, handcuffs and the rest. This wasn't Ben in his house, this was Constable Benjamin Fields.

Still, he was making the tea, and there was something right about that.

Toby sat at the table and waited, torn between wanting Ben here and wanting him gone.

'Here,' said Ben, putting the brew down in front of him.

The awkwardness Ben usually displayed around him was hidden behind a mask of formality. Considerate but distant. As Toby sat he watched Ben, the graceful but manly way he moved around the kitchen and took his place opposite. One hand on the table, his thumb tapping, the other hand holding onto the mug's handle. Long, big thick fingers and hands that matched the rest of him. He was so close.

'How long until I can talk to him again?' Ben asked.

'Your guess is as good as mine.' He blew across the surface of the mug. 'About what he said…'

'About you being at the cemetery?'

He nodded, putting the mug down. 'He was referring to the funeral, not to today.'

'That's what I thought, but…'

'But what?'

Ben sipped his tea, his green eyes holding his attention. 'Where were you this morning, Toby?'

'You think I'm some firebug now?'

'I didn't say that, but if I go back to the station and haven't asked the right questions, then what kind of cop would I be?' Ben's jaw tightened.

Toby tongued the back of his canine tooth. Ben was right. As always. 'I got to the station just before eight. I was there until eleven then we turned out.'

He wrote in his pad. 'And you have no idea about your dad's whereabouts before we arrived?'

'If he went to the cemetery, he went after I left, but he's not a fire-starter. I didn't see him or anyone else on the way to the cemetery this morning. You'll have to look for another suspect.'

He regretted the defensiveness in his voice. What must he have sounded like?

Guilty. That's what.

He'd always been guilty. That's why he kept his mouth shut as much as possible. But keeping quiet would not help him or his dad right now.

Ben took another sip of his tea, his expression dark and serious, then pushed the cup away. He closed the pad and stood up from his chair.

Ben couldn't leave thinking his dad had done this.

'Dad was there to visit Mum's grave. That's all.'

'Perhaps, but it's also a coincidence that on this day, where your dad was, there was a fire. Put yourself in my shoes—'

'I'd rather not,' he said quickly. He couldn't bear to imagine how Ben saw him.

Ben flinched. 'Suit yourself. I'm going to ask around if anyone saw your dad or anything suspicious up at the cemetery. It's routine. And if he becomes lucid again, call me. I want to talk to him.'

He poured the rest of the tea down the drain. Toby didn't move. His hand wrapped around the mug, the heat from the water distracting him from the doubt shooting into the base of his skull. What if it had been Dad?

Ben headed for the door but stopped before leaving the kitchen. He looked at the marked wall, then to Toby. 'You sure you two are safe here?'

'It was an accident.' Was he practising his defence? 'I've disconnected the gas since then.'

Ben didn't speak. What was there really to say? But there was a look, not pity but real, heartfelt concern, the way Ben had looked when their mothers had died. Ben had given him so much even then, but there was nothing he could have given in return. He had to escape it.

He stood and headed to the family room. 'I'll let you know when he improves. Show yourself out.'

And he retreated into the other room and sat with his dad, unnoticed and unrecognised, not moving until long after the front door closed.

Chapter Three

Three days after the fire and they were still no closer to finding the arsonist. No tip-offs. No one had seen anything useful. One person remembered seeing Bob heading out that way, but they couldn't recall if he'd been carrying anything other than flowers. It didn't sit well with Ben to consider Bob Grimshaw a suspect. Then again, he'd been accused of thinking the best of people before and look how well that had turned out.

He'd planned on seeing Toby again to ask if Bob remembered anything, but he'd been kept busy attending a domestic dispute and filling in paperwork. Then there were patrols and stopping speeding drivers. Monday vanished and the fire-starter was still no closer to being found.

When Ben's shift ended, knowing it was still unsolved agitated him more than the prickly heat of the late summer afternoon. He'd find Toby the next day and see what else he had to say.

He walked alone to the pub—Leila said she'd catch him up—and he took his time along Main Street to the Cooee Hotel. The sun was still above the horizon; thanks to daylight savings there'd be hours of light left. Even so, twilight couldn't come fast enough. His favourite part of the day. He enjoyed the way the heat sank into his bones as the stars came out and melted the stress of the working day.

Most of it anyway.

Here he had time to think, time to process, a moment to breathe. Not like Sydney. At twenty-five he'd already felt exhausted, going from work to the gym to somewhere out and getting to bed late and getting up early to do it again. Piece by piece he'd been chipped away until there wasn't much left that he recognised of himself.

Or of the person he'd been with.

But that was done now, long past, and he didn't regret coming back. The career path might not have been the same but Echo Springs was home. If only he had someone to share it with.

He entered the pub, already busy at six, and greeted people as he headed to the bar to buy a pint. Trading hellos, some jokes and a bit of news, he almost felt like he wasn't one of the town's police officers. He was just another member of the Echo Springs community. No one commented on his work or the fact that he was gay—at least not within earshot. Some of them had a problem with one or the other, or both, but they wisely kept their mouths shut around him. And it's not like he was the only gay guy in Echo Springs.

Toby's eyes met his at the same time Ben looked over. Whether it was the atmosphere, the warm feel of belonging or—as was most likely—the effect of seeing Toby, he smiled on reflex.

Toby blanched, and that was enough to scare away his grin and remind him that things were not all good in Echo Springs. After all, he was investigating Toby's dad for arson, accidental or otherwise. Bob sat at the table with Toby and his aunt, Narelle. He seemed lucid now, but as Ben came over to talk to them, pint in hand, Toby's eyes widened.

Fear? Panic? A plea?

Ben indicated with his head for Toby to follow him. He could talk to Bob the next day, especially if tonight his mind was functioning, and give the family this time together. Bob was telling his sister a joke, and then another old-timer joined the table and started chatting to him. He hoped for Toby's sake that Bob continued to enjoy his evening.

He chose a spot by a window, far enough out of earshot. He put the untasted beer on the table. He'd wait to hear what Toby had to say before drowning the aggravation scratching in his throat. The table they stood at was small, forcing Toby to come close. Being this near to him, the heat radiating off him, the black t-shirt taut across his chest, his curly hair...

Damn.

He took a drink anyway.

'Bob's looking in fine form,' he said after he'd swallowed.

'Today's been a good day. Thought it might help to bring him somewhere familiar.'

'Seems to be working out.'

Toby watched Bob, which gave Ben time to watch Toby. Not staring but glances, studying the hard line of his jaw, the accented curve of his lips, and that perpetual line of worry across his forehead. No mistaking how much of a man he was now, and how distant.

Time to be Officer Fields and get the hell out of there. He'd see Leila tomorrow.

'I read your report,' he said. 'I was going to come see you.'

'Same. I've spoken to Dad and he said he was at the cemetery by himself. He went soon after I left for work and then was back by half-past ten. He remembers because he got home to watch the start of the match. The fire began after that and he didn't see anybody nearby.'

'He'll repeat this if I ask him?'

Toby's eyebrows raised as he dipped his head. 'You think I'm lying?'

Ben's hand tightened on the glass. If it shattered, he doubted he'd feel it. 'I'm just asking the question. I need to hear it from him too.'

He sighed. Hard. 'You can talk to him tomorrow. I'm off-shift so I'll be there.'

'Fine.' He drained the glass.

Toby had already stepped away but he stopped and turned, his top lip pinned in distaste. 'You really think he had something to do with this, don't you?'

This was the Toby he'd become used to, the one who'd taken away his friend and replaced him with an embittered bastard.

'I'm doing my job. I don't want to believe that your dad would be capable of it, but if you were me and he was the only person you could find who'd been at the scene at the time—'

'But he wasn't there at the time,' Toby said, coming closer than before. Ben forced himself to stay rooted to the spot. 'If you really did read my report, then you'd know that the fire couldn't have started before eleven. The way it burned, the speed with which it ate up the grass, it's not possible.'

'Assuming your Dad got back when he said he got back.'

'There could have been someone else at the cemetery. Did you smell petrol on Dad when you came to the house? Did you find anything that could suggest it was him?'

Leila had done a quick search outside the house without Toby knowing and she hadn't found anything suspicious. It wasn't conclusive though, and they'd need a warrant to do anything more thorough. By which time any evidence would probably be gone.

Toby was nothing if not protective.

'He's not the man he used to be. Things change. And what with it being the anniversary—'

Toby stepped in closer. 'You're wrong, and if you were a half-decent cop, you'd stop going down this useless line of enquiry and start looking at other options.'

Blood jack-hammered in his temples. Toby had always doubted his ability as an officer. Ever since he'd slunk back to Echo Springs, he'd put up with the disappointed looks Toby flung his way. Not that it should have mattered what Toby thought; it had been years since Toby had wanted anything to do with him. If anything, Ben had been too lenient, too easygoing and blind when it came to Tobias Grimshaw and his father.

Blind Ben Fields...

His insides cracked rather than thawed. He levelled his voice as much as he could. 'I'll be at your place first thing tomorrow, whether Bob is with it or not.' He marched past Toby and wrenched open the door.

The suffocating evening heat rushed to envelop him. He stalked down the road towards home, thoughts tumbling over themselves, stirring up the past so all he could think about was how he'd run back to Echo Springs, a failed cop from the city going to where expectations were lower. And Toby was one of the first people he'd seen. From the looks he'd given him, he'd already known. They'd all known.

'Ben!'

That sounded like Toby but it wouldn't be him. Toby had never chased him down in his life.

'Ben! Stop, for god's sake!'

That *was* Toby. He shuddered to a halt. He needed to fortify himself, but the heat melted his defences. Whatever argument they had now, it was going to wound deep.

Toby came around to stand in front of him. He was a couple of inches shorter than him, but Ben had always considered Toby the bigger man. He rose to his full height and crossed his arms in front of his chest.

'I'm sorry.'

Ben flinched. This was not the Toby he expected.

'What I said was out of line. I was...I was protecting my dad.'

How many times had he heard arguments like this from misguided and fooled loved ones? 'And would you protect him even if he was an arsonist?'

'If he was an *arsonist*, I'd absolutely hand him over. You know what it's like. If there's one bent cop, it gives you all a bad name. It's the same for us. We spend our time putting out fires; to have one of our own go around starting them... But trust me, please, it's not him. I believe Dad.'

'But how can you be sure?'

'I've checked the house myself. There's no spare fuel lying around. None of his clothes are covered with it. There'd be some smoke residue on something. The place would stink. I know my stuff.'

'Unlike me.'

'That's not what I said.'

'But it's what you think.'

Toby didn't say anything. He never said anything, nothing that mattered. Anyway, Toby said more with his eyes than his mouth.

'I've had enough of this. I'll see you tomorrow when I do *my* stuff.'

He walked away but Toby grabbed his arm.

'You're a good cop, Ben, but you need to let this go. Dad's not your guy.'

He expected anger on Toby's face but instead there was a vulnerability that he was unused to seeing there, an openness that attempted to drain Ben's heart of its anger. He jerked his arm out of Toby's grip and tried to weave around him but Toby got in his way.

'If I were a *good cop*, whoever started this fire would already be caught, so don't patronise me.'

'I'm not patronising you, Ben, I'm trying to help.'

'Since when have you ever wanted to help me, Toby? Since when have you ever given a shit about me?'

He hadn't meant to say it but it came out with such force. Even so, he didn't regret it. The only regret he had about it was that Toby didn't speak, only confirming what he'd known all along. They may as well have been strangers.

'We should be working together—'

'But instead you're stopping me from following a line of enquiry that any other cop would follow just because it concerns your father.'

'Wouldn't you do what you thought was right to protect someone you love? *Didn't* you?'

There it was again, the assumption that what he'd done, the thing that had brought him scurrying back here, had been for love. He'd been betrayed, done his job and still ended up worse because of it. No one believed him that he had no idea about Jared dealing. He wouldn't have believed it himself, but it was the truth. Yes, he'd been blind, stupid, ignorant. But never corrupt.

What the hell did it matter now?

Except it did matter, and right now it mattered a lot. Tobias Grimshaw judged him every day because of it and was now trying to use it against him. 'You want to work together on this? Then I'm going to speak to Bob now. You can chaperone, I don't care, but I'm doing this.'

He spun on his heel and headed back to the pub. Toby wouldn't lie about what Bob had said, or at least he'd once known him well enough to believe that, but it was now a matter of principle. A good cop never rests, justice never sleeps, serve and protect, all that stuff.

And pride wouldn't let him retreat, not even when Toby seized his arm.

'Get off me, Toby, touch me again and I'll do you for assault.'

Pathetic. Using the law like that to defend himself because his feelings were hurt.

'Ben, not tonight,' Toby said, running beside him. 'I'm asking you, as a friend.' It sounded like he meant it.

'We're not friends,' he said, spitting out the word, and marching into the pub.

A hollowness chiselled through his chest as he ripped open the door and strode over to Bob's table. Cold, unfeeling, but managing to put on an imitation of a smile, he peered down at the group. Their laughter tapered off as they noticed him and said their cautious hellos.

'Mr Grimshaw, do you mind if we have a chat?'

'Of course, Ben, always got time for you.'

Just like old times.

The Grimshaws' place had been a second home when the two families had spent so much time together. His father—a police sergeant—and Bob—the fire chief—had been good mates, but it was Mary and Ella who'd been the closest, ever since they were girls. When all six of them were together it wasn't two families, it was one, and they'd been so happy. Thinking of what they'd lost, acid tears scalded the back of Ben's eyes.

The old-timer gave his goodbyes, and Ben took his seat. Narelle stayed and Toby joined them. His expression clouded over with more gloom than an approaching storm.

'I suppose you want to ask me about that day at the cemetery, too,' Bob said.

'Afraid so.'

'Well, there's not much else I can tell you that I haven't already told Toby, but sure.'

He repeated what Toby had said, not word for word but in a rambling, story-telling sort of way. Ben asked questions to test Bob's story but it held, as did his memory. Worry replaced the anger on Toby's face in anticipation of the moment when Bob would no longer be himself. Some of the tension in Ben's shoulders unwound.

'And you didn't see anyone else out there at the time? Didn't notice anything unusual?'

'To be honest, I was focused on visiting my Mary, I wouldn't have noticed a herd of cattle if they'd been standing next to me. But as far as I remember, and the memory isn't as good as it once was,' he laughed, 'I don't think there was anyone else there.'

'And you didn't smell anything?'

'Now, Ben, I was a fireman for thirty-something years. If I smelled a fire, do you think I wouldn't have noticed?'

'Just checking, Mr Grimshaw,' he said, his lips softening into a smile. 'How'd you get out there?'

'I walked.'

'Bit of a long way, isn't it? Especially with the heat?'

'Well, I had no other way of getting there.' He leaned closer and whispered. 'They've taken my licence away, don't you know?' He winked at him before sitting back. 'Narelle was busy that day and Toby...where were you? I can't remember.'

'At work, Dad.'

'Oh, yeah,' he frowned to himself. 'Funny, I'm sure I saw you but...nope, it's gone. Must have been someone else.'

'Who was it? Where did you think you saw Toby?'

'Nah, forget it. Wasn't anyone.'

He glanced at Toby and the huffy look he got before he rolled his eyes told him that Toby knew what was coming next. Not that he could really imagine Toby would be the arsonist.

'Well, that seems fair, Mr Grimshaw. Sorry to have interrupted your evening.'

'Anytime, Ben. Can't be too cautious. Whole town could go up if we're not careful. Never seen the place so dry.'

'Let's hope it never comes to that.'

'Yeah, Echo Springs has seen enough tragedy,' he said, then paused and looked down. Was that it? Had Bob used up the last of his good times and was now lost in the fog? Ben stood to go, but sat down again when Bob looked up. 'I said a prayer over Ella's grave too when I was there. I wanted you to know that.'

His heart ached as the memory of his mother's death yanked on it from across the years. Maybe he should have brought flowers for Mary's grave as well. Next year. He cleared his throat. 'Thanks, Bob. I visited her too on the day, twice. Brought Dad with me the second time.'

'You're a good son. I've asked Toby to come with me, but he refuses. I'm sure he has his reasons.' Bob took a swig of his beer. 'You'd think it was the least he could do.'

'Are we done here?' Toby snapped.

Toby had never wanted to talk about their mothers' deaths when they happened, and then after the funeral he'd shut Ben out of his life. Had Toby ever talked about it? With anyone? Ben had wanted to be there for him, but he'd spurned his sympathy and his love. That memory was almost as unhappy as finding out his mother had died. No matter what he'd tried, Toby had remained resolute, and there were only so many times he could be rejected before he got fed up with being kicked.

'Yeah, I'm done.' He shook Bob's hand. 'Thanks for your time. Hope you enjoy the rest of your evening.' He nodded to Narelle, ignored Toby and left the pub, texting Leila that he'd gone. Right now, he needed to get home, have a shower and forget about Toby for the rest of the night. He gave a derisive laugh. He may as well try to summon rain.

Chapter Four

Toby's nightmares supplied the screams. The terror-filled high-pitched wailing rang in his ears while Ella and Mary burned. They marched out of the shadows inside the flames, their bodies charred but their faces still visible. They weren't alone. More townspeople emerged—his dad, members of his crew, Ben!—and ambled towards him as their shrieking raised louder. He searched for an escape but they surrounded him. Their screams… ringing… ringing… ringing… as they called his name.

'Toby!'

He jerked awake, sweat soaking his body and his heart jack-hammering inside his chest. Smoke alarms shrieked, wood crackled and popped, and the cloying stench of smoke roused him more than smelling salts. He'd woken out of that horrifying nightmare and into a whole new one. They had minutes to get out.

'Dad!' he shouted, jumping out of bed, grabbing his phone and sprinting down the hall. His hand touched the wall and he snatched it back from the roasting heat. Minutes or seconds?

'Dad!'

He ran down the hall. The roof creaked and splintered, as wood cracked in the blaze. He covered his nose and mouth with the crook of his arm, and bent low to avoid the smoke filling the house. He glimpsed inside the kitchen, the flames more intense and swarming there, giving off an oily sheen. He glanced at the floor to confirm no body lay on the ground before hurrying on. His dad wasn't in the bathroom either and his room at the back of the house was empty. Wherever he was, he wasn't inside.

Toby rushed through the open backdoor in the laundry, grabbed a pair of shorts out of the washing basket and burst into the fresh air, coughing to clear the smoke out of his throat. He rang emergency services and gave the details. His gaze swept across the backyard.

His dad wasn't out the back but he shouted for him anyway. He hadn't checked the family room and a hard knot solidified in the middle of his chest. He'd rescued people from burning houses before, how could he not have done a full sweep? He turned to re-enter the house but the roof caved in, forcing him back. The flames feasted on their wooden home crammed with junk. Pulling on the shorts, he took the chance and raced down the side of the house, dodging flames and searching among the grass. Someone talked to him through his phone, but he hung up when he heard the approaching sirens. Sweaty and singed, he broke free from the house's reach and into the front yard, slamming into his neighbour.

'Ian, have you seen Dad?'

Ian's hand latched onto his sweaty arm and pulled him away. 'He's with us,' he said. 'We found him out the front. He said you were already out here but when we couldn't find you… Are you okay?'

He extracted himself from the grip. 'I'm fine, I'm fine. I need to see Dad.' His lungs hungered for clean air, expanding like giant balloons then abruptly emptying.

The house crumbled behind him as neighbours emerged to gawp. He couldn't think about what he'd lost, or what he'd almost lost. Bob sat in the grass. He was calm and whole. The weight in Toby's chest plummeted to the bottom of his stomach, almost taking out his knees. He staggered over to Bob. When he reached him, he sank to the grass. Bob sat with his palms open, pink and weeping, but he didn't recognise him.

'We tried to move him but he refused.'

The fire tanker arrived. Adrian jumped out first and grabbed the hose, while Lewis hung back, got everything working and tried to control the crowd. A second tanker would arrive soon. Maybe he should help, but his legs refused to budge. If he couldn't save his own house, what kind of fire-fighter did that make him?

Dad must have had the same thought. When he saw Adrian in his gear and the hose snaking across the lawn, he rose to join him.

'We're staying here, Dad.' He grabbed Bob's forearm as high above his burns as possible and applied enough force to keep him down.

'But there's a fire!'

'I know,' he replied softly. 'But they don't need us right now. We're second shift.'

Thankfully, this placated him and he sat back down, content to watch the fire consume the property. The heat against Toby's back was all he needed to know that it still raged. They should move away but the drive had gone out of him. Lewis and Adrian did their job, the water and the foam working to beat down the flames. Neighbours milled too close for their own safety. Someone handed him a t-shirt, not that he needed it. The adrenaline, the heat rolling off the house, the earth still hot from a scorching day…he'd never be cold again.

A paramedic—Steph—appeared next to him with her kit.

'Bob,' she said, 'can you hear me? I'm going to look at your hands.'

He didn't acknowledge her. Transfixed, shadows danced across his lined face as he kept the blaze in his eyes.

The fire devoured their home but Toby felt like he was inside a glass box. Protected. Untouched. But forced to stay.

Someone talked to him but he couldn't hear them.

'Toby, have you got any injuries?'

Was that Steph? Had she already asked that question?

'Umm…no,' he said, not sure he understood what he was responding to.

He refused oxygen, hands examined him but he stumbled away from them and faced the fire. The red flames battled to stay alive as Adrian mastered them. But his eyes were drawn to the point of their strongest retaliation. His head filled with the screams of ghosts, and out of the fire and the smoke that erupted into the night air, the faces of Ella and Mary flew towards him.

Startled, he screwed his eyes shut, protected his face with his hands and spun, slamming into the warm and solid body standing behind him. He released a shaky breath.

'It's okay, Toby. It's okay.'

Strong, thick arms circled him and hugged him. His own rapid pulse faded as he listened to the reassuring heartbeat now filling his ears. Time stopped and he wasn't there any longer. There was a long stretch of blessed nothing and eventually he could breathe again. He inhaled deeply and a familiar scent filled his lungs as he lifted his head. When he opened his eyes, it was to look into Ben's gentle eyes.

Thank god you're here.

A fist punched his heart, strong enough to push him out of Ben's arms. He wiped his nose with his forearm, and staggered back. He couldn't depend on Ben for support. He couldn't fall into that trap. He'd denied himself that when he'd needed it years ago and promised never, no matter how much he wanted it, to seek solace in Ben's arms. If he knew the truth, he'd hate him.

It was better this way.

'Toby, please...' Ben said.

But he refused to hear it. He walked over to his dad who sat in the back of the ambulance. His father was his priority now. Lewis and Adrian had the fire under control, despite the stench of ash and petrol. The next thing they had to do was find out how the hell it happened.

'Dad,' he said, but Bob didn't notice him. In shock? Or just...gone?

'His burns aren't severe but we've given him painkillers,' Steph said. 'We'll transfer him to hospital for further assessment. I'd like you to come with us, Toby.'

Narelle appeared by his side, in her dressing gown, and out of breath. 'Are you two okay?' She pulled him into a hug and he allowed himself to relax into her arms, the adrenaline finally draining and his body ready to collapse. Her voice cracked over her whisper. 'I thought I'd lost you both.'

He sniffed, fighting back the tears. Her embrace was fierce but it wasn't like his mother's had once been. And it didn't do for him what Ben's had.

'I'm fine,' he choked.

'Toby, can we talk?' Ben was there. 'We need a statement.'

He sighed. Anybody but Ben. Wasn't he meant to be off duty? When he straightened out of his aunt's arms, he saw he was right. Ben wore shorts and a tank top. Behind him stood Matty and Smithy in their uniforms.

'Auntie, can you go with Dad, please?'

'Are you sure you don't need looking over?' Steph asked.

He put up his hands. 'I'm fine. The shock's passed. Nothing wrong with my lungs. I'll be over later if I feel funny.'

'Please do,' she said. 'Don't be a hero.'

A hero? If his throat wasn't scorched raw, he'd laugh. He looked at his dad, glassy-eyed and unaware of what was going on. Or perhaps he was trapped in his memories. At least he was quiet and calm.

Narelle climbed into the ambulance with Bob and the paramedics and they drove away. Toby was left with three police officers and a whole bunch of drama-loving onlookers. He tried to ignore Ben and the suspicion that must now be running through his mind. But it wasn't that which occupied his thoughts. It was how good it felt to be held by him, how calm and reassuring and...and...safe. His body yearned to be surrounded by him again. It was intoxicating. It always had been.

He crossed his arms to stop himself from shivering.

Matty took the lead. Toby refused to meet Ben's eyes—not that it mattered. Ben's gaze was as hot and insistent as the fire inside the house. Toby recounted what had happened from the moment he woke up to getting out of the house. There wasn't a lot to say, and the little he told them revealed how little he'd done. He hadn't fought the fire. He hadn't rescued anyone.

What use was he?

'You're lucky to have gotten out of there alive,' Matty said. 'From what we've heard, your dad was already outside when you got here. Any idea how he burned his hands?'

Though Matty had asked the question, Toby glanced at Ben. His face was neutral and he gave no outside indication that he thought Bob was behind this whole thing, but even he had to admit it wasn't looking good. Could his dad really have done this? And if he did, could he have started the fire at the cemetery too?

The fire in the kitchen from months earlier had been an accident, surely, and he'd been safe since then. He'd disconnected the gas, hidden the matches, and checked the electrics for any shorts or exposed wires. But he couldn't, with hand on heart and looking straight into Ben's green eyes, say he knew how this fire had started or who had started it. Not yet anyway. All he had was faith that his father would never do this. Never knowingly at least.

And that was the problem.

How much was Bob aware of these days?

'I've got no idea,' he said, and his head and body slumped.

Chapter Five

Ben and Matty shared a look. They needed to talk to Bob. Toby wasn't giving them anything else and there were witnesses still to talk to.

'We're done here, then,' Matty said. 'I'm going back to the station to hand over to Leila. Smithy will stay to set up the scene. Toby, do you want a lift to the hospital?'

'No.'

Ben shrugged at his colleague. Matty raised his eyebrows but didn't waste his words on a second try. He knew Ben would hang around as long as necessary. His shift was starting soon anyway, and Matty would be happy to hand this investigation over to him and Leila. They'd talk to Bob.

Toby didn't acknowledge Matty as he left, instead choosing to watch as the firefighters extinguished the last of the flames and picked through the wreckage. His arctic silence, and the waves of hostility coming off him, helped freeze Ben's tongue. He'd wait for as long as he had to. And right now he wasn't sure he trusted himself to speak. The relief of Toby being alive fluttered at the top of his throat.

By the time the guys had doused everything, dawn light smeared itself across the horizon and the appearance of the house changed. Electric lights had been set up to illuminate the area. It appeared every bit the crime scene it now was, but a softer hue entered the house and painted the husk as less stark, less horrific, yet with a daub of melancholy. The weatherboard walls transitioned from cream to black; holes appeared higher up and exposed the bones. Where it still stood, the tin roof had buckled. Somewhere inside the house, they'd find the rest of it covering the floor. The house had given up everything, exhausted everything, and now its life had ended.

At least there were no bodies to retrieve.

A chill trickled down Ben's spine and he shivered.

The last of the neighbours disappeared. Now it was just Smithy and the fire crew, and before long even the firefighters packed up and moved off, with consolation and pats on the back for Toby. Smithy walked away to cordon off the area. Toby remained grim and unmoving. Ben strained against the silence and shifted his weight from one leg to the other.

'You don't have to stay.' Toby's voice cracked.

'I want to,' he replied. 'I want to make sure you're alright.'

'Keep the suspect under surveillance?'

Another fight. When Toby had ended up in his arms, he'd believed for a fleeting moment that they might have a chance at a different relationship. He wished someone else had been called out to that fire the other day.

'Is that an admission of guilt?' He half-meant it as a joke but regretted it immediately.

'No,' Toby shot back, then he exhaled long and heavy. His energy seeped out and he sagged. 'I'm sorry, I don't know what I'm saying. My head's all over the place.'

Ben stuffed his hands inside his pockets. 'Maybe we should get out of here. I'll take you to see your dad.'

'I don't think I can see him right now. What if—'

What if Bob had really done this? It would be easier if he had. Lawyers would argue reduced competency and he'd probably never see the inside of a jail cell. He'd be committed though, and perhaps that was the right thing for him now. But Toby didn't need to hear that, and Ben wasn't yet on duty.

'No one got hurt, that's the main thing.'

Toby walked off, towards the house, as if he hadn't heard him, and Ben was obliged to follow.

'Toby, you can't go in there.'

'It's my home.'

'It's also a crime scene.'

'Are you worried I'm going to tamper with the evidence?'

Ben hurried to stand in front of him.

Toby stared at him, a haggard look that, with the smear of ash and soot on his face and his already dark and brooding eyes, struck Ben as panicked. But then the scowl returned. 'I want to see what's left and where it started. This will help with *your* investigation, whether it incriminates my father or not. Accompany me if you're so concerned.'

Belligerent as ever, Toby diverted around him towards his home's soggy remains. Ben kept up. As much as he wanted to handcuff the bastard and drag him away, he could use Toby's knowledge at piecing this together. A proper investigation would be carried out in a few hours but it couldn't hurt to check things now. At least he hoped not.

Only a few of the walls still stood, as did a small part of the roof. Toby seemed unfazed at the risk of anything falling on him, picking his way through as he went. They entered from the front of the house; half the doorframe remained. They navigated their way down the hallway, the floor warm and damp, and headed to the kitchen. The side of the house was now open to the outside. A few sticks of charcoal, what had once been cabinets or chair legs, and the twisted remains of a metal oven were all he recognised.

'The fire felt strongest in here when I searched for Dad,' Toby said, looking around. Ben wasn't sure what he was looking for. It was just debris and kindling to him.

'Dad's room is down the hall. Mine's up here. The gas was disconnected, but this doesn't look like a gas fire. There would have been an explosion of some sort, a whoosh that even I would have woken up from.'

'I remember you being a pretty heavy sleeper.' Happy memories of sleepovers intruded into his mind, even the times when he'd lie awake and watch Toby sleep. How many times had he done that and wished he'd reached over and touched his bare chest or woken him with a kiss? He pined for those days.

'Times have changed,' Toby said quickly.

Right. Back to the present. Back to the investigation. 'Smoke alarms?'

'Yeah, that's what got me up.' He crouched. 'There are signs of accelerant here, here, and here.' He pointed to big patches on the ground, darker than the rest. 'He really went to town with the stuff.' He ran his fingers through the stain and sniffed them.

'What is it?'

'Petrol. And it's black as black here under the window.'

'Maybe that's where he started pouring it.'

'Weird spot. And it's haphazard.' He massaged his right earlobe. 'Even so I'd say it was poured in from outside the house.'

'That's where they found Bob, right?'

'But it's not logical—'

'You think Bob would be logical about this? He looked pretty out of it when we saw him.'

'That was shock. It doesn't make sense that he'd set fire to the house, or even that he had the capacity to. It's not him.'

'Who knows what he's going through?'

He rose off his haunches and faced him. 'You think he did it, don't you?'

For once, it sounded like he wasn't trying to start a fight. If anything, he wanted reassurance, wanted someone to say that yes, his dad had set fire to the place and nearly killed them both.

'It's possible.'

He sighed, an awful defeated sound like a bull with a broken leg too exhausted to rise. Toby trudged down the hall. He scanned the scene from the floor to the remaining walls and into the roof. Wherever there was anything left untouched—books still on shelves, photos in frames in their vibrant colours, even if a little smoke-damaged—Toby ignored them.

They'd done a tour of the rooms and ended up back at the front of the house in Toby's room. Half the room was still intact, if a little sodden. Smithy came to check on them, questioning Toby's presence inside the crime scene. Ben explained they were doing a preliminary search and that he was helping the investigation.

'Just don't contaminate anything more than you already have,' he said.

When Toby turned away, Smithy eyeballed him, a hard look on his face, before storming off. He might have a point. Toby shouldn't be in here. But as he was about to guide Toby out, his eye landed on a faded football sitting on the shelf. It couldn't be the same one. He leaned closer and saw the message he'd written there nearly twenty years ago.

Happy 12th b'day Toby. Ben.

The words were in his young hand and the memory of writing them fluttered up, along with the tension he'd felt at wanting to write 'love Ben' instead. The other kids had thought Toby too small to play footy with them, but seeing how much he wanted to join in stirred a sense of injustice in him. Being the tallest and fastest kid on the team, he'd refused to play if they didn't let Toby join. They'd relented and he and Toby were friends from then on.

'Dad couldn't cause this much damage.' Toby startled him out of his memories. This room was full of them and he'd gotten distracted. He put the ball back on the shelf. Toby didn't comment. 'I would have heard him.'

'Leave it for the statement, Toby.'

The football brought out the protectiveness in him, but Toby didn't take the advice.

'There are no matches, no drums of petrol, no hose, nothing. If he'd done any of it, there'd be something left lying around. He didn't have time to get rid of it all. Someone else did this.'

'Then who?'

Arson wasn't something that people did for no reason, even if they were deranged. What reason would anyone have to burn down the Grimshaws's house?

'Someone with a thing against firefighters.'

'You haven't pissed anybody off lately?'

Toby wasn't called Grim for nothing.

'I might not be the most cheerful bastard in town, but I don't go around picking fights.'

'No one in your crew? No ex-lover whose heart you've broken?'

'There isn't anyone worth worrying about.' His lips sealed. He'd already said more to him in the space of a few minutes than he had in a year, but past relationships were no-go with Toby. There might not have been any, at least none of any importance. Toby was well known for being one of the most unattainable men in town, a fact that, to his shame, Ben found a relief.

'If it's not random, then maybe it's got something to do with that case I worked on with Erika, the meth-lab explosion. They could be trying to get back at me for the help I gave her. Maybe they think I know something about Peter.'

Erika Hanson's brother was still missing. He was involved in the drug trade somehow but there'd been no new leads on his disappearance. But it wasn't Toby who'd figured out it wasn't Peter's body in that fire, it was Erika. Ben doubted the gang behind the explosion—two of whom had been captured by police—had much of a beef with a town firefighter.

'Even if they thought you knew something, why go for the cemetery too?'

Toby scraped his fingers through his hair. 'What does it matter? All I know is Dad didn't set fire to the house. And when the investigation is done, you'll be as sure as I am that someone else tried to kill us.' He walked away.

Goosebumps rose along his skin. It was easier to think this was an accident than that someone wanted Toby dead. 'Where are you going?'

'I need to see Dad, but first I'm going to grab a shower at the station. I stink.'

'Use my place and you can borrow some clothes.' The words were out before he could stop them. It was being in this damn house. 'It's closer than the station and I can drive you to the hospital after.'

Toby rubbed the back of his neck, his arm raising up and his bicep bulging. The moisture in Ben's mouth evaporated. What was he doing inviting Toby to his house?

'It's not a good idea.'

'I'm going there anyway. We may as well go together.'

'Hoping to extract something else out of me? Wrap up a case so it's done and dusted, and you don't have to look for who really set fire to my house?'

If there was one thing that churned his blood, it was having his integrity questioned, and Toby knew how to do it every time.

'Keep pushing me, Toby, and you'll see how much of a cop I really am,' he snarled, more annoyed at himself for slipping so easily into lusting after Toby when he was meant to be on the case. 'I've given you the benefit of the doubt already. If I'd pushed harder, your Dad would have been brought in for questioning sooner.'

'You haven't got any evidence that it was him.'

'No, but we've got witnesses and he was at the scene.' Ben held up his right thumb then counted on the rest of his fingers. 'He had opportunity and maybe—just maybe—the anniversary of his wife's death was enough of a motive. We all know how often the switch in a firefighter's head gets thrown so cut the bullshit because right now,' he stabbed the air with his index finger, 'I am really close to arresting Bob on suspicion of arson.'

His chest heaved with leaden breath, his fists clenched and his body readied to launch at a physical attack. He would fight, he would fight anyone who dared to doubt his abilities as a cop, especially after what he'd been through to atone for Jared.

Jared had kept him in the dark, and blinded him with false love. All that dealing, the lies and betrayal. Even when he'd done the right thing and brought about his arrest that hadn't been enough. His colleagues suspected him of being culpable too—guilt by association or wilful ignorance. Their contempt followed him from the locker rooms, down the halls and out onto the street. No matter how clear the evidence, he'd not been a good enough cop to see that his boyfriend was a drug-dealing scumbag. That's why there'd been no one else since. No one could suggest that Ben Fields was blinded by love.

And yet here he was, letting Toby roll him over.

I'm a fool.

'He didn't do it,' Toby said between gritted teeth.

'Then we'll find that out, but either way, I'm going to question him and regardless of whether you come with me or get there yourself, I'm leaving now. It would be in your best interest to not be here or else you might be suspected of tampering with evidence.'

'You really do have a suspicious mind.'

Whatever. His insult left no mark. 'I'm a cop, Toby, I'm saying how I see it. And right now, do yourself a favour and follow my advice.'

Toby glared at him and the silence stretched, filling with unspoken recriminations. Would he have to strong-arm him out of the house?

'Fine, let's go,' Toby said, exiting the house, leaving Ben to seethe.

A few deep breaths later and they got in Ben's car. He drove in silence; and for once Ben preferred it. They lived on the same street, a few blocks apart, but the short distance was enough for the anger to bubble and fill his head with toxic fumes. What-ifs and what-could-have-beens dissolved in a sulphuric cloud. What remained was distilled into the pure thought that had always been there but he'd suppressed.

Toby didn't care about him. Toby probably didn't even like him. And that was okay, if that was how it was going to be. Thinking they'd shared something over a decade earlier wasn't the basis of a relationship. It never had been and it never would be. He'd allow Toby to use his shower, lend him some clothes if he wanted them, but that wasn't anything he wouldn't do for another member of the community if they needed it.

Perhaps some more than others. He'd never had much cause to deal with the bikies and drug dealers and other members of Echo Springs's criminal underbelly in any way other than as a police officer. But Toby would be in and out of his house in little more than fifteen minutes.

Thirty max.

And once he was out, and they'd questioned Bob, that would be it. He'd go back to avoiding the dark looks and keeping Toby Grimshaw from having an impact on his life. To hell with him and his dad. They deserved nothing more than equal justice under the law, whether guilty or not.

They pulled up to his house and Ben got out, slamming the car door. He opened the house and stepped aside for Toby.

'Bathroom's down the hall, third door on the left. I'll get you some clothes. There's a clean towel in there.'

Toby grunted. He guessed that was some form of agreement, maybe even thanks. He was down the hall and behind a closed door in no time. Ben shook his head. How had it gone so wrong?

He went into his room and picked clean clothes out of the drawer that might fit Toby. Accidents and ashes: was that all there was between them? When their mothers died, a wall went up that Ben had spent too many years waiting to come down. His initial attempts to break it down had met with steel that patience hadn't eroded. All those years wasted. But to never talk about it, to never have it resolved…

Could he press the issue now? His timing was terrible, but he'd waited for the right moment before and it had never come. Toby couldn't run now. Couldn't hide from it. And no matter how badly it might hurt to hear it, what was he still holding on to? A childhood fantasy built on nothing but daydreams and crazy ideas. Toby Grimshaw didn't know how to love. That had been burned out of him. What was a little more pain?

It's now or never.

Chapter Six

Ben's bathroom was as neat as Toby expected. Ben had always been like that, his bedroom tidy with everything in its assigned spot, his bed always made. He probably kept his hair buzzed because it reduced the risk of any follicle getting out of place. His bathroom was exceptionally clean, no toothbrush left out, no hair missed, towels folded on the rack, soap clean and in its dish.

A model home for a model cop.

Toby turned on the water and stripped while it heated, resisting the urge to open the cabinets to confirm what he already knew. Ben would have that ordered too. Probably alphabetised. Toby might not have been the same, he'd have a few bits and pieces left out—or at least they used to be before the bathroom burnt down—but he wasn't a slob. Yet being here, in Ben's house, somewhere he never thought he'd be, he didn't measure up. And being here brought mess into Ben's life.

Quick shower, then I'll go.

As he stepped under the spray, the water needled into his muscles and scoured the exhaustion and the worry. He focused on the water's sting before his skin numbed. At this moment, all he had to do was wash, clean away the stink of smoke, and have it disappear down the drain. A long, hard and loud breath vibrated out of him, the sound dislodging something he'd held onto since waking in terror.

His dad didn't do this. There was no way. The timing, the slapdash approach—he'd been the fire chief, for god's sake. The investigation would confirm his innocence, if they were smart about it. And Bob would give his side of the story and everything would be fine.

Well, as fine as anything could be now that they'd lost their home.

And the small matter of someone trying to kill them.

Adrenaline shot through his spine before it dissolved under the heat. He had no idea who would want him dead. He kept to himself, except with his crew. Was it some old vendetta with his dad? Had he put out the wrong fire? Had he helped the police lock up someone who now had him on their shit list?

He'd have to go back through the investigations he'd run. The most recent was the one with Erika and her brother, Peter, who they'd all thought had been killed in a drug lab explosion. Erika was a coroner: she had discovered the body wasn't her brother's. That still bothered him, that someone would go to the trouble of faking Peter's death. And that the guy was still missing. But Toby hadn't had much to do with what Erika had uncovered. Why go after him? And then there was the question of why they'd bother setting fire to the cemetery as well. That's if the two fires were connected. A quick recall of the fires during his life in Echo Springs raised nothing suspicious.

Other than the one that had blackened his mother's body beyond recognition.

Ben's mother's too.

Though the water stayed hot, it didn't warm the chill inside him. He finished washing and shut off the water, grabbed the towel and dried himself. Ben had never confronted him about the deaths. He'd never so much as looked at him funny, never blamed him, questioned him…nothing. That was his own fault. He thought if he could keep Ben away, he'd be able to hold onto his guilt and protect Ben. Eventually he'd stop loving Ben.

But that hadn't happened.

Ben knocked. He probably wanted to get to the hospital so he could question Bob.

'Hold on,' he called out, wiping the last drops off and slicking back his hair before opening the door.

Ben's fist gripped a set of clothes. His hands were covered in sweat and ash. Toby's gaze drifted to Ben's eyes glaring at him from beneath a stern brow. He seemed ready for something, a lecture, a reprimand. This was Officer Fields, one of the most upright and principled men he'd ever met, in or out of uniform.

Ben's eyes swept down Toby's chest, his gaze lighting sparks that burst behind Toby's sternum, showering down around already hard nipples, stirring the turmoil swelling in his belly and landing to ignite a fire in his groin. Being looked at by this man, as much as he wanted to deny himself, brought with it such pleasure that he wanted to drop the towel and let Ben devour him in his entirety.

Coming here was definitely not a good idea.

'Thanks for the clothes,' he croaked.

Ben handed them over, but didn't let go. 'Listen, I—'

Their eyes locked and those knots of tension from the accident were replaced with a different kind, one he was far too familiar with. Every time he saw Ben was a moment of exquisite torture, hoping yet not hoping he would look over, come near, touch him. He existed in this permanent yes/ no state that only intensified when Ben looked him in the eye. But if he was honest, he was more yes than no at those moments.

Or rather, hell yes.

Whatever Ben had been about to say didn't make it out of his mouth. As Toby's gaze dropped to Ben's lips, the memory of them being so soft yet firm came to the fore. If only he could try again, wipe out the years between them. Why not?

You know why not.

'I want you to know that however this happened, I'm glad you're safe,' Ben said. 'You and Bob.'

Toby's heart purred at the gentleness in Ben's voice.

'Don't go getting soft on me, Ben.' He broke eye contact, and pulled on the clothes, but instead of them slipping out of Ben's grasp, he held on and came with them. He couldn't look up, couldn't bear to see what was in Ben's eyes, and how he would inevitably destroy it. But being this close again to Ben's arms, remembering that moment outside the house when he'd been held and safe and warm…god, it *did* things to him. He wanted it. He *needed* it.

He retreated but Ben's arm slipped around his waist and the space between them vanished. He should have resisted but whatever his mind ordered, his body disobeyed. And then Ben's lips were on his and thought ceased. There was nothing but lips on lips, body pressed against body, and the inner peace of knowing that this was right, that this was what he needed. Desperate yearning reached out from his chest as his fingers spread behind Ben's head, along his prickled scalp. Toby kissed him harder, their tongues touching, caressing, and he released a deep moan.

He was taken back to that time by the springs, when their families had been alive and whole, and he'd been so happy, having Ben there to be his friend, and thinking that perhaps one day if they left Echo Springs, they could go somewhere and love each other the way he wanted them to love each other. He could wait a few years, and then they could live out the fantasy that he'd built in his head, of their forbidden love given free rein in Sydney where it was not such a *thing*. Where they could just be Ben and Toby. Together. And when Ben had kissed him, it confirmed his secret hope. He'd given him a gift in those furtive, desperate yet tender kisses when they'd gone off by themselves. Those kisses, followed by childish and horny groping, then more, and those weeks had been filled with bliss.

Until the accident.

Then he'd denied all contact and wouldn't give Ben a reason why he'd wanted him one moment but not the next.

But he hadn't stopped wanting Ben. He'd wanted it at the right time when things could be better, could have space to grow. He wanted time to think, and this was no more the right time than it had been ten years ago.

He stopped kissing Ben. Or at least he tried. He shouldn't be doing this, shouldn't be doing this with Ben. But he kissed him again, their lips in sync and it felt so *right*. Couldn't he have this forever?

No!

Sorrow and guilt flooded through him and drowned that love, that *feeling*, he'd kept locked away. He pulled back, wrenched the clothes out of Ben's hand and used them to disguise the tenting in the towel.

'What the hell?' Ben shouted, still leaning forward and his mouth wet with their saliva.

'I'm sorry,' he said, his lips tingling. 'I shouldn't have kissed you.'

'But I kissed you.'

'Then I shouldn't have kissed you back.'

Ben's hands covered his face and his fingers massaged his forehead. The sound of his harsh breath amplified. 'This is ridiculous. You're telling me you felt nothing?'

'It doesn't matter what I felt. It was wrong.' His free hand rubbed his sternum.

Ben backed up and straightened. 'Wrong?'

The tone couldn't have been clearer. 'Not how you think I meant.'

'No, but kissing me has always been *wrong*, hasn't it? Ever since we were boys.'

'It's not like that. I mean, we can't be together.' Why couldn't he accept that this wasn't going to work? His heart ached at seeing the distress on Ben's face. If it hurt this bad now…

'Because it's *wrong?*'

'Because you'd get hurt.'

'Don't you think I can take care of myself?'

He couldn't speak. He was too much of a coward and Ben didn't know what he was asking for. Better to have some of Ben's animosity and still hope than to expose all and live in complete desolation.

'Let's talk about this once I'm dressed.' He shut the door quickly, before Ben could jam his foot in, and before he broke and they kissed again.

Ben's fist struck the door. 'Goddamnit, Toby!'

Toby hurried to dress in Ben's clothes—they fit as best they could—and warmth blanketed his body, inside and out. They even smelled like him under the lemon-fresh detergent. He folded up the clothes he'd come here in. His hand smoothed over the letter secreted into the pocket of the borrowed shorts—the one thing he'd really gone inside the house for after the fire was extinguished, the thing he'd been able to snaffle without Ben seeing.

He took a few deep breaths, but didn't stay longer than he should, as much as he wanted to avoid what was to happen next. Ben's questions hadn't changed in ten years.

Perhaps now he deserved some answers.

When he opened the door, Ben wasn't there. Caution slowed him as he padded down the hall. He stopped at the door to Ben's room and watched him dress in his uniform. Toby gripped the doorframe, his hand moulding to the wood as he fought to stay where he was.

His trousers already on, Ben shielded his skin beneath a layer of official blue. Ben ignored him, but he had to know he was being watched. To think that muscled body had been, only moments ago, pressed against his own. They could be lying naked in that bed, making loud, desperate love to each other, but instead he was forced to watch Ben dress and close himself off as surely as each button hid his chest. Words jammed into his throat, stopping his pleas begging him to not put on the uniform. Once he did, they were back to being cop and civilian.

But what could he say to rescue this? Uttering his own sins risked too much.

Ben finished the last of the buttons and tied his boots. Transformation complete. Officer Fields reporting for duty.

'Let's go.' Ben pushed past him and walked to the front door, showing him his back.

He couldn't bear this. No matter how close they got they always finished up further apart. Distance heaped upon distance until there wouldn't be a planet big enough for the both of them.

'That's it? You don't want to talk?'

'What's the point? It'll be more crap and I'm sick of taking it. It's never been right between us. I couldn't take it then and I can't take it now.'

He stepped forward. 'At least let me explain.'

'I'm not interested.' He yanked open the door and held onto the handle. 'I want to get you to the hospital and then get the hell away from you.'

If Ben hated him so much now, he'd hate him worse if he knew the truth. Toby's fist tightened over the clothes, and the letter crumpled. He denied the words that readied to fire from his mouth, swallowing them down again and burying them so deep he hoped they'd never emerge. Ben didn't need to know what happened.

'It's probably for the best,' he murmured.

'No, you don't get to say that!'

'Then what do you want me to say?' Toby shouted.

He surged forward until Ben's face was so close to his that it would have been nothing to kiss him again. Nothing and everything. 'I want to know why we can't be together, why you won't even try. Why you wouldn't then?'

His eyes shot to the wooden floorboards. It would have been better to say nothing but those words were as tenacious as weeds. 'You wouldn't want me if you knew what I'd done.'

Ben folded his arms, the muscles tensing and rippling. 'What did you do?'

He dragged his fingers through his hair and pulled at the roots. He'd said too much already. Some secrets were never meant to come out. He broke for the door, but Ben seized his arm as he passed.

'What did you do?' he repeated.

'Forget it, Ben. Forget everything. I need to see Dad.'

Chapter Seven

Toby's fingers drummed on the bonnet of the car. Ben had two options: take Toby to the hospital or watch him go.

Should he have demanded Toby tell him what the hell he'd done that was so bad? Perhaps—especially if it were illegal—but maybe he'd been given the chance to extricate himself without implication from whatever it was. He'd already gone through that once before.

But this was Toby, and he'd go through anything for Toby.

Anything to be kissed like that again.

Anything to be loved by him.

He locked the door behind him and walked to the car; Toby climbed in. An agitated silence filled the already hot car as they drove the short distance to the hospital. Questions and unspent desires kept them company like blowflies buzzing at the base of the windscreen. Ben pressed his foot to the floor, travelling at just above the speed limit. His hand gripped the gearstick, the closest he could physically be to Toby, who held himself tight against the door. Ben chewed his tongue like it was a gnarled dog toy. They couldn't arrive soon enough.

After checking in at the front counter, staff directed them through to Emergency. Bob sat on a hospital bed with his bandaged hands resting in his lap. Narelle wasn't there, but Leila stood talking beside him. Whatever they'd been discussing was forgotten mid-sentence as they entered. She eyed Toby as she passed him. He ignored her hello and focused on his father.

'How are your hands?' he asked, picking them up gently.

Bob snatched them back. 'Why'd you do it?' The skin around his eyes quivered as he demanded answers. His lips pulled back from his teeth as distress gouged lines into his forehead.

Did Bob mean… Ben stepped closer to Toby.

Toby blinked, his head swivelling between his dad and Leila. 'Dad? What are you talking about? What's he been saying?'

If Leila had any misgivings, she hid them behind a mask of official neutrality. Her words marched resolute from her mouth. 'Bob says you lit the fire at the house.'

Ben's stomach hit the floor. Bob must be mistaken.

Toby's eyes searched his dad's face, his hand gripping Bob's forearm. 'Dad, what is this? I was asleep, remember? I came outside to find you.' His voice jittered as he reasoned with him.

'I saw you running. That's why I went outside. That's why I chased you.'

Toby tried to say something, anything, but nothing came.

'Bob, are you sure?' Ben asked. 'If you saw Toby set fire to the house, why didn't you stop him?'

'It was already up, it was already lit. I heard a sound and went into the kitchen and the fire was already…but there he was at the window and he ran and I chased him…it was him!' He pointed at Toby with a gauze-covered hand. 'He thinks I don't know it but I saw him. He was running but I couldn't get to them in time, but he got out.' Bob's eyes turned glassy and stared into a past none of them could see. 'At least Toby got out. But Ella and Mary—' He covered his face with hands; the bandages caught his tears.

Bob's cries summoned spirits that scratched the back of Ben's neck with their bony fingers, coaxing goosebumps to pucker along his skin.

Toby slumped next to Bob, one arm draped over his shoulder, but he offered little comfort.

Leila indicated with a jerk of her head that he should follow her. They left father and son and went a little way down the corridor. Once out of earshot, Leila confirmed that Bob had told her the same story. 'We have to bring Toby in.'

He tugged at his bottom lip with his thumb and forefinger. Bob might not always be a reliable witness but they had enough to at least arrest and question Toby. But was that enough?

'It was hard enough to believe Bob could have done this, but Toby? He said the fire would have started in the kitchen, probably petrol poured in through the window, so that matches Bob's story, but maybe he's confused.'

'How does Toby know this?'

'We searched the house.'

Her eyes bulged. 'You searched the house? Together?'

'Yes.'

'You were with him the whole time, right?' Her brow raised, propped up with a hint of hope that the answer he'd give would be the correct one.

He hesitated.

Her eyes closed and her head tilted back.

'I only turned my back on him for a second,' he hurried to clarify. 'There wasn't enough time—'

'This is not good, Ben.'

She didn't have to tell him that. 'Crap.'

She groaned. 'I agree it's probably unlikely Toby's our guy because he doesn't seem that sort, but we can't ignore what Bob said.'

'I liked it better when Bob was the suspect,' he muttered.

'Maybe they both are. Unless Toby lit the one at the cemetery too.'

'He couldn't have.'

'Are you sure?'

His credibility had—yet again—taken another bruising, but he'd done due diligence when it came to this aspect of the investigation. 'I've asked around. It wasn't possible for him to light that fire, then get back in time to attend it.'

'I hope you're right.'

He was. Too bad he couldn't be so certain about anything else when it came to Toby. 'So, what do we do now?'

'Bring Toby in for questioning. He's already given a statement but maybe he'll change it.' She paused and gave him a look, the kind given when someone's dog dies.

'What?' he asked.

'Do you think it's possible this is because of what happened to your mothers? Has he snapped?'

He crossed his arms over his chest. 'Are you asking because you're worried about him or you're worried I'll snap too?'

'Don't be ridiculous,' she scoffed.

'There's your answer.'

'But how do you *know* Toby didn't do this? You two haven't been close since you were kids. He barely registers your existence.'

He studied the scuffed floor. He thought he'd known Jared and that had been a disaster. For a cop, he'd been far too willing to trust the people he loved. Could Toby lie to him about this? Was Toby not who Ben thought he was? Venomous snakes writhed in his stomach, striking and sinking their poison into him.

Hadn't Toby already confessed to something terrible?

'You're right,' he said. 'I can't know for sure. It's a feeling.'

'I know about your feelings where Toby's concerned. Maybe you should give this case a rest. I can take over.'

Heat flushed up his neck. 'No,' he said. 'I have to do this. If I can't do my job despite my feelings for the guy, then what kind of cop does that make me?'

'A human one.' She placed a hand on his arm and squeezed. 'But look, if you get any more compromised, I'm telling you to get off the case. I'll go above you if I have to. It's for your own good. Got it?'

Knowing she was looking out for him helped calm him. 'You won't need to, but I appreciate it.'

'Any time. Ready to do this?'

He took a deep breath. He needed a shower, a break between the fire and the upcoming interrogation, and something to wash away the feeling of Toby's body against his. What had he been thinking, kissing Toby like that? He'd wanted a sign that the distance could be crossed, but secrets blocked their path.

When they reached the cubicle, Narelle had appeared, telling them that Toby's uncle was waiting out the front with the car. She implied that they were ready to go.

'Tobias William Grimshaw, you're under arrest for suspected arson. You do not have to say or do anything but if you do, it may be used in evidence against you,' Ben said in a level tone, while his body numbed.

'What?' Narelle snapped.

Toby shut his eyes. 'You can't be serious.'

'Based on what Bob's said and your proximity to the scene, this is something we have to do. Now you can either come without any fuss or in handcuffs.'

Narelle rushed to interject. 'You can't believe what Bob said.'

Leila took over. 'So far he's the only witness, and he's been pretty lucid throughout his time here.'

'But he's got dementia.' Narelle gestured to her brother, who paid them no attention. 'He's confusing one event with another. Toby's already told you what happened. He came out after Bob.'

While Leila reasoned with Narelle, Toby's eyes met Ben's. They shone with defiance but also an assertion. *You know this is wrong.*

His heart froze and the expression wiped from his face. That kiss, their past: obliterated. There was nothing he could have done differently, except not be the officer on this case. However, he was a cop, and, for better or worse, Toby was now a suspect.

'Narelle, that's enough,' Ben said. 'Please take Bob home, we have his statement. Toby, let's go.'

Narelle's mouth flapped open and closed, while her hands fidgeted, seeking something to grab. She had probably believed they would disregard Bob's admission.

Toby clasped her shoulder. 'It's fine. Look after Dad. I'll be home soon.' He handed Narelle the clothes he'd been wearing after the fire. 'Please take these with you.'

Ben stopped him. 'Sorry, Toby, we need them for evidence.'

Toby relinquished his hold with a shake of his head. Ben handed them to Leila, who slipped them into an evidence bag she pulled from her vest.

'You're making a mistake,' Narelle hissed, fixing him with a stare that could wither a crop of wheat.

Don't I know it.

Toby came without a fuss, walking between him and Leila down the corridor and out of emergency. Medical staff cast looks as they passed. Some busied themselves, others openly gawked. The news that Toby Grimshaw had been arrested—whether guilty or not—would have ripped through the town by the end of the day, if not within the hour.

In the car park, Ben marched him over to the back of Leila's patrol car and held the back door open. Toby climbed in without speaking but disappointment flowed from him; Ben knew he was blaming him for not doing his job properly. Toby couldn't see that the situation was impossible and any officer would have to do the same thing.

Or perhaps he regretted the kiss because it hadn't distracted Ben from the arsonist in front of him.

Chapter Eight

The interrogation room measured little more than three metres square. Chips and gouges marred the beige walls. The fluorescent lights overhead emitted gloom. Toby rubbed his eyes with the heels of his hands. When he took them away, he sought the clock on the wall beside him and watched as it slowly drifted into clarity. Quarter past nine. *Was it still only morning?*

'You sure you don't want a lawyer?' Ben asked as he and Leila sat opposite him.

He nodded. He was innocent. Someone else had lit the fire, and within a few hours they'd have found something to prove that. Hopefully before the four hours they were legally allowed to hold him for were up.

Leila's eyes sparked as she studied him, her enjoyment obvious. The two of them hadn't been on the friendliest terms since she returned to Echo Springs. He couldn't think why; they'd barely spoken. Her stare would have made a guilty man squirm. But not him. He had nothing to hide.

At least not about this fire.

The cop he really worried about was Ben. Impassive, statue-like, *cold* Ben. The Ben he liked the least. The Ben that spurred him to do better. The Ben that brought out those misguided, want-to-make-him-proud-of-me feelings. He sat straight behind the steel-topped table, with his palms resting on the edges of a pad of paper. A pen lay next to his right hand, ready to be picked up and used to record whatever he said.

'Right, let's go back to the beginning,' Leila said. 'Tell us what happened this morning.' Leila pulled out the pad she'd used to write down his earlier statement. She needn't have bothered; there'd be no difference in his story.

There should be no reason he wouldn't be out of here in ten minutes, maybe fifteen. Give them the statement; get the hell out.

'The smoke alarm woke me and—'

'What time was that?' Ben cut in.

'I don't know,' he snapped before his brain lurched out of its haze and reminded him aggression wouldn't get him out of here any sooner. He tried a more conciliatory approach, ignoring the sour taste in his mouth. 'I guess it was about four-thirty, maybe quarter to five.'

'So, you looked at a clock?' Ben's dismissive tone whipped him.

The skin at the top of his chest heated as anger burbled beneath the surface. He swallowed hard to keep it down, annoyed at himself at how quickly it had risen. They were trying to get to him. They'd use whatever cop tricks they had at their disposal to trip him up. Leila wanted him to be guilty, but it sounded like Ben did too. 'I looked at my phone when I got outside and it was almost five so I worked backwards. Can I go on? The sooner this is over, the sooner you can get back out there and find who really did this.'

Ben scribbled while Leila flipped through the pages of his older statement. The rustle of paper and scratch of the pen were the only sounds while they ignored him. Toby wanted to reach across the table, grab Ben's face and reason with him. Instead he closed his hands into fists and tried to rein in his frustration.

Eventually Leila looked up and marked a place on the page with her index finger. 'You said that the fire was already going strong when you woke. Why didn't you wake up sooner?'

'I'm a heavy sleeper,' he said, ignoring Ben's lift of his head and subsequent stare. 'The fire was going when I woke up. I smelled the smoke and felt the heat so I jumped out of bed, grabbed my phone and called for Dad as I ran down the hall.'

'Where were you running?'

'To Dad's room.'

'Did you stop anywhere?'

'The kitchen.'

'Why the kitchen?'

'That's where the fire felt the strongest. I saw the flames, checked Dad wasn't there, then kept going.'

'How are things with your Dad?' she asked.

He flinched at the hand-brake redirection. 'What do you mean?'

'Your relationship. It must be strained considering his health.'

He bit hard on his tongue, the sting darting out to pierce the red bubble inflating inside him. 'Our relationship is fine. He's not that bad.'

'So, he doesn't have dementia?'

Ben rearranged himself in his seat.

'Yes, he's got dementia. You've seen it. The whole bloody town's seen it.'

'Does that bother you?' she asked. 'People knowing?'

'I couldn't give a rat's arse what the town thinks.'

'That's strange considering how much of yourself you commit to the place. Has looking after your dad made that difficult? Do you resent him?'

He shook his head, using the motion to distract from the long exhalation he needed to clear his thoughts. This from someone who hadn't been back in town more than five minutes. And considering her background, she had the nerve to question his dedication and paint him as someone who cared more about appearances than helping people.

She's trying to rattle me.

She wanted him to admit to things that weren't true. He took another deep breath.

'I don't resent my father. If anything, I wish I could do more for him. It's not been easy.'

'Would it be easier without him?'

'That's not what I meant,' he said harshly. 'He's done it tough. Lost his wife, now losing his memory and who he is. It's hard to watch but I bet it's harder for him.'

Leila stared back at him but he held her gaze. She didn't know the debt he owed his father. Caring for him was the least he could do.

'Whatever you're implying, he's not a burden and I wouldn't change anything.'

'Let's return to the fire,' Ben said.

Toby eased back, surprised to find himself so far forward over the table. Leila smirked and it took every bit of restraint to stop from sneering at her. The angrier he got, the more likely it would be they'd pin him for something.

'What can you tell us about the fire?' Ben asked.

'I think it started in the kitchen. The fire had consumed most of it and gone into the roof and through part of the house. I don't think it had been lit long before I got there. I could still smell the accelerant. Petrol.'

'How can you be sure it was petrol?' Leila asked.

'Because I'm damn good at my job, and any idiot could detect the smell.' There was no point in being civil with her; it didn't work. 'Can I go on?'

Ben nodded, putting his hand to his mouth and dragging his finger across his bottom lip.

Toby looked away. Focusing on Ben's lips was not going to help him now. Not that it had ever helped him. If only they could go back a few hours.

Or years.

'I called for Dad as I ran down the hall. I checked his room but he wasn't there. I then ran out the open back door. The roof collapsed behind me soon after. I cut around the house and then a neighbour got me and brought me over to him.'

'Who called the fire brigade?' Ben asked.

'I did. I called from inside the house.'

Ben jotted this down.

'Can anyone confirm any of your side of the story?'

'Only the people who saw me come out of the house. No doubt Dad knows something.'

'Why do you say that?'

'I'm sure he saw someone. You know, the guy you two should be out pursuing instead of wasting time here with me.'

'Bob was pretty emphatic it was you,' Leila said.

'Then he's mistaken. He often gets like that. Ask his doctor.'

'What did you do after the fire?' Leila took over the questioning.

'I waited until the fire was extinguished. One of your officers put up the crime-scene tape, while I went inside the house. Ben came with me.'

'Why did you go into the house? It was a crime scene.'

'I wanted to help with the investigation and to see what was left.'

'Constable Fields says there was a moment where you were out of his sight. What did you do?'

He looked to Ben but he had his head down. The muscle in his jaw twitched.

He couldn't—

Before now Toby assumed Ben was just following procedure, as galling as it was, but now he saw the truth. Ben believed he was sitting across from the arsonist. The air was stripped from his lungs and took with it a piece of him he hadn't realised was still there, the part of him that thought Ben might love him.

He dragged his hands off the table and steadied them on his thighs. They already had the letter so there was no point in denying it. Revealing its existence exposed him more than he cared. The one thing he'd saved from the house. The one secret he wanted. But what did it matter now? That kiss. This distrust. He should have thrown the envelope in the fire. He would have if he had known it would lead here.

If that was so, then why did he hesitate to tell them about it now?

'I grabbed a letter.'

Leila continued. 'And you didn't tell either officer you wanted this letter?'

'I didn't think it was any of their business.'

'But it was important enough to contaminate a scene for. Surely you knew it was a dumb move.'

'You don't have to tell me that,' he barked. 'I've been to more of these than you, Leila.'

Her eyes narrowed as she readied to pounce. '*Constable Mayne*, thank you. But I don't see what could be worth the risk.'

'I wasn't thinking about procedure, alright?' He thrust forward over the edge of the table. 'I wasn't thinking about what was right or wrong, just that I had to go back for the letter in case it got destroyed. The roof had fallen in and the place was dripping with water, but I had to get it.'

Ben cleared his throat. 'And did you?'

He nodded. They'd look at it. They hadn't searched his clothes already or else they wouldn't be going down this line of questioning. Ben would know what it was the moment he saw it and that should be enough to clear him. But a part of him didn't want Ben to see it. Especially not now. Saving it had meant nothing.

'Where is it?'

It was a simple question, but answering it came with so much gravity it crushed him.

'Where is it, Toby?'

If only I'd let it go up in flames. If only I'd stayed in the car.

'You've already got it. It's in my shorts in the evidence bag.' He'd extracted the letter from a metal tin hidden in his top drawer, leaving everything else behind. It was still in the same envelope, the paper yellowing, the edge torn. But after he'd retrieved it, it had crumpled, and creases that hadn't been there before now marred its surface and the letter within. He'd taken such good care of it, but now…

'And what's in the letter?' she asked. She thought it would be something incriminating. Perhaps it was.

His chin jutted at Ben. 'Ask him. He knows all about it.'

Chapter Nine

'What the hell, Ben? What's in the letter?'

Leila had called a break after Toby's revelation stole his ability to speak. There was only one letter he could think of. They now stood in the corridor, the air warmer than a moment ago. He leaned against the wall and closed his eyes. Tiredness seeped into his bones.

He kept it.

'It's from me,' he said. 'I wrote it to him when we were younger. It was soon after our mothers died.'

He'd forgotten the exact words, but he remembered how a storm raged inside his chest when he wrote it. He'd railed against Toby's denial, shouting out his desperation, disbelief and pleas, but it hadn't done any good.

Eventually the storm passed and left him behind, sopping and miserable.

'This keeps getting better.' She walked a small square on the floor. 'The guy is going to be your downfall. He's incriminating you every step of the way.'

'It wasn't him.'

'From where I'm standing, it is. Think about this.'

'I am.'

'No, you're thinking about *him*. What you're not thinking about is him being a *suspect*. He was at the scene. He's got motive.'

'Because his dad has dementia?' He massaged his forehead. Was he being thick? Could Leila see this more clearly than he could? 'That's not enough. I know you think he's pulled a fast one over me, but I would not be comfortable standing up in court to justify charging him with the fire.'

She shook her head. 'You're an idiot.'

'That's enough, Leila.'

'He's bad news.' She raised her voice. 'And now he's trying to take you down with him. You think you'd have had enough of guys trying to ruin your career.'

Toby would have to care about him for that to happen.

'This is different. This is nothing like Jared. You don't like Toby so you're trying to pin it on him.'

'If the arrogant firefighter's boot fits.'

Toby might have kept his retrieval of the letter a secret, but he understood why he hadn't. Or at least he thought he did.

'Let's see what comes back from the crime scene,' he said with a lot more confidence than he felt. 'We'll keep him here a while longer, but I'm telling you it wasn't him.'

'Why are you so sure when everything tells you otherwise? What if he started the fire and then grabbed the letter to throw you off the scent? Couldn't that be as plausible?'

Cold burrowed into his chest. Could Toby really be that deceptive? That malicious? That good an actor?

A sigh rumbled out. 'You're right.'

'I am?'

'He's a suspect and our history, as messed up as it is, shouldn't cloud that. But I'm still not prepared to charge him further. He can go back to the cell until his time is up or unless we find something else that's more substantial.'

'You're making a mistake.'

'Then I'm the one who'll wear it but as leading officer that is my decision.' He'd decided. She couldn't persuade him otherwise. 'Is that a problem?'

Rather than get pissed off at him, she smiled. 'I hope you know what you're doing.'

His nose wrinkled. 'Let's get this over with.'

He opened the door and walked over to Toby. Standing a foot away from him, looking down as he looked up, Toby's body relaxed a little and his lips parted, not in readiness to attack, but in softness. Toby probably thought he was free to go. That relief wouldn't last. Ben's words took longer than expected to come out. 'We're going to take a break while we go check up on a few things. Please go with Constable Mayne.'

Toby's eyes bulged as he looked from Leila to him. His hands slammed onto the table as he leapt to his feet. 'The real arsonist is getting away!'

Ben ignored him and spoke to Leila instead. 'Please take Mr Grimshaw to a cell.'

'Come on, Ben, please. You can't believe it.'

Leila intercepted him as he tried to get closer. She tried to direct him with her arm, but Toby remained with his eyes fixed on Ben. Hurt blazed in them. Ben's mouth dried.

'There's no way I would have set fire to the house, not for any reason in the world, you know that.' His voice vibrated from between his clenched jaw, and the lines between his eyes deepened.

Ben's heart shivered, sensing danger.

Leila tried to lead him away and at first he followed but then he spun back.

'If you felt anything for me, you wouldn't be doing this.'

I've heard that before.

He didn't reply. He couldn't. Instead he forced himself to watch as Leila pulled Toby out of the room. He wore the same horrified look that Jared had when they'd taken him away. History repeating itself? He hoped not, but he wouldn't allow himself to be blinded again. He needed an open mind about this, even when he wanted to find a dark hole to crawl into and never leave. To have his trust torn up again…

What am I doing wrong?

His legs wanted to buckle and he could have sat. No one would have bothered him while he gathered his emotions and shut them down. But he had fewer than four hours in which to find something to keep Toby in a cell—or to set him free.

★★★

Ben pulled up in front of the remains of Toby's house, and walked across the half-yellow, half-black front lawn. Smithy spotted him and left with barely a nod of his head. He'd put in the extra hours and Ben had called ahead to relieve him. He took it as his due; at least he wasn't hanging around. Leila would arrive soon to monitor the scene, but Ben wanted to get in early to speak with the arson investigator. Despite the fact that his colleague and friend was currently residing in a cell, the investigator offered his hand when Ben arrived at his side. At least someone could be professional.

'How'd it start, Carl?' he asked, knowing the answer already but wanting the confirmation.

'Petrol, poured into the kitchen.' He wiped the sweat off his forehead with the back of his hand. Even so it left a smudge of soot across his skin. 'Sprayed or splashed otherwise it would have been hard to get it up so quickly. I wouldn't be surprised if accelerant had also been added to the roof.'

'Sounds like someone really wanted the place to go up. Any idea who?'

He chuckled. 'That'd be your job, Ben. But look at this.'

Carl led him out the front door and around the right side of the house to what had once been the kitchen wall. He pointed to the ground at a strip of scorched earth leading away from the window towards the road.

'A trail?' Ben asked. It continued for a few metres before stopping. Surely he would have been seen, especially if Bob had been shouting at him.

Carl nodded. 'Whoever lit the fire was heading that way and probably in a hurry. They were sloppy. My guess is they poured the fuel in through the window, chucked a heap of it on the roof too and then lit it, carrying the container and whatever was left away with them. Some would have spilled out and whoever it was would have been lucky to get away without singed hair.'

Bob said he'd seen Toby through the window. But if so, was there time for him to evade Bob and double back to emerge out the other side of the house? No one had seen him leave the house through the back door, but wouldn't someone have seen him running back? And where would he have dumped the container with the fuel?

They had to widen their search.

'What about his clothes?'

'Smoke-damaged probably, unless he was unlucky and they got burnt too. Could be a bit of blow back, ash stuck to it, that sort of thing. They'd stink too.'

Toby hadn't worn a shirt until later but he'd worn shorts. Not that Ben had paid much attention to their condition. He'd been too busy holding Toby, his solid, lean body pressed against him. Whatever their state, he could have had a second pair lying around and dumped his damaged ones. Forget circumstantial; Toby being the arsonist was sounding about as flimsy as a paper hat in a cyclone.

'How'd they get the window open?' he asked.

'Bob and Toby probably left it open. Do you lock everything up?'

Ben raised his eyebrows.

'Oh, guess you would, being a cop. But not these guys. Would have been easy enough to put a hose through the opening.'

'Fingerprints?'

He shook his head. 'The window's gone. The frame's turned to charcoal. I'm hoping to find some matches. They usually help. Mind you, if they're local, there's not a lot of choice of which brand to buy. Everyone in town probably has the same type in their drawer. I'll keep looking though.'

'Thanks.'

He jotted down a few more notes, but his concentration struggled under Carl's scrutiny. The investigator tilted his head and his closed lips bulged as if he held back a swarm of questions.

He's going to ask about—

'Have you arrested anyone yet?'

Ben's molars scraped against each other. He didn't look at Carl; he kept his pen on the pad, although his writing couldn't be said to resemble anything coherent. 'The investigation is ongoing.'

'Oh yeah? So, my mate Toby's not sitting in a cell?'

No point avoiding it. He flipped the pad and tucked it away. 'Word travels fast.'

'That's Echo Springs for you. Toby would rather bite off his own foot than start a fire, especially with his dad in the house.'

'I'm following procedure,' he said. 'I hope you're doing the same.'

Carl's smile slipped and he closed the few inches between them. 'You wouldn't be questioning my integrity, would you, Ben?'

'No more than you'd question mine.'

Ignoring Carl's glare, Ben slipped the pen into his top pocket and turned at the sound of Leila's car pulling up out the front. Grateful for the distraction, he went to meet her. He gave Leila a recap of what Carl had said, cut down any of her scoffs and eye-rolls when it came to his suppositions, and then said goodbye. She'd stay and work on gathering evidence and write a report. Meanwhile, Ben was keen to talk to the neighbours. They might prove to be the witnesses he needed. Then he could get Toby out of that cell, and find out who had tried to kill the Grimshaws.

He knocked on the neighbours' door, which opened after the first rap of his knuckles. Sharon and Ian Cooper, both in their fifties, and a fixture of the local community organisations, greeted him and bundled him inside. Ian retreated to the kitchen to boil the kettle. Ben had barely taken a seat on their couch before Sharon started talking.

'We couldn't believe it when we saw it.' She tucked a dirty blonde curl of hair behind her ear. 'The home of a firefighter going up in flames! Wait, *two* firefighters because Bob used to be one, of course. Before he got sick, I mean.'

'Do you have much to do with the Grimshaws?' he asked.

'We say hello when we see them, and we try to keep an eye out for Bob.'

'Any problems?'

'We've seen him go wandering down the street—haven't we, love?—but he's looked pretty *compos mentis*.'

'And the last time was...?'

Her lips pursed before her eyes widened and mouth opened. 'A few days ago. Same day you showed up at the house. What was *that* about?'

The temptation was obviously too great not to ask for the full story though Sharon had probably already mentioned their visit to a half-dozen people.

'Just a routine enquiry,' he said, keen to keep her moving.

'Hartley says that to us when we ask him things.' As well as being two of the town's 'concerned' citizens, Sharon and Ian were Detective Senior Constable Hartley Cooper's aunt and uncle. Ian was Sergeant Cooper Senior's brother—a good reason to keep it friendly. 'Still no word on Peter Hanson's whereabouts?'

'None I'm afraid.'

'Erika must be so worried. She's such a lovely girl, good for Hartley, even if she has been through some tough times.' Sharon obviously didn't share her brother-in-law's harsh opinion of Erika. 'That Mabel was always a hard one to deal with, but Peter seemed to have the magic touch. And after all he did for her, to just vanish like *that*.'

'We're still working on it, but right now I'd like to know what you saw this morning.'

Sharon didn't seem to mind the redirection. 'There's not much to tell really. I'm a pretty light sleeper—Ian snores.'

'Rubbish,' her husband interjected as he came into the room with a tray. Despite the dig, he smiled benevolently at his wife and handed out the tea. He seemed very different from his brother.

'What time did you wake up?' Ben prodded, putting the cup on the table and pushing it away.

'I was half-awake sometime after four—Ian's snoring rattles the windows— and I tried to get back to sleep but then I heard, well, the fire really.' Sharon blew on her tea. 'At first I thought it might have been in our house so I jumped out of bed—I woke Ian too—but we couldn't find any damage. Then I looked out the window and saw what was happening next door so I call the fire brigade, but they already knew about it.'

How Toby had the presence of mind to search for his dad, get out of the house and call the fire brigade staggered him but didn't surprise him. Toby was nothing if not an experienced firefighter.

'Can you describe what you saw?'

She took a sip, enough to wet her lips as the steam still rose off the surface of the tea. 'We look out onto what I think is Bob's room at the back, but I can see their kitchen too. The fire was worse there. I was worried it would leap across to us.'

'Any reason?'

'There was fire on the other side of the fence, not in the house, but on the ground too. It wouldn't take much for ours to go up in flames too.'

If that were the case, then that matched Carl's report, and she must have looked up after Bob had scared the arsonist away.

He leaned forward in his chair. 'Did you see anyone?'

She shook her head. 'Did you, hon?'

'I was already out the front so I didn't get a good look,' Ian said. 'But I ran into Bob.'

'And did he say anything to you?'

'He was wandering at that stage, staring up at his house. I think he was in shock.'

At least no one had so far implicated Toby.

'Do you know where Toby was?'

'I asked Bob but he was off in his own world. I was about to run into the house but…well, I heard the sirens.' Ian shrugged. Heroism had its glory but it didn't come without risks. It also often went hand in hand with stupidity. Ian had done the right thing. 'I went looking for Toby down the side of the house and that's where I met him. He was shouting for Bob and the relief on the kid's face…heartbreaking, especially as Bob didn't even register him.'

A dull blade twisted in Ben's heart. If Bob had died, Toby would have lost both parents. And instead of letting Toby celebrate the fact that his dad was still alive, Ben had thrown him in a cell.

If only Bob hadn't said he'd seen Toby light the fire.

'Did you notice anything strange about his appearance? Any burns or ash, or a particular smell?'

'He was shirtless,' Sharon said, a little too quickly before the glint in her eye vanished. 'That was about it. No shoes either, his hair a mess, but then it always is.' Her nose wrinkled. 'No smell. Mind you, hard to get the stench of fire out of your nose. I think we go a bit crazy when that's in us, worried about whether the whole town is going to go up in smoke.'

Two fires within a week during a dry spell and here he was locking up firefighters.

Innocent firefighters.

He pressed on. 'Have you noticed anything unusual the past week? Anyone hanging around the place?'

Ian sat back, resting the mug on his paunch.

'I don't know if it's unusual or not,' Sharon said, pausing to take a mouthful of tea. 'But yesterday, I'm sure I saw Toby walk down the side of the house. It was fleeting but I was in the kitchen and looked up at that moment to see him peering into one of their windows. I was hoping to catch him to ask him about the cemetery fire—my dad's buried there, you see—and I hadn't been able to get out to look at the damage myself. So, I dried my hands and hurried out to catch him—he's so busy I rarely get the chance to talk—and when I got outside I called out but he'd disappeared.'

Ben's body stilled, inside and out. Any sudden movement might muddy the recollection and this was the first witness, other than Bob, who might have seen anything of use. 'And you're sure it was Toby?'

'Same black hair. I didn't get a good look at his face but...' The curl fell forward and she tucked it back again. Her fingers continued the loop and hovered in front of her lips. 'I *assumed* it was Toby.'

'What time was this?'

She took a second to answer, her eyebrows furrowing. 'About two,' she answered absent-mindedly. 'When you think about it, he would have been at work, right?' She looked at Ian and reached out to take his hand.

'And Bob wasn't home?'

'No, Narelle had picked him up about an hour before. I meant to go see Toby later that evening, but I got distracted. Next time I saw him was at the fire the next morning.'

Ben's pen moved as fast as his heart agitated inside his chest. Either Sharon had seen Toby—and in which case, why was he there at that time and what was he doing?—or she'd seen someone else. Someone who could be the arsonist.

'Thank you, this is very useful,' he said, rising from his seat. 'If you remember anything else, please let me know.'

She rushed up off the couch. 'Have you seen Toby? We thought he would have been around by now. We wanted to offer our help.' The lightness with which she'd greeted him had fallen away, replaced with the concern of someone who wanted absolution.

He couldn't give her that. He had his own forgiveness to seek.

He smiled, hoping it would offer some reassurance. Sharon couldn't have known this would happen. 'He's helping us with our enquiries, but I'll be sure to pass on your thoughts.'

If he ever speaks to me again.

***

He was missing something. It flitted at the edges of Ben's consciousness, taunting him with its vague presence, but every time he tried to focus his attention on it, the answer darted into the shadows. Toby was innocent but he was connected to this in some important way. As much as he disliked holding Toby in a cell any longer than necessary, he needed to talk to Bob.

He pulled into the driveway and the front door opened as soon as he got out of the car. Narelle guarded the entrance with her arms crossed beneath her bosom. 'Well? Where's Toby?'

'Perhaps we should go inside before we start talking about this.'

'The neighbours already know what you've done. How could you arrest Toby? It's ridiculous.'

He resisted the urge to scrub his face in his hands. Instead he ignored the question and the accusation. 'Has Bob changed his story?'

'He's asleep. He was distraught and tired himself out.'

'If you want to help Toby, then I suggest you wake Bob so I can talk to him again.'

She huffed through her nose and her lips puckered, but she motioned for him to follow her into the house. He took a seat in the family room. He couldn't fault her for her loyalty to her nephew. In fact, he'd always liked Narelle, but right now she was someone else ready to have a go and he was running out of patience.

Voices murmured down the hall. He hoped Bob was lucid enough for this conversation.

'Where's my son?' Bob asked as he came into the room. His usual smile was gone, replaced with the stern glare of the fire chief he'd once been. Ben stood up to not feel so small beneath that reproach.

'He's at the station. We're holding him while we check out parts of his story.'

'You've got the wrong guy.'

'So people keep telling me,' he said, sitting back down. Bob sat opposite with Narelle hovering to the side. 'Do you remember what you said at the hospital about seeing Toby lighting the fire at the house?'

'I never said that.'

Ben looked at Narelle, but her closed face told him he wasn't going to get any support from her. 'I'm afraid you did. Twice. You said you'd gone into the kitchen and saw Toby outside the window.'

'I was confused. It wasn't Toby, but it was someone who looked like him.'

'But that's not what you said.'

'Then I'm changing my story,' Bob boomed, whether from the affront at having his authority questioned or in frustration.

Witnesses changed their stories all the time, often when they realised they'd implicated loved ones. Unless Bob could offer him something new, he'd come across as an unreliable witness.

'You won't do Toby any favours if you're protecting him when he's done something wrong.'

'That boy would never harm me or anyone, so I'm telling you, I didn't see Toby out the window.' Bob's jaw jutted forward. 'I came into the kitchen. The fire was already lit. I looked out the window and a face looked back at me. The bastard got a shock and took flight. I called out to Toby, and then ran out of the house to catch the perpetrator.'

Each statement, fired in a casing of rebuke, struck Ben's core. Wounded, he spoke softer but he had to continue. 'Can you describe him?'

'Black hair, white guy. Hard to tell really because I didn't have the best view but...but he looked like Toby but it wasn't Toby.'

Toby, but not Toby.

Ben sat back in his chair, not speaking, not moving, letting the words filter through his head. If Bob was changing his story, then the description matched that of the guy Sharon had seen. And as he held that thought in his head, his stomach shrivelled and sank into murky dankness, taking the last of his breath with it.

It can't be him.

He wiped his palms along his legs. 'The other day, after the fire at the cemetery, you said you saw Toby there too. Did you?'

He frowned. 'I went to the cemetery?'

Narelle moved at the edge of his vision.

Bob pinched the bridge of his nose, muttering under his breath. 'I can't remember. I can't remember going to the cemetery.'

'It's alright,' he said. 'So, you're saying it wasn't Toby who lit the fire at your house?'

'That's right. So, will you let him go?'

If his suspicions were correct, then they needed to be looking elsewhere. He knew where to start. He stood to go.

'Well?' Bob demanded. 'What will you do with Toby?'

'Nothing,' he said. 'If you're changing your statement and as we've been unable to find any other witnesses to Toby starting the fire, then he's free to go.'

Bob spluttered. 'And what about catching the guy who really did this? Should we be worried he's going to come for us again?'

Bob wasn't the target. That was one thing he could be certain about. 'Based on new evidence, I'm confident we'll arrest a suspect soon, and I believe you're no longer in danger. However, please keep an eye out for anyone looking suspicious.'

He exited, ignoring the stunned looks on their faces. They might hate him but arresting Toby wouldn't be the worst thing he'd done in all this. Not after what he'd come to realise. Toby was innocent and had to be released.

But if he were in a cell at least he'd be safe from the man who was trying to kill him.

Chapter Ten

The cell door clanged open, releasing some of the stagnant air from the confined space. Toby's eyes had traced the walls for hours, following the lines of scratches and graffiti, running over the cracks and chips in the paintwork. He hadn't been able to rest; the worries of what they'd use to incriminate him and how his dad was coping gnawed at him. So he'd watched the walls, partly to be sure they weren't closing in any further.

Ben stood in the doorway. In one hand he held Toby's phone; in the other the bag containing his shorts.

And the letter.

Has Ben read it? Or does he remember what he wrote?

He turned back to the wall. Keeping quiet was the best thing for him at this stage. If only he'd done that before. Or at least asked for a lawyer. Playing over the interview in his head, there'd been too many moments where he'd sounded guilty. Perhaps not beyond a shadow of a doubt but enough to tarnish his reputation.

'You're free to go,' Ben said when it became obvious Toby wasn't going to speak first.

His heart thudded into his throat, but the tight hold he kept on his jaw stopped it from getting any further. He should be happy about this. He was free. Exonerated.

But he'd been innocent all along.

And Ben hadn't believed him.

His heart slid back down to where it belonged, leaving behind an oily slick as he levered himself off the bench and head for the door.

Ben gave him his phone and offered him the bag. Toby looked at it then stared ahead. He didn't want to see any regret in Ben's eyes, or any hint of an apology. They were past that. He might have been the one to push Ben away in the beginning, but Ben had fixed the distance in place.

'I don't want it.' Toby knew the letter off by heart, but without that visual reminder those assertions of love would fade.

Can't come soon enough.

Ben's hand lowered.

Toby left the cell, but he'd not gone far before Ben's words brought him to a standstill.

'Has anyone followed you lately?'

He snorted. 'So, you finally believe me when I say it's not me or Dad who's been lighting fires?'

Ben couldn't meet his gaze and for one traitorous second he felt sorry for the guy. Ben had made a mistake—a monumental mistake—and it was easy to see he felt bad.

But that and five bucks didn't go far these days.

'Your neighbour saw someone by the house yesterday, and your dad now says it wasn't you he saw out the window, but instead someone who looks like you.'

'And you want to catch the person who tried to kill us? Like a real police officer?'

Ben's eyes flared, searing through the shame, before his gaze weakened and sank to the floor.

'Do you want an apology? Right.' His chest inflated and he raised his head. 'I'm sorry for falsely accusing you of being the arsonist. And I'm sorry you lost your house. If you could answer my question, I'd be grateful because if something happened to you again—'

The words stuck in Ben's throat, but the way Toby was feeling it was like they stuck in his. A lump bulged in his neck, built from rage and pride, but then the concern on Ben's face and the way he'd said 'again' dissolved it. For how long would Ben hang around? For how much longer would he care?

He spoke before Ben could continue. 'I haven't noticed anyone following me or felt watched. Do you think we're in danger?'

Ben rubbed his forehead. 'I think your dad's safe.'

His pulse boomed in his ears, as loud as Ben's meaning.

'But I'm not.'

'I don't know, but you need to be careful.'

His breath shortened, and his chest constricted as adrenaline galloped through his body. He raised his hand. 'Wait. Are we in police protection territory here? If you think someone's after me, shouldn't I have more than a few bits of advice from Echo Springs's finest?'

Ben gave a crooked smile, his dimple appearing briefly before fading away, along with his ability to look Toby in the eye.

'Who is it, Ben?' He stepped closer.

'I don't know. Not for sure. But...look, I think it'd be safer if you took a holiday out of town for a few days.'

His heart jerked. If he was a target, he couldn't stay with Narelle and Frank. But he hated the idea of running. Whoever was doing this wanted him scared—and he wouldn't give the arsehole the satisfaction. He'd stay at the fire station. Surrounded by firefighters was the safest he could manage.

He swallowed the panic and kneaded the back of his neck. 'Look, I'm grateful for the concern, but I'll take my chances. Just catch who's doing this.'

Ben's face closed and he was Constable Fields again. 'If you see anyone acting suspicious, call me.'

Toby nodded. He almost relented and asked for the letter, thinking that somehow it would offer him some safety, or at least some comfort. He'd sought solace in its simple and honest words many times over the years, remembering when there'd been hope and promise in their friendship, if not a relationship. But what good were a few words in blue ink now? He left Ben—and the letter—behind.

Once out the front of the lock-up and away from Ben, the reality of what had happened—and what could yet happen—crashed on top of him. He walked, but his legs didn't move easily. The town's attention on him, even when there was no one there, caught at his heels. He walked the streets to see his family, and a wave of pity, curiosity and wariness bore down on him.

But it paled against someone wanting him dead.

Dismissing the worst of his unease, he broke into a sprint, Ben's larger-sized clothes dancing on him as he ran. He had his own at the station, but everything else had gone up with the house. He was going to have to buy a lot of new things.

And a new house.

Thank god the insurance was paid up.

His father, aunt and uncle were waiting for him. He listened to their outrage about the foolishness of the police, but he didn't have it in him to stoke their anger. He was more concerned about who was after him. The thought dogged him as he excused himself and set a course for the station, despite assurances they'd given him the day off. He'd feel safer there, and his family would be safer too.

At least he'd not been responsible for anyone's death this time.

Just the destruction of property.

Carl was at the station house and gave him the rundown of the investigation. He had no suspicions that Toby had anything to do with the fire, but he couldn't find any identifying evidence of someone else.

'A bloody amateur,' Carl said.

But whoever it was had been professional—or lucky—enough not to leave behind any hard evidence. No fingerprints. No blood. Just a lot of fuel.

He leaned back in his chair. His hands smoothed through his curly hair then tightened into fists. He let go with a long breath and the four legs of the chair touched the floor. 'I'm starting to think the fire at the cemetery has something to do with me, too. You've not seen anyone who looks like me around town?'

'Nah. Will tell the team to keep an eye out. We've got your back.' Carl gave his shoulder a squeeze and a shake. 'Police doing much? Apart from arresting the wrong bloke?'

'Ben suggested I leave town.'

'I bet he did. So you can't sue for wrongful arrest.'

He shook his head. He'd already had enough of his family thinking the worst of Ben. 'I think he's worried.'

'Good. If you need a place to stay, you're welcome at mine. Plenty of room.'

'Thanks, but I think I'll sleep here until they catch this psycho.' He didn't want to endanger anyone else more than necessary.

Carl stood and turned towards his desk. 'I need to finish this report for the cops, but shout out if you need anything. Sorry about the house, mate.'

He still didn't have a home and he still had a madman after him, but here, at this moment, he had help.

Chapter Eleven

'Jared Matthew Fairfax. Released on parole three weeks ago,' Leila read over Ben's shoulder as he sat looking at the screen. 'This your guy?'

Jared had served two years of a four-year drug charge handed down during a time when judges were going hard on dealers, even those on their first offence. The political winds had changed since and blown him back into Ben's life. Jared stared out at him from his mugshot, the hard set to his jaw warring with the tension in his eyes.

'Not my guy, but *the* guy, possibly.'

'Pretty—in a drug-dealing, ruin-your-life kind of way. Hope he was good in bed.'

He tried not to think about it, but had to admit the sex had been good—when everything had been good.

'And you never noticed the resemblance?' she asked.

He leaned forward, looking for where Jared was meant to be now and which station he reported to. He was definitely *not* looking at what had been staring him in the face for two-and-a-half years.

'Don't ignore me, Strawberry.' She nudged him before gesturing at the monitor. 'The guy's the spitting image of Toby. No wonder Bob got confused.'

'Dark. Broody. That's it,' he said, rather weakly, as he picked up the phone to call Newmont police station. Post-release, he discovered, Jared had gone home to his mother in his hometown about two hours away from Echo Springs.

Leila waited while he spoke to an officer on the other end and told them the situation. They'd pick him up—if he was there—but Ben said he'd head out there anyway. He wanted to talk to Mrs Fairfax.

Details given, he jabbed the disconnect button, and flung the phone on the desk.

Leila relaunched her attack. 'I bet if I put the two of them in a line-up, you wouldn't be able to tell them apart. Is he as short as Toby?'

He rolled his eyes. 'Five-foot-eight is not short.' Yes, he knew how tall Toby was. It was a cop thing.

She cocked a brow. 'Come on, they could be brothers.'

'Will you give it a rest? If you're going to be like this, you're not coming to Newmont.' He hunched forward and poured his focus into the screen in front of him. He wrote down the address, but he was certain he'd remember how to get there. Other memories of Jared were surfacing, why not this one?

'Just a bit of fun, man.' She popped him on the arm. 'That's why you dated Jared in the first place, isn't it?'

Blood charged through his veins, and raised the heat beneath his skin. She was trying to make this easy for him, but he didn't deserve it. 'This isn't funny.' His hands closed into fists to stop himself from shaking. 'Because of me, Toby nearly died. Whatever Jared's got in his head, he's coming after me and he's doing it through Toby.'

Leila leaned closer and bumped her head to his. 'It's okay, Ben. We're going to catch him.'

His heart eased its hammering. His hands opened and he exhaled. She was on his side.

'You talked to him about Toby then?' she asked.

'We got really close.'

Shame sluiced through his body, and concentrated low in his belly, dissolving time and distance to expose what an idiot he'd been. At the time Jared had helped dress a wound he hadn't known was bleeding. The haze around their relationship had been strong enough that Ben didn't see he was living with a drug-dealing arsehole. But then the evidence mounted and he'd been forced to act. How could he have been so blind? How had he allowed himself to become so compromised—professionally and personally? Jared tried to convince him it was a lie, but then, faced with too much proof, he said he'd wanted to keep Ben safe from it all.

Bile smeared the back of his throat and he swallowed to wash it down. 'Obviously I regret that now.'

'Don't be so hard on yourself. Be grateful you got out of it relatively unscathed.'

Unscathed was a stretch. His colleagues—he couldn't say friends anymore—from his previous station might not have laid a hand on him but he'd suffered their distrust. That's why he'd ended up back in Echo Springs. Now there was nowhere else to run.

He had to make this right.

He picked up the keys and Leila followed him out. He drove, heading south on the highway as Echo Springs quickly gave way to open plains and the broad clear sky. They were quiet until about half an hour down the road.

'So, Jared gets out of jail, decides to pay you back by killing your old flame—ha! How poetic—and then what? Kills you too?' Leila said.

He grimaced. 'Sounds about right.'

'But instead we catch him, you're a hero and Toby falls into your arms.' She swooned… before miming sticking her finger down her throat.

He snorted. 'I think that boat has not only sailed, but struck an iceberg, caught on fire and everyone on board has been eaten by sharks. I stayed in Sydney after training to keep away from Toby, but I left there to escape the shame of Jared. Perhaps it's time to go back again.'

'Echo Springs not big enough for the both of you?' she said. 'As much as Toby grates on me, he obviously hits you in all the right places. Have you ever actually tried to have a conversation with him? Or is it all longing looks from across the pub?'

'He thinks I'm a screw-up.' It was easier to stare into the distance than look her in the eye.

'Really? He said that?'

Flashing back through as many of the interactions with Toby he could remember, he admitted that those words had never crossed Toby's lips. But still, that's what he thought.

'He doesn't need to say it, he just has to…look.'

If those dark glances and open glares didn't communicate disappointment, then what were they about?

'Why would he think you're a screw-up?'

He rearranged himself in his seat; the belt cut across him too tight. 'Apart from arresting him? Jared.'

'Did Toby know him?'

'No, but the whole town knows why I came back. And there's nothing Toby values more than professionalism and integrity—which I blew.'

'Sounds like you got a bit of your own back when you charged him with arson.'

'Uh, we charged him with arson.' No way was he alone in the blame. 'You practically salivated at the thought.'

'I bet you liked the idea of him in handcuffs too,' she purred. 'Look, when this is over and you've saved the day, I'm sure he's going to have questions. Maybe it's time to suck it up and face this once and for all.'

His thumb thudded against the top of the steering wheel. Hadn't he already tried to talk to Toby? 'It's a two-way street. Toby hasn't exactly wanted to spend time around me.'

Even if he did kiss me back this morning.

Right before he'd thrown him in jail.

'But he admitted to me this morning that he's done something terrible.'

'Really? And it's not the fire?'

He shook his head.

'Then what is it?'

The highway veered west through dry country with not a cloud to shield them from the relentless sun.

'I've got no idea.'

★★★

The local cops phoned when Ben and Leila were less than an hour away from Newmont; they couldn't find Jared and he hadn't shown up for a meeting with his parole officer. An arrest warrant had been issued and they were searching for him. With Jared having relocated close to Echo Springs and with his whereabouts unknown, Ben knew they had found the culprit. Leila called Echo Springs and told them to be on the lookout—especially around Toby. Jared's mother hadn't seen him but Ben still wanted to meet with her.

Jared's mother's house sat behind a low hedge surrounded by well-cared-for grass. Rose bushes grew in her garden beds, and the trunks of four evenly spaced palm trees blocked the view from the two windows at the front. Cream wooden slats ran around the box home, and the corrugated roof had stained a burnt umber. Patches of green paint peeled off the eaves jutting over the windows and the brown door.

It was much as he remembered.

He and Jared had visited once in their relationship, doing a tour of their hometowns. That they had grown up near to each other had seemed like fate. But his dad hadn't approved when he brought Jared around. Bill Fields, ex-cop, had one of his typical gut reactions and after the visit he didn't mention Jared again.

Once Jared was out of his life, things had resolved between Ben and his dad. One good thing among many. Jared was in his past. No contact. No looking back. And with any luck he'd never have seen him again.

A bitter taste scraped the back of his tongue as he knocked on the door.

Val Fairfax opened the door. She had always been a small woman, but she'd gotten thinner since the last time he saw her. An inch of grey showed at the roots of her auburn hair. Weary hazel eyes took in his uniform before rising to his face; recognition flashed and the set of her mouth changed from slack resignation to a hint of relief before it fell. She stood aside to let them in.

No resistance.

His heart ached for her.

She herded them into the sitting room and plonked herself down in a scuffed soft leather couch, gesturing that they could sit in the armchairs. Her gaze fixed on him once introductions were out of the way.

'I've already told the others I haven't seen him since last night. I have no idea where he's gone.'

'We know,' he replied. 'How has he been since he got out?'

She broke the look and smoothed her hand back and forth over her throat. 'I barely talk to him. He lives here but…but I find excuses to stay away from him. I guess that makes me a bad person.'

'You've given him a place to stay, probably when no one else would,' Leila said. 'You've done more for him than anyone else, considering the situation.'

'I try.' She picked at a hole in the arm of the chair, ripping off a bit of leather before letting it drop and brushing it off. 'I tried. And when he was with you, Ben, I thought finally he'd come good. It wasn't until later I learned he was still up to his old tricks and I worried…' She sighed. 'I worried he was going to take you down with him.'

Everyone had seen Jared for what he was. Everyone except Ben. He'd been so desperate to replace Toby that he had been willing to accept anyone, no matter what.

'It wasn't your fault,' he said. 'He was good at hiding things. Have the police searched his room?'

She nodded. 'But you can look too. They said he's been lighting fires. I was surprised because I've never known him to do that. Lighting joints, sure, but burning down the bush, setting people's homes alight…I guess I don't know him at all.'

She led them down the hall to Jared's room. One curtain had been pulled back to reveal an unmade bed with clothes littering the floor. Jared's childhood room had been neater the last time he'd seen it. Ben couldn't tell what was the result of Jared's general untidiness and what the police had overturned. From experience, however, much of this would have been Jared's doing. It had been their biggest source of conflict: Jared's messiness.

That was, until there were more important things to fight about.

'He spends most of his time driving,' Val said. 'He'd check in with the parole officer and then disappear for hours. I didn't ask where. I was glad he was gone. I wish I'd made more of an effort.'

'He had everything he could have hoped for and he threw it away,' Leila said. 'Wouldn't you say, Ben?' Leila might have been trying to comfort Val, but her words rang inside Ben's head, sounding through his emptiness.

'You did your best,' he said.

If only he could believe that of himself.

Val wiped her eyes and walked away. Leila went with her. Ben slipped on protective gloves and searched the room. It smelled of Jared, a rich, sharp, citrus scent that knocked him back to the moment they'd met at a bar.

His head had turned at his cologne and he'd gasped as he'd looked into Jared's eyes. Jared had been close enough and the hungriness in his gaze had been a turn-on. Plenty of guys had shown their interest, and he'd gone home with his fair share of them, but Jared's bravado and determination had won him over that first night.

He'd gone willingly and Jared had devoured him. Consumed him to the point where he sat in the belly of darkness, unable to get out, to face the truth about who he'd become involved with. He hadn't cared how fast he'd fallen or for much else about Jared, seeing in him the fulfilment of a fantasy.

He'd tricked himself into believing it was love, and brushed aside the concerns that niggled at him. Late-night phone calls, Jared's resistance to introducing him to his friends, and the endless last-minute cancellations. He'd only agreed to move in together after Ben gave him an ultimatum. He'd worried Jared was having an affair; ultimately that's how he'd discovered Jared's real line of work—tailing him late at night only to see him meet known offenders instead of a hookup. A relationship built on deception, and Ben had been complicit. He'd fallen so hard that it had taken him an age to climb out and see the desolation surrounding Jared.

And here he was standing ankle deep in it again.

He sorted through the clothes on the floor, throwing them on the bed after he picked them up and sniffed them for fuel. The first few pieces were all about the citrus, but a pair of shorts and then a black t-shirt gave off a whiff of fuel.

He bagged them and left them at the door.

He didn't find a phone or anything else that could provide a clue. Whatever Jared was up to, he'd have knowledge of it with him. If they found his car, they would find him and they'd find the evidence. There was nothing else to do here.

He picked up the bags and cast a final look over the room. So ordinary. The messy room of someone he had loved, a son who a mother loved, yet Jared had used their love as the best cover.

Did he love me?

It didn't matter, not now, and perhaps not even then. It had been temporary. He'd given plenty to Jared in the hope of having him return his love, but he'd known it wasn't meant to be.

All along he'd wanted Toby.

And now he'd put Toby in danger.

Chapter Twelve

Toby couldn't stay at the station house. There were no emergencies, not even a cat to rescue from up a tree. And while he sat there, someone was out there stalking him and stealing his life from under him. His legs jittered while he fumed over how little he could do, until eventually he had to get out. He returned to make a start on the ruins of his home now the police were finished with the scene.

As the sun sailed across the sky, Toby lost himself in the gradual sorting out and discarding of his family home. The neighbours, a few off-duty firefighters and people who had barely said two words to him his whole life all helped. They left the personal stuff to him, but everything that could be saved was stacked elsewhere or packed into plastic tubs. The rest of it—the fallen-down roof, the stripped walls and burnt-out kitchen, a bathroom that would never be resurrected—they tore down and carted to the front lawn ready to be lobbed into skip bins.

People talked and shared the work. Every now and then they came to ask for his permission to do something but otherwise they got on with it. A lump hardened in his throat at those times; he was surprised at how much he craved their kindness.

He'd starved himself for so long, believing it would be better and safer for everyone if he stuck to his job and nothing else. He had destroyed lives when he was younger. He hadn't wanted to do it again.

Looks like he'd failed anyway and now someone wanted him dead.

And Ben knew who it was.

By the end of the day, the home had emptied. His uncle came by with the car to take the things of value back to their house, and neighbours stored the few surviving bigger items in their backyard. Only the shell remained, ready for demolition. Desolate as it was, ghosts still haunted its ruins.

'Do you want a lift to the station?' his uncle asked, wrenching Toby out of his dark musings.

'Nah, I'll walk.'

'You sure it's safe?'

'I'll be fine,' he said.

His uncle opened his mouth to say something else, but Toby held up his hand. 'And yes, it's safer if I don't stay with you guys.'

'I hope you know what you're doing, Toby.' He clapped him on the shoulder. 'We'd never get over it if anything happened to you.'

That's because you don't know the truth.

'You've got nothing to worry about.'

He slipped out of his uncle's protective grip and walked away before he tried to change his mind. But when he arrived outside the station house with its pale bricks and large garage doors, he couldn't go in.

The lights were on, people were inside and there'd be work to do, or he could train in the gym, then grab some food, take a shower, immerse himself in that side of his life and hide the shame and the guilt. But he wasn't ready to go back to that yet.

If ever.

He retreated, heading south through Echo Springs's streets as the calm of dusk descended. He watched for anyone watching him, but his concentration drifted. His thoughts dwelled on the events of the night before and on how much he'd have gone to his grave not saying.

And how much Ben wouldn't know.

He navigated to Ben's house and knocked on the door before he could stop himself. He screwed his feet to the ground. Ben had to know how his mother had died.

Footsteps thudded on the wooden floor on the other side of the door, which opened to reveal Ben wearing a pair of long gym shorts and a tank top. The clothes—or lack thereof—exposed his muscles, especially his arms and chest. A light covering of hair crested the top of his shirt. Toby forced his eyes up, despite wanting to indulge himself a little longer. It'd been a long time since he'd seen even this much of Ben's body, and back then he hadn't been this built. But Toby was here for a reason and it wasn't to salivate over Ben's biceps. He licked his lips and swallowed.

'Toby,' Ben said. 'Ahhh… how are you?' He smiled and his dimple deepened. Its appearance pinged Toby's heart. Perhaps it would be better to focus on his chest after all.

He rubbed the back of his neck. 'Can I come in?'

Ben stepped aside and Toby brushed past him, aware of the heat coming off him. The wounded dog inside himself wanted more than consolation, it wanted fierceness, strength. He cleared his throat and walked into the family room, but couldn't decide whether to sit or stand for this. He hovered, waiting to follow Ben's lead.

'Wanna beer?' Ben asked.

Within seconds a cold bottle of courage appeared before him and he took a swig. The bubbles flushed his throat. He took another long drink.

'Long day?' Ben said, nodding to the bottle and sitting down on the couch. He perched on the edge with his hands clasped around the neck of his untasted beer.

'Cleared the house today.' Toby sat in the armchair to Ben's right.

'I'm sorry,' he said. 'That must have been tough.'

He rolled the bottle between his palms, the cool glass soothing his raw skin. 'It was necessary. Actually it felt good.' He drank again. He'd need another at this rate. 'It's one way of clearing out the clutter.'

'Still, I'm sorry it was done the way it was. You could have asked me for a hand with the spring-cleaning. I'm pretty good with a feather duster.' He laughed but it came out stilted. Had Ben always been this uneasy around him? 'I suppose you're here for an explanation.'

Toby blanked, taking a second to figure out what Ben was talking about. He'd been so focused on what he'd wanted to say that he'd forgotten about the arsonist.

'Did you find who did this?'

Ben took a drink and Toby recognised that slow swig and strain in his neck which had nothing to do with swallowing a mouthful of beer. Ben placed the bottle on the table and twisted it by its neck, pouring his focus into the inanimate object.

'Ben? Who did this?'

He locked his fingers together and popped his knuckles. 'There's no easy way to say this. His name is Jared Fairfax and he—'

Nails gouged into Toby's chest. Adrenaline rushed to fill the wounds.

'Your ex!?' He slammed the bottle on the table and jerked to his feet. 'What the fuck?' He gripped the back of the armchair. Ben's ex—that lying, cheating son of a bitch—had tried to kill him.

He'd seen the worthless prick when Ben had brought him to town and had disliked the guy without ever having been introduced. It wasn't until later he'd learned his feelings were justified.

Ben gulped down more beer.

Toby's skin buzzed. He held tight to the chair to keep grounded. 'So that sack of shit is the one doing this?'

'He's on parole and has been staying at his mother's over in Newmont,' he said in a flat tone. 'He's out to get me back for what I did to him.'

'Then why didn't he burn down your house? Why go for mine?'

Ben tapped his thumb against the neck of the empty bottle.

Why would Jared know anything about him? Why would Jared use him to get at Ben?

You know this is your own fault, don't you?

If he'd cleared this up years ago, then Ben could have moved on and not dated this psycho. He would have hated Toby, but then he wouldn't have gone for his doppelgänger.

Yeah, he'd seen the resemblance. That's why he hated Jared so much.

The bastard had stolen his place.

'You want another?' Ben asked, getting up and heading for the kitchen.

'Ben?' He followed. 'Why is Jared coming after me?'

He opened the fridge but instead of reaching for another beer, he stared inside as if the broccoli and the apples could give him the answers.

The waiting squeezed Toby's ribs until they ached. But he had to hold back and let Ben do this in his own time.

Man, it killed him.

Ben closed the fridge and faced him. 'Because of what you meant to me.'

The breath shuddered to a halt in his throat.

Had he heard that right?

Past tense.

'Meant?' The word scraped from his tongue.

Ben ignored his question, reopened the fridge, grabbed another beer and walked away.

'What did you tell Jared about us?' he asked to Ben's retreating back.

'He knew there wasn't an us, but he knew what you meant to me and what happened.'

But Ben didn't know everything—like why Toby had ended it.

Ben sank into the couch. 'I guess he figured those feelings were still there, and that hurting you was the best way to hurt me.'

'And those feelings aren't there anymore?' He dragged the question from the depth of his stomach, bringing to the surface the fears that had sunk to the bottom. At least Ben didn't look at him; his skin had probably gone pale.

Ben stared at a spot on the wall. 'What good are they, Toby? What good have they ever been? I wanted you so badly that I went out and got a copy— a shit copy I admit—but a copy nonetheless. I knew he wasn't you...' Ben buried his head in his hands.

Toby hurried around and sat on the coffee table in front of Ben, took hold of his hands and pulled them away from his face. A shiver rushed under his skin.

'You have nothing to feel bad about, Ben. You weren't to know what Jared would be like.'

'You don't understand.' He shook his head. 'I thought I'd got him out of my life and dealt with my failure.'

'What failure?'

'Don't patronise me, Toby.' Ben withdrew his hands.

'I'm not. What are you talking about?'

He stood and marched away. 'The way you looked at me when I slunk back to town, you needn't have bothered. I couldn't have felt any worse about myself.'

The air punched from his lungs. How could Ben have ever thought that? 'What's got into you?'

'You thought I was a screw-up.' Ben's lips crinkled. 'I know how highly you regard your own integrity. The idea of losing that sickens you. It wasn't hard to see you thought I'd lost mine.'

Where was this coming from? He scrabbled through as many memories of Ben as he could find; all he saw was how few there'd been since his return.

'I really didn't.' He crossed the room, but his approach brought Ben's arms across his chest. Toby placed a hand on his arm anyway. 'When you came back I was worried. I hated the idea of you with that dickhead and then to hear what he'd done and how he'd endangered your job—because I know how much you love it—how low he must have brought you.'

'When I moved back, all you said was, "I'm sorry to see you back".'

'I was.' Even if a big part of him—the part that was currently gunning like a V8 engine—had rejoiced to have him near again. 'You should have been in Sydney, doing what you love, rather than being back here.'

Ben unfolded his arms and scratched his throat. 'So, if you don't think I'm a failure, then why stay away from me?'

Toby had come to give Ben answers, but now the moment was here, the words stayed locked inside. He stumbled back.

Ben closed the gap almost immediately. 'I want to know because I can't take it anymore. These past few days, as bad as they've been, they've brought us together more than in the past decade. Before this we could get through our days with barely seeing each other, but after this is over I can't go back to that. I don't want to.' Pain contorted Ben's face.

I did that. I'm the one who's brought this suffering.

Ben advanced, forcing Toby to retreat until his back hit the wall. With nowhere left to go, he had to surrender.

'There's something I've kept from you, and when you hear it I don't know what you're going to do.'

Ben towered over him. His eyes pleaded for an answer. 'What could you have done that was so terrible? You used to tell me everything and then you stopped. You shut me out.'

His stomach turned seeing how much he'd hurt Ben, remembering how much it had hurt to deny him.

Toby hugged himself.

I had to.

'It was the only way I had of holding on to what we shared. It mattered too much to me to destroy it and...' He took a deep breath that opened the locks to his secrets. 'And because of that, I never told you what really happened when our mothers died.'

Ben straightened, the mask descending to show a face clean of emotion.

Please, anything but this.

'They're dead because of me.' Toby beat his chest, hard enough to rattle his ribs. 'I caused the accident.'

Ben walked across the room. 'No, you didn't.'

'It's true.'

'No, it's not,' Ben said firmly. 'Your mum was driving too fast, she swerved and lost control of the wheel. The car left the road, flipped, slammed into a tree and burst into flames. Both Ella and Mary were killed, but you survived because you were in the back wearing a seatbelt.' He rattled off the facts like he gave testimony at an inquest. Official. Distant. 'I've seen the report, Toby.'

'Didn't you ever wonder why she swerved? On a stretch of road she'd driven on for nearly twenty years?'

Ben shrugged but it didn't come easy. 'Maybe when I was younger. Maybe when I later read the report. But I've seen enough car crashes to know that sometimes it's dumb luck.'

'That's me. Bad-luck charm.'

'You gave a statement. You said you didn't know what she saw.'

He bit his bottom lip. 'I lied.'

Ben scraped his fingers over his scalp, again and again. What Toby would have given to take Ben's hands and hold them still. To ease this.

'We argued,' he said.

'About what?'

'About you and me and us.'

'I swear to god, if you say this is my fault I'm throwing you out of here.'

'No, no, no. You're blameless in all this. All you did was give me what I'd always wanted. It was my fault what happened after.' He scraped one thumbnail over the end of the other, catching at the little nicks and breaking them down. 'The three of us were in the car, and your mum asked if I knew why you'd been acting so strange the past few days. Loved up, she called it. And I guess I wasn't thinking, or maybe I was feeling the same way, realising that what had happened between us was what I'd wanted, I... I told her.' His throat strained with the truth to come. 'I told both of them.'

Ben collapsed onto the couch. 'What did you say?'

'I said I hoped it was because you were in love because I was feeling the same way. It took your mum about half a second to realise what I meant and she broke out in this—' The anguish over keeping Ella's happiness from Ben scoured his body. It could have been Ben's last good memory of his mother, but Toby had kept it.

Maybe he'd been jealous.

'She broke out in a big smile, a great gasp, it was... God, she looked so happy. She reached behind and took my hand and squeezed. It was like how those close families around town look when the daughter from one marries the son from another. Except it was for us.'

Ben wiped at both eyes with the heel of his palm. 'You should have told me,' he whispered.

Toby's heart stung from bottom to top. He dug his fingers into his chest and kneaded the muscle. 'I know. I wanted to but then...then you would have known what else happened.' He breathed out. 'My mum took longer to grasp it. Ella explained and Mum lost it. Called me all the names under the sun, you too, and then blamed you and Ella, saying it was her fault you had turned out that way and how now *her* son was trying to corrupt me. It was just...horrific.'

His knees weakened and he had barely enough strength left to stay upright. He'd relived that moment so often over the years, and every time there'd been a twist of acid to go with it, a poison that tried to cripple him. Speaking it aloud, and to Ben, almost floored him. But Ben had to know the rest.

Toby straightened, sweeping back a few fallen curls. He sniffed. 'I couldn't believe that these hateful things came out of Mum's mouth. I tried to reason with her, but she wouldn't listen. She kept going on and on and on, getting more worked up. And Ella wasn't having any of it. She defended you and tried to convince Mum it wasn't something to be angry about. But it got worse, and all these other things came out about their friendship and then they were screaming at each other. It was so bad and then...and then Mum lost control of the car.'

Warm dizziness swirled through his head. His eyes slid closed but that didn't stop the ghosts shrieking. In fact they wailed louder.

'Ella screamed and told her to watch out, but by then it was too late and the car jack-knifed. It was a mess. I got knocked out.' Toby thumbed his left bicep where the break had been. 'Your mum was thrown out the windscreen while mine was broken over the steering wheel. When I came to, I screamed at her to wake up, but she was dead. Then I saw the flames and dragged myself out of the car, over to your mum.' He swallowed a few times to wet his mouth. 'I got to her but she... The car went up and burned my mother's body, but I dragged Ella's with me as far as I could. I wanted you to have her back. But... oh god... but I had to leave her behind.' His eyes stung in a ring of tears barely held back. 'I'm sorry, I had to leave her.' He wiped his nose with the back of his hand.

'Eventually the police and the firefighters came. I got to safety, but I could still see the fire burning, and I kept thinking how I'd caused this. And how I'd killed your mother.'

His breath shuddered through his body and emerged into a thick silence. The cicadas in the summer evening, the whirr of the fridge, and the slow creaking of the roof and the floorboards became louder. Toby had crushed Ben beneath the weight of his revelation. Standing with his back against the wall, he dared not approach.

But the quiet stretched and his heart, stripped of energy from the recounting, thrummed in nervous anticipation.

'I'm sorry,' he said.

'Please leave,' Ben whispered. He stared at the floor with his hands holding his head.

His heart froze, casting a chill through his body that hardened him into ice. Cold. Empty.

No, not this. It can't end like this.

'Ben, talk to me.' He risked a few steps closer. What he really wanted was to fall at Ben's feet.

'No!' he shouted. 'Leave. I won't ask again.'

He shivered. How could this happen? 'But—'

Ben launched off the couch and strode past him to the front door. Opened it. Waited. Eyes ahead. His free hand bunched into a fist.

I've blown it.

Ben vibrated where he stood. Ben wouldn't ever use unjust force against him, but Toby didn't want to be strong-armed out of a cop's home. His feet dragged on the way to the door, pausing in front of Ben, but Constable Fields was already moving and using the door to herd him out.

Toby found himself on the front step. Ben was closed to him—perhaps forever—and night had fallen over Echo Springs.

Ghosts stalked the land.

The darkness hid a man who wanted him dead.

And tomorrow was on the other side of a very long night.

★★★

The Echo Springs Hotel was quiet, even for a Tuesday night. A few regulars held up the bar, others played a game of pool. Apart from a couple of nods hello, they left Toby alone to nurse his beer in a booth as far as possible from everyone. He couldn't go home, wasn't ready to go back to the station, so this was as good as it was going to get. And the drink gave him something to do besides wait outside Ben's door like a stray dog whining to be let in.

He should have kept his mouth shut. He took a long drink, the full-strength brew landing on top of the one he'd had at Ben's. But rather than drown his sorrows, they pushed them to the surface, sloshing about on top of foamy waves.

Had he really thought Ben would understand? He'd revealed he'd been the one to get his mother killed. How else was Ben meant to react? He squeezed his eyes shut, his hand covering them as if he could make it all disappear and go back to how it was before.

But before what?

'Mind if I sit?' Erika Hanson said.

He wiped his hand down his face, about to tell her to leave, but she was already sitting and dumping a stack of papers and files on the table in front of her. She didn't look at him, her focus on the pages, no doubt searching them for some sign of her missing brother. At least Erika was the sort of person to not in—

'Want to talk about it?' she asked without looking up. She shuffled through a couple of pieces of paper, pen in one hand, its end tapping away.

If he said no, she'd leave it at that. After the short time they'd been working together, he at least knew that about her. He appreciated her professionalism and her dedication, and if he said he wanted to be left alone, she'd accept that without being insulted. Problem was, he *did* want to talk about it. The words burbled up inside him, a desperate panic to pour out and have someone listen and hear what he had to say. All these years keeping it locked up and spilling it once to Ben hadn't been enough.

So he told her.

And she listened.

She didn't flinch when his voice cracked or when he wiped away half-formed tears, or fill the silence when he fought to hold himself together. And when he finished, when he told her what had happened to Ben and how much he'd meant to him, she waited until he'd stopped talking. Her hand hovered above his for a second before she lowered it and their skin touched.

'You know you didn't kill them, right? And there's no way Ben could think that either.'

'You didn't see the look on his face.' He cringed at the memory of it. He could have lived with his guilt if it had meant he'd never see that pain on Ben's face again.

'I carried the guilt of my parents' death for years,' she said, withdrawing her hand. 'Not only had I survived but I'd failed to save them too, and that made it worse.' Her parents were another statistic for country road deaths. The numbers hid the awful impact on the town and those left behind. 'But it wasn't true. It wasn't my fault they died, just as it wasn't yours.'

He didn't want to play tit-for-tat over who caused their parents' deaths, so he kept quiet. As far as he was concerned he'd ignited an argument that had blown his mother onto a suicidal crash course and taken Ben's mum with her. He was culpable.

'Ben knows that too,' she continued when he didn't respond. 'You've given him a shock, that's all. He needs time to process it.'

'But it would have been better if—'

'A lot of things would have been better if other things weren't done first. It doesn't matter. You do what you have to do to survive and then you deal with the consequences later.' She got a faraway look in her eyes before shaking it off and coming back to focus on him. 'Ben will come around. His heart's too good to hate, and considering how he looks at you, he could never hate you. Not in a million years.'

Fingers stroked his heart before they shoved their nails in. If what she said were true, then he'd wasted too many years holding on to this secret, keeping Ben's mother's final moments to himself, dissolving as much of the old Toby as he could in the hope that there'd be nothing left for Ben to love and he could move on.

But Ben hadn't. Unless now it really was too late. Erika might be right, but she couldn't know for sure. He should have told Ben when they were younger, and then none of this would be happening. He could have done it if he hadn't been terrified. Then his house wouldn't have burnt down and Jared wouldn't be after him.

Shoulda. Coulda. Woulda.

Idiot.

He drained the beer, hoping it would quell the impotent rage boiling inside him. *This is all your fault.* He shoved the voice aside, and grabbed a stack of Erika's pages. 'What are you looking for?'

Better to distract himself with her problems than dwell on those of his own making. She didn't answer for a while, and he could feel her eyes on him, but he was done with self-pity. He'd blown it. Time to move on and assault the next problem head-on—whatever that was going to be—and hope Ben found it in his heart to forgive him one day.

Chapter Thirteen

Ben's ringing phone reached into his sleep and dragged him out of tortured dreams. He smacked his hand down on top of it, and ground the sleep out of his eyes.

It had taken an age to fall asleep, what with the heat and Toby's revelations replaying through his head. Only when he'd decided on his next course of action had he drifted off. He was going to be on night shift so he could afford the lie-in.

He held the phone in front of his face.

Six-thirty am. Dispatch calling.

Fat chance of sleeping in now.

'Fields,' he croaked.

'Major fire incident. All officers to attend.'

His heart punched into his throat. Jared. Toby. He was awake now. But the nightmares had followed him out.

'On my way.'

He leapt out of bed, pulled on his uniform and ran out the door into a hot wind. He inhaled smoke and his lungs squeezed to expel the air.

Jared had picked a good day to wreak havoc.

Ben sped to the station and rushed inside. Two officers followed in after him but the others were already there. Superintendent Stuart greeted them, her face bleak as she outlined the situation.

'We've got multiple fires surrounding the town.' She pointed to three points on the map, one in a paddock, one in scrub and the other in a broad area in the south. Burn-off hadn't happened for about three years; it was a surprise this hadn't come sooner.

'You four, you're to position yourselves here on the Mitchell from the north and stand by ready to stop traffic. There's a fire crew stationed there battling that blaze. The wind is pushing it away from us so that's not the main threat to Echo Springs, but if it shifts we're going to be in trouble.'

She pointed to the south. 'Here's the biggest fire and it's blowing our way. Officers from Newmont are redirecting traffic at this point but I want a blockade at this junction. No one leaves town from this road. Only emergencies get through.'

'Regional support?'

'Units are coming in from the surrounding towns but they're taking time. Fire Rescue volunteers have been called up and the firefighters are coordinating them. Helitax has already dropped a load on this fire,' she indicated the blaze in the west, 'and a team has nearly knocked that one out. I want the rest of us on crowd control. Emergency vehicles have to get through, everyone else gets out of the way.'

'Suspects, boss?' Hartley asked.

The superintendent looked at Ben. 'Fields?'

All eyes turned to him. Did they know this was his fault?

'Jared Fairfax.' He picked up a wanted flyer from his desk and displayed it to the team. 'Twenty-six-year-old Caucasian male, black hair, one-hundred-and-seventy-three centimetres tall. Car registration CC33GF.' He passed the paper around and they jotted down the description. 'Former drug dealer, out on parole. I sent him down so he's come for revenge. He hasn't been seen at his mother's house in Newmont since early yesterday. We suspect he's responsible for the fire at the cemetery and the one that destroyed the Grimshaws's house. We don't know if he's armed but assume so. Anything else, boss?'

'I want him caught, Fields.' The superintendent's eyebrows raised, her demand clear. 'He's your responsibility and I want him found before he can do any more damage.'

'Yes, boss.'

They had their orders. The officers dispersed. Leila came up and squeezed his arm but there was no time to chat. He jumped on the phone and called Jared's mother.

'What's he done?' Val's voice quavered.

'We believe he's lit fires around Echo Springs and they're threatening the town.'

'He never would have done something like this before—'

Before he'd been sent to prison.

Too bad he hadn't stayed there.

'Can you think of anywhere he might go?' he asked.

'I've tried calling him but his phone's off. I'm sorry, I don't know where he is.'

He'd tried too and the trace on Jared's mobile hadn't worked either.

'If you think of anything, please call me.' He hung up and walked over to examine the map.

The southern fires had spread and advanced on the town. They hadn't yet jumped the highway and joined forces to create a wall of flame, but if the wind kept up, Echo Springs was as good as charcoal. But the placement bothered him. It made sense for Jared to light one in the west as he'd come that way from Newmont. Even so he'd poured his efforts into the one in the south instead. Had he known what the wind was going to do?

Ben roved over that section of the map, and his eyes stopped on the springs that gave the town its name.

And the spot where he and Toby had first kissed.

Shivers scuttled up his back and crested his raised shoulders before a chill spilled down his chest.

He'd told Jared about it.

That's why the fire was worse there.

But where was he now?

Most arsonists liked to watch the effects of their crime, see the rush of activity as they wielded power over life and death. While Jared wasn't the stereotypical pyromaniac, he'd want to watch this. He'd want to make sure…

'Toby,' he whispered.

He grabbed his keys and hurried to the fire station. The garage doors were open; the tankers and pumps deployed. The offices buzzed with phones ringing and people coordinating teams on the ground. Smoke wafted through the air. He searched for Toby.

'Can I help you, officer?' a female volunteer asked.

'Where's Toby Grimshaw?'

'He's at the springs with three crews.'

The muscles at the base of his skull knotted into a fist. His breath stopped and everything dimmed. *He's fighting that fire thinking I hate him. What if Jared gets him?* Black crept along the edges of his vision. He fought for breath. He had to get out there. He inhaled and the world solidified.

'Send a message to them,' he said. 'The arsonist is coming for Toby.'

Chapter Fourteen

'Bring it back in, Toby.' Adrian's voice crackled through the radio.

Toby didn't respond. The water ran out and he switched the hose to pump foam, blacking out a section of the ground. He'd attacked the fire's flank but barely contained it. His muscles ached after nearly two hours up and down the highway. Two other teams were stationed further along this line, holding back the blaze that erupted out of the heart of Echo Springs's namesake. Gum trees exploded as their oil superheated, and a carpet of flames swept across the grass. Coal-grey smoke billowed, casting embers and ash into the sky.

If he'd died in the house fire, then Jared wouldn't have done this.

Sweat poured down his skin as the heat rolled over him and through the suit. He bunched his shoulders, trying to dislodge the knots that bulged across them. Aiming the hose at the base of the flames, he swept left and right but failed to find a rhythm. His hands were sprained from holding on for so long.

'Toby!' Adrian shouted. 'Inside now or I drive off without you.'

His breathing laboured through the mask that kept the toxins out of his lungs. Clamped over his mouth and nose, it itched. He was tempted to rip the damn thing off. Five minutes without it would do the trick. He blasted the ground with one more jet, then jogged to the tanker.

Adrian started packing up the hose and yanked it out of his gloved fist. 'Get in the cab.'

Anger clawed the backs of Toby's aching eyes. He shoved Adrian against the truck. 'Watch it.'

He reared up, and their helmets bashed together. 'Quit acting like a dick with a death wish. Get in.' He jerked his head in the direction of the cab and continued storing the hose.

Toby squeezed his fists. Adrian couldn't speak to a superior—to him!—like that. He was about to ream him out, but Adrian finished packing and stormed around to the other side of the truck and climbed in. The engine roared to life. He had no choice but to get in or get left behind.

He slammed the door and Adrian drove. The tanker kicked up dust and dirt as its tyres tore up the paddock, bumping over uneven ground, setting a course ten minutes down the highway to refuel. Toby pulled off his helmet and mask, then shook his hands free from his gloves and unzipped the front of his coat. Cool air blasted through the air-con vents but heated blood thundered through his temples.

'You ever talk to me like that again—'

'You keep behaving like this and there's not going to be another chance.' Adrian watched the road ahead. 'You'll die out there if you don't pull your head in. Nobody wants that.'

The tirade Toby had been about to unleash died on his tongue.

'Here,' Adrian said, chucking Toby a bottle of water from the seat in between them. He reached forward and snatched a packet of electrolytes from the dashboard. 'And this.'

He did as he was told, ripping open the sachet and pouring it into the bottle. He put it to his lips and his raw throat instantly soothed. The more he drank, the more he wanted. How much fluid had he lost today? He'd fought the fires while Adrian stayed at the tanker. Those had been Toby's orders. They were going as fast as they could but the fire seemed to be growing. What if he couldn't stop it?

He lowered the empty bottle and tightened the lid.

'More.' Adrian thrust a second bottle at him.

'I'm fine.' He propped his elbow on the window and rested his head on his knuckles. The blaze roared in the wing mirror.

'You're staying behind at the pump,' Adrian said. 'You're not in the right frame of mind to do this.'

He stared out the window across paddocks yet to burn, at homes yet to be destroyed. More lives to be ruined.

'What's going on with you? It's not like you to put yourself in harm's way.'

'We're firefighters.' His voice ran as flat as the highway. 'We do this all the time.'

'That last sector you got too close to the head instead of sticking to the flank. You only needed the wind to change suddenly and you'd have been engulfed. That was a rookie error, Toby.'

His neck flushed and the skin around his throat prickled. He covered his mouth so Adrian couldn't see him cringe.

If Adrian hadn't shouted at him through his headset to fall back, he wouldn't have noticed if the direction changed. He'd been too busy thinking about Ben ordering him out of his house.

He'd been so angry.

He shut his mouth. Arguing with Adrian wouldn't do any good. They needed to refill the tanks and get back out there. Hopefully by that time the Elvis helicopter would be ready to drop a load from the sky.

Adrian eased up on his nagging, but the crew at the pump had heard the barrage over the radio. He took their ribbing, biding his time until he could get back out there. One of them asked if he was alright to continue.

'He's fine.' Adrian answered for him, ignoring his narrowed glare. 'He's staying with the tanker this time, aren't ya, mate?'

The bossy bastard's smile punched him in the gut.

'Like hell I am.'

'It's either that or you stay here. Your call, Grim.'

He bristled. They knew he hated that name. Luckily they didn't use it often. Only when he deserved it. The other crew watched him and waited, and for the first time in his career, he felt like telling them to get stuffed. The job could go to hell. What was the bloody point of being here any longer?

But Adrian's you-know-I'm-only-looking-out-for-you grin matched the ones the other guys wore. The muscles in his jaw eased. He wasn't ready to smile but he was ready to return to work.

He sucked his teeth. 'Whatever,' he said and their laughter pushed him to the tanker.

The drive to their sector was done in silence but the tension had eased. They passed the McCormacks' hundred-year-old homestead, empty now that the fire had gotten so close. Their cars were gone but a motorcycle had been left abandoned in the driveway. They hadn't wanted to leave but the danger was too great.

Adrian suggested a different section of the advancing fire and Toby got them as close to it as they could get on the sealed road before cutting across the paddock.

'Here's good, don't you think?' Adrian asked.

Toby hit the brakes and killed the engine. Adrian jumped out of the cab first, taking his equipment with him, and slammed the door.

A wet ball of shame lodged at the back of Toby's throat. His head hit the headrest and his eyes slid closed. Exhaustion scraped his bones. He'd been fighting on all fronts and battle weariness had set in. Despite this, Adrian should be the one to stay behind while he stood in front of Jared's anger. But now the guys knew he was struggling and their confidence in him had crashed.

It would have been better to keep silent and take the truth about Ben's mother's death to the grave. What use was a firefighter who couldn't be trusted to do his job? But he struggled on. The fire was only getting worse.

He slid out of the cab and his boots hit the dirt. He leaned in and grabbed his protective gear and the radio burst to life.

'Unit four-zero-four, message from the police. Be on the lookout for suspected arsonist. They say he's coming for Grimshaw. Recommend unit withdrawal. Do you copy?'

Something hard and round jabbed between his shoulder blades. He froze with his hand hovering over the transceiver.

'Turn around, Toby. Slowly.'

The pressure on his back abated as he was given room to back up and turn to see a shotgun levelled at his chest. Jared's finger rested on the trigger.

The radio squawked again. 'Unit four-zero-four, do you copy?'

This was the first time he'd seen Ben's ex up close. His tense eyes were the colour of river water after the rains. His hair was a little shorter and straighter than Toby's. They were evenly matched in size and height, although Jared's shoulders were broader and his biceps slightly bigger. Adrian's bushfire mask covered his mouth and nose, and he'd claimed his coat.

'What did you do to Adrian?' he asked.

'He's fine,' Jared said. 'Grab your mask and don't try anything stupid.'

He reached back for the yellow mask, his eyes searching for anything he could use to protect himself from Jared's attack. Water bottles and a helmet weren't enough.

'Quit stalling.'

The shotgun prodded him and his spine stiffened. He turned and Jared signalled for him to put on the mask; the air flowing into his lungs became easier to inhale, even if his breathing was shallow.

'What now?'

'We're waiting for someone.'

Dread pitched into his stomach like a tree crashing to the ground.

Ben, please don't come.

'He won't come. They're too busy protecting the town, you know, the one you're intent on destroying.' His voice didn't come out as scornful as he'd intended; the mask muffled some of the sound, the rest quivered on his fear.

'He'll be here. He's nothing if not dependable.'

Jared motioned for him to move away from the truck and towards the edge of the fire. The heat intensified and sucked sweat to the surface of his skin. He could try to grab the gun, but the gear weighed him down. He was likely to get shot in the back before he'd turned ninety degrees.

'You've got it wrong!' He shouted over the roar of flames. 'There's nothing going on between Ben and me.'

I'm going to die out here.

'Stop there. That's far enough.'

Flames licked at the ground a metre from his feet.

'Did you hear me? Ben and I are not together.'

Desperation scratched up his throat. He wanted another chance.

I never told him I loved him. I thought he'd know but I never said it.

'Shut up, Toby.'

The gun barrel jutted into the base of his skull. His heart galloped around inside his ribcage, yanking air into his lungs. He didn't want to die but if the opportunity came and his death meant saving Ben's life, he'd take it.

Chapter Fifteen

Ben spotted the tanker parked in a paddock and dwarfed by the inferno. In the distance two figures moved against a backdrop of crimson flame and jet-black tree trunks. Heat waves distorted their bodies, making it impossible to tell who they were, but that was definitely Toby's unit. His foot slammed the pedal to the floor, and the patrol car tore up the distance. The siren wailed. As he got closer, the figures moved towards the flames, and he lost sight of them.

No! No! No!

He cut into the paddock, the tyres sinking dangerously low into the dirt, but he gunned the engine and pushed through as the dust flew. He skidded to a halt behind the truck. He drew his weapon and lowered his body out of the car, searching for signs of movement. The car door shielded him as he slipped out into an intense heat. His shirt, weighed down by a bulletproof vest, was plastered to his skin.

Backup was on its way but this looked wrong. Two people had been there but now they were gone—and he'd hazard a guess that one of them was Jared. No firefighters operated the hose, and a motorbike lay discarded behind the back of the truck. No wonder they hadn't found Jared's car. Continuing his scan of the area, he spotted two legs jutting out from the other side of the tanker. Checking he wasn't about to be ambushed, he broke his cover and ran. Adrian lay unconscious on the ground, blood wet in his hair and on his forehead. His hands had been cuffed to the side of the truck.

Shunting his gun to one hand, Ben felt for Adrian's pulse. His touch roused the firefighter and he groaned.

'Adrian?' he shouted.

He lifted his head lazily, his eyes fluttering open. Fear bulged in them and he scrambled to get away.

'It's okay, mate,' Ben said. 'You're fine. What happened?'

Adrian's chest heaved as he got control of himself, then he doubled over and coughed. How much smoke had he inhaled?

'Some guy came at me—' He coughed and spat black spit. 'From behind. I didn't get a good look at the bastard. Get me out of these, will ya?' He rattled his hands. 'There'll be some bolt cutters on the tray above my head.'

Ben grabbed the tool and opened its jaws.

Adrian pulled the cuffs taut. 'He's taken my jacket and my mask. Where's Toby?'

'Not here. I think he's been taken hostage.' He applied pressure and the link snapped.

Freed, Adrian struggled to stand.

Ben helped him up. 'Backup's coming.'

Adrian leaned against the side of the truck. 'If they're in the fire, then they don't have long. Things can change fast in there and it's only getting worse.'

'Then I'm going in.' He turned to leave.

Adrian grabbed his arm. 'It'll be suicide, Ben.'

'I'm not leaving Toby in there to die. You do what you can but I'm going after them.'

Maybe Jared will take me and let Toby go instead.

'At least take some protection.' Adrian opened the back of the truck and pulled out a coat and a mask. 'Use them. I'll try to keep the fire at bay but we're up against it.'

Ben put on the gear and crept to the edge of the truck. He peered around into the forest fire, the land undulating as it deepened towards the springs where it descended into a fiery amphitheatre. Smoke wafted out and in the gloom he spotted a man-shaped shadow ahead. Only one. His palms sweated, making the hold on his Glock shaky.

He marched out of his cover, his weapon pointing in front of him. Navigating around burning patches of ground, he struggled to define distances and details. He tensed, ready for the shot that'd blow his head off. Flames roared around and over him, glaring down at him as he advanced. The figure stayed where it was, sharpening as the smoke thickened, thinned, then parted to reveal not Jared, but Toby.

The breath he'd been holding exploded out of his lungs. Toby. Alive. His hands were up, his helmet gone, but he had his coat and the mask kept him from suffocating. Behind him waved claws of yellow, orange and deep red that lashed out to snare him and drag him into hell.

But where was Jared?

'Are you alright?' Ben shouted, coming closer.

Toby's eyes widened, but he needn't have worried with the warning. Jared edged out from behind him, enough to reveal the shotgun levelled at Toby's head.

Ben's pulse resounded through his body in measured and certain beats. Faster than normal but steady. Police training kicked in and he fixed Jared's head within his sights; it was the only part of him clearly visible.

Neutralise the target.

Minimise fall-out.

What if he hit Toby?

Nerves burbled in the bottom of his stomach, and he tightened the grip on his weapon. He breathed as deeply as he could to suppress the rising fear until it muted enough for him to relax his hold. He sharpened his focus and readied for a clean shot.

With their mouths and noses covered, they could have been twins—if not for the crazed look in Jared's eyes, and the urging in Toby's.

He strengthened his stance. He wasn't leaving alone.

'Lower your weapon or Toby's dead,' Jared barked.

'Don't do it, Ben,' Toby shouted. 'He'll shoot you.'

Jared's eyes darted to Toby, and Ben used the distraction to inch closer. 'How's this going to end, Jared? Backup is on its way. The fire's getting worse.'

'It doesn't matter. I'm not going to jail again and neither of you are leaving here alive.'

Ben cracked a vertebra in his neck. 'Let Toby go. He's got nothing to do with this.'

'I want you to see your lover die,' Jared's gravelly voice yelled at him. 'I want your heart ripped out of your fucking chest knowing it's all your fault.'

The words struck his heart. He fought to hold onto the gun.

'He's not my lover.'

Toby arms tensed and rose higher.

'I've seen you together.' His eyes narrowed.

'Then you were watching the wrong people. We're not even friends.'

Defeat washed over Toby's face and he closed his eyes. Ben's chest constricted. They had to survive this and then Ben could explain. Hopefully Toby would listen.

'So why was he at your house?'

Inch by inch, he narrowed the distance between them. 'Because I had to tell him about you setting fire to his place and almost killing him and his dad.'

'You expect me to believe you two have nothing going on?'

How much had Jared seen? Had his face peered through his window the moment he kissed Toby? Or did he assume?

Toby's arms sagged. 'That's what this is about? Jealousy?'

Jared jammed the gun barrel into Toby's back. 'Shut up,' he leered. 'Ben ruined my life so he could be with you. He couldn't wait 'til I was behind bars so he could come fuck you.'

'I suppose he planted the drugs as well,' Toby spat.

'Toby, shut up.' Ben was still too far away to intervene if Toby goaded Jared into firing his weapon.

Toby rounded on him, facing him down, forcing Jared to raise the gun higher and aim it nearer Toby's face.

'Don't you dare move,' Jared said.

'So it's Ben's fault you were a drug-dealing scumbag? Ben's fault you dated a cop and used him as cover?'

'I loved him.' The gun punctuated Jared's declaration.

'Bullshit. Do you know the damage you caused? Do you know why he's back here? Because the cops in Sydney thought he was bent. Guess whose fault that was.'

The muscles surrounding Ben's spine pulled tighter. Toby was defending him. He wasn't just buying time. His voice carried more than fury. He was ready to do battle on Ben's behalf.

Jared inched back as Toby advanced. Ben crept closer, watching the flames, watching the gun, watching for a clean shot. He heard the scrape of boots on gravel behind him and lowered a hand to his side to tell them to wait. Jared and Toby remained fixed on each other, and their positions began to shift.

'Do you know what Ben's been doing back in Echo Springs? Rebuilding his life after you nearly destroyed him.'

'Good. He deserved it. He was meant to stand by me, but instead he dobbed me in.'

Ben ignored Jared's whining for what it was, a desperate attempt to avoid owning up to problems of his own creation. But Jared wouldn't take Toby's gibes much longer. He'd lash out if cornered. Toby would say the wrong thing and make the hell they were already in worse. As the pair argued, Ben used Toby's distraction to narrow the distance between him and Jared.

'How dumb do you have to be?' Toby said. 'Ben gave you everything. And all you gave him was pain and humiliation.'

'What about you? The way he talked about you, you'd think you were the bloody Messiah, but you didn't treat him any better. When we came here, I wanted to punch your face in for what you did to him.' They kept moving, Toby gaining ground, Jared giving it, until their back and forth brought Ben behind Jared's back. He had a clean shot. He just needed to take it.

'Maybe if I had, he could have gotten over you.' Jared jabbed the gun in Toby's face again, and Ben's finger slipped in front of the trigger. 'Then I wouldn't have spent two years locked up. Do you know what it's like for a fag in jail? Especially one who dated a cop?'

'You want pity? You forced him away for what? Money? Power? You're pathetic.'

Jared braced the gun against his body. 'And you're dead.'

Ben's heart punched into his ribs and he thrust his gun into Jared's back. 'Drop the gun, Jared,' he bellowed. Rage surged through his body and flowed into his hand, increasing the pressure on the trigger. Jared's head turned and his eye shimmered with impotent fury.

It'd be so easy.

But Toby grabbed the barrel of the shotgun, angled it up and wrenched it from Jared's hands. He flipped it and stepped back out of Jared's reach.

Jared lunged for Toby but he swung the gun and clocked Jared across the chin with the rifle butt. His head snapped back with a loud crack and he collapsed to his knees.

A breath fired out of Ben's lungs. He was impressed at Toby's speed.

Ben holstered his weapon and ripped out his handcuffs but before he could slip them on, Jared roused out of his stupor, charged Toby and slammed into his stomach, carrying him forward, away from Ben, away from safety. The shotgun dropped to the ground and the two of them tumbled over each other, propelled by Jared's shock attack. They plunged into the burning scrub.

Fire rose and the cracking of burning branches covered any sound of their fight.

Ben's body hardened like he'd been encased in concrete, and he stared at where Toby had been.

Gone.

His brain rebelled. It wasn't possible. He stumbled forward but three sets of hands grabbed him and forced him down. Officers rushed past him, their thundering feet carrying them to peer into the terrifying maw of the inferno that had consumed Toby. He fought to break free but there were three of them and only one of him.

'You're not going in there, Ben.'

'We have to save him.' Was that him? He sounded so distant.

'Leave it to Adrian, alright?'

The firefighter ran past, dragging the hose and searching the blaze. Why did he hesitate? He knew Toby was in there. What was he waiting for?

'Get out of here,' Adrian shouted. 'The fire's getting worse.'

Ben looked up, looked around. The flames had grown taller, looming over them and threatening from above as well as below. Sweat cascaded over his skin. He tasted slate. Toby was still out there. There was still a chance.

Officers heaved him away, but he resisted as much as he could, never taking his eyes off that spot.

Losing Toby was not possible. It couldn't happen. Not because of him.

'Come on, Ben. We have to go,' Mac said.

His heart wrenched from his chest and incinerated in the fire. He was left with cinders and soot. He should have shot Jared. If he had, Toby wouldn't be fighting for his life. He'd have had a chance to explain, to say sorry, to say thank you.

They hauled away a shell.

But then Adrian hollered, fired his hose and disappeared into the gully. Ben wrestled free and hurtled towards the edge, watching, hoping, as Adrian cut a path through the blaze. He shot after him, and followed the black path until he reached Adrian returning with Toby under his arm.

Relief shattered Ben's body but Toby had lost his mask and he collapsed to the ground, even with Adrian's support. Ben dropped beside Toby's body. His fingers dug through the warm dirt and hefted Toby into his arms.

He jogged up the crest and out of the fire. His colleagues tried to help him but he wasn't letting go. Toby's suit scalded the exposed skin on his hands.

But it didn't matter.

Only Toby mattered.

Chapter Sixteen

A day in the hospital and Toby was back out fighting the fire. Discharged against medical advice. He had to get back to fighting the blaze that was still raging across parts of Echo Springs. He and Carl were out extinguishing the last of the fire on a scrap of land to the south of the Buchanans' property. An old wooden shack had been caught in its path.

The fire hadn't engulfed it completely, burning down the rooms on the right of the building but leaving those on the left largely intact: smoke-damaged and blackened but still standing. The flames had been beaten back and Toby entered the house to get the last of them, not to save the remains of the house, which had been abandoned long ago, but to ensure no embers were left behind.

Down a short hall, he passed into the kitchen, half of it blackened, the other half still resembling a lived-in abode. An old wooden table and two chairs, then behind that in the wall an old stove and beside that—

He hollered for Carl, dropped the hose and ran over to the body slumped against the wall. He shook off his glove and reached under Peter Hanson's neck for a pulse but the grey-tinged skin and still chest were enough of a sign that looking for life was pointless.

His body was as flat and drawn-out as it could be to get away from the fire and smoke. His right arm was handcuffed to the stove, the skin bruised and bloodied from where he'd tried to pull himself free. Chained, he couldn't escape. And he couldn't have got down low enough to avoid the smoke. Death would have been inevitable.

This was going to break Erika's heart.

'Jesus,' Carl said from behind him.

'Can you do the final sweep?' he said, getting up and walking outside to call the police. He'd been foolish enough to believe they were going to get through this blaze without a death—Jared excluded. Guess he'd been wrong.

The cops were on their way. Meanwhile, he and Carl returned to putting out the flames as they licked their way across the paddock. When the patrol car arrived about forty minutes later, he and Carl were done and ready to move on. Hartley stepped out of the car followed by Erika carrying her bag. Although the victim was her brother, she was still the town's forensic pathologist. And she'd want to see this for herself.

He left Carl to pack up the tanker and walked with Hartley and Erika over to the house. Hartley's hand slipped into Erika's.

'I'm sorry it's like this Erika,' he said as they followed him down the hall. They'd left Peter as they found him. Hartley stopped at the edge of the table, close enough to see Peter's body, but Erika continued right up to her brother and crouched down next to him. She felt for a pulse as well, and then her hand moved to lightly stroke her brother's face. She sniffed and her head raised, her shoulders slumping forward before stiffening. Hartley went and knelt behind her, placing a hand on her shoulder. She turned her head towards it and looked at the handcuff that had stopped her brother from escaping.

Her hand hovered over it and then closed into a fist. Toby came closer then and saw the gouged nail marks along Peter's wrist.

She stood and turned to Toby. 'Thank you for finding him. Now I know whatever he'd gotten involved in, he'd been forced to do it against his will. Thank you for giving me that.'

He didn't know what to say in response so he hugged her. 'Will you two be okay from here? Carl and I have more work to do.'

She nodded. 'I've got Harts and we've got work of our own to do here as well.' With any luck, Peter's body and the scene would give her the answers as to who had done this to him, but for now she could stop wondering where he was.

He gave her hand a final squeeze and nodded goodbye to Hartley. It was on the end of his dry tongue to ask how Ben was doing but now wasn't the time and there were fires still to fight.

★★★

Toby blasted the ground with a jet of foam and extinguished the last embers. Fire controlled and contained.

'It's done?' Adrian sidled up to him.

He nodded, surveying blackened earth, charcoal stumps and a sky laden with smoke. After three days, it was out.

If the rains ever returned, they'd see such colour.

He must be tired if he was thinking about flowers.

'I think we've earned a drink.' Adrian nudged him and they stamped back to the tanker, loaded it up and hit the road.

Fatigue swamped him as he collapsed into the passenger seat. He hadn't fully recovered after his short stay in the hospital, but though he struggled to keep his head up, he couldn't rest yet. His need to see Ben intensified, sitting on his chest like a tonne of ore.

Adrian drove them back to town and pulled into the station. Another tanker had returned and was parked in the garage. They went inside and joined their mates, welcomed by whooping and hollering at a job well done. They wanted to celebrate. He wanted to find Ben, but they wouldn't take no for an answer. They shoved him into the shower, and he washed the stench of smoke and the remains of ash out of his hair and skin. What if Ben had meant what he said to Jared? They weren't lovers or even friends.

Twenty minutes later his teammates corralled him down the road to the Echo Springs Hotel. He'd have a drink then go. He'd need the liquid courage. He couldn't bear the weight anymore. Better to know once and for all.

But the hotel was packed and they entered to applause and shouts of appreciation. Carl kept a firm grip on his arm as he cleared a path to the bar to order their drinks. His plans of sneaking away after one drink folded as he accepted the handshakes and the pats on the back. His energy dwindled after five minutes. He rubbed his eyes but he couldn't dislodge the exhaustion.

He breathed deep to brace himself—dreading another minute of this— and inhaled the smell of beer and sweat and...leather.

Warm, sun-soaked leather.

His head swam as the intoxicating scent coaxed him into opening his eyes. *Ben!*

His mouth curled into a broad smile, parting his lips, and a breathlessness stole through his lungs. Emerald eyes shone down on him and that dimple—that ensnaring dimple—furrowed his cheek. His arm slipped around Toby's waist, his head tilted down and their lips met.

The crowd fell away as Toby's eyes closed and he leaned into Ben, out of sheer relief at releasing a love long withheld. Lips fitted to lips as their soft, strong touch launched a torrent of sparks into his desperate heart. His hand reached behind Ben's head. He would never let go.

Until Carl nudged him—he was a dead man—and broke the spell. The chattering of the pub, quieter than before, rushed back in along with an awareness that flushed his cheeks. They were now the centre of attention.

'Looks like thirsty work.' Carl offered him a beer.

Ben pulled back but didn't let go, his smile looking a little too pleased with himself and unfazed by everyone's scrutiny. And while Toby wanted to get back to kissing him, he didn't want an audience. They needed to talk anyway.

'Drink it yourself, mate.' He slipped his hand into Ben's and pulled him through the crowd and outside. Knowing looks and mostly smiles followed them. It helped that Ben's hand fit so well in his. He squeezed harder, as if he could take an imprint for a memento. Just in case.

Once outside he didn't stop until they'd reached the garden and found a quiet spot beneath the shade of low-growing trees. But Ben didn't want to talk. He pressed him against a trunk and his devouring passion crashed into him. Need stampeded through his body and plunged into his groin, churning up the desires he'd only stoked with his imagination. The feel of Ben's arms, the hunger in his lips and the press of his pelvis brought a moan to his lips. Oh god, he wanted it. When they'd kissed at Ben's house, stopping had nearly killed him, but knowing it could have been taken away from him had made it easier. Did he have to fear that now?

He raised a shaky hand and placed it on Ben's chest, using all his willpower to push him away. Their lips were the last to separate. 'Stop,' he panted.

Ben's breath heaved and his wild eyes twinkled. Had he forgotten?

'Don't you want to talk about what happened?' Toby asked, still struggling to fill his lungs. His legs quivered; the tree stopped him from dropping.

Ben frowned at him. 'He's dead. Did you...do you blame me for what happened?' He stepped away.

A hook yanked on Toby's heart. 'What? No! You're not responsible for what Jared did.'

The last he'd seen of Jared he'd been plunging deeper into the heart of the blaze. If he screamed, Toby hadn't heard him, not over his own desperate breathing and scrambling to get out. Then Adrian appeared and guided him back. When he saw Ben, he'd collapsed.

Ben's eyebrows deepened as he scratched the back of his head. Toby couldn't wait to run his hand over that buzzed scalp and brush away the worry.

'And you're not pissed at me for falsely accusing you or your dad? Or for putting the whole town at risk and nearly getting you killed?'

He'd be lying if he said it hadn't hurt that Ben hadn't trusted him. But their past hadn't been the shining example of faith it could have been. It was something they could work on. 'I wish those things had never happened but I'm not going to hold them against you. Did you really tell Jared that stuff about me?' His thumb kneaded his left palm. Dirt still lay in the lines.

Ben shrugged. 'I thought he was the one but when I told him about my past with you, I knew that wasn't the case. Telling him felt like a betrayal to you, that I'd somehow killed our memory.'

He took Ben's hand, pulling him closer. 'You know it wasn't your fault, though, right? Why I kept away? Are you sure you can…that you're…'

Christ, how was he going to say this without completely ruining it again?

Ben squeezed his hand. 'You didn't kill her. You didn't kill either of them. And you didn't cause the accident. All you did was tell her the truth about how you felt.'

His heart stuttered. 'About how I still feel.' He sighed. 'But the way you looked when I told you. I thought you'd never want to see me again.'

Ben stroked the back of Toby's hand. 'It was a lot to take in, but I didn't blame you. I kept thinking how awful you must have felt and how long it must have weighed on you to keep it secret. I should have tried harder. I let you down.' The stroking stopped and Ben hung his head.

How could he think he ever let me down?

Toby reached up and placed his hand on Ben's cheek, lifting his head so he could see his eyes shimmering. 'You saved my life. How about we call it even?'

Relief broke across Ben's face and his smile returned. Toby grabbed the front of his shirt and pulled him down to his lips. Ben readied for a kiss but Toby paused, revelling in the faux indignation in Ben's eyes. He laughed. 'I love you, Ben Fields.'

Toby kissed him, softer and slower than before, and his heart bloomed, a green shoot emerging out of the desolation to heal a dry land that had lain barren for far too long.

Epilogue

Four months later…

'Are you sure it's this way?' Toby skittered down another bank of rocks. When Ben suggested they come to the springs, he'd expected it would be to where they'd first kissed. He hadn't expected it to look so unfamiliar. The rains had encouraged some life back to the land but a lot had changed in ten years.

Ben halted a few metres ahead, his long stride having carried him further down a path only he knew. His shoulders slumped. When he turned, his lips had bowed into a pout. 'You mean you don't remember?'

Goof.

Toby rolled his eyes, causing him to miss his footing and slip. His arms flailed as he skidded over sand and stones and slammed into Ben's chest. He was saved from hitting the dirt but the air punched out of his lungs. Looking up into Ben's smiling face, it took even more effort for his breath to return.

'If you wanted a hug, you only had to ask.' Ben wrapped his arms around him and squeezed, hard and rough.

Toby laughed. 'Get off, Strawberry.'

Ben bent close to his ear. 'Anything you say, Grim,' he growled. His breath tickled his ear and roused more than the hairs on his skin. Ben pecked him on the cheek and released his bear hug, substituting it for a firm grip on Toby's left hand, and returned to his mission through tree stumps and charcoal shrubs. Splashes of green, white and red caught his eye as nature returned. But as they descended deeper into the gully and towards the water, the forest thickened. His footsteps crunched over a carpet of grasses and scrub and leaf litter. He'd known the whole forest hadn't been lost but to see this much…

'You didn't tell him the exact location, did you?'

Ben gave him a sly smile and continued towards the river, rounding a boulder taller than Ben.

There it was.

Their place.

The trees had grown bigger, the reeds thickened, but there was no denying the C-shape of the pool, smaller than the more popular locations farther upstream, and its position beneath the shadow of three giant triangular rocks. He could even hear the laughter.

He strolled alongside Ben towards a flat rock jutting over the edge of the pool. They'd lain there with their friends and he'd stolen glances at Ben's long body, wishing he could touch his tanned skin. Furtive looks lengthened until Ben noticed and winked. His heart had flapped in his throat like a caught trout gasping for air.

'I'm surprised you could find it again.' He'd never returned after his mother had died.

'I came here a lot,' Ben said, 'hoping I could find some answers about what was going on with you.'

Toby squeezed his hand.

'After the fires, I wanted to find it again. It took time. We'd have come sooner but our schedules haven't been the greatest.'

It was one drawback of both partners doing shift work. Much of their time had been spent rebuilding Toby's house and helping Narelle care for his dad. And Ben was trying for a promotion too, so he was putting in extra hours. Thankfully they had all those times when they woke up together or he fell asleep with his head in the crook of Ben's arms.

Ben slipped the backpack off his shoulder and pulled out a picnic blanket, laying it down on the rock. He removed his tank top, exposing the built chest and abs and the light brown hair that extended past the waistband of his shorts. Desire rumbled deep in Toby's belly, so long denied it reared easily now, knowing it could be sated. To think that this man was his: beautiful, strong and caring. He bit his lip.

Ben saw him gawping and made his pecs dance, a dumb move that brought out his smile and the heat to his cheeks. He reached forward and pawed at Toby's shirt.

And I'm his.

He allowed Ben to pull his shirt over his head, then once freed, rushed forward and kissed him hard. He'd never get tired of Ben's lips. He had ten years' worth of kisses to collect.

'What was that for?' Ben asked when he was finally allowed to take a breath.

'Like you need a reason.' He sat on the rug and pulled off his shoes and socks while Ben settled next to him and busied himself in his bag.

Toby leaned back and looked across the water, memories flowing around him of not only the first time they kissed—behind *that* gum tree—but the time they'd made love behind the middle rock. He blushed. Quick, frantic, but fun and gentle and...

He leaned forward to cover his hardness. Perhaps they needed a repeat. That is if Officer Ben could overlook the indiscretion. He grinned and opened his mouth to suggest the idea, but his lover's smile was cautious as he looked at the letter in his hand.

Cold water trickled down Toby's spine and dripped into a cavern where light and life struggled to emerge. He'd wondered if Ben had kept it, but he thought it too dangerous to ask. If he didn't know for sure, he could pretend it had never been written.

Stupid but still...

'I was wondering what you did with.'

'You're not pissed I've got it?' A shadow stole across Ben's eyes.

'Why? You wrote it.'

'To you.' He paused. 'This was dumb. Forget I mentioned it.' He started to put it back in his bag, his body closing away from him like a torch fading into the gloom.

Panic prickled in Toby's chest. He'd faced deadly fires but the darkness hid his terrors. He needed Ben's light but he had to be the one to reach for it. Toby grabbed the letter and opened it.

Ben's blue scrawl bled out of the past. The words had started to fade—both on the page and from his memory—but combined they brightened.

'Dear Toby.' Pain clamped a fist around his throat. He'd never read it aloud before, frightened to be overheard and certain he couldn't have got through it without doubling over in anguish. But that was then. He cleared his throat and his voice broke free. 'All I want is to know that you're okay. There's not much else I can hope for now. We used to tell each other everything.'

Ben scooted over to sit behind him. His arm slipped around his waist and his chin rested on Toby's shoulder. The warmth from Ben's skin spread through Toby's back.

'I know you must be hurting because of the accident. I know because I'm hurting too. But it's worse because I don't have you. Why can't we get through this together?'

Pressure mounted behind his eyes, holding back tears he'd shed in private when his sorrow had become too great. God, how he'd wanted to tell Ben. He closed his eyes and breathed, leaning into Ben's warmth so it could ease the chills rising through his body. Ben knew now and Ben still loved him. The warmth grew and the tension in his eyes eased. He blinked and his vision cleared.

'It hurts so much to see you and not be with you. You won't answer my texts, my emails, my calls. All I see is you but you look through me. Please, Toby, I love you. Ben.'

The water burbled over the rocks as it flowed into the pool. The leaves rustled in the trees as a light breeze buffeted the gully. Sunshine cascaded down to dance across their skin. Magpies sang.

And Ben's heart beat against Toby's back.

'What do you want to do with it?' Ben asked, his hold still tight.

The letter had been a part of him for so long. Knowing that Ben had loved him—even without him knowing the truth—had been a glimmer of hope. Not strong enough to guide his way out, but bright enough to know there was one.

But now it showed a lack of faith—the faith of a boy and a man who'd failed to accept the love offered in his darkest hour. He had no such lack of faith now. The past unlocked its shackles from his heart and emerged into a bright future.

A future with Ben.

'I love you, Ben.' His whisper shook with the weight of his affection. He folded the letter and tore it in half then again and again. He opened his hands and the fragile pieces caught and scattered on the wind. He relaxed into Ben's arms, sinking into the comfort that he gave so freely.

Consoler, protector, lover.

He reached behind to rub the back of Ben's scalp, enjoying the soft sandpaper feel on his palm and the way that Ben leaned into it and moaned.

'I love you too, Toby.'

Also by TJ Hamilton

Buying Thyme
Finding Thyme

Echoes of the Past

TJ Hamilton

For my daughter, April.
Please, never tame your wild spirit.

Chapter One

According to the laws of attraction, Leila Mayne knew she should have never been a police officer at all; a cleaner or kitchenhand was all she should have aspired to. Despite all the obstacles she had overcome since coming back to Echo Springs, she would always be reminded of where she came from, and today was going to be one of those days.

'Mayne?' the man asked while eyeing off her light-blue name badge. 'You're not related to Ned Mayne are you?'

'Yep ... he's my dad,' Leila replied without lifting her eyes from the traffic fine she was writing out—but she could imagine his reaction. She'd seen this scene play out many times since returning to her home town of Echo Springs, this time as a sworn officer of the law.

His voice was familiar. Probably from one of the many parties her parents held as a kid. 'Now Mr Coleman ... I've only fined you for failing to stop at a stop sign.' Using the end of her pen, she pointed to the rear of the ute. 'I need you to get that left brake light fixed within the next twenty-four hours or else you'll receive a defect notice for that too. You have twenty-eight days to pay this fine, or fill out the details on the back if you want to contest the matter in court.' Leila delivered her rehearsed speech while tearing the man's copy of the fine from the book before folding it in half to hand over to him. 'Have a nice day, and drive safe.'

He gave her an empty smile and his three missing teeth on the left formed a black hole through the scruffy grey of his beard. His well-worn Ford ute was laden with concreting gear, which Leila knew was sitting well past the safety distance at the back but she chose to let that one slide altogether to satisfy her own need to prove she was not a total asshole.

As she walked back to her patrol car, she heard Mr Coleman call out from his window. 'Great! This is all the town needs, a Mayne with a badge!'

The old off-white ute kicked back into life with a low moan and squeaked as if in pain when he drove away from Leila. She'd known it was coming. The comment—they always had to remind her of where she came from. But it was her choice to come home after finishing her training at the Police Academy in the spring, and this was the kind of response she was prepared for. Head held high, she got back to the comfort of her air-conditioned Mitsubishi Lancer. It was the glariest police car within the fleet and all the cops hated it so she was always the one to be stuck with it. It was mainly hated because it wasn't a four-wheel drive, but also because its blue-and-white chequered pattern took up the entire side panels, making it stick out like a sore thumb around town. But Leila knew she was going to have to do more than drive the gaudiest police car to get the respect of her fellow officers from the Echo Springs police station, so the hit to her pride was mild. She was alone on the streets for the first half of her shift, a rare luxury. As the lowest-ranking officer of the station, Leila was hardly ever left alone, but with Constable Sam Chalmers out of action today with a busted knee from a local cricket match, she'd finally been given the all-clear to go out for a few hours on her own.

★★★

Growing up in the housing-commission area of Echo Springs and having a surname like Mayne meant life was going to throw its challenges at Leila. Her dad, Ned, was known around town for being violent and drunk, usually at the same time. She held onto the times when he was sober, usually the week he came home from a stint in prison with a positive attitude about starting life in a new direction. That was, until a mate came past to celebrate his release, and then the cycle started again.

'Echo Sixteen,' Leila said into the car's radio piece.

'Go ahead Echo Sixteen,' came the amplified sound of a voice through the speakers.

She recognised the voice of Ben Fields, the only cop she felt completely comfortable around. He was coming onto shift that afternoon. Luck had shone light on her day.

'Are there any outstanding jobs?'

Pinching between her eyes, she braced for the response and hoped the news was positive.

'No outstanding jobs, Echo Sixteen.'

Hearing the news she was hoping for, a smile threatened to spread across her face but she bit it back and maintained her composure before talking into the radio again.

'Copy that. I'll head to the Terrance residence for a welfare check on Brayden.'

'Copy, Echo Sixteen,' Ben replied.

Her grin exploded.

***

Leila drove to the outskirts of town, where the green grass noticeably decreased and red dirt battled to take over anywhere it could. Both metaphorically and physically, the surrounding environment in this part of town had a harder edge. But to her, this was home.

She pulled into the driveway of Brayden Terrance's house, three hundred metres away from the house where she had grown up.

On his fourteenth birthday, Brayden Terrance had been standing in court for the fourth time in a year, this time for stealing a motorbike. The local magistrate, Bruce Northcott, ordered that he take part in the new youth justice initiative or face being transferred into the Northern Territory juvenile justice system. All the kids in town were terrified of being transferred out of New South Wales and into the notoriously harsh system in the north of Australia, so the threat was taken seriously. Leila had offered to be Brayden's support officer—given her family's history with his, she thought it might help—and despite many discussions surrounding the need for her 'transparency' and 'ethical practice', the boss of Echo Springs Police finally agreed to it. With Brayden's oldest brother, Jayden, already serving a lengthy sentence, this was a combined effort to prevent the same thing happening again.

'Echo Sixteen, going off at fifteen Ricardo Street,' she said into the radio before hooking it back up.

'Copy, Echo Sixteen.'

The house was white fibro with brown trim, and sat about a foot off the ground; typical for the area. Leila adjusted the uncomfortable vest crammed with her arms and appointments, and gave three hard knocks on the closed front door. The thud of footsteps came from inside, the gait too wide to be Brayden's. The smile threatened again, but she pushed the emotion aside to remain professional.

The door burst open with enough force to start the country's next cyclone and six-foot-and-four-inches of brawn stood in front of her; a frown furrowing his forehead with deep lines.

'I knew it was you with that stupid police knock,' he grunted.

Leila rolled her eyes. The frown slowly dissipated from the giant and a smile seeped into its place.

'Come here, Lah Lah,' he said, throwing his arms around her, pulling her through the doorway.

She chuckled and hugged him back. 'Do you have to call me that?'

She wished Hayden Terrance, her lifelong friend, ex-boyfriend and now worst nightmare, would take her a little more seriously while she was in uniform, but she'd missed his big arms so much. He'd almost doubled in size since she left for the academy four years earlier. They were only eight months apart in age, but suddenly he seemed years older.

'I had to come home and see this for myself.' Holding her out in front of him, he eyed her up and down. 'I would've thought you'd look a bit bigger with all this shit hanging off you, but you're still a little runt. You do look a little taller though, I have to admit.'

Words struggled to make an appearance, but looking into the green eyes of her childhood sweetheart was something she wanted to savour, so she didn't mind the moment's disability.

Her eyes scanned the muscles on his arms and she squeezed them with a laugh. 'Are you on the gear or something? Your arms are like cannons.'

Hayden looked down at them and smiled. Raising an eyebrow, he teased, 'Like the gun show, hey? Nah, I don't need to touch that shit. It's just called going to the gym and becoming a man.' He tensed a bicep. 'Plus, my dad was a big guy too, remember?'

The mention of his dad punched a big hole into Leila's chest, and Hayden bit his top lip in frustration, obviously regretting mentioning him too. Uncle Mick had been a man-mountain and her dad's best friend. Six years earlier, he'd died in the back of a police truck while being transported to a prison in the city, launching a state inquiry into the way the local police had treated Mick in the moments before his death in custody. Given the profession she'd entered, and the people she now worked with, it was a subject that made everyone uncomfortable.

'I miss your dad every day,' she said, finding her voice again. 'Especially being back here.'

Hayden nodded. 'Me too, Lah Lah. Anyway, how's my little brother going? I heard there's this new thing you've got happening for the young ones, and you're now his support person or something? How long have you been back in town?'

'Almost twelve months.' She failed miserably at pretending she wasn't counting them. The gruelling challenges of the Academy were a picnic compared to facing a town where her family and her colleagues were well acquainted, for all the wrong reasons. Climbing Mount Everest would have been an easier path to take in life. But just like reaching the pinnacle of the mountain, the ease of the descent was in sight; so long as she avoided the occasional avalanche—in the form of her father. 'I get my first stripe in a couple of weeks so I'll no longer be on my probation. The boss already lets me go out on my own though and treats me like a striped constable.'

'You've been here that long already? Mum didn't tell me you were home until last week.' Leila knew. She'd made Hayden's mum promise not to tell until she was ready to face him again.

'Where *is* Brayden by the way? His curfew starts in half an hour, so he better be home soon.' Leila glanced around Hayden to see if she could spot a sign of Brayden being home.

Hayden smiled again, but while once she could read all his varying smiles, her separation from him meant she could barely even guess what this one meant.

'Thank you for trying to help him,' he said. 'I don't want him to turn out like the other boys have in my family.' He placed his hand on her shoulder, and suddenly became the boy who'd protected her all her life. 'But you can rest your knickers, he's just out the back … Mum's really proud of you, you know.'

She nodded in reply. His words reminded her why joining the police force was the right thing to do. She had to come home and show the other kids how it *could* be done. This is where she was supposed to be. She'd fought hard to be here, in the town where she belonged. Now that Hayden was back as well, she could almost believe everything would be all right.

Chapter Two

'Still drink coffee without milk?' Hayden asked while pouring boiling water into coffee cups.

Leila couldn't help but stare at the flex of his arms as he poured. She cleared her throat, pondering the crass jokes from all the guys at the station about what her coffee said about her sexual preferences. She was more tolerant of it than she thought she'd ever be. The misogyny, subtle and overt, was ever-present, but in an industry geared towards men she was not about to start a feminist revolution, so she chose to ignore it without biting. There was a lot she'd underestimated about herself since joining the police force.

'Is there any other way to drink coffee?' she said finally, letting a smile roam freely on her face.

Hayden snorted and shook his head. Leila caught the dimples that only ever made an appearance when Hayden found something really amusing. Earning them was like wearing a badge of honour. The twenty-five years spent growing up together meant she could read his face like a book, as she was sure he could hers. It was sometimes intrusive, yet there was such familiarity in Hayden's actions that Leila relaxed more than she had in years.

'You've always been the one to do things differently,' Hayden joked and sat next to Leila at the square kitchen table. 'Is it what you imagined it would be—being a cop?'

Raising the cup to her mouth, Leila blew into the steaming coffee. 'I imagine it's much like becoming a parent; all the ideas and training won't even come close to preparing you for the actual reality of it. Nothing can prepare you for being a cop until you experience it for yourself. I mean people avoided me when I was growing up but this is a whole new ball game. *Everyone* avoids me. It's like I've got leprosy or something. No one trusts me anymore. Do you know how that feels?' She glanced up into Hayden's eyes and suddenly regretted feeling so at ease around him. 'Things are different from this side of life,' she tried to explain. 'You start to see the world for what it is. I just wish people would learn to behave themselves so my job would become obsolete. But we both know that's not going to happen so there has to be the good people in the world to stop the bad.'

'Not all cops are good people, you know.' His words had an edge of anger that made her wince. 'Why did you come home, Leila?' It was the question she was hoping to avoid.

Their gaze remained fixed on one another for a moment, and Leila was the first to look away. 'I could ask you the same thing.' Her words almost passed under her breath. Hayden didn't answer so she buckled. 'I had to come back to Echo Springs. It was the right thing to do.'

'The right thing for *who?* You could have been a cop in the biggest city in Australia; far away from this place. I bet you got good grades at the academy too, so you could've gone anywhere you wanted. But you chose to come back here? Why? Haven't you punished yourself enough for growing up in this shithole? You had an opportunity to break free; that's what you told me you were doing. You told me you'd never step foot back in this town when you left me in it, remember?' Hayden ran a hand through his hair in frustration.

'What do you mean I left you here? You could've come for me, but you didn't, you just let me go. So I stayed away.'

He was calmer now, sipping from his coffee cup. 'You didn't want to be *you* anymore. You didn't want to be Leila Mayne.'

'I didn't hate my name. I hated everything it was a product of.' She looked down, bringing the coffee cup to her lips to let the hot liquid wash away any regret. 'I can't explain why I wanted to come back … it's just home.'

The truth was, she wished Hayden had come and saved her, but looking at him now, it was clear their paths had grown so far apart that there might as well have been a continent between them. Footsteps on the back deck brought a welcome interruption. Brayden's face appeared around the door and Leila smiled. Brayden walked into the room with an unusual spring in his step, but when Brayden slapped his older brother on the back as he passed, Leila understood why he was happy. As she got up to hug Brayden, he stretched out wide, pretending not to go anywhere near her vest full of weaponry. Rolling her eyes, she warned him not to tempt fate.

'You should see Leila's right cross, bro,' Brayden said as he punched the air in front of him with his fist.

Hayden's eyes met Leila's. She shrugged and grinned. 'There's a lot you don't know about me now, Hayden Terrance.' She turned her attention back on Brayden. 'You're going to get a good night's sleep tonight so I can kick your ass again tomorrow morning, aren't you?'

'You're on, and better keep your fist up this time.' Brayden tapped the right side of his face with a clenched fist, ducking and weaving as if in a boxing ring.

She laughed, loving how far Brayden had come in the Youth Justice Program. Taking the last sip of her coffee, Leila rinsed the cup. As she watched the last of it wash down the sink, she imagined for a moment that her feelings for Hayden could be rinsed away that easily too. But for now she sighed under her breath and strived for a more casual conversation. 'Thanks for the brew, Haydog. Good to see you again. Are you staying in town for long?'

'I'll walk you to your car.' He deliberately avoided her question by opening the door, then burst into laughter at the ridiculous patrol car sitting in his driveway. Had she been so strong a distraction when she first arrived that he hadn't noticed before?

'It looks like something that belongs in a circus parade! What are you supposed to do with this piece of crap? Who you stopping in that tin can?' He laughed harder.

Leila raised her head as high as she could. 'I'll have you know this car did just fine in the last pursuit I was in with my partner. We got the shitbags in the end. Some idiots from north came into town to pinch cars. If it weren't for me and my partner Ben, there wouldn't have been a pursuit. We're the ones who kept the pursuit alive long enough for the highway team to get here. We pushed this little thing so hard, it was steaming by the time we got back to the station.'

As she talked, Hayden opened the driver's door for her but then shut it again before she could get in. 'Sorry, I'm sure you don't need me opening your door when you're the authority around here.'

'Why did *you* come home, Hayden?' she asked.

He shook his head but a rueful smile slipped out. 'I wanted to come and check on mum and Brayden.'

Leila opened the car door to get in. Winding down the window, she replied, 'Well, it's good to see you anyway.'

Hayden leaned into the open driver's side window, causing her to look around the streets, checking if anyone saw. He clocked her reaction and stepped back.

'Are you going to tell me how long you intend to stay around?' she tried, one final time.

'Let's not try to complicate things between us. I could be gone tomorrow if I see everything's going well out here.'

His phone rang in his pocket. He pulled it out and looked at the screen. 'I better get this,' he said as he kissed his index and middle finger and pointed them towards her.

As Leila reversed out of the driveway, she realised the distance between her and Hayden was more like planets than continents. She glanced in her rear-vision mirror as she drove away, torn between wanting him to stay longer than a night, and wishing he'd never come back.

Chapter Three

Ben looked up from the front desk as Leila walked through the front doors of the station. 'What's up? You look like you've won the lottery and your cat's been run over at the same time.'

Leila managed to break out of the filthy mood she'd been in for the entire ride from Hayden's place and chuckled. 'You don't miss a beat, do you?' she replied. 'I don't know how you're not lead detective in this place.'

'So are you going to tell me what's happened? Or is it *who's* happened? Does this have anything to do with the last address you called off at?' Ben raised an eyebrow.

Her game was up and she knew it. 'I just saw Hayden Terrance.'

Ben's eyes lit up. 'Ah, the *elusive* Terrance brother. I thought you never wanted to see him again?'

'I didn't expect him to come back so quickly. I only let Aunt Sue tell him I was home two days ago.'

Ben frowned. 'Well that either speaks volumes or it's just a terrible coincidence.'

'What's for dinner tonight? Whose turn is it to choose tonight's pub meal?'

Ben finished filling out details of a case on his screen and turned his attention back to Leila. 'Do we need a night out tomorrow to get your mind off this?'

Leila had never been close to Ben in school, in fact they hadn't really got along at all, but Leila's transition to the law gave them a commonality that they'd bonded over in the past twelve months.

'Sure, but I can't go to the pub knowing he's around.' Leila slumped into the office chair with a huff. 'So it has to be a very low-key night at home. No going anywhere. Just you, me, and … Toby?' she teased playfully.

'I don't know if I'm ready to include him into our crazy nights just yet. I'll only invite him if you promise not to break out the karaoke machine ever again.'

'No promise of that!' Leila laughed.

The sergeant's voice boomed out from behind the two-way mirror at the back of the station. 'Mayne. Fields. I've got tonight's taskings for you.'

Leila and Ben got up immediately and went straight into his office.

'Now that Siobhan is here to man radio, I want you out on the truck with Mayne,' Sergeant Cooper said to Ben.

'I want you guys to make some extra patrols around the vicinity of Far Trail Road tonight, the Bulls' Run end. Matty and Smithy said they saw some cars that look like they don't belong out there. They've been hanging around town for a few days, so keep your eye out. With Hartley gallivanting off overseas with his ladyfriend,' the Sarge grunted, 'Detective Senior Constable Hudson is taking on most of the pressure of the drugs investigation. That means everyone else keeps an extra sharp lookout.' He scowled.

Leila winced. Calling Detective Senior Constable Hartley Cooper's trip to the states 'gallivanting' was a bit harsh, given that he was helping his girlfriend, Erika Hanson, escort her elderly grandmother to a specialist hospital for treatment. Erika had been left to do it alone after her brother was killed, horribly, in a bushfire some weeks earlier. But it was no secret that the Sarge didn't exactly approve of his son's love affair with the cool and professional Erika. Still, everyone was pleased Mac finally got to work as a detective— something he'd been gunning for for a while.

'Sure, Sarge,' Ben replied, taking the paperwork with the list of areas for them to patrol.

The Sergeant directed his attention to Leila. 'How's the Terrance boy going?'

'So far he's turned up to every boxing session and went to two group sessions at the PCYC this week,' she replied.

Sergeant Cooper nodded. 'Good to hear. I hope we've got third time lucky with those boys.'

Leila's jaw clenched. The bosses were purposely testing her, and she needed to stay professional. She hated it when anyone related Hayden to his brothers. Hayden wasn't the shiniest example of an upstanding citizen, but he'd never been in serious trouble with the law like the rest of his family. If anything, he was the only one who had shown any type of prospect of breaking *out* of the family cycle. But the bosses never seemed to understand that, and with her limited rank and experience within the force, she wasn't about to challenge the Sergeant's opinion anytime soon. Instead, she bowed out of the battle and replied as calmly as possible, 'I actually think he's got a positive future ahead of him. It's all about empowering kids like Brayden, Sarge.'

From the cluttered paperwork across his desk, Sergeant Cooper looked up with an implacable expression. She continued, 'If there are enough people behind Brayden to make him believe he has a future, he's going to make better choices.'

Was that a hint of a smile in Sergeant Cooper's eyes? 'I hope you're right, Mayne.'

She'd pushed her rank's boundaries enough for one conversation, and made a brisk exit from the Sergeant's office before she ran her mouth off any more.

★★★

'Gee, Coops sounded really optimistic about Brayden Terrance.' Leila's voice dripped with cynicism. 'Even with how much Brayden is trying, Sarge still doubts him.'

Ben laughed. 'Wait till he hears about Hayden being back in town. I doubt he's going to be too happy about that, especially after Brayden's been doing so well.'

'What do you mean?' she snapped.

Ben fastened his seatbelt and started to reverse out of the car park. 'Brayden has been doing really well without the influence of his brothers around. I just know it will make everyone edgy, waiting to see if he can keep out of trouble with Hayden here.'

'Hayden's nothing like his brothers, and Coops knows that. He's just forgotten, and so have you, obviously.' Her voice cracked in frustration, and confusion about why she felt the need to defend Hayden so desperately. What if he had changed in four years and she no longer knew him like she used to? She'd changed too, in the most dramatic way.

'Just remember, for as long as your old man and Mick Terrance were young troublemakers, Coops was here cleaning up their mess. He's got a reason to be pessimistic about the fourth Terrance he's had to deal with in his policing career,' Ben said bluntly.

If anyone else talked about her family like that, Leila would be infuriated, but Ben presented the facts without any prejudice.

'They can all get lost. If I can change opinions about my family name, then anyone can.' Leila watched the darkened empty streets outside her passenger window, waiting while Ben took his time to respond.

'What if Hayden's been in some trouble that you don't know about?' he finally said. 'Have you ever *accidentally* looked up Hayden's file while you've been the buddy of his little brother?'

She shook her head. 'It's too risky. I already have the boss expecting me to do something wrong because of my family. Imagine if they caught me looking up Hayden's profile.'

'Why would they care about you looking up the details of Hayden Terrance when you have such an important role with keeping tabs on his brother? Are you avoiding any feelings for Hayden? People have watched you two together since you were kids. Why the change of heart?'

She couldn't make eye contact with Ben. 'Why all the questions? Do you think he *has* been in trouble? Do you know something I don't?'

Ben shook his head. 'I don't know. You know I never really had much to do with him or his family until I was in the job. All I know is that curiosity would have gotten the better of me by now. Especially if I had the expression you had on your face after seeing the guy today.'

Chapter Four

Hayden looked at his watch before glancing at the side mirror again. The drop car was late and he had no way of contacting the driver. He couldn't turn his phone on in case it set off a ping—the cops were always on his tail and paranoia tugged on the back of his neck. Rolling his head back, he stretched his shoulders up until he felt in control of it all again. He hadn't asked for any of this; it was thrust on him because of his brother. The carnage in this town wasn't his choice. 'Just this once,' Jayden promised him. Hayden swallowed as he thought about all the city's crooks who were willing to make a house call for Jayden if he refused his brother's orders. His brother's threat hadn't just been for him either … he'd implied it could be aimed at their mum, at their little brother, too, if things got out of Hayden's control. Jayden's warning about handing over Jacinta Buchanan's mines to his harder criminal associates from the city hadn't left Hayden's mind since he threatened it. What was he to do? He couldn't let it happen and since his brother was incarcerated, Hayden knew he was powerless to stop it. There had been so many times Hayden wished he shared a surname with someone else. Instead, he seemed destined to a life of dodging cops and finalising deals that were out of his hands.

Seeing Leila again had ignited a fire inside his chest. He pushed her out of his mind, but couldn't shake the contentment of being around her. He couldn't have just packed up and left, recreated himself the way she had. He was clever, but not smart the way she was.

A red Hyundai hatchback pulled up behind him; it was the car he was waiting for. Running his fingers through his hair, he got out of his Holden and pressed a button on the key to open the boot.

Hayden glanced around the dirt track that lined the boundary of a property where their drugs were manufactured. The bushland was thick with olive greens and the occasional spattering of brown. The landscape, from the deep red dirt to the dark green of the trees, all seemed hostile, trying to claim back its place.

A short, heavyset guy got out of the car, reaching for a bag on the back seat. Hayden nodded, but that was it. No names. No talking.

Hayden took the bag and a phone, which contained all the contacts Jayden thought he would need. He threw them straight into the boot, then got in his car and took off down the dirt track, speeding further and further away from town. The track ran along the border of Jacinta's sheep station, Bulls' Run, a place he'd known all his life.

When he and Jacinta were kids, they'd come down to these parts of her family's land, far from the prying eyes of her parents, and play anything from cops and robbers to cowboys and chiefs for hours in the old abandoned dug-outs. Sometimes her older brother Jamie and Mac Hudson had joined them, along with Jayden, although the older boys were forever trying to lose him and Jac and Brayden, who was still just a little kid tagging along. Jacinta's parents never approved of the Terrance kids, and wanted her well away from them, but Jacinta had never listened. Hayden struggled with using her property behind her back. Maybe he could pay his brother a visit again, to ask if they could relocate the lab to somewhere else, despite already knowing the answer. Unless he found a better location than the abandoned mines—which there wasn't—Jayden would just say no. One day Hayden would work up the courage to say no to his brother, but until then family was family. It's not like Jayden would hurt him, his own blood. But Jayden would hurt other people, and keeping his own mouth shut kept people like Jacinta safe.

He pulled up to the entrance of the mine shaft and got out of the car, grabbing the bag and the facemask next to it from the boot. He replaced the filters at the end of the mask and pulled it over his head, adjusting it until it felt comfortable, before making his way towards the abandoned mine tunnel, bag slung over his back. The opening looked more like a supersized wombat hole, and Hayden had to bend slightly to make his way through the darkened entrance. A round white pipe ran along the ground from the opening, pulling dangerous air from within the mine. The distant sound of glass chinking got louder further into the old mining tunnel, and became clearer when he reached an open room with trestle tables jam packed with glass tubes, bowls, hoses and steaming substances straight out of a mad sci-entist's den. Through his newly filtered mask, Hayden could still make out the harsh smell of fumes when he walked past to the lab cook, Larry. Larry, also masked, nodded at Hayden briefly but turned his attention straight back to the bubbling triangular jar. The ends of his bushy ginger beard wisped around the edges of the apparatus.

'I hope that's finally the ephedrine I need? This whole batch will be fucked if I don't get it into the mix ASAP.' His voice was muffled through the mask.

Hayden nodded and dumped the bag on the ground.

'No! Not there! Jesus Christ, Hayden. Do you want to fucking blow us both up? Put it up the back on the bench near the barrel.' Hayden reacted quickly, grabbing the bag and putting it to the back of the room. The room was filled with enough hazardous material it could create an outback Cher-nobyl if it exploded. Hayden hated the claustrophobic space.

'When will this be ready?'

'Well if you give me a hand here for a few hours, I'd get it done a lot quicker,' Larry replied.

Hayden shook his head in disgust, 'Sorry Larry, you know my deal. I'm not having blood on my hands. This is your dirty work.'

Larry's shoulders shook with amusement, 'That's where you're wrong, kid. The blood is already on your hands. Now get some gloves on, grab me that bucket from the back and measure out forty grams of ephedrine on the scales.'

Hayden sighed. The fear of knowing Jayden's threat was very real angered him. Jayden would send his crew into town to pay him a visit if he didn't do the drop. Protecting his mum and Brayden was paramount to Hayden's very being. He knew once Jayden's associates rolled in, even Jayden himself wouldn't be able to stop the cyclone of criminality. Those type of guys were the ones who broke the law because they got a kick out of it. They were the soulless who had seen the inside of prison walls, and for them nothing compared to the thrill of the hunt. Hayden had seen them in action at clubs in Sydney. After one visit to see his brother, Hayden knew his brother was no longer the person he grew up with. Ever since their father died, Jayden disappeared more and more. Or was he always bad, but his father knew how to help Jayden keep it contained?

He picked up a pair of red welding gloves and slid them on. Larry passed him a white bucket that once stored pool chemicals. The room had a dampness to it, which Larry said was ideal for keeping the chemicals at a consistent temperature. There were three sets of scales on the back trestle table, all layered thick with grime. Wiping the digital screen on the front, Hayden opened the duffles to lift out one of the many zip-locked bags of white powder; the crucial ingredient to making ice. He pulled the bag apart to unlock the air trapped inside, and a subtle plume of particles arose out of the bag, reacting with the air and creating a low fizzle that was only just audible. Hayden held his face away, tipping the powder into the plastic tub on the scales until the numbers climbed to forty. He re-zipped the plastic bag and dropped it back into the green duffle bag before tipping the powder into the bucket and handing it back to Larry. He turned to leave, no longer wanting to be part of the process.

'All yours, Laz,' he said, walking back past the drug cook. 'Can we get this finished up by tomorrow night so that we can get the hell out of here again? The cops will notice the different cars around town so we need to get in and out quickly.'

'I don't want to speed up the process, Hayden. It will compromise the quality. You know what your brother's like. He hates moving shit gear.'

Hayden glanced back at Larry, who was stirring the white bucket. The fizz of the mixture was clearly visible on the surface of the bucket's rim.

'Laz, just get it done before we get noticed. No doubt we'll be back here again in a few weeks if it's anything like the last lot that came out of here.'

Larry waved Hayden away and continued the procedures he had perfected over the past twenty years as a suburban pharmacist turned professional drug cook.

Hayden got back into his car and pulled off the mask, shoving it under his driver's seat. He drove back into town and pulled up at the front of Clayton's Chicken Shop. It was finally safe to turn his phone back on and he went straight to the photos, scrolling back past the recent photos of late nights in darkened clubs, binge drinking and people who never quite felt like friends. When he found the last photo he had of him and Leila together, he stopped. He had his arm around her, kissing the side of her temple as she smiled so hard her eyes almost squinted shut. There was a blur of colour in the background and it took him straight back to that night at the local carnival, when they were happy together. Right before everything went wrong.

Chapter Five

Leila turned the music up in her modest two-bedroom home, trying anything to drown out the unwanted thoughts of Hayden. She yearned to see Hayden for longer than the twenty minutes they'd spent together, so even the driving beat couldn't quell her anxious tummy. The morning's boxing session and group breakfast with Brayden and the other kids in the justice program had done its best to keep her mind from wandering too far, but it was the time at home alone that Leila feared most. She needed to stop thinking about Hayden. The bass to 'Rebel Girl' by Bikini Kill caused the old windows of her fibro house to rattle. She smiled and started dancing to the heavy drumbeat. This was exactly what she needed; her favourite punk music. Listening to this, she felt far from the straight-laced officer she tried to be at the station. There would always be something inside her that needed to break the bounds of her conformity and rage against the colleagues she felt so separate from, and feminist punk music did the trick.

Dancing in her living room, Leila began folding the pile of washing she'd ignored for the past three days. When she was finished she wrote her list of groceries needed to entertain Ben and Toby later that night. She was nervous about having her best friend's boyfriend over at her house, knowing the pair had only just reconciled after their rocky past.

Hayden's mum, Sue, was working in the deli department when Leila arrived to order the necessary items to make her favourite grazing platter. She had discovered the joy of a platter at the Academy, when the girls in her dorm made several of them during a marathon Netflix night. It was a lightbulb moment for Leila. To anyone else, grazing platters meant nothing, but to Leila they were what real grown-ups did—and something her family never would.

'I'll have two hundred grams of prosciutto, thanks Aunt Sue,' Leila said with a broad smile.

Sue's eyes ignited. 'Are you making one of those fancy platters of yours for anyone special?'

Leila knew Sue was referring to Hayden, and noticed the instant disappointment in her eyes when she told her, 'Yeah, Ben and Toby are coming over. Netflix and a cheese board with friends, what more could you want?'

Sue shrugged once. 'You kids these days. We never had none of this Netflix stuff or cheese platter thingies.'

'Maybe things would have been different if there were?' Leila couldn't stop from spewing the cynicism of her childhood.

Sue looked at Leila through the glass display cabinet, disapproval in her eyes. She had only started ordering in this particular cured Italian meat when Leila came back home. Not many people in town either knew or cared for such delicacies. Measuring two hundred grams, Sue wrapped up the sliced meat and handed the parcel over.

'No amount of Netflix would've stopped our good times, kiddo. We're just not those kind of people. Could you imagine your old man and Mick sitting down to watch movies together?' Sue said.

A light flush stained Leila's cheeks and she smiled. 'I guess not.'

Leila wanted to avoid talking about Hayden, but Sue was having none of it. 'Hayden said you came by the house in uniform. He's very proud of you, you know. It just takes people a little getting used to seeing you in the blue. You know that. But I told him it's still the same girl underneath the badge.'

Nodding, Leila replied, 'I didn't expect him to come home so soon.'

Sue's arched eyebrows screamed *I told you so*. Leila knew deep down he'd come home as soon as he found out she was here.

'Are you coming past your mum's tomorrow night? She's going to get a few roast chooks from the shop and I'll bring a potato bake. You should bring one of these fancy platters,' Sue asked before Leila said her farewell.

Leila didn't often wish she were on duty, but she did now. She already had an invitation, but was trying to avoid it altogether. How could Sue sound so pleasant when she talked about their families' version of dinner together? Her mum's idea of cooking was to buy roast chicken from the takeaway shop, and the rest of the night would be ruled by booze, a bonfire in the back yard, and an evening-ending fight; verbal or physical. Dinner was always a mask for the rest of the night's proceedings. Cath had other priorities—the end of the bottle. Leila had dodged going to her parents' place 'for dinner' for the past year, and was grateful to all the other guys in the station for taking the call-out to her house whenever there was a disturbance and she was on duty. But Leila knew there was more she could do to help her family's struggle with alcoholism. She was an only child, so it was up to her to change the future of the family name. It was only a matter of time before she had to accept that responsibility completely.

'I'll see how I go. I've got a few things I need to do tomorrow. I'll pop over if I have time,' Leila sidestepped.

Sue smirked. They both knew Leila was lying and had nothing else to do.

'It would be nice for your mum if you came over, love. She said she doesn't get to see you much, even though you're less than five kilometres away now.'

Leila contemplated replying with a comment about the effect her parents had on her policing career or the effort they'd made to see her when she lived in the city, but she knew the consequences, so she let her rebuttal go.

'I'll do what I can to come past,' she replied.

Leaving the supermarket, Leila was grateful to make it to the car without running into anyone else she knew. As she drove through Main Street, all the little things in town reminded her of Hayden, drifting in and out of her mind like a montage. She was adamant she could fill the place with new memories, but who was she kidding? Everything she knew about Echo Springs included Hayden in it.

Driving past the bowling club, a memory flashed of the blue-light discos the police used to run once a month. It was the place where she and Hayden had shared their first kiss—right in the middle of 'Promiscuous' by Nelly Furtado, at the end of the night. All the kids in town would count down the days until the next blue-light disco. It provided the same type of escapism that the Cooee Hotel brought to the working class on a weekend.

Leila needed to look into why the discos had stopped. It had been something so positive when she was growing up, and she could really sink her teeth into a new project. Anyone growing up in Echo Springs these days had little choice for social outlets other than skipping school to hang out at the brand-new skate park or driving out to the pools at Echo Springs ... if someone had a car. Smiling to herself, Leila knew this was part of why she had needed to come back here, to help the next generation flourish. She couldn't bring herself to see more kids like Brayden end up part of the system just because they thought they had no other option.

With her hands full of groceries, Leila carried her keys between her teeth. Walking up the ramp to her front door, she tried to navigate the bags and keys but it took her a solid four minutes of looping her hands through all fifteen-odd bags of shopping to carry it all at once, so she was hesitant to put down either handful. Pausing at her front door, Leila sighed and conceded defeat, ready to drop one handful of groceries.

'You look like you could do with an extra set of hands?' She instantly recognised Hayden's voice, and a flush threatened her cheeks.

How convenient. Hayden delicately took the keys from her mouth, and she obliged without objection. She couldn't bring herself to look him in the eye; not after thinking about him constantly all day.

'It's the gold key ... and thanks,' she said, only focusing on the keys in his hands—his big, strong hands.

Not that she was totally surprised, but where had Hayden suddenly appeared from? She watched him covertly, blissfully, while he picked out the gold key to unlock her front door. Excitement swirled through her body. This was exactly what Leila had been avoiding all day.

Chapter Six

Hayden offered to take some bags from Leila, but she pulled away stubbornly and continued through the opened front door. He followed her, amused at the sight of her strung with plastic bags.

'Mum said you moved into old man Walker's place,' he said.

Leila's pride in her house was everywhere, from the colourful rugs and the mismatched orange and brown couches, to the retro paintings of wild-life on the walls. This was not the old Leila, and he was confronted by how much she'd matured and evolved. It was demoralising yet captivating, and Hayden couldn't work out which Leila he preferred.

Following her into the kitchen where she dumped the shopping onto the chequered red and white linoleum floor, Hayden wanted to offer help, but didn't want to be rejected again, so he stood back, feeling unnatural as he tried for casual. Her long dark hair draped loosely around her shoulders like it always had, and Hayden craved running his fingers through it. She wore little denim shorts and a black singlet peeking out from an unbuttoned red and black men's flannelette shirt, and Hayden couldn't avoid staring at the curves of her body. She'd always drawn his touch and their absence had only intensified his need. But where did he start when there was so much that hadn't been said?

Leila rummaged through the shopping, pulling out the contents from the plastic bags and placing them across the original yellow laminate benchtops of her retro kitchen.

'Wow, this kitchen hasn't changed since I sold old man Walker some chocolates for the school fete when I was about ten,' Hayden laughed. 'I used all the money I earned in fundraising that year to buy lunch at school for the next month. How did I think I was ever going to get away with that?'

Leila looked up at him for the first time since he'd walked up to her front door. 'Did you really spend school fundraising money on canteen food?'

'Yeah, don't you remember I was banned from school camp the year our class went to the gold fields?' he asked.

She shook her head. 'I thought you were there for the gold fields camp?'

'Nope.' Hayden also shook his head. 'I spent about sixty dollars that was supposed to go towards the school, and my parents had to cover the cost of the four boxes of chocolates I'd sold.'

How could she not remember? These were pivotal parts of his childhood, parts that shaped him to be the person he was today: the person who knew better than to get caught.

'You expecting company tonight, or do you still eat enough to feed a third-world country?' Hayden eyed off Leila's haul of food.

It was a smart-ass comment and he wanted to stop himself, but there was so much he wanted to know about the new Leila. How else was he to react, now that Leila had materialised back into his life?

'I've got friends coming over tonight for a Netflix night.'

'Cool,' he said as nonchalantly as possible. Who were the friends?

'Are you going to Mum's tomorrow night?' She changed the subject.

Hayden shrugged. 'Apparently I have no choice.'

'Me either,' Leila chuckled.

Finally, there was a sliver of hope; they were still the same people, despite their different paths in life. 'Those two will never change. Mum and Cath will do anything to get us together in the same room.' Leila laughed, and he liked it so he continued. 'Remember the year when we weren't talking because I got caught smoking at school and you hated me for it?'

'I didn't hate you for getting caught smoking. I was mad when you gave up football to hang out with your brother's loser friends.'

Everyone in school knew they could buy pot from Hayden's older brother, Jayden, and Leila always hated him for it. When Hayden started hanging in Jayden's crowd, she was repulsed by the sight of him.

'It was the same time you were hanging around with that scrag, Michelle Carpenter.'

'Is that really why you weren't talking to me? You know, nothing ever happened between me and Michelle? She was only ever a friend.' Hayden dared a smile.

'Well I heard something *very* different. I heard she was your first.' Leila slammed the bottle of green olives on the countertop so hard the glass jar cracked in her hand. The juice spilled out over the floor, along with droplets of her blood.

Hayden moved in to help but Leila glared at him with intense fury, her eyes vivid green. He didn't understand what she was so mad about; she was the one who left *him*. She wanted nothing to do with *him*. Now it was *her* who had come back to Echo Springs to live her life when he was just managing to get on with his, without her in it. *He* should be the one who was angry.

'Just go, Hayden,' she said. 'I don't know what you've come here for anyway. Just go—leave me alone. This town is too small for us both to be back here. I can't even go out with my friends in town, knowing you're here.'

'Fine.' He would leave. He didn't know why he was here either. 'Have it your way. You always have. I'll be staying far away from the shithole pubs in this town, don't worry. This is a joke. I don't know why I bothered.'

Chapter Seven

Leila's chest tightened when she looked at the deep cut on her palm. A pool of thick blood formed and then cascaded over either side of her hand as her heart pumped faster. *Shit.* She wrapped her hand with a tea towel that Ben had given her with the quote 'I use the smoke alarm as a timer' written across it in black; a housewarming gift from five months earlier. She immediately regretted soiling it, but it was the first thing she had to hand. Getting into her car, she rushed to get to the doctor's surgery on Main Street before they closed.

The receptionist greeted her with a warm smile. Her full cheeks rounded like inflating balloons on either side of her grin and her pale blue eyes had an instant kindness to them that steadied anyone who walked through the clinic's doors in a crisis. Mrs Carpenter glanced at the blood-soaked cloth Leila was cradling and hastily buzzed the intercom for the doctor's room, and Leila was immediately drowned in guilt knowing her injury was caused by anger at this pleasant, helpful woman's daughter.

'Sorry to interrupt, doctor. I have Miss Leila Mayne in Surgery Room One as soon as you can see her.'

Mrs Carpenter came around from her reception desk and assisted Leila into the surgery room to the left of the small foyer. The doctor walked through a door opposite at the same time.

'Miss Mayne, what have you done to yourself?' Doctor Evans, the same doctor who delivered Leila, eyed off the blood-stained tea towel wrapped around her hand.

'Just a flesh wound, Doc,' she casually replied. 'I don't know my own Hulk strength sometimes.'

'Sit up on the bed and we'll take a look at the damage.' The doctor waved towards the tall consultation bed while he grabbed a trolley of medical equipment. 'Why do police in this town always seem to hurt themselves more when they're *off* duty?'

As the doctor unwrapped the tea towel, Leila's head spun and she felt the colour drain from her face.

'How about we get you laying back?' the doc said and guided her back on the bed before unravelling the final bit of tea towel. 'Yep, you've got yourself good, Leila. I'll have to give you a local and make sure it's properly cleaned out before I stitch you back up.'

Leila's head spun with wooziness, but she hated being vulnerable, so she covered her eyes with her arm. 'Yeah, whatever you need to do.'

She felt four pin pricks and blessed numbness in her hand as the anaesthetic worked its magic. 'So how are you enjoying being back in town?' Dr Evans asked.

'It's good to be home, but it's hard. I wonder why I bothered ever coming back here when it was easier to just stay away from the place.'

'Then why did you come back?'

Leila sighed. It was the one recurring question she really revolted against, but she needed to keep talking to keep her mind from the doctor scratching around in her numb palm. 'I guess I just wanted to come back and make a difference. Plus, this is my home. It always will be, no matter how much I try to hate it.'

'Then make a difference and ignore the naysayers,' he said.

Under the cover of her arm, she caught Doctor Evans peering above his thin glasses at her. She smiled. Yep, that's exactly what she wanted to do. Screw Hayden Terrance, or anyone else for that matter. She *did* come back here to make a difference. She felt as if she could run for the next female prime minister of Australia, until the doctor suddenly pulled on her skin and she felt it. Sharp pain.

'Oh that hur—'

Chapter Eight

As Ben walked into the doctor's room, Leila flashed a crooked, groggy smile from the bed.

'Here's my knight in shining armour. I love you, Ben Fields,' she slurred.

Ben looked at Dr Evans with a puzzled frown. 'I thought you only had to give her a local anaesthetic?'

The doctor nodded. 'Yep, but she almost passed out when I had to pull a large piece of glass out of her hand, so I decided to give her twilight anaesthesia. Now that she's coherent, sort of, she's had an interesting reaction to the pain medication.'

God, she *adored* Ben. A horrifying thought struck her 'We're still doing Netflix night, aren't we? I want to watch *aaaaall* the movies. I can see every freaking colour on the spectrum right now.' She scanned her un-bandaged hand across the room, following a shooting star.

Ben looked at the doctor again for answers. The doctor shrugged. 'This should wear off within the hour. It's just a combination of the anaesthesia with the heavy dose of analgesic. Some patients will present with a euphoric-like state, and she's one of the lucky ones.' Doctor Evans smiled before finishing writing notes on his computer. 'I certainly didn't want her driving home.' Ben smiled politely and put his arm out for Leila to take. 'Come on, princess.'

Leila squinted. 'I'll never be anyone's *princess*.' She emphasised the last word while trying to point her index finger towards Ben, but couldn't manage to control it. It just ended up circling within the vicinity of him.

'Wasn't I your knight in shining armour two seconds ago?' Ben teased.

Remembering was harder than she thought it should be. 'Oh yeah …
I guess you are … okay … but I'll only ever be *your* princess. No one
else's, okay?'

'Okay,' he said, still holding his arm out.

Leila linked her arm through Ben's and cradled her bandaged hand
against her chest.

Miraculously, they made it all the way to his car.

'I really mean it,' Leila said again as she grabbed Ben's face between her
palms—one bandaged. 'I really love you in my life.'

Ben laughed and gave her a quick peck on the lips. 'You are forgetting
one minor detail about which team I bat for right?'

Leila flopped back against the seat and blew out to make a raspberry sound
between her lips. 'So what, we can't love each other just because you're gay?
I could've told you you were gay years before you ever confirmed it. How
could you not eye off all the hot boys at school? Toby Grimshaw—prime
example. He's like a delicate cut of beef from one of those fancy gourmet
butchers in Sydney.' She licked her lips.

Ben buckled Leila into her seat and shook his head in amusement. 'My
boyfriend is more than just a piece of meat, I'll have you know.'

'Whatever you say.' Leila found herself reflecting on Toby's athletic physique, the way that all the girls swooned at school. Ben closed her door and
walked around to the driver's side.

'He's always been a hot hunk of a man,' she said, slapping at Ben as he
started the car. 'Go you!'

'That's funny, coming from a person who was adamant Toby was an
arsonist a couple of months ago.'

Meandering thoughts flowed in and out of Leila's head all the way home:
How she had managed to become the very thing her family despised and
redirect their former hostility towards police. She was surprised when she
first heard her mum come down hard on someone when they called police
'pigs' around her. She was proud to think her family were trying to be better
people because of her. But so far, her attempts to reconnect with her family
on a personal level had proven to be just as difficult as ever.

'You're a breath of fresh air, Mayne,' Sergeant Cooper had said after she
completed her first investigation, resulting in a conviction and suspended
sentence. She smiled wide, as Ben pulled into her driveway.

'Okay, princess, your chariot has arrived. Wait there a sec and I'll help
you out,' Ben said as he got out of the car. But Leila was no wilting flower

and opened the car door before he could stop her, face-planting on the ground a few seconds later. Ben started laughing when he heard her laughter. With her ass high in the air she formed a really terrible version of the downward dog pose, which made her laugh even harder.

'Oh love, you're a mess,' he said and he tried to pull her from the ground. 'Let me look at you.'

Ben brushed the dirt off Leila's cheek. 'I'm surprised you haven't grazed your face. You look considerably intact for the sound your head just made when it connected with the concrete.'

Ben assisted her up the ramp to her front door. The ramp, an adjustment Mr Walker had made when he started to rely on a frame, suddenly didn't seem as ridiculous as she had first thought.

Placing Leila delicately onto her orange couch, Ben took off her shoes. He swung her legs around as she flopped back against the cushions she'd made out of Australian vintage tea towels. 'The flying swallows look fantastic,' Ben said as he eyed off the flock of seven blue porcelain swallows sprawling across the wall above her television. It was the last thing she remembered him saying before she allowed the darkness to take over her tired mind.

★★★

Leila opened her eyes slowly to find Toby and Ben sitting on the couch adjacent to her, their legs intertwined as they watched television. She smiled as she turned her gaze towards the TV. A young River Phoenix walked on train tracks with three other friends carrying rucksacks.

'*Stand By Me*—god, I love this movie,' Her thoughts were clearer than they had been a few hours earlier.

'Ah, Sleeping Beauty awakens,' Ben teased.

'Enough of the princess references thanks.'

'You were a princess an hour ago.'

'Was not.' Her green eyes snapped to Ben. 'It was the drugs.'

'Yeah, the stuff Doctor Evans had to give you because you passed out at the sight of blood? You were only at that terrible car crash the other week, where the guy no longer had a head, and you were fine.'

'Nice details,' Toby quipped.

Leila rubbed her unbandaged palm against her forehead. 'I don't know what's gotten into me either.'

'You've been weird since Hayden's been back.'

'Who's Hayden?' She bit down on her smile, but failed miserably. 'He's not going to be a problem anymore. I've been thinking a lot today.'

'Did that hurt?' Ben teased her again.

She rolled her eyes. 'Very funny. I've realised I have so much to be thankful for, there's no point adding drama to the equation.'

She caught sight of the coffee table with a beautifully arranged grazing platter.

'Wow, this spread looks amazing,' she said.

'You can thank Toby for this one.' Ben and Toby shared a smile.

'Let's break out the good wine. I feel like we have to celebrate.'

Ben frowned. 'I don't think that's a good idea, Leila. Only a few hours ago you were as high as a pixie and confessing your love for me.'

Leila screwed her nose up. 'I was just happy to see you. I feel perfectly fine. I have a little cut on my hand, barely a graze.'

'But you're on some strong antibiotics.' Ben tried another approach but it was all in vain as Leila jumped from the couch, popping a green olive in her mouth, and made her way to the kitchen.

Ben shook his head and followed her into the kitchen. 'I've never come across someone so pig-headed.'

Toby laughed. 'She's always been that way.'

'*Oh my god*, these olives are amazing. Who did the marinade?' she called out.

'Well after you attempted to marinate the olives with your own blood, I figured a good dose of vinegar and garlic would bring them back to life again. Can't waste the Sicilians, they're too expensive.' Toby pushed his new friendship with her.

Leila laughed loud. 'Hell yes they are! Bloody brilliant thinking. I knew there was reason to like you.'

★★★

Once she finished off a bottle of her favourite twenty-dollar Shiraz Grenache from the Barossa Valley, Leila was desperate to head down to the Cooee Hotel for a dance.

'Like hell, Leila! You're not going anywhere. Who knows what you'll do in this state.'

She shook her head. 'I'm fine. We're going out.'

'How many fingers am I holding?' Ben held up three fingers in front of her.

Leila frowned. 'Are you serious?'

Ben huffed in frustration. 'Doc Evans had to ring me to get you because you were flying high and now you want to go out? Are *you* serious?'

'Yes I am. It's exactly what the doctor ordered so get your dancing shoes on because we're going out.'

'Only for an hour, and then we're going home whether you like it or not,' Ben succumbed.

'Ooh we're a '*we*' now, are we?' she replied with a teasing sing-song.

Chapter Nine

Leila was relieved to see the Cooee was quiet for a Thursday night. There were the usual regulars of the pub, but the Thursday dart crowd was absent for once.

'Why aren't darts on tonight?' she asked Karen, the publican.

'Barry Saunders passed away last week, so they're saving this week's match to coincide with his funeral and naming the competition in his honour,' Karen replied.

'Oh no, that's really terrible, Karen. I didn't realise.' Ben clearly didn't know about the death either, which was unusual for their profession in this small town. 'That's a really moving gesture from the Darts Association. How are the Saunders kids?'

'Rick and Josh are on their way back from the city to be with their mum,' Karen replied.

As the trio got their drinks from the bar and made their way to the beer garden at the back of the pub, Leila couldn't help searching to make sure she wouldn't run into Hayden. It was the last thing she wanted. Ben pulled her over to the darkened table under a big tree, furthest from the door.

'You sure you're alright to be out, Leila?'

She shot him a look of annoyance, but she could tell he wasn't about to let it go.

'I'm just making sure you're okay. Stop being a bitch about it!' Ben said.

Leila took in a deep breath and checked herself. 'I promise we're here for one hour. As soon as we've finished these drinks, we'll head inside, commandeer the jukebox and dance before we all turn into pumpkins and have to go home.'

Ben took a sip of his drink and agreed. 'Thank god there's no footy on tonight, or else we wouldn't be putting any music on.'

'I'm not dancing,' Toby added.

Ben smirked. 'Neither am I. A chair dance is all I manage while pixie here jumps around like an idiot. It's always cringeworthy dancing … but entertaining. You're in for a treat.'

Leila chuckled. It was true. She only cared what the town's people thought of her when she was in uniform.

Uniform-Leila was different from off-duty Leila, and she worked hard to maintain the ability to switch between work and home. Her upbringing and now her adult career choice gave her unique insight into the town—and a unique position both when she was at the station, and when she was hanging out at the pub.

Leila sculled the rest of her drink and slammed it on the table a little harder than intended.

'Ease up on the glass in your hand, Leila. You only have that one left for the next two weeks, best you look after it,' Toby warned.

She gave him a slight nod, got up and made her way back inside, not waiting to see if the guys followed her. With a quick detour past the bar, Leila ordered herself another drink before making a bee-line for the digital jukebox. She used the touchscreen to flick through the album covers, stopping at 'Push It' by Salt-N-Pepa. 'Oh shit, yes.'

The moment the unforgettable cow-bell beat started, Leila busted out her best moves, singing along as loudly as possible.

'Here, catch,' she said to Toby as she threw her handbag at him.

Leila could feel the combination of wine and prescription medication, and let it carry her through 'the running man' and 'the sprinkler' right through to 'the worm'. The song was a classic favourite of hers and she just let the joy of the beat take over. When the final digitalised chords finished, Leila heard a loud clap in the distance and dramatically threw herself forward in a bow. She had impressed at least one of the patrons and was pleased, regardless of how embarrassed Ben and Toby might be. As she rose from her bow, she saw not her two friends, but the bulky figure of Hayden leaning against the doorway, clapping and grinning. She forgot to breathe. His sandy waves were tamed more than usual and the grey V-neck tee he was wearing shaped his chest perfectly.

Leila turned to Ben and Toby, exaggerating a look of shock as she briskly walked towards them. 'Right, well that's perfect time to call it a night then. I've got my dance in, so we might as well get out of here early.'

As Leila grabbed her handbag, she gulped her second drink. Ben and Toby finished their drinks and also got up to leave.

'Hey, stop, Leila,' Hayden called out after her.

She didn't look back; she couldn't. If she did, she would stop. His hot grip wrapped around her wrist as he caught her un-bandaged hand on its backwards swing.

'You're really injured?' He sounded concerned.

'As if you give a shit, but yes I am.'

'Hang on a minute, you told me to get away from you and leave you alone.'

'I also told you to stay the hell away from the pubs, but you seem to have ignored that request.'

Leila turned to Ben and Toby, who were waiting a few feet in front of her.

'Come on, Leila. We're going, remember?' Ben said.

Leila glanced to the sky, hoping advice would drop onto her from above.

It was Toby who now sounded annoyed. 'Ben, I think we should give these two space to work their shit out. I'm tired.'

Searching between the stares of Ben, Toby and Hayden, Leila was losing the battle between her heart and her head.

Hayden's voice was deep and silky, with a hint of sadness beneath it. 'Leila, I don't understand why you're trying to avoid me. I thought it was going to be nice to see you after all this time, but obviously you don't feel the same.'

She wished she was brave enough to tell him how happy she really was to see him, and how it scared the shit out of her at the same time.

'I just want to talk to you, you stubborn shit.' Hayden's voice was more frustrated than angry.

She shot a look to him. His heat was kind of sexy, in a challenging way.

'Ben, it's fine. Go home. I'll call you tomorrow.'

'Drink?' Hayden offered.

Bemused, shocked and slightly inebriated, she managed an eye roll for an answer before following him to the bar. As she walked away from Ben and Toby, she faintly heard Toby reassuring Ben that she was more than capable of looking after herself in this town. It made her smile that Ben cared so much.

Chapter Ten

As Karen poured from the bottle of Glenfiddich straight onto ice, Hayden glanced across at Leila as she fiddled with a disposable coaster.

'You hit the hard stuff now? I never thought I'd see the day.'

'What's that supposed to mean?'

'Your old man should've had shares in a whiskey distillery by now.'

Leila shrugged. 'I guess the job does that to you.'

'Being a cop makes you want to drink? Why would you work in a career that forces you do something you've hated for so long?'

Karen handed over their drinks and walked to the other end of the bar, leaving Leila and Hayden alone in the unusually quiet pub. Hayden didn't know what to say. Leila took a solid gulp of scotch and turned to him with softened eyes.

'So I haven't asked you what you've been doing with yourself for the past four years?'

Hayden paused; he couldn't exactly tell her he'd been doing everything to avoid running his brother's criminal enterprises in Echo Springs while Jayden served out his sentence at Silverwater prison in Sydney. Remembering life before his brother was convicted of armed robbery, Hayden talked about the programs he was helping to run at a government-funded recreation centre in Sydney.

'I've been teaching some of the disadvantaged kids from the city to learn how to cook and get the basic skills needed to step into an apprenticeship,' he said with a burst of pride tingling within.

Leila sparked up. 'Really? That sounds wonderful. You've always been pretty good in the kitchen, so it really suits you.'

He quickly extinguished his misguided pride, realising the hypocrisy of his fake reality, and replaced it with a stark reminder of where his life was now. All Hayden wanted to do was give kids from vulnerable neighbourhoods more options in life, but all he did by delivering the drugs was perpetuating the problem. He was now the bad guy and he hated himself for it, but he'd hate himself more if anything happened to Brayden and his mum like Jayden had threatened.

She took a sip of whiskey. 'Where do you live? Do you like the city?'

'It's alright, but it's not home,' Hayden confessed. 'I live with my Uncle Ray for now. I've been thinking of moving out. Rent's too expensive in Sydney to get my own place. I don't earn much from the centre. Mum was talking about living with me, but then the judge made Brayden stay in this shithole.'

'Yeah, sorry. That's because I put my hand up to be his buddy.'

'It all makes sense now.'

Most of what he told Leila was true, except he hadn't been at the centre as much as he wanted. The income he got from his brother barely covered the cost of living, and everything else was deposited in a family trust.

After his dad's death, his mum had pushed hard for an inquest, using local legal aid, writing letters, shit he'd never seen her do before. Six months later, his family had ninety thousand dollars. It was a moment of consolation to mask the hole his dad left. Hayden didn't know if she'd always planned to put the money away, or if she'd planned to give it to her kids, but the day she got the cheque, Jayden was arrested and the trust was established.

Over time, his mum had grown cautious about their windfall, and protective of it. She didn't want it to go to them until they had proven they could handle it. For Jayden, the account became the perfect hiding place for his drug proceeds. Hayden used a burner account to transfer money into the family's trust at the same time the account's interest was added. If they didn't touch the money, the cops couldn't prove it was dirty. At first glance, it was a separate insurance payment. Make it regular and make it predictable, Jayden told Hayden.

He knew how foolish it was to trust Jayden, but his desire to keep out of the family business meant following instructions, keeping his head down, and not involving himself too deep.

From his first arrest to his latest armed robbery charge, Jayden's cunning evolved; he grew harder. Hayden was trapped by loyalty but also, more and more, by the fear of what his brother would do if he opted out. Being back in Echo Springs was the only way Hayden controlled the drugs in and out of town, and he could ensure his family, his mum, was safe. He was convinced Jayden intended for the money to go further, really helping his brother and mum set up themselves up for a positive future. Maybe it could mean a fresh start in a new town.

Maybe Hayden was just as good at lying to himself as Jayden was at lying to those around him.

He sat with Leila at the bar for the next hour, enjoying her loosened tongue. She talked about everything from how badly the Rabbitohs did in the last season of NRL to the cost of petrol in the city, avoiding anything deep and meaningful. The more time Hayden spent with Leila, the more he realised his life had barely moved on since he'd last seen her. He was in limbo, stumbling through the motions of life without her. It was never his choice to leave things the way they had and he hadn't fully recovered from the aftermath of their sudden break-up. Leila's life, on the other hand, had grown exponentially; she'd developed into a strong woman and left the girl she once was in her dust.

What would their relationship look like if he had gone after her to rebuild everything he lost the day she left town? Or was it better to just forget what had been and bury himself in the present? He knew just the person he needed to speak to, and he was due to pay his brother a visit anyway.

Leila's eyelids had started to lag every time they closed.

Hayden pushed off the barstool, reaching for her hand. 'Come on, I'll walk you home.'

Her left brow pulled inward. 'I can walk myself home, you know.'

Even drunk, she was still so proud. It entertained him. 'I'm sure you can. I'm just being polite, Lah Lah.'

Her shoulders relaxed. He'd always wanted to take care of her, she'd probably just forgotten. She got up from her stool and stumbled back slightly. Hayden caught her elbow.

'Yep, definitely walking you home.'.

'I'm not drunk, it's the stupid anaesthetic the doctor gave me,' she explained. 'I probably should've stayed home.'

'Anaesthetic? How badly did you hurt yourself? I knew I should've stayed.'

Leila looked down at her hand. 'I think the doctor said I have twelve stitches. Apparently I missed any tendons, nerves and arteries though.'

'Oh, that's a positive.'

She was still the stubborn annoying girl who thought she didn't need anyone. But Hayden knew better.

'See ya, Kaz,' Leila called out as she left.

On the five-block stroll back to Leila's house, Hayden tried to avoid asking what he really wanted to know, but the closer they got to her house, the more the questions pushed against the inside of his skull, until he couldn't keep them inside anymore.

'I honestly didn't think I was going to see you again. You didn't have to suffer on your own, you know.'

'Who said I was suffering?' She didn't look him in the eye.

'I don't know why you would ever come back after...' He stopped himself from talking about what was really on his mind.

'I ask myself the same thing every day, don't worry.'

'Then what changed to make you come back?'

She kicked at the ground slightly as she walked.

'I couldn't let everyone I love screw up their lives. I came back to help change it, and prove to the town that we're not scum.'

'I've never thought our families *were* scum.'

Leila's eyes snapped to his. 'Neither did I, but I worked out that we were the only ones who didn't think that. I can't have my family's name go down like that in this town. I'm the only child, so it's up to me to change it.'

'And you thought becoming a cop was going to be the right choice in this situation?'

'It's worked so far, hasn't it? Your brother is a perfect example of why I came home. He's a good kid. He just needs positive guidance.'

Her words whipped him in the face. How could she insult his family, his mum, even himself? Sure, Brayden was a reckless kid, and he reminded Hayden of young Jayden. But what else was his Mum supposed to do? Realistically, a kid like Brayden probably needed someone on him twenty-four-seven.

'Mum is doing her best, but she can't be everywhere at once.'

'Then why aren't you here?'

Hayden stopped. 'I was coming back. I just had things to sort out in the city first.'

'Things that were more important than your brother?'

Truth was, he had to make sure his other brother kept his associates well away from his family.

'Come on, let's keep walking, we're almost at your house.' Hayden didn't reach out to touch her or guide her, he just kept walking.

A few metres along, Hayden opened the gate of the waist-height wire fence and allowed her to walk through first. At her front door, she rummaged through her bag for her keys.

'Thanks for walking me home, it was really nice of you.'

'Do you ever think about her?' He couldn't stop himself.

She didn't answer.

Hayden reached out, cradling Leila's elbow and pulling her to him. She didn't fight it and he reached for her chin. With a hooked index finger, he pulled her head up slowly. She watched his dark eyes, searching deep in them until their lips finally met. Memories flooded back to him, the exact reason he'd never been able to keep away, would never be able to stay away—this. This passion. Her tongue found the warmth of his; she tasted like every colour of the rainbow. He gripped her waist and pulled her into him, deepening the kiss. Everything about her fit perfectly into him and they both knew it. He breathed her in, and rubbed his nose against her cheek. She pulled back and his mind, quiet while kissing her, was bombarded with questions again. 'Hayden,' she whispered.

'I didn't think I'd get to do that again,' he smiled.

'We can't. Not after—' He pressed his fingers against her lips to stop her from talking.

'Don't think too much into this, it's just a kiss. I wanted to see if you still kissed like you used to.'

She pulled herself away and unlocked her front door. She had her phone in her hand and he took it from her.

'Here, I'm putting my number into your phone. If you ever need to use it, I'll be on the other end waiting.' He handed it back to her before she could react.

'Goodnight,' she finally managed.

She made her way through the doorway, and he watched her for a moment before turning and walking back down her ramp. There was always going to be a connection between them, no matter how much he wished it away. Every fibre in his body sparked whenever she was around and although he told himself it was wrong, she was selfish, she was a *cop*, she allowed herself to feel all of it. Being wrong never felt so right.

Chapter Eleven

Leila woke up overwhelmed with happiness, despite the throbbing in her hand and head. She didn't know why she'd convinced herself that it was going to be hard to be around Hayden. The only things stopping her were her own insecurities, so she decided to let them go and see where things took them instead.

The first thing Leila had to do was deliver her doctor's certificate in to the superintendent at the station so that they could get a replacement officer sent over from Bourke for the next couple of weeks until her wound healed enough to go onto light duties at the station. They were already short-staffed with Hartley Cooper away overseas.

She struggled getting on her usual jean shorts because of the thumping coming from her bandaged hand. She cursed her temper for getting so out of control. She *could* move on from this; she didn't need to be angry.

Forgoing shorts, she opted for a black maxi dress for ease and comfort in the heat. Getting any type of shoe on was also impossible so she slipped into black slides. Leila attempted to do something with her mane, but failed even getting it up into a hair tie with one hand. Again, she conceded defeat and let her hair flow for the second day in a row. Quickly dusting her cheeks with bronzer, she stared at her refection for a moment. Hating being useless and vulnerable, she took a deep breath and exhaled long and slow before heading out the door, ready to take on the world.

Deciding to walk instead of driving, Leila hit the footpath with a bounce in her step. As she turned the corner, she noticed the car of Detective Senior Constable Mac Hudson driving towards her. The car pulled over and the window came down as he pulled alongside her at the kerb.

'Thought I better give you a heads up about what you're about to walk in to at the station,' Mac said.

Leila frowned. 'Really?'

'Smithy saw you with Hayden Terrance last night,' he continued.

'So what?'

'So what, Leila? Do you realise how much of a conflict of interest it is when you're the buddy of Brayden Terrance? Everyone back at the station knows about it too, so I'd say the Boss will want to speak to you about it.'

'Why did Smithy think it was so appropriate to tell everybody about my business anyway?'

'Maybe you need to be more discreet in future?'

'Discreet? I've done nothing wrong. Hayden and I can't even share a drink at a pub before we're suddenly fucking? This town *is* bullshit!' Vaguely, she remembered Hayden saying something very similar the day before.

'Apparently you shared more than just a drink when he walked you home?'

'Are you serious? Smithy was spying on me? What a fucking creep! I think that's more of a concern. Him being a creepy Peeping Tom!'

Mac shrugged. 'Take that up with the Boss, but when you stand at your front porch kissing the guy you agreed not to have any association with, the Boss is going to want to know about it, and will have something to say about it. You know how it works, Leila.'

Mac was right. The fog of alcohol and prescription drugs had completely clouded her judgement. There were reasons why she couldn't be with Hayden. If it would cost her the career she had fought so hard to acquire, that was a compromise she wasn't willing to make.

★★★

Leila walked through the station as quickly as possible. She felt Sergeant Cooper's eyes pierce her skin as she passed his office on the way to see the superintendent. Standing at the closed door to the boss's office, Leila paused for a moment before giving three hard, swift knocks. *Act confident*, she encouraged herself.

Superintendent Katherine Stuart called out, 'Come in.'

With her head high, Leila stood at attention in front of the boss's desk. 'Ma'am, I have something I need to confess.' She ran the risk of sounding insubordinate.

Superintendent Stuart trained a firm gaze on Leila, her mouth pursed, before she said, 'Take a seat, Mayne.' She continued scrawling her pen across the paper in front of her.

Leila waited while the superintendent finished signing paperwork. Katherine snapped the lid on her fountain pen and folded her hands in front of her. 'Go ahead then,' she said.

'Well, I have to disclose that I was with Hayden Terrance last night, and although it appears that some people believe we were intimate—not that it's anyone else's business, if I can be completely frank—but I can assure you I wouldn't jeopardise my position with the Youth Justice Program by getting involved with Hayden Terrance in a romantic way.'

The superintendent was quiet for at least four seconds longer than Leila was comfortable with.

'I have been a young woman before, and I know what it's like to have your heart and your head pull you in two different directions,' Katherine said. 'If you need me to remove you from the program, I can, and will completely understand in doing so.'

'No. No. Honestly, that won't be necessary, Boss. My heart bleeds blue. My job will always come first. But I'd like to know why Constable Smith thought it was okay to follow me? There are questions with his motive there. What did he expect to find me doing?' She wasn't going to be judged.

'He was on his way to Ricardo Street at the time for a curfew check. It wasn't Constable Smith who put the complaint in.'

'There's an official complaint already? On what grounds?'

'Sergeant Cooper felt that we needed to remove you from the program.'

Leila shook her head in disbelief.

The boss put her hand up. 'But I didn't sign off on the paperwork until I had spoken with you. I want you to know that you will be interviewed during the week about it, so take some time at home. Rest your hand and think about what's best for you.'

Leila studied the Boss. She was a striking woman. Ben always said she had very horse-like features, but Leila liked her. She was strong and fearless.

'Are you happy, ma'am?' Leila dared to ask.

It was a risk to speak so candidly to the highest-ranking officer in the station, but Leila needed her professional perspective.

Katherine smiled. 'Of course I am. The Command's stats are all trending down, our Youth Justice Program is on top of juvenile delinquency, and break-and-enters are sitting at an all-time low.'

'No, I mean, with everything you've achieved in life? Would you do everything the same if you had a chance to repeat it?'

'You want to know if I have ever sacrificed love for this job?'

Leila nodded sheepishly.

'Sometimes, everyone has moments of reflection where you wonder what the right choice was, but for the most part I have accepted my decisions and haven't looked back.' The Boss folded her hands into one another and she leaned across the desk. 'You are a fine young constable. You're sincere and committed and I have every confidence that you will make it as high up the ranks as you want to go. But you're going to have to really weigh up what you want out of life. You can create change; you've said so yourself. And if you feel that you've achieved that already and there's nothing more you *could* do, then you've answered all your questions for yourself.'

Leila knew she hadn't finished everything she'd set out to achieve in Echo Springs, so the decision wasn't difficult.

'I will have to associate with him to some extent, ma'am. Our families are tight, and I am still Brayden's buddy.'

'I'm well aware of that, Mayne. I'll leave it up to you to determine the level of acceptable association with Hayden Terrance. But please, I implore you to come and talk to me if a line has been crossed. My door is always open to you.'

Leila nodded and softly smiled. She handed over the doctor's certificate and signed the paperwork the boss had for her to cover the days off.

'As soon as Doctor Evans gives you the all-clear to come back to work, I'll get you to work from the PCYC. Sergeant Garrison said the number of kids coming in has increased significantly, so he needs more help. I think you'd be great down there.'

'That won't be forever though, right? I still want to manage cases as an OIC before I go into a job that I'll end up retiring in.'

Superintendent Stuart laughed. 'You can come back and run an investigation as soon as you do a re-shoot and defensive training to lift your restrictions. You'll need clearance before that though. The doctor said you've got a deep cut in your palm. It might take a bit more time to recover than you think.'

'I don't think it's that bad, ma'am.'

'Any type of hand injury has to pass the grip test, remember.'

Leila was over the lecture from her superior and smiled in defeat.

'Thanks, Boss. I promise to let it heal properly,' she said and briskly left the office.

As she walked out of the station, Leila let the hot sting from the sun set into her skin. She normally hated being away from work, but maybe a few days off were just what she needed to clear her head and get her priorities straight.

Chapter Twelve

Hayden filled out all the requirements of the visitor request form at the front counter of Silverwater Correctional Complex. He slid the clipboard into the drawer and the warden on the other side pulled it through to his side of the protective Perspex barrier.

He looked over the details and smiled an insincere smile. 'Hayden, just take a seat and I'll put the request through. Get comfortable, this might take a while to process.'

It was the usual deal, but still the quickest way to get approval. Jayden's visitation requests were less frequently accepted than Hayden's and could take days, or weeks, to get a response. Their main source of communication was via the phone Jayden had smuggled into prison. Their in-person visits were so infrequent that Hayden knew his brother would be edgy.

Hayden watched the morning program on the TV in the waiting room. A guy he recognised from the last visit came out with his black labrador. They walked straight to Hayden and he tensed; he'd handled some of the pseudo-ephedrine only the day before. The dog happily sniffed its way around him, wagging his tail in delight, wanting to please his handler with a find. But he didn't slow. Hayden gave the guy a smile hoping to pass it off as self-assured. The sniffer dog continued waving his nose in every direction, before cheerfully moving off in another direction. The handler acknowledged Hayden and nodded before making his way back to the double doors. Hayden began breathing normally again.

Twenty painfully slow minutes later, the warden came back out to the shielded reception area. He pressed on the button, amplifying his voice through the speaker. 'You've been approved for a boxed visit with your brother, Hayden,' he said.

A 'boxed' visit meant no contact, and he wasn't surprised. The warden put a lanyard with keys attached to it into the drawer and slid it back through.

'Put this on and lock your wallet, phone and any other personal items into the lockers behind you. I'll meet you at the double doors to take you through to be screened.'

Hayden pulled a packet of cigarettes, lighter, keys, wallet and a phone out of his pockets in two handfuls and dumped them into the locker. They'd all be checked while he was in the visitor's room, but he couldn't care less. The phone Hayden had on him was the one used to talk to his family around Echo Springs or in the city; he had a separate phone for everything else. He was becoming a regular drug dealer with multiple phones and he hated the world he was in.

As he walked up to the door, it buzzed open towards him. After he was through, it clicked shut and the warden escorted him to the scanning area. He took his brown boots and socks off and put them on the conveyor belt to the X-ray and stepped into the scanner.

'Arms at forty-five from your body and your legs shoulder width apart,' the warden called out from behind another barrier, this time protecting him from the scanner. What was this machine doing to his sperm count every time he used it? All the little worries about this life Jayden had thrust upon them kept piling up.

Once the hum of the scanner slowed, the warden called out, 'You're right to step out now, Mr Terrance.'

He collected his shoes and socks from the end of the conveyor belt and slid them back on, bending down to pull on his boots.

The inside of the correctional facility wasn't dissimilar from the inside of a hospital ward—just with a harder edge. The prison wasn't respected or looked after, like a hospital was. The walls were scuffed with black marks, possible signs of a struggle. Some of the windows had words scratched into the plastic. 'FUCK PIGS' and 'DOGS DIE' seemed to be the two favourite quotes.

The warden stopped at a door with a small square window. A sign under the window read: 'Private Room'. Hayden walked in and the door was shut and locked behind him. In front of him was a half-wall, the top half plexiglass, with a bench underneath it and a chair pushed up to the bench. The other side of the window had the same thing: bench and a square metal box fixed to the floor as a seat. Jayden hadn't arrived yet so Hayden took a seat. He looked around, locating the camera. He hated being watched.

Jayden's familiar figure swaggered up to the window in front of him. Another, bigger, prison officer followed close behind him. Dressed in a green tracksuit, complete with white and green Volley tennis shoes, Jayden looked even more intimidating than he did on the outside. His hair was shaved tight against his head, enhancing the darkness in his eyes. He was pale, but whether due to emotions or lack of sunlight, Hayden couldn't tell. Jayden chewed on a toothpick, a substitute for the cigarettes he was no longer entitled to smoke. The effect added to the thug look he had going on.

'You have one hour. Everything you say will be recorded,' the guard said, as Jayden sat on the metal box. The speaker on the side of the window picked up the sound from the other side of the thick protective glass.

They stared at one another until the guard disappeared, studying in silence. Jayden's deadpan look broke into a smirk. 'You're looking good, kid. You been on the gear or something?'

'Why's everybody saying that? Haven't any of you pricks heard of hard work?' Hayden spat back. 'That's right, you wouldn't know hard work if it hit you in the face.'

Jayden laughed.

'So to what do I owe the pleasure?'

'I've seen Leila,' Hayden volunteered.

'How's she doing? Does she look hot in uniform?' Jayden winked.

'She's doing pretty well.' He paused. 'I want to move back to Echo Springs.'

'And?'

'And I really want to give things a proper go with her.'

Jayden's glare spoke loud and clear.

'All for a girl? Didn't think you had it in you, little brother.'

'She's not just any girl and you know it.'

Jayden's jaw clenched before he nodded and mulled the toothpick in his mouth around at the corner. He sighed loudly and moved in to lean against the metal bench below the window. 'How's that baby brother of ours doing? How's Mum? I told her I wanted her to head back to the Springs. I could tell she missed the place.'

'Yeah, she did. Leila's really trying to help Brayden. She's risking a lot to be his buddy in this Youth Justice Program. He's staying out of trouble.'

'She'll be risking a lot if she gets involved with you. She won't give up her job for you, Hayden. I don't think you quite get how the world works. You're two different people. You'll never be together again.'

'You don't know shit. Plus, I don't trust what I'll do if I ever see her with someone else.'

Jayden's nostrils flared. 'Is Ned still a useless drunk?'

Hayden shrugged. 'I haven't seen him since I've been back. I almost don't want to go 'round there ... I wonder whether our folks would've ended up like that if dad was still around.'

Jayden smirked. 'I don't know how Leila ended up so vanilla with parents like hers.'

Hayden didn't laugh, even if he agreed. 'My future's with Leila.'

Jayden reached up to his toothpick and flicked it between a couple of his teeth, his cold stare not wavering.

'Don't know how well that's going to go for you, mate? But it might be good for her to have someone to help her mess of a family.' He tongued the toothpick. 'I know a couple of blokes who might be able to help cure their disease.'

Hayden held his breath, controlling the rage. 'I'm going to do what I was doing in Sydney and start cooking classes for the kids of Echo Springs. It will help Mum get out of the supermarket, and start something for herself too.'

'You're not going to use any of *Dad's* money for that are you, Martha Fucking Stewart?'

Hayden pulled his shoulders back. He could feel the cameras on him from behind and it tempered the simmering fury inside. 'I had a life before you came and destroyed it, so did Mum. I'm not letting you destroy whatever future the rest of your family has left. That's where I draw the line. Time's up, buddy.'

Jayden tilted his head back, and Hayden couldn't tell if he was preparing to run at the glass with full speed, like a lion in an enclosure. But Jayden physically steadied himself with a roll of the shoulders.

'For fuck's sake, you sound like Mum.'

'Is that such a bad thing?'

Hayden continued to stare at his brother, a snarl in his top lip. Jayden replied with an equally ferocious glare, a stare-off through the security glass.

'Fine! Fuck off to your picture-perfect life on the outside. I won't be rotting in here, just remember that. I'll be building my crew. So before you come crying back to me when it all blows up in your face, just remember this day.'

Hayden got up from his chair, no longer in control of the vehemence inside him. He thrust his finger sharply, hitting the window in front of him.

'It's not my fault you got put in here. I owe you nothing, Jayden. I'm going to live my life with a mother who needs me, a girl who deserves me and a younger brother who craves an example like me.' Hayden stared into the pit of Jayden's dark eyes to remind him he would always be superior. He would never do the things that Jayden did, but it didn't mean he wasn't capable of it, which made Hayden more of a threat.

'I suggest you clear everything out of Echo Springs within a month or I'll be calling in some of my own favours owed by old friends.' Hayden knew this would pique Jayden's interest.

Hayden had helped tie up his dad's loose ends after he died, and some of those ends were attached to heavy hitters in town, and they all respected the stoic young man in a time of turmoil—while Jayden had hidden from it, and word got around quick.

Jayden shrugged. Hayden turned and knocked on the door behind him, signalling the end to their conversation. As the warden opened the door, Jayden spoke. 'Hey,' he said.

Hayden stopped and turned to look at his criminal brother.

'Dad always said you were the one who would make him proud.'

They stared at each other for a minute.

'Fuck you,' Hayden said and stepped out of the visitor's room.

Chapter Thirteen

'Is he still here?' Ben asked immediately, when Leila answered the knock at her front door.

She rolled her eyes. 'Obviously you've heard the town's news? The boss already knows I was kissing Hayden on my doorstep last night. Now she's made me pledge my allegiance with the Big Blue Gang, and everybody gets a say in who I can and can't sleep with.'

'Wait? What? You kissed him?' Ben's brow rose. 'I was just joking. I didn't actually think you would go there.'

Leila looked around the empty street behind Ben and quickly pulled him inside. She shoved the door shut with the back of her bandaged hand.

Ben sat on the brown couch to the left and Leila flopped onto the orange couch with a sigh. 'I almost forgot what it was like to kiss him.'

'And you're happy about this because? Christ, Leila! You're in serious trouble. Listen to how you talk about him after one damn kiss. If you screw him, you're screwed!'

Leila's green eyes snapped to Ben. 'Who said I was going to do that and why is this suddenly every other bastard's business?'

Ben tilted his head dramatically to the side as if he knew her game was up. Was she that obvious?

'I've made a choice,' she maintained. 'I'm putting Hayden on ice and I'll be focusing on the job. What else can I do? The Boss made her position very clear, and Coops already put in a formal complaint to have me removed from the program.'

'You could always leave the force...'

Her heart skipped a beat. 'Are you serious? I couldn't if I tried. I've worked too hard to get people in this town to take me seriously. I can't give that up yet, I'm not finished.'

Ben smiled. 'Then it sounds like you've answered it for yourself. But you're not going to leave the poor guy hanging forever, right?'

She grinned. 'If he runs, I'll just have to go after him and drag him back to the Springs like a cave woman.'

'If you're sticking with the job, then I seriously don't know how you're going to keep yourself off him until you're *finished*,' Ben said, complete with quotation-mark fingers.

'The job will be a distraction until that day comes.'

Leila exited the conversation by standing up from the couch to walk to the kitchen. 'Spritzer?' she called out.

'How long have you got before your hand heals and you're back on operational duties?'

'Couple of weeks. The boss wants me to go to the PCYC to work when I come back.' Leila deflated a little, her shoulders slouching as she poured them both a drink.

'You'd be great down there. You've done amazing things with Brayden. The Boss uses him as her poster boy to the board, you know, and you're her star officer.'

'Really?' It was a risk for the superintendent to put her faith into a new Probationary Constable when Leila hadn't proven herself yet.

'I still want to be a lead on a big case before I retire, just so you know.'

'I don't think it's the worst thing in the world if you don't solve a big case. Do you really want to end up like Sergeant Cooper, all cynical and one fatality away from full-blown PTSD?'

She chuckled and handed Ben's drink to him, holding hers out ready for a salute.

'Cheers,' she said. 'Here's to living to serve and fighting for love ... eventually.'

She clinked their glasses together and knocked back the contents.

'I don't exactly see you fighting for your love right now, just so you know,' Ben added a moment later.

'I am fighting ... fighting to stay away.'

★★★

Leila added baked fig with honey and ricotta to her extra-special grazing board. Going the extra mile for her mum's gathering was not so much about impressing everyone but showing them that they could all be better people if they just tried a little harder at life. Cath had tried, stayed off the sauce for a few years, giving Leila a slim shot at a normal life, but with Ned's drinking only getting worse, she'd fallen off the wagon and stayed off.

Leila placed the large, round bamboo tray full of cheese and savoury goods carefully in the front seat of her blue Ford Focus. Driving over to her parents' house, she took deep breaths, digging for strength within. She counted while she breathed; *five, four, three-with-a-pause, two and one.* Tonight would be the perfect test to see how she would go being around Hayden without jumping straight into his arms.

Hayden was standing in her parents' driveway when she pulled in, casually smoking a cigarette. She hated smoking, but Hayden made everything sexy. He butted out his cigarette into an ashtray and exhaled smoke, his lips puffing perfect rings into the air between them, before walking towards the car. Leila's hand had started to ache, and she let him open her door for her. 'Hi,' she said instead of a thank you, and walked around to the other side of the car. Hayden smiled and shook his head.

'Do you need help to bring anything in?'

'I've got a bandaged hand, Hayden, I'm not an invalid.'

'Is it still PC to call someone an invalid? Isn't disabled the correct term?' Hayden said as Leila opened the car door, reaching in to grab the platter.

She ignored his gibe and composed herself long enough to steady the platter in both hands, her bandaged hand acting as the balancer underneath.

'Wow, that's an impressive-looking platter. Mum was right. You definitely give my culinary skills a run for their money.'

'It's not exactly cooking, it's all about placement and presentation.' She smiled up at him.

He watched her walk up the two steps of the front veranda to the cream-coloured weatherboard house. 'I can see that.'

As she got to the front door, Hayden reached around her, quickly opening the door. His hand knocked clumsily against her elbow and the entire platter tilted on the balanced hand underneath. As she felt the platter tilt, she took two steps forward to balance it back again. Miraculously she didn't drop it, and she blew out a sigh of relief.

'Shit! Sorry, Lah Lah.'

'You big shit!' she said. 'You're so bulky, you hardly know how to move your own body properly.'

He laughed. 'I wouldn't want to jeopardise that platter-thing, so I'll just wait right here.'

She relaxed a little. 'Is it too much?'

'Definitely!' Hayden chuckled. 'Your dad's not going to have a clue what any of that is. Not that he'd have a clue anyway. He's already rotten drunk and singing in the back yard. That's why I came out the front for a smoke. I don't even think he'll make it through to food being served.'

She breathed in, trapping her emotions inside as much as possible. It had been a long time since she had to deal with her parents and their addiction, so she wasn't sure how to react.

Hayden reached out gently, wrapping his strong fingers around the top of her arm. 'Remember, my old man would've been out there with him. And the only reason Mum's not, is because Dad died.'

Her eyes shot straight to him. Why was he being so forthright about his family all of a sudden?

'I just wasn't expecting Dad to already be at the train-wreck stage. I thought I'd get here before that happened.'

'I'll get the door for you, shall I?'

She nodded, finally accepting the offer and he opened the door, holding it wide for her. The front room of the house stretched the entire width, featuring the lounge and dining rooms, and a small kitchen. The carpet, a bold brown floral pattern from the seventies, reminded her of the hours spent dancing on it when they were kids, while her parents partied in the back yard. As a high-functioning alcoholic, Cath always managed to keep the house clean. Even with all the pain and anger associated with her parents, Leila still felt comfort when she walked into these rooms. Cath and Sue were at the dining table as Leila walked into the room. They both beamed with joy when they saw her.

'Poss!' Her mum called out. 'Wow! That looks beaut, love. Here, do you want me to take it for you?'

Leila pulled the platter towards herself, shaking her head aggressively. 'It's okay, Mum, I've got it.'

'Well come over and put it on the counter … Get in here, Ned! Poss's home,' she called loudly.

Leila inhaled, but before she could take another breath Ned staggered in, bouncing off the doorway of the back door as he launched towards her. 'Poss, I haven't seen you for ages. Give your old man a hug.'

Leila didn't answer. She came by at least once a fortnight, but each time she'd see Ned collapsed in a drunken stupor on the couch through the front curtains and couldn't bring herself to open the front door.

Ned tripped over his feet and crashed messily into Leila. He caught the edge of the bamboo tray, sending it flying across the room, dropping its precious cargo everywhere. The marinated olives fired into Leila's face like shotgun pellets. The ceramic bowl they were in smacked into her forehead with force. Time slowed as the beetroot dip sprayed out of its container, covering three of them and the wall like a blood splatter. The hummus and crackers crashed to the floor. Baked figs whacked into Ned's face. The tray landed on the lino floor, spinning around and around in the echoing silence.

If she were a different person, Leila would have laughed. She wanted to laugh. She wanted to be the person who could find the humour in the drunk-clumsy actions of her father.

But she wasn't.

She smiled at her dad, who was frozen on the spot, and went to grab a cloth. Brayden walked through the front door, confronted by the sight in the room.

'What the fuck happened here?' he said.

Hayden hit him across the back of the head. 'Hey, watch your language.'

'Have you reported?' Leila's attention was immediately drawn to Brayden.

Brayden held up the printed receipt to confirm his bail compliance.

'Did you tell them you were going to be here tonight, in case they go to your house?'

He shrugged a reply and looked to the ground. She could see Brayden was getting annoyed, but bail wasn't supposed to be fun.

'Remember, you have to play by their rules. We want you here with us, and not in juvie.' Leila reminded him.

Hayden chimed in. 'She's right mate, you can't mess around anymore.'

'Can you call them and let them know for me then?' He gave his devilish grin and Leila instantly buckled.

'Only if you give me a hug,' she teased and held out her arms, oil dripping from her fingers.

'Get lost,' he said and escaped to the kitchen to get himself a drink of lemonade.

Sue picked the tray up and started placing the crackers back onto it again. Hayden leaned down to help her. Cath held onto the side of Leila's arm. 'You know your dad would be really embarrassed right now. He wants to get better, you know.'

Leila looked at her mum. 'Don't do that, Mum.'

Her mum frowned. 'Do what?'

'Lie. You don't need to lie for Dad. He's a drunk and always will be.'

Her mum looked sympathetically at her. 'He just gets nervous when he knows you're coming around. He still struggles with who you are around town.'

Leila could feel anger rising. 'Being a cop is what I do, it's not who I am.'

Her mum searched her daughter's eyes.

'Your dad was talking about signing up for AA.'

Leila held her hands out, showing the mess strewn across her body. 'And how's that going for him, Mum?'

'I've still got some of your old clothes in the cupboard of your bedroom. Why don't you go and get yourself cleaned up? We'll sort out the mess here. Don't worry, Poss. I'll order some chooks and Sue's got her potato bake in the oven. We'll still all have a nice night.' She offered a smile.

Leila felt Hayden's stare from across the room, and smiled meekly at her mum. This wasn't her mother's fault. Her anger wasn't directed at Cath, or even her father. She was just angry at their choices, their life, and her own stubborn ambition. Why couldn't she just be happy as a check-out chick in the supermarket or a hairdresser, like everyone else in her high school class? Whatever the reasons, she wouldn't have fought for this life so ferociously if it weren't for her parents, so she still owed them some gratitude whether she liked it or not.

Chapter Fourteen

Her old bedroom had an unused musty smell to it. The bright walls would always remind her of the day her mum got wasted and decided to spontaneously paint her room candy pink. As an eight-year-old she had thought it was magical when her mum did things impulsively, but as a teenager it served as a reminder of her mother's addiction. Her mum hadn't even remembered that she had done it when she sobered up the next morning, yelling at Leila instead. So as a teenager she plastered the walls with any poster she could get her hands on, erasing the memories as much as she could.

A large Harry Potter movie poster sat proudly above her bed; the books and movies were a favoured form of escapism during adolescence. Posters of all the actors from *Gossip Girl* hung across the largest wall in the room, next to posters of Drew Barrymore, Lucy Liu and Cameron Diaz in various poses as Charlie's Angels. Her bed still had the original cover on; a sky-blue watercolour pattern with white daisies. Nothing had been touched in here since she left home seven years earlier when she moved out to live with Hayden. She sat on her bed and peered around the room. She sighed; her mum *did* try, and Leila hardly took notice of the good. Why did her mum leave her room as it was? In a way, did Cath grieve the loss of her daughter?

Opening the big vintage wardrobe—which would look great in her own home—Leila opened a drawer to find the Green Day t-shirt she had forgotten she even missed until now, and chuckled. Under it were some Bonds hoodies and other t-shirts she had also forgotten about. As she opened the drawer below, Leila closed her eyes and prayed to find the missing blue velour track pants she had loved so much. When she opened it, there was only a short denim skirt, ripped at the bottom, and a few scrunchies scattered. She held the skirt up against her waist and moved back to look into the full-length mirror beside the door. It could work. She stripped out of her shorts and singlet, wiping herself down with her dirtied top, and pulled her old denim skirt on. Sliding into her old Green Day shirt, Leila made her way over to the wooden desk that doubled as a dresser, and picked up her old brush. She blew off the dust and tried to brush some of the oil out, which only spread it through her hair more. Looking in the mirror, she realised it was a futile effort. The olive oil wouldn't come out unless she showered, so she awkwardly threw her dark waves up into a top-knot with one of her old scrunchies.

She slid back into her shoes, folded her dirtied clothes and opened her bedroom door. Taking one last look back at her old room, she slowly closed the door behind her.

Hayden caught sight of Leila when she walked back into the lounge room. 'Someone's bringing back the noughties,' he laughed. 'I remember how much you loved that t-shirt. You'd wear it for days without showering during the school holidays. Here.' Hayden handed her a towel to wipe the oil from her face.

'I used to wash. Not like you! I remember Uncle Mick had to hit you with a hose a couple of times because you hated showering during the school holiday.'

'It's call holidays for a reason.' Hayden shrugged.

'Thankfully that's one habit he's grown out of,' Sue said. 'His room stank when he hit his teens. In fact, all the boys' rooms were gross.'

Cath held up a couple of twenty-dollar notes. 'Hey Brayden, love. Can you pop up to Clayton's and grab us four chooks. That's a good lad.' She didn't give him the opportunity to answer before she dumped the notes into his hand.

Brayden's shoulders slouched and his head drooped. 'But I just walked all the way here from Bradman Place! Hayden, can you drive me down to the shops?'

Hayden nodded. 'Come on.' He walked towards the front door, grabbing his keys from the dining table on the way.

Leila helped her mum and Sue clean up the remaining bits of cheese from the floor.

'You'll have to make this again for us, Poss. It looked lovely,' her mum said, offering a smile.

'I will.' Leila tried smiling back.

Cath brightened, and a shard of guilt pierced Leila's heart.

'I like your earrings, Sue. They're not from Echo Springs are they?' Leila asked.

'No, love. You don't find these around here anywhere. Hayden bought them back from his trip to see his brother today. They're pretty neat, huh?'

It was a sixteen-hour round trip and yet he managed to look well rested. Why did he drive there and back in one hit?

'He drove to Sydney and back today?' Her thoughts spilled out of her mouth.

'Yeah, he left last night and just got back an hour ago. Said it couldn't wait and he had to go.'

What couldn't wait? Even as kids, Leila and Jayden had never seen eye to eye. The very mention of Hayden's jailbird brother made her stomach turn acid and sour.

Sue brought the vacuum cleaner to life, the sudden sound breaking Leila out of her spiralling thoughts.

'Would you like a drink, Poss?' Cath waved a cleanskin bottle of wine at her from the kitchen. Leila dropped the last of the cheese chunks into the bin and shook her head. 'No thanks.'

Cath frowned. 'Come on, Poss. Lighten up a bit.'

'I had a bit too much to drink last night, and I'm on some strong antibiotics, so I'm good. Really.'

'Best reason to have a drink is to clear a hangover,' Cath said as she poured out a glass for Leila anyway.

'Spoken like a true wino.' Leila took the glass without sipping it and smiled at her mum. 'It was a joke, Mum.'

By the time the dining room and kitchen were in order again, Hayden and Brayden had walked back through the front door, bags of roast chickens from Clayton's in their grip.

They placed them on the kitchen bench and Hayden made his way back to the front door as he pulled out a cigarette from its packet. Leila looked at her mum, waiting to see if she needed more help. Instead Cath nodded at the door, encouraging her to follow him. 'Go on then, I'm sure you two have got plenty to catch up on.'

They did, but the officer Leila had become had questions, and she was going to get some answers. With a glass of wine in her hand, Leila smiled at both her mother and pseudo-aunty, and made her way to Hayden.

Hayden sat on one of two plastic chairs at the front of the house. She took the other. A thick hedge had grown over the railing at the front, narrowing the width of the sitting area. A short round table separated them.

'That look on your face when your old man sent that platter flying...' Hayden's eyes pinched in the corners as he grinned.

'You must be tired after your big drive. I don't know how you're still standing.' Leila watched him from the corner of her eye.

Hayden nodded as he drew on his cigarette. 'I won't be having a late night, that's for sure.'

Leila paused. Did she really want the answers or should she just drop it? She couldn't drop it.

'Your mum said you went to see Jayden.'

Hayden nodded.

'That's a long way to just visit your brother.'

Hayden watched her. 'Is this an official interview, officer?'

Her eyes snapped to him. 'Everything is suspicious in my world. Even you.'

He laughed. 'Well, what a time to be alive.'

'The only reason you visit someone in prison over phoning them is because you want to tell them something ... covertly.'

'Is that right?' He was mocking her.

Leila looked back out to the street, full of doubt. The job made her distrusting of people and far too quick to judge. Had she read this all wrong?

'How about you use your copper contacts to see the footage from my visit with Jayden for yourself instead of interrogating me,' he said, getting up to walk back inside.

Leila let Hayden walk past her without glancing in his direction, acknowledging her haste in accusing him of something so quickly. Why did she have to push for answers when she wasn't completely sure she wanted to know anyway?

The table was set when she wandered back inside, with Sue's famous potato bake proudly taking centre stage. Leila tipped her warm wine into the sink, and decided to pour herself a fresh glass. She did want to loosen up around her family. Why couldn't she just relax around them like she did when she had a drink with friends?

Brayden sat impatiently while Cath prepared the rest of the roast chickens, spreading out cut-up pieces in single-use oven trays. Taking a sip of her drink, Leila watched Sue smother the salad with a bottle of dressing, soaking the lettuce, tomatoes and onion, and smiled. Sue had always poured so much dressing it made everyone squint from the sourness. One gathering, Sue was beside herself when she couldn't locate the beloved dressing. It wasn't until they found a newly crawling Brayden with the contents of it poured all over him that they'd realised where it had gone. The poor kid stank of the stuff for days after that. There were plenty of happy memories Leila had of her family, she'd just forgotten how to remember them.

Hayden walked back into the room. 'Ned looks too comfortable to disturb.' Everyone understood the subtext of Hayden's comment. For the ease of their night together, it wasn't such a bad thing if he was left to sleep off his intoxication. Leila wanted to believe he could break this beast. She couldn't give up on him—like everyone seemed to.

They all sat down at the table and Brayden started grabbing at pieces of chicken, placing them on his plate. Hayden sat back to wait. Sue gave Hayden a wink, acknowledging her middle son's chivalry. It didn't go unnoticed by Leila, and she couldn't keep from meeting his eyes, their gaze locking as food was passed around in front of them. There was so much she wished she could talk with him about.

He smiled; heat rose up her neck. There was no denying their chemistry. But Leila knew the consequences of crossing that line. Was her career worth giving up the love of her life?

Chapter Fifteen

The thumping finally brought her back to her senses. Her ears rang and her head pounded. She looked around. There was nothing but dust. She couldn't breathe. What had happened? Why couldn't she breathe? She grabbed at her throat but couldn't feel anything. She was numb all over. Something wet slid down her face. Looking at her hand, she saw blood. She was bleeding? From what? Where's Mum? Hayden?

'Hayden!' she called out. 'Mum!'

No one answered back. She called again. Suddenly the earth beneath her shook. What the hell had happened?

'Hayden!' she screamed.

The sound of her own voice woke her suddenly and she stared into the darkness of her bedroom.

Everything was silent and she could breathe again. Her forehead was dampened from sweat; her heart pounded in her ears.

'It was just a dream,' she whispered into the night air.

Leila got up and headed to the kitchen, pouring herself a glass of water. She stared out the window above her sink into her moonlit backyard beyond. The subtle light cast shadows across the two citrus trees in the middle of the grassed area. Leila hadn't felt alone in a long time but Hayden's return had shifted something in her and she couldn't deny it any longer. She went back to her bedroom and found her phone. Checking the time—two am—she fought the urge to find Hayden's number and call. She scrolled through the contacts and paused, focusing on his name, the nine digits taunting her. She really shouldn't. She couldn't. She tapped *call*. Pressing her phone to her ear, Leila tried to settle her pounding heart. The phone rang once, twice, three times…she should just hang up. But he'd see that she'd called in the middle of the night anyway—she was in it now.

'Hey. Is everything okay? What's happened?'

His sleepy voice made her smile. He sounded soft, gentle, vulnerable. She sat on the edge of the bed, imagining he was next to her like he used to be.

She wanted to tell him how much she still loved him, but stopped herself from completely drowning in her raw emotion. 'Everything's fine. Well, it's not fine. But I'm okay. I just had a nightmare and wanted to talk to someone. It's late though. You just drove back from Sydn—'

'Leila. It's fine. I told you I'd always be here.' He paused. 'Did you want me to come over?'

'Yes,' Leila said without hesitation.

'Okay,' he replied and abruptly ended the call.

What had she just done? She put the phone on the counter and slapped her uninjured hand against her forehead. Why did she just do that? Why couldn't she just keep her mouth closed and thoughts to herself? She'd had nightmares before.

Leila hurried around her bedroom, throwing the strewn blue uniform and other clothes into her washing basket and quickly kicking her work boots into her wardrobe. She paused. Why was she fussing about the bedroom so much? There was no way he would ever be in her room. She wouldn't go there. Not tonight, or any night. *You invited him over in the middle of the night!* Sure, she felt like she needed company after having bad dreams, but why her old flame? The old flame her supportive boss had very compassionately told her to stay away from?

There was a quiet knock at her back door and Leila jolted upright. *That was quick.*

Pausing for a moment at the door, she talked herself through the next moments. She definitely *not* going to kiss him. She was definitely *not* going to touch him. She was definitely going to remain in control. Opening the door, she took a deep breath. Hayden's dark eyes were shadowed and his brow was furrowed. The light of the moon highlighted his strong, angular jawline. Her fingers twitched with the urge to trace it.

The silence lingered, but she didn't know how to break it, how to defuse this loaded moment. She had no idea what to do, and then Hayden saved her. He saved them both by stepping forward, throwing his arm around her and pulling her in to him. His lips caressed hers as he kicked the door shut behind him with one swift move. Leila was powerless to do anything but kiss him back. His lips were soft, stubble rough, and he held her securely, as if he never wanted to let her go. He offered her everything she yearned for. Their bond was stronger than her will. Lifting her off the ground, he helped her wrap her legs around his waist, securing herself to him. Her arm slid around the back of his solid neck and the fingers of her bandaged hand touched the side of his face delicately. He proceeded carefully as their kiss deepened, walking towards her bedroom, the very room she wanted to avoid. She peeked between lashes as he lowered her gently onto the bed.

The weight of him brought so much comfort, she could almost cry from the pain of missing him. He pulled back and looked into her eyes.

'I've wanted you to call me because you needed me since the day you left. I've missed everything about you,' he said.

A tear threatened to spill from the corner of her eye. She didn't want to trek back over their history, but she couldn't move forward without talking to him about everything they lost.

Reality kicked her right in the gut. 'We can't do this. I don't know if I can ever do this. I feel like I can't let anything in again. Not after Kaylee.' Leila finally said the one word she had vowed never to speak again.

She sat up, drawing her knees to her chest. Hayden stared at the ground, sitting next to her on the bed.

'I can't believe it's been four years,' he replied.

'I haven't been able to say her name for four years.'

She was unprepared for the wave of relief that washed over her body from the simple act of speaking the name of their daughter, the unborn baby they had lost.

She looked into his dark eyes. 'I'm ready to talk.'

Chapter Sixteen

Fully clothed, Hayden pulled the sheet over them and they sunk into Leila's bed together, his eyes fixed on her. Finally, comfortable with the pillow arrangement, they faced each other and Leila began.

'I hated my body for the pain it caused you.' Her words sounded like they came from the deepest part of her sadness, but they brought confusion.

'What do you mean the pain it caused *me*? It's no one's fault, Leila. Even the doctor kept reminding us of that. Plus, you were feeling every bit of pain that I was.' He paused on that for a moment. 'Well obviously you were feeling a lot more than me, but I don't understand why you didn't just talk to me about it?'

She shrugged. 'I couldn't.'

'So you ran?'

'The alternative was to jump off the Springs bluff. So I thought leaving town would cause the least amount of pain for our families. I'd already done enough by losing Kaylee.'

Hayden reached out then, cupping her face, drawing back a piece of her hair. A tear slipped down her cheek and she pinched her eyes shut.

'The counsellor warned me you might've been experiencing some dark thoughts. But I didn't believe her until you said you were leaving. You were always good at masking your pain. I was floored when you said you wanted to move on … without me. The thought of not being with you just wasn't in my realm.' He sighed. 'I had my brother's crew watch you for a while in the city, to make sure you didn't do anything to yourself.'

'Did you really? I should be angry, but I don't blame you. I just wish *you* came for me.'

'You told me you hated the sight of me. Said you couldn't be reminded of our daughter every day.'

Nodding again, Leila started to cry in earnest. 'What else could I do? My insides were rotten. I didn't understand how my own body could punish me so cruelly.'

'The counsellor said it was really common for you to react the way you did. She said it was best to let you come back to me when you were ready. I just didn't think that would be four years later.'

'The same counsellor encouraged me to find a passion and dive into it, to heal.'

He almost felt it possible to chuckle. Leila had done exactly what the psychologist suggested, left and become the opposite of everything she'd ever known.

'I had to leave. I didn't think I could survive another day being in this town, remaining in the lifestyle we were born into, being near the nursery we set up together. One minute we were going to be parents, the next it was gone. All that was left was a whopping big void of emptiness. So I thought if I was ever given the opportunity to be a parent again, I wasn't bringing another child into the environment *we* were raised in … so I left. To find who I could truly be.'

Hayden slid his eyes from hers, guilt pulling him into a vicious undertow.

'I don't think I'll ever meet anyone like you. I would've been the proudest father in the world to have a daughter with a mother like you. You're more resilient than I gave you credit for. I just thought you were being selfish.'

'I was. I left you with a big mess to clean up, and you did it all without me.'

Leila's tears continued to flow like a stream down her cheeks. The water pooled on his chest where she curled into him. He held her while she let all the pain fall from her. He continued to hold her without moving for the next twenty minutes, lying while she sobbed. He didn't ask any more questions. He didn't force her to talk about it further, he just kept her safe in his arms. She was vulnerable and open, and even though she was in pain, he couldn't help treasuring these small moments with her.

'I think we might've been too young to become parents anyway. I would never have become a cop and you wouldn't have been able to explore your passion for food.'

Again, Hayden pushed against the current of guilt that was ready to sweep him away. Did Leila have the right solution all along?

'So why *did* you come back if you wanted to escape everything so badly?' It was a risk to ask again.

'I still don't know. Maybe it was you. Maybe it was the home I missed. It's hard to be exact, but something drew me back. I knew I'd be a good cop here. It wasn't going to be easy, but it just felt right.'

'I think about her so much whenever I come back here. I saw a couple of little girls crossing the road to Echo Springs Primary the other day. She would've been getting ready to start school soon. I think about whether she would've had dark wavy hair, just like her mum's. I wonder about how many teeth she would've lost by now. I imagine she would watch the football with me, cheering on the mighty Dragons in our matching jerseys. I can't help but imagine what life would have been like with Kaylee in it.'

She looked up at him with tear-soaked eyes.

'I feel like I'll never get over how cruel it all felt. Having to register her. Having her on public record. I tried talking about her once, two days after her death, but the nurse looked at me as if I were some overreacting teen with a first-world problem. I didn't feel like we were given the same set of grief rules as anyone who loses a real baby.'

He drew a deep breath, his chest lifting her cheek.

'She was a real baby. Her heart beat the same as anyone else and our blood pumped through her veins. I never thought about how you must've felt betrayed by your own body, and then everyone's opinion of you. My experience was nothing like that. I should have come with you.'

'There was no way you were coming with me at that point.' She held her head up to meet his eyes finally. 'I wanted you to come *for* me. Don't get that confused with coming *with* me.'

Hayden's cheeks expanded with a wide smile. He never thought he'd understand the reasons why she left. He never thought any reason she gave would be good enough. But just hearing her words helped him understand the pain she'd been holding onto for all these years.

'My dad's been looking after her, I reckon. I'm glad we put her with him out at the cemetery.'

Leila's tears started again. 'There's nowhere I'd rather her be,' she replied and buried her head back into his chest.

'I catch mum talking to her angel statue in the garden sometimes. You know the one she said was Kaylee the day she bought it. She says Kaylee was always destined to be an angel.'

'Great, so your mum always thought I was going to miscarry?' she said bitterly.

He looked down at her, knowing she was speaking from pain. Losing their baby changed their life forever, and until now, Hayden never thought they would recover from it. Maybe they still wouldn't; but talking about it had shifted something between them. His decision to stand up to his brother suddenly felt imperative.

Hayden watched the full moon beyond the window, as Leila's tears dried and her body relaxed into sleep. She was all he'd craved for years. His arm was beginning to tingle from a lack of circulation, but he didn't want to let her go again. Not now, not ever.

Chapter Seventeen

Hayden's eyes slowly adjusted to the light streaming through the curtains. It took him a couple of seconds to work out where he was.

The air was thick with the smell of frying bacon and he smiled. This was everything he'd hoped for and something he'd thought he'd never have again. Walking into the kitchen, he found Leila trying to cook with one hand. His chuckle caught her attention. She smiled with an animated look of defeat.

'I feel so useless,' she laughed.

'Here, let me help.' He took over and she allowed it without hesitation.

'I'll make the coffees. I can do that much.' She gave a soft smile.

Moving around the kitchen with her felt effortless. Their bodies were in harmony with each another, like they always had been.

'Did you sleep okay? Sorry if I kept you awake with the tossing,' she asked.

Frowning, Hayden looked over at her and shrugged. 'Didn't feel a thing. Slept like a baby.'

Their eyes met on *that* word; it still had a sting to it. Hayden tilted his head slightly, and smiled his apology. She nodded in reply to everything he couldn't say out loud.

Leila set the round white table in her kitchen as he finished plating up their breakfast feast. It was all so natural, but he wouldn't break the spell by daring to say it out loud.

Hayden was beaming when they sat down together.

'I forgot how much you grin all the time,' she teased.

'When life makes you smile, you go with it.' Hayden said and cut off a big bit of bacon before shoving it in his mouth.

He could see her grimace from the corner of his eye, and decided to take smaller bites.

'So there is a snag in this whole situation that I need to talk to you about,' Leila said as she put a piece of toast in her mouth, munching on it for a moment.

He knew where she was going with this. Even Jayden had called it: her job changed everything. He cursed his brother under his breath for both causing his snag and being right about it.

When she finished her mouthful, she continued, 'I love being back around you again, believe me. But—' She paused. 'I just can't. For Brayden's sake. It took a lot for me to convince the bosses and board of authorities I was going to remain impartial with Brayden. Being with you compromises that.'

Nodding, Hayden took another bite of his bacon and looked out of the kitchen window, fury eating away at him. He could feel her watching him.

She huffed. Loudly. 'So, you have nothing to say about it?'

He shrugged. 'What is there to say? I agree. I knew this would be the case, and Brayden needs someone like you in his corner. That's as important to me as you are.'

'Right. Okay.'

She straightened in her chair, as if a weight had been lifted, and took a sip of her coffee.

'But it's not forever … I mean, eventually the bosses at the station will see that you're a decent person, and as soon as I've got my stripe I'll have a bit more respect and… Well. Then—'

Hayden put down his fork to place his hand gently on top of hers. 'Lah Lah. It's fine. Until three days ago I never thought I'd even be present in the same room with you again. I need time to process this too. Let's just focus on Brayden and we'll see where we end up.'

Leila giggled, which struck him as odd, until he realised she'd been nervous about talking to him. Two years of working for his brother had made a world's difference to his own ability to handle stresses.

'Okay.' She smiled, filling her mouth with a fork full of egg and toast, and took the conversation back to the town and safer ground.

'So it sounds like you're planning on staying a bit longer then?' Leila asked after their discussion of Hayden's plan to help with his mum's garden.

He smiled, 'Yeah. You could say that. I don't have much dragging me back to the city. Not like I have anchoring me here anyway.'

'What about the community centre and your cooking classes?'

TJ HAMILTON

He shrugged. 'I thought I might use what I've learned in the city and get the courses for the kids started out here. The kids around here could really do with it. I know we did.'

She agreed. 'The kids out here definitely need it. They have fewer opportunities to engage in courses like that compared to the city kids. These boards full of authorities and brass with their privileged ideas seriously have no idea what it's like to grow up out here. They finally come on board when kids end up their customers. I mean, we were lucky to end up how we did. You think about our friends. How many of them have stayed out of prison, or weren't charged with something in their life? It's fuck all. We were lucky.'

Hayden drank the last of his coffee. She was right. He thought of everyone from their high school class who had either ended up incarcerated or on the end of a bottle. Hayden hadn't given it much thought until now; it was just life—until his younger brother started going down the same path. When he left town he saw how life could be for those outside Echo Springs. Leila's passion for making change for the next generation sank into his skin, deeper. He could do the same. It was only by pure luck that he wasn't already in prison, and his work on his brother's behalf was a ticking bomb before he too became another statistic of the Springs.

'Well, you've just given me more reason to stay and start something positive for the kids. Who's running the PCYC at the moment?'

Leila laughed. 'The PCYC is a bit of a joke at the moment. Garrison is down there. Do you remember him?'

'Yeah, I do. Isn't he the copper who was caught drink driving and crashed his car when he ran from the booze bus?'

Leila nodded. 'Exactly. Now do you see the problem?'

'How do cops like that stay in the job?'

'They get shoved away to a place like the PCYC to be forgotten about while the kids in this town continue the vicious cycle and the bosses in the city question the failure.'

Hayden laughed. 'What a delightful and honest system to be part of.'

'Hey.' Her eyes snapped to him. 'I understand its faults. But it's still a system that serves good in the community, okay. Most cops I know are outstanding people who do amazing things on a daily basis.'

He wanted to burn in all that fire. She had always been destined for this role, he was only beginning to see. Ever since they were small kids, she was the peacekeeper between his brothers and their families. If there was anything unjust happening in the school yard, she was the first one to stand up and make sure the issue was sorted out properly. Whenever fights broke out at lunch, everyone would stand and inflame the situation by cheering on the fight, but not Leila. She would be the first person to dive in and break it up, putting herself between the fighters, no matter how much bigger the kids were. But she differed from other police; she understood the unspoken code of silence their part of town was built on. It was the only thing Jayden had ever liked about her. Many times it was Jayden involved in a fight, and Leila broke it up, in spite of the threats of what Jayden would do if she got in the way. But when the teachers finally arrived, she wouldn't tell them who the culprits where, giving the bloodied and bruised opponents the opportunity to flee the scene. He would never admit it, but Jayden even respected her for it. It was this shared childhood that set her apart from other cops, the 'blow-ins' from out of town. They didn't understand the marrow in the bones of Echo Springs.

Hayden helped with the clean-up after breakfast and watched Leila as she stacked the last of the plates away. He'd tried to resist her, but he couldn't stand it any longer. He strode across the room grabbed her by the waist, spinning her around to pull her into him, kissing her as if his life depended on the air she breathed. She fell straight into his kiss. She didn't fight it. In these last few hours, he'd found himself falling back in love with her again, almost as if he never stopped. Had he?

His hand dwarfed her face as he cupped the side it, fingers running into the back of her hair. Twisting her waves, he let them fall again between his fingers. Everything about her body was soft, and he wanted to rip her pyjama shorts and singlet straight off. But the anticipation was heady, and he wanted to savour every step. He was the first to pull back this time. Running his thumb along her bottom lip, he grinned at the plump softness. He knew how much he loved her, and that made him cautious. He couldn't lose her again. He might as well cut out his own heart and continue living without it, because that's all life would resemble.

'I think it's best if I use the back door and slip over the fence to the Michelsons' behind you,' he said with a smile.

'Just be careful. The last thing I need is for you to be implicated in a suspected home invasion.'

He laughed. 'Would you like me to go and knock on the door of Mr and Mrs Michelson and ask if it's okay with them if I climb their fence to come and see you?'

She considered the idea with a dramatic tilt of her head. 'I'm trying to decide which is the lesser of two evils. If I see Mrs Michelson tending to the roses behind my washing line, I'll be sure to mention something to her. As long as she doesn't tell her sister, Marcy though. The moment Marcy finds out the whole town will know before sundown. I need to think about the best plan of attack with this. Welcome back to the country.'

She smiled, and he couldn't help smiling back. There was intimacy here, knowing each other, knowing the town. It was comforting.

'I'll call you later then?' he said, as he gave her one more kiss on the lips.

Their whole future was in her nod and smile.

Chapter Eighteen

Leila waited for the sting of the midday sun to settle before pulling on her runners for an afternoon jog. The excitement coursing through her body had Leila thinking she could run an entire marathon instead of her usual five kilometres. She filled up her water backpack and threw it over her shoulders before carefully selecting her favourite playlist for the trek. Popping her earbuds in, she started the distance tracker on her phone and slid it onto her running armband before heading out the door. This time, Leila took the track around Bulls' Run, to push herself and reach all the way to Echo Ridge Lookout.

Running through the streets, she waved to the motorists who passed her, eager to be out of town to focus on her pace and breathing. TLC drowned out her thoughts as they sang about creeping around to hide a love affair. How appropriate. Before Hayden came back, she thought she had healed her old wounds and severed all but one or two strings she held on to him with. But those final remaining strands of love were held so tight that nothing could ever cut them. The possibilities in her future dominated any obstacle in her way.

Finally, the houses spread further and further apart until there was nothing but barren scrub and bushland surrounding her. She took a walking track veering from the dirt road, cutting through the bush directly towards the lookout.

Small pale-green salt bushes lined the track, scattered in clumps of three or four. Beyond the salt bushes, naked grey trunks of mallee trees stretched to the sun with their finger-like branches; their sprays of green beginning to form at the very tops, signs of life returning to the bush after the devastating fires that had torn through only recently. The branches waved at the sky, pleading for the rain to come down upon them—much like the rest of the inhabitants of the outback. The red dirt was soft enough to lessen the impact of each pounding step Leila took, striding towards her goal. Besides the odd remnant of a snake's slither or the distinctive three divots caused from the bounce of a kangaroo's paw, the track was rarely used. In the heat of summer, the only people game enough to hit the fifteen-kilometre trail were the native fauna, crazy backpackers or young constables who may have lost their mind in love. Leila wore a hat to shield her from the afternoon sun, but her singlet did little to protect the bare top of her chest. It stung from both the sun and the heat resonating within her chest. The dry air made it impossible to draw a deep breath so Leila slowed her pace and stretched her arms above her head, opening her torso to allow the maximum amount of oxygen in. Eventually the heat was too much and Leila knew she had been overambitious. She slowed to a walk and pulled her phone from her armband, clicking open the tracker to check her distance. Only seven kilometres into her run and she was disappointed with herself. She took her earbuds out, pausing for a second or two to catch her breath. There was nothing like running in the bush. The clear air and isolation just couldn't be replicated anywhere else. This *was* her home and at times like this, right here, it was the *real* world. Why would you want to be anywhere else? Leila pulled her water tube from her pack and took in a couple of mouthfuls, enough to wet the inside of her mouth. The water cooled her chest as it slid down. Should she continue on or just turn back?

She stopped to listen. The isolation of the bush was interrupted by the rev of an engine in the distance. She tilted her head to gauge where the sound was coming from. There weren't any homes out here, only Jacinta Buchanan's sheep station. Jacinta wouldn't have the sheep up this end of her station already, surely? There was barely any feed on this side of her property this time of the year. She listened again. The car sounded like it might be having engine problems, so she headed towards it in case it was some unsuspecting tourists with a beat-up four-wheel drive. They all passed through Echo Springs looking for 'the authentic outback experience'. She'd been called out many times to rescue a carload of young backpackers in the middle of nowhere when they decided to head out into the bush without the slightest understanding of the terrain.

She left the track and cut through the bush, weaving through the salt bushes, eucalypts and mallees. The engine was definitely heading towards Bulls' Run. If she didn't know better, she would say it was right near the old mines that dated back to the gold-rush era. Still possibly tourists. They wouldn't know they were trespassing onto private property. Through the copse of trees in the distance, Leila began to make out a sleek white Audi. Not the car she was expecting. She slowed and edged closer, stopping behind some trees to get a better look. She couldn't make out the person sitting in the driver's side. Did Jac Buchanan just buy a very new, very fancy car? No, there was no way Jac would be able to afford that. Last time she'd checked, Bulls' Run was treading water to stay afloat. Her cop instinct flared to life and she inched closer, keeping concealed. Crouching down, she waited.

Someone appeared at the tunnel of one of the mines and she lowered herself even further behind the scrub at the base of the tree. She squinted to try and bring the emerging figure into focus.

'Brayden?' she whispered.

Why on earth was he out here with a white sports car that was worth more than the average mortgage in town? He carried a black duffle bag over his shoulder and walked towards the car.

'Shit.' She swiftly ducked down again when Brayden glanced out across the scrubland.

She peered back through the branches, watching him in the passenger seat while the other figure, a man she'd never seen before, struggled to get his fancy car to kick over. They shared an exchange and the driver waved his hands in the air. He hit the steering wheel with both hands and got out of the car. She saw him clearly enough now: he was bald with a beard and wore a white t-shirt with a red S on the front. Her heart pounded like a bass drum in her chest. Everything about this was sinister.

Carefully taking her black cap off so its peak didn't expose her, she glanced up to see what the driver was doing. He was occupied by a conversation on his phone. If only she were able to hear what he was saying. She contemplated getting closer again, within earshot, but twigs breaking under foot was too great a risk at this distance. So she waited, unsure.

Her phone! Reaching slowly down, she nudged it to the side of the tree trunk, wary of not pushing it too far. Using the fingers of her bandaged hand to hold it steady, she zoomed in enough to see the unknown man pixelated on her screen. Checking that the phone was still on silent, she took four or five shots of him as he paced along the outside of the car, talking on his phone. He got back into the Audi and tried again to get the engine to click over. This time the car responded to its desperate occupants, and the engine roared to life. The driver smiled, his brilliant white teeth clearly visible through the scruff of his beard. Still with the phone open on camera mode, and its zoom pushed in as far as it could be, she fired off shots of the car as it circled. She rolled to the other side of the trunk and focused on getting the car's number plate as it drove down the narrow dirt road. The dust thrown up obscured the yellow and black plate, distinctly registered to New South Wales.

When the car was out of sight, she looked at the photos on her screen while leaning back against the trunk.

'What the hell are you doing, Brayden?' she said quietly.

The weight of disappointment sunk deep into her chest, burrowing into her like a wild animal. Should she take a closer look at the old mine? No. Not without some backup. Tombstone courage was one of the ten fatal errors she was taught over and over at the Academy, until it finally branded itself into the brain of every officer. Making sure all was clear behind her, she made a dash back towards the walking trail and ran home as fast as her legs would carry her.

Chapter Nineteen

Leila's mind refused to still. While in the shower, she let the water wash over her, numbing her hot skin, bringing her body temperature back down. Along with the water, she tried to blink away the image of Brayden, praying that her mind was wrong about recognising him. But she wasn't, it was him and no amount of hope could change that. He was doing so well. Had she been deceived all this time? There were a few holes in his day where he wasn't being monitored. It would be ignoring his rights to monitor him around the clock, but even Hayden himself said Brayden needed that type of supervision. Was juvenile detention the best place for a kid like Brayden? Kept away for his own good?

If only she'd gone closer to see what was in that mine. Could it be something completely innocent and she'd just become cynical, as her days in the police force progressed? No, she knew better than to be naive. There was no good reason for a car like an Audi or a kid like Brayden—with a duffle bag—to be in an isolated area of the bush. One thing was for sure, she had to get to the bottom of it before Brayden made the biggest mistake of his life and she could no longer protect him from her own colleagues.

She got out of the shower and wrapped one towel around her head, another around her body. As she picked up the phone from the bathroom basin, it pinged to signal a message. It was from Hayden, and despite her troubled mind she grinned wildly. He had added a Snapchat filter over a photo of him, a filter she only recognised from when Brayden showed her his own photos from the app she refused to download. In the photo, Hayden draped his arm around his Mum's old dog, Max. Hayden had dog ears and nose with a long tongue hanging all the way out, mimicking the real dog's tongue next to him. She laughed. Stretching her phone out, she took a selfie of herself in her towel, complete with bandaged hand wrapped in a plastic bag. She paused before sending it. Was it too much? She wouldn't know anymore. Back when she and Hayden were together, selfies weren't a thing, neither was Snapchat. Her hand pressed send before she gave it a second thought. Before she had made it to her bedroom, another message pinged back in reply, reading: *I'll be over in 5 mins.* An emoji face with its eyes wide open.

She laughed again and replied: *Unlike some others, I've been out for a 10km run and now have things to do.*

Watching the three ellipsis scroll to show Hayden was replying, she unravelled the towel from around her head, scrunch drying her dark locks in anticipation of his response.

He replied with: *Show off! Catch ya later x*

Still smiling, she closed her messages, returning to her phone's home screen. She opened her photos and the pictures from the mine filled the screen. Her flash of happiness was quickly replaced with apprehension about what might already be known about Brayden and whether she was too late.

It was almost six, so she messaged Ben to see if he was on shift tonight. He quickly replied with a 'yes' and she asked if he wanted her to deliver him some dinner.

Can't you stay away from the place? It's only been four days! Ben replied.

I'm bored. She wrote back. And then followed it up with: *Plus, I miss you.*

Ben was replying back. She watched the rolling dots: *lol I'll be back in the station in halfa. I'm on the truck with Tracey Anderson, from Bourke tonight. She hates Indian, so can you bring me a medium Chicken Vindaloo from Echo Taj?*

She chuckled. Ben's solution to Tracey's complaints was a pretty normal type of response. When cops find something you dislike, she thought, they'll exploit it until you crack, then back off a little. Weaknesses were fair game in a job that required a few extra layers of skin than most.

Leila threw her phone onto her bed as she passed to get dressed. Once in track pants and a singlet, she called the Echo Taj Indian restaurant—the only Indian restaurant in Echo Springs—and placed her order.

After her long run, Leila drove instead of walking. When she pulled into the motel with the Indian restaurant attached there was the Audi, parked outside one of the rooms.

The bravado this guy had by staying in a small town was impressive and alarming. She looked around the empty parking spaces, checking for surveillance. Could cops from the city be here to investigate? The carpark was empty, but Leila made a mental note to get details of all the people staying at the motel. Her takeaway order was ready and waiting in a white plastic bag, on the counter at the rear of the restaurant. Leila passed three rows of tables to the takeaway counter, which also doubled as a bar. There were people sitting at a table to the right. She could just make out their shape, but didn't dare look in their direction. Mrs Chopra smiled from behind the cash register. She was draped in a dazzling pink sari with gold embellishments.

'Hello, my dark fury. You know, I remember the moment when you came into this world.'

Leila nodded, trying her best not to appear bored with the story, but the details were so ingrained, she could retell it after ten shots of tequila.

'Your mum was about to go into the operating theatre to have a caesarean when I came and crashed the party with a baby wanting to arrive feet-first and took Doctor Evans away.'

Leila smiled as Mrs Chopra told the story of Leila's arrival into the world.

'And then you screamed the entire ward down all night, Leila. You always had a great set of lungs on you. You know your name means—'

'Nocturnal,' they both said in unison.

Vijay, Mrs Chopra's youngest son after five girls, walked out from the kitchen. 'Mum's not trying to tell you about how you're half an hour older than me again—as if you've never heard it before?'

Leila laughed. 'Some things are nice to stay the same.'

'Mum, can you please go talk to Dad? He's complaining that you've moved his bag of cumin seeds again.'

Mrs Chopra patted her son on the back as she passed him. She didn't see the sad smile Vijay sent after her.

'How's everything going with your mum?'

He shrugged. 'She's getting worse. She has the same set stories she remembers people by, but the specialists in the city said it's only a matter of time before they will lessen too.'

'How much longer can you defer med school?'

Vijay tilted his head, unsure. 'I have to go back soon, so Misha is going to come back. The problem is, I don't want to go. I'm the most qualified in my family to help care for Mum so I feel obligated to stay.'

Leila's heart sunk for her friend.

'What about getting your med school done and then you can come back to Bourke Hospital to do all your placement out here? That way you'll be back with your family. Our town always needs good people like you coming back here and understanding what we're up against.'

Vijay laughed. 'It's not that dire out here, Leila. Plus, it's my duty as the youngest to make sure I care for Mum and Dad, so that's what I'll do. Med school can wait and Echo Springs isn't going anywhere. My intention is always to come back. This is home.'

Leila smiled and said, 'Yep, I get that. That's why I'm still here.'

She handed over the money and Vijay gave Leila her change. Taking the plastic bag of goods, she turned, clocking the bald guy from the Audi seated with a bearded man with his back to her. The Audi guy looked in her direction. She had two options: avoid the eye contact and quickly look away or acknowledge it and look directly at him. She chose the latter and greeted him with a polite nod and smile. But inside, her smile was anything but polite and she wanted to scream a warning at the top of her lungs.

She got back into her car and waited for a moment, composing herself. Did he suspect her of being a cop? Leila felt like her entire demeanour would give her away. Her heightened alertness alone screamed cop, not to mention her terrible effort to look casually in his direction. As she was scrolling through her phone to call Ben, there was a tap on her side window, making her jump. The Audi guy smiled from the other side of the glass. Even with a scruffy beard and bald head, the man's smile was dazzling, brilliant white. Leila put her window down just enough to make a ten-centimetre gap at the top.

'Sorry to startle you, love. I was just seeing if you know of any places around town to go where there might be some fine young ladies such as yourself?'

She would've been flattered if she didn't know better. Sliding her phone out of view, she casually responded.

'It's a Saturday night, so I'm sure the two pubs will have enough action for you. What brings you to a town like Echo Springs?'

The man smiled without baring his teeth. Was he onto her?

'A mate of mine is from out here. Raves about the place all the time, so thought I'd come and see it for myself.'

'Oh really? What's his name? I might know him. Everyone knows everyone out here.'

'He's not out here anymore. He's actually banged up, which is why I wanted to come and make sure his family are all okay.'

Leila knew exactly who he was talking about and didn't want to push the conversation. This guy already knew too much about her for her liking.

'Well, I better get this food back before it gets cold. Enjoy your stay in Echo Springs.'

The man bared his teeth in a smile this time. 'I'm sure I will.'

Heat inflamed Leila's chest. She could feel the heat pouring from her skin so she quickly started the car and pulled out of the carpark. The man stepped back but didn't go back inside the restaurant, watching her as she drove away.

She glanced in the rear-vision mirror as she pulled away. She knew she was up against the clock now, and she knew it reeked of Jayden Terrance.

Chapter Twenty

Leila parked her car at the back of the police station within the gated compound, and raced inside. Ben and Tracey were in the muster room at the rear of the building, a room full of computers on desks for police to write statements and finish their investigation reports. Ben's smile quickly fell off his face when he saw her.

'What now?' he asked.

'Nothing,' Leila replied, shooting a glance at Tracey. 'Shall we go and eat this in the kitchen so that the smell doesn't annoy Trace?'

Ben looked sceptical, but followed Leila into the kitchen and dining area. They unpacked their food and Ben grabbed a couple of forks from the cutlery drawer.

'Now are you going to tell me what the hell is going on?' He talked low, taking a seat next to Leila at the table.

Leila, still watching the door to the kitchen, spoke equally as quietly. 'There's something going on out at Jacinta Buchanan's property, at the old mine sites.'

'Okay? I think they're already onto it because our taskings have all been out to Far Trail Road.'

'So have you been out there?'

'Not yet. I keep getting tied up with other jobs. But what's this all about?'

Leila paused. Should she confess everything she knew, including Brayden's involvement?

'I saw a car up that way today when I went for a run, and then I just saw the same car again in town. The guy talked to me. I think he's an associate of Jayden Terrance.' She omitted the information about seeing Brayden.

'Oh,' Ben said. 'Are you going to tell Mac about this? Or at least write an intel report on what you've seen?'

Leila shook her head. 'I want to double check everything before I go putting my foot in it with the wrong information.'

Ben frowned again, clearly unconvinced.

'Don't look at me like that. I'm not going to do anything stupid. You just know what Coops will be like if he gets wind of any of this.'

This time Ben couldn't argue with her. They both knew all too well what Sergeant Cooper was like when he was on the warpath about something; his blinkers came on and he was hyper-focused, sometimes to the detriment of himself and the case.

Ben ate down to the few last mouthfuls of his vindaloo when a call came over the radio broadcasting throughout the station speakers—there was a domestic assault occurring. Scoffing down the last of the meal, Ben wiped his brow, damp from the heat of the dish. Tracey came past the doorway.

'Come on Fields, that's the same place we were at earlier for the noise complaint with that party,' she said as she rushed past the door.

Ben rolled his eyes at Leila. 'As if I didn't know that already,' he muttered.

Leila waited to hear the sound of their car pull out of the carpark before she made her way out of the kitchen to see who else was around for the night. Thankfully, the sergeant on duty wasn't Cooper but Sergeant Bob Baxter.

'Hey Sarge,' she said as she walked into the sergeant's office.

Sergeant Baxter smiled, his big bristly moustache spreading across his top lip like a sandy-coloured broom-head. 'Hi Leila. How's that hand of yours? I heard you have at least a couple of weeks off?'

She smiled back. 'It's good, thanks. That's kind of why I came in. I've got a couple of resubmits sitting on my work-off, so I thought I'd get them cleared before they became overdue and I end up having to fill out a report on why I didn't finish them in time.'

Sergeant Baxter pinched his mouth in a smile and nodded to agree. 'Not a bad idea, Leila. If you get those cases back through to me, I'll look over them tonight before Coops comes back on shift in the morning.' Sergeant Baxter gave Leila a wink and she smiled back; Sergeant Cooper was strict with quality control of all cases, but Sergeant Baxter was less so. He came from the 'just get the work done efficiently' side of the rules.

'Thanks Sarge, I appreciate it.'

Leila headed back towards the muster room, passing the locked door to the detectives' office. She had to conjure up a plan to try and somehow get access to the room, to find out how much the detectives already knew. Opening up a screen on the nearest computer, Leila sat down and typed in her username and password. She went straight in to look up the registration plates of the Audi.

'Alpha, Romeo, November. Six, four, eight.'

The registration came up as a hire-car company in Sydney. Leila took down the details of the hire company, writing them straight into her phone's note section. She knew it wasn't going to be easy to find out who this guy was. If he was a serious criminal, on Jayden's level, he wouldn't be driving around in a car that was linked to him. Because her searches in the system were audited, she added the registration details into a noise complaint at the motel, and included an incident number from the last day she worked, to prevent her being detected. With every keystroke recorded in the policing system, Leila risked getting caught. Leila kept herself logged into the computer, but locked the home screen and made her way to the kitchen to a vending machine that generally had a mind of its own. Wedging two one-dollar coins into the opening, Leila got them stuck at just the right moment. Out of the corner of her eye she clocked a person coming, and jumped.

'Shit, Sarge, you startled me.'

His smile widened underneath his moustache and his heavy-set physique rumbled with a chuckle. He held out the empty cup in his hand, pointing it towards the sink.

'Just making the last coffee. The doctor said I need to cut back on my six coffees a night. I'd like to see how he goes on night shift after twenty-four years.'

Leila banged on the vending machine for effect. 'Hey, has anyone used this tonight? There are some coins stuck in here. I just wanted to get a can of coke and a chocolate bar to keep me going for the next hour.'

Sergeant Baxter shook his head. 'That bloody machine is useless. The bloke was only out here fixing it, two nights ago.'

A twinge of guilt niggled her for being the cause of the machine's failure this time.

'Do the Ds still have their social club fundraising chocolates and drinks in their office?' She kept her breathing careful and natural.

'Yeah, they sure do, love. Go grab the keys from my desk. Here, can you grab me one of those honey nougat bars?' He handed her a two-dollar coin.

She smiled. 'Sure thing.'

There was only a small window of time to get into the room and gather all the information she could. Opening the top drawer, Leila grabbed the bulky keys among the loose paper and visitor passes, and headed back along the corridor to the detectives' office. Sergeant Baxter passed as she unlocked the office, humming a tune that Leila didn't recognise. The detectives' room was dark so Leila flicked on a light and shut the door behind her. Pulling her phone out of her pocket quickly, she flicked the camera open and raced to the whiteboard where details of the detectives' latest investigation hung. She started snapping away at the timeline of events and correlating photographs. So far, they believed the activities around town were drug related, and that more than one operation had come into conflict in Echo Springs. No medals for intelligence there; most of the trouble in town was due to drugs. One photo stopped her. It was a picture of her and Brayden boxing together at the PCYC, followed by a series of photos of Brayden hanging around town, mainly talking on his phone. Leila kept snapping the pictures and file photographs across the board, until another photo made her pause. It was a custody photo of Audi guy. Brett Pearce, read the name underneath. His photo was among a group of other possible players involved in the drug distribution around town. Two of them were the bikies Detective Senior Constable Hartley Cooper had caught a few weeks back; although in prison now, they had clammed up about their boss. Leila's eyes darted desperately around the whiteboard, her phone lowered as she searched for the one face she prayed not to find.

But there, sitting alongside his own mother, was Hayden.

She froze. Squinting her eyes shut, she took in a breath and couldn't bring herself to read the writing underneath. She turned to walk to the small fridge in the far corner and grabbed a can of coke. Dumping the coins into the honesty tin, she also took two chocolate bars and made her way out of the office. She paused at the door and flicked the door's lock to unlock it and flicked the light off.

It all made sense in the timeline. Why had Hayden come home now? It was well known in the station that Jayden Terrance was likely a high-level supplier of meth, so when he was put away, it only made sense that his younger brother would take over.

Threatening tears pushed against the back of Leila's eyes as she walked back down the corridor to the sergeant's office.

Sergeant Baxter looked up at Leila as she entered, keys and chocolates in her hand. 'What's the matter, Leila? You look like you've just seen a ghost or something.'

She blinked hard and laughed off the suggestion. 'You don't seriously believe all those rumours about the figure that wanders around the cells in the custody area do you?'

'Rumours? Not rumours, I saw it for myself one night in custody,' he replied.

Leila shivered. 'Until I see it for myself, I don't believe it, but I think someone just ran over my grave.'

Sergeant Baxter's left brow raised. He smirked. 'Yep. That's him alright. That's what the ghost does. He does shit like that all the time.'

Leila shook her head while putting the keys and chocolate bar on the desk. 'Well I'll get this work done and I'm out of here.'

Thank goodness.

'Sing out if you need anything,' he said, unwrapping the chocolate bar.

Leila slowly walked the corridor, the lump in her throat hardening. But Leila had become a master of hiding pain since losing her daughter; deflecting the subject to numb the rawness. Pausing at the door to the detectives' office, she wondered if she should just look one more time. There might be more to it? She hadn't snapped a photo of Hayden and his mum. *Wait.* She stared ahead. *Why was Aunt Sue there too?*

Looking around her, Leila quickly opened the door and closed it behind her. Flicking the light on, she saw her can of coke on the desk near the whiteboard. *Careless, careless, careless.* She inhaled and held it as she made her way over to the board. The moment of truth about her love, laid bare on the investigation board.

A photo of Hayden from his father's funeral sat beside one of him visiting his brother in prison. Next to those two photographs was one of Sue, taken by the local newspaper when she was named employee of the year at the supermarket. Underneath each photograph, their personal details were written out in in black marker. Below that read: NIL INVOLVEMENT. The pounding in Leila's chest released like a strained coiled spring. Tears of relief slipped down her cheeks; she wiped them away with the back of her hand. She took as many photos as she could of the board and grabbed her can and chocolate bar, locking the door behind her before anyone could see her.

Chapter Twenty-One

Hayden flicked through the *Echo Daily* newspaper as he ate his toast smothered with strawberry jam, just like his father used to, paying close attention to the classifieds and hoping for a bargain item. The usual furniture, televisions and lawn mowers were listed along with a few boats, cars and motorbikes. Hayden continued scrolling through the list before hitting the real estate section. His brow pinched inward at how long some of the houses had been on the market for, including Leila's rental.

'Morning, love.' Sue patted him lovingly on the shoulder as she passed to switch the kettle on.

Dressed in a lightweight robe, singlet and track pants, Sue stretched side to side as she prepared her morning cup of coffee.

'I didn't hear Brayden leave this morning,' she said mid-yawn. 'I've been having such a great night's sleep since you've been back, love. But you've always have had that effect on me.' She kissed the top of Hayden's head and got the milk out of the fridge. He stretched back to give his slight mum a single-armed embrace in return.

'That kid almost didn't go to boxing this morning,' Hayden said, still frustrated. 'I had to kick his ass out of bed. He looked rough when he woke up, like he had no sleep or something. Do you ever look through his phone? You do have a right to, you know. He's only fourteen and in more trouble than most kids his age, so he just has to deal with not being trusted.'

Sue continued making her cup of coffee. Shaking her head, she replied, 'Love, there's no use fighting with that boy. You know what he's like, and my life just becomes more stress than it's worth. Thank goodness for Leila doing what she's doing with him. I couldn't cope with him getting locked up and sent away.'

'Well then, I will be getting him to hand over his phone as soon as I see him next. If he's looking like he hasn't slept all night when he's on curfew, then I can only imagine the shit he's looking up.'

Sue blew out a long breath. 'I hate to bloody think. It was bad enough finding porn DVDs with you and your brother, let alone this internet stuff now.'

Hayden laughed. 'All of those were Jayden's, by the way. I just watched them. I'm not that much of an ass man.'

Sue shook her head and screwed her face in horror, taking a seat at the kitchen table next to Hayden. 'Yeah, I still don't know if you needed to watch Anal Bandits One, Two and Three to understand the Volume Four that I found in the DVD player every time I tried to put a movie on.'

After Hayden recovered from his mother's blatant honesty, he changed the subject. 'I see they still have the old Town Hall up for sale.'

'Yeah, that silly Mayor Zangari wants way too much for it. That's why they can't sell it,' she replied. 'Someone told me that the council were asking almost half a million for it. You can't expect those sort of dollars in a town like this.'

Hayden nodded, taking in all the details. Sipping her coffee, she watched him for a moment.

'Why are you so interested anyway?'

His dark eyes lifted from the page. 'I wouldn't mind having a chat to the Mayor about what the Town Hall could do for the kids in our town.'

Sue smiled widely. 'How about you sell your pitch to me first then?'

'You know the cooking classes I was running in the city at the community centre?'

Sue nodded.

'Well I've seen the success they had in town, and I reckon all the kids out here deserve the same opportunities. That PCYC is useless. There's no programs for the kids to stay out of trouble. Obviously, cooking is just the start. There's a lot the kids could be offered. The government has plenty of funding for programs that I would apply for. I've done a bit of research and a proper youth centre is something our town desperately needs.'

As Sue drank her coffee, he caught her adoring stare and smiled sheepishly. She put her hand on his strong arm and rubbed her thumb along the ridge of the muscle on his forearm.

'Love, that is one of the best things I've ever heard. If you can talk that Mayor down to two hundred K, I'll invest Dad's money for your project. You have a beautiful heart, Hayden. I'd love to see you do good things for this town.'

Hayden stared at her, speechless. A flood of emotions from the time after his dad died washed over him. He could take the drug money Jayden had been putting in and invest it back into the community. Hayden felt less and less intimidated by Jayden as he continued making his plans. Maybe he was being reckless, but this was a risk he was prepared to take. He told himself he was ready to take Jayden on, head first.

'I wouldn't need all of it, Mum. I'd just need enough to get a deposit for a mortgage and business start-up loan from the bank.'

Sue shook her head. 'Bullshit. You know what banks are like to a family with a name like ours. No, son. This is something your father would want to see you succeed in. You're having as much as you need.'

'I'd repay you though,' he said, mainly convincing himself.

Sue nodded in response. 'I know you would, my love.'

Hayden finished the last bit of his toast and got up, putting his plate in the sink.

'How's Leila's hand anyway? Brayden's just not the same without her dragging him to boxing in the mornings.'

Hayden's smile spread across his face before Sue had finished the question. 'We talked about Kaylee the other night.'

Sue's eyes widened. 'Really? Leila actually talked about her? Well I never.'

Hayden chuckled. 'Yeah, I know. I mean, I knew she took it hard with the way she just took off, but I never really thought about how she felt towards her own body. She really hated herself. I wish I went after her harder when she needed me.'

'Love, there was nothing anyone could've done for her. You know Leila better than anyone. She was never going to let you get close. I'm just glad she's talking to you about it now.'

Tears formed at the bottom of Sue's eyes. She wiped the pooled tears with the back of her index finger. Hayden reached around his mum and pulled her into his body.

'Mum, you don't need to cry anymore. Leila and I are in a really good place now. What we had never left—either of us.'

Sue choked back a sob from his words.

'Ah Jesus, Mum. You're a bloody mess,' he laughed.

'I've hoped this day would come. Wait till I tell Cath.' Sue squeezed her son tight. 'Now go get this project of yours started so that you two can turn this town around together.'

Chapter Twenty-Two

The sun had risen well into the sky by the time Leila woke up. She could sleep anywhere at any time, which always helped with working shift work. Mac and Hartley called her part feline.

She reached across to check her phone. No messages. A lump niggled in her throat. Hayden hadn't responded to her message last night. She shook the thought; he was not involved in anything his older brother was doing to this town. She didn't need to worry about jeopardising her position within her command. They *did* have a shot together after all—Hayden was not one of the bad guys. She always knew it, but the confirmation made it all taste so much sweeter. Maybe that was why she could sleep ten hours straight.

She was glad Hayden hadn't pushed the issue about coming around the night before. But there was something unsatisfying that he hadn't pushed for it either. Having sex with Hayden was the final piece of the healing puzzle … and she still didn't know whether she was ready for that yet. She didn't trust how she would react to being intimate … and vulnerable. Even though he was the one person she trusted with all her heart, there was still something about her body that she needed to protect herself from. What if her body deceived her again? She couldn't risk it. Not yet.

Leila got out of bed, heading straight to the computer in the second bedroom of the house. She opened the photographs she had taken of the detective's board and began printing them off one by one. She needed to spread everything out to get a clear picture of what the detectives were on to, and what was missing from the picture.

Grabbing Blu-tac from her desk drawer, Leila started sticking the pictures along a blank wall in her home office, emulating the detectives' investigation

board at the station. She added the photos she'd taken of Brayden and wrote
the name of the hire company the Audi was rented from and then stood back
to inspect the timeline of events. Definitely drugs. With someone like Brett
Pearce in town, it meant there was a drop happening. She shook her head,
eyes gazing over the photos of Brayden.

'Fuck, Brayden. What have you got yourself involved in?' she said aloud.

The duffle bag must have been a bag of cash. Was he keeping a cache out
at the Bulls' Run mines? It all made sense. No one ever went near the mines,
so it would be the perfect place to store cash from the proceeds of crime. But
the cops weren't onto this information yet, so she needed to get to Brayden
before her colleagues did. Closing the door on her pseudo-investigation
room, Leila opened her phone and sent a message to Brayden: *How was boxing this morning? I miss kicking your ass already!* She signed off with an emoji
with its tongue sticking out.

Brayden didn't reply; he must be getting ready for school. He hated school,
but he only needed to stick with it for one more year and she had plans to get
him into a trade apprenticeship. School just didn't suit some kids, and Brayden
was a prime example of why trades were a good alternative to stop kids slipping through the cracks and adding to the unemployment stats across town.

By the time Leila finished eating a bowl of cereal and drinking a cup
of coffee, she'd decided to pay Brayden a visit at school. The absence of a
response from him had her on high alert. It wasn't like him to not reply. She
sent Hayden a text next.

*Did Brayden go to boxing this morning? I'm going to drop past school to pay him
a quick visit today.*

Hayden instantly replied: *Had to drag his scrawny ass out of bed for boxing.
Must've gone straight to school. When you see him tell him to get back to me! The
little shit isn't answering his phone!!*

Leila was instantly uneasy, and she'd learned not to ignore her intuition.
Discovering facts before jumping to conclusions was how she was supposed
to think, but there was something just not right about this whole scenario.
She didn't want to alarm Hayden yet, and replied back: *lol will do. Do you
have plans later?*

Again, the reply was immediate: *Thought you'd never ask.* Complete with
a row of love hearts.

Leila smiled. Her heart was consumed by Hayden, only subsumed by the
drive to keep Brayden safe and out of trouble.

She cursed Jayden under her breath as she got dressed. His influence had his baby brother tied up in all of this, and she knew Hayden was going to be furious when he found out.

Getting in her car, Leila drove past the motel to see if the Audi was still there. Brayden's unusual behaviour had coincided with Brett Pearce's arrival. There was no sign of the Audi at the motel. She drove around the main street, supermarket and pubs. With no sign of the Audi anywhere around town, she headed to Echo Springs High School, in desperate hope that Brayden would be there when she arrived.

Parking the car and walking into the reception office of the school, Leila was greeted by Tamara, a bubbly girl she used to go to school with.

'G'day Leila. How's that hand? I heard you had to take time off work because of it.'

Leila smiled politely. 'Yeah, it's all good now. I cut it on a jar of olives of all things. I'm such a klutz.' She quickly changed the subject. There was no time to waste. 'Hey, I'm just coming in to see Brayden. I won't distract him and pull him out of class, but I just want to come and observe how he's doing while I'm off work.'

Tamara looked perplexed. 'But we had an email from you saying he was going to be absent due to his performance review with the justice program. I have it printed out here.'

Leila was stunned. What email account? How did anyone have access to her work or home account? Tamara came back with a piece of paper in hand and laid it across the wooden reception counter. Leila looked first to the email address. It wasn't her account.

'I don't have an account like that,' she said pointing to the email: constableleila@gmail.com.

'Oh. I didn't even think to check that. It all looked legit to me. As soon as I read your name, I thought it was you. He's a bloody sneaky kid, that Brayden.' Tamara had turned red in the face.

'Look, so that we're both not in hot water for this little situation, I'm going to go and find him, and drag him back in here before the day's out and anyone knows what's happened.'

Tamara's smile was full of gratitude. 'Thank you, Leila. I feel a bit stupid.'

Leila put her hand on Tamara's. 'Don't beat yourself up about it. Like you said, Brayden's a cunning little shit sometimes, so let's just sort this out quick smart.'

Leila made a dash back out the door, pulling her phone from her pocket as she walked quickly. Hayden answered after three rings.

She didn't let him speak before jumping in. 'Hey, Brayden's not at school.'

'What?!' Hayden's voice was raised.

'But don't worry, I'm going to find him and bring him back here,' she tried to reassure him. 'So if the police come past, just tell them he's with me, okay?'

'Why would the police come here? What's going on, Leila?'

She could hear the concern in his voice, but she held back from telling him more.

'Nothing. I'm just worried someone from work will be onto him for not being at school. It's all part of the program. If they see him around town, he's going to be in breach of his program conditions.'

'I'm going to look for him too then,' he replied.

'You don't have to do that, I'm sure he's just out at the lookout, smoking or something.' She was trying her hardest not to tremble, fear for Brayden setting in deep.

'Yeah it will be something alright. I'm going to wring his neck when I find him. Call me if you get to him first.'

Leila was about to reply with the same request when the call ended abruptly. She checked the phone to be sure, staring at the black screen in shock. Hayden was going to be angry, but she would rather it was him than one of her workmates who found Brayden.

Chapter Twenty-Three

After spending the day driving around town without any success, Leila made her way back home. She even went as far as driving out to the old mines, but there was nothing out there and no sign of anyone having been there at all. The rough surface of the gravel road made it almost impossible to locate tire tracks or footprints. She was hesitant about going into the mine, and decided at the last minute not to go. Running around all day and not eating or drinking had left her light in the head.

As she rounded the corner into her street, a patrol car drove towards her. The highbeams flashed to indicate they wanted to chat. She gulped in a deep breath and held it there as she wound down her window. She was relieved to see Ben on his own. He frowned when she pulled up beside him.

'A couple of the guys said you've been driving around town like a crazy woman today. What's going on?'

She looked down, trying to avoid lying to his face. 'Nothing now. I couldn't find Dad earlier. He went wandering off as drunk as anything and Mum has been beside herself.'

Ben's eyes softened. 'I'm sorry, Leila. That must be really hard.'

If only Ben knew the truth to his words. Blowing out a puff, she replied, 'Yeah, but he's home and tucked in bed now so I'm going home to do pretty much the same thing.'

'Fair enough. If anything like that happens again, just call us to help okay?'

Leila smiled, her insides crammed with guilt.

'We're busy enough in this town without worrying about people like my old man. I had it covered, but thanks all the same.'

Within Ben's car, the radio began broadcasting a job for a theft at the bottle shop. Ben listened and looked back at Leila with a grin.

'Same shit, different day,' he said before waving and driving off.

Leila pulled into her driveway. With a heavy heart she made her way into her house. Despite all her best efforts, she couldn't stop Brayden from making mistakes that could ruin his entire life. If he went into juvenile detention for longer than a few months, she knew he would be lost forever. The pain her Aunt Sue would go through was a weight on Leila's shoulders.

She swung the door open to find Hayden sitting on her couch in the lounge room. He got up and hugged her tight the moment she entered. She held onto him. The hug wasn't one of reassurance. Hayden's body was tense under her touch, and everything was far from alright. She looked up into his eyes. There was darkness there.

'He's gone to the city,' Hayden finally said.

'What? … How? … Why?'

'I had a call from my Uncle Ray. Brayden's crashing at his, and he'll be back tomorrow night. He's a stupid kid who wanted to go for a joyride and wag school.' Hayden was unconvincing, but Leila wasn't willing to step away. 'I'll go and get him tomorrow if he's not home.'

She held on tight, but the secrets between them created distance.

'He's more trouble than he's worth, that kid.' Hayden tried to crack a smile.

There was nothing either of them could do now.

'But what about his curfew? What if they go 'round to check on him tonight?'

'Mum knows what's going on and she'll be telling them he's with me. His conditions are that he needs to be in the presence of a responsible adult if he's out. And I'm the responsible one in the family, remember?' He winked playfully.

Leila chuckled and held him tighter, agreeing with him more than he knew. Hayden was the responsible one, and her workmates' board confirmed as much.

'I don't know how I feel about harbouring a criminal in my home for the night,' Leila teased.

Hayden frowned. 'I don't get it.'

'Well if you're supposed to be with Brayden, and you're not. You're basically breaking the law. And I don't know how I feel about hiding a lawbreaker in my home.'

Hayden kissed the top of her head as he laughed. 'Then that makes you a co-conspirator, Constable.'

Leila couldn't help but grin. 'You got me there.'

Hayden bent down and whisked Leila off her feet, holding her easily. She kissed him as he walked towards her bedroom, letting her love for him free. She felt wild, untamed, her senses alight with anticipation. In a time of need, they came together, like they always did, and everything was like it should be—everything was right.

The closer they got to the room at the end of a long corridor, the more their kiss deepened. She wished she could just fall into him and become one being.

He laid her gently onto her bed, and she held his face between her palms, never wanting to let him go. He hovered above her before moving himself around, arranging his strong, broad body over hers. Her legs wrapped around his waist, pulling him to her. He ran his hand down the back of her thigh, all the way to the hem of her shorts, sending a multitude of electrical spasms across her body. With her eyes closed, Leila could see bursts of light under her lids every time Hayden's lips met hers. He trailed his lips, soft and supple, along her jaw, his stubble gently grazing her skin. He slid the left singlet and bra strap down her shoulder, and followed with his mouth.

Leila wasn't afraid. She savoured every ounce of the building sensuality, releasing her past with each heated breath she exhaled. Hayden cupped his hand behind her back and pulled her top up over her head, leaving her lilac bra on. He paused for a moment, and she watched as he took her all in. His eyes glistened in the evening light.

Not a word was uttered between them before they fell into each other for the rest of the night, replacing her pain with something brighter, softer. It coursed through her veins and love exploded throughout her body.

Chapter Twenty-Four

Leila woke before Hayden, making full use of the morning's stillness to take in every inch of the beautiful, naked man lying beside her. She didn't realise just how much she'd missed him until she had him again.

Being completely naked with Hayden hadn't had the effect Leila was worried about. Instead of making her feel insecure about her own disloyal body, it brought a sense of calm she'd been yearning for but unable to find.

She gently draped a leg around him as he lay on his side facing her.

Their night together was everything Leila hoped it would be, and more. A weight had been lifted, her pain soothed by her intimacy with Hayden.

Leila's gaze was drawn back to his lips as they twitched. She grinned so hard it almost hurt her face.

His sandy-coloured eyelashes flickered slowly, dark eyes peering into hers.

'Good morning.' His sleepy voice was music to her ears.

'Good morning.'

They stared for a moment longer, drinking each other in.

'I love you,' she said, without hesitation.

His eyes pinched at the edges as he beamed. He launched at her, taking her by surprise, and they rolled into one another with a crash of passion.

'I never stopped loving you,' he whispered and nibbled on her earlobe.

She giggled like an idiot and the world melted away again.

The day was almost coming to a close by the time Leila and Hayden drew breath from one another. She had never felt more alive. His talent in the bedroom had only matured. Leila begrudgingly put it down to the experience he'd had with other women in the time they were apart. But everything that had happened before now had made these moments more perfect. What they had could never break again.

'I'm going to shower and try and fix us something to eat, considering we haven't eaten all day,' Leila said and gave him one more kiss on the lips before dragging herself away.

'Oh, but I have eaten all day.' His eyes were alight with humour.

She couldn't help but laugh. Tempted to just climb back into bed with Hayden, she dragged herself to the bathroom before it was too late. She passed the closed door to her office where her makeshift investigation time-line sat, and the magic of the morning slipped away. How was she going to approach it with him? She had to tell him. It was his family. But it was also her career she would be jeopardising.

The warm water of her shower washed over her. She dipped her head back under the stream to let the water rinse the heat and sweat from her body. Closing her eyes, she also tried to wash away the test the very near future was going put on them as a couple.

Hayden's big hands slid around Leila's naked waist and she opened her eyes under the stream. The shower sat above a candy-pink porcelain bath from the seventies. The bathroom's seventies vibe was complete with light green tiles with little frogs sitting on lily pads. It was Leila's favourite room. She'd added a bold green banana-leaf shower curtain to modernise the features and complement the colour scheme. A long Devil's Ivy plant hung from the corner ceiling, flowing all the way to the floor. Hayden didn't seem to notice, concentrating on squeezing a handful of gel into his palm and lathering it all over Leila's soft skin.

Her skin still prickled from heightened sensitivity and she squirmed under his touch. She tried to focus on their life outside so that she wasn't just swept back into their consuming passion again.

'Hey. There's something I have to show you.' She tried to pull back from him, but he wouldn't allow it.

'Okay, but first—'

She interrupted him before he could finish. 'No. This is serious. Focus for a minute.' She held his hair-covered face in her hands.

He rolled his eyes and pouted like a kid.

'There's more to Brayden that I haven't told you about,' Leila said.

The first hurdle of their choices was upon them, and Leila wondered how many more times they would come up against this, when both Hayden's brothers were engaged in criminal activity and she was the law.

Leila rinsed the remaining soapy foam from her body and got out first, grabbing a soft white towel to wrap around her body. She tried to prepare herself for how Hayden was going to feel about seeing his baby brother implicated in something that might also have something to do with his older brother. She started towel-drying her long dark locks when Hayden turned the shower off and joined her. She passed him a towel and wrapped hers around her head in a turban before walking along the hallway, completely naked. She loved how she felt about her body again. Knowing how much Hayden loved it had helped her to love being in her skin again. As strong and independent as she may have pretended to be on the outside, Leila was forced to admit how much sexier she felt after allowing a man to worship the body she had despised for so long.

Leila threw on a pair of sweatpants and singlet—her usual house attire—by the time Hayden came into the bedroom. His clothes were strewn across the floor, and he picked up his shorts and Nike t-shirt.

'So tell me what's been going on,' he said.

She grabbed his hand and led him to her office. Opening the door, she stood in front of her timeline of photographs spread across her wall. Hayden's eyes bounced across the names and faces.

'What is this?'

'It's the investigation the detectives have on drug supply in town, naming Jayden as the main suspect … and it could possibly involve Brayden.'

Hayden got closer to the photos Leila had taken at the mine site, pulling one off. It was the one with Brayden carrying the duffle bag from the mine. His nostrils flared and she could see the fury building.

'The detectives don't have these photos.' She indicated the photos of the white Audi at the old mines. 'I took them when I went for a run the other day.'

Hayden looked at her.

'I've got to go into the city and get Brayden,' he said. 'My brother won't stop until the kid is balls-deep in this shit-fight. I can't let Jayden destroy my brother's future.'

'What shit-fight? Did you know what Jayden was doing?'

Hayden stuck the photo back onto the wall. 'I've tried to stop this from happening for a long time, but you know what Jayden's like. I'm going to put a stop to it for good, like I should've done from the start. I'm not going to let drugs and crime ruin what's left of my family.'

'Then you should have gone to the police. They have Jayden locked up anyway, so who cares what you tell them to keep him there. He obviously has little regard for the system if it hasn't slowed the operation after him being locked up.'

'You think going to the cops would've stopped him? Nothing would stop Jayden. He was just born bad, and metal bars won't stop him from being just that. I'm paying my brother a visit and then I'm getting Brayden and bringing him back home. I'm not having this anymore.'

Leila offered a slight smile to Hayden. She'd made the right decision. He'd reacted exactly how she'd hoped he would. She knew he would pull Brayden out, and they could begin the rest of their lives. Once Hayden had his own family's problems sorted, Leila knew she wouldn't have to adjust her moral compass again. Her dedication to the job was too much to ever risk this type of behaviour, but considering her ties to the Terrances, this just felt right.

Chapter Twenty-Five

Hayden pushed the car beyond the speed limit as he raced towards the city, desperate to find his baby brother and stop the dictatorship of his older brother once and for all. The sun rose from the edge of the horizon, the road to the city vast and flat with barely a tree in sight. You could almost make out the curvature of the earth, it was so desolate and bare for as far as the eye could see. Then a dramatic change as the mountains grew higher and the road travelled up towards the clouds. It was a punishing drive through the ranges until the road reached the other side and flattened out once more.

Eight hours later, and an hour before the prison's visiting hours started, Hayden arrived in the city. He pulled into a truck stop and showered to freshen up. He didn't want to give any reason for the wardens to deny him access to his brother, and presentation was one way they would try to stop him.

Arriving at Silverwater Correctional Complex with half an hour to spare before visiting hours began, Hayden made his way to reception to enter in the details for his request.

After an hour's wait and the usual screening processes, Hayden was let in to a no-contact room. It was just as well because Hayden didn't trust what he would do to his brother with the amount of uncontrollable rage coursing through his body.

As soon as he saw the shadow of his brother approaching with the distinctive swagger, Hayden stood up, showing his towering size to his shorter, older, menacing brother. Jayden smirked when he saw Hayden standing.

'You leave Brayden the fuck alone, or else I'll go to the dogs and have you stay in here forever!' Hayden shouted at the window.

Jayden didn't sit, but the warden next to him commanded he take a seat or else the visit was over. No longer in control of his life inside these walls, Jayden sat without challenging the demand. His top lip curled into a snarl at Hayden.

'So your little girly's already got an influence over you, has she? Brett said she's still a hot piece of ass. He reckons it's no wonder you bailed on me.'

Hayden's blood boiled in his ears and he beat against the toughened Perspex barrier with both fists. 'IF YOU COME NEAR HER, I WILL GUT YOU!' he roared.

Two guards immediately opened the door behind Hayden, physically restraining him either side.

'YOU GO NEAR ANY OF MY FAMILY AND YOUR LIFE WON'T BE WORTH LIVING, YOU PIECE OF SHIT!' Hayden continued to bellow as the guards dragged him from the room. 'I HOPE YOU ROT IN HERE!'

The prison's chief governor insisted on speaking to Hayden once he'd calmed down, summoning him to his office. Hayden obliged, knowing full well this would be his official ban from visiting the prison. Entering the modest grey-blue office, Hayden took a seat as directed.

'You want to tell me what that was all about? We take threats to our inmates very seriously in this facility, so you might want to start explaining the reasons for the outburst before you're charged with menacing behaviour.'

Hayden stared at the governor, unfazed by the threat of legal action. It had been worth it to Hayden. He'd seen the moment of fear pass across his brother's face. Jayden knew Hayden's capabilities; he wouldn't be taking the threat lightly. Evil ran in their family, whether Hayden liked it or not. With every Terrance, there was always something bubbling just below the surface, waiting to break out with the right provocation, and Jayden would know it was in Hayden too.

'How surprising. You don't want to talk? Well let me just say this, young man. You may not be a customer of mine, but by the sounds of your recent conversations with your brother, I'd say you're a bee's dick away from getting to know me a whole lot better.'

Hayden's rage was still teetering close to the edge, but he controlled it enough to reply with, 'Is that all? Unless you're going to charge me, I would like to go, thanks.'

'Oh, and before I leave, you might want to confiscate the phone I have in the locker. I think you'll find everything you need on that.'

Hayden was crossing a line they said never to cross, but what choice did he have?

'You will have an indefinite suspension, prohibiting you from coming back to this facility, Mr Terrance. Please gather your property from the front desk and never return, am I understood?'

Hayden nodded. 'Loud and clear,' he replied, and left the office to be escorted out of the building.

He heard the governor pick up the phone before he was even out of earshot.

'Seize the phone from the Terrance kid immediately.'

Hayden jumped back into the car and turned on his other, everyday phone. A message instantly pinged from Leila. *Brayden is home. I'm at your mum's house now. He's not leaving my sight.*

Hayden smiled at the welcome news. He was so grateful for Leila. What if this kid was really becoming more trouble than he was worth? He shook the thought; if he wanted to start helping the other kids in town like Brayden, he needed to stop thinking like this. Of course they were all worth it.

He replied back with a message to Leila: *Thanks for being there. I'll see be seeing Jayden in an hour then I'll head back home. Love you xx*

He felt a twinge of guilt about lying to her, but what he was about to do had to be his secret from her forever.

If he was to keep the city bikies out of town, he needed to pay them a personal visit. It was a risk he was willing to take to protect everyone he loved.

Chapter Twenty-Six

Leila sat with Sue in her kitchen while Brayden slept off wherever he'd been. Leila attempted to explain her extra interest in Brayden as something happening in the mentoring program, but she knew Sue wasn't buying it.

'So how about you cut the crap about this justice program and you tell me exactly what's going on with Brayden.' Sue took a sip of her tea.

Leila avoided direct eye contact.

Sue pushed further. 'Is it because he went to the city? Is he in trouble with the cops? Is that why you can't tell me?'

Leila's eyes flashed to Sue's. 'No, he's not in trouble … yet. But he's going to be if we don't keep an eye on him. We can't let him out of our sight, okay? I won't be able to help him if the cops find out what he's been up to.'

Tears threatened. Brayden's welfare was important to her, but the position he'd put her in was excruciating. Sue delicately placed her palm over Leila's bandaged hand resting on the table.

'Thank you, Leila,' she said. 'I don't think you understand how grateful I am that you're in our life.'

A tear slipped down Leila's cheek. Being seen within the community as something positive was all she'd ever wanted. But doubt tugged at the back of her neck. At what cost did she earn this understanding? She was pushing against her own ethics to keep Brayden out of trouble, and it would cost her career if anyone found out what she knew but hadn't disclosed to her superiors.

Sue pulled Leila into an embrace when her tears kept coming. She stroked the back of her hair and Leila's tears fell freely without a sound.

'Thank you for not acting on whatever information you have. I can't imagine how you must be feeling. I'm just sorry my boy is the one doing this.'

'If it wasn't your son, I wouldn't be feeling like this,' Leila replied.

'I know, love. You are one special kid.'

Nothing else needed to be said. Leila's allegiance to her family would always be stronger than her job. Were her bosses right all along? Would people like Leila never fit the mould?

'Hayden said you have a statue of Kaylee in the backyard. Can you show me?'

Sue pulled back.

Leila, now uncomfortable, shrugged. 'It's funny how you can miss someone who you didn't even know.'

Sue's chin quivered, tears welling in the bottom of her eyes.

'We all think about her every day. We think about you too.' Sue sniffed and blinked the tears. 'But I feel better knowing Mick would be looking after her up there.'

Leila didn't necessarily buy into heaven, but she was really sure Mick and Kaylee would be in the same place if there was one.

'Come on, I'll show you my beautiful granddaughter,' Sue said as she pulled Leila up from her seat, leading her to the back door.

The yard was lush with green tropical plants lining the back deck, and the grass beyond the deck looked fluffy and inviting. It had never looked nice when she was a kid. The harsh outback sun and lack of rain meant things got brown and crusty pretty quickly. But Sue's backyard now looked like the houses on the other end of town, where people could afford to pay for the council's high water rates.

'Wow, Aunt Sue, this looks beautiful out here.'

Sue looked back and smiled. 'This is my happy place since my Mick left, and I stopped with the booze. With the boys always off busy, and your mum, well—' Sue didn't continue talking about Cath Mayne, and Leila was happier for it. 'I just find I'm really enjoying coming out here and seeing the new life around me.'

'Well you've certainly turned this place around. I can't believe how beautiful it all looks.'

Sue pointed to a garden bench under the towering gum tree in the far corner of the yard. Next to it sat a beautiful little garden statue of an angel, wheeling a barrow full of flowers. The angel was childlike with her hair falling in ringlets around her shoulders and plump cheeks. Her feathered wings draped behind her like a cape and she wore a crown of flowers around her head. For a statue she was perfect and Leila beamed. Sue watched Leila carefully.

'I like to think of her helping me out here when I'm gardening. I can feel her and Mick around me whenever I'm out here. I talk to them a lot. I tell them everything that's going on. That's Mick over there.' Sue pointed to a statue of an eagle perched on top of a set of sculpted rocks at the opposite side of the garden bench.

The eagle's neck was stretched high, its wings also stretched behind like the wings of an angel, but slightly held out from its body, as if it were ready to take flight at any moment. He watched out across the garden like a protector, regal and powerful. It was everything her Uncle Mick had been and more. Both statues were perfect, as if commissioned especially by Sue.

'I can't believe you didn't show me sooner. I love them,' Leila said.

Sue shrugged. 'Love, I don't think you've been ready to come and see them until this very moment.'

She took Leila's hand. 'But I'm glad you're here now.'

They took a seat on the bench together and looked out over the garden Sue had worked hard to produce.

'You know you could make a business out of this. If you can turn this old dust bowl into an oasis, imagine what you could do to all the backyards in this street.'

Sue laughed. 'Thanks, love. But do you know how much hard work and money this takes? I don't think the people on this street would have that kind of money to spend. Plus, I can't even get your mum to water the cactus and succulents I bought her.'

Leila sighed. All she'd ever wanted was her parents to be a bit more like Sue. Exhaustion washed over her.

Sue watched her for a moment.

'Why don't you go home and have a good sleep, love?'

Leila squinted out of one eye.

'I'll watch him. Trust me. That kid won't move from there for at least another twelve hours. You know how that boy can sleep.'

Leila's four good hours of sleep after Hayden left to drive back to the city still hadn't made up for the sleep she'd missed out on the night before.

'I'm really glad to see you and Hayden back together again,' Sue said, interrupting Leila's wicked thoughts.

How did she know so much already? Did Hayden tell her everything? Did her face give everything away?

Sue read the shock in Leila's face.

'Oh … *oh* … if something has happened, I can assure you, I didn't know you were *together* together. I just thought you were back talking.'

Leila started giggling and shook her head in amusement. 'It feels like no time has passed at all. I know that sounds clichéd, but I forgot there was ever a time apart, the moment we were *together* together again.'

Sue couldn't wipe the joy from her face.

Life suddenly felt as vibrant as the garden in front of her, as if her own happiness had made it blossom. Leila yawned again and rested her head on Sue's shoulder. Sue put her arms around Leila's face and patted her cheek.

'Go home and get some rest. I've got the day off, so I'm not going anywhere. That boy is getting a good talking to whenever he decides to get up.'

'I don't think he realises just how close he was to losing everything he's worked so hard for in the past few months. Go easy on him. He's just a kid that's been influenced by the wrong kind of people.' And with a sliver of reluctance, Leila went home to wait for Hayden to get back from the city.

Chapter Twenty-Seven

It took Leila longer than normal to settle. Her body ached from the additional physical activity she had been getting in the past couple of days. Something strummed in the back of her mind but she blew it off. She rolled her eyes and finally settled into a position where she was comfortable enough to fall asleep.

It felt like no time had passed at all when Leila woke up to Hayden's face in front of her, his eyes wide.

'Hey,' she said, rubbing her eyes. 'What time is it? I feel like I've just fallen asleep.'

'It's just past four. Mum's been trying to call you. She's frantic, and driving all over town.'

Leila's heart thumped hard. 'What? Why? Where's Brayden?'

Hayden shrugged. Disappointment was awash across his face and Leila was overcome with anger at herself for leaving Sue's place.

'Mum went to check on him when he hadn't woken, and he wasn't there. We think the little shit climbed out the window.' Hayden shook his head in frustration.

Leila climbed out of bed quickly. 'Well, let's go look for him then.'

'I think I know where he will be,' Hayden replied.

Leila pulled on some shorts and threw a shirt over her singlet. She slid into her Doc Martens, not bothering to lace them up, and rushed out to Hayden's car, which was openly parked in her driveway. At this point Leila didn't care who saw it there. She knew the superintendent would understand, given the circumstances.

They hit the dirt road towards Bulls' Run when Leila's phone rang. It was the superintendent.

'Hi, Leila. I need you to come on duty to man the station. I know you're restricted, but everyone's been called in. There's been an explosion at the old mines on Jacinta Buchanan's property. We have no idea of casualties or anything yet. I'm on my way out there now. Sergeant Cooper and the detectives are already out there with the firies. Our suspicions are that it was a clandestine lab, but we'll go over that at the debrief. All I need you to do is head into the station to manage it for me.'

The blood drained from Leila's face. 'Brayden.' Her throat clenched when she tried to talk.

'Leila. Leila! Are you there?' The superintendent's voice was breaking up as the phone slipped from Leila's hand.

There was a plume of smoke in the distance. 'What's that?'

'Drive, Hayden! Brayden's in there,' she screamed.

Hayden flattened his foot to the accelerator and they sped closer to the scene, Leila nearly hyperventilating in the passenger seat. Why couldn't they go faster?

'What's happened, Leila?' Hayden asked, but they both knew the answer.

Through the trees, she saw the flashing lights of the fire, ambulance and police cars surrounding the entrance to the mine. They rounded the corner and came to a screeching halt. Leila couldn't feel her legs hit the ground. The white Audi was mixed in with the emergency vehicles. Her whole body trembled.

Toby Grimshaw stepped out in his full yellow fire-retardant suit and helmet, and caught Leila as she ran towards the site. 'Leila, what are you doing? You can't go in there. It's unstable! We can't get near it yet.'

'BUT BRAYDEN'S IN THERE!' she screamed again.

'How do you know that?' Toby looked confused.

Superintendent Stuart came over to the commotion Leila was causing. 'Leila. You were asked to man the station,' she said.

'But I think Brayden Terrance is in there,' she cried.

Ahead, two officers fought to stop Hayden from entering the mine. Sergeant Cooper was threatening to arrest him. Leila noticed Jacinta Buchanan looking on in horror.

'I think you need to tell me what's going on, Leila.' Superintendent Stuart brought Leila back from the brink of panic.

The ground rumbled beneath them and someone called out in the distance, 'it's gonna bl—', but before they could finish, a shock wave rolled through the air, the force throwing everyone to the ground. The debris partially blocking the entrance to the mine hurtled out like missile fragments.

Everything was black. Leila tried to pull herself out of wherever she was. Her ears were ringing and she couldn't see.

'Hayden!' Leila screamed, but she was unsure if she made any sound.

Rocks of all sizes landed like mortars around her; she could feel the thump, but everything was silent. Leaves from the trees floated through the air, some of them blackened, others glowing red embers. The air was thick and Leila couldn't breathe. She coughed and staggered towards the emergency vehicles. Coops pushed to his feet in the distance, a mix of blood and dirt sliding down the side of his face.

'HAYDEN!' she tried to yell, but she still couldn't hear anything. 'HAYDEN!'

There were three people on the ground in front of her. One of them was Hayden, but he wasn't moving.

'Hayden! Hayden!' She threw herself on him. He didn't move. Blood ran from his nose and ears. His face was pale from the dust.

'Oh my god, no! Hayden, wake up!'

Police training kicked in and she started checking for vital signs. Pressing her fingers to the side of his throat, she felt a light pulse. He was alive! Suddenly, she was a robot, feeling breath from his mouth with her cheek. It was faint, but it was there. She slapped his cheek and rubbed his sternum with her knuckles to rouse him. His head began to move, and she shook him until his eyes began to flutter open. His lips moved, but still she couldn't hear. Her heart surged with relief.

Chapter Twenty-Eight

Leila's lips moved. He couldn't hear anything, but Leila was there and the sense of relief saturated his aching body.

Brayden!

'Brayden,' he said, but couldn't hear himself.

Leila was trying to say something again. His legs were heavy when he tried to move them. He looked next to him and saw one of the coppers on the ground. He wasn't moving. Leila followed his glance, and jumped across to her colleague, pressing her fingers to his throat.

Sounds hummed through Hayden's ears in waves like helicopter rotors. He tried to push off from the ground, but his muscles wouldn't obey. Finally forcing himself to sit up, he found strength to lever himself with his arms. Looking down at his legs, there were spots of blood coming through his jeans from tiny rocks hitting him like shotgun pellets.

There was another copper on the other side of him. He too was trying to get up. Blood was dripping down the side of his face and Hayden was guilty of causing this; it was his fault these guys looked like this. They were doing their job by putting themselves in harm's way to stop him from dying. Suddenly he was angry for being such a pig-headed dickhead and found every bit of strength to pull himself up to help the guy next to him.

The ground rumbled again. Hayden looked across to Leila, who was pumping the chest of the cop on the ground. The mine was going to explode. Strength rushed back into his body, greater than he'd ever felt. In one swift move, Hayden held his hand out to the cop next to him, pulling him up as he collected the guy Leila was trying to resuscitate and threw him over his shoulders. He gripped onto Leila's hand and ran. Just as the line of flashing cars appeared through dust, a wave came behind them like a steam train. He launched himself behind the fire truck, dragging Leila with him as a ball of fire rolled above. The heat of it stung his back as he lay on top of Leila to shield her. The ball of fire hissed as it hurtled into the air, craving more oxygen as it rushed higher and higher. It finally ran out of fuel and puffed into a ball of smoke, sending ash and embers everywhere.

Hayden looked down to find Leila staring up at him. She held his face between her palms, and tears streamed down her cheeks. Brayden had been in there, but he was so guilty to feel so relieved that she was safe. Leila pushed Hayden off her and called out for someone to come and help Smithy, before she prepared to start giving him compressions again.

Her eyes lit up. 'There's still a faint pulse. He needs oxygen,' she yelled.

Two paramedics raced over to Smithy and the firies sped to their battle stations, preparing to fight the fire that had quickly ignited in the surrounding scrub from the explosions.

'Come and grab the trolley from the back of the ambos and we'll run it back to these guys to get Smithy in the truck,' Leila yelled at Hayden. He could finally make out her words. They ran towards the open ambulance and Leila pushed the stretcher out, her bandaged hand working as if it were healed. Her adrenaline must've kicked in, he realised. They ran back to the two paramedics tending to Smithy.

'Thanks, Leila,' one said. 'We all have to get four points around him and on the count of three, we'll lift him up onto the stretcher. I'll grab his head.'

Next to Hayden, Ben jumped in to help.

They gripped onto Smithy's uniform, and the paramedic holding his head counted, 'One, two, three.' Smithy was up and on to the stretcher. The ground was too rough to wheel the stretcher back to the ambulance so all four held a handle and they fast-walked him over to the truck. The paramedic at his head started pumping the oxygen ball as they went. They slid the stretcher into the back and the two paramedics jumped in to continue working.

'I can jump in and drive you back into the hospital,' Ben said.

'But you just bore the brunt of that explosion too, Ben. We don't want to lose all of you,' Leila said with a frown.

He shook his head. 'I'm fine. I just want Smithy to be okay. Laura's pregnant, and I promised her on their wedding day that I'd always bring him home.'

Hayden dropped his head. This was all his fault.

When Leila spotted Hayden's expression, she said, 'I would've run towards that mine if Toby didn't stop me.' Leila looked at the crew in the back. 'I'll drive. I'm fine, I didn't even black out,' she lied. 'You guys both get in and I'll drive you all back to town. There's nothing we can do out here.'

The ambos nodded at her and she hopped into the driver's seat. Hayden jumped in beside her and Leila drove as fast as possible along the dirt track.

This type of bravery and kinship in the face of danger was new to Hayden. He hadn't witnessed people behaving so gallantly and selflessly for one another. For the first time, he respected the guys in blue. Glancing at Leila, his emotions were a swirling concoction of guilt, respect, pride and grief.

He had caught a glimpse of her world, and everything his family had done to the town now smacked him in the face like the explosion he had just experienced.

Chapter Twenty-Nine

Hayden's arms remained wrapped around her on the hospital bed when they were given the all-clear by the emergency staff. Thankfully, Hayden's leg wounds were superficial and their hearing had almost returned back to normal. Smithy's condition had been lifted from critical to stable, and Constable Matt Hutchins was getting stitched up before he was also cleared to leave. Leila was grateful for the outcome, but she knew Hayden would've been fighting his demons. Jacinta Buchanan, the landowner and a friend of theirs from their school days, was in hospital as well. She'd been knocked out by the second blast.

A heavily pregnant Laura Smith ran through the ER doors, tears streaming down her face. The nurses guided her to her husband, reassuring her that he was now stable but not out of the woods just yet.

Hayden and Leila looked at one another. News travelled back to them; the Boss had found Brayden's hat inside the Audi. They'd contained the site to begin a recovery process. The police rescue squad was on its way from the city, complete with the cadaver search dog. Leila was grateful for the information, but also wished she didn't have access to it.

Just like Laura Smith moments earlier, Sue Terrance burst through the ER doors and raced towards Leila and Hayden. Hayden instantly let go of Leila and jumped up, grabbing his mum. His strong arms enveloped her into him. She wailed and her knees buckled under her.

'It's not true, it's not true!' she howled.

Leila cried and stretched her arms around Hayden and Sue.

'I'm so sorry, Mum. I tried to stop him.' Hayden's voice cracked.

★★★

Five days had passed since they'd located and recovered Brayden's body, and Sue was still refusing to leave her bedroom. Leila didn't think it was physically possible to only go to the toilet twice in ten days, but apparently extreme grief could do that. They'd found the bodies of Brett Pearce and a Larry Donaldson, apparently the drug cook, in the mine also.

'Did you know him?' Leila dared to ask Hayden.

Hayden took her in for a moment. 'I did actually. Not a bad bloke given his occupation. I don't know if anyone will miss him though. He didn't have family.' Then he shrugged and walked off.

'Mum, are you dressed yet? The car's going to be here soon to pick us up,' Hayden said gently into Sue's closed bedroom door.

Leila appreciated how handsome Hayden looked in a dark suit, despite the fact that she had only ever seen him like this at funerals. She put her hand on his shoulder, giving him a soft smile.

'I'll go and talk to her,' she said.

He nodded. 'Thank you,' he said and kissed her on the lips.

Leila didn't know what she would do without the comfort of Hayden right now, and her heart bled more for Sue. She opened the door quietly to find Sue, dressed in a simple black dress with a thin white trim around the edges, sitting on the edge of her bed. Leila sat next to her on the bed. Sue immediately gripped Leila's hand.

With her eyes closed, Sue whispered, 'I don't think I can do this. I've had to bury too many people. I didn't think Bra—' She choked on a sob.

Leila squeezed Sue's hand tight. 'We're going to be right here with you. I'm not letting go all day, okay?'

Sue looked at Leila through bloodshot eyes. Hayden poked his head around the door and joined them on the bed, sitting on the other side of his mum. He held her other hand and repeated what Leila had just said.

'We're not letting go, all day.'

Tears slipped down Sue's bare cheeks. Through the windows, Leila saw the black Ford from the funeral home pull into the driveway. Hayden looked at his mum. She nodded back at him, and they walked out of the house, helping Sue into the car while the funeral director held the door open for them.

The trip to the cemetery felt like hours. Selfishly, Leila wished she could have Hayden next to her right then, but Sue's need for support far outweighed her own.

There was a larger crowd of people than they thought would gather around the grave for the ceremony. A small pop-up tent protected guests from the heavy clouds, threatening rain The hearse sat at the end of the pathway, waiting for Hayden and the other boys to carry Brayden to his final resting place. Leila's dad, Ned, looked smart ... and sober. He waited for the car to pull up behind the hearse before he opened the door on Leila's side. Leila climbed out first and hugged her dad tight.

'I'm so sorry, baby girl. I know how hard you were working with the young fella,' he said into her ear.

Did he? Did he really understand the frustration she faced trying to prevent this from happening? Whatever the answer, Leila was happy her father had finally made the effort to stay sober for Brayden's funeral.

Leila and Sue made their way over to the graveside and took a seat in the front row beside Cath, who also looked surprisingly fresh. Leila noticed her superintendent in full ceremonial uniform and nodded at her. They both knew she didn't need to be here, and Leila was really grateful for what the superintendent's presence meant to a family like the Terrances. Next to Superintendent Stuart was the head of the Justice Program, the Honourable Chief Justice Howard, from the city. Leila looked at Sue to see if she recognised the kind of people who were paying their respects to her son. But Sue was staring at the ground, unable to bring herself to look in the direction of the coffin sitting in the back of the hearse.

The casket was perfect for Brayden. Dark mahogany with silver trim, it had a majestic feel about it that suited the vibrant young man in eternal rest inside. Tears fell down Leila's cheeks as her father and Hayden led the pall-bearers in carrying Brayden.

The headstone facing away on the other side to Brayden marked his father's resting place, and Leila was glad they'd pushed to purchase this plot. It was important for Sue to know Mick wasn't far away. Leila recognised the fresh grave of Barry Saunders from the Darts Association, who was only buried a month earlier, only a few metres away. She wondered how his boys were doing. It was a weird thought, but Leila's mind wandered anywhere but where she actually was. Reality hurt too much. Everything Brayden represented—youth, hope and a bright future for others—was now about to be buried. She had failed him. She had failed the system that tried to protect him. Most of all, she had failed her Aunt Sue.

***

The rest of the graveside service was a blur. Sue's only request was that they didn't lower Brayden's casket until she had left.

'No one should ever watch their child go into the ground,' Sue had said at the funeral home. She had immediately stopped and apologised to Leila, who had assured Sue it was fine, but it just sent Sue into another spiral of anguish and they'd had to stop the meeting altogether.

Cath offered to go with Sue to the Town Hall for Brayden's wake, while Hayden stayed back and made sure Brayden went to his final place in peace.

Leila thanked the superintendent for coming, and the Chief Justice, who both told her how sorry they were the program hadn't been successful in stopping Brayden from making the wrong decisions.

'The program will continue to work for other kids in town. We'll all work harder together to stop this from happening again,' Leila answered.

Superintendent Stuart nodded and gave Leila a hug. 'Come and see me as soon as you feel like you're ready to come back to work. You always have a position to come back to, Leila.' The superintendent turned to Hayden. 'And Hayden, you've been nominated by Constable Matt Hutchins for a commander's commendation for your actions on the day of the explosion.'

Hayden ran his fingers through his hair, embarrassed.

'According to Hutchins, if it wasn't for your quick thinking before the second explosion, none of you would be alive today,' the superintendent insisted.

His family had been the cause of the explosion, and his youngest brother was the sacrifice for it all. Leila was glad Corrections had rejected Jayden's application to attend the funeral. Neither she nor Hayden had the heart to tell Sue it was Jayden's drug lab that had killed her youngest son.

The superintendent looked between Hayden and Leila and said, 'I know you have the support of each other, but remember there are specialised support networks that you can access through the police, Leila. And you can request that Hayden get support too.'

Leila nodded. 'Thanks ma'am.'

Although Leila knew she would have some disciplinary actions to face for the questions she had answered during the detectives' investigation into the clandestine lab explosion, she was grateful she still had a job to go back to. She had compromised her job to help Brayden. Would it have helped him if she had told the police? These questions swirled through her head over and over. She'd answered the detectives truthfully, and admitted to seeing Brett Pearce's Audi at the mine during her run and then again in town at the Indian restaurant, but stopped short at telling them about seeing Brayden or taking photos of the detectives' investigation board. Those details would serve no purpose to their investigation. Brayden was dead because of it, and she was the only one who had to live with that.

Hayden held her hand when they were the last ones remaining under the marquee, and together they watched as the funeral staff lowered the wooden casket, covered in bright yellow flowers of every kind, into the deep earth below. Leila turned to hold on to Hayden when the sight was too much for her. His body jolted as he silently cried.

When the motor that lowered the casket stopped and Brayden was laid to rest, Hayden said, 'Goodbye, you little shit,' and kissed a yellow rose before throwing it into the hole.

Leila did the same, but said, 'I love you, Brayden. Look after your niece for us.'

Chapter Thirty

Three weeks after saying goodbye to Brayden, Hayden wanted to surprise Leila with a picnic in his mum's backyard oasis. There was so much Hayden wanted to tell her, and their grief had subsided enough to see the sun shine on their life again.

'Let's go and sit in mum's backyard,' Hayden said and guided Leila up the driveway of Sue's home.

'Good idea. There's something we need to talk about,' she replied.

What secrets had she been keeping from him?

They walked into Sue's backyard and the sight made Hayden smile. His mum had gone out of her way to set a basket on top of a rug; eager to help push love in the right direction. Cushions clustered at one corner of the patchwork rug and a vase of flowers from the garden sat next to the basket of goodies.

Leila smiled. 'This looks like it should be on the set of *Farmer Wants a Wife* or one of those dating shows on TV. Did you do this?'

'With a little help from mum,' he said, winking.

They headed straight to the rug, and Leila made herself comfortable against the cushions and pillows. The lush line of arching giant bird-of-paradise palms along the opposite fence flourished despite the harsh weather conditions. The whole yard was blooming and Hayden instantly felt himself relaxing.

'Those palms of Mum's have gone crazy. I didn't think you could grow plants like that out in the bush,' Hayden said.

'Well actually, your mum told me that these bird-of-paradise palms would spread like a bushfire out here. We have the perfect conditions for this species apparently. They're from Africa. Same environment as Echo Springs.'

He couldn't bring himself to tell her everything, to ever tell her about going directly to the bikies' club house in the city to warn them that Echo Springs was his patch now. When they'd laughed and pointed guns at him, he told them to sort it out with Jayden if they had a problem or come and find him themselves if they weren't satisfied with the answer. Hayden hoped his brother would pay heed to his warning. Hayden was not only tougher than his father, and Jayden had witnessed it first-hand, but Hayden was smarter and Jayden knew it too. Hayden's priority was to protect the town from his brother, and he would stop at nothing to keep it safe.

Leila looked across the stretch of green paradise. It was nice to finally have good things that were cared for by one of their parents.

'Did you see my how good my dad has been looking since the funeral? I even saw him at the supermarket the other day. I don't think I've ever seen him in a supermarket my whole life.'

Hayden nodded. 'He's been going to AA meetings at the church once a week for almost a month now. He didn't want you to know until he reached his ninety days. Apparently that's a big deal or something. But ever since he fell over that night and smashed your platter across the room, he wanted to cut the drink and do the right thing by his only kid.'

Leila choked on her laugh. 'I was such an asshole then. I'm sorry. If anything, Dad knocked me down a peg or two, and it did me some good.'

Hayden laughed while he stretched his arm around Leila, resting it behind her head on the cushions. She folded into him. They fit perfectly together.

'You were always going to come out a good person, Leila. No matter what the world threw at you, you were always going to take it on and win. So it's understandable if someone like you ends up an asshole for a while. I knew you would come good eventually.'

'Huh,' she smiled. 'You did not think that. I distinctly remember you telling me a month ago that you never thought you'd see me again.'

He chuckled and gripped onto her. 'I think I had to tell myself that for a while. It made me feel better.'

She sat up and looked at him. 'See, I *was* an asshole. I will never freak out and take off on you again. I promise. No matter how hard it gets.'

He stopped laughing and glanced at her. 'There is something I haven't told you.'

Would they ever stop keeping secrets from each other?

'I bought Town Hall.'

'What?' Her eyes were the size of saucers.

'Town Hall has been up for sale for a while so I made an offer and the Mayor and I came to an agreement.'

Leila stared at him, 'Okay,' she gulped. 'And what are you going to do with this?'

'Well, this is where I think you'll get cranky.'

She frowned with anticipation.

'I've been working with your boss and the juvenile committee, and I pitched a program that could work with the centre I'm building at the Hall. With their support and funding, I'll be able to offer courses that help to get kids into apprentice jobs.'

Leila looked like a deer in the headlights.

'Mum helped me buy the Hall. It was Dad's money, but after everything that happened with Brayden, it just felt like the right thing to use it for. Mum finally had a spark in her eye. Even your mum and dad want to come on the books to work as the hall's cleaner and maintenance manager. Mum said she can run gardening classes, and I'll teach them about cooking. Your boss said you can run programs there for the kids and stay in the police for as long as you like. There's never been anyone like you in this town.'

He knew she didn't see herself as special, but everyone else did. 'Kath Stuart sees what a difference you make to the kids. To have them see someone who's grown up from their side of life and still make something good of themselves, is important. Your boss really believes in your work and the positive difference it's making to the community.'

A pained look crossed her face.

'So what did you want to talk about?' Hayden asked hesitantly.

'I'm pregnant,' she blurted.

He sat up straight.

'What?' His mind raced wildly, desperate to hold onto one emotion long enough to register it. 'But … we … what?'

Leila held his face between her palms.

'I've felt sick for about a week, but with everything we've been through in the past couple of weeks, I thought it was stress. I'm only just four weeks pregnant. It's really early so I think we need to just be careful and not get our hopes up too much just yet. I don't have the best track record of keeping pregnancies.'

'Leila, you never have to go through anything alone ever again. I will never let you. This is the greatest news. You're allowed to be happy, you know.'

Hayden instinctively put his hand out to touch the magic growing inside his beautiful girlfriend's belly. He jumped to his feet, pulling Leila with him. Then, while holding her hand, he crouched in front of her on one knee.

'I never want to spend another day without you not knowing how much I love you, and how much you give me the air inside my lungs. Leila, will you let me be your husband?'

She grinned, a tear escaped from the bottom of her eyelid.

'I just told you not to get excited just yet. What if—'

'Sssh, Leila. We are going to be a family again, and we're doing it right this time. I never want to live my life without you in it. I don't have a ring, but we both know I wouldn't get it right anyway ... so what do you say? Let's make this official and commit to forever.'

She hesitated, and Hayden was suddenly beset with doubt. Could he have misread everything he thought he knew about her?

'I want nothing less than forever with you. Of course I will marry you,' she replied and he leaned up to her for a kiss. Leila leaned down to him, then stopped. Hayden watched her for a moment, equally stunned by her beauty, but frozen with fear of something being wrong. 'What's wrong?' he asked.

'I don't know. It's all too much. The pregnancy, marriage, Town Hall being yours.'

'Ours,' he affirmed.

She smiled. 'Let's just try this again tomorrow.'

'Leila, I never want to wait another day without knowing you're mine forever. This day, and every day, we are doing it together.'

She smiled, but the tears slipped down her cheeks. He stood and wrapped his arms so tightly it would be physically impossible to let her go.

'Let's crack open this amazing hamper and see what Sue has done for us. We should go and see the Hall later, you can tell me all about what you've got in store,' Leila said while rummaging through the wicker basket.

'It's Brayden's Place by the way.'

'Pardon?' she replied.

'It's what the centre will be called. His friends always called this house Brayden's Place. It was a safe haven for a lot of kids when we were growing up. So I thought it would help kids feel comfortable. I want kids to see what they're capable of and what happened to him can happen to them too.'

'It's perfect,' Leila said and folded back into Hayden.

They were two halves of each other, their love crucial not only to their lives, but to the town they each vowed to save.

Three months later

Hayden guided his blindfolded mum down the stairs of the back deck and out onto the grassed yard. Cath and Ned Maine stood, still slightly awkward in their newfound sobriety, but endearingly happy to be living in the moment.

Leila stood next to her parents, her hand gripped tight with excitement around her mother's. She purposely wore looser tops lately because she didn't want to share their expectant news until they were confident. Both she and Hayden were still erring on the side of caution with allowing themselves this happiness.

With his hands on his mum's shoulders, Hayden assisted her over to the garden bench.

'What on earth are you kids up to?'

Hayden untied his mum's blindfold, saying, 'Okay on the count of three, I'll drop the blindfold and you can see.'

'Alright, alright. Hurry up, the suspense is killing me. You're going to give me a heart attack,' Sue demanded.

Leila and her parents tried not to giggle and make noise.

'One, two, three.' Hayden lowered the blindfold.

Hayden had added a new large rock formation behind the bench. It rose up alongside the rocks where Mick's eagle sat with honour. Sitting proudly atop was a statue of a lion, its mane flowing, but its face was tilted slightly, almost playful. It looked lovingly across Sue's much-loved garden.

'Oh. It's beautiful, Hayden. It's just like him.' She turned to kiss Hayden and noticed Cath, Ned and Leila standing behind her.

'Surprise!' Ned laughed.

'There is just one more surprise, mum,' Hayden said as he guided her over to the bench. 'But you might want to sit for this one.'

Both Cath and Sue screamed at the top of their lungs, which set off a flurry of dogs barking in the distance. The commotion triggered a flock of sparrows to fly into the air in a rolling formation and Leila looked up at the beautiful sight.

She closed her eyes and took in the memory as she heard her dad's laughter bellow into an echo across town.

'You bloody beauty!' he roared.

Also by Shannon Curtis

Runaway Lies
Heart Breaker

Available in ebook from Escape Publishing

Enamoured
Enraptured

Hope Echoes

Shannon Curtis

*This book is dedicated to all those farmers who are doing it tough,
and who have to battle the banks as well as a changing environment
and challenging political landscape. You have my respect, admiration,
gratitude and awe.*

Chapter One

Jac Buchanan jolted at the dull roar that echoed across the paddocks. She dropped the clamp she was positioning on the pipes she'd just glued together, and swore. Ray, her kelpie cross, started trotting to and fro, staring off into the distance and barking a warning. Jac picked up the clamp and quickly set it on the pipes, then placed the connection gently into the trench.

Heart pounding, she pushed her hat back to wipe the perspiration off her forehead, then lowered it against the glare of the sun. She stared into the distance. What the hell was that? Her gaze snagged on a plume of black smoke that trailed up over the ridge. *Oh. Crap.*

She picked up her shovel and tossed it into the tray of her red ute, then ran up the rise to the base of the windmill she was repairing.

She scanned the horizon, her eyes widening when she saw the flash of orange in the distance, followed by the muted *kaboom*. 'Bloody hell.' It looked like something was happening down at Dick.

Ray barked excitedly and scampered along the ridge line. She whistled as she ran back to the ute. Within minutes she was bumping along the track that led to the far paddock gate. The ute shuddered as she rolled across the cattle grid, not slowing down at all. Tyres skidded on the track, kicking up a cloud of dust, red under the hot afternoon sun, as she drove across the paddocks, angling cross-country for the gates. Ray barked from the back, and she checked her mirror to make sure the dog was still in the tray. He was.

She crossed the four outer paddocks, then shuddered along the dirt track in the direction of what now seemed to be a rising cloud of dark smoke. Otherwise the sky was clear, cloudless. She kept an eye out for any stray roos, braking hard when one bounded alongside her car for a few metres before cutting across the track.

She shook her head grimly. Bloody roos. Fence-mangling, bumper-denting bloody roos.

She crested a rise in the track, her jaw dropping when she saw what lay below. Pulling the ute to a shuddering stop, she grabbed the satellite phone from the car's centre console, and ran. *Bloody friggin' hell.*

A white Audi was parked near Dick's entrance. Jac's frown deepened. The mine had been closed for years—long before she was born. Who the hell reopened it? Damn it. Smoke billowed out of the entrance, and flames licked along the wooden beams that supported the structure. She held up the phone and dialled Scott Nielsen, her station manager.

'Jacinta, did you hear—'

'Yeah, I heard. There's a fire out here at Dick. I need you to bring the tanker, ASAP.'

'Dick?' Scott was silent for a moment. 'I don't understand.'

'Neither do I, Scott. I have a car parked here and nobody with it, and Dick is going up in flames. Bring the tanker, I'll call the firies.' She disconnected the call, and then called Toby Grimshaw, the local fire inspector for the rural fire brigade and good friend to her father.

'Grimshaw.' The voice was rough, deep, as though the smoke of too many bushfires had given his throat a permanent husky tone, and she was so glad to hear it.

'Toby, it's Jac. We have a fire here at Bulls' Run, on the south-west range. Dick's mine entrance.'

Bulls' Run sheep and cattle station spread out over a number of old copper mines, and her grandfather had named them after the tunnels used in *The Great Escape*—Tom, Dick and Harry, with a George closer to home. Grandma got to the name the others, being Brandy, Sherry and good ol' Ginny. Grandma's wish to name them after the ladies' Saturday evening sippers had been a running joke in the family, but the local community had adopted the names—when anyone remembered they existed.

'Brushfire?'

Jac hesitated, eyeing some of the bushes that were even now catching fire. 'Some brush, but this—I don't know what this is. Looks like an explosion of some sort inside the mine.'

'Inside the *mine*?'

Jac could understand his surprise. These mines hadn't been used in over two generations. 'Yep.'

'Okay, I'll get a unit out there.'

'Toby—' Jac bit her lip, shaking her head. 'Toby, someone's in there. I have a car parked here, and nobody in sight.'

'Stay out, Jac. Those supports are old and rotting, and you'd be looking at a tunnel collapse at any time. Then we'd have to look for you *and* whoever else. Stay put until we get there—but call in the cops. We might need them.'

Toby disconnected the call, not giving her the opportunity to argue. Jac held the phone to her forehead. God, this was awful. Someone was in there, possibly stuck, and she had no way of knowing who, where, or how many. She put a call in to the local police station, and caught Ben Fields, an old acquaintance, and quickly explained what was going on. He told her he'd organise assistance, but to stand clear and wait, then he hung up.

Wait. Jac shook her head. It was a twenty-five minute drive just to the Bulls' Run front gate, with another five minutes at a good clip to get near the house, and a ten- to fifteen-minute drive over a dirt track along the fence line to get to this point. Even if the cops and firies ignored all legal speed limits, they'd probably only shave off about fifteen minutes from the full trip. Whoever owned that car didn't have another half-hour to wait for help to get to them. She approached the entrance, squinting through the smoke.

'Hello? Anyone in there? Can you hear me?'

She ducked, trying to get under the arching flames that were being caught by the soft breeze outside. Despite her repeated calls, nobody answered.

She ran back to her ute and pulled out the shovel she'd used earlier that day. Ray was barking and whining, wanting to get in on the action, but she ordered him to stay. She didn't want her dog running into the blaze.

Jac hurried over to a small burning shrub and scooped up some dirt, shovelling it over the shrub to cover the flames. She made her way closer to the entrance, trying to kill each flame she encountered. Her eyes began to itch, and she coughed at the smoke. In moments, her eyes were blurry and it felt like razors were attacking her throat. She had to back away. Whatever was burning inside, it wasn't ordinary smoke that was coming out. Black smoke. This wasn't a bushfire. She shrugged out of her plaid shirt and tied it over her nose and mouth as an improvised mask, then did what she could to control the blaze from spreading. She slapped at the burning embers that drifted through the air to land on her arms, singlet top and jeans.

Jac turned when she heard the engine of the approaching tanker over the roar of the flames. She saw Scott's grim face through the window and waved him over.

'I don't know what's burning down there,' she yelled hoarsely, 'but it doesn't seem like your normal wood fire.' Scott shrugged out of his shirt and did the same as Jac, tying it around his face as a mask before heading to the back of the tanker.

Jac helped him unravel the hose. They moved in unison, dragging the hose out to the entrance of the tunnel. Scott braced himself, planting his feet shoulder width apart, and she ran back to the tanker to turn the red wheel.

They'd run this drill a hundred times, despite Scott's complaints that they knew what they had to do. As soon as she heard the water enter the hose, she ran up to help brace Scott against the force. Scott flicked the lever open, and water spewed from the outlet, spraying over the brush near the entrance. She didn't know how long they stood there, but it seemed they were winning the battle against the spreading fire.

'Try to get closer,' Jac called out to him.

Scott shook his head. 'Are you crazy? We don't know where the source is—this fire could have been burning for days.'

'There are people still in there,' she yelled back at him. He glanced over his shoulder at her, his face shocked. He looked back at the fire, and she could feel his shoulders tense. Slowly, they crept forward, aiming the stream of water at the entrance of the tunnel.

The ground shuddered, and a fireball rolled out of the entrance. Scott dropped the hose and turned, diving to the ground and taking Jac with him. She landed heavily as flames bucked and roiled over the top of them.

In the distance, she heard the scream of the rural fire brigade sirens, battling for supremacy over the shriek of police sirens.

'We have to get out of here, Jac,' Scott yelled over the roar of the flames.

Jac stared in horror at what was now a plume of fire blazing out of Dick's entrance. Someone was down there. Bloody hell.

A spray of water hit her in her back, a force that left her breathless, and she realised the hose was whipping around like a snake on crack. She rolled over to her feet and staggered to it. She dodged it briefly, then pounced, gritting her teeth as she wrestled with it.

'Get your arse over here, Scott,' she hollered, rolling with the hose.

Scott swore loud in frustration, then pounced. Together, they regained control of the hose, each getting to their feet to train the water at the fire once more.

The rural fire tanker pulled up, a cloud of dust billowing out before them. Jac sighed in relief when she saw the volunteers alight, all coated up.

Most of the crew jumped into action, running around to the tank of water that looked at least double the size of the Bulls' Run tanker. She saw Toby Grimshaw on the radio, barking orders back at command.

She turned to look at the fire. It burned at least two storeys high, now.

Yeah. They were going to need more trucks.

Minutes later, the police arrived. She recognised Constable Smith, a guy who'd been a couple of years behind her at school, as he stopped to speak to the Toby, and from the looks of their expressions the conversation was serious.

Smithy went back to the police car and leaned in through the window to snag the radio. She couldn't hear what he said, but he bent his head, listening. He responded once more, then dropped the radio and jogged over to her.

'We need you to step back, Jac,' he told her, arms out.

'Someone's in there,' she told him, using her chin to indicate the tunnel.

He shook his head. 'If they're still alive, we'll find them, but we need to stand clear. This looks chemical.'

Jac frowned up at him. 'What?'

'That's not a wood fire, Jac. We'll start working on trying to get access, but this looks like a chemical fire, and until we figure out what kind of chemicals, we need you to stand clear.'

'I'm shutting down the water,' Scott yelled, then ran back to the tanker. In moments the weight and pull of the hose lightened, and she could consciously relax her arms and shoulders. Smithy ran to the back of the police car and opened the trunk, reaching in for some masks and yellow slickers. He ran back and offered her a mask. 'Wear this, but stand back. When the paramedics get here, they'll look you over.'

'I'm perfectly fine,' she muttered to him, and he smiled.

'Humour me.'

She stood back, mask sitting awkwardly over her face, and she watched the rural brigade go into hazmat mode.

More vehicles turned up, and flashing lights pulsed into the dimming sky. A car came jolting along the track, and her eyebrows rose as Hayden Terrance climbed out the car. She hadn't seen her buddy for ages, but he didn't even look in her direction, his attention solely focused on the burning tunnel.

Leila Mayne was with him, her face drawn as she too tried to get toward the entrance. Jac called out to them, but her voice was muffled by the mask. She took a step forward, and Scott put his hand on her arm. She shot him a glare of frustration, then lifted the mask to call out to them. Hayden was now fighting with two of the cops, trying to get to the mine entrance despite the obvious fire hazard. She frowned. Why—?

She heard the yells, could make out only one word. Brayden. Her blood chilled in her veins, and she glanced in horror at the inferno. Oh, god.

She lifted the mask off her face, and took a step toward Hayden and called out to him, and then the ground shook. The mine entrance exploded, the force throwing her back, and then everything went black.

Chapter Two

Mac Hudson braked, then got out of the car to open the gate. He drove over the cattle grid, then stopped the car again in order to get out and close the gate behind him. He didn't want old man Buchanan to have a rupture over cows running loose. The man ran on a short fuse these days.

He slowly drove up to the mine site, or what was left of it, the car rocking over the rough dirt track. He shook his head. He hadn't been out to Bulls' Run in years, not since his friend Jamie Buchanan left to serve in the army.

The property was deceptive. The track that connected the homestead to the highway was well graded, and relatively smooth to drive on. Getting around the property was a different story. Sometimes the drive was little more than kangaroo or cow trails through the scrub. On this occasion, though, it was clear to see there'd been recent activity on the track.

The car edged over the rise, and Mac braked. *Bloody hell.* The sun had yet to crest Echo Ridge in the distance, and the landscape still wore the purple haze of a dawn. It felt like another warm day on the horizon. He stared down at what remained of the mine entrance. The scrubby trees and bushes ended in a defined ring with a diameter of about twenty metres, which dipped about two metres below ground level, as though God had reached in and pulled a plug, and everything had subsided. There was a small, taped-off opening in the ground. The yellow tape that had been staked around the site fluttered in the warm breeze. He could see the charred wooden supports that were strewn about, but the mouth of the mine was now gone, as though it had never been there.

Mac gaped at the view. He'd heard the stories—from Leila, from the rural fire crew, and something dozy and slurred from Smithy as he recovered in hospital, but nothing quite prepared him for the reality of it.

He could remember playing out here with Jamie. Remembered playing forts, cowboys and Indians, cops and robbers—hell, he even remembered playing bloody Robin Hood and his merry men, thanks to Jamie's sister.

This, though, looked post-apocalyptic. Something moved to his right, drawing his eye. Jacinta Buchanan sat on her dusty yellow trail bike, looking at him, her gaze hidden by the shade of her Akubra and her sunglasses. He hadn't noticed her in the gloom as he'd pulled up.

He strode over to her, and she slung her leg over the back of the bike to stand and face him. Good. He'd intended to swing by the main house after he'd had a look here in order to interview her. She was saving him a trip. He eyed her from behind his sunglasses. In so many ways she was so familiar—same ponytail, same taunting lift to her chin, and yet she somehow seemed so different to the annoying tomboy who'd followed him and her brother around the bush. His gaze drifted over her. She'd always been tall. Gawky. Like a colt still growing into its legs. Well, she'd definitely grown into those legs.

His lips firmed. She was Jamie's sister, and now a person of interest in the case of three suspicious deaths on her family's property. Noticing the line of her legs, or how the denim of her jeans cupped her tight butt, or even how the indent of her waist seemed to enhance the slight curves of her breasts and hips would only get him into trouble he didn't want.

'Aren't you supposed to be in hospital?' He'd gone to interview her the night before, only she hadn't been in her bed on the ward. He could see the white of a bandage peeking out from beneath the band of her hat.

'I checked myself out,' she said, her voice low and husky. Her mouth was turned down at the corners, and there were grooves around it. Her face looked pale beneath her tan, her brown hair tied back in a loose ponytail at the base of her neck, with tendrils escaping. Truthfully, she looked like she'd just rolled out of bed and tied it back as an afterthought. He frowned. She also looked tired, and in pain.

'Do you think that was wise?'

Her mouth tightened. 'I needed to be here.'

To cover up her tracks? To see what damage she and her cronies had done? 'Why?' He'd learned the best way to get the answer was to ask the difficult questions—no matter how much he didn't want to know. And in a small town, where everyone knew everyone else, there were plenty he didn't want to know. Mac didn't want to slip handcuffs on friends or family, or drag them down to the lock-up. But that was part of being a country cop in the town you grew up in. You inevitably arrested someone you liked, knew or respected.

Jac blanched at his question, and her brows drew down. 'Did you hear that Bra—Brayden was in there?'

He didn't miss that rough catch in her voice, as though she was talking through a virus. 'I heard.' He waited. He noticed she didn't mention the two other guys who'd been found.

She turned to look at the dip in the ground, and he saw the tear roll down her cheek before she brushed it away. 'God, it was so horrible.'

He looked briefly at the dent in the ground. 'What happened?'

She shook her head. 'I don't know. I was over at the dam, fixing a pipe, and heard this explosion…'

She covered her mouth, as though trying to hold back a sob. 'God, he was so young,' she wailed softly.

Brayden's body had been recovered, along with two other bodies, both adult males. One of these was the driver of the white Audi who'd since been tentatively identified as Brett Pearce, although DNA confirmation was still pending—but that took months. The fire, though, was a different matter entirely. It looked like a rudimentary drug lab had been set up down there.

On Buchanan land.

He stared down at the Buchanan in front of him. Most of the older folk in town knew about the defunct mines of Bulls' Run, but these days not many of the Echo Springs community would remember exactly where they were, they'd been unused for so long. He knew, but he'd been a regular visitor out to Bulls' Run before Jamie had left, and had caught hell plenty of times from old Tom Buchanan for playing out near the mines.

The Terrances, too, had been regular visitors. He knew them well. All those boys were bad news, and now the youngest, Brayden, was dead.

'What was Brayden doing here, Jac?' Mac tried to keep his voice calm, casual, burying his anger and disappointment beneath the facade of professional courtesy. Jac shrugged, shaking her head. 'I have no idea,' she answered.

He turned to look at the plughole in the ground, hiding his disappointment from her. She was covering up for the Terrances, damn it. Hadn't he and Jamie told her enough times to steer clear of that family of juvenile delinquents? Only they weren't kids anymore, and the trouble that followed the Terrances was no longer juvenile, but very adult and very dangerous.

'Come on, Jac. You don't expect me to believe that, do you?'

'What?' she asked, her forehead dipping between her brows.

'Three people died on your land, Jac. You expect me to believe you know nothing about it?'

'Yes,' she exclaimed, then startled. 'Did you say *three?*' She removed her sunglasses to stare at him. Mac watched her closely. Her shock seemed genuine.

'Oh, you didn't know?' He knew she hadn't been informed about the other bodies, so he was interested in her reaction. The charred corpses had been removed from the scene while she was still in hospital. 'Brett Pearce was found inside Dick as well.'

'Who's Brett Pearce?' she asked, surprised horror creeping over her face. She tilted her hat up, revealing more of the bandage that was wrapped around her head. 'What were they doing here?' Her tone conveyed the same frustrated curiosity he felt.

Unfortunately he'd learned in this job never to take anything at face value. He pursed his lips. The firies had discovered the remains of a secret meth lab, but the Sarge had decided to withhold that information for the time being. 'We don't know,' he lied. 'Do you?'

Jac shook her head again, wincing as though the movement hurt. Damn it, she should have stayed in the hospital at least another day. He knew, though, that once Jac made up her mind, a nuclear blast couldn't shift her.

'No. I didn't even know Brayden was out here. I haven't seen him in months.'

'Does Brayden usually come out here?' he asked.

She shook her head. 'He hasn't come by the house, not for ages.' Her expression darkened. 'Dad made it pretty clear he didn't want him or his brother visiting anymore.'

Mac nodded. Tom Buchanan was a grumpy old bastard. He could just imagine how that conversation must have gone. For once he and the old man held a similar viewpoint. The Terrance brothers were a bad influence, and Jac shouldn't have any involvement with them.

'What about his brother, Hayden? Aren't you two close?' He had to force the words out of his mouth. Jamie would be spitting nails if he heard his sister's name in connection with that particular Terrance brother. He still remembered the Christmas party when he'd had to break up a scuffle between his friend and Hayden Terrance—after he'd hauled Jac off her brother's back.

Jac shrugged. 'If by close you mean friends, then yes, we're close, but I haven't seen Hayden in months, either.' She gestured to the land around them. 'I have a station to run, Mac. It doesn't leave much time for socialising.'

Thank Christ for that. He'd promised Jamie he'd look out for his mate's little sister, and he realised now he wasn't doing a very good job of it. He rarely saw her in town, usually a wave as she drove by. He hadn't had a conversation with her in—hell, months. He'd figured no news was good news when it came to Jacinta Buchanan. Now he was beginning to realise how wrong that assumption was. He'd hate to think what trouble she could get herself into if she applied herself. Running illicit drugs out of the mine was bad enough. 'Did you know Leila Mayne is back in town?' He didn't know why he mentioned it, the words just popped out.

Jac nodded. 'Yeah. She was here the other night when—' She stopped talking, her blue eyes darkening as her gaze fell on the burnt hole in the ground.

'She and Hayden are seeing each other again.' He tried to say the words gently. He knew at one point Jac and Hayden had been really tight. He'd hate for her to be hurt by Terrance, and wanted to prepare her for the undoubted disappointment that usually followed the man. God only knew what Leila saw in him.

Jac's eyebrows rose. 'Really? That's ...' He stared at her closely. Damn, when had she gotten so good at the poker face? He couldn't read her as easily as he used to. 'Interesting,' she said slowly. 'Yeah. Interesting.'

His eyes narrowed. Did that shake any loyalty she had to Terrance? Enough for her to tell him what was going on?

A low drone had them both turning around, and he watched as one of the battered utes of Bulls' Run bounced across the paddock toward them. It took a few minutes, but finally the vehicle pulled to a stop and the Bulls' Run station manager, Scott Nielsen, alighted.

'Mac,' the man said, dipping his head in acknowledgement. 'How's it going?'

Mac waved casually. He knew the guy enough to greet him on the street, but not much further beyond that. The man had started working at Bulls' Run after Jamie had left for his basic training. 'Scott. Just swinging by to look at the damage, and to get Jac's statement.' He turned to stare at her pointedly. 'Seeing as she left the hospital before I could interview her.'

She screwed up her nose. 'I hate hospitals.'

Scott shook his head as he approached. 'You could have blown me over when your dad told me you were back home. You sure you're all right? You took quite the hit to your noggin.'

'You were here, too, weren't you?' Mac asked, and Scott nodded.

'Yep. Although I wasn't as close to the blast as Jac was. She was knocked out cold.'

Mac's jaw tightened at the mental image of the girl who'd pestered him to play rendered unconscious.

'I'm fine,' she said brusquely.

'Well, your father wants you back at the house. Marion's turned up, and he's not happy.' Scott glanced between them, and then shifted a little closer to Jacinta. Mac noticed the almost proprietary move as the man put his hand on Jac's shoulder.

'What's new?' she sighed. She turned to Mac. 'Are we done here?'

Not by a long shot. 'You go ahead. I'll get Scott's statement,' he said, 'and then I'll swing by the house and get yours, and say hi to Tom while I'm at it.'

Jac met his gaze for a moment. 'Dad's not really in the mood for visitors, these days.'

Mac's lips curved. 'What's new?'

Jac kicked the stand down, and gently swung her leg over the back of the bike, wincing. Her head ached. She glanced out across the paddocks. The sun had finally inched over the ridge, and lavender hues were disappearing as the tangerine streaks of light stretched across the red earth and green scrub.

No. Ached was too subtle a word. Her head throbbed like the Echo Springs Town Hall floor at a blue-light disco. Did they even do blue-light discos anymore? She didn't know. That seemed so fun, so frivolous, and she couldn't remember the last time she'd been fun or frivolous. She walked across to the kennels and opened the gates, letting the dogs out into the run. She filled up bowls, wincing as she had to bend down, and the thump in her head got stronger. In minutes she'd put the food out for them, and she ruffled Ray's neck as he ran around her legs. The other dogs were working dogs, but Ray—well, Ray had been the runt of the litter, and she'd had to beg her father to let her keep him. She'd never admit he was her pet, though. Not where anyone could hear her, anyway.

She walked gingerly up the steps to the house, her boots thunking on the wraparound timber veranda. She almost put her foot down on the third slat, and caught herself just in time. There was a portion of the wood that was rotten, and she hadn't gotten around to replacing the bloody thing yet.

Just one more thing to add to the endless to-do list at Bulls' Run.

'I don't want your bloody eggs!'

Jac stopped at the back door and grimaced as she heard her father's roar. Uh-oh. Ray stopped next to her, his ears pricked forward.

'Well, then, you don't get breakfast,' a woman's prim voice answered in response, and Jac's eyebrows rose. Wow. Marion Morrison had a little bit of sass in her.

The widow had approached her for a job as a cook and housekeeper on the station. With Jac doing a lot of the farm work, she didn't have the time, energy or inclination to do laundry, cook, or wash up after everything else she had to do. Money was tight, but they'd managed to come to an arrangement that included free board for the woman. The only problem was, she hadn't yet told her father about the new arrangement. With everything that had happened, it had completely slipped her mind.

'I'll get my own damn breakfast,' her father muttered.

'I'd like to see you try lighting that stove,' Marion chirped back, and Jac's jaw dropped. Oh, now that was brutal. She could just imagine her father turning an apoplectic shade of plum purple. She toed off her boots and hurried into the house, hanging her hat up on the hook on the wall just inside and letting the screen door slam loudly behind her to let them know she was there. She winced as the sound added to that blue-light disco in her head. Ray whined outside the door, then lay down on the mat. Her father's rule was no dogs in the house.

'Morning,' she called as she walked through the laundry to the kitchen.

'Just the person I want to speak to,' Tom Buchanan called back to her. He eyed the bandage around her head. 'You look terrible.'

'Thanks, Dad,' Jac said, her tone dry. At the moment, the bandage seemed to be all that was keeping her brain from exploding.

Tom stood behind the chair at the head of the table, his one hand resting on his hip, his features tight and angry. 'What the hell is she doing here?'

'She's the cat's mum, Tom,' Marion said as she dished some eggs and sausages onto a plate and set it on the table. 'I have a name, and if you use it and show me some manners, you might even get coffee.'

Jac blinked rapidly. The woman had a death wish. Nobody talked to Thomas Buchanan that way. 'Uh, I thought Marion could help us out around the house,' Jac explained in a rush. She smiled at Marion. 'I thought you'd be coming later,' she said to the older woman. Like, after she'd had a chance to explain things to her father.

'We don't need help around the house,' her father snapped.

Marion's eyebrows rose as she eyed the overflowing hamper in the laundry. 'Are you sure? This place looks like it needs a good clean.' She crossed to the curtains that ran the length of the kitchen, and started pulling them back, letting the morning sunlight pierce the gloom. Dust motes danced in the light. And for that one little action, Jac wanted to hug her. Tom Buchanan didn't like the curtains opened. Not since his accident.

Her father's face showed his surprise at Marion's comment, then his anger. 'We've never needed anyone before. Jacinta and I are perfectly capable of looking after ourselves.' He turned to Jac. 'And maybe if you spent more time in the house and less time running around the farm, you'd see that. Let Scott do his job.'

Jac gaped for a moment. 'Geez, Dad. Would you say that to Jamie?'

Her father's frown deepened, if that were possible. 'What's Jamie got to do with this?'

Marion indicated the seat at the table, and Jac sat, scooping up the cutlery. She held the knife and fork in her fists, too angry and sore to force her appetite awake. 'You wouldn't tell him to focus on bloody housekeeping, if he were here.'

'Well, no, he'd be looking after the farm.' He stated the fact so simply, as though it was obvious.

Jac's shoulders sagged. She couldn't get angry with her father. He'd grown up in another time, and had no idea how much of a chauvinist he could be. She mentally counted to ten.

'Well, Jamie's not here,' she said quietly, and started cutting into one of the sausages on her plate. The knife squeaked on the plate. 'So I'm—' She hesitated, and avoided looking at the pinned sleeve of her father's shirt where his arm used to be. She didn't want to say anything that implied she was doing the jobs he no longer could. 'I prefer looking after the farm, Dad. I'm better at that than cooking, and you know it.' She met his gaze. She'd tried to do a roast on Sunday. It came out looking like a tree stump after a bushfire.

'We're not a charity case,' he said roughly, lifting his chin.

'And who said you were?' Marion exclaimed. 'This is my job, Tom. I don't do this out of the goodness of my heart.' She eyed him up and down. 'I'm nice, but not *that* nice.' She sighed, then lifted her chin. 'I need this job.' She turned back to the stove, and held up a plate. 'Now, do you want breakfast or not?'

Tom was silent for a moment, then grumbled under his breath as he pulled out the chair and sat down. 'Fine.'

'Fine, what?'

Jac's eyes rounded. Ever since her father had lost his arm in a tractor accident three years earlier, he'd become angry. Bitter. She tried to avoid upsetting him, but she seemed to have a knack for doing just that. She'd never speak to her father the way Marion was speaking to him now.

'Fine, Marion,' her father muttered. The woman eyed him expectantly over her shoulder. 'Please,' he said with a growl. He glared at Jac over the table, and she dropped her gaze and hurriedly put the morsel of sausage into her mouth to hide her shock. They ate in awkward silence.

Jac looked up in relief when she heard a vehicle outside. Ray started barking. Her father looked up, frowning.

'Who the bloody hell is that?'

'Mac Hudson would be my guess. I ran into him out near Dick.'

Heavy boots clumped across the wooden veranda, and Jac heard the rap of knuckles on the screen door jamb, then a chuckle and some thuds. He was patting Ray.

'Come in,' she called out, and within moments Mac entered the kitchen, his hat in his hand. She tried not to stare. Just like she tried not to stare every other time she saw him. She couldn't help it, though. He looked so tall and tough in his dark trousers and collared shirt and tie. His light blue shirt was still crisp across his broad shoulders despite the slowly climbing mercury, a twenty-minute drive from town and tramping about a crime scene. That didn't surprise her, though. Mac had always been more than presentable, growing up. That's why he was so popular with the ladies. She'd had such a crush on this guy when she was a teenager. But she wasn't a kid anymore, and had long outgrown the flights of fancy of a romantic young girl who'd watched her brother's best friend play the field ... but she still remembered those fantasies, about him staring at her with those cool green eyes, opening those full lips and saying—

'I'll take your statement now, if you can spare the time.'

Chapter Three

Mac watched as Jac blinked rapidly, then nodded. 'Uh, yes. Of—of course.' Were her cheeks rosy? Damn, was she fighting off an infection from the cut on her head?

She rose from the table, and he nodded at old man Buchanan. 'Tom, how's it going?'

'How do you expect?' Tom muttered, using his knife to indicate out beyond the bank of kitchen windows. 'Someone's blowing up my damn property.'

'Yeah, well, we'll get to the bottom of it,' Mac assured him.

'I don't want to see any of those Terrance boys cross my fence line again,' the older man said.

'Dad—' Jac protested.

'I mean it, Jacinta. Their father was no good, and those boys take right after him. No more.'

Jac's lips tightened, and she left the table. Mac noticed she didn't agree to abide by her father's dictate. She jerked her chin at him, and he followed her through the kitchen to the hallway, and then into the living room. He watched as she walked with a loose-hipped lankiness, shoulders back, her messed-up ponytail ending mid-back. The plaid shirt she wore looked vaguely familiar. He could have sworn it was Jamie's, at one point. They entered the room, and she paused briefly to draw back the curtains to let light filter into the room. Jacinta started walking toward the couch, then changed direction and sat in one of the armchairs. He took the lounge, and watched as she settled herself. She rested her ankle on her opposite knee, and tilted her head back against the armchair's backrest.

'What do you want to know?'

His eyebrows rose at her abrupt question, and she rubbed her forehead. 'Sorry, I lost a day in the hospital and have so much to do...'

'Why don't you tell me exactly what happened?' He pulled out his notebook, and then listened carefully as she told her story. Every now and then he'd stop her to ask a question, to clarify a detail, but mostly he let her talk.

Her voice was calm, husky, but with a catch whenever she spoke of Brayden. Whatever she was involved with, he didn't doubt she mourned the young boy's death. He closed his notebook with a snap when she was finished. She didn't once mention the lab, the Terrance brothers, or how she was involved with the operation. He glanced down at his black shoes. He didn't want to arrest Jacinta Buchanan, but he couldn't understand how this could happen right under her nose without her knowing anything about it. He looked over at her.

She looked exhausted. Her complexion was pale, her blue eyes ringed with dark shadows. 'You should rest,' he told her.

She shook her head. 'Got too much stuff to do.' She fidgeted with the bandage wrapped around her head. He still found it hard to think about her being knocked unconscious. She was normally so lively, so bubbly, but here, today, she was a shadow of her former, annoyingly chirpy self.

He tilted his head. 'Can't Nielsen take care of a few things for you?'

She dropped her hand in her lap, and her eyes narrowed. 'Why? Because you don't think I'm capable of doing it myself?'

Mac straightened, already sensing the minefield he'd accidently wandered into from the way she glared at him. Just like when he'd told her girls couldn't be Robin Hood. He instinctively placed his hat over his lap, remembering the outcome of that particular discussion, so long ago. 'Uh, no, that's not—'

'Because I *can* work this station, I don't care what everyone else thinks.' She'd leaned forward in her chair, and try as he might, he couldn't stop his gaze from briefly sliding down to see her oversized plaid shirt draping forward, revealing a glimpse of navy tank top and cleavage.

Jamie's little sister had cleavage.

He snapped his gaze back up to Jacinta's. Gawd, whatever you do, don't look. She'd neuter him. Jamie would neuter him. He'd be a walking, neutered mess. He hesitated when he saw her expression. She looked fierce, but it didn't quite hide her vulnerability, her sadness. His gaze slid to the door. It must be tough, living with Buchanan since he'd lost his arm. He knew from his folks that Jacinta's father had pretty much shut himself off from everyone, and was rarely seen in town.

'How's Tom doing? Really?'

Jacinta sagged back against the chair. 'He's angry,' she said quietly. 'So angry. I can't blame him. What happened to him—it just wasn't fair.'

'You found him, didn't you?'

He still remembered when he'd heard the news. He'd been sitting at the bar at his parents' hotel when they'd all heard the wail of the ambulance. Tom had had an emergency amputation at the site. He'd been lying trapped under the tractor for hours before Jacinta went looking for him. By that time it was pretty clear he'd lose his arm. Must have been an absolute nightmare for Jacinta to witness. Of course, it had been worse for Buchanan to experience it.

She nodded, then looked up at the ceiling, blinking rapidly. She cleared her throat. 'Yeah. Sometimes he has good days, but mostly they're bad. He finds his limitations… frustrating.'

Mac nodded. He could appreciate that. Tom had always been a fit, robust man, and had worked hard. Without an arm … yeah. He could see why Tom would feel frustrated. Jacinta rose from the chair, giving him a silent cue to leave. He stood, but hesitated. He looked at her directly. This was Jacinta. Jamie's sister. She seemed so … tired. He felt the weight of that promise he'd made to Jamie the night before he'd left for basic training at Kapooka. He'd promised to keep an eye on her, keep her out of trouble. Well, he apparently sucked at that, and had to do better. She weaved a little on her feet, and he caught her arm. Her muscles tensed under his grip.

'You know—you know you can talk to me, right?' he said to her, his voice low.

Jac's eyes widened as she stared up at him. 'Uh, yeah. Sure.' She looked a little confused, her voice low and husky, but her features softened at his words.

He stepped closer. She was so tall, he didn't need to duck his head to maintain eye contact. 'No, I mean it. If you need anything, if something's troubling you, you can call me. Day or night.' He eyed her intently. 'I know Jamie's sometimes hard to get hold of, so if you need a stand-in big brother, call me, okay? I'm available.'

Jac blinked. 'Big brother…' she repeated.

He nodded. 'Yeah.' He snapped his fingers. 'While I remember, Mum and Dad send their regards, and want you to come into town for a visit.'

Their mothers had been close friends, before June Buchanan had passed away suddenly from a brain aneurism.

Jac smiled faintly. 'Well, say hi right back to Uncle Pip and Aunty Daph for me.'

'When can I tell them you'll pop in?' he pressed her.

'Uh, probably next week. I've got a feed order due in at the co-op.'

He nodded, then realised he still held her arm, that they were standing very close—so close that her loose tendrils seemed to have a static energy, reaching out to touch his shirt and arm. He raised his hand to tuck the strands behind her ear, but stopped when he realised what he was doing. He turned it into a casual gesture of farewell. 'No worries, I'll let them know.'

He followed her through the house to the back veranda. He found himself gazing at the long panel of red and brown plaid fabric that obscured the shape of her butt from his view, and then shook his head. No staring at her butt. No staring at her boobs. Butt and boobs were out of bounds. Jamie would tear him—

Jac turned to give him a brief smile as she opened the back door, and his gaze dropped to her boobs. God, he deserved everything Jamie could dish out. He smiled tightly, then strode out the door, his gaze fixed firmly ahead of him. Eyes forward, just keep your eyes—

'Whoa, avoid that bit, I have to fix it,' Jac said, grabbing his arm and pulling him to the side. He glanced down and saw the warped and cracked boards, and then nodded. And definitely did not look at her boobs.

'Thanks.' He slid his hat on as he crossed the dusty yard. He lifted a hand to wave farewell at Tom, who was walking out toward one of the sheds. Mac wasn't sure if Tom was waving back, or shooing flies from around his face—or flipping him the bird. He decided to take the gesture as a farewell. Mac climbed into his car, and for a moment he stared at the tall young woman who'd followed him out. She leaned against the veranda post, one elbow braced above her head. Her messed-up ponytail hung over one shoulder, and one of her long legs was bent casually and crossed at the ankle. He wondered if she realised she wore mismatched socks. She was tired, she was in pain, but there was something so damn dauntless, and yet so relaxed that it gave her a quiet air of confidence he hadn't noticed about her before. She'd grown up, and grown comfortable in her own skin.

He didn't know what trouble she'd gotten herself into, but he hoped it wasn't too late to pull her butt out of it.

★★★

'Hey, Dad,' Jac called, scrambling up from the seat in the office and hurrying down the hall after her father. She'd spent the day catching up on paperwork and bills—which generally meant shuffling bills from one pile to another because you needed money to pay bills and she didn't have any. She'd hoped that going over invoices and orders and doing a little more research on her special project would be easier on her head than bouncing around the property on a bike or a ute. Sadly, though, trying to come up with a plan to wring money out of red dust made her head ache just as bad.

Her father halted in the hallway and turned back to her. He'd already changed into his pyjamas and robe, his feet encased in slippers. For once, his face looked a little less … sour. She hoped it had something to do with the delicious roast-chicken dinner that Marion had made for them before retiring. Hmm. Maybe the way to a man's heart really was through his stomach.

If that was the case, she was monumentally screwed and should prepare herself now for a solitary life.

She clasped her hands in front of her. 'Have you had a chance to think about my idea?' she asked gently.

Her father pursed his lips. 'I don't see there being any use for it,' he said. 'I think Scott is right. Trying to diversify our activities at the moment, when we're still trying to claw ourselves back from the drought, seems a little risky.'

Jac frowned. 'Scott said that?' She thought he'd been tepidly encouraging when she'd raised it with him.

Her father nodded. Jac sighed. 'I think it's probably the very reason why we should do it,' she said.

'I don't know, Jacinta. We're talking a lot of money in the setup, when we already owe so much.'

'But I think the bank would lend us what we need,' she argued gently. 'Solar farming isn't some weird and wacky pseudoscience myth. We have a great area to do it, and we'd be less reliant on water…'

'I don't—'

'What if I got some information together for you, and scouted out the property for a suitable site. There's no cost involved in that, and then we could look at our options,' she interjected, hoping to stop her father from completely shutting her down.

Tom Buchanan sighed as he looked at her, and she didn't pretend she wasn't praying. 'What does your brother think?'

Her fingers clenched, and her brain clicked through a number of responses ranging from 'who cares?' through to 'let me ask' and 'why do I bother?'. She pasted a smile on her face.

'Good question,' she answered. 'Next time we talk, I'll run it by him.'

Her father nodded. 'Well, I think you need to do more research. We'll talk about it later.'

He turned and shuffled off to his room, and she stood in the hallway, watching with pursed lips. Just once, she'd love it if her father would consider letting her take on some real authority, and give her some room to do what she wanted with Bulls' Run. What was the word? Oh, yeah. *Trust.* She wished her father trusted her with the farm.

'At least it wasn't a flat-out no.' She sighed, trying to find something positive as she switched off the office light and padded down the hall in her socks. Within minutes she'd slipped out of her clothes and into her robe, and padded down the hall to the bathroom. She turned the light on, and startled when she saw her reflection in the mirror.

'Oh, hell.' She clapped her hands over her mouth. Why hadn't anyone told her she looked so crap? Her face was pale, with dark bags under her eyes. Her hair was—god, what the hell was going on with her hair? An oily bird's nest. She shuddered, then tilted her head, frowning. She was sure she'd washed her face that morning, damn it. She hadn't been able to shower, because of the bandage, but had she been walking around with that dirt streak down her cheek all day?

Including when she was talking with Mac?

Embarrassed horror flooded through her, and she covered her face with her hands. Ugh. She looked about as good as a cane toad getting cosy with a cricket bat. And she'd sat across from Mac looking like this. She was definitely going to die a spinster.

No wonder he'd suggested she consider him a stand-in brother. Not that she was considering him anything else, mind you. Macarthur Hudson was the love-'em-and-leave-'em kind of guy. He might be hot, but he was not boyfriend material, as many of the broken hearts around Echo Springs could attest. She rolled her eyes. Boyfriend. That sounded so … teenagey. At her age, she needed a man-friend, not a boyfriend.

Mac was a man. And a friend.

She covered her eyes. Gawd. No. Stop thinking about Mac.

She raised her hands and gently unwrapped the bandage from around her head. She winced as she peeled off the dressing and peered at the abrasion on her head. For the amount of blood she'd lost, it was a surprisingly small wound.

She disrobed and stepped into the shower, sucking in her breath as the cold water hit her. Whatever Dad thought, she was going to organise solar panels for the roof. It'd be nice to have hot water without having to run a generator.

She showered hurriedly, shampooing her hair a couple of times to remove all of the dirt. Once finished, she raided the first-aid items in the mirror cabinet to redress her wound, but left the bandage off. She gently squeezed the excess water from her hair and then ran a comb through it, hissing as each snag sent a mini throb over her scalp. She popped an aspirin, then finished towel-drying her hair. Within minutes she was back in her room, and combing her hair in front of her dressing table and mirror.

She eyed the photographs stuck with clear tape to the frame of the mirror. There were some of her parents, of her and Jamie, of Jamie, Mac and Jayden Terrance, of her with Hayden and Brayden… She fingered one in the corner. Young Kelsey. Her dorm mate looked happy in this photo, taken three days before Jacinta had found her body in the shower block at school, dead from a drug overdose. Damn, but she missed her friend. And now she'd lost another one. Sure, Brayden was much younger than she was, but she'd treated him like a kid brother when the Terrances had first lived on the property while Mick Terrance worked as a station hand. Then, after they left, Hayden had ridden his bike from the house at the edge of town to the Bulls' Run property over the school holiday breaks when she was home from boarding school, with young Brayden dinkying on the back.

She moved a photo of Brayden down next to Kelsey, her shoulders drooping under the weight of her grief. They'd been so young, so full of life, and now both of them were gone.

The images started to blur, and she brushed at her tears as she slid between the sheets of her bed, sighing as she finally lay her head against the pillow. She was so ready for sleep.

Two hours later, Jac sighed in frustration as she glared up at her ceiling. Sleep. That's all she wanted. Sleep. The aspirin had kicked in, her head was no longer throbbing, she could just close her eyes and drift off.

She squeezed her eyes shut, trying to imagine sheep jumping over the fence, only to constantly see the fireball that had been Brayden's death. Tears rolled down her cheeks. He'd been so young—fourteen. Too young to die, especially so horrifically. His smiling face kept morphing into the burned husk of a skeleton she imagined they'd found, and then into the lifeless face of her friend, Kelsey, slumped against the cold tiles. God, stop thinking of that.

She turned her mind to Mac, and his questions. Something bothered her there, but she couldn't quite put her finger on it.

A low drone rumbled across the yard, and she turned her head to look at her open bedroom window. She frowned. No, that wasn't her imagination, there was definitely something out there.

She pulled the covers off and swung her feet down to the floor, then padded over to the window. Pulling the curtains aside, she peered out into the darkness.

The three-quarter moon had risen, and the landscape was bathed in silvery purples. She cocked her ear, listening hard, until she heard the noise again. That was definitely an engine—a car of some sort.

Her lips tightened. It wasn't Scott. His truck sounded different. If there were more kids out there getting drunk or stoned, she was going to put a stop to it. Three deaths at Bulls' Run were three too many.

She dragged her jeans on over the silk boxer briefs she wore as pyjamas, and a loose t-shirt over her crop top. It was late August, and while the days were warming up, the nights were still chilly.

She hurried down the hallway until she padded out onto the veranda and tipped and shook out her boots from habit, then slipped them on. She paused, glancing around.

There. She could see lights in the distance. Car lights, jolting over the ground. Geez, they were a fair way out. Why didn't kids hang out near the springs, like she and Hayden had done as kids?

She jogged over to the ute parked near the maintenance sheds. Keys were always kept in the ignition, or hooked on the sun visor. Within minutes she was bouncing across the paddocks into the darkness, her mouth set in a grim line. Bloody hell. Had Brayden told all his mates where to go to get wasted without supervision?

She drove along the tracks, stopping at the gates along the way. Looking at the angle they were driving, it looked like they'd taken the third gate from the road. Bulls' Run had a number of gates along the highway, just to make it easier for feed deliveries or stock collections. That gate was far enough away from the main gate that they wouldn't have heard the entry back at the main house. If she hadn't been awake at the time, she probably wouldn't have heard them driving out. Sheep moved in huddles, disturbed by her car, and she kept her eye on them. She didn't want a group to run across the track in a panic.

It took her a moment to realise the car had stopped moving. She drove around to it, frowning as it remained stationary. They'd have to have seen her lights. She braked to a stop about four metres away from it, her headlights trained on it. A white four-wheel drive with dark tinted windows.

'Hey, you're trespassing,' she called out as she climbed out of the cab. She strode toward the car, hands on hips. Bloody teenagers. Were they hiding in the car? Yeah, they oughta be scared.

'If you don't clear out of here right now, I'm calling the cops, and then your parents.' She stopped in front of the driver's window, then peered through the glass. The seat was empty. She frowned.

'Where—'

Something moved in the reflection of the window, and she turned, just in time to see the fist before it hit her face, and then she didn't see anything.

Chapter Four

Mac rested his elbows on the bed, and stared at the woman beneath the covers. Jacinta's complexion was pale save for the blue bruise on her left cheekbone and temple. His stomach clenched. She looked so vulnerable beneath the white woven blanket. She had a slight smattering of freckles over her nose, freckles that he hadn't noticed so much against her tan, but they were now distinct against her pale skin.

He reached over and gently smoothed back a lock of brown hair that had fallen over her brow. Jac had been brought in unconscious to the Echo Springs hospital. His stomach muscles clenched. How the hell had this happened? It was freaky, seeing her so still. So … inert.

Her dark eyelashes fluttered, and he removed his hand from her forehead. Her eyelashes fluttered some more, then flickered open. Relief flooded him as he met her groggy blue-eyed gaze. He'd never realised how beautiful those eyes were until they were covered by the cloak of unconsciousness.

Her eyebrows dipped, and she winced a little as she blinked. 'Wha—?' She made a move, and he placed a hand on her shoulder.

'Easy, Jac. Don't move.' He leaned over and pressed the buzzer by the hospital bed.

'Where am I?' she whispered, her voice husky. She gazed around the room in confusion, then glanced back at him. She stared at him for a moment. 'Am I—is this a dream?' she whispered in wonder.

He smiled reassuringly at her. 'No, Jac. You're in Echo Springs hospital.'

'What happened?'

'I was hoping you could tell me that.'

A nurse bustled into the room and smiled at Jacinta. 'Well, hello there, Sleeping Beauty. How are you feeling?'

'Sore,' Jacinta rasped, and the nurse nodded.

'I can imagine. Let me get you some water, and I'll fetch the doctor to come have a look at you.'

Jacinta looked at Mac. 'How did I get here?'

Mac winced. 'Scott found you out in a paddock, unconscious.'

She raised her hand to her cheek, and her lips firmed. 'Someone hit me.'

Mac stilled. 'What?'

'I heard a car, saw the lights, so I went out to tell whoever it was to get off our land—'

Mac frowned. 'You went out to face down trespassers by yourself?'

'I thought they were teenagers, like Brayden,' she argued.

He closed his eyes. 'Why would you think that?'

She frowned. 'Why wouldn't I? Who else would be out there?'

'Oh, I don't know, hunters, maybe?' Or maybe more guys like Brett Pearce...

She shook her head. 'Most of them around here know to ask permission, first. No hunter is going to venture onto private property to hunt without permission, and all our gates are clearly marked.'

'What if it *was* friends of Brayden? Didn't you think that maybe it would be dangerous for you to talk with them?' He tried to work the conversation around diplomatically.

'I never thought teenagers would hit me, Mac,' Jacinta muttered.

'Did you see who hit you?'

'No, it happened so fast.'

'So you can't identify him? Or her?'

She frowned. 'I think it was a him.' She raised her hand to touch her cheek. 'He hit me with his fist.'

Mac pursed his lips. 'He hit you with his fist, but you didn't see him in front of you?'

She shook her head, then winced. 'No,' she said in a low voice. 'I pretty much turned to face whoever it was, but all I can remember is turning into the fist in my face... I didn't see anything beyond that.'

How convenient. Was it someone connected to the drug operation? Retribution, perhaps, for losing their lab? She had to know, surely, yet she wasn't telling him anything he could use.

The doctor entered the room and smiled.

'Ah, you're alert. How do you feel?' He pulled a pencil light out of his pocket.

'Sore,' Jac muttered.

The doctor flashed his light in her eyes, and asked her to track some movements. Mac stepped out of the room to let the man examine her, and bumped into Scott Nielsen.

'Is she awake?' Scott asked, his expression taut with worry.

Mac tried not to resent the man for his concern. He nodded. 'Yeah.'

'Did she say what happened?'

Mac turned back to look at the doorway. 'She reckons someone hit her.'

Scott frowned, then shook his head. 'There was nobody else out there.'

Mac glanced at the man, his expression intent. 'Tell me again. What happened?'

'I woke up when I heard the ute start up. By the time I got out of bed and looked out the window, she was bumping along a track. I couldn't figure out what she was doing, but when I didn't hear her return I got dressed and drove out after her in my truck. When I got to her car, she was out cold on the ground. I thought she'd tripped over—the ground was pretty rough, and even though she had her headlights on, there were dark patches in the uneven areas.'

Mac frowned. 'Did you see anyone else out there?'

Scott shook his head. 'Nope. Didn't see anyone, didn't hear anyone. Just Jac.' Scott hesitated, then rubbed his chin. 'You don't think she was maybe sleepwalking, do you?'

'Is that something she does?'

Scott waved his hand. 'I know she talks in her sleep, and she can be restless. She wandered into the kitchen one night and then didn't have any memory of it the next morning...'

Mac kept his expression calm. Scott knew she talked in her sleep. Had found her in the kitchen one night. He could feel his muscle tick in his jaw. So what if Jac was sleeping with the station manager? She was a grown woman, now. It shouldn't matter who she spent her nights with.

It shouldn't, and he refused to wonder why it kind of did.

He nodded. 'Okay, thanks.'

The doctor stepped out into the hallway, and lifted his chin when he saw the men waiting.

'She's had a bump to the head, and the scans we took earlier indicate a mild concussion, but in light of her recent visit, we'll keep her in overnight and monitor her, just to be on the safe side. I'll come back and check her in the morning, but for now she's staying put.'

Mac nodded. 'Thanks, Doc.'

The doctor glanced between the two men. 'Will one of you come back tomorrow when she's released? I don't think she should drive, in her state.'

'I will,' Mac responded quickly, then looked at Scott. 'I'll take a statement from her and drive her home.'

'I can pick her up if you like, save you a trip.'

Mac's lips tightened into a smile. 'It's no trouble. Besides, if she's here, she might need you to do her chores back home.'

Scott's lips pursed. 'Yeah, sure. Okay. Well, I'll see you tomorrow. Let me know if you change your mind.'

Mac nodded, then waited. Scott looked between him and the doctor, and then Jac's door. 'She should probably rest, right Doc?' Mac asked casually. He didn't want to look into why he felt this inclination to insert a little distance between Jac and her handsome station manager. It was instinctive, and he was happy to go with it.

The doctor nodded. 'Yeah. We'll be waking her up during the night to check on her, so whatever shut-eye she can manage is for the best.'

Scott cleared his throat, then nodded. 'Okay. Well, I'll be off.' He jerked his chin at Mac, and then sauntered back down the hall.

Mac looked at the doctor. 'I might just pop in and have a quick word, but I'll be back in the morning for her.' He handed the man his card. 'Call me if you need to.'

The doctor nodded, sliding the card into his coat pocket before wandering on down the hall.

Mac stepped quickly into the room. It was darker, now, the main light switched off, with just a small light on over her bed. Jac was lying in the bed with her arms folded, and damned if she didn't have a pout on.

'I want to go home,' she said.

'You can't,' he told her firmly.

'I hate hospitals,' she cried softly. He fought back a smile.

'Suck it up, Buchanan. It's just for one night.'

Her eyes shone, as though she was fighting back tears, and he frowned as he approached her. 'Hey, it's okay, Jac. It's just for one night, you're going home in the morning.' He put his hand on her shoulder, giving her a casual, friendly pat of assurance.

She blinked rapidly, tilting her head back as though working against gravity. 'I just want to be home in my own bed,' she said.

'And you'll get there, just let these guys look after you for one night,' he told her. His lips curved. 'I never knew you could be such a wuss. What's so big and scary about a hospital?'

She flicked her gaze to his. 'Mum went into a hospital, and never came out,' she said in a low voice. Then she shrugged. 'Before the other night, I hadn't been in a hospital since Dad's accident.'

Mac closed his eyes. *You dick.* Her aversion to hospitals made so much sense now, as did her rush to check out the last time she'd been in. He was a prime idiot for not thinking of it before. Bloody hell. And he was now a detective.

Dick.

He opened his eyes, and rubbed her arm. 'I'm so sorry, Jac. I didn't even think…'

She sniffed, then lifted his chin. 'It's not your fault. Not your problem.' She made a half-hearted gesture toward the door. 'I'm fine if you need to go.' She flicked him a quick glance.

Pig's arse, she'd be fine. She'd developed quite the poker face, but he still knew her well enough to know when she was trying to brazen her way through something when she was anxious. Like when he'd borrowed *The Amityville Horror* from the video store and he and Jamie had watched it, along with Jac—until she'd bolted from the room.

He hooked the leg of one of the visitor's chairs with his foot and dragged it over. 'Nah, I can hang for a while,' he told her. He positioned the chair close to the bed and sat down, raising his feet to rest on her bed.

'Make yourself comfortable,' she said dryly.

He grinned. 'Thanks, I will. Hey, did you hear the Black Cockatoos made the finals?' The local cricket team was having a stellar season.

'Really? When's that match?' Jac said through a yawn.

'Two weeks. They have a bye this weekend.'

'That's nice,' she said softly. She moved her hand out from her side, and he reached for it, his fingers sliding between hers. She gave him a gentle squeeze in acknowledgment.

'Uh-huh. First time in seventeen years we've made the finals. They're talking about making it a bit of an event,' he said, eyeing her. She blinked slowly.

'Really? Like how?' Her words were slow, and she yawned again.

'Oh, barbeque, cake stall, raffles—they may even get Dave Baker's band to play.' He kept talking in a low voice, and gradually her blinks got longer and longer, her breathing deepened, and her hand relaxed in his. After a while he stopped talking and just sat there in the low light, holding her hand as she slept. He brushed his fingers over her knuckles. Her skin was surprisingly soft. Smooth. Silken.

He scooted his butt forward in the chair so that he could tilt his head against the low backrest, and stared at the perforated ceiling.

Scott thought she'd been sleepwalking. Can you drive a vehicle in your sleep? He didn't know. His head rolled to the right so he could look at her, and his gaze was drawn to the bruise on her cheek. Had she tripped and fallen? Or had someone really attacked her?

His hold on her hand became firm. If it was the latter, god help the bastard who dared to lay a hand on her, because he'd make sure the guy lived to regret it.

Mac flinched awake. He could hear yelling down the hall. He glanced over at Jac. Her eyes were still closed, her chest rose and fell in a regular rhythm beneath the thin hospital gown.

And he was staring at her chest. Mac blinked, and sat up—oh, crikey, his neck ached—and he looked toward the door. What was going on? He swung his legs off the bed and strolled to the door, rubbing the back of his neck. There was more yelling—although the words were indistinguishable.

He strode down the hall, stretching his neck, and stopped at the door to Casualty. Constable Ben Fields wore a bored expression as he cuffed a man to a bed. Mac walked through the swing doors, and Ben smiled when he saw him.

'Hey, Mac. What are you doing here?'

'Jac Buchanan got knocked out at Bulls' Run, and I was just, uh,' he frowned, 'interviewing her. She's fallen asleep, though.'

'Hey, I wan' sumpin' to eat,' the man hollered from his bed.

Mac looked at him. 'Hey, Jim. What brings you here?'

Jim Howard was the town's mechanic and frequent visitor to the Echo Springs cells on a Friday or Saturday night. He was also one of Mac's father's friends.

Jim smiled serenely. 'I think I broke my leg.'

Ben shook his head. 'Sprained ankle, methinks.'

Mac eyed the cuffs and raised his eyebrows. Ben grimaced. 'Found him fighting Gerry Sinclair. He was still a little … testy, when I got there.'

Mac's lips pressed together. Jim was usually a good bloke, but when he got a drop in him, he could be a rowdy mongrel. Still, his father would insist Mac be completely fair with the man. 'Jim, why were you fighting Gerry?'

'He accused me of trying to run over his old lady,' Jim exclaimed, his expression showing his offence at the suggestion.

Mac flicked a glance at Ben, who gave a slight shrug. His shoulders lowered a little. Ah, damn it. 'When did this happen?' he enquired casually, then held up his hand at Jim's frown. 'Sorry, when does Gerry *think* this happened?'

'Just before this bugger picked me up,' Jim said, gesturing toward Ben.

'So you were driving,' Mac said, his voice low.

'Well, how else am I going to get home?' Jim responded.

'Did you hit Gwen Sinclair with your car?' Mac was already tugging his phone out of his pocket.

'No!' Jim exclaimed. 'And I wasn't trying to, either.' The man sniggered. 'Not without a bullbar, anyway.'

Ben closed his eyes and shook his head, then looked at Mac. 'They were tussling on the street. When Gerry talked about "hitting" his wife, I thought he meant with a fist, not a car.'

Jim snorted. 'I'd need knuckle-dusters for that, and I'm fresh out. That woman has a jaw the size of—'

'Jim, were you driving tonight?' Mac interrupted, knowing full well the size of Gwen Sinclair's jaw. He hoped, prayed the man would have enough sense to think about his response.

'Hey, I was on my way home, minding my own business,' Jim stated. 'Then Gwen jumped out in front of me. Didn't know a woman her size could move that fast, frankly. She's damn lucky she's still in the land of the living, if you ask me.'

Mac shook his head, then held out his hand. 'Keys. Now.'

Jim blinked, and awareness slowly flared within his glazed eyes. 'Wait—'

'No. Now, Jim.' Mac's tone was firm.

Jim grumbled under his breath as he pulled out his keys, and slipped the car key off his ring.

'All of the cars, Jim,' Mac said brusquely, knowing too well who he was talking to. The man had a yard full of clients' cars, but also a couple of cars he used as courtesy vehicles to rent to clients while their vehicles were in the shop for repair.

'But that's my business, Mac,' Jim protested.

Mac leaned down so he could meet the man's eyes on the same level. 'Then perhaps you'll think next time you drink and drive. Hell, Jim, you could have hit Gwen Sinclair—or anybody else, for that matter. I don't know the full details, but knowing Gerry, if all you walk away from this with is a sprained ankle, then consider yourself lucky.'

'How am I supposed to work?' Jim snapped, his hand tightening into a fist, the cuff clanging against the bed rail.

'Be thankful you live another day to worry about having to walk, mate.' He glanced at Ben. 'Breathalyse him, and request bloods and urine. I'll go talk with the Sinclairs.'

'Don't be such a party-pooper, Mac,' Jim whined. Mac shook his head as he walked down the hall toward the exit. 'I'll tell your father,' Jim called out to him.

Mac turned, any good humour he felt for the man leaching away. 'You do that.' He'd deal with his father—later. He left the hospital, jaw clenched. Jim was drunk. No question. And he'd been driving around town. Bloody hell. The man was lucky he hadn't driven into a tree or a pole—or worse, somebody else. Anger had him clenching and unclenching his fists. The amount of times they'd arrived at a scene of carnage on the highway because people thought they could drive with a blood alcohol level that made it difficult to form a sentence, let alone operate a vehicle...

This was one of the perils of working in a small town. Inevitably, you had to deal with someone you knew. These people were generally his friends—until he had to arrest them. He'd learned a long time ago to set low expectations to avoid disappointment—and there *was* disappointment. Every time he had to haul a friend's butt into jail for beating up his wife, or driving drunk, or stealing, or dealing drugs ... Believe the worst of people, and you typically couldn't go wrong. Jayden Terrance had taught him that lesson. Once knockabout friends... until he'd arrested the man.

He slid into his car and stared at the single-level block building. Jac was in there, and his conscience pricked at him for leaving her alone... He sighed. He'd have to have that talk with her. That one where he told her he knew illegal activity was going on at her property, and he knew that she was involved. He just hoped she'd make it easy on them both and confess.

He started the car and pulled away, calling into the station to let them know he was on his way to the Sinclairs' to check on Gwen and get their side of the story.

And then he'd have to go home and tell his parents that Jim would be arrested and likely lose his business ... He could just imagine his father's reaction.

Sometimes being a country cop sucked.

Chapter Five

Jacinta slid the t-shirt on over her head, and was pulling it down when she heard the door open.

'Oh, sorry,' a deep masculine voice said behind her. 'I'll come back later.'

She yanked the garment down and turned to face her visitor. 'It's okay, Mac. What are you doing here?' At most he would have seen her back, and that was nothing to get embarrassed about, yet a soft warmth crept over her cheeks. She was super-conscious that the night before she'd slung clothes over her pyjamas, and wasn't wearing a bra beneath her clothes. Or knickers. Not that that would shock Detective Casanova here.

She eyed him surreptitiously as she reached for her jumper. He looked … tired. No, not so much tired as weary. Her cheeks heated again. She'd fallen asleep on him. Well, not *on* him… Images sprang to mind about what falling asleep *on* him could look like. Oh, god. That was so wrong. She blamed it on the knock to her head. Yeah, that had to be it.

'I'm taking you home today. Has the doctor released you?' His lips quirked as he removed his hat. 'Unless you want to check yourself out again…?'

She pulled the jumper over her head. 'No, he's released me. I can't wait to get out of here. I'm so tired.'

His eyebrows rose. 'Rough night?' The concern in his voice touched her, and she preoccupied herself with smoothing the jumper down over her hips. He'd stayed with her. Well, until she'd fallen asleep. That was sweet. She'd felt … cared for. Which made her feel all kinds of awkward.

'Uh, the nurses came and woke me up every hour or so…' And shone a light in her eyes, and wanted to talk. She understood what they were doing, appreciated it, but now she was really craving a solid sleep. She picked up the headache tablets the nurse had given her—they were ones easily bought over the counter, but she'd been given some at breakfast, and some to tide her over during the day.

Then his words sank in. 'You're taking me home? What about Scott?'

Mac's expression became impassive. 'I thought he might need to do some of your work this morning, so I figured I'd save him a trip.'

Jac paused. While she was hesitant to put Mac out—it wasn't like Bulls' Run was a regular visit for him, not since Jamie had left—she appreciated the fact that someone would be at the station to do her chores while she was away. She didn't want her father to stress.

'Thanks,' she said, then slid her feet in her boots and walked to the door without tying her shoelaces. It hurt her head too much when she bent down.

'Laces,' Mac said, pointing to them. 'You'll trip.'

'I'll be fine to walk to the car.'

His eyes narrowed, and then his gaze drifted to the butterfly stitches on her temple. He tossed his hat on the bed.

'You could just ask, you know,' he murmured as he hunkered down and started to tie up her boots.

'I didn't want to be a bother,' she said, looking down at his bent head. A memory of him doing the exact same thing when she was seven and he was eleven flashed through her mind, and that same sense from the night before, that one of being cared for, filled her, warmed her.

And then he tied her boots together. 'Mac,' she cried in protest, cuffing him gently across the back of his head. 'You're so juvenile.'

He chuckled as he undid the laces and tied them correctly. 'You're so gullible.'

She rolled her eyes as he rose, and for a moment they stood so close, she could lean forward and brush against him.

Which was so *not* what she was going to do. What the hell was she thinking? She rubbed the back of her head as she stepped back. She was going to blame these little mental side trips to fantasyland on the knocks to the head.

'You ready to go?' he asked. 'I can come back later, if you need to rest a little more.'

She shook her head gingerly. 'No, I'm good to go.'

She followed him out in silence, then squinted at the too-bright sun outside. The glare prompted a tiny little throb. She wished she had her sunglasses. Fortunately, though, it wouldn't be long until she was home, and could flop into her bed.

She stared out of the passenger seat while Mac drove them through town. She leaned her elbow on the window frame and covered her face as they drove past the supermarket. A number of people were already out doing their shopping, and she could just imagine the gossip her trip home in a cop car would generate.

'Thanks for doing this,' she said quietly as Mac turned out onto the highway.

'No problem. It gives us a chance to talk.'

Really? He wanted to talk? A secret thrill rushed through her. He seemed … determined. Not so much brotherly as deliberate. Intent. They'd seen each other more, had talked more, in the last few days then in the eighteen months since her brother's last visit. Did seeing her without Jamie's presence finally show her as more than a pseudo-sister to him?

'What—' Her voice came out in a squeak, so she cleared her throat. 'What about?' God, she hoped that sounded casual. Calm.

'About Dick.'

It took her a moment to realise he was talking about the mine. She wrestled the images in her mind into a more PG-rated picture.

'Uh, okay. What about … Dick?'

He slid a sideways glance at her. 'I thought I'd give you the opportunity to tell me what's really going on.'

Uh… 'What do you mean?' Her frown deepened, her confusion making the throb in her head ache more. Perhaps he was talking about his body, after all? Did he know about her teen crush? That maybe, if she had a few beers and he caught her in a weak moment, she might admit she still had a residual flare of attraction for him? That could be either all kinds of mortifying, or the beginning of something very adult. He'd never asked her out—he'd asked out pretty much every other single, available and age-appropriate woman in Echo Springs, but not her … She wiped her palms on her jeans. His expression was so deadpan, she couldn't gauge where his mind was at. Did he want to talk about them? She was trying to ignore it, but hey, if he was prepared to address it, she could. But she sure as hell wasn't going to mention it unless he said something first.

He turned his attention back to the highway. 'I mean the real reason Brayden was in that mine shaft.'

She shut her mouth. O-kay. Not an *I-think-you're-hot* conversation, then. She took a deep breath, trying to will the colour back from her cheeks. 'I don't know,' she said, shaking her head. 'I didn't know he was out there, and I don't know who this Brad Perse is—'

'Brett Pearce,' Mac corrected.

She made a gesture with her hand. 'There you go, I can't even get his name right. I don't know what they were doing...' Her voice trailed off, and she turned to Mac. 'You don't think Brayden was gay, do you? Not that there's anything wrong with that, mind you,' she said hurriedly, 'I just didn't get that impression from him. Wow.'

Mac's lips pursed. 'Brayden and Brett weren't gay.'

'Okay, well, I don't know why they were there or what they were doing.' She tilted her head to the side. 'Did you ask Hayden? Does he have any idea what was going on?'

Mac's gaze narrowed as he eyed her briefly. 'Are you trying to find out what Hayden Terrance has told us?'

She shrugged. 'Kind of. I can talk to him directly, I guess. I want to attend Brayden's funeral, but that's not really the best time to bring this up, is it?'

'Just tell me, Jac.' His voice held such resignation, such disappointment, that it stopped her for a moment. She turned a little more in the seat to face him fully. There was something going on here, a tenseness that she was only just becoming aware of, and she'd bet the last of the Bulls' Run funds that it had nothing to do with the undercurrent of an attraction it seemed only she felt.

'Tell you what, Mac?' she asked carefully. She was wracking her brain, but she couldn't figure out what it was he seemed to want to hear from her.

'I *know*, Jac.'

'Know *what*, Mac?'

'I know about the meth lab,' he exclaimed, his knuckles turning white with frustration on the steering wheel.

Shock hit her like the mine explosion. 'What meth lab?'

'The one that the Terrance brothers and Brett Pearce set up in Dick.'

Her jaw dropped for a moment, stunned surprise and horror filling her. No. No. It couldn't—Hayden and Brayden wouldn't ... She shook her head. 'I don't believe you.' Her voice came out nearly hoarse.

'Toby Grimshaw confirmed it. Jac, you had a hazmat team out here, for crying out loud.'

'No, no, no,' she said, and continued to shake her head. There was no way—*no way*—that was true.

'Yes, Jac,' Mac said, nodding at her.

'Hayden wouldn't do that,' she said, her voice gaining strength. 'Brayden wouldn't, either.'

'Seriously?' Mac shot her a glance, his green eyes incredulous. 'None of the Terrances are choirboys, Jac.'

'I know that,' she snapped. 'I know Hayden's done some shonky stuff in the past, but there is no way he would do this, not with Brayden, not to me...'

'Your father fired his father for drinking on the job,' Mac argued. 'You think he wouldn't use you guys, even for just a little payback?'

'That was years ago,' Jacinta exclaimed, 'and those brothers kept coming out to Bulls' Run to hang out with us. You should know, Jayden was one of your friends, too.'

Mac pulled into the Bulls' Run's main drive and braked hard. 'Which is why I know what they're capable of,' he retorted, unbuckling his seat belt with a ferocity that surprised her. He was out of the car and stalking to open the gate with a speed that showed just how angry he was.

Jac folded her arms, her lips tight. Damn it, he was so wrong.

In moments he was back in the car and driving through the gate, only to stop and get out again to close the gate behind him. She shook her head. No, she wasn't going to do this. She was too steamed.

She got out of the car. 'I'll walk from here,' she said, slamming the car door shut.

'Get in the car, Jac,' Mac muttered as he strode around to the driver's door.

'No. I'd rather walk, thanks,' she snapped back at him.

He glared at her over the roof of the car, his features harsh with an anger she'd rarely seen him show.

'Get in the car, or I will cuff you and take you back to town,' he told her in a low voice.

She gaped at him. 'Are you serious?'

He braced his hands against frame of the car, his forearm muscles flexing as he gripped the car tightly.

'There was a meth lab operating right here on Bulls' Run, Jacinta,' he said quietly, and so calmly it had her stopping in her tracks to listen. 'You expect me to believe you didn't know anything about it? The kind of operation that could happen in a place only someone with an intimate knowledge of your property would be familiar with?' he said, using his fingers to list off his points. 'You're trying to tell me that A: it could continue to operate right under your nose without you knowing, and B: that you couldn't use profits to help you keep the farm?'

She stumbled back as though he'd pushed her. 'Bloody hell,' she whispered. 'You actually think that, don't you?'

He squinted up at the sky for a moment. 'It's no secret that you and your dad are in financial trouble, Jac.'

Her shoulders sagged. 'Take a look around, Mac,' she said, waving to encompass the broad landscape. 'Pretty much everyone in this area has financial trouble. But ... drugs?' Hurt washed over her. That last image of Kelsey, the one she hated but seemed burned into her memory, flashed through her mind, and she shook her head—to shake it out, but also in instinctive, reactive, visceral denial. 'How could you think I'd be involved with *drugs?*' The very thought was so offensive, it made her eyes burn.

He pressed his lips together, as though trying to bite off some words. 'That burn, Jac, that explosion from the other day, the one that sent you flying and incinerated your little mate,' he said, and this time she couldn't blink away the hot tear that rolled down her cheek, 'that was from a well-established laboratory.' His right fist clenched. 'We're not talking a couple of cones of weed. We're talking methamphetamines, drums of stuff, liquid, that built up gases that caused such an explosive reaction it changed your landscape.'

She folded her arms, hugging herself as though she could use the movement as a shield against the suspicious ring of fact in his words.

'That stuff didn't just appear there. It had to be carted in. Driven in. If it wasn't done in bulk, it was done over time, in repetitive trips, and you say you know nothing about it.' Mac shook his head. 'I don't believe you.'

She held herself tightly, trying not to splinter under the harsh distrust those words held.

'I didn't know,' she whispered hoarsely.

Mac shook his head, his expression closed. 'Get in the car.'

She hesitated, but seeing the grim look on his face, she didn't want to challenge his patience. She got in the car.

They rode up to the house in a cold, deafening silence. The centre console separated them, along with some sort of computer system, but it may as well have been an ever-increasing chasm. She could feel the chilled distance growing between them with every bump and lurch of the car.

Mac braked in front of the house, and a cloud of red dust that had followed them from the gate billowed up and enveloped the car for a moment, enclosing them in a red shroud of silence. She almost felt stifled, before it gradually subsided.

If it had been 'Mac' driving her home, he would have driven around the back, like all of their friends. No, she finally got it. 'Mac' wasn't driving her home, it was Detective Sergeant Macarthur Hudson doing the honours. In a freakin' squad car, no less.

The front door opened, and her father stepped out. Today he wore a collared shirt, his sleeve pinned to his side. His expression was curious at first, then relieved when he saw her in the front seat. He lifted his hand and waved.

Jacinta waved back. He looked … well, he looked almost happy to see her, a slight smile on his face. She caught her bottom lip between her teeth. It had been so long since she'd seen anything remotely like a smile on his face, it was a bittersweet experience now. 'You can't mention anything to him,' she said, keeping her gaze on her father.

'Jac—'

'Please,' she said in a whisper. 'He can't know about this. He can't be stressed out about it—this would send him back over the deep end.' And he'd only just managed to crawl back to the ledge. It wouldn't take much to push him back into a depression. 'I've bought the mortgage. I'm the land-owner of record, so you need to discuss this with me, not him.'

Mac's sigh was gusty. She smiled at her dad, but her words were for Mac. 'This—we didn't do this, Mac. There's another explanation, and I intend to figure it out, but it's not us.' She grabbed the door lever, then hesitated, then turned to look him in the eye. 'There is no way I would ever get involved with drugs,' she said to him, low and fierce and oozing as much sincerity as her indignation would allow. Hurt gradually burned away under the swell of anger. How could he think such a thing? After Kelsey… no. This just didn't make any sense whatsoever.

She got out of the car, and slammed the door shut with more force than necessary.

Mac lowered the window and looked out at her. 'We're not finished, here, Jac. We need to talk.'

'Count on it,' she said, and walked toward her father. Hell, yeah, there were plenty of things she wanted to say, but for now she was too angry, too sore, and too tired to properly formulate a logical position. No, at the moment she'd probably rant, rage and then hit Mac, so saving that discussion for another time worked. 'Later.'

He nodded, but it was obvious he wasn't happy. Well, great, because she definitely wasn't feeling like Susie Sunshine at the moment, either.

Mac put the car into gear as she strode up the stairs to the veranda. Tom Buchanan frowned. 'Isn't Mac coming in for a visit?'

'Nope.'

He looked at her. 'Are you okay?' There was a concern in his voice, a tremor that showed his worry.

She hugged him. 'Yeah, I'm okay. The nurses had to keep waking me up through the night to check on the concussion. I'm just tired.'

He hugged her back. 'I'm glad you're okay, kiddo. Go rest, Scott and I can take care of everything today.'

She hid her face in his collar, battling tears and the urge to sob. It was such a relief to hear him talk about working, something she hadn't heard, hadn't seen from him, since he was wheeled out of the hospital, his arm a stump, and a bitter, pained expression on his face.

'Thanks.'

She took a deep breath, gave him an extra squeeze, then stepped over the third plank and walked into the house without a glance over her shoulder at the squad car slowly driving out of the yard.

Mac closed the gate behind him, then drove back toward town. He hit the steering wheel with the flat of his palm.

That conversation hadn't gone the way he'd expected it. Even when faced with the facts, Jacinta hadn't admitted guilt. He still didn't know who had attacked her the night before. Was she protecting them? Was she so scared of the guys she was working with that she would shield them from the law? Was she ready to go to jail for them?

Jamie would be furious. Mac felt he deserved to cop some of that fury. He'd promised his mate he'd look after his younger sister, and now look what had happened. She was working with criminals, violent men who wouldn't think twice about killing her or her father if they didn't get their own way.

'What was she thinking?' he muttered. Maybe that was the problem. Maybe over the years she'd done a number of favours for the Terrances until setting up a meth lab and supplying stock to Sydney seemed like an acceptable thing for her to do. A little cash on the side to keep things going...

Mac pulled into the parking lot at the back of the police station and sat there for a moment. What was he going to do about Jacinta? She wasn't like

Jayden Terrance, a natural-born felon who manipulated those around him and betrayed them to benefit his own self-interests. Jayden had deserved everything that came his way, but Jacinta? Jacinta deserved his help.

Mac exited the car, his mouth tightening as he walked into the station. For now, he had to figure out who else was involved in this drug operation. It wouldn't surprise him to hear Jayden Terrance was high up the chain— but he wouldn't be top dog. No, the guy was a sociopath, granted, but he wouldn't be the kingpin. Mac shook his head. Maybe he could get Jacinta to turn on the men who were using her, using her farm? He just had to figure out the leverage.

Mac walked into the muster room and nodded at Ben Fields. Ben leaned back in his chair.

'Hey, how is Jac?'

'Sore,' he said shortly, then shrugged. 'Grumpy. How is Jim?'

Ben shuddered. 'Still sleeping it off. What about Gwen?'

'Not a scratch, fortunately. Jim missed, but only just, from what she and Gerry tell me.'

Ben rose, and looked about the empty muster room before making his way over to Mac. 'Hey, do you really think Jacinta is involved in what went down with Pearce and Terrance?'

Mac eyed the younger man. 'You know I can't really discuss that with you...' he said. There was a drug epidemic in Echo Springs, and so far the organisers had managed to evade the law. They'd captured two members of the gang who seemed to be running things, but apart from vaguely threatening references to 'the Boss', the pair had clammed up. The Sarge wanted to limit certain information getting out—they still had no idea who was involved, only that it was a decent-sized operation. He'd finally been given the green light to interview Jacinta—which he'd have to do properly, and soon.

Ben nodded, holding his hand up. 'Sure, no worries, it's just—' The constable grimaced. 'I know you know Jacinta. I know Jacinta, too. She went to the same boarding school in North Sydney as my first girlfriend—long story,' he said at Mac's arched eyebrow.

Mac knew Ben was gay; he'd gone to a Raiders football game a few weeks earlier with him and his partner, Toby.

'I guess I'm trying to say—this really doesn't sound like Jacinta.'

Mac sighed. 'Yeah, well, I thought that about Jayden Terrance too, until I had to arrest him.'

Ben grimaced. 'Jayden Terrance should be your exception, not your standard.'

Mac shrugged as he backed toward his office. 'And yet Jim is sleeping it off in the cells after driving under the influence, and a meth lab exploded at Bulls' Run. I've learned you can never presume to truly know anyone, because sooner or later, they'll disappoint you. I'm sure if you talk to Leila, she could tell you the same thing...'

'We've all got a story like that, I guess,' Ben sighed as he turned back to his desk.

Mac unlocked the door to the detectives' office and stepped inside. He switched on the light as he closed the door behind him, then looked at the whiteboard. It was peppered with photographs of persons of interest, diagrams and timelines. He picked up the rubber ball from his desk and bounced it against the door, staring at the information, trying to get a flash of inspiration, a fact they could follow to find out who was behind the drugs in Echo Springs. Who was dealing it?

He bounced the ball against the door again. Constable Leila Mayne didn't know this, but she and Hayden were under surveillance. Leila was on leave, dealing with the aftermath of Brayden's death, but also as part of a disciplinary action after she'd confessed some of the information she'd initially withheld from them. And didn't that just suck. Another woman he knew and respected being drawn into the web of lies that surrounded Hayden Terrance. So far he hadn't had any hits. He did know that Hayden had visited his brother Jayden, down in Silverwater prison. He knew they'd argued, and that Hayden hadn't had any contact with Jayden Terrance since. He also knew a phone had been confiscated, and he was currently awaiting intelligence from that phone.

He just had to connect the dots between Jacinta and Bulls' Run, and Jayden Terrance and the druglord he was working for.

Back to the drawing board, as they say. He bounced the ball again, then turned back to his desk. Grimshaw's report on the fire sat there, about two centimetres thick. The guy was nothing but thorough. Maybe, if he knew the volumes they were talking about, he could start tracking the goods... He sat down at his desk, and got to work.

Chapter Six

Jacinta hugged Hayden Terrance, her arms holding him tightly. 'I'm so sorry,' she whispered through her tears. She stood back, wanting to avoid staining his dark suit. Brayden's casket sat on the gurney above his grave. Sue Terrance was walking toward the hearse. Brayden's mother refused to watch her youngest son being lowered into the dark hole.

'Thanks for coming, Jac,' Hayden murmured. His face was drawn, and lines surrounded his mouth and eyes that hadn't been there the last time she'd seen him. His younger brother's death had aged him. Hayden shook his head. 'You've got nothing to be sorry for, kiddo.'

She tilted her head, her smile sad. 'He died on my property.' She had plenty to feel sorry for.

'He died on my watch,' he corrected her, his expression firm. 'This isn't on you, Jac.' He frowned, and lifted his hand to tilt her chin a little further. She'd tried to hide the bruise under a tonne of makeup, but seeing as she rarely wore the stuff, she didn't think she'd been that successful. 'What the hell happened to you?'

'Long story.' She caught her lip, glancing over her shoulder. A number of people were queueing up to pay their respects. She leaned closer to him. 'I—I need to talk to you,' she whispered.

Something flickered in his eyes, a knowing, and a realisation crept over her. He knew. Hayden knew something about his brother's death, about the meth lab at Bulls' Run. Her mouth opened a little. He lowered his hand, then nodded.

'Yeah. Raincheck?'

'Of course,' she said, patting his arm. 'Now is so not the time.'

Leila Mayne approached them, looking slender and stylish in her fitted black slacks and black singlet and sheer blouse. Jacinta smiled. She was so happy to see these two back together. When Hayden had dated Leila in high school, he'd seemed so happy, so relaxed. She always thought Leila was such a good influence on him. Better than Jac could be, anyway. Sure, these two had had their obstacles to overcome, but it was nice to see her childhood friend find his place with this woman.

'Hi Leila,' Jacinta said, and hugged her. Leila hugged her back gently.

'We all appreciate you being here, Jac,' Leila murmured.

Jac smiled, tears still fresh on her face, as she left the couple and walked across the cemetery to her ute.

A figure detached from the back of the crowd, and she frowned at Mac as he started to walk toward her. She held up her hand. 'Not today,' she said firmly. 'Today is for Brayden.'

Mac came closer. He looked so tall, so strong, in contrast to the shaken community around him. He wore a charcoal grey shirt and black trousers, and not for the first time she thought a business shirt enhanced the breadth of his shoulders, the leanness of his hips. There was an undeniable strength in the man. His green eyes were solemn in the mid-morning sunlight, his lips pressed firmly together. Those lips…

Fine, the man was hot. And she was all sorts of desperate if she was eyeing a cop at a friend's funeral. And this time she couldn't blame a bump to her head. Brenda Durrant, one of the mourners, called out softly to Mac, and he lifted his hand in a casual wave. Jacinta didn't miss the flirtatious smile, the hopeful look in the woman's eyes, or the disappointment as Mac, oblivious, turned back to face Jacinta. Brenda's smile tightened, but she walked back toward the cars with the rest of the mourners.

Mac's eyes drifted to her cheek. 'How's your head?' he asked quietly.

She hadn't expected his expression of concern. 'Uh, fine.'

He lifted his hand to her chin, much like Hayden had, and yet her body reacted so differently, as though every nerve ending had switched on. Her heart skittered in her chest, and her breath hitched, before she forced herself to exhale. His hand was warm against her skin. He tucked a tendril of hair behind her ear, and she shivered at the contact. Something warm surged through her, something smooth and wicked that awoke at his touch. Desire.

Heat flickered in his eyes, and then he blinked, and an impassive shutter came down over awareness in his gaze. His hand lowered. 'We need to talk,' he told her quietly.

And just like that, his words killed any warmth and desire she was feeling. He needed to talk, because he thought she was a drug runner.

'Not now. I'm on my way to Brayden's wake.' She needed to pay her respects to Sue, Hayden and Brayden's mum. She wasn't about to talk about the explosion, or what Mac thought was her part in it. That would be too painful, and too infuriating, to handle at the moment.

He scanned her face, his gaze so intent, as though he was trying to peel back the layers to reveal her secrets. He reluctantly nodded. 'Fine. We'll talk another time.'

She took a step, then turned back to him. 'Don't think I'm putting you off,' she told him, frowning. 'I am more than willing to talk with you, just not today.'

'I understand,' he said, glancing at the funeral party behind him. She nodded, then continued to stride across the graves.

Hours later, Jacinta braked, then switched off the engine and stared at the dirt and patchy tufts of grass. This was where someone had hit her. She climbed out of the cab. She'd changed into jeans and a shirt as soon as she got home from the funeral, and was so happy to be out of the heels she'd worn for most of the day.

God, the funeral. What a sad, depressing time. Sue Terrance was devastated. She shuddered when she thought of Hayden's mum all worn and ravaged. She didn't want to think about it. Didn't want to think of their loss, of Brayden's shining smile permanently darkened.

No, she wanted to get the bastards who'd pulled him into that situation, and who thought they could use her home as a bloody drug operation.

And then she'd make them pay.

Jac put her hands on her hips and walked around a bit, eyeing the ground. The sun was dipping low, the sky blazing with fiery orange and peach as the indigo of dusk crept in. She checked behind her truck, eyeing the gauge of the tracks, then walked out in front. She was pretty sure the other vehicle had been right here. She crouched down.

There was a pattern here, one that didn't match her tyres. She rose and put her foot next to it, trying to get an idea of the size. It had three central lines, the middle of which had a zigzag groove.

She glanced back in the direction of the highway. She knew where they'd entered… She turned back again. 'But where were you going?' she mused softly. There were other mines throughout the property, but whoever was driving would be taking a circuitous route if they were heading toward one of them.

She eyed the tracks again. They stopped where she was, and then it looked like they'd turned around. She followed them for a bit, and then halted. There was yet another set of tyre tracks. This pattern looked like more of an interrupted wave down the three centre panels.

Two vehicles? Maybe one belonged to Scott. He'd been the one to find her and bring her in. But had he seen the other car, or had it left by the time Scott arrived?

She frowned as she walked back to her truck, and then started to drive back toward the highway. The third gate was for organised deliveries. It wasn't a common thoroughfare, and the gate had a lock on it, so she wanted to check it out.

It took several minutes of bumping along the track, and she shook her head. She still couldn't believe someone had the balls to just drive onto Bulls' Run property, and then knock her out when she approached. Anger had her clenching the steering wheel just a little tighter. Son of a bitch. The shock of the incident was beginning to wear off, and fury was building in its place.

She hadn't been out this way for weeks. Months, even.

She pulled up in front of the gate, and frowned. The chain and pad-lock hung between the gate and the post. She climbed out of the car and approached the gate. Everything looked normal. She placed her hands on the gate and sighed. Then how the blood hell had they—

The chain wobbled with the tremor she'd set off in the gate when she touched it, and that's when she saw it. She leaned down to lift the padlock. The shackle was positioned over the top of the slide, but not connected to it. Son of a bitch. The damn thing wasn't locked.

She squeezed the shackle into the slide until she heard the click as the mechanism engaged. She shook her head, not at all confident that it would keep her trespassers out. She got back into the truck and headed home. She was determined to make it as difficult as possible for her midnight visitors.

She was going to need a bigger lock.

Mac pulled up around the back of the house, and braked. Jac was talking to Scott. As she spoke, she tossed a ball into the air, hit it with a cricket bat, and her dog ran after it, pouncing on it in the dirt, only to bring it back to her feet, and she'd repeat the process. There were two vehicles parked in the yard, and Tom stood on the back veranda, watching.

Jac turned to face Mac, and she rested the cricket bat on her shoulder as she leaned back against the bonnet of her car.

Well, he guessed he didn't expect her to throw confetti at his arrival. He climbed out of the car and walked up to the veranda.

'Hey, Tom,' he said, holding his left hand out.

Tom reached out with his left hand and shook it. 'Mac. What brings you out here again?'

'I needed to have a word with Jac—about the other night,' he said casually.

'Oh, okay. Is everything alright?'

He remembered Jac's comments about her father's stress levels, and pasted a smile on his face. 'Just getting some more information, that's all.'

Tom shook his head. 'I tell you what, I'm not happy we're getting so many trespassers.'

'Neither am I, Tom. Not happy that Jac got hurt, either,' he said quietly.

Tom nodded, his expression grim. 'We need to sort this out, Mac.'

He nodded. 'We will.' He just hoped Tom wouldn't be devastated when they did. The screen door clanged behind him, and Mac peered over Tom's shoulder. He smiled when he saw the woman who'd caused tongues to wag in town when she'd moved out to Bulls' Run.

'Marion, how are you?'

'Good, Mac. I don't suppose the old grump here offered you something to drink, did he?'

Tom made a scoffing sound. 'Haven't had a chance yet, woman.'

'Well, at least one of us can remember our manners. Can I get you a drink? Lemonade? A cup of tea?'

Mac smiled as he shook his head. 'No, I'm right, thanks. I just want to talk with Jacinta.'

Marion's eyebrows rose. 'Oh, really?' Her curiosity was obvious.

'About the other night,' Jacinta said as she walked over to the bottom of the veranda steps. She turned to Scott. 'You know what to get now?'

Scott's lips firmed, and he nodded. 'Yeah. Want me to stick around?' he said, gesturing toward Mac.

Jac shook her head, and Mac was momentarily distracted by the movement of her ponytail. 'Nah. I can handle him. You head on into town, and call me when you get back.'

Scott nodded, then leaned in. Mac looked away, but not quick enough to miss his kiss on Jac's cheek. Marion raised her eyebrows once again, and then Mac heard Scott's truck start up, and he turned.

Jac trotted up onto the veranda and placed the bat and ball against the side of the house, avoiding the section of warped and splitting wood. She beckoned him. 'Come on.'

Mac frowned. 'What?'

'I've got to go check some sheep out in the west pasture,' she said, her gaze darting to her father before meeting his again. 'You can come with me, and we'll talk on the way.'

Mac glanced toward the house. He guessed anywhere they talked inside, there was the possibility that Tom might overhear. He felt that at some time Tom would have to be advised of what was going on, but for now, if Jacinta was more prepared to talk where her father couldn't hear, he'd go along with it. For now.

Hell. The things he did for this woman. He nodded, and trotted down the steps toward her red, dust-covered ute. 'Fine.'

She whistled, and her dog came bolting around the corner, tongue hanging out of his mouth. The dog jumped up into the back of the tray, and she slammed the tray gate shut, then got into the vehicle without further comment. He followed suit.

Mac twisted in his seat once they were underway. Jac had flung her hat on the window ledge between the cab and the tray behind. He could see her dog through the rear window, lurching from one side of the vehicle to the other as he surveyed the landscape. Mac turned back to Jacinta.She had donned her sunglasses, and her red shirt sleeves were rolled up. The top three buttons of her shirt were undone, and he saw the neckline of a green singlet.

Tendrils of hair framed her face. He noticed how some strands of her hair were lighter than others, touched by the sun and burnished a warm copper colour.

He noticed the faint lines around her eyes as she looked out through the windscreen. Whether they were born from the narrow focus of determination, or relaxed good humour, he couldn't tell. Right now, though, she seemed determined.

He noticed the firm press of her lips, the lift to her chin that lengthened the line of her neck ... and the indent of her collarbone and the smooth skin of her chest. His gaze dropped and he noticed the swell of her breasts yet again. He frowned. He was noticing her breasts a lot.

He told himself he noticed these things because he was a detective, and that was his job. But the growing awareness of her body, the tightening in his groin—that had nothing to do with his job and everything to do with a physiological response of a man admiring an attractive woman. He needed to get out more. He'd been so involved with the drugs and related crime in the area that he'd let his social life slide into the background. Obviously that was a mistake, though, because now he was seeing Jac as a woman, and not the irritating brat he'd grown up with. Scott Neilsen definitely saw her as a woman, judging by the way the station manager had looked at her when he'd approached them earlier. Mac shook his head as he remembered the guy offering to help Jac with *him*. No. They'd known each other for that long, they could handle it, thanks. He wasn't going to wonder why he was feeling so proprietary toward Jac. He just was.

'So, you'll handle me, huh?' His voice was low, and he tried to keep it casual, enquiring, only it came out just slightly flirtatious to his ears.

It must have been flirtatious to Jac's ears, too, because she shot him a quick glance, and he noticed the bloom of colour in her cheeks, the way her blue gaze brightened with the curiosity of a woman about a man.

He should have been mortified, should have just focused on the professional, but that little part of him that harkened back to his cave-man ancestors experienced a flare of satisfaction and triumph at her looking at him like something more than honorary family.

She gaped a little, then snapped her mouth shut and nodded. 'Yep. I own Bulls' Run, so I'm the one you take this up with.'

Her words made him frown. 'When did you take over the farm? I don't think any of us knew you were running it.' At least, not by herself. He hadn't spoken to Jamie for a few months—his mate being in a war zone meant regular communication was challenging.

Her lips curved in a wry half-smile that he found attractive, and all Jac. 'I said I took on the mortgage. I didn't say I run the farm.'

His eyebrows rose. 'There's a difference?'

Her smile subsided as she nodded, keeping her eyes on the track they were bouncing along. 'When my father's involved, you bet there is.'

Mac glanced out the window. Some of the paddocks they passed had a sheen of golden grass, but many were big red-dirt fields with patches of green scrub. The dams weren't quite dry, but they were low. Hay bales spotted the area, and sheep and cattle grazed lazily, or lay in the shade of some of the trees, depending on the paddock.

He shook his head. 'That's a lot of responsibility for a—'

'Careful,' she warned, holding up a hand. 'If you say woman, or girl, so help me I'll smack you.'

'I was about to say anyone under thirty,' he told her airily, mentally making a note about her attitude to sexism. She'd always been a tomboy, always ready to show she could do as much, if not more, than her brother and their friends. He'd never considered her as a delicate desert belle—she had a right hook that could convince him otherwise—but perhaps that was his problem. His gaze toured over her body. She was long and lean, with curves that drew his eyes where his hands wanted to be. The day before, at the funeral, she'd worn a straight black skirt and a navy blouse, and it was probably the first time he'd seen her out of jeans in ... years.

He hadn't realised how slender her waist was, or how curvy her hips were, when she wasn't wearing the baggy guys' shirts and the slim, straight jeans that showed off the long, firm line of her legs.

She shrugged, and he had to force himself to look away from the swell of her bosom. 'When Dad lost his arm, we missed a few payments. We talked about re-financing, but the bank was taking the line that Dad was the owner of record, and was now no longer "able" to work the land,' she said, emphasising the word with a twist to her lips. She changed gears when they hit a smooth section of track.

'Like that was what he needed to hear after losing his arm, that he was technically disabled.' She shook her head, then took a deep breath. 'So I took on the farm.'

'And Jamie?'

She flashed him a quick look, and he was struck by the sadness he saw in her eyes. 'I had to borrow from him so I could purchase the farm. He was happy to give it to me. He's got no interest in being a farmer, Mac. He's bought a place down in Sydney. Near the beach, if you can believe it.'

Mac stared at her. 'Seriously?' He didn't quite know how to react to that. He missed his best friend, but Jamie had been away for some time, had travelled ... he guessed he could understand why his friend didn't want to come back home to Echo Springs. It wasn't exactly a town of excitement and adventure, not after whatever Jamie would see serving in the Australian army.

'Yeah. He didn't tell you?' She turned her attention back to the track. 'He visits us when he can, but then spends some time at his place.' She grimaced. 'Dad doesn't know, though.'

Mac's eyes rounded. 'You don't think Tom needs to know your brother isn't coming back home?'

She rolled her eyes. 'I think Dad has enough trouble coping with the fact his daughter is doing what he can't. He's never really seen me as being the one to take on the farm.'

'He can be old-fashioned, sometimes,' Mac allowed. 'But it's a hard life for anyone, Jac, man or woman.'

'Can you see me behind a desk?' Jacinta scoffed. 'I like it here, Mac. I love it. This is my home, and I want to make a good go of it.'

He shook his head. Jacinta would be facing an uphill battle with Tom, with the banks, hell, any of the shearers that had to take orders from a woman...

'What does Scott think?' he asked carefully.

She shrugged. 'He doesn't know. He doesn't need to know.'

'You don't think he'd like his girlfriend being his boss?'

She frowned. 'I'm not his girlfriend,' she said, surprised. 'And it's got nothing to do with me being a woman. Most of the men I come into contact with, I've already worked with for years, and they don't really have too much of a problem. No, it's not about gender.'

He blinked, trying to process what she was saying, but all he was focusing on was 'I'm not his girlfriend'. But she had been so touchy about his comment before... 'I don't get it, then,' he admitted.

She braked as they came up to a number of sheep huddled on the track, and pressed her hand to the horn. The sheep slowly started to shift.

'It's Dad. It's not that a girl is taking over—although I'm sure he'd prefer to have Jamie working here than me,' she said, and rested her elbows on the steering wheel as she turned her head to face him. 'It's got nothing to do with me being female. It's the fact that I'm doing what he *can't*. I think even if Jamie were here, there would be some friction, but Dad...' She hesitated. 'I'm his daughter. I think he feels guilty for not being able to do what he used to do, for not being able to look after me, and that I have to do it, and look after him. Losing his arm—he's had to question what, exactly, he *can* do. He's had to fight his way through so much pain, and yeah, there have been some really dark days...' The shadows in her eyes hinted that perhaps even those words were an understatement for her experience. 'I mean, can you imagine your whole livelihood hanging in the balance because of a freak accident, and possibly losing the land that generations before you built up... that you may not be able to pass on to generations to come... It's screwed with his mind. Hell, do you know it took me being in hospital for him to try milking the cow again? That was a huge step forward.' The sheep cleared the track enough for her to move the car forward, and they continued on their way.

He arched an eyebrow. 'How did he do?'

She beamed. 'He did *good*. Apparently it took him a while, but he now knows that's something he can still do—one handed, no less.' He heard the pride in her voice. Then she shrugged. 'I'm just warming his seat. He'll get there. He'll figure out one arm doesn't maketh the man. He just needs some time. Then he can tell the banks where to shove their disabilities.'

'Well, I guess you were never one to take the easy way,' he muttered, slightly in awe of her and her attitude. He'd never guessed things had been so dire, so dark out at Bulls' Run. Sure, it was a known fact that Tom had gotten even grumpier, but whenever he'd seen Jac in town, she'd been smiling and chatting to folks, and seemingly happy.

She chuckled, a sound that was low and husky and curled deep inside him, grabbing his attention until the dust, the flies, the heat, the spring that poked him in the back every time they went over a bump or through a dip, all faded until there was just Jac and her sexy little laugh and seductive smile.

'Yeah, well, the harder you work, the better the reward,' she said.

He had to look away. She was beginning to sound like her own person, a person he wanted to talk more with, to understand a lot better.

'Where are we going?' he asked, glancing about. She'd mentioned something about the west pasture, but if he had his bearings right, she'd driven slightly north.

The smile slid off her face, and he immediately noticed its absence.

'We're going to visit Harry,' she told him.

'Harry? As in the tunnel, Harry?'

'What about the sheep?'

She nodded. 'We'll also check on the sheep,' she said. 'But I want to check on Harry first.'

She pulled the ute over to a fence that had run along the side of the track, then braked when she reached the old, rusty gate. She twisted in her seat to face him.

'I didn't have anything to do with what happened at Dick,' she told him firmly. Her expression was so earnest that for the first time he found himself entertaining the possibility that maybe he'd gotten something wrong. 'But something *is* going on.' She glanced around, and his eyebrow rose as she

leaned closer. 'The other night, someone knocked me out—on my property,' she said.

Her voice dropped to almost a whisper. Why, he had no idea, unless she
didn't want the sheep to be distressed by their conversation.

'Do you sleepwalk?' he asked abruptly, and she blinked and jerked back.
'What?'

'Do you sleepwalk, Jac?'

'No.'

'So you weren't out driving around in your sleep?'

She frowned. 'Uh, no. I was fully awake and aware of my surroundings—
why would you think I was sleepwalking?' She gasped. 'Did Dad tell you the
flu meds story? I swear, he tells that to everyone. It happened once, and I've
never had that particular brand of meds since.'

'Do you talk in your sleep?'

'No.' Her gaze flickered. She exhaled, a sound that conveyed her exasper-
ation. She waved her hand casually. 'Maybe. When I'm really tired, I might
talk—but I don't walk in my sleep. Why would you think that?'

Because your 'boyfriend' told me so. He wasn't quite sure what to believe,
and aside from coming straight out with 'are you sleeping with Scott
Nielsen?'—a question he would have to admit had nothing to do with his
investigation and everything to do with a fast-developing fascination with
this woman—he'd have to hold his own counsel until he could figure out
the truth of the matter.

She waved her hand. 'Anyhoo, when I got back from the funeral I went
out to where I got hit—'

'You *what?*'

Chapter Seven

This time it was Mac who leaned forward, stunned.

'I went out to where it happened—'

'Why did you do that?' Didn't she care about her own safety? If what she was saying was true—which meant putting aside Scott's comments for the moment—she'd happened upon an intruder, who had struck her, and knocked her out cold. Anger, surprising and swift, roared through him at the thought of her defenceless and vulnerable to the likes of the men whose pictures were on his investigation board. These guys didn't play around.

She frowned, confused. 'Why wouldn't I do that? Someone was on our land, Mac. Something is going on here, and I need to find out what it is.'

'Then you call *me*,' he exclaimed. 'You don't go playing amateur sleuth and start hunting down these people on your own.'

Her lips firmed. 'Would you say that to Jamie? That he should call you in? Step back and let you do your "thing"?' she said, making quote marks in the air with her fingers.

'Jamie is a commando, Jac. I would step back and let *him* do *his* thing. He'd be way more dangerous out there than anyone he'd encounter.'

'And he's my brother. He's taught me a thing or two about self-defence. So did you, remember? Stomp, jab and twist...?'

Instantly, he got a headache behind his eye. 'The best self-defence is to avoid the situation where you'd need it,' he muttered.

Her nostrils flared, and she actually looked like she was mentally counting to ten. 'Mac, what do you expect me to do?' She gestured outside the window. 'Take a look. There is nobody out here.'

'That's my point,' he exclaimed. 'There is nobody out here. What if these guys came for another visit, and you're out here all by yourself?'

'What I mean is that you can pretty much see or hear them coming. I went out yesterday, knowing I was safe.'

He folded his arms. There might be an element of truth to what she was saying, but he didn't have to admit it. Or like it. 'And what did Miss Marple find on this little sleuthing excursion?'

She gave him an exasperated look, then sighed. 'I found tyre tracks. At the time, I saw the car—it was a white four-wheel drive, with dark tinted windows. Imported,' she sneered. 'I reckon I could pick out the make and model,' she offered.

He arched an eyebrow. 'You want to pick the car out of a line-up?'

She smacked him lightly on the arm. 'You know what I mean.'

He guessed he deserved that. 'Okay, so you think you can identify what kind of car—was there something unique or interesting about it? Or do you think it looks kind of generic, and that you might find it's a common vehicle for people to drive?'

Her shoulders sagged, and she glanced out the window. 'I think it's the kind of car lots of people would drive, but,' she held up a finger, 'it was new. No scratches, not so dirty... it was a new model.'

'O-kay...' he shrugged. Without a licence plate it would be hard to track, but he'd store the detail away for future reference. 'Anything else?'

She nodded. 'I reckon they came in through one of the gates on the high-way, further down, so I went to check it out—'

'Jac,' he whined, pinching the bridge of his nose. She was killing him.

'The gate is supposed to be locked—we generally only use it for a stock delivery, or some feed, and Dad, Scott and I all have keys. The gate is sign-posted for trespassers, but it's not used often so we lock it. There are plenty of other gates for folks to come through...'

'I take it it wasn't locked?' he surmised.

'They must have picked it open, then just left it hanging so it *looked* like it was locked. I thought it was locked until I got right up to it.'

He tilted his head back against the car seat and gazed out of the window as he pondered her words. He looked at the rusty gate in front of them.

'So why are we visiting Harry?'

'Once we cross this fence, we're on the back lot,' she told him. 'No pad-docks, just free range. No gates, no cattlegrids... Lots of tunnels. I know where these guys are coming in—and when Scott gets back from town we're going to make it a lot more difficult for them to get onto Bulls' Run—but I don't know where they were headed.'

He looked at her. 'You want to search your property?'

She nodded. 'Yep.'

'That's ... twenty-three thousand acres,' he said in surprise.

'Twenty-seven thousand, actually—we have an easement beyond that.'

'Twenty-seven thousand acres...' he said, turning his gaze to the land-scape. 'You want to drive around twenty-seven thousand acres and look for criminals.'

'Yep—unless you have a chopper at your disposal?' she suggested hopefully.

He shook his head. He wouldn't be able to commission one for that pur-pose. He frowned. 'Why?'

She looked down at the dash. 'Because Brayden Terrance is dead—a fourteen-year-old boy who was a friend of mine, and who should have been safe on my property,' she said. 'Because someone came on my property in the middle of the night and thought he could hit me. Because someone was making drugs on my property ... and because you think I had something to do with it.'

The last was said so quietly, but he heard her pain, the hurt that was laced with anger. He regretted causing that, but honestly, he still couldn't rule her out. Not factually, anyway, with a logical explanation for his commander that wasn't 'I feel it in my gut'.

'I have to do my job, Jac,' he said, just as quietly. She nodded, but her lips pressed together.

'So, let's do it,' she said, lifting her chin toward the gate. 'Hop out and open the gate.'

He sighed, then undid his seatbelt and climbed out of the cab. He fum-bled with the latch—it looked like it hadn't been touched in years. He had to press against the gate and give it a shove, using his shoulder and hip for added force. He grimaced when he heard the cotton of his shirt tear, felt the give in the fabric, as he pushed the gate open.

He glanced at the ripped shirt and dirty trousers as Jac drove through, a smirk on her face.

'City clothes, mate,' she called through the open window. 'They don't hold up on a farm.'

'You just want to tear my clothes off me,' he retorted as he closed the gate and climbed back in the truck.

'Don't flatter yourself,' she sniggered.

Four hours later they were sitting on the tailgate of her ute with Ray flopped out between them. Jacinta handed Mac a bottle of water from the esky that was tied in at the end of the tray, right next to her toolbox. She always stocked it up after breakfast. You never wanted to get stuck out somewhere without water. She poured a little into her hand and offered it to Ray, repeating the process until he had drunk what he was interested in.

'Thanks,' Mac said, lifting the bottle.

She nodded, then tilted her head back to sip from her bottle. The water wasn't cold, but was still refreshing enough after what they'd been doing.

She lowered the bottle and eyed Mac. His white shirt looked filthy. So did his pants for that matter. God, she hoped those shoes weren't expensive.

'Okay, so that's George done, Harry, and Sherry. Dick was blown to kingdom come, so that just leaves Tom, Brandy and Ginny.' She counted the tunnels off on her hands, juggling her bottle of water as she did so.

'I need to call in to the station,' Mac said, holding up his mobile and moving it around. 'But I don't have service.'

'You can use my satellite phone,' Jac offered, jumping off the tailgate and walking back to the cab. She reached into the centre console and grabbed the satellite phone from the charging port connected to the cigarette lighter, disconnected the cord, then walked back to hand him the phone.

'Ta.' He keyed in a number, and then held the phone to his ear.

Jac clicked her tongue, and Ray sat up, then jumped down as she stepped away from the vehicle to give Mac some privacy. She walked a little bit, and Ray trotted along beside her, sniffing around some of the silver cassia before heading over to flop down in the shade of a mulga tree.

She heard Mac swear lightly behind her, and turned. He grimaced. 'Dad's been trying to call me.'

Jac shrugged. 'So call him back.'

'Nah. I know what he wants to talk about. I'll leave it until I get back to town.'

'Why, Macarthur Phillip Hudson, are you avoiding your old man?'

He grimaced. 'One of his mates was brought in the other night, and I may have had something to do with charges being laid against him.'

'Um-mah. Bet Uncle Pip isn't happy about that,' she said. Mac's parents ran the Echo Springs Hotel, and she knew Pip Hudson well enough to know he was staunchly loyal to his friends—her father included—and woe betide anyone who messed with them. Including his police detective son, apparently.

'I don't have the luxury of applying the law when and where I feel like it,' he said. 'If you break the law, I have to uphold it. Dad's mate broke the law.' Mac shrugged, as though the logic was simple and obvious, and it was—for someone who was as black and white as Mac.

'But you can use some discretion, right? Like letting someone off with a warning as opposed to a ticket...?'

He arched an eyebrow. 'Are you planning on speeding into town?' He held out the sat phone to her.

She smiled, shaking her head as she took it off him. 'You know what I mean.'

He leaned back against the tailgate and braced his arms either side of his lean hips, his broad shoulders rolling slightly forward with the movement. 'Sure, but if we're talking drunk driving, or even drug manufacturing,' he said, gesturing to the landscape, 'I have to investigate. I can't turn a blind eye, no matter how much folks might want me to. I live in this community, and I want to make it safe for those I care about.'

There was something in his voice, a resignation that gave her pause.

'It must be hard when you have to police your friends and family,' she said slowly. For the first time she tried to put herself in his shoes.

'Part and parcel of being a country cop in your own community,' he said, dipping his head.

'I never really considered what your job must be like, sometimes...,' she admitted. She couldn't imagine what it might be like, the things he'd see. She occasionally got the local paper when she was in town, and would read various stories about so-and-so being arrested, or such-and-such a crime being committed, but had never once really thought that it would be Mac having to do that unpleasant job of arresting people he knew, maybe even liked.

He winced. 'The worst was when I had to give my mum a ticket.'

Her eyes rounded. 'You didn't. Aunty Daph?' she gasped.

'Yep. Speeding. When I was a constable.'

'You gave your own mother a ticket,' Jacinta repeated, shaking her head, shock and amusement warring with each other until amusement one. She tried to bite back a smile.

'What was I supposed to do? I had Sarge in the squad car with me,' he said, raising his hands, palms up.

'Man, I bet it sucked to be you that night at the dinner table.'

'Tell me about it. I ended up having to go to the Cooee for a meat pie,' he said, referring to the Echo Springs pub.

She chuckled, and Mac smiled reluctantly. He looked more relaxed when he smiled. Younger. As though for a moment he could discard the weight of his job.

She sobered. 'I guess—I guess I can understand why you would think ... what you did,' she said quietly. She didn't want to put his suspicions into words again, it still made her angry, but ... 'I suppose if I found out there was a drug lab on my friend's property, I'd be a little suss about it too.' She shifted to stand in front of him. 'For the record, you're wrong, by the way. And I'm. Going. To. Prove. It.' She prodded him gently in the chest to emphasise each word. She noticed there was very little give beneath her touch, his skin firmly muscled beneath the fabric of his shirt.

He shifted, relaxing his thighs slightly so that she now stood in between them.

'And just how do you expect to do that?' he asked silkily.

She realised they were standing close to each other. *Really* close. Despite the day's heat, the tramping over hills and down through gullies, she could still smell traces of his aftershave, all mixed with a musky scent that was pleasant and ... sexy? Gawd, she must have it bad. Any other guy, and sweat smelled like, well, sweat. Mac, on the other hand, smelled wickedly delicious. And the heat coming off him...

'I'm going to find out who *is* behind it,' she told him airily, hands on her waist.

His gaze went from challenging to serious, and he grasped her hips gently, pulling her forward until his gaze was on level with hers. She was tall, and she knew he was tall, but this close, this quiet and still, she was beginning to get a sense of how powerful and all-encompassing his presence was. Her heart started to pound a little faster in her chest.

'Be careful, Jac. These guys are dangerous. If you see *anything*, you call me. Don't approach them.'

His green eyes were steady, resolute. He was so damned concerned, and if she'd only admit it to herself, his worry made her worry.

'What do you know that I don't?' she asked in a low voice, focusing on his gaze. He blinked, and his expression became shuttered.

'You know I can't discuss that with you,' he said, his voice low.

She frowned. 'Why?'

'Because you're still—'. He bit the words off. 'Because I'm a cop investigating illegal activity on your property,' he told her.

'You *still* think I'm involved?' she said, a little louder than she meant to. She'd been half-joking before. 'Damn it, what do you think I'm doing out here?' After all the time they'd spent together that day, inspecting as many mines as they had, he still thought she could be party to this drug operation. 'Why would I invite you to search my property with me if I was guilty?' She tried to step back from him, but his grip tightened on the belt loops of her jeans, preventing her from retreating.

'Hey, I have to do my job. You could be leading me on a wild goose chase, dragging me *away* from where the action is, for all I know. I have to be objective.'

Oh. Wow. 'Screw you,' she said, shoving against his chest, breaking his hold. 'You know me better than that,' she said, holding up a finger at him. 'I have *never* had *anything* to do with that rot, and never given you reason to think I have.' She pivoted on her foot toward the front of the vehicle. She was tempted to let him bloody well walk—

His hand grabbed her arm, pulling her back as he rose from the tray. His face was tight with fury. 'Do you think I like this? Do you think this is easy for me? I *wish* this hadn't happened, or if it had to, that it happened anywhere but here. I don't have the luxury of telling my sergeant or the public prosecutor that she's okay, I know her, she wouldn't do this. I'd be replaced in less than a heartbeat.'

Damn it. Every single time he voiced his suspicions, it hit her like a barb.

She stepped closer, her chin jutting forward. 'You said it the other day— you're like a stand-in big brother. You know me *that* well. Do you honestly think I would let drugs onto my property?'

'I'm not here as a big brother, Jac—'

'No, I get it. You're here as a cop—'

'I'm here...' he said, his voice hard with frustration. He gazed down at her face, his green eyes dark and stormy with anger, but something in her eyes arrested him, and he stared at her intently. 'I'm here,' he murmured huskily, and dipped his head.

Chapter Eight

Mac pressed his lips against hers, felt her swift intake of breath, and then her lips relaxed against his. He opened his mouth wider, deepening the kiss. Her hands came to rest on his chest, and he slid his arms around her slender waist, pulling her gently to him.

She moaned softly against him, and his heart thudded at the sound. Her hands started to slide up toward his neck. She tasted delicious, all honeyed warmth and fiery spice. Something thudded into his hip, and Ray started barking excitedly as he jumped around them.

He lifted his head, surprised at what he'd done. That so wasn't planned. Judging by Jacinta's stunned expression, she hadn't expected it, either. Ray jumped up again, as though wanting to join in the play.

Play. Yeah, he'd like to play with Jac, but not in a way that was at all childish or innocent.

He swallowed as he stepped back. 'I'm—'

Sorry. The word tripped on his tongue. It was the polite thing to say, after kissing a woman when she had no idea it was coming, but for the life of him, he couldn't quite get the word out. He wasn't sorry. Hell, he wanted to go back for more.

With Jamie's kid sister.

Bloody hell.

'Uh, no, it's ... fine,' Jacinta said, although her expression looked confused. Well, he could relate. It's just that she'd had this look in her eyes, this hurt, this vulnerability that he knew he'd put there...

And yeah. That kiss was all about offering moral support. Completely platonic.

Not.

She jerked her thumb toward the car. 'We should, uh, get going.'

'Yeah.' Before he did something stupid, like kiss her again.

And again.

They had to pass each other to walk around to their doors, and did an awkward little two-step. He halted, and gestured with his arm. 'After you.'

She pasted a smile on her face and skirted around him, then strode along to the driver's door.

He closed his eyes and shook his head. Gone was the easy conversation, the occasional teasing from before. Had he made it awkward?

The car started up, and he heard the grate of an awkward gear change. Of course it was bloody awkward.

He sighed, opened his eyes, and walked around to the passenger side.

The entire trip back to the house was ... torture. Mac mentally berated himself. He was a cop. He had a job to do, and at the moment Jac was part of that job. He had no business kissing her.

Getting involved with a suspect was ... bloody stupid. He had to figure out what was going on, and Jacinta would be exonerated—or incriminated.

She was younger than him. Oh, not that much younger, but sometimes he felt so old, so cynical, and she... well, she still seemed so... *young*, so trusting.

And she was Jamie's sister. His mate wouldn't be happy to know Mac had hit on his kid sister.

He straightened. Ah, crap. She was seeing Nielsen. Okay, so they seemed to have a special relationship if Nielsen knew her nocturnal habits but she didn't consider herself his girlfriend. He slid his gaze toward her. He hadn't realised she was so open and free with her intimate relationships.

Not that he was being critical—that would make him the ultimate hypocrite, what with his own track record.

But he realised he didn't know very much about Jac and her relationships. She'd gone off to boarding school in North Sydney, and he and Jamie had been sent off to a boarding school in Campbelltown, just outside of Sydney. Neither of them had attended the local school, like Leila Mayne and the Terrances.

Jac pulled into the yard and stopped the car.

'Uh, look, Jac—'

'Hey, Jac!'

Mac frowned as Scott Nielsen strode out of the larger maintenance shed.

'Scott. Did you get the goods?'

Jac had climbed out of the car before Mac could say anything else. Mac followed, but at a slower pace.

'Yeah. I'll do the job tomorrow,' Scott answered.

She lifted her hand. 'No, I'll head out now and do it.'

Scott frowned. 'What's the rush?'

The screen door slammed, and Mac turned to see Tom walk out onto the veranda.

'I'd like to do it ASAP,' Jac said. 'I'm going out to check some of the fences tomorrow, so I'd prefer to do it now.' She put her hands on her hips, and Mac noticed she'd crossed her fingers. He realised his body shielded her from her father's eyes, and that Scott couldn't see her hands.

Almost despite himself, his lips quirked. She still crossed her fingers when she was telling fibs. It was adorable.

And not something a detective should find at all cute in a suspect when she was being deceitful. He cleared his throat, and Jac glanced over her shoulder, and immediately folded her arms at his meaningful glance.

'We'll take your truck,' she called out to Scott, then started to walk off.

'I'll be back tomorrow morning,' he told her, and she halted, her expression surprised.

'Oh? I thought—' She broke off, but her cheeks grew heated, and he would have loved to know what thoughts were running through her head to give her such a warm, rosy hue.

He grinned. 'I need to just clarify a few details.'

'Oh. Well, I'll be heading out early,' she said to him, as though to discourage him.

'How early?'

'Seven,' she said straight away.

He managed to keep the smile on his face. 'I'll see you at six forty-five, then.'

He'd have to get up at sparrow's fart to do it, but he'd be there.

Jac's jaw worked, as though she was talking and didn't realise her voice wasn't working. She eventually closed her mouth and nodded.

Mac watched as she strode off with the station manager toward another vehicle in the yard, his eyes narrowed. Then he turned and found Tom giving him a similar look.

'Need to clarify things, huh?'

Mac nodded. 'Yes, sir.' If she'd talk with him. At this rate, it might be a very quiet excursion.

'You just spent half the day with my daughter, and didn't get things clarified enough?'

He glanced over his shoulder as the other ute pulled out of the yard. 'Not nearly enough.'

Tom glanced between him and the car, then nodded. 'See you tomorrow, then. I'll let Marion know you'll be here for breakfast.'

'I heard,' Marion sang out from inside the house.

'Of course she heard,' Tom muttered. 'She's got ears like a bat.'

'I heard that, too.'

Mac's lips twitched as he started to walk back toward his car, but halted when he heard Tom call his name. He turned.

'I'd suggest you dress down for the occasion,' Tom said, pointing to Mac's ripped shirt, and then sauntered back into the house.

Mac grimaced as he fingered the ripped fabric. He liked this shirt.

He'd kissed her. Jac drove the spike into the ground and twisted it deeper.

'Are you all right, Jac?' Scott asked, curious as he watched her attack the sensor she was spearing into the ground.

'Fine,' she muttered. She stood back to check her handiwork. A little to the left. She jerked her chin to the one she'd already placed on the opposite side of the track. 'Can you get behind that one so we can make sure they're lining up?'

Scott strode over and hunkered down, guiding the sensor until it faced hers. She nodded, then walked back a little ways to lay out the cable. The sensor would be hooked up to a solar panel. If anything interrupted the signal, her laptop would ping back at the house. If their internet connectivity was working. It could be a bit patchy, sometimes, but she hoped it would be sufficient to catch the alert of any intruders.

'Do you think this is necessary?' Scott enquired gently.

'The new padlock is a start,' she said, gesturing to the big, shiny lock and thick chain that now adorned the gate, 'but only if nobody uses bolt cutters. If they drive through, though, we'll know.'

'Yeah, but...isn't this overkill?'

She stood, panting, her hands on her hips. 'I got knocked out in the middle of the night, Scott. On our property. Three people were killed in an illegal meth-lab explosion. You tell me. Do you think it's overkill?'

Scott's features stilled. 'Meth lab?'

She nodded. 'Yep. That's what made Dick blow, apparently.' She closed her eyes. 'God, that sounded normal inside my head. That's what made Dick explo—forget it. That's why Brayden died.'

She opened her eyes in time to see Scott glance up and down the road. They'd had one car pass since they'd started working on the gate. Damn it, now she'd made him anxious.

'Look, I know it's a bit to process, but I'm working on sorting it out. Don't worry, we'll be fine.'

She started gathering the tools, and Scott bent down to pick up the hammer. She'd placed a number of sensors along the track. A roo or a rabbit, maybe even a possum, could set off one of the sensors, but she figured if all of them went off, she could be sure it was more likely to be an intruder and not a kangaroo deciding to follow a track instead of jumping across it. She was thinking of getting some cameras set up, but she still had to figure out how to find the money for them, and how to get them to run. That was going to take a little more research, which all needed to be done on their slow and patchy internet connection.

'What does Tom think?' Scott asked quietly.

'He doesn't know,' she said, then turned to look at him. 'And I don't want him to know. Not yet. I don't want to get him worried. Okay?'

Scott stepped toward her. 'Don't worry, Jac. You can trust me.' He stood directly in front of her, eyeing her closely. 'Is that why Hudson keeps coming out?'

She nodded. 'Yeah, he's investigating Brayden's death, and the meth lab.'

Scott dipped his head. 'I see.' He rubbed his lip, then lifted his head to meet her gaze. 'You know you can talk to me, about anything, right?'

Jac's eyebrow rose. This seemed like another version of a previous conversation with Mac. 'Uh, yeah, I know.'

'I want to help, Jac.'

She smiled. 'Thanks, Scott.'

He tucked a hair behind her ear, and she tried to stand still for it. 'I want to help, because I like you, Jac.'

Jac blinked. O-kay. 'Uh, I like you, too, Scott. I think we work well together.'

'I think we could do lots of things well, together,' he murmured, and leaned forward to kiss her.

Jac's eyes rounded as his lips pressed against hers, and for a moment she hesitated, waiting for that same heat, that same zing of attraction she'd felt with Mac. But all she felt was a guy's lips on hers. She raised her hands to press against his chest as she leaned back. 'Whoa, there, cowboy.'

He lifted his head, and his expression smoothed so quickly she almost missed his frustration. 'I'm sorry, I just—I like you, Jac.'

She swallowed. 'Uh, I ... like you, too.' She frowned. 'I'm just not sure how much.'

Scott's smiled. 'I surprised you.'

She nodded. 'Uh, yeah, you did. I really wasn't expecting that.'

Again. Two guys kissing her out of the blue on the one day. Had she stepped into some alternate universe?

He fingered the collar of her shirt. 'Was it a good surprise?' He grinned hopefully.

Uh... 'I'm still trying to figure that out,' she said truthfully, then bit her lip when she realised that probably wasn't what he was hoping to hear.

His lips twisted, before he forced a chuckle. 'Well, I guess I'll have to work on it, then.'

'Uh...' She wasn't sure how to react to that.

He lifted the hammer. 'Come on, let's head back. I think we've finished for the day.'

She nodded. 'Yeah,' she said slowly.

She sat in the cab quietly for the ride back to the house, stunned. What the hell was going on? First Mac, with his infuriating comments and his— oh, my god, so hot kiss—and now Scott, a man she respected and considered a close friend, and his not-as-hot kiss. She felt like she'd stepped down into a rabbit hole and everything was being turned about on its head.

She slid a glance in Scott's direction as he turned into the yard, and he caught her gaze. Winked. She smiled tentatively, then jumped out as he slid the gears into park.

She thought she'd been confused earlier, after Mac's kiss. She chewed her lip as she strode across to the veranda and toed off her boots before stepping over the third plank and entering through the back door. That kiss had been ... a surprise. It had shaken her to her core. Mac was like ... what? Another big brother? She snorted as she entered her bedroom. No. Not after that kiss. There was no way she could look at him in that light again. He'd been all heat and muscle and sexy lips. God, no wonder he was so popular with the ladies. She stopped in front of her dresser and eyed her reflection in the rectangular mirror that hung on the wall behind it. Her face was red. She fanned herself. Damn, even thinking about it was getting her hot and bothered.

And he still thought she was guilty of running drugs, of setting up a lab that had killed people. She eyed the photos on her mirror, and Kelsey's image caught and held her attention. Kelsey was sixteen when she died. Memories of that day still haunted her, and she'd sworn—after seeing what they'd done to her friend—that she would never, *ever* do drugs.

And Mac thought she was involved with this drug thing. The photo of her friend blurred, and Jac brushed away the tears falling down her face. Her gaze fell on a photo of Brayden, and the tears started falling faster.

'Never again,' she murmured.

'Jacinta, dinner will be on the table in ten,' Marion called down the hallway.

She blinked, and wiped at the tears. 'Okay. I just need to clean up,' she called back. She eyed the photos on the mirror. She hated drugs, she hated what they'd done to her friends. She'd lost too much to the toxic crap. Well, she was going to put a stop to whatever the hell was going on at Bulls' Run. These guys had no idea the trouble coming their way.

She took a deep breath, held it, then let it out. She turned back for her door, scooping up her robe as she made her way to the bathroom, her socked feet stomping resolutely across the timber floorboards. She was going to prove to Mac once and for all that she was innocent, damn it.

Mac sat down at the formal dining table, and met his father's gaze.

'Peas?' Daphne Hudson offered the bowl of green peas to her son.

Mac nodded and smiled. 'Thanks, Mum.'

'I'm surprised to see you here,' Pip Hudson remarked as he speared slices of roast lamb with a fork and served them to his plate.

'It's Thursday night, Dad,' Mac said calmly. 'Family night. Why wouldn't I be here?'

There were no guests staying at his parents' hotel just then, but the street bar was still open for business, and the dull noise of chatter still carried through the walls. His mother took the plate of meat and offered it to Mac, who accepted it while he could. If the conversation was going to go the way he thought it would, he wanted to eat before he ... couldn't.

'So, darling... how's work?' his mother asked conversationally.

'Busy,' he replied. 'Long hours.' He never really talked too much about his work—with anyone. He sure as hell wasn't going to tell his mother about meth labs and drug dealers. The dark side of the town had already touched her life recently. Jac and her brother weren't the only kids his parents had pseudo-adopted into the family. His friend Peter Hanson, and Peter's sister, Erika, were also much loved, and Peter's recent death had devastated his parents. Erika was currently overseas with Mac's colleague, Hartley—a connection Mac hadn't seen coming—and his mother missed Erika a lot. She didn't need to know about the trouble going on with Jac, too.

'Oh? I hope you're getting some down time,' she said, passing him a plate of honeyed carrots. 'Are you seeing anyone?'

The ladle for the carrots slipped out of his hand, and clinked against his plate. He retrieved it gently. 'Ah, no. No time, really.'

Maybe that was why he was carrying on like an unprofessional idiot by kissing Jac. He hadn't dated a woman in months. Echo Springs wasn't really a hub for the single ladies, but he wasn't lying when he'd told his mother he was busy. He was so involved in this investigation, and getting acquainted with this new role of detective while Hartley was away, he hadn't really missed going out with some feminine company.

'I spoke with Jim Howard. He's looking at a suspended licence.' His father poured gravy over the food on his plate.

Here we go. Mac nodded. 'He's bloody lucky.'

'Swear jar,' Daphne Hudson said, pointing to the big jar on the mantelpiece.

Mac nodded. 'Sorry, mum.' He pulled a note from his wallet. He figured he'd set up a tab for the night.

'He needs his licence, Mac. How is he supposed to drive those cars to find out what's wrong with them? How is he supposed to drive them to test the repairs?'

Mac shrugged. 'He'll have to figure something out. Legally, of course,' he said, cutting into his meat and popping it into his mouth. He loved his mother's cooking. 'Delicious,' he said, and winked at her. She smiled as she began to eat her own meal.

Pip frowned. 'He could lose his business, son.'

Mac didn't reply immediately, but chewed as fast as polite table manners would allow before eating some more. Tramping around Bulls' Run had made him hungry.

Maybe kissing Jac, too. But no amount of his mother's roast lamb would satisfy his desire for a woman he couldn't, shouldn't have.

'Did you hear me, Macarthur?'

Mac nodded as he took a swig from the glass of beer at the side of his plate to wash his food down. His father was using his full name. He must be pissed off.

'I heard. Did Jim mention *why* his licence was suspended?' He scooped up a forkful of peas and met his mother's eyes as put them in his mouth. She was watching him with a perplexed frown on her face. Probably wondering when eating went out the window and inhaling food became a trend.

'He was a little over the limit,' Pip said, shrugging. 'He made a mistake, didn't realise that last beer would put him over.'

Mac coughed and had to hit his chest to get the food past his disbelief. He winced. 'Uh, Dad, he drove, and he was over the limit. He nearly hit Gwen Sinclair.'

'That woman would have done more damage to the car than he could do to her,' Pip said, pointing at Mac with his fork.

'Pip,' his mum chided.

'That woman is the size of a—'

'Pip,' Daphne admonished, her tone severe. His dad dipped his gaze to his plate.

'Well, she is,' he muttered.

'And she's got just as much right to walk along a street without being hit by a drunk driver as anyone else,' Mac said, before scoffing some roast potato. Oh, man. His mum made the best roast potatoes.

'Drunk,' Pip muttered. 'Jim can hold his bloody liquor. It was just that last beer...'

'Pip,' his mother chided.

His father sighed. 'I know, swear jar. I'll pay it later.'

Mac sighed. 'Jim blew 0.32. That's way more than a last beer. That's like the last seven beers. And he *drove*. He was nearly involved in hitting a pedestrian. So his licence is suspended—that's actually pretty light, all things considered.'

Daphne held up a finger in a silent request to be excused, and rose from the table to walk back into the kitchen.

'My own son,' Pip said, shaking his head.

'I was doing my job,' Mac muttered.

'Well, maybe you should go do your job now,' his father exclaimed. 'Keep our streets safe, son. I can hear someone jaywalking on Main as we speak.'

'Why does everyone expect me to just turn a blind eye when their friends break the law?' Mac exclaimed right back.

'Some people might like to know you have their backs,' his father retorted.

'Did you ever consider that my upholding the law *is* me having your backs?' Mac glared at his dad.

'I think we need some space,' Pip said, his chin jutting forward.

'So do I,' Mac said, jabbing some more meat with his fork, and then popping it into his mouth as he rose from the table. He looked at his plate. Three-quarters eaten. Well, at least he ate.

He walked into the kitchen and his mum bustled over to him with a Tupperware container.

'Dessert. Apple and rhubarb crumble with custard.' She handed it to him.

He smiled. 'Thanks, Mum. Dinner was great.'

'Don't worry about your father. He needs to get things off his chest, but he'll calm down.'

'Yeah, I know,' Mac said ruefully. His mother hesitated.

'What?' he asked.

'I bumped into Sue Terrance at the supermarket,' she said quietly. 'That poor woman. She doesn't deserve any of the grief the men in her family have dished out to her. Hayden sounds like he's trying to make a good go of it, though.'

He nodded, but remained noncommittal. He'd heard Terrance was trying to start up a youth program, and Leila was helping him. It was too early to call the man an angel, though, as far as he was concerned.

His mother looked beyond him to the dining room, then met his gaze again. 'She mentioned that Brayden might have been involved with drugs— is that right?'

He sighed. 'Mum, I can't talk about an ongoing investigation...'

She lifted her chin. 'Well, I want you to check on Jacinta. I worry about her out there, so far out of town, especially with what's been going on. I promised her mother we'd look out for her.'

Mac nodded. He remembered June Buchanan, and the close friendship the two women shared. After June's death, Daphne Hudson had shopped with Jac for her graduation outfit, had attended mother-daughter events on June's behalf, and had visited her regularly on the farm until Jac was old enough to drive into town on her own.

'You may need to prepare yourself, though, Mum. I can't say much, but it's not looking good for Jacinta with all this business going on at Bulls' Run.'

Daphne's eyebrows rose. 'Jac? And drugs? Our Jac?' She snorted, then shook her head. 'No, not our Jac.'

'Mum, we don't know anything for sure—'

'Well, I know this for sure. That girl would rather burn that property to ash than get involved with drugs.'

'What makes you say that?' he asked brusquely. Of course his mother would defend Jac. In her eyes, Jacinta Buchanan could do no wrong.

'One of her school friends died from drugs,' Daphne said soberly.

Mac frowned. 'I don't remember hearing anything about this. When did it happen?'

Daphne waved a hand. 'Oh, you and Jamie were at school. Jacinta found her after she'd passed. It shook her up pretty bad, though, poor thing.'

'I didn't know,' Mac said thoughtfully.

'Well, I don't suppose it's the normal topic of conversation,' his mother pointed out primly.

Mac smiled. 'Yeah, I guess not.' He leaned down and kissed her again on the cheek. 'Thanks again, Mum.'

'See you next week,' she said, patting him on the cheek. He glanced over his shoulder toward the dining room, and his mother waved her hand again. 'Don't worry about him. He'll be fine.'

'I'll believe it when I see it,' Mac murmured, then strode through the kitchen to the back door.

It wasn't until he was at home, spoon in his mother's apple and rhubarb crumble, that he thought about her words.

That girl would rather burn that property to ash than get involved with drugs.

Well, he guessed they'd have something to talk about on their drive, after all.

Chapter Nine

Jacinta looked up from the boiled egg she was about to lop the top off when she heard the knock at the back door.

'Come in,' her father called without looking up from his bacon and eggs.

Footsteps clomped through the back hall and Mac entered the kitchen. Jacinta's knife went straight through the cone end of the egg, and her father frowned when the top of the egg landed on his plate. She mouthed an apology and quickly used her fork to steal it back.

'You don't need to knock, Mac.' Her father indicated the other setting at the table. 'You're as good as family.'

Jac focused on sprinkling a little salt on her egg. Mac didn't kiss her like family. Heat rose in her cheeks, and she tried to hide her face by sipping from her coffee mug. You weren't supposed to have hot and sexy dreams about family.

'Thanks, Tom. Appreciate that.'

She noticed he wore jeans today, along with a grey t-shirt that looked soft from repeated washing. How could the man look even better in jeans than he did in his work clothes? She glanced down at her own stained jeans and the well-worn denim shirt she'd appropriated from Jamie's wardrobe before he left. Ugh.

Marion lifted the frypan off the stove and brought it over to serve Mac some bacon. 'Do you like your eggs boiled, fried or scrambled?'

His eyebrows rose. 'What a choice. I'll go with fried, if that's easy enough.'

She winked as she smiled. 'Coming right up.' She cracked two eggs into the pan, then lifted the coffee pot from the bench. 'Want some coffee?'

He nodded. 'Please.'

Her father held up his own mug as Marion poured the dark liquid into the mug in front of Mac. 'I'll have a top-up, too, while you're at it.'

Marion tilted her head.

'Please,' her father said hurriedly. She arched an eyebrow. 'Marion,' he added.

'Of course,' she said demurely.

Jac watched as Marion placed her hand on his shoulder and leaned over to pour him coffee. Was her father ... *blushing?*

'So, all went well last night?' Mac enquired as he started to eat his breakfast.

Now *she* was blushing. Those dreams... She nodded as she dropped her gaze to her plate. 'Fine.'

'Nothing ... untoward?'

'Nope.'

'Good.'

'Yep.'

Her father glanced between them. 'So. Fences, huh?'

'Yep,' she said, as Marion served Mac his eggs.

'I've made you a packed lunch,' Marion said, pointing to a container on the kitchen bench.

'Thanks, Marion,' Jac said, surprised. She hadn't expected the older woman to do that.

Marion waved a hand as she bustled over to the sink. 'Oh, it's no trouble.'

'What is Scott doing while you're off galliva—checking fences?' her father asked.

'He's checking all the gates along the highway,' Jac informed him, then sipped more coffee. 'Then he's got to round up the sheep in the south paddock, because the dipping contractor will be here in a week.'

'Oh. I might go with him, then,' Tom suggested.

Jac coughed into her mug, then set it down on the table. 'That sounds great,' she said, sincerely. 'I'm sure Scott would appreciate your help.' Her father was going to ride along. She tried not to dance in her seat. Marion winked at her over her father's shoulder, and Jac hid a smile as she stood to clear her place at the table. Mac scooped up the last of his eggs, then did the same. Jac leaned over and kissed her father on his cheek. 'See you later.'

'So, which fence are we checking first?' Mac asked as he followed her out the back door. She stepped over the third plank, and then pointed at it in

silent reminder to Mac, who also avoided stepping on the weakened timber.
She really needed to fix that. Soon.

She leaned down to pick up her boots and tipped them over to shake. 'I'll
figure we'll head out—holy mother of god,' she shrieked, jumping back as a
small brown snake fell out of her boot and onto the veranda.

Mac yanked her back behind him as the snake's body uncoiled. In what
seemed like a blur of movement, Mac grasped the cricket bat that leaned
against the wall, leaned down and slid the spine of the bat under the snake.
Lightning fast, he scooped up the snake and flung it off the veranda. It
made a thud when it landed on the ground three metres away, and then it
slithered into the bush, away from the house.

Jacinta sagged against the wall of the house as her father opened the
screen door. 'Did you just scream?'

'Snake,' she rasped.

'Where?'

'Gone.' She waved in the general direction of Mac, who was returning the
cricket bat to its spot, and then beyond to where the snake had disappeared.

'It's not gone under the house, has it? I don't want the bugger to pop up
somewhere else inside—like the dunny.'

Mac shook his head. 'No, it's gone in that direction.'

'Well, I guess those solar snake repellers don't work, after all,' her dad
said. Jacinta shot him an exasperated look, and he nodded. 'Fine, we'll get
that vermin mesh you were talking about the other day. You can have your
snake soother after dinner.' He winked before heading back inside.

'Snake soother?' Mac queried.

'A whiskey after dinner,' Jacinta told him. 'My grandfather started the
tradition, because Grandma almost fainted one year. Gave her a whiskey to
calm her down. She actively went looking for one the next year.'

She gently kicked over both boots, then picked them up by the sole and
shook them over the railing. She was relieved to find there were no more
unwelcome visitors in her shoes.

Scott trudged around the side of the house, and looked surprised when he
saw them all standing on the veranda. 'Morning folks. What's up?'

'I just found a snake in my boot,' Jac told him. She felt a little awkward
seeing both Mac and Scott in front of her, after the events of the day before.
Scott glanced about, then up at her.

'Are you okay?'

She nodded. 'Fine.' She pointed in the general direction of where she'd last seen the snake. 'He was only a little one. He's gone off that way, so I'd keep all the dogs in, just for a little bit, and give him time to escape.' She looked over at Mac, who wore a faintly amused look on his face. 'Let's get going,' she told him. She slipped her shoes on, then trotted down the steps to her car.

She had to lock her knees a little. While snakes were not uncommon, it was still a little nerve-wracking to find one in your boot. She shuddered. Thank god she always shook them out. She'd hate to think what would have happened if she'd slipped her foot in without checking first. She eyed the tall man striding along next to her. He'd used his body to shield her. She swallowed. That had been … brave. She blushed, remembering her shriek. Hell, she'd have climbed up over him, if he hadn't moved so fast. He probably thought she was such a wuss. Her legs were still trembling, just a little. She clenched her hand into a fist. Enough of that. Snakes, schmakes. Wasn't the first one of the season, and it wouldn't be the last. She was just caught by surprise by that one. She lifted her chin. Besides, she already knew he thought the worst of her. Adding fraidy-cat to the list wasn't going to make a difference. Her lips tightened as she remembered his words from the day before. She reached for the ute's door handle, and realised her hand was trembling.

'Why don't you drive?' she suggested suddenly across the tray of the ute.

Mac's lips lifted a little. 'Shaky, huh?'

'No,' she lied. 'I just thought if you drive, then you can go wherever you like. That way I'm not taking you on a wild goose chase *away* from the action.' She injected her words with frost. Damn, that had stung.

He arched an eyebrow as she threw his words back at him. Then he shrugged. 'Fine.'

They walked around to the opposite sides of the vehicle, and she climbed in. The sooner they got going, the sooner she could get rid of him.

Mac shook his head, slightly incredulous, as they bounced along the track. He'd tussled with a brown snake. Sure, snakes were part of the territory out this way. They even got a few in town. He and his dad had had to remove the occasional reptilian intruder that had slid into the hotel over the years, and he'd encountered a few out this way with Jamie… A smile lifted his lips as he remembered the cute little Irish dance skips Jac had done when she'd seen the snake. His smile fell. Thank god she shook out her boots. He shuddered at the thought of what could have happened.

'Do you normally find snakes in your boots?' he enquired.

She shook her head. 'No. I found a redback spider once. That's why I always check.' She patted her chest. 'But that definitely gave me a shock.'

His gaze dropped to her chest. Oh, god, he had to stop doing that. He turned his attention back to the track—although calling it a track was being generous—as she continued.

'We don't normally see them anywhere near the house—we clear out the garden, don't leave anything around they can hide under, and this year Dad wanted to try these new solar snake repellers—they don't seem to work, though.'

He frowned. 'Really?'

She nodded. 'It's been so dry this winter... I mean, if we'd had lots of rain, and saw the brush come back a little, with birds and mice and spiders, I could understand, but we haven't, so...' She shrugged.

'Does everyone put their shoes out on the veranda?' He had seen a number of shoes, but wasn't sure who owned them.

'Yep.'

'And the snake picked your boot,' he murmured.

Jacinta nodded. 'Yep. I'm surprised it didn't die of asphyxiation—I've nearly worn these boots to death.' She frowned. 'Do snakes smell?'

'With their tongues,' he said absently.

Jacinta made a gagging noise. 'Ugh, that's worse. It had to taste my foot odour.'

Mac chuckled as he gazed out at the landscape. 'So, tell me, how do we get to Brandy from here?' They were coming up to a fork in the track.

'You don't remember?'

He shrugged. 'It's been years, Jac.' That's why he'd thought she was involved—she knew where all the skeletons were buried, figuratively speaking. She indicated the right fork, and he drove on.

They were silent for a while, and he looked at her a few times. She'd fixed her gaze out of the passenger window, and looked quite prepared to spend the trip in utter silence.

The shock of the snake had worn off, and now she was freezing him out.

He turned back to the track. Classic Jac. Every time she got pissed with him or her brother, she'd give them the silent treatment.

Back then, he'd enjoyed the peace that came with it. Now, though, not so much. Especially after the kiss. He wanted to talk with her. He wanted to listen to her. He wanted to find out more about her... He'd enjoyed the day before. Mostly. He'd learned she was easy to talk to, and had a great sense of humour. He racked his brain, trying to think of a way to break the ice—because apparently saving her from a brown snake wasn't enough to thaw her chill.

'I saw Mum and Dad last night,' he said conversationally.

She nodded.

O-kay. 'They said to say hi.'

'Say hi back.'

He grimaced. 'Well, Dad and I aren't really talking, but I'll pass it on to Mum.'

She folded her arms. 'I understand how your father feels.'

He pressed his lips together. He guessed he'd opened himself up to that one.

'Jac, I'm just trying to do my job,' he said, sighing.

'Stop the car.'

He shook his head. 'No, I'm not going to let you storm off on me—'

'Stop the car—we're here,' she said louder.

'Oh.' He braked, then eyed the opening of the tunnel. It was set into a low hill, and even from here he could see the tyre tracks at the front. 'Stay here.'

He shut off the ignition, then climbed out of the cab, scanning the area as he did so. They were in the middle of a range of hills, without the clear view to the horizon. Plenty of places for someone to hide a car, or a number of trucks. He started to walk slowly toward the mouth of the tunnel.

Then he heard the car door slam behind him. He halted. Turned.

Jacinta was strolling toward him. She, too, was scanning the vicinity.

'I told you to stay in the car.'

She rolled her eyes. 'Yeah, but you didn't really expect me to, did you?' She passed him. Today, her shirt was tucked in at her waist, and he could see the swing of her hips. He shook his head as he caught up with her.

'Stay behind me, then,' he muttered, then wagged a finger at her frown. 'And yes, that one I do expect you to do.'

He pulled her behind him, then sidled up to the tunnel. The opening wasn't quite big enough for a car, but he couldn't assume the tunnel was empty. He stopped at the opening, using the supports as a shield. He peered inside. There were lights strung between the supports, all the way in, although they currently weren't on. He eyed the ground. Car tracks led up to the opening, and then smaller tracks, as though they were using a gurney or trolley, led inside. He pulled out his mobile phone and snapped a couple of photos.

Jacinta pointed to the tracks. 'They're the same as the ones from the other night.'

He looked over his shoulder at her. 'How can you be sure?'

'Three small tracks in the centre, the middle one with a zigzag pattern. It's the same,' she murmured confidently.

His eyebrows rose. 'Since when did you become a tracker?'

'I read a lot of Nancy Drew books as a kid.'

'Of course you did,' he muttered. He glanced back at the car. 'I think you should go back to the car. Pretty please?'

She was about to protest, then stopped. 'You know, that's not a bad idea.' He watched, surprised, when she jogged back to the car. That had been a lot easier than he thought it would be.

He turned back to the tunnel, unclipping his holster as he stepped inside. He put his hand on the butt of his handgun, and was about to step further when he heard the familiar, quiet click of a safety release. He halted, then turned to face Jacinta, who was just entering behind him, holding a rifle.

'What are you doing?' he hissed.

She gave him a confused look, as though it was obvious. And maybe it was, but he hoped he was wrong.

'I'm your backup,' she hissed back, lifting the rifle as though he couldn't see it.

'Are you crazy?'

'Think of me as your partner,' she told him in a low voice.

'You are not my partner. You are not even a cop,' he whispered back to her, wanting to shout the words instead.

'If you think I'm just going to let you wander in there unprotected, you've got another think coming.'

His eyes rounded as he lifted his own weapon. 'I'm not unprotected.'

'And now you've got me and Jane,' she snapped back in a whisper.

'You named your rifle Jane?'

'Well, I actually named her Calamity Jane. I just call her Jane for short. What do you call your gun?'

'I don't have a name for my gun,' he growled. 'Because I'm a professional, I don't name my guns like pets or kids. I'm trained for this. You're not. Do you even know how to use that thing?'

Her eyes narrowed. 'Gee, it's been a while. Mind if I use you for some target practice?' She rolled her eyes. 'Of course I know how to use her.'

His eyes rounded. Her. She called her rifle a *her.*

'Now, are we going in or not?'

He gritted his teeth. He didn't know what was worse, having her follow him into a potentially dangerous situation, or her sitting outside in the car with a loaded gun. 'Come on,' he muttered, 'but stay behind me and do exactly as I say—and for god's sake, don't shoot me.'

He turned away, and although he heard her mutter something, he didn't quite catch the words—but 'shoot' was definitely in the mix, along with 'misery'.

He crept forward. The further they went into the tunnel, the darker it got. The tunnel seemed to pitch down at an angle. He fished his torch out of his trouser pocket and kept it low to the ground to minimise stretching the light, just in case there anyone was further inside. He noticed the pipe running along the ground, the white PVC a stark contrast against the dark red earth. He trained the light up the walls, and stopped when he saw the lights wired from one post to the next. He had no idea where the switch was, or the generator, but these lights definitely weren't from the original mine. No, they were a recent addition. They wandered a little further, and the air started to smell distinctly unpleasant. Mac about-faced, grasped Jacinta's arm, and walked them both outside toward the ute.

'What? Why aren't we going in there?' she asked.

'I've seen enough,' he said. He checked his phone, his lips tightening when he saw there were no bars. 'I need your phone.'

Jacinta reached inside the cab and removed the phone from the centre console. 'Here.' She eyed him as he punched in the numbers. 'There's something in there, isn't there?' she whispered.

He nodded. 'And it's toxic as hell.'

Her eyes glistened. She turned away from him, and she slid the rifle into the space behind the seats in the cab. Her shoulders were hunched as she stepped away. He made his call, and told his sergeant of their discovery. Several long minutes later, he hung up.

'Now what?'

He turned to face Jacinta. She looked devastated. 'Now, we wait.'

'Is it—it's more drugs, isn't it?' She wrapped her arms around her waist.

The pipe that was installed to help draw out the fumes from the lab, the harsh smell of chemicals indicating the lab was in recent use, the newly installed tunnel lighting … it all showed a significant investment in this operation. 'Yeah.'

'Those bastards,' she whispered. She straightened, her fists clenching. 'I want to burn it to the ground,' she said, and strode to the back of the ute. He jogged around as she lifted up the lid on the tool box. She withdrew a box of matches as she reached for the jerry can that was strapped in against the side of the tray, and his eyes rounded. Good grief, she actually meant it.

He placed his hands on her arms, preventing her from lifting the container of fuel. 'Uh, you can't do that, Jac. That's destroying evidence.'

'I can't let that poison get out on the streets,' she told him firmly, although she let go of the fuel.

'It won't,' he assured her quietly. She turned around to face him, and although her face was pale, her expression was grim.

'How can they do this?' she said, staring past him at the tunnel. 'Damn it. How dare they come on to *my* property and use it like their own? And *drugs*,' she cried, her hands rising to clench in her hair. 'Drugs.' Her hat fell back off her head, onto the tray of the vehicle.

'Hey, we'll stop them.' He reached out to grasp her shoulders, and found she was trembling. Whether it was from fear or rage, he couldn't tell.

'I hate them,' she whispered fiercely. 'They've made me a party to this. I want to make them pay. For Brayden, for Kelsey, I want to hurt them so damn bad.' She uttered the words through clenched teeth.

Okay, so rage it was. His brow dipped, and he stroked her arms, trying to calm her. 'Is Kelsey your friend from school?'

Her gaze snapped back to meet his, then flickered back to the tunnel, before finally coming to rest back on him. She nodded, and this time the tears fell. 'She was my best friend.'

'Tell me,' he said, his tone gentle.

She wiped her nose with her sleeve, but she couldn't seem to stop the tears. She brushed at her cheeks a few times. 'She liked to party. A lot. And there's not a lot of opportunity for that at a Catholic boarding school in North Sydney, so she used to … use.'

He brushed at a tear on her cheek, patiently waiting for her to continue. She sucked in a shuddering breath. 'God, I haven't talked about it since it happened.' He nodded, then waited.

'I found her in the shower block,' Jacinta whispered. Her breath caught in her chest, and Mac instinctively stroked her hair back from her face, trying to soothe the torment he could see twisting her features. 'She snuck out

after I fell asleep, and when I found her, she was already gone.' Her eyes
squeezed shut. 'She'd been there for hours, by herself, so co-old.' Her breath
hitched again, and this time he pulled her to him, holding her as she sniffed
into his shirt.

He held her like that for a while, keeping her against his chest, smoothing
his hand down her back.

'You never mentioned it,' he said quietly. 'I had no idea.'

She shook her head into his chest, then drew back a little. 'I didn't want to
talk about it. Every time I do, I think of how I found her, how she looked…
I'd rather remember her alive than dead.' She sniffed, and lifted her chin, her
gaze direct as she looked up at him.

'I hate what drugs do, Mac. I hated how they changed my friend when
she was on them, I hate that drugs stole her from me, from her parents, and
robbed her of her future. I hate that it's done the same with Brayden. You
have no idea how *angry* I am that someone has done this on my property,'
she said in a low, hoarse voice that more than adequately communicated her
rage. 'I don't do drugs, and I don't want them anywhere near me, near my
home, near my family or friends.'

He met her gaze. She was practically vibrating with fury in his arms.
Despite finding a second lab on her property, of having to stop her from
destroying evidence, of the coldly logical brain that said there was an argument for her being involved, he had to listen to what his instincts were
currently screaming at him.

'I believe you,' he told her softly.

She stared at him for a moment, then nodded once. 'About bloody time.'

Chapter Ten

Jacinta watched from behind the police tape boundary as what looked like the full force of the NSW police force descended upon Brandy. Scott and her father were being interviewed separately, and she'd just completed her third interview. Her clothes had been tested for chemical residue, but she was clear, as she'd only been in the tunnel, and hadn't entered the area where the 'cooking' took place. She shook her head. She was learning way too much about meth manufacturing. Still, being given the all-clear wouldn't prevent her from burning these clothes when she got home, just to be on the safe side.

She watched as a tall, broad-shouldered figure emerged from the tunnel, clothed head-to-toe in a white hazmat suit. Even though a mask obscured his face, she instantly recognised Mac's physique, the way he walked, the way his shoulders and hips moved as he stepped into the temporary outdoor shower setup, and was momentarily obscured from view. It was several long minutes before he emerged from the blue tent, dressed in navy cargo pants and a dark blue t-shirt with the NSW Police insignia on the left breast and 'POLICE' emblazoned on the back. The clothing gave him a dark, authoritative air as he stopped to talk with several officers before making his way over to a middle-aged woman whose default expression seemed to be resting bitch face. He spoke with her, and although it didn't look exactly like an argument, it definitely looked like an intense discussion.

They both turned to look at her, and Jacinta tried to look as innocent as possible, under the circumstances. It was hard to get past the anger. She'd just been told that the area was toxic. As the cooking occurred underground, it looked like Brandy would have to be destroyed. The local council would be advised, which meant Bulls' Run would be put on a contaminated properties

list until testing showed the property was clean. They'd have to call in the
EPA to test the livestock in the nearby paddocks, but Mac had assured her
that they seemed far enough away that it would be unlikely they'd come into
contact with any fumes or chemicals. Still, it meant they'd have to spend a
bit of money on the property clean-up. Once the police had cleared out all
the chemicals, she'd have to call in a clean-up crew to decontaminate where
possible, and then a demolition crew to pretty much bury Brandy.

On top of that, she knew that while Mac might believe she had nothing
to do with this narcotic nightmare, they still had to convince the rest of the
investigation team, the superintendent, the public prosecutor and anyone
else who was considering laying charges against her and her family for having an illegal meth lab on their property.

She glanced over at her father. His face was grim as he listened to the officers, and every now and then he raised his hand to his forehead, as though
he was fighting off a headache.

She turned to where her station manager was talking with some officers.
Scott didn't look that much better. He looked like he was going to puke. She
bit her lip. The sun was setting, they'd been out here the whole day, and it
didn't look like the cops were going to leave any time soon. She folded her
arms as she leaned back against her car, her hands clenching and unclenching
around her shirt sleeves.

What was she supposed to do now? What *could* she do? She couldn't go
into the tunnel—not that she really wanted to. One part of her wanted to
see it for her own eyes. Another part of her wanted to run in the opposite
direction, and she still battled that tiny little seed that wanted to blow the
damn meth lab sky high.

She'd overheard some of the officers talking. Apparently this site made
Dick look tiny in comparison. Something about a record haul. Her hands
tightened again on her sleeves. They were going to sift through the Buchanan
financial records, and there was already a team searching the main house,
from what she'd been told. Two teams had also been dispatched to the other
tunnel entrances, but they'd received word those tunnels were clear.

Thank God for small mercies. This was it. Brandy and Dick. She shook
her head, her shoulders slumped under the disbelief. Who would do this
to them? She had to find them. No, she had to look after the farm. It was
going to cost a small fortune to decontaminate the sites, so they could stand
a chance of using the land in the future. Was now an appropriate time to
go back and feed the dogs? Drugs. Damn. Brayden had died because of this.

She raised a hand and rubbed her forehead as an ache started to build. Following a train of thought to a logical conclusion was impossible when those thoughts were bumbling around inside the tumble dryer that her mind had become.

'Come on, I'll take you home.'

She looked up, not realising Mac had approached her. 'Oh? I can go?' The t-shirt he wore complemented his tan and revealed the bulge of his biceps, the corded strength of his forearms. His dark hair still looked a little wet, and shone in the lights that were being set up and switched on around the site. His dark hair, tanned skin and dark shirt all served to make his eyes, in contrast, look bright. Arresting.

'Under escort,' he clarified. 'Your father and Scott will follow once we're done with them here.'

He seemed so … businesslike. So … detached. She started to walk around to the driver's door, but Mac stepped in front of her. 'I'll drive.' His broad shoulders blocked her view of the site, and she could almost pretend the local police units weren't out in force. That it was just them two, and he wanted to drive her home.

With pretty red and blue lights flashing like an intimate party for two.

Gawd. Maybe she'd unwittingly caught a sniff of those chemicals inside. She sighed, but didn't argue as she backed up to the passenger door and slowly climbed in.

Mac reversed out of the crime scene, and had to flick on the headlights as the gloom crept in, chasing away the pretty sunset.

'What happens now?' she asked as he drove carefully along the track. She eyed his hands on the wheel. He had big hands. His grasp on the wheel was light, though. Controlled. She blinked, forcing herself to look away from those big, strong, gentle hands.

'There will be an investigation,' he informed her.

She nodded. 'Good.'

'We'll have to investigate everyone at Bulls' Run, to discount you from the suspect pool,' he told her in a low voice.

She shrugged. 'Fine. Bring it on. We've done nothing here, and we've got nothing to hide.'

'Well, now would be a good time to let me know … anything,' he suggested.

Jac looked at him. 'There's nothing to know, Mac.' She indicated herself. 'What you see here is what you get.'

His green gazed flicked over her, pausing on her curves. She wasn't going to blush, she wasn't going to—damn it. Warmth bloomed in her cheeks, and she became supremely conscious of her body, of how she sat. She straightened a little, and his gaze fell on her breasts briefly, before he looked back out the windscreen.

'I'm just saying, if there was something—'

'I thought you said you believed me,' she said, frowning.

He nodded. 'And I do.' Then he shook his head. 'God knows how I explain that to my boss, because there's no evidence to back up that conclusion...'

She gaped at him. 'Are you kidding me? Apart from the location of this lab, there is nothing to link me to the operation, so there's no evidence to back up the other conclusion.'

'Which is why you're all going to spend tonight in your beds, and not in the lock-up.'

'How long do I have to put up with these accusations?' It was tiring. Annoying. Disheartening.

Mac sighed. 'I'm sorry, Jac. I do believe you don't have anything to do with the operation, but somebody does, and we have to find that somebody.'

She leaned her head against the window, and a sneaky exhaustion stole over her. She just wanted this all to be over with. No more accusations. No more strangers on her property. No more friends dying. 'Well, hopefully with all the stuff you've found today, you'll find that somebody—and make them pay.'

'Well, hold that thought. I want you to remember it when we do find out who is responsible—and we will.' The determination in his voice was laced with something else; a tension, or was it a warning?

'What do you mean—roo!' she called out, bracing her hand against the car's dash as a large red kangaroo bounded out of the shadow of a mulga tree, jumping alongside the car as it tried to cut across the track.

Mac braked hard, yanking hard on the wheel, and the ute swerved to the right, narrowly missing the kangaroo that seemed oblivious to their presence. Jacinta's eyes narrowed, peering through the dimming light. Come sunset, the roos were bouncing all over the plains.

'Bloody roos,' she muttered, then turned to look at Mac. He was scanning the area to the sides of the vehicle, keeping his eye out for more. His square jaw was set, and the muscles on his forearms, the bulge of his biceps, flexed as his grip tightened on the steering wheel. She tried to regain the threads of their conversation. 'What do you mean, hold that thought?'

Mac looked at her, then twisted in his seat to face her properly, his broad shoulders blocking the view through the driver's side window, darkening the cab a little. 'I mean, Jac, that Brandy is not easy to find.'

'So? Isn't that the point of hiding a lab—you put it in a place not so easy to find?'

Mac's lips pursed—he had very mobile lips, she'd noticed—and he hesitated, as though trying to find the right words. She sighed.

'Spit it out, Mac,' she told him. 'I can handle it.' They knew each other too well to tiptoe around difficult conversations, and she was beginning to find his special brand of non-existent tact annoyingly refreshing. They'd had enough discussions over the past couple of days that she felt she could handle pretty much anything that came out of his mouth.

His mouth. Her gaze dropped to focus on his mouth.

His lips quirked. 'Okay, fine.' He met her gaze directly. 'I was a regular visitor to Bulls' Run, and even I had trouble remembering where Brandy was. You had to give me directions. Only someone who knows the property really well would be able to pull off setting up a drug lab inside her.'

'No, Mac,' she protested, shaking her head. 'I thought you said you believed me.'

'I do,' he agreed. 'But you're not the only one at Bulls' Run.'

'No,' she cried out, thumping the palm of her hand on the dash. She was dropping the 'refreshing' part of her earlier description, and leaving his assertions at just plain annoying.

He arched an eyebrow. 'I thought you said you could handle it.'

'You're saying that my dad, or Scott, or hell, Marion, is involved.' Flipping heck. She could feel the mini mental explosions going off in her head at the thought.

'I'm saying there's a distinct possibility, and you need to prepare yourself.'

She held up a finger, frustration gripping her tightly. 'No, you need to find out what is really going on before you start accusing my family of this.'

'Whoever is involved has more than a passing knowledge of your property,' he told her.

'Well, then you'd have to include every shearer who's worked for us, all the contractors who come out—heck, you'd probably need to throw Jamie into the mix, too.' She raised her eyebrows meaningfully. 'Oh, and *you* can explain that to my brother—but you have to let me be there so I can watch him deck you.'

'Jac, think about it—'

'You're saying that either my father, or the guy who has worked by my side for the last four years and is one of my close friends, or that sweet little lady who makes my dad smile for the first time in ages, is behind this whole operation.' Was she the only one here who thought this sounded cluster-fudge crazy?

Mac wore a resigned expression, and shrugged, his shoulders rolling with an almost graceful movement. 'Yeah, I guess that's exactly what I'm saying.'

'Oh, you're driving me nuts,' she exclaimed, clenching her hands tight. 'How is it that you immediately assume the worst of everyone?'

'I don't assume the worst,' Mac argued, then he shifted. 'I just suspect.'

'You thought I was involved, and now you believe I'm not. Why can't you extend that same faith to Dad? And Scott and Marion?'

He stilled for a moment, then leaned forward, his green eyes dark and serious. 'Because I know you, Jac,' he told her simply.

Her eyes narrowed. 'But you knew me before, when you assumed, sorry, *suspected* the worst of me.'

'Well, I've had the chance to get to know you better, now,' he clarified. His gaze drifted down over her, halting briefly at her breasts before touring over the rest of her. The temperature in the car seemed to rise incrementally with each sweep of his eyes over her body. 'And I want to know more,' he said quietly.

'More? Like what?' She braced her hand against the dash, feeling like she was standing on shifting sand. The way he was looking at her ... well, it was confusing as all heck.

His lips curved. 'Like what you do to relax,' he suggested, shifting closer. 'Like what kind of music do you listen to, like what books you read now...' She watched his arm as it slid along the backrest of her seat, his massive body moving closer. 'Like what your favourite food is.' Each time he uttered a sentence, his voice got quieter. Deeper. 'Like how you want to be kissed...'

He dipped his head, and instinctively she lifted her chin. Their faces were so close, she could feel the soft gust of his breath against her cheek, her lips. Her pulse rate quickened, and she could sense the warmth emanating from his body. The things he was saying, the way he was saying them—it was a seduction of its own, the idea that he was interested in her. Like, *interested*, interested.

'That doesn't sound—' she swallowed, 'brotherly.' Her gaze kept flicking between his eyes and his mouth, and she could almost feel the heat from his sexy smile as his lips curved wider.

'Not at all,' he agreed, then lowered his head to close the distance between them.

Her eyes fluttered closed as his mouth pressed against hers. His arms slid around her, pulling her torso against his. God, he felt wonderful, so big and firm... Her hands slid up his arms, caressing those biceps before trailing up over his broad shoulders.

She moaned as his lips parted hers, and the taste of him, the smell of him, filled her senses. His hands slid over her, caressing her, making her writhe against him. Her heart thundered in her chest, and she could feel the strong throb of his heart beating in his chest.

The sensations he awoke in her were so new, so unfamiliar, and yet so instinctive, so natural. He was all-enveloping, all-consuming, and she could feel herself slowly slipping under his sensuous spell, surrendering to his touch...

Losing herself to Mac's touch.

Mac.

His hand trailed down her back, and he leaned in closer to cup her butt.

A horn sounded, and they both jerked apart, startled. Jac's heart stuttered in her chest. Mac was panting, and he raised his elbow.

'I bumped the steering wheel,' he told her, his breath escaping in a breezy chuckle.

Jacinta glanced between his elbow and the steering wheel, then grabbed the door lever. Mac frowned.

'Jac, wait—'

She shook her head as she climbed out of the car. 'No, we can't—we can't do this. I'm going to walk.'

She'd kissed Mac. What the hell was she thinking? What the hell was *he* thinking? That shifting sand turned into quicksand, sucking her down.

'Jac—'

'No. I need to think,' she called as she kept walking, arms waving as she spoke. Her thoughts were a chaotic mess inside her head, and all she knew was that Mac was the prime source of that chaos. 'I need space, I need air—and I need everyone to stop kissing me!' She strode up the rise, leaving the car well behind her.

'First he wants to be a brother. Then he's kissing me,' she muttered to herself. 'And what do I do about Scott?' She gestured with her hand in the general direction of where she'd seen her station manager last. 'Do I actually think Mac would be interested in anything with me? Is this serious for him, or am I just another age-appropriate chick in convenient proximity? If we did anything, are we talking about a proper relationship, or just a bit of fun?' She hesitated, hands on her hips. 'Oh, and I bet that would be a lot of fun...' She shook her head and continued to stride over the rise and down toward the house. 'And how would that affect our relationship? I mean, if this—whatever this is,' she said, making a big circular gesture with both hands, 'dies, how do we face each other after? How do we talk to each other? Gawd, what would Jamie think?'

Mac watched her stomp away. She was literally stomping, little puffs of dust erupting with each footfall. He scratched his head, and turned to look at the empty passenger seat next to him, and then back at the woman who now seemed to be having a conversation with herself, complete with hand gestures.

He sat for a moment, stunned. What the hell happened? One minute they were locking lips, the next she was trudging her way across the Western Plains to get away from him. Admittedly, that wasn't the usual reaction to one of his kisses.

He winced. He'd done it again. Kissed Jac. Jac Buchanan. And it had felt so natural, and so damn good... and too damn short. What was it about Jac that one minute he could be arguing with her, and the next he wanted to kiss her? No other woman had that effect on him, and frankly, it wasn't something he enjoyed.

Okay, he enjoyed the kisses. A lot. He shook his head. Too much. He just—he didn't know what the hell he was doing. Not with Jac. Any other woman, and he knew how things worked, knew what he had to do, knew to set the expectations, knew when to put a brake on if things were getting a little heavy. With Jac—well, he was operating blind. One thing he did know was she wasn't the kind of girl to hang out with for a good time, and then walk away from.

Not that it wouldn't be a good time with Jac... he was sure it would be a darn good time. He closed his eyes. And there he went again. She wasn't a casual booty-call kind of girl, and with his job, that was pretty much what he looked for. No strings. No responsibilities. No commitment. His job could be all-consuming. Long hours, some really crappy situations... and there was always the risk of being injured or killed in the line of duty with his work. 'No strings' was as much for him as the woman he was actively *not* involved with.

And Jac—Jac had strings that could choke the life out of him. Their families were so closely entwined. Hell, his parents were her honorary aunt and uncle. Jamie was his best friend. And Jac was too sweet. After the things he'd seen, he felt old and jaded next to her optimism and innocence. He wasn't relationship material, and if he kept kissing Jac, he'd want more. And then, at some point, he'd disappoint her, or hurt her, and he didn't want to do that to Jac. Not to mention how it would affect the bonds between the Buchanans and the Hudsons.

Anything with Jac had to be avoided at all costs. He put her car into gear, and then pulled back onto the track. He had to focus on the job. Find the guys behind the meth labs, shut down the whole operation, and move on with his next investigation. Then he would avoid Jac, and put all temptation behind him.

That was the plan. Focus on work, not the woman.

His lips firmed. She'd defended her friends and family. He should have expected that. While her loyalty was commendable—it was equally attractive and annoying, how fiercely she defended those close to her—it could get her into trouble. Focusing on his job didn't void his vow to protect her, though. He'd tried to tell her, but he still didn't think she understood. Whoever was helping Jayden Terrance and his cronies set up drug labs at Bulls' Run had an intimate knowledge of the land. That meant someone close to Jac was involved. Someone she trusted. Focus on the case. That was the plan.

His chin lowered as the car topped the rise, and he could see Jac stalking up the steps of the back veranda. He would keep an eye on her, make sure she was safe.

Damn, he'd stuck to the plan, what, two seconds? He was so screwed.

Chapter Eleven

Jac bounced over a rut, then drove up over the tiny rise at the edge of the track, getting some air between her motorbike's tyres and the ground, before thudding back down to make contact with the dirt once again.

'Yah! Yah!' she called out, causing the cows to change direction. She leaned to the right, letting the rear tyre kick out so she changed direction on a dime, then headed toward that one cow that seemed to think she could go against the traffic of the rest of the herd.

She whistled, and Ray raced around, barking, and the cow reluctantly altered direction.

The sounds of the other hands she'd hired for the round-up brought a grin to her face. Bikes, trucks, whistles, barking and the occasional swear word peppered the air. This was a soundtrack she'd grown up with, and it was always fun doing a round-up.

It was also handy for distracting her from her almost obsessive thoughts about a certain dark-haired detective.

It had been four days since the discovery of the meth lab in Brandy. They'd been told they could continue the normal day-to-day operations of the station, but the mine was still a crime scene. There was a large-scale deconstruction operation going on as they removed all of the stock and paraphernalia. Mac had been out at the site, but had dropped in at the house each day—or so Marion had told her. Jac had been out, busy with catching up on the tasks she'd set aside to go meth-lab hunting with Mac.

But now they'd found it, and things were being cleaned up. She'd started to relax. The police could sift through her records, could search her house, but she wasn't worried because she and the Bulls' Run family had done nothing wrong.

Take that, Mac Hudson. She planted one foot on the ground, spinning the wheel on the ground so that red dirt sprayed everywhere, and gunned the motor as the bike sprang off at a different angle.

She still couldn't believe he thought one of the others was involved with this drug business. She whistled again, signalling to Ray to turn and run around the bank of the herd, getting them to shift toward the gate of the pen.

Once they got them contained, she and the hands would tag them and check them over for general health. An EPA representative would be out to do some tests, and once they got the results they'd be able to organise transport to market—provided the test results came back negative for contamination. She hoped that would be the case. They couldn't afford to lose so much stock, or the income they could provide to the station. This whole thing was keeping her awake at night—along with thoughts of Mac. Okay, maybe horny little fantasies, too, but the stress of dealing with the consequences of the meth labs at Bulls' Run was enough to keep a narcoleptic awake.

She revved her motor, using the louder noise to help move the cattle in the direction she wanted. She grinned as the cows herded through the gate, and nodded when Steve, an Indigenous teen, waved at her, click-counters in hand. Leila Mayne had mentioned the young man needed a job, and Jac needed the help, so it had been perfect timing. For the last two days the teen had arrived on time, followed instructions, shown an interest in the work, and shown a good sense of humour—all things she'd told Leila at the end of each day when the woman rang to get a report on her charge. Her lips tightened. Jac still hadn't spoken with Hayden. He'd tried to call her, but she wouldn't, couldn't talk to him just yet. She needed to calm down a little before she had a sit-down chat with her friend.

Jac killed the engine as one of the contracted hands ran the gate closed. She looked up at Steve where he'd found a perch on the top of the fence. 'How many?' she asked.

Steve glanced down at the counter. 'Two hundred and ninety-three.'

Jac frowned. 'Really?' There were supposed to be more heads out this way.

Steve held up a second counter. 'Yep.' She smiled, impressed he'd taken a second counter. 'Okay. Two hundred and ninety-three it is.'

She turned as Scott stopped his truck and leaned his arm on the window frame. 'How'd we do?'

Jac winced. 'We've lost over a dozen. I'm going to ride out and have a quick scout along Duck's Gully.' The gully was dry now, but when the rains came the gully filled with water, and ducks were known to paddle. Not for a while now, but the name had stuck.

'Want me to come with you?'

Jac smiled. She was still finding it a little awkward, being around him after that kiss, but he was definitely making more of an effort to spend time with her. But it didn't need two of them to scout for cows, not when they had to test all the stock here. 'Uh, no, I'll be fine. Can you get the guys to start checking their tags? And we'll do another count. Pull out any that look sickly, and we'll take it from there.'

Scott nodded, put his truck into gear, then hesitated. 'Say, we've been working like Trojans for the last few days. Do you feel like having a drink when we get back? I'll bring the beer...?'

She bit her lip. She wasn't sure how she felt about Scott—or Mac. They were each so different, and they made her feel differently. Mac could be infuriating. Annoying. Challenging. Sweet. Too damn sexy for his own good... and Scott, on the other hand, was easy. Comfortable. Relaxed... and good-looking in his own way. She never thought either of them would show any interest in her, so she was surprised and more than a little confused when they did. But Scott was right. She had been working everyone pretty hard since the discovery at Brandy, and they'd always shared a beer and had a chat to unwind after a big day. Maybe the company of a man other than Mac was exactly what she needed. 'Sure. That would be great. I'll see you back at the house after dinner.'

Scott flicked his hat with his finger, his lips curving into a smile as he drove off.

She turned back to Steve, who looked like he was trying to hide a smile. 'Can you make a note of the numbers, then reset for a third count?'

He quickly wiped the smile off his face and nodded.

'Good. You could call it quits after that, if you like.' She smiled. 'An early mark. You've done well today, Steve. Thanks.'

He ducked his head, and Jac pretended she didn't notice his blush. 'Thanks, Jacinta.'

'No worries. See you tomorrow.'

She whistled for Ray, who came racing around the pen and jumped up on the back of her seat. She took off smoothly, careful not to dislodge her dog, and rode off in the direction of Duck's Gully.

She had to crest two hills before heading down into the mouth of the gully. It was wide—a dry riverbed, actually. But it had started as a gully, and general erosion had widened it to its current layout.

She slowed down, cruising along the floor of the riverbed. Down here, with yet another sunset colouring the skies with the apricot streaks and a blue-grey blush creeping in, it was quiet. Peaceful. The dry banks reached a height well above her head, so it was like entering a hushed haven.

Mac would like this place, she thought idly, then sighed. She had to get him out of her mind. Every now and then she'd have a flash of memory, of him kissing her in the car, or that first time, at the back of the ute. She was fantasising about it happening again, but these fantasies involved them both being horizontal. Preferably naked. No car.

And then she'd start to stress. She hadn't heard Mac's name linked with another woman for a while, but that didn't fool her. The guy was a player, and she had no intention of being another notch on his bedpost. Besides, when they weren't arguing, she enjoyed their talks. She'd gotten closer to him in those drives out around the property. When he wasn't being an infuriating douche, he could be quite funny. And deep, with his need to make his community safe. He was as dedicated to his job as she was to the farm. She couldn't help it, she was fascinated by the man.

He was a complex, contrary mix. He could be so distant and cool when he was working, yet so tender and considerate, like when he'd stayed with her at the hospital. Or smoking-hot-sexy, like he'd been when he'd kissed her. She didn't know what to do about him. Her. Them. He was a friend. He was Jamie's best friend. If it didn't work out, things could get messy. And did she want things to work out? Was she ready for that? There were things she still wanted to do with the farm. She needed to cut down the debt attached to the property—a debt that would balloon as a result of the meth-lab clean-up and property decontamination. She needed to help look after her father. He was so worried, after learning about the drug activity. He was even doing some fence inspections along the highway, which was both fantastic and distressing. Not many guys would sign up for this kind of life. She didn't have the time to date anyone, let alone forge a relationship, and she was used to being her own boss—well, as much as she could be with her father around. And who said anything about a relationship? Mac wasn't the marrying kind. The man was a born bachelor.

And up until a few short days earlier, he'd considered her a sister and had never looked twice at her. She could handle brother Mac, had managed to handle him all these years, but she had no idea how to handle sexy Mac. Scott was easy. Mac was … a challenge, one that left her feeling a little unbalanced, and a little out of control. If there was one thing she needed at the moment, it was to feel like she had *some* control over her life. Besides, Mac thought her father, Scott or even poor Marion could be involved with the drug operation—which was just pure bonkers.

Jac frowned. Maybe she should just try to weigh up the good versus the bad. So Mac's suspicion of her family was … bad. His kisses, on the other hand, were good. No. Bad, because the kisses changed everything, and she wasn't sure if she was ready for change. She could lose a friend. Brother. Whatever. Scott was supportive and loyal to her family … good. His kisses were—well, they weren't *bad*. Maybe she just needed to try again with Scott, when her head wasn't already in a tizz from Mac.

She followed a bend in the gully, and skidded to a stop. Ray toppled off the bike and rolled when he hit the ground. He shook the sand off as he rose to his feet. Jac stared at the carnage in front of her, her mouth opened in stunned horror.

Cows, calves … she rapidly counted them. Twenty-one, twenty-two, twenty-holy mother of god, twenty-three. They lay where they'd fallen, flies buzzing around the puddles of blood that had pooled under and around the bodies.

She cut the engine and swung off the bike, letting it drop to the ground as she stepped away. *Oh my god.* Tears blurred her vision as she staggered over to the first corpse. She dropped to her knees. *What the hell?*

She reached over and touched the dead cow's shoulder. The poor thing. She sniffed, then scanned the body. What had happened? How had she died? Jacinta leaned over to look at the sightless eyes, and froze when she saw the bullet hole in the forehead. Turning slowly, she looked at all the other animals.

They'd all been shot. Her hand rose to her mouth. Why? Why would someone do that? Cows were … harmless. Docile. Generally. This was such a *waste*. She swallowed as she rose to her feet and backed up toward the bike. They'd been shot.

When? She hadn't heard any shots. Not that day, not the night before… She wasn't a vet, she had no idea how to tell how long the animals had been dead. Hours? Days? She bent and hauled up her motorbike as she tried to swallow her tears. Why? Why this senseless killing? There was so much damage…

She swung her leg over the bike and kicked the starter. She tried to whistle a couple of times, then just ended up calling Ray over as she revved the bike and tore up an incline. She cleared the ridge, Ray running behind her, and headed back to the house.

She needed to call Mac.

Mac picked up the sheet of paper that the printer had just spat out, and walked over to whiteboard. He snagged a bit of sticky tape and stuck the photo he'd just printed next to Jayden Terrance's mug shot.

Detective Brent Pocock leaned his hip on the spare desk that Mac had set up for the visiting officer from the drug squad in Sydney.

'He's not the prettiest lad,' Mac commented.

Brent shook his head. 'Nope.'

Mac folded his arms and stared at the image of Graham Toohey. Apparently the phone confiscated from Hayden at Silverwater prison had coughed up a big fish. 'Jeez. It seems incredible, and yet…not.'

He'd already had an interesting discussion with Hayden Terrance. The man was being surprisingly cooperative. The guy had been furious to learn of the discovery of a second drug lab at Bulls' Run. Actually, ballistic might be a better description for his reaction. If Mac had any doubts about Hayden's friendship with Jac, they'd been put to rest when the guy had agreed to an interview, and given up whatever information he could in order to protect Jac and her father. The problem was, Hayden had been given the phone he'd turned in, and all numbers had been pre-programmed. He didn't know any names, but he did recall seeing a guy visiting his brother at the prison, once. The man had been leaving just as Hayden was arriving. There was no contact, no discussion, but Hayden thought he could identify him if he saw him again. Mac and Brent were currently waiting for Hayden to come in to the station to see if this photo matched the guy Hayden had seen at the prison.

Brent sighed. 'We've been trying to nail this guy for years. That phone is the first time we can link Toohey's operations with Terrance at Silverwater—and if your contact can identify him, that's another nail in the coffin. Then you guys found those meth labs…' Brent shook his head. 'That's going to cost Toohey millions. We're getting close.'

Mac nodded. Toohey was a renowned underworld figure. Murder, prostitution, drugs… you name it, the guy was into it. And he was nasty. Leader of the Black Demons motorcycle gang, which had been responsible for several drive-by shootings, and was currently in a war with the Chinese gangs in Sydney, as well as some of the gangs up in Queensland.

Brent looked over his shoulder. 'We had no idea he had a base this far out of Sydney.'

'We've had an increase in overdoses, from here to Cobar and Bourke,' Mac told him quietly. 'We've also had a lot of drug-related crimes... break-ins, assaults, arson, some significant biker activity. We had what we thought was a smaller meth-lab explosion a few weeks ago ... turns out it was a cover-up of an execution. Whoever was running things here didn't want anyone setting up a rival operation. The murderer ended up dead and my colleague caught two of the other guys...'

Brent was nodding. 'Suspected associates of Toohey, but like Terrance, we've never been able to prove the connection.'

Mac shook his head. 'One of our own, an Echo Springs man, ended up dead as well, in a bushfire, after the bastards tried to use him as their chemist then left him to rot. Even so, we never expected to find the stuff was being made right under our noses.'

Brent shifted to look at the area map on the wall next to the door. 'And the property owners?'

Mac hesitated. 'Generally, they're good people. Great, in fact. I've known them for years. The daughter now owns the property, and I really believe she's not involved.'

'But?' Brent asked, glancing at him.

'But the site is not an easy find on that property. That would require a detailed knowledge of the mines and shafts. Someone out there knows what's going on.' Despite being a regular visitor to the property, Hayden had needed the second site to be pointed out to him on a map.

Brent shifted to look at the photos. Mac had had to put up shots of Jacinta and Tom Buchanan, as well as Scott Nielson and Marion Morrison.

'What about the old man?'

'He lost his arm in a tractor accident three years ago. The farm's got some massive debt—but that's not uncommon in this area. I don't like to think he's involved, but they need money, so it's a possibility.' Mac hated the fact that he had to lay it all out like that, that they had to assess the cold facts. 'He's got no criminal history, though, that would suggest he even has contacts.'

'Financials? Any significant deposits?'

'Nope. Same goes for Nielsen. No criminal history, modest bank account... He was employed by the family a little while before the accident, and has been living on-site in the station manager's house for the last four years.'

'And Ms Morrison?'

Mac sighed. 'She cooks a great breakfast. She puts up with Tom. She's lived in the area for as long as I can remember, and became a widower about twenty years ago. Husband died of cancer. She was recently hired by the family as the cook and housekeeper, and moved out to the farm after the discovery of Dick.'

Brent's eyebrows rose, and Mac's lips quirked when he realised how it sounded. 'All the tunnels have names. Long story. Dick was the first lab we discovered when it blew up.'

'So what made you think to look for another?' Brent put his hands on his hips, assessing the investigation board.

'Actually, Jac—Jacinta Buchanan,' Mac amended, 'drove that search. She was attacked one night on the property, after Dick blew—' He shut his eyes when Brent lost his battle not to smile. 'She invited the police onto the property to help with the search for further illegal activity.'

Brent rubbed his face. 'How easy is it to access this property?'

Mac shrugged. 'Like most of the farms here, they'll have gates and signs, but there's nothing that will actually stop folks from trespassing. Their home gate is always unlocked. They've started to beef up the security on other access points, though.'

Brent tapped one of the pictures that had been taken of the lab found in Brandy. 'This is big. Judging from the quantities of hydrochloric acid, red phosphorous—jeez, look at all the sodium hydroxide—this is a superlab. Toohey would have been raking it in.' Brent glanced over at Mac. 'He's going to be mega-pissed it's been shut down.'

'Hopefully he gets riled up enough to make a mistake.'

There was a knock at the door. 'Come in,' Mac called.

Ben Fields opened the door quickly and peered around the jamb. 'You have a visitor out the front.'

Mac's eyebrows rose, and he followed Ben through to reception. An image of Jac popped up in his mind. He hadn't had a chance to talk with her since the car ride back from Brandy. He'd stopped by each day, but she was always out ... somewhere. He knew what she was doing. She was avoiding him. He sighed. He'd made her uncomfortable, and he hated that. He wanted that easy camaraderie back from when they'd toured her property. He wanted his friend back. He missed her. Sure, he was attracted to her, but he also just plain *liked* her. Knowing his luck, though, it would be Hayden Terrance out there. He waved a greeting to Julie Sponberg, the administrative assistant and receptionist for Echo Springs police station. He smiled when he saw his mother standing at the desk, a cling-wrapped plate in her hands.

'Mum, what a nice surprise.' He gave her a kiss on the cheek, and accepted the plate she held out to him.

'I heard you've been busy out at Bulls' Run, so I thought I'd drop off something for dinner.'

He grinned as he glanced down at the plate. Chops and vegies. 'Thanks, Mum.'

'Oh, and I had a tin of lemon bars, but Ben said he'd look after them for you.'

Mac shot Ben a dry look, and Ben casually backed away into the office. 'That's nice of him,' he said loudly.

'Anything for your mum, Hudson,' came Ben's mumbled reply. Mac assumed he was already tucking into the bars.

'So, what's happened?' Daphne Hudson enquired as she adjusted the strap of her handbag on her shoulder.

He gave her a look. 'Mum, I can't talk about it.'

His mother frowned. 'I swear, if I have to read it in the paper along with everyone else, I won't be happy. Is Jacinta all right?'

Mac looked down at the plate and smoothed over the cling wrap. 'She's fine.' She was better than fine. She was funny, and feisty, and ... avoiding him. He nodded. 'Yeah, she's ... good.'

'So she's safe?'

'Mum, do you think I'd be here if she wasn't?'

'Well, I don't know, dear. You don't talk much about your job,' she pointed out.

'Mum, I would protect her with my life,' he assured her. He heard some radio chatter in the background, and stepped toward the main door.

Daphne's eyebrows rose. 'Well, that's a bit dramatic. Are you sure everything's okay?' She walked up to the door with him, and hesitated, her hand on the door pull. 'I know you're hurrying me out.'

He winced. 'Sorry, Mum. Like you said, things have gotten really busy here at the moment. I have to get back to work.' He and Brent had to discuss the next step in tracking down Toohey and find some rock-solid evidence.

'Well, I've got to get back to work, too. We've got a guest from Sydney staying with us for the next couple of days.' Daphne folded her arms, not looking in the least bit ready to leave. She gave him a patient look, and he nodded.

'Everything's fine, Mum,' he told her. 'Jac's fine, Tom's fine—hey, did you know Marion Morrison has moved out there?'

'Oh, yes, the CWA ladies haven't stopped talking about it.'

'They're being nice, aren't they? Marion's a good egg.'

'Of course she is, she's exactly what Tom needs right now.'

Mac halted. 'Sorry? Are you ladies playing matchmaker?'

Daphne scoffed as she opened the door to leave. 'Don't be silly. We're all too busy trying to sort out your love life to worry about Marion and Tom.'

He gaped as she closed the door and walked down the ramp toward the street.

He shuddered at the thought of the CWA ladies plotting his social life, and turned back to the office. He had to step aside as Ben ran out, his hat in his hand. Brent was right behind him.

'We just got a call about a murder out at Bulls' Run,' Ben called out as they passed him. For a moment Mac felt his heart squeeze in his chest. He handed the plate to Julie and ran after them.

Chapter Twelve

Mac stood with his hands on his hips, staring down at the body.

'A cow.' It wasn't a question. He didn't need to confirm that he was, indeed, looking at a bovine.

'Twenty-three cows, to be exact.' Jac stood with her arms folded, her face grim.

Mac chewed his lip for a moment. '*This* is the murder that was called in?'

She indicated the cow corpses. 'Well, I don't think they passed away from natural causes—do you? Of course it was murder.'

He ducked his head and leaned forward, just for a moment, as his stomach muscles clenched. He sucked in a breath, trying not to puke.

Jac frowned. 'Are you okay, Mac?'

'Fi—' His voice came out a little pitchy, so he cleared his throat. 'Fine,' he said, reassured when he hit his normal baritone range. He wiped the back of his hand against his brow, then looked up at Brent and Ben. Ben grimaced at the carnage. Brent had that same look on his face as when Mac had told him the first lab's name was Dick.

Mac cleared his throat, then turned away from Jacinta as if he was looking at the crime scene. He closed his eyes and sucked in a breath, trying to calm his racing heart.

She's okay.

He raised his hand to his chest, waited as his heart rate slowed from a gallop to a brisk trot. For the duration of the car ride, he'd agonised over what he might find. Tried to mentally prepare himself for the worst, all the while praying for a better outcome.

Thank you, Jesus.

'I can't believe they did this,' Jac said as she skirted around the dead cow. He held up a hand, halting her progress. If she came any closer, he couldn't trust himself not to grab her, hold her tight, and never let her go. In front of a constable and a detective. While working a scene.

She's okay. He kept repeating the phrase, over and over in his mind, as he blindly surveyed the scene. *She's okay.*

When he'd calmed down enough to frame words in a logical order, he turned to face her. 'Generally, we class murder for people,' he told her, trying to keep his tone even and gentle. Calm. Like this was all completely normal, and he wasn't putting himself back together, piece by piece. 'Animals... not so much.'

Jac put her hands on her hips, so delightfully frustrated, so damn adorably alive... 'These animals were killed. Shot dead. For no good reason. Someone trespassed—again—and this time they murdered my cows.'

He held up a finger. 'Destroyed property,' he corrected.

Her eyes narrowed. 'Whatever. The point is, somebody did a very bad thing, and I want them caught.'

Oh, bless her. The words sounded so righteously, indignantly sweet.

'I want to find them,' she said in a growl. 'I want to hunt them down. I want to brand them with a hot poker, and then I want to hang the bastards— then put a bullet through their brain and see how they like it.'

So ... sweet. He frowned. 'One, if you hang them, they're already dead so shooting them after that is pretty much the definition of overkill, and two, that's like ... slightly illegal, Jac. But I appreciate you want justice,' he added.

'I've had it, Mac. These guys—they've used my property to produce drugs. They've attacked me,' she started counting off their crimes on her fingers, 'they killed Brayden—and those other two—and now they've shot my cows. Apart from this being just so cruel and evil and—and just plain *mean*, do you know how much this is going to cost me? With the cost in getting this property cleared off the contaminated list, and the lost income from these cows, these guys are slowly ruining me.'

'Look, we don't even know if it's the same people,' Mac said, although he had his suspicions.

She jerked her thumb over her shoulder. 'I looked around while I was waiting for you. Found the tyre tracks. Three central lines, middle one zigzag. It's the same guys.'

He sobered as he glanced along the gully floor. He was beginning to think the snake in the boot may not have been an accident, either.

He looked up at Brent, who nodded. Mac turned to Ben. 'We'll need the kit from the boot,' he told the constable. Ben grimaced, but turned and went to get the field forensics kit from the back of Mac's car.

Jac stood there, looking magnificent in her dusty black jeans, white and green plaid shirt and blue singlet. Her brown hair fell in a tangled ponytail over her shoulder, and red dust covered her from top to toe. Her brown Akubra hat looked worn and dusty, and her blue eyes were stormy with annoyance.

And she'd never looked so damn beautiful. He wanted to check her over for himself, assure himself that she truly was all right. God, he had it bad. He pointed to the top of the gully. 'I'll need you to exit the crime scene, please. I'll see you back at the house.' Where it was safe, and away from any stray, cow-killing bullets.

Her mouth opened as though to protest, then she looked at the cows in the gully, and made a face. 'Okay,' she agreed, and trudged up the gully walls to her bike. He watched her go.

Brent made his way down toward him, and turned to look at the cows. 'I'll help you walk the scene, if you like. Take some photos, extract some bullets...' He shook his head. 'This is seriously messed up, though.'

Mac nodded, watching as Jac climbed onto her bike, kick-started it, and rode off.

Brent made a noise that sounded like a cross between a sigh and a chuckle. 'So that's the owner, huh?'

'Yep.'

'Man, you are so screwed.'

'Yep.'

'It's going to be okay, Jac,' Scott said, and then took a sip from his beer bottle. They were sitting on the steps to the back veranda, watching the sun set. Ray sprawled across the bottom step of the veranda.

Jacinta smiled grimly. 'I want this to stop, Scott.'

He nodded. 'I know.' He shifted closer to her on the step, until his hip brushed against hers. 'We can sort this out, you and me. It will be all right.'

She sipped her beer. 'Thanks, Scott.'

His arm slid around her shoulders, and she shot him a sidelong glance. His face was close to hers, his blue eyes serious. 'I think, at the moment, that we should stick together. No more going off on your own, okay?'

She frowned. 'I don't want to be afraid to walk around my own property, Scott. They've already stolen so much from us, I don't want to give them my security, my freedom.'

He nodded. 'I know, but … those cows, Jac? Someone *shot* them. We should just leave all that investigating to the police. Don't get involved.'

Jac's lips pressed together. 'Scott, this is our home. I want to make it a safe one.'

Scott's gaze flickered. 'I like hearing you talk about it being *our* home,' he said huskily. 'It gives me hope.'

Ray rose to his feet, shook himself off, then trotted over toward the gate. The dog started to bark. Probably saw a rabbit.

Jac hesitated, conscious of Scott's body so close to hers. Um… that wasn't what she meant. Scott lived at Bulls' Run, just like she and Tom did, and just like Marion now did. She didn't mean 'our home' as in Scott and hers, like they were a couple, or something. But how did she say that without causing him embarrassment, or hurting his feelings? 'Uh, well—'

Two cars crested the low ridge, headlights on as they turned into the yard. Jac rose, relieved at the opportunity to put some distance between herself and Scott.

She smiled and waved as Ben Fields climbed out of the squad car, and Mac and the other guy got out of Mac's car.

She knew the other guy had a name, that she'd been introduced to him at the gully, but she'd been slightly distracted with checking out Mac when he'd arrived, looking all ferocious and stern.

Now, though, he just looked grim and tired.

He slammed the car door shut and strode toward her. The others followed at a slower pace.

Mac climbed the steps. 'Can we talk?' he asked briskly. 'Privately?' he shot a quick glance in the direction of Scott, who narrowed his eyes at the comment.

She nodded. 'Yeah, sure—'

She gasped when he grasped her hand, guided her around the third plank on the veranda, then opened the door and stepped inside her home. She could hear the other detective introduce himself to Scott, but then her attention was on the tall, broad-shouldered man who seemed to be dragging her through her house.

Mac strode down the hallway, and nodded at her father when he passed him in the kitchen.

'Mac,' Tom greeted him, without looking up from the *Cattleman's Weekly* he was reading.

'Tom,' Mac replied, and continued on down the hall. Jac had to run a little to catch up. She could smell dinner in the oven. She had no idea what Marion had prepared, but it smelled delicious. Jacinta thought they were headed for the living room, but Mac continued on down the hall to open her bedroom door.

He pulled her quickly inside, and she opened her mouth to ask him what was going on, but he turned her, backed her up against the door and kissed her.

She gasped, and he took advantage of her open mouth, employing his lips and tongue in a hot kiss that stole her breath, along with any intention of resisting. He cupped her cheeks, and she moaned softly as he slowly slid his hands into her hair. He tilted her head back to improve the angle of the kiss, his hips pressing against hers.

She reached for his shoulders, pulling him closer, her fingers twisting in the cotton of his business shirt as she kissed him back. His shoulders were so broad, and she could feel the muscles beneath flex as he moved, his arms sliding around her to pull her even tighter against him.

Her heart thudded in her chest as though she was running a sprint race, and she gasped when she felt his hand against her breast. He lifted his head, panting, then leaned his forehead against hers as he slowly lowered his hand to her waist. She shuddered at the caress, and gulped in some air.

They stood there for a moment, breathing. Silent. Mac swallowed.

'I needed to do that,' he whispered.

She opened her mouth, but couldn't think of a response. He'd fried her mental circuits with that kiss. 'Uh...'

He shook his head, pulling her against his chest in a tight embrace, and she felt the weight of his chin against the top of her head. 'When I heard about a murder at Bulls' Run...' She felt him shudder in her arms, and she slid her arms around his waist to instinctively offer him comfort, a small measure of reassurance.

He huffed brusquely, then loosened his hold on her. He stepped back a moment, and looked down at her. She was shocked to see the rawness in his eyes, the stark emotion that was both power and vulnerability. He lifted a finger. 'Just for the record, don't use the word murder unless we're talking humans, okay?'

She nodded. 'Uh...'

He nodded once, then leaned down and pressed a quick hard kiss against her lips, then pulled her away from the door.

'Good talk,' he said, and stepped out of her room. She sagged against her bedroom wall as his footsteps thudded down the hall. She raised her fingers to her lips, realised she was trembling.

That kiss... She swallowed. That kiss had been amazing. Powerful. Hot. As though he cared. Deeply.

Her eyes wide, she tilted her head up to look at her bedroom ceiling. She ... wanted to kiss Mac some more. And maybe not just kiss. And he apparently wanted the same with her. Heat bloomed in her cheeks, and a slow smile curved her lips. Mac liked her.

Sounds filtered down the hallway. Marion and her father arguing. The mens' voices outside on the veranda. Yep, the world was still turning. She shook her head slightly, trying to clear the sensual haze Mac had created with that kiss. She should get back out there.

It took a couple of attempts to get her legs moving.

She walked out to the back veranda, then halted. Everyone was gathered on the decking—and all avoided the third plank. She really should fix that. She met Mac's gaze briefly. He seemed ... calm. As though he hadn't just kissed the socks off her. Jacinta's brows dipped, just a little, then she noticed her dad was carrying an overnight bag, as was Marion. Jacinta raised her eyebrows. What on earth ... ?

Her father flexed his wrist, as though to get a comfortable grip on the straps of his bag.

'I have to visit the doc in Bourke,' he told her shortly.

'I'm driving him,' Marion said, just as shortly.

Jac stepped forward, concerned. 'Is everything all right?' She reached out to touch his arm.

Her father's stern expression broke into a brief, reassuring smile. 'Everything's fine, kiddo.'

'Physically, anyway,' Marion huffed. She held out an envelope to Jac. 'Can't say the same about him mentally. I found this when I was cleaning his room. He "forgot" he had an appointment,' she said, glaring at her father.

'Dad, it's for tomorrow afternoon,' Jac exclaimed as she scanned the letter.

'I can reschedule,' Tom suggested hopefully.

'For when? The twelfth of Never?' Marion asked archly. She jerked her chin at Jacinta. 'Read it. He's already put it off twice.'

'It's just a routine scan,' he muttered, turning to Marion. 'I don't want to leave Jac alone, not when all this stuff is going on.'

Jac frowned. 'Dad, you have to go. These specialist appointments are hard to get. It might be months before you can get back in.'

'I don't like the idea of you being here all by yourself, not with everything that's been going on,' her father stated.

'I'll be fine,' she told him, although for the briefest moment anxiety flared at the idea of being alone at night. She had a flash of memory of the night she was hit out in the paddock.

'I'll stay with her.'

Jacinta's eyes rounded at Mac's sudden offer.

'What?' she asked, surprised.

'What?' Scott repeated.

'Really?' Tom asked hopefully.

'Yeah, sure, I don't mind. I'll sleep on the couch' Mac said, shrugging. As if it wasn't a big deal. Jacinta blinked.

'I'll go set it up for you,' Marion offered, and dropped her bag with a thud on the deck as she bustled inside the house.

'Uh, I could stay...?' Scott offered.

'Uh...' Jacinta glanced between the two men.

'Oh, that's okay, Scott. If Mac's happy to stay, that should be fine. Besides, we've only got one couch,' Tom said, straightening his shoulders. He turned to Mac. 'If you're sure...?'

'Yeah, it's fine,' Mac said, nodding.

'Well, thanks for that, Mac. Appreciate it,' her father said, and smiled.

Mac smiled back. 'What are friends for?'

Friends. Mac sighed, waving as Brent and Ben rode off in the squad car, the headlights catching rabbits bopping across the track. The feelings he had for Jacinta went way beyond the friend zone. He winced as he watched the car disappear into the night. Brent and Ben still had to log and dispatch the evidence they'd recovered from the cows, and he felt a little guilty that he wouldn't be there to help—not that the guys had any issues with it. He'd had a quick discussion with Brent out at the car. The Sydney detective found the whole scenario highly amusing, apparently.

He gently scraped his thumb across his eyebrow. What was he doing? What was he thinking? Spending the night with Jac? Alone?

He was making damn sure she was safe, that's what he was doing. What had happened with her cattle—that was disturbing. Someone was sending a message, whether it was a retaliation for the meth-lab discovery before Toohey and his gang moved on, or a sign for more sinister things to come. He needed to talk with Jac—properly. She'd managed to anger an underworld figure who'd now slaughtered some of her livestock.

And they had other things to talk about. He looked back at the veranda. Jacinta was hugging her father, then Marion, while Nielsen looked on with a sour expression. Mac lifted his chin. It was time they stopped pussyfooting around and put all their cards on the table. He was prepared to admit it. He wanted Jacinta. Did she want him?

Yeah, they needed to talk. His shoulders sagged. Except, he didn't really do talking. Not that kind of talking. That was ... awkward. He usually walked in the opposite direction when a woman wanted to have that kind of talk with him. Maybe ... maybe they could just go with the flow. See where things went. Not make an official case out of it?

He was scared to talk with Jac. Not because she might hit him—although he wouldn't put it past her, but because ... she might not feel the same way about him. This was the first time he'd walked on this side of the relationship fence, and he really was stumbling along without a clue.

He strode back to the house and shook Tom's hand in farewell as Marion drove her car from around the side of the house.

'Drive safe,' he called as Tom climbed in, and Marion waved back.

He turned back to the veranda in time to see Nielsen saunter off in the direction of the station manager's house, his hands in his pockets.

And then there were two.

Jac stared at him for a moment, and gave him a shy, tremulous smile. She turned and walked around the back of the house. Minutes later he heard the stuttering start of a generator, and lights came on in the house. Jac walked back around to the veranda. Mac followed her into the kitchen.

She looked over at him as she donned oven mitts. 'Marion's cooked a pasta bake, apparently.'

He nodded. It smelled good. Jac turned back to the oven, so he crossed to the cupboards to help set the table. It wasn't until they both sat down that he was struck by the domesticity of the situation, and how natural it felt.

She handed him a ladle, and in moments they were quietly eating their meal.

Surprisingly, it didn't feel awkward. Mac glanced up briefly. It felt ... companionable. They chatted briefly about the local cricket team, her father's medical appointments ... Marion.

Jac shook her head. 'I swear, there's something going on between those two,' she said, referring to her father and Marion.

'Is that a problem?' Mac enquired gently. June Buchanan had been a lovely woman, and a great mother. He knew both Jac and Jamie missed her terribly.

Jac shook her head as she rose from the table, carrying her now-empty plate and cutlery over to the sink.

'Not really. I mean, it takes a bit of getting used to, but ... she's good for him.' She started running water into the sink, and Mac rose and brought his plate and cutlery over to the sink.

'You know, he's started to do a little more around the property.' Jac leaned close to him. 'He's started shaving every day, now, instead of maybe once a week,' she whispered. Mac smiled at the comment, and grabbed a tea towel that hung from the oven handle to help with the clean-up.

'So you're okay if...'

'If ... they started something?' Jac paused, then shrugged. 'I just want my father to be happy. Whatever that looks like, I'll support it.'

He frowned, and tilted his head to look at her curiously. 'Why did you hire Marion?'

Jac grinned. 'It was either that, or we'd starve. I don't cook.'

'But ... why now?' He was trying to sort out timelines in his head. Could Marion's sudden interest in the farm, and Tom Buchanan, be as a result of a connection with the illegal activity?

Jac sighed. 'When we have a muster on, or the shearers are here, I have a cook. During the off-peak times, though, it's just me and Dad. Scott lives in his quarters, so I was looking after everything here, and I couldn't do everything by myself.' She glanced at him briefly. 'I'm also a terrible cook.'

His eyebrows rose. 'What? You? How could that be? I distinctly recall you baking a chocolate cake that was quite special when you were what, thirteen?'

Jac groaned. 'Stop. That was an easy mistake for anyone to do. Salt and sugar look a lot alike.'

Mac chuckled as he helped put away the kitchen items. 'Well, it was definitely an experience.' He hung up the towel, and followed her down the hall to the living room. 'Have you spoken to Jamie lately?'

She nodded. 'Yeah, I managed to catch him last night on a video call. Obviously he was worried when I told him what was going on, and he's frustrated that he's all the way over in Afghanistan and not here with us. I told him you were working the case, and he was happy to hear that.' She walked in to the living room then halted.

The sofa had been made up into a makeshift bed, with a towel folded neatly on the arm.

'Ah, right. Well, here you are for the night. You know where the bathroom is... You go ahead and take the first shower,' she offered. 'I'll go after you, then turn off the generator.' Jacinta folded her arms, then smiled as she started to back toward the door. 'I'll, uh, leave you to it.'

'Jac, wait,' Mac said, holding up a hand to prevent her from leaving. 'Can we ... talk?'

Her eyes narrowed, and she looked at him askance. 'What about? Because you said you wanted to talk earlier and we ... didn't. Quite.'

'That's what I wanted to talk to you about.' He clasped his hands in front of him to prevent himself from reaching for her. He could do this.

She dipped her head. 'Let me guess,' she said quietly. 'You're regretting it because I'm Jamie's sister, and you're worried how that will shake out with Jamie, and how it will affect our families. You're annoyed because you pride yourself on being a professional, and kissing a person of interest in one of your cases is not considered professional. You're worried how we're going to stay friends if whatever this thing is doesn't work out... that this,' she said, gesturing between them, 'would just be a whole host of trouble.' She raised her eyebrows as she looked up at him. 'How am I doing so far?'

He rubbed his chin, surprised. 'Ah, pretty good, actually.' He blinked. Freakishly insightful, in fact. As though she could see inside his brain.

'Did I miss anything out?'

He winced. 'Well, there's always the nature of my job, how it's pretty demanding, and doesn't leave a lot of time for ... personal stuff.'

She nodded. 'I see. You think I can't handle being in a relationship with a cop? That I'm a little too sheltered, and you're a little too cynical?'

He gaped at her. 'How do you do that?'

'Do what?'

'You know what's going on in here,' he said, tapping his temple. She'd pretty much laid out all of his concerns in a logical, ordered fashion.

She gave him an exasperated look. 'Because what you're worried about is pretty much what's worrying me.' To hear that she shared his concerns was like a weight crushing on him.

He tilted his head. 'You're worried?' So she could see the dangers, too.

She smiled, and her expression was both sweet and sad at the same time. 'Of course I am. We have known each other for all of my life, Mac. You think I don't realise the risk involved if we—' she said and then hesitated, as though trying to find the right word, 'if we changed our relationship?'

'Do you want to?' The words were out before he could stop them, and he kept his expression calm, despite the twist in his gut as he waited for her answer.

She bit her lip. 'Do you?'

'I asked you first.'

She was silent for a moment. 'I don't know,' she whispered finally.

He pursed his lips. Well, at least she was being honest. And pretty much expressing everything that was going on inside his head. He shoved his hands in his trouser pockets. Hell, this was a lot harder than he thought it would be.

'What about … you?' She sounded casual, yet the question was loaded with a nervous tension he couldn't miss.

'Uh, like you said, there are all those things to consider…' He swallowed. He couldn't remember the last time he'd had this kind of conversation with a woman. Had he ever? He'd wanted to have it out with her. He'd wanted to talk about this—because he was the kind of guy who preferred to tackle things directly.

He looked at her, and she chewed her lip, waiting for his response.

All he had to do was tell her how he felt. Jamie flashed into his mind. His mother, how she considered Jacinta like the daughter she'd never had … his work. 'Like you said, this could be a whole lot of trouble. I—I'm not sure if I'm ready for a wife, or even a girlfriend—'

She nodded. 'I get it. I'm not looking for a boyfriend, or a husband…' She laughed softly. 'I mean, I have a farm, you have the force—how would that work? I'm not sure if I'll ever be ready for that kind of relationship.'

He opened his mouth for a moment. Then frowned. 'You … don't?'

'No.' She smiled as she took a step toward him. 'Look, it sounds like while we both maybe kind of like each other, we're not prepared for anything more … yet.'

'Uh, maybe.' He kind of wanted more, but wasn't sure if he was ready to take that leap of faith just yet.

Jac winced. 'Well, that's a great boost for my confidence,' she muttered.

'No, I mean—'

She held up a hand to interrupt him. 'It's okay, Mac. You're smart, you're hot, but you're not really husband material, are you?'

His eyebrows rose. Husband material? That was a *huge* leap.

She stepped up close to him. 'I think maybe we should stay friends, keep it simple. What do you think?'

He chewed on his lip. She made sense. A lot of sense. His brows dipped. 'That's really ...' His voice tapered off.

'Mature?' she suggested. 'Reasonable?' He nodded. Both would fit. She smiled. 'I have my moments. So, what do you say? Friends?'

She held out her hand toward him, and he stared at it for a moment. Jac was right. This approach made a whole lot more sense. It preserved their friendship, and nobody would get hurt in the long run.

He nodded. 'Sure.' He reached for her hand, and clasped it gently. Her hand felt so dainty in his, and he could feel the slight tremble in her fingers. He flicked his gaze up to meet hers, saw the confusion, the sadness ... the tiny flare of attraction.

He didn't know who made the first move, only that suddenly she was in his arms, and they were kissing. He lifted her up, angling his head to deepen the kiss as her legs wrapped around his hips. He walked the few steps to the nearest horizontal surface—the sofa—and followed her down.

She moaned, a sexy, husky sound that curled inside him and brought him to attention. Her fingers fumbled with his buttons, and he slipped the shirt off her shoulder, stroking the smooth skin that wasn't covered by the strap of her singlet. She growled softly as she worked at his second button, then, frustrated, she yanked at the cotton, and he heard the buttons clink as they hit the coffee table and floor.

'Oops, sorry,' she gasped, then started to kiss his neck.

He groaned at the sensation of her lips and teeth nipping at his skin, could feel himself tightening in his trousers. 'Don't worry, I have plenty.' He dragged the shirt down her arms, and she writhed under him in a very pleasing way as she freed her arms. He took her lips again, hands trailing over her body. He broke the kiss, panting.

'Wait, what happened to being just friends?' he gasped.

'We're being very friendly,' she panted, and they kissed again. He slid his hands around her hips, cupping her butt and bringing her flush against him.

Jac pulled away for a moment. 'Wait—are you sure? Do you really want this?'

He nodded as he met her gaze. 'Oh, I want this. Do you?'

She smiled. 'Hell, yeah.'

She pulled his head down for a deep kiss, and he growled softly as he kissed her back.

They were in so much trouble.

Chapter Thirteen

Jacinta opened her eyes. A large, warm, heavy hand lay on her breast. She lifted her head to peer down. And a muscled thigh lay over her hips. Her lips curved as she looked at the large naked man who slept on the sofa with her.

Oh. My. Gawd. They'd done it. Heat rushed to her cheeks. She and Mac had made ... trouble.

Her smile broadened into a grin. Mac was very good at making trouble. She sobered. But now what? Would he regret it? Did *she* regret it? She thought about it for a moment. Nope. She glanced up at the living-room window. The sky was lightening. As much as she wanted to stay here with Mac, she had some chores to do.

Slowly, gently, she slid out from underneath him, gathered her clothes, and tiptoed from the room, wincing. She was feeling muscles she hadn't used for a very long time. After a quick shower she hustled out to the dogs and fed them, then hurried across to the pen where Mary, their milking cow, spent the nights. As she sat down on the overturned milk crate, she tried to focus on what she was doing, and what she needed to do that day.

With the reassuring sound of the milk hitting the pail, Jac found herself thinking about the gloriously muscled hunk asleep on her living-room couch. Last night had been ... wow. Rough and tumble, sweet and tender... her cheeks heated again when she thought about what they'd done.

She couldn't remember having that kind of experience before. Hell, she wasn't a virgin, but ... with Mac it had been different. Fun, but also ... she frowned. Meaningful. Emotional.

And she wanted to do it again. She wanted to do it tonight, and every night into the foreseeable future. She even wanted to do it in the day.

Her frown deepened. They were supposed to keep things friendly. No emotional entanglements. She'd told him as much.

But how many friends did she ever spend the night with, making love? Zero.

Mac was special. Sure, annoying. Frustrating. Irritating. But ... special. Her stomach pitched, like she was on a roller coaster at the Royal Easter Show. Did she really think she could sleep with Mac Hudson and go back to pre-shagged-Mac life? She put her hand up to Mary's flank as the cow shifted.

God, what the hell had she done? What happened now? Mac would leave, and could go shag any other woman he so desired. Her mouth dropped open. What if he went and shagged Brenda Durrant? How would she feel about *that?*

She'd feel like her heart was ripped out of her chest.

'Fudgerooney,' Jac breathed. She swallowed. She loved Mac Hudson. She hit her forehead with the base of her palm and swore. Mary shifted, and Jac automatically reached out to stroke the cow's flank. 'It's all right, Mary. I'm just realising what an enormous twit I am.'

She patted the cow as she rose. Well, she couldn't say anything to Mac, not after what they'd said last night, not after what they'd *done* last night... You can't make love to a guy and then tell him you love him. That would just completely ruin the buzz. She swallowed as she lifted the milk pail and trudged back across the yard. She'd told Mac they were just going to be friends. He wasn't ready for anything more serious. That much had been obvious from their discussion last night. Bed buddies, maybe. A relationship beyond that? Nooooope.

She hesitated at the back door. Maybe, in time, that would change? Hope soared in her chest. Maybe, if she just kept things calm and casual, he'd come around. Maybe fall in love with her right back. She closed her eyes briefly. God, she hoped so.

She walked into the back hall and through to the kitchen, then almost dropped the pail. Mac stood at the bench, sipping coffee from a mug. His hair was tousled, his shirt was open, his chest—Jac swallowed as she stared at his glorious chest. She felt like she'd just walked into a domestic sex fantasy.

Mac smiled when he saw her, his lips curving in a hot, provocative smile, his green eyes flashing with wicked mischief, and he sauntered over to her, placing the mug on the table as he passed. Her mouth went dry, watching that muscular body come closer.

'Morning,' he murmured, taking the pail from her and putting it on the bench, then leaning forward to kiss her, his hands cupping her face.

Oh, God, it was happening again. Heat, fire, want, desire, a mind-stealing need that took over her. She raised her arms around his neck, opening her mouth to her kiss. This was the Best. Morning. Ever.

He kissed her languorously, as though he had all the time in the world to explore her mouth. He eventually drew back, and kissed her lightly on the tip of her nose. 'I have to go into the station,' he said softly, 'but I want you to take it easy. Be safe.'

A warmth spread through her at his concern, his protectiveness, and she smiled up at him. 'I love you,' she said softly.

Uh-oh. Her eyes widened. Had she—? Did she—?

He stilled. Blinked.

'Uh,' she uttered, scrambling for something to say. 'I mean—'

'Thank you...?' he said tentatively.

Jacinta blinked. Er... 'You're welcome,' she responded automatically. What? She blinked. You're welcome? *Thank you?*

Mac stared at her for a moment, his face blank, then he jerked his thumb over his shoulder. 'I should get going,' he muttered.

Jacinta clasped her hands in front of her. 'Yeah, I have to ... do something.' She half-turned, her mind blank.

Mac leaned forward, drew back, then pressed a quick kiss to her cheek. 'I'll call you.'

He walked out of the kitchen, his open shirt billowing behind him. Jacinta turned around and gently hit the wall with her forehead.

I love you. What was she, some kind of idiot? What happened to letting things play out, and keeping that little nugget of humiliation to herself?

And who the hell says *thank you* to a declaration of love?

Mac gripped the steering wheel and tried to shake it as he drove along the highway.

Thank you? She'd said I love you, and he'd said *thank you?*

'You stupid, stinking, bloody idiot!' He thumped the wheel. Bloody hell. He'd frozen. No, he'd choked. He'd felt the words bubbling up inside him, and he'd choked. He'd never said them to a woman before. Never.

He was such. An. *Idiot.*

Last night had been ... too much. He'd been more honest, more open with Jacinta the night before than he'd ever been with a woman. He'd made love to her, and it had been, well, pretty fantastic, actually. He'd even *snug-gled* with her. Usually he was up and out the door before the woman woke up, but Jac had beat him to it. And when she'd walked in, all rosy-cheeked and walking sunlight, he'd wanted to hold her close, cherish her.

And then she'd said she loved him.

He shook his head. He'd handled that badly. He'd handled it monstrously bad. Sure, she'd surprised him. Hell, she'd shocked him, but … she loved him. Despite his annoyance at himself, a little kernel of warmth flared. Jac Buchanan loved him.

Gawd, what was he going to do now?

He pulled into the police station parking lot, and walked into the office. Julie blinked when she passed him in the hall, but he kept walking. He entered his office, and Brent Pocock looked up. The detective's eyebrows rose as Mac walked over to the cupboard in the corner and pulled a fresh shirt off a hanger. He quickly changed shirts.

'Did you—'

'Don't ask,' Mac muttered. He didn't want to talk about it. Couldn't talk about it. Didn't want to admit how monumentally he'd screwed up. On so many levels.

Brent nodded. 'Okay. Uh, I got some intel this morning about Toohey.'

'Yeah? What?'

'Well, word on the street is he's got a big deal going down. He's been in talks with the leader of the Coffin Dodgers motorcycle club up in Surfers Paradise.'

Mac buttoned up his shirt. 'Okay. And?'

'Well, Toohey seems to have left Sydney, and they think he's meeting the guy up near the border for an exchange.'

'Yeah?'

'Yeah. But it's not drugs.'

'What is it?'

'Guns.'

Mac frowned. 'Huh.'

Jac placed her rifle behind the seat in her ute, and turned to face Scott. 'I want you to go back out to the cows. We'll need to dispose of them. I'll be by in a couple of hours to give you a hand.'

'What are you going to do? Maybe we should stick together?' Scott said, squinting against the morning sun.

No. No more being or not being with anyone. 'It's fine, Scott. I'm just going over to just beyond the west paddock to scout out a potential site for some solar panels, and I'd rather do it on my own.'

Because right now she didn't want to be around a man, talk to a man—and definitely not talk about the non-relationship she and the man were in. She whistled, and Ray came running around the side of the house, leaping onto the back of the ute. She closed the tailgate with a little more force than usual.

'Why don't we leave that for another time? Your old man doesn't seem sold on it—'

She stared at him coolly. Oh, that was right. Scott had said something to her dad. 'We disagree at the moment. Isn't the first time, won't be the last, but we generally work out a compromise. See you later,' she added, to prevent further conversation.

She wanted some time to herself, some time to think. Some time to wallow in her abject humiliation over confessing a love that didn't seem to be returned.

Scott nodded. 'West paddock, huh?'

She nodded as she climbed into the cab and started the car. 'Yep.'

She put the car into gear and drove off, bouncing along the track. A brief glimpse into her rear-vision mirror saw Scott driving his own vehicle off in the direction of Duck's Gully.

She turned her focus back to the track. Her knuckles whitened on the wheel. She'd ruined everything. She'd made something that was supposed to be fun and casual way too serious and heavy. She shook her head. She knew Mac felt something for her, but he'd been hesitant to commit to anything. Had she just been fooling herself into thinking she could handle a no-strings-style relationship? She sighed. She wanted more than just one night of sex with Mac. She wanted the conversations. She wanted his time. She wanted ... something he wasn't ready to give her.

'You are an idiot,' she muttered to herself, eyeing the landscape. She realised she was driving past the spot where she'd been attacked the other night. She brought the vehicle to a stop, and frowned. She twisted in her seat. The gate they'd used was back that way, and Brandy was off this way... she eyed the area. But this guy hadn't been headed for Brandy. Or if he had, he was taking the scenic route.

'So where were you going?' she wondered aloud. She sat forward in her seat, scanning the ridge in the distance. If you kept driving in this direction, you'd eventually hit the base of Echo Ridge. There was nothing out there except... her eyes widened.

'The caves.'

She put the truck into gear and changed direction. There was a cave system within the ridgeline. They eventually linked up with the springs that gave the town its name. But the caves out this way were rarely visited. Mainly because it was a bit of a slog to get there, and there were much better caves, some with thermal springs, closer to town.

It took her over half an hour to get there. The track was almost non-existent, with plenty of grassy shrub to drive through. If she got up to twenty kilometres an hour, it was a good stretch.

She slowly drove up a ridge, and braked, her blood running cold.

A white four-wheel drive was parked a little way away from the cave.

Mac leaned back in his chair and looked over at Brent. Hayden had come in and identified Toohey as the man he'd seen at the Silverwater Correctional Complex. Since then, they'd spent hours poring over phone and financial records, and still nothing. 'So nobody's seen Toohey for five days?'

Brent shook his head. 'Nope. Our man on the inside said Toohey received a call and chucked a tantrum that would make my two-year-old nephew look like an altar boy.'

'He heard about Brandy,' Mac surmised. He frowned as he calculated the timeline. 'Like, straight away,' he murmured.

'What?'

'Five days. That's the very day we found Brandy.' He started flicking through the phone records, scanning the dates. He'd requested the phone records, but they only went up to the day before the discovery. Jacinta had given the phone company permission to hand over all of the data, as she had done with the banks—it had been faster than waiting for a warrant, and she'd wanted to clear Bulls' Run of any suspicion. Whatever he'd asked for, she'd made it available.

He reached for his phone, and after several long minutes was able to speak to the person he'd been dealing with at the phone company, and requested all records between then and the day the meth lab at Brandy had been discovered. He hung up and looked at his watch.

'I caught her on her lunch break, so she's going to go pull the records now and email them.'

Brent's eyebrows rose. 'Wow. That's really fast.'

Mac shrugged. 'We got lucky.'

Brent smiled and waggled his eyebrows. 'Again.'

Mac shifted in his seat. He didn't want to talk about the other time he'd gotten 'lucky' today. Didn't want to think about it—but it was on constant repeat in his mind.

'I don't want to talk about it,' he muttered.

Brent sniggered. 'You don't have to, it's written all over your face.' He indicated the records they were sifting through. 'I have to say, she's very cooperative.'

Mac nodded. She was also a whole lot of trouble. An email notification popped up on his screen, and he clicked on it. The phone company data.

'I'm thinking of grabbing a bite to eat. Wanna come with?' Brent asked.

Mac nodded. 'Sure, I'll just—' He frowned at the records as someone knocked on the door. Brent rose to answer as Mac leaned forward on his desk. He knew Jac's number off by heart, and could see the entries of the calls he'd made from her phone. There were no calls on the landline, and there were two more satellite phones linked to the account. One of them had made a call during the afternoon—when Tom, Scott and Marion had been informed of the discovery, and en route to being interviewed.

'What's Toohey's number again?'

'It ends with two-zero-four-one.'

'Son of a bitch.' Mac rose from his desk and picked up his keys. 'I know who called Toohey.' He glanced at the door. Ben was there, and as his colleague opened his mouth to speak, he was shoved aside, and Hayden Terrance stuck his head in.

'I was on my way back in from picking up a second-hand industrial oven at Dubbo, and I reckon I saw that guy, Toohey. He was driving in the opposite direction, and it was only for a brief moment, but I'm pretty sure that was the same guy I saw at Silverwater,' Hayden said, his face grim.

'Where did you see him?' Mac asked as he brushed past him on his way out of the office.

'Out on the Mitchell Highway,' Hayden replied, falling into step behind him.

Mac started to jog. Bulls' Run was off the Mitchell Highway.

Jacinta crept up to the back of the vehicle, trying to keep below the line of the tailgate. She held Calamity Jane in her hand, and she gripped it tightly as she paused, crouching, behind the car.

She glanced down at the track. Three centre lines, the middle one with a zigzag. She swallowed, her heart thudding in her chest. She peered around the corner of the car to the side mirror. She couldn't see anyone in the driver's seat. She skirted along the side of the vehicle, keeping low, until she reached the driver's door, and slowly rose to peer inside. The vehicle was empty.

She glanced toward the cave. She couldn't see inside, it was so dark. She didn't know where anyone was, or how many of them there were. She pulled out the screwdriver she'd removed from her tool box and slid into her boot, and stabbed the front tyre. She smiled grimly when she heard the faint hiss of air escaping. Try driving away now, you bastard.

She scurried in a wide curve toward the mouth of the cave, putting her back up against the rock wall. She listened. A cockatoo flew overhead, and she could hear the faint rustle of wind through the clumps of grass, the soft whine of a mosquito, but other than that, nothing.

She peered around the lip of the cave. It took a few moments for her eyes to adjust to the dim interior. It was empty, but at the back she could see the flutter of light. A tunnel.

The light was getting fainter and fainter. Whoever was carrying it was walking deeper into the ridge. Was this yet another drug lab? She couldn't believe it. She pulled the satellite phone out of her back pocket, and dialled Mac's number. She didn't hesitate as she started to back away from the cave, her eyes trained on the entrance.

It took a few rings, but Mac answered the call.

'Jac! You need to—'

'They're here,' she said quietly, firmly into phone.

'What? Who?'

'The white—'

A hand snaked around her mouth, cutting off her words as her wrist was grasped so tightly she had to drop the phone. Eyes widening, she tried to swing the butt of her rifle around, but whoever grabbed her let go of her wrist and caught the gun. She could hear Mac's voice, tinny and indistinct, calling from the phone she'd dropped to the ground.

She raised her foot and brought it down in a fierce stomp, catching her assailant on his foot. She heard a harsh curse word, felt the grip tighten on her mouth. She launched herself backward, barrelling into the hard body behind her, tumbling them both to the ground.

The grip on her face lessened, and she dug her elbows in fierce jabs, until the grip relaxed enough for her to break free and rise to her feet.

'The caves, Mac,' she screamed. 'The—oof.'

Her ankle was grabbed, and she hit the dirt on her stomach. She twisted, kicking at the guy who was now trying to claw his way up her legs. Her eyes widened. He had a tattoo of a spider across one side of his bald skull and face. She tried to wriggle away, and managed to kick him in the cheek.

'You bitch,' he roared.

She rolled, her arms spread to try and give her traction to crawl away. Her hand touched the barrel of her rifle and she rolled again, swinging it with force against his face. His head whipped back, and his grip relaxed as he fell off her, dazed.

Jacinta scrambled to her feet and cried out in frustration when she dropped her rifle, but didn't turn back to pick it up. This guy was twice her size, and she wouldn't win in a tussle. She bolted along the track toward her car on the other side of the rise. She wrenched open the door as she heard the guy roar behind her. Her fingers trembled around the key in the ignition, and she heard Ray growling from where she'd secured him to the tray of the ute. She glanced up. Spider-faced dude was running toward her, his expression so fierce she almost peed her pants.

Ray started barking, interspersed with a deep, guttural growl. She finally got the engine to start, and she slammed the car into reverse.

The guy skidded to stop, then ran back to the white car. She saw another man emerge from the cave. He was taller, thinner, and carrying a big, nasty-looking gun. Jacinta yanked on the wheel, turning the car in a tight circle, then changed gears, bursting forward as the driver's side mirror shattered, followed by a crack that reverberated along the valley floor.

She pressed her foot down on the accelerator, crying out when she drove over a bump so fast she hit her head on the ceiling of the cab. She didn't bother with the track, but drove across country. She swerved a couple of times, kicking up a big cloud of red dust. Another shot rang out, and she whimpered as she heard the thud the bullet made as it hit the ute. But she kept driving, kept up the dust cloud, kept dodging the bullets.

Her heart thumping painfully in her chest, Jacinta checked her rear-vision mirror. The white car had dropped back a little. She shook her head. She should have punctured all of the damn tyres. As it was, one deflating tyre would slow them down, but not stop them.

By the time she crested the hill close to home, she was frantic. She needed to call for help, but her phone was on the ground out by the cave. Scott was in the other direction, at Duck's Gully. The closest phone was the landline at the house. She glanced in the mirror again. The white car was still there, although the distance was slowly growing.

She didn't slow down for the gate, but rammed it. The chain snapped, and the gate sprang open as she bounced her way through it. She skidded to a stop at the back veranda, and could hear the gunning of the other car as it roared up the rise. Jacinta almost tripped as she burst out of the car, and reached around to release Ray's lead.

'Come,' she called to the dog as she raced toward the house. She slowed down long enough to collect the cricket bat as she ran past it, and leaped over the third plank. Ray ran up behind her as the car sped into the yard. Spider-faced dude didn't even wait for the car to stop. He launched himself out of the moving vehicle and ran toward the veranda.

Jacinta opened the screen door and ushered the dog inside, her pulse thundering in her throat as she followed. She could hear the thump of the man's footsteps as he ran up the steps and across the veranda. She heard the crack, and then the scream of pain. She whirled around. He'd fallen through the rotten wood. Partially. One leg was below the veranda, and the wood surrounding his thigh was red with blood. He tilted back his head and roared with enraged pain.

He glared at her, and Jacinta saw the pain-crazed look in his eyes as he reached behind him and pulled something out of the waistband of his jeans. She saw the handgun, and reacted, swinging the cricket back for six and out. She caught his wrist, heard the crack of bone and his scream as the gun was smacked out of his hand. She then hit him across the cheek. His head whipped to the side, and she saw his eyes roll back in his head as he slumped, unconscious, onto the deck.

Jacinta backed into the house, pulling the screen door shut and locking it, then doing the same with the back door. She couldn't remember ever having locked it before. She started running through the kitchen, then screamed as glass shattered behind her, and she heard the crack of a rifle. She dived for the floor as Ray barked excitedly. It took her a couple of attempts, but she managed to whistle to the dog. He hunkered down, his eyes on Jacinta as she commando-crawled along the hallway.

A high-pitched whiny scream got louder and louder, and she realised it was sirens. More bullets peppered the bank of glass windows, and she crawled toward the hall. Ray did the same, just like she'd trained him to herd sheep. As soon as she got beyond the kitchen she rose to her feet and scurried down the hall. Her father kept a gun locker under his bed.

The sirens wailed louder, and she could hear the scud and squeal of rubber on dirt. She changed direction and headed for the front door. There was only one other guy, and the cars were headed around the back. She reached for the front door and yanked it open, running out into the arms of a man.

She screamed, then sagged when she realised it was Scott. 'Oh, thank god,' she sobbed, leaning into him.

He tsked lightly. 'You should have stuck with me, Jac.' She looked up at him, and that's when she saw the gun in his hand.

Chapter Fourteen

Mac used the car door as a shield as he trained his weapon on the man currently firing on Jac's home. He wore his vest, as did the other officers, but the more protection, the better. 'Freeze! Drop the gun, and turn slowly.'

The man halted, then looked over his shoulder at the four police cars that had pulled up behind him. His expression clearly showed his anger and frustration. Mac didn't turn, but he was pretty sure Hayden had followed them out there. He just hoped the guy had enough sense to take cover.

'Drop the gun, now,' Mac bellowed. He kept his eye on the weapon. It was a large calibre hunting rifle.

The man's shoulders sagged, and for a moment Mac thought they had him. Then he saw the man's wrist shift position on the rifle. 'Gun!' Mac yelled out to the other officers as the intruder whirled and raised the rifle to his shoulder in one fluid motion.

All of the officers reacted, and the noise was deafening as the bullets were fired. The man's body jerked and jolted, as though electrocuted, before he dropped the rifle and slumped to the ground.

Heart thudding, weapon trained on the man on the ground, Mac raced over and kicked the rifle away from him. His caution proved unnecessary, though, judging by the lifeless stare of the dead man.

He looked up at the house, frowning. A shape was slumped on the deck, but it didn't quite make sense. Mac raised his weapon and carefully approached the veranda. It took him a moment to realise it was another man who had fallen through the rotten patch of the deck. He didn't know whether the man was unconscious or—

A scream tore through the air, and Mac flinched, recognising the voice. Jacinta. He signalled one of the constables to take over his position. Mac ran along to the end of the veranda and peered around the corner of the house. Nielsen held a struggling Jacinta, his arm across her torso, a gun to her head.

A dog barked from inside the house, and there was repeated scratching on the front door.

Rage and fear were a galvanising combination. Mac jumped over the veranda railing, his weapon trained on the man.

'Let me go,' Jacinta yelled, writhing in Nielsen's arms. Mac's eyes narrowed when the man jerked her against his body, and twisted to face Mac.

'Drop the weapon,' Mac said, his voice calm and controlled. Inside, though, agonising dread gripped him at the sight of Jacinta in the arms of a violent criminal. *Make her safe.* The dread was swallowed by a cold, unflinching rage at the man who dared to put Jacinta in danger.

'Stay where you are, Hudson, or I'll shoot her,' Nielsen called out.

Mac shook his head. 'If you shoot her, you'll lose your bargaining chip.' He took another step, but halted when Nielsen cocked the gun.

'I swear to god, I'll do it,' Nielsen growled.

Mac was conscious of the team of officers hustling through the yard and taking up positions. Hayden bounded around the ring of officers, but skidded to a stop when Scott shifted to keep an eye on him.

'Stay back, Terrance, or I will kill your friend.'

The muscles in Mac's jaw flexed. Hayden's presence was against all protocol, but he didn't have time to call a halt and clear the area. He had a feeling the guy wouldn't budge, anyway.

'You hurt her and you're a dead man, Nielsen,' Hayden growled, his fists clenched. Okay, so at least he and Terrance agreed on something.

'Back down, Terrance,' Mac called, and Nielsen glanced back toward him, just as Mac hoped he would.

'Why, Scott?' Jacinta cried. 'What is going on?'

'Everything would have been fine, Jac, if you'd just left things well enough alone,' Nielsen grated. He ground the barrel of the gun into her temple.

'He's the one who's been working with the drug runners,' Mac told her.

Jacinta shook her head. 'Why, Scott?' she panted. 'Why did you help them?'

Nielsen laughed. 'I'm one of them, Jac. You have one of the biggest land holdings, and it was perfect for our operation. It didn't take much to wrangle a job here. It's been quite a profitable operation.' He scanned the yard, eyeing the officers who were slowly advancing toward him. 'Stand back,' he hollered, and changed the position of the gun to beneath Jacinta's chin.

Mac held up a hand, and the police officers halted.

'Let her go, Nielsen,' he told the man in a low voice. 'It's not too late for you. You can cut a deal.'

Nielsen laughed bitterly. 'Do you think I'd last two minutes in prison if I did? Toohey has people everywhere.' If Nielsen didn't release Jacinta, he wouldn't have to worry about Toohey. Mac's shoulders tensed, although he kept his grip relaxed on his gun.

'Let Jacinta go,' he repeated. He edged a little closer.

'No. I want a car, and then this little lady and I are going to take a drive.'

Not on his watch. Mac kept his eyes on Nielsen. 'Jacinta, I want you to stay calm,' he called to her.

'I'm calm,' she muttered as she writhed again, trying to break free of Nielsen's grip. Even as a hostage, she had to be contrary. Mac held up one hand, palm out in a placatory gesture.

'It's going to be okay, Jac,' he said in as soothing a voice as he could muster. 'Just think happy thoughts.'

She frowned, looking around the yard. She opened her mouth, and he shook his head to prevent what he was sure would be a smartarse remark. 'Think about Jamie, and the times we used to play together,' he said, sliding his foot a little closer, and shifting his weight. 'All those things we both taught you,' he said meaningfully.

He almost sagged with relief when he saw understanding flash through her eyes. His palm out, he raised a finger. 'I want you to let her go, Nielsen.'

'Screw you, Hudson,' Nielsen snapped back. 'Where's my car?'

He raised another finger, as though cautioning. 'I need everyone to calm down,' he said, as he slid his foot forward again.

'I'll calm down when you give me what I want,' Nielsen shouted.

Mac nodded. 'I understand,' he said, raising his third finger.

Jacinta brought her boot down sharply on Nielsen's foot. As he jerked forward, she jabbed him forcefully in the ribs, and then grabbed the wrist that held her and twisted it under.

Mac launched himself at them in a low tackle, getting under Nielsen's arms and body-slamming him into the dirt. Jacinta fell and rolled away. Nielsen roared with rage and tried to sit up, but Mac blocked the hand holding the weapon, and the gun fell to the dirt as Mac swung at the guy's face. Mac's anger turned into white-hot rage. There was a satisfying crunch of bone as his fist connected with jaw, and he reared back and let fly with another two fierce, brutal jabs, before Ben called out to him.

'She's clear, Mac. She's clear.'

A gun entered Mac's peripheral vision, and he looked up at Brent Pocock. Brent nodded as he trained his gun on the bloodied and dazed man on the ground. 'We've got him, mate.'

Mac rose to his feet. He wanted to hit the guy again, the bastard. He turned to Jacinta, and caught her as she ran to him.

'It's okay,' he whispered, hugging her close and stroking her trembling back. 'You did good.'

She clutched him to her tightly, and he felt like he'd come home. 'You're going to be fine.'

Jacinta huddled in the blanket as Marion and Aunty Daph fussed over her. The house was a crime scene, so they weren't allowed to sleep there that night—or the next few nights. Mac had called Aunty Daph, and she had been driven in a squad car to the Echo Springs Hotel.

She scratched her nose, her hand still beneath the blanket. She and Hayden had had a long chat, too. He'd been horrified when he'd learned about the second lab and the weapons cache. He'd admitted his part in the lab at Dick; it had been partly so that he could make sure she was safe, and partly because his brother had threatened to use Brayden if Hayden didn't do as his brother instructed. He told her how his brother had played him, telling him that if Hayden was in control then at least the real thugs from the city wouldn't be moving in to his town. But as it turned out, Jayden had never really been in control, and once Toohey had seen the potential of the mines he'd expanded rapidly. After seeing those other men in action today, and the violence they used so easily, she could understand why Hayden felt he'd had to get involved, and how he'd tried to protect her. He'd made some mistakes, and lost his younger brother in the process, but after he'd come to help rescue her, she felt she could forgive him. Even in the midst of making his mistakes, he'd made them with the intention of protecting her from Jayden and his brutal associates. Poor execution, but best of intentions.

She watched as Pip Hudson patted her father on the shoulder. Her dad and Marion had arrived home several hours after the excitement had concluded. The police had still been present, so the explanations had been long and comprehensive. They'd been shocked and dismayed when they saw the bullet-riddled house. Her father had been furious when he'd heard about

---

Scott, and Mac and Ben Fields had had to prevent him from driving into town to the lock-up and 'dealing with him'.

Jacinta shuddered. She still couldn't believe it. Scott. He'd taken the job at Bulls' Run specifically to help set up the operation.

'Here, drink this,' her father said, handing her a mug. She obediently raised it to her lips, and almost choked on the fiery liquid.

'Oh, my god, Dad,' she rasped. 'Whiskey?'

'I reckon you deserve a double dose. What happened today was worse than any snake sighting.' Her father sat down at the dining table next to her. 'How are you doing, kiddo?'

She gave him a weak smile. 'I'm a little wobbly,' she admitted. Every now and then she'd get the shakes. God, she'd been so damn scared.

'I'm not surprised.' Her father slid his one arm around her shoulders and hugged her close. 'I'm glad you're here,' he told her, his voice rough and husky.

'Me, too,' she replied, squeezing him back. He chuckled. 'Wait until I tell Jamie you took out an underworld figure.'

Jacinta grimaced. It turned out that Spider-faced dude was the head of the operation. Some guy called Toohey something. Or something Toohey. He was currently in hospital with a lacerated leg, a broken wrist, a broken jaw and severe concussion. Considering he was pretty much caught in the act of trespassing with a firearm, he was going to jail for a very long time, as was Scott. She'd told Mac and his detective buddy that she'd found them out at the caves, so they'd sent a team out to investigate. It turned out there was a weapons cache large enough to mount a third-world coup. The charges were piling up.

She didn't want to think about what could have happened if the men had decided to use more than the weapons they'd had on them. As it was, her dad had joked about letting the police use the shearer's quarters as a temporary station. Homicide were currently out there to investigate the death of one of the intruders, and forensics were out there to work the scene. The Gang Squad, Drug Squad, the Counter-Terrorism Unit and some other divisions had all sent personnel to assist.

The back door slammed, and she looked up to see Mac stroll into the kitchen. Everyone greeted him, and she smiled shakily. He'd removed the dark vest, but he still wore his white business shirt. There were a couple of streaks of red dirt from when he'd tackled Scott. His sleeves were rolled up to expose his muscular forearms, the colour stark against his tanned skin. She thought she'd never seen him look so fit and strong—unless it was when he was leaping over the railing of her veranda, a lethal-looking gun in his hand with the intense look of an avenging, pissed-off angel ready to do damage. She'd seen him at work—pretty much every minute she'd spent with him since Brayden's death—but she'd never seen him look so dangerous as when he'd come for her.

Now, though, his handsome face was tired but relaxed, his smile gentle when he saw her.

He walked over to her and placed his hand on her shoulder. She found the contact warm and supportive, and wanted to curl up in his arms. Her fingers tightened on the blanket around her shoulders. She was turning into a pathetic sook. She craved the touch of a man who wanted only to be friends. She couldn't help it, though. She chewed her lip. Tomorrow, she'd grow a spine. Today, she wanted his touch. Mac looked at her father. 'I need to talk with Jac,' he said. 'I just need to clarify a few things.'

Ugh. So no cuddles, no touchy-feely realisations of a returned love. No, he wanted to discuss the case.

Tom Buchanan gave him a shrewd look, then nodded. 'Sure. You go … clarify.'

Mac looked down at her. 'Would you mind?' he asked gently.

She shook her head. 'Sure.' She figured there would be plenty of interviews over the coming days, and this was just the start. She rose to her feet, and smiled when Aunty Daphne bustled over.

The older woman held out a key to Mac. 'I've put her in room twelve,' she said.

Mac accepted the key, then put his arm around Jacinta as they walked to the door that led to the hotel's front of house. Jacinta glanced over her shoulder. The room was silent as the others watched them leave. Marion's hand was gripped in her father's, and Pip had his arm around Daphne. She raised her eyebrows, and the couples turned to each other and started talking, while keeping their gazes on the departing couple, as though they were trying for a level of normalcy. Jac shook her head. It would take a while for any of this to return to normal.

She leaned into Mac's side, enjoying the moment of being held by him, if only for friendly support. They walked up the carpeted stairs to the first-floor hallway, and along until Mac stood in front of room twelve. He unlocked the door and pushed it open, stepping aside to let her in first.

She crossed to the queen-sized bed and turned to sit down on it. Mac closed the door behind him, and came to sit next to her.

He clasped her hand. 'How are you?' he asked.

'Okay,' she told him.

He arched an eyebrow, and she sighed. 'Fine. I'm a little shaky.' She brushed at the tear that trickled down her cheek. 'Go ahead, call me a wuss. That's what I feel like at the moment.'

He chuckled as he drew her close. She let him, ducking her head so she could rest against his broad chest. His heart beat, strong and regular, beneath her ear, and the rhythmic thump relaxed her.

'You just took out the head of a crime syndicate, Jac. Wuss is not a word I'd use to describe you.'

'Yeah? What would you use?' She lifted her head to peer at him. She needed to know exactly where she stood with this man.

He gazed down at her, then slid his hands up to cup her cheeks. 'Strong,' he whispered. 'Amazing. Smart. Beautiful—'

'You think I'm beautiful?' she asked, surprised.

He smiled. 'Sexy, too.'

Her cheeks warmed as his hands slid into her hair, and he gently drew out the elastic that held her ponytail. 'Go on,' she said, trying to keep her tone casual.

He chuckled, a low, husky sound that slid over her skin like a lover's caress. 'Frustrating, irritating, trouble, pain in the a—'

She thumped him in the shoulder. 'Mac.'

He wheezed with laughter, then sobered as he gently threaded his fingers through her long hair. 'I was so scared for you,' he whispered, scanning her face as though ensuring she really was okay. 'When I realised Nielsen was involved, and then when we were in the car and you called...' He swallowed. 'We could hear you struggling.'

She bit her lip. 'I didn't realise. I thought he'd disconnected the call.'

'I thought I was going to have a heart attack when we heard the shots,' he told her, his expression grim, the emotion in his eyes raw and vulnerable.

She reached out to pat his leg. 'I'm okay,' she said, trying to take away the residual panic she saw.

His lips quirked. 'Are you trying to comfort me?'

She smiled. 'That's what friends are for, right?' The words fell out naturally. This was what he wanted, after all.

His smile fell, his face serious as he shook his head. 'No. Not friends.' He tipped his head forward until his forehead gently touched hers. 'My heart stopped when I saw you with Nielsen. All I could think about was making sure you were safe.' He swallowed, and his hands clenched a little in her hair. 'I thought I was going to lose you, and I couldn't bear it.'

Her heart rate picked up a little, and her breath hitched. She was afraid to speak, afraid to interrupt the moment... afraid of what he would or wouldn't say.

'You're not just a friend to me, Jac,' he whispered, angling his head, bringing his lips close to hers. 'I don't want to have some sort of casual, easy-come, easy-go relationship with you.' His green hot gaze kissed her skin, so full of resolve, so full of heat. 'I'm all in.'

Jacinta could feel her smile dawn within her, a happiness that spread outward, bursting to full-blown joy. She lifted her chin the fraction of a millimetre required to press her lips against his, and kissed him. He let her, drawing her close. She lifted her arms around his neck, the blanket drifting off her shoulders. He kissed her back, his head angling, deepening the kiss from tender to sultry. He drew back, but only enough to meet her gaze.

'I love you, Jac Buchanan,' he told her quietly, his sincerity adding a weight and warmth to his words that made her want to hold them to her heart forever.

She smiled, her gaze drifting from his lips to his glittering gaze. 'Thank you,' she said simply.

His eyes narrowed, and he chuckled as he took her lips again in a hot kiss. She laughed huskily, and felt the world tilt as he lowered her to the bed. 'I always knew you were trouble.' He kissed her gently. 'Marry me.'

Her heart skipped a beat. 'You want to marry me?' That was more than she'd dared hope for...

He nuzzled her neck. 'I want you. Today, tomorrow, and forever after that. Besides, how else am I going to keep you out of trouble?'

She punched him lightly on the shoulder, and he laughed into the dip between her neck and shoulder, his warm breath setting off a ripple-effect of nerve-endings awakening throughout her body. He lifted his head to meet her gaze, his eyes serious.

'I love you. Marry me.'

'Yes,' she breathed, then laughed between the triumphant kisses he planted over her face and neck, until he took her lips in a soul-searing kiss that touched her even more deeply than his beautiful words. She kissed him back, and their lips and tongues tangled. The kisses became longer, steamier, and she caressed his jaw as she pulled back to look up at him.

'I love you,' she whispered, surprised that joy could be borne from such a dark day. She'd been so devastated that morning, so heartbroken. She'd been frightened beyond belief, and now she was so happy she could burst. Happy, and hopeful for the future together.

He gathered her close, his gaze lit with a love that mirrored hers. 'I love you, too.'

'Even if I'm a so-called troublemaker?'

He grinned. 'Oh, you're definitely trouble. Nothing so-called about it. It's okay, though. I'm a police officer. I can handle trouble.' He kissed her in that sweet, sensitive spot on her collarbone, and she shuddered.

'Show me.'

And so he did.

* * *

From our authors

As always, I couldn't have done this without my husband, Mark, who takes care of all things techie and listens to me ramble about characters and plot-lines that are as real to me as he is. Thankfully he loves me and knows I'm not insane. Thanks to my two beautiful boys, Jacob and Nathaniel, for doing the same—it can be tough sometimes to have a mum who lives in another world! Thanks to my family and close friends—especially my parents, Kerril and Jim, my sister Kirrily and my gorgeous friend, Helen, who when I told them I was asked to take part in writing this series and was all full of doubts, told me I had to say yes. They were right. A writer needs a family of writing peeps all their own and I have some of the best. Thanks to my writing friends—Liz, Laura, Chris, Marnie, Frana, Helena, Anyo and Anita. I couldn't have gotten here without you. And a big shout out to all my friends in Romance Writers of Australia—you are inspiration and mentor rolled into a big ball of supportive writerly love. Thank you. I also need to mention my agent, Alex Adsett, who was so excited when she was approached about me writing a book in this series and believed whole-heartedly that I could hold my own with such great fellow authors, that she made me think I was the Little Engine that Could. You are the best agent ever, Alex. Thanks also have to go to Kate Cuthbert at Escape, who took a chance on asking a brand new Escape Artist to be a part of this series with such talented established authors. You make me feel like I can shine. And finally, thanks to my fellow Escape Artists, Dan, Shannon and TJ, who made being part of this project a joy. I had so much fun creating this town with you guys and discussing the ins and outs of life in a northern NSW country town and workshopping the ups and downs of character and story. You guys are the best and I hope to have the pleasure of working with you again in the future.

—Leisl Leighton

Thanks to my good friend Nikki Logan for the many hours she spent cri-tiquing this book, providing untold feedback to bring it up to a publishable standard. I'm so grateful to have someone like you in this business. Thanks to Kate Cuthbert from Escape Publishing for giving me the opportunity to be a part of this series, and to Laurie Ormond for the editorial support to make it shine. Trueman Faulkner for his time in giving me the facts on what really goes on in the life of a firefighter. (And any errors are mine.) My fellow authors—Leisl Leighton, TJ Hamilton and Shannon Curtis. It's been fun working together to create a whole new world where our characters can fall in love. And finally to my husband Glen who gives me the freedom to do what I love—and who, thankfully, loves what I do as well.

—Daniel de Lorne

I'd like to thank my extended family in the bush for the inspiration and experiences that led to this story, as well as Leisl Leighton, Daniel de Lorne and TJ Hamilton for being a great bunch of brainstorming, entertaining and talented writers to work with! I'd also like to thank the team at Meth Lab Cleaners Australia, for the information and assistance they provided in the research for this novel. You guys are fantastic.

—Shannon Curtis

The fictional town of Echo Springs has a neighbour in Bourke, a small town in north-west NSW. Bourke has been first in Australia trialling a Justice Reinvestment Program, which brings the community together with service providers to find better partnerships in reducing offending and making the community safe. You can find out more about the Maranguka Justice Reinvestment Program, including ways to support it, at justreinvest.org.au.

Leisl Leighton is a tall redhead with an overly large imagination. As a child, she identified strongly with Anne of Green Gables. She's a voracious reader and a born performer, so it came as no surprise to anyone when she did a double major in English Literature and Drama for her BA, then went on to a career as an actor, singer and dancer, as well as script writer, stage manager and musical director for cabaret and theatre restaurants (one of which she co-owned and ran for six years). After starting a family Leisl stopped performing and instead began writing the stories that had been plaguing her dreams. Leisl's stories have won and placed in many competitions in Australia and the US, including the STALI, Golden Opportunities, Heart of the West, Linda Howard Award of Excellence, Touch of Magic and many others. Leisl lives in the leafy suburbs of Melbourne with her two beautiful boys, lovely hubby and overly spunky dogs Buffy and Skye, and likes to spend time with family and friends. She is addicted to the Syfy channel, and her shelves are full of fantasy and paranormal books and sci-fi DVDs. She sometimes sings in a choir, has worked as a swim teacher, loves to ski, can talk the hind leg off a donkey and has been President of Romance Writers of Australia from 2014 to 2017.

Website: leislleighton.com, Facebook: Leisl-Leighton-Author

Twitter: @LeislLeighton

Ruin. Romance. Redemption. That's the magic trifecta **Daniel de Lorne** promises readers of his books. Whether it's irresistible vampires, paranormal paramours, or hot everyday men, Daniel's books go for the heart. In his other life, Daniel is a professional writer and researcher in Perth, Australia, with a love of history and nature. All of which makes for great story fodder. And when he's not working, he and his husband explore as much of this amazing world as they can, from the ruins of Welsh abbeys to trekking famous routes and swimming with whales.

Website: www.danieldelorne.com, Facebook: danieldelorne

Twitter: @edanieldelorne

Shannon Curtis has worked as a copywriter, business consultant, admin manager, customer service rep, logistics co-ordinator, dangerous goods handler, event planner, switch bitch and betting agent, and decided to try writing a story like those she loved to read when she found herself at home after the birth of her first child. Her books in both paranormal and romantic suspense genres have won awards nationally and internationally, judged by both readers and writers. Now she spends entirely too much time daydreaming about hunky heroes and malicious murders—for her books, of course! She loves reading, loves writing, and loves hearing from her readers, so visit her at shannoncurtis.com and say hi!

TJ Hamilton is a crime expert, writing professionally for varying platforms of media and entertainment. As a former police officer for the New South Wales Police Force with a BA in Criminology, TJ has carved a solid understanding of the macabre over the past fifteen years. TJ's passion for storytelling developed after leaving the police force where she used her knowledge to create stories of mystery and intrigue. She has won the coveted Scarlet Stiletto Award for the Sisters In Crime and was shortlisted for Endemol-Shine's ROAR: Smart For A Girl initiative to develop women writers for screen. TJ's work has been published in various news mastheads, including News Corp's *Daily Telegraph* and *Sunday Telegraph*. TJ now works in script development for television, providing story consultation with production companies such as Playmaker, CJZ and Hardy White.

LET'S TALK
ABOUT BOOKS!

JOIN THE CONVERSATION

HARLEQUIN
AUSTRALIA

@HARLEQUINAUS

@HARLEQUINAUS